THE WORLD OF ASSASSIN'S CREED® VALHALLA

JOURNEY TO THE NORTH—LOGS AND FILES OF A HIDDEN ONE

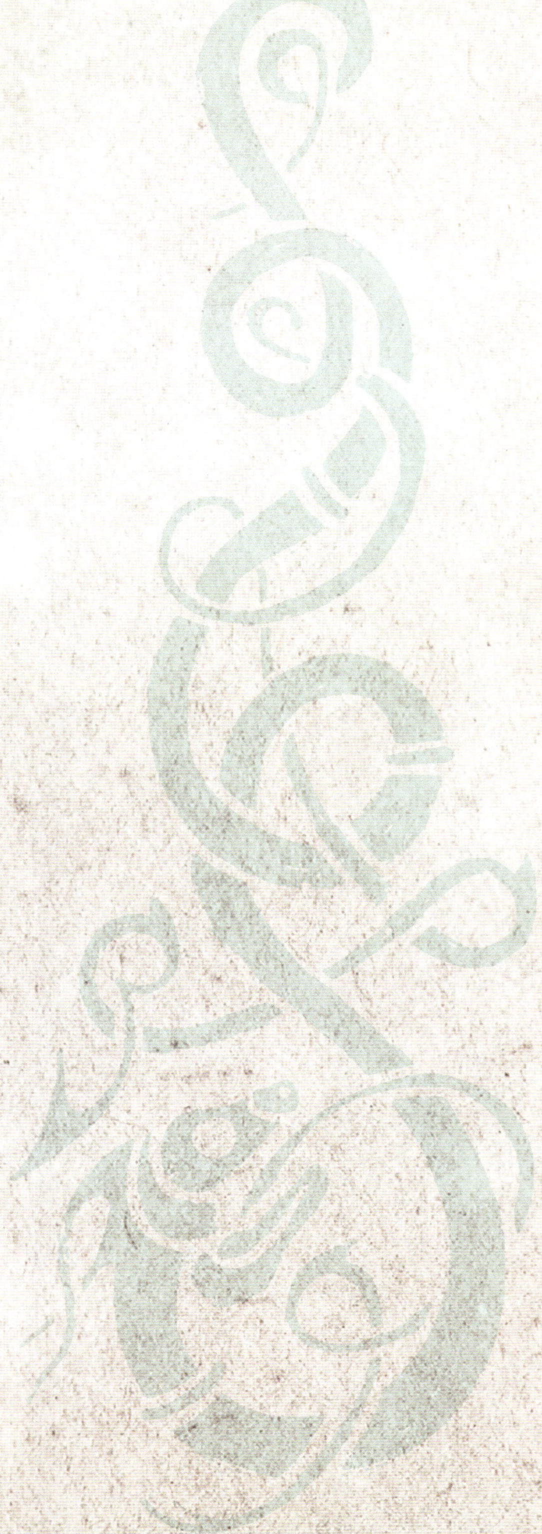

THE WORLD OF ASSASSIN'S CREED® VALHALLA

JOURNEY TO THE NORTH—LOGS AND FILES OF A HIDDEN ONE

FROM THE RECORDS OF **HYTHAM**
AS COLLECTED BY **RICK BARBA**

DARK HORSE BOOKS

President & Publisher
Mike Richardson

Editor
Ian Tucker

Assistant Editor
Anastacia Ferry

Designer
Sarah Terry

Digital Art Technician
Allyson Haller

Special Thanks to
Caroline Lamache, Fatiha Chellali, Laura Ducos, Thierry Noël, Florence Baccard, Louis Barraud, Jacob Liutkus, Nadja Iman Binte Azmi, Clément Neel, and Elisa Lemercier.

THE WORLD OF ASSASSIN'S CREED VALHALLA
JOURNEY TO THE NORTH—LOGS AND FILES OF A HIDDEN ONE

Published by Dark Horse Books
A division of Dark Horse Comics LLC
10956 SE Main Street | Milwaukie, OR 97222

DarkHorse.com
Facebook.com/DarkHorseComics
Twitter.com/DarkHorseComics

First edition: June 2023
Ebook ISBN 978-1-50673-523-8
Hardcover ISBN 978-1-50673-521-4
Deluxe Edition ISBN 978-1-50673-522-1

1 3 5 7 9 10 8 6 4 2
Printed in China

MIX
Paper | Supporting responsible forestry
FSC® C016973

TABLE OF CONTENTS

INTRODUCTION

This is my official record of our brotherhood's engagement with the Order of the Ancients in the northern kingdoms of Norway and England in the years 872 to 878 CE.

With the apparent demise of my master, Basim Ibn Ishaq, the job of reporting these momentous events has fallen solely to me, Hytham the Acolyte. I openly admit that I am not privy to all that Master Basim has seen and heard, but I will attempt to faithfully discharge this duty of account to the best of my ability. Before I start, however, let me point out one thing increasingly clear to me:

We Hidden Ones have been absent far too long from this darkening island.

The Order of the Ancients operated unfettered in England for four centuries, dating back to the Roman withdrawal, and thus we've had much catch-up work to do. To this end, I decided to share intelligence with my Viking hosts, especially any info gathered from my nascent network of agents in England's festering cities. Working with the Raven Clan, I felt we could make significant progress together.

As Mentor Rayhan once wrote to me: *Work in the dark of oppression, serve the light of freedom.*

Our story begins in Constantinople, where Basim and I first met the Norse warrior-prince named Sigurd Styrbjornsson. There, we served as his "shepherds" (as he called it) through our homeland, the Abbasid Caliphate. Sigurd found us fascinating and often joked that we seemed part of a "brotherhood of shadows"—a designation that hit much closer to truth than he realized.

Sigurd, in turn, shepherded us north to his own homeland of Norway. This sojourn served our greater purpose of countering the spread of the order through Anglo-Saxon Christendom and the Norse regions, purging its evil wardens and minions from those northern lands. Once there, we met Sigurd's Viking kinfolk, countrymen who called themselves the Raven Clan.

One of the very first we met upon our arrival was Sigurd's adopted sibling, Eivor. By all accounts, Eivor was an extraordinary warrior with almost preternatural physical skills as well as hidden depths—a perfect candidate, certainly, for apprenticeship in our ranks. And yet, when Basim gifted her with a sacred wrist blade almost immediately, it seemed premature. I feared that without extensive training and the proper devotion to our creed, Eivor would misuse the weapon.

Indeed, Eivor immediately strapped the blade to the wrong side of her wrist! I was appalled.

But as my mentor duly reminded me—it is not the weapon itself but the mind wielding it that counts most.

Even as Eivor affixed her bracer incorrectly—and mocked our missing fingers as a "mistake"—Basim was forgiving of tone, and generous with his guidance. In truth, I should not have doubted. Eivor was a *remarkably* adept learner. She wielded the Hidden Blade with surprising skill . . . quickly mastering even the artful timing of our ledge and air strikes! Her ability to execute stealth techniques so swiftly was humbling. Those took me many weeks to master, I'm embarrassed to admit.

And so, please bear with me as I recount the following story by way of introduction to Eivor, as I find it both illustrative and significant:

One day, not long after Ravensthorpe was founded in England, Eivor stopped at my tent.

I was staking out perimeter measurements and hewing support posts for the Hidden Ones bureau I hoped to build. I'd explained how my brotherhood needed a base of operations for tracking our enemies in England. I listed the major cities infested by the order—Lunden, Jorvik, and Wincestre—and described (perhaps a bit too vigorously) how this vile cult spreads its plague of illusion.

"This is our sole purpose," I exclaimed, "to liberate the body and spirit of man from unnatural shackles!"

Eivor was a bit taken aback by my passion, I suspect, but graciously offered to help. Indeed, over the next few days, Eivor provided supplies, raw materials, and the labor I needed to build our Bureau. The final edifice ended up far more aesthetically pleasing than I'd dared hope—for such a peripatetic people, Vikings build remarkably durable structures, and exhibit an unerring eye for clean lines.

In thanking Eivor, I reemphasized our common cause, and how tightly our concerns overlapped. I implored Eivor to actively assist those in need—beneficent actions are their own reward, of course, but grateful people may also reveal clues that can help us track down our foes. In particular, I pressed Eivor to target Lunden, where the order was operating without restraint. Eivor agreed to take it up with Raven leaders.

At that moment, something about Eivor's essential persona—a deep well of sincerity—reminded me of how Basim so quickly saw something that he trusted implicitly. Inspired by this, I decided it was time for my new partner to take a step forward in consciousness. I led Eivor directly across the Nene River from Ravensthorpe to a cliff's edge. There, I invited her to experience our brotherhood's most sacred and exhilarating ritual of initiation—the Leap of Faith.

At first—like most initiates including myself—Eivor was reluctant to jump. But once I did, she followed almost immediately!

Afterward, her response was as I expected: "I felt madness and vigor and a purging of fear!" she exclaimed, acknowledging that it was indeed a "gift" as I'd promised. This rite, I explained, dated back more than a thousand years to before the birth of the Christian Jesus. It was a rite that had long steadied us in our resolve.

Eivor pointed out her own people's yearning to rule a land they could call their own. But I dissuaded her from any notion that this desire was even remotely comparable to the order's ambition—that twisted, dishonorable, unprincipled urge to subjugate. In fact, as I told Eivor, I felt our purposes were perfectly aligned! The Raven Clan neutralizes potential foes by forming alliances in good faith and building trust; meanwhile, we Hidden Ones work in the shadows to rescue England from a deepening rot.

Yes, the darkness of oppression had been spreading unchecked far too long. It was time, we agreed, to serve the light.

Over time and many missions, I've developed a level of trust with Eivor that I find not only strategically valuable but also personally gratifying. I'm not a warm or gregarious man by nature, but I must say—the depth and intensity of Viking friendship and familial bond is unlike any I've encountered in my extensive travels.

Frankly, I find it somewhat appealing.

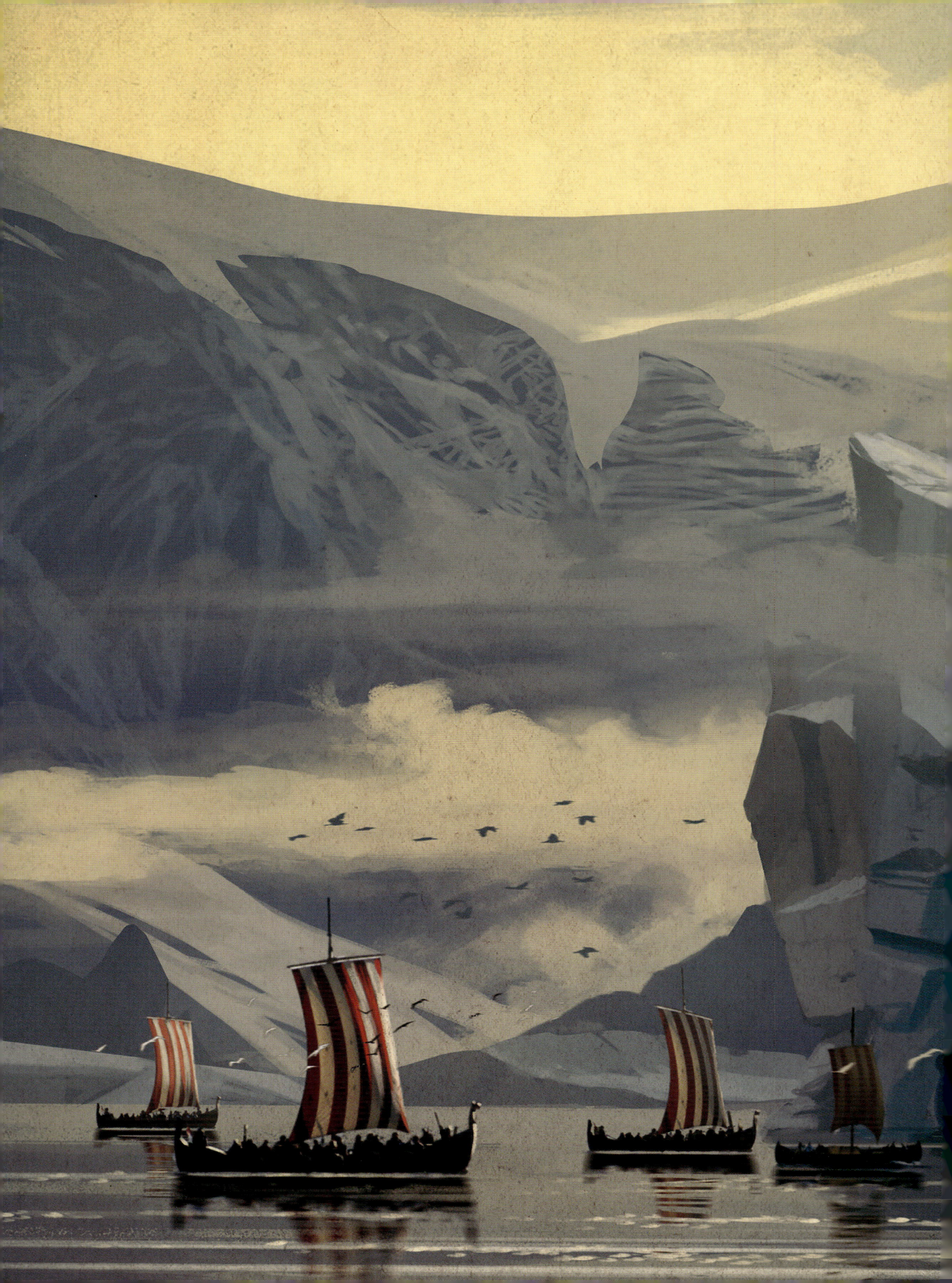

CHAPTER ONE

VIKING CULTURE

Membership in the Hidden Ones requires far more than just physical training. After all, our creed requires us to blend seamlessly into places we visit, some quite foreign. Such discipline demands a solid familiarity with local custom and lore. As a result, acolytes and masters alike spend countless hours studying foreign cultures and history. When Master Basim was called to spearhead our countermoves against the Order of the Ancients in northern Europe, we started with an immersive review of travel accounts from that region archived in the Imperial Library of Constantinople—my first visit to that temple of knowledge.

I must confess, wonder struck me like a thunderbolt—very nearly debilitating—when I first entered the library's grand atrium. I'm a scholar by temperament, and spending days surrounded by one hundred thousand volumes . . . well, it was like a magician had conjured my personal paradise. Did you know the imperial collection includes a scroll of Homer's collected works, one hundred and twenty feet long, inscribed in gold ink by the Levant's finest calligraphers? I can think of no document more sacred.

And yet, foraging through troves of parchment chronicles, Basim and I were forced to rely on clearly flawed transcriptions of Viking oral tradition as well as sketchy Frankish and Saxon accounts of barbarous Viking behavior to construct our initial cultural overview. Of course, these misconceptions were challenged when we first met Sigurd on that dock in the Golden Horn and then swept away after our Rygjafylke arrival. In Norway and England, my own eyes and ears have provided so much context.

This chapter provides a distillation of my findings, both scholarly and observational, on Viking culture. Keep in mind that, like all Hidden Ones acolytes, I kept a careful journal of daily observations. We do this to help construct a chronicle of the events, people, and cultures encountered in our assignments.

THE VIKING EXPANSION

The Norse homeland to the north features a starkly beautiful but often frozen and forbidding landscape. Jagged white peaks drop into silver fjords carved in the coastline like an artisan's engraving—so unlike the fiery escarpments of my Levantine homeland, the deep red rays on the mountain of fire, Jabal Farhar. Soils along Norway's coastland and southern rim are lush and fertile but aren't enough to sustain a growing population. European "scholars" typically depict the Viking expansion as a barbarian blood lust for plunder and glory. But the Viking expansion southward into Anglo-Saxon and Frankish territory was more likely an entirely practical attempt to settle more arable land and pasture.

One other element of Norse society probably came into play. In Norway, the wealthiest and most powerful jarls control vast estates. Ancestral land cannot be divided and thus is inherited by a single family member. This leaves many Norse descendants with a burning desire to acquire land of their own. With limited opportunities in the northlands, these folk have little choice but to seek fortune elsewhere.

EXPLORING THE WORLD

Viking maritime skill is truly legendary. Chronicles I've reviewed suggest that Norse explorers and traders have reached coastal regions all the way from Norway, rounding Jabal Ṭāriq to the Levant and beyond, even finding routes east to the Black Sea. Again, the first Viking I ever met was Sigurd Styrbjornsson. He and his longship crew had circumnavigated Europe, sailing nearly 5,600 Roman miles from their native Norway to Constantinople.

However, while Vikings display remarkable skill at navigating open seas, they actually prefer river travel, exploring inland channels instead of skirting shorelines. Traveling via interior waterways often requires portage—a process where crews drag their boats ashore and haul them overland to skirt obstacles such as waterfalls or dangerous rapids. I've personally witnessed Viking sailors carry a longship on their shoulders more than a mile to the next navigable stretch of water!

PRE-VIKING BRITANNIA

Back in Rome's imperial heyday, a Roman legion was as invincible a military unit as the world had ever seen. When Emperor Claudius invaded England in 43 CE, his army rolled over the ragtag British tribes that tried to resist. By 87 CE the conquest was essentially complete, with Roman control extended over all but the island's far north and west. Rome called the new territory Britannia.

In 122 CE, Emperor Hadrian oversaw construction of a massive defensive wall (often called Hadrian's Wall) that extended coast to coast across England's northern neck. This imposing barrier established the northern boundary of Roman rule. It helped control trade flow and the economy in Roman Britain, and—perhaps most importantly—stood as a commanding monument to Roman might for three centuries.

But eventually, administering such large provinces while defending them from hordes of hostile tribes drew down the resources of the Western Roman Empire. By 410 CE, Rome had withdrawn all its garrisons from Britannia, leaving behind hundreds of imperial structures and a yawning power void. This void was quickly filled by native Picts and Celtic Britons, and then an

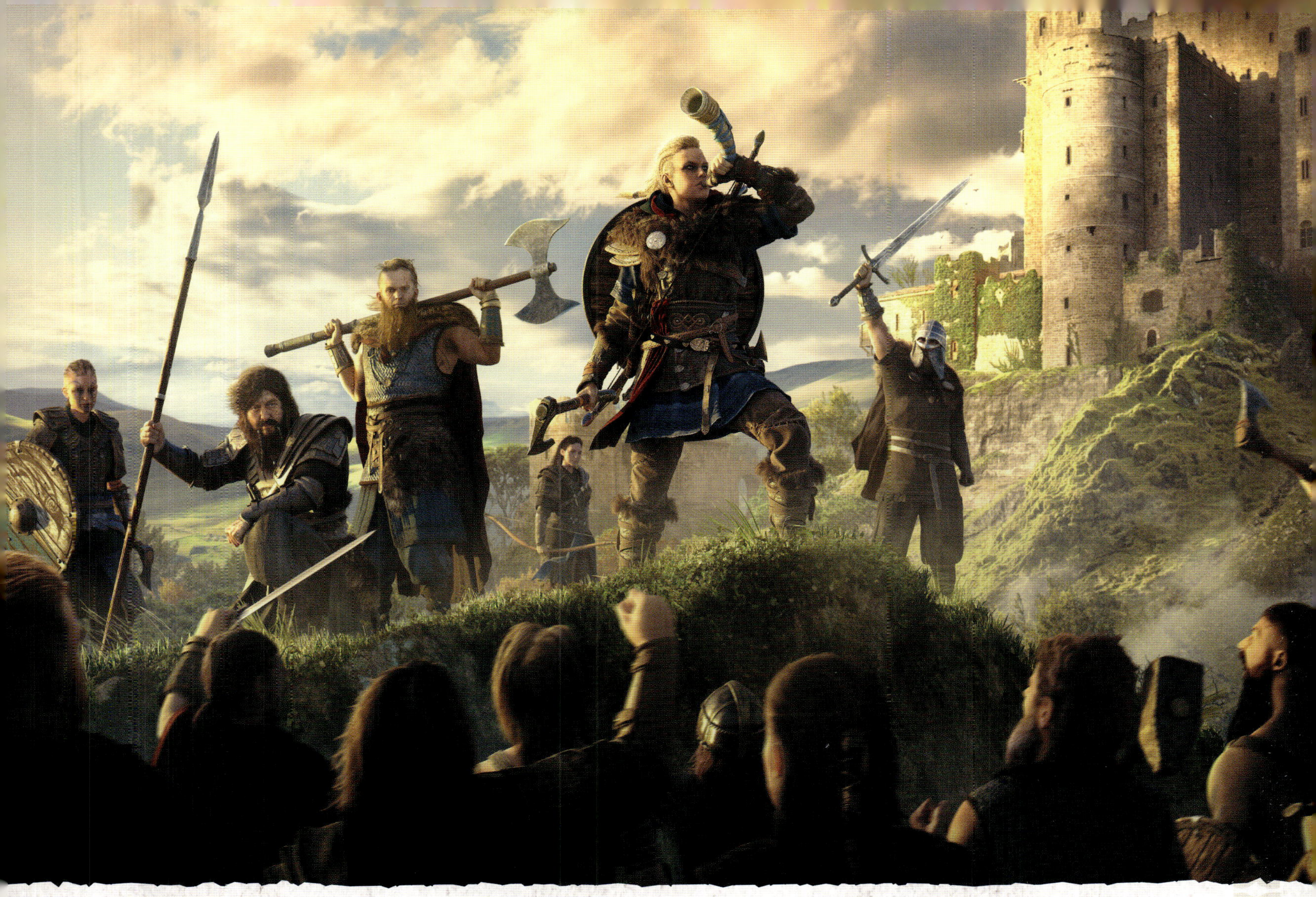

influx of Germanic tribes flowing across the sea from the continent—primarily pagan Saxons and Angles, and a later wave of Christianized Jutes.

VIKING ARRIVAL IN ENGLAND

The earliest Viking moves into England typically involved small raiding parties. One or two longships would probe coastal or upriver settlements or monasteries, looking to plunder and leave. But sometime in the 860s CE, a legendary Viking jarl named Ragnar Lothbrok led a much larger war band of warriors into England, seeking to conquer territory and establish permanent settlements. Ragnar's string of successes ended when he lost a decisive battle to the Northumbrian king Aella . . . who promptly tossed his captured Viking foe into a pit of snakes.

THE GREAT HEATHEN ARMY

When word of Ragnar's tawdry, dishonorable execution reached Norway, his sons—Halfdan, Ubba, and Ivarr the Boneless—rallied a large cohort of Viking warriors and set out for England to seek revenge and reclaim their father's conquered lands. Anglo-Saxon Church propagandists called it the Great Heathen Army, hoping to stir up a powerful, pagan-hating resistance across Christian England. But the Ragnarssons embraced the derogatory name with a fierce glee.

Ironically, Halfdan's so-called heathens included fighters from Norse settlements across Francia, Friesland, the Scottish islands, and Ireland. In those areas, Viking settlers (many who'd been there for decades) often had to convert to Christianity before they could trade goods with Christians or boost their social status in Church-dominated territory. Thus the army's "throng of pagans" actually included a considerable number of Christians!

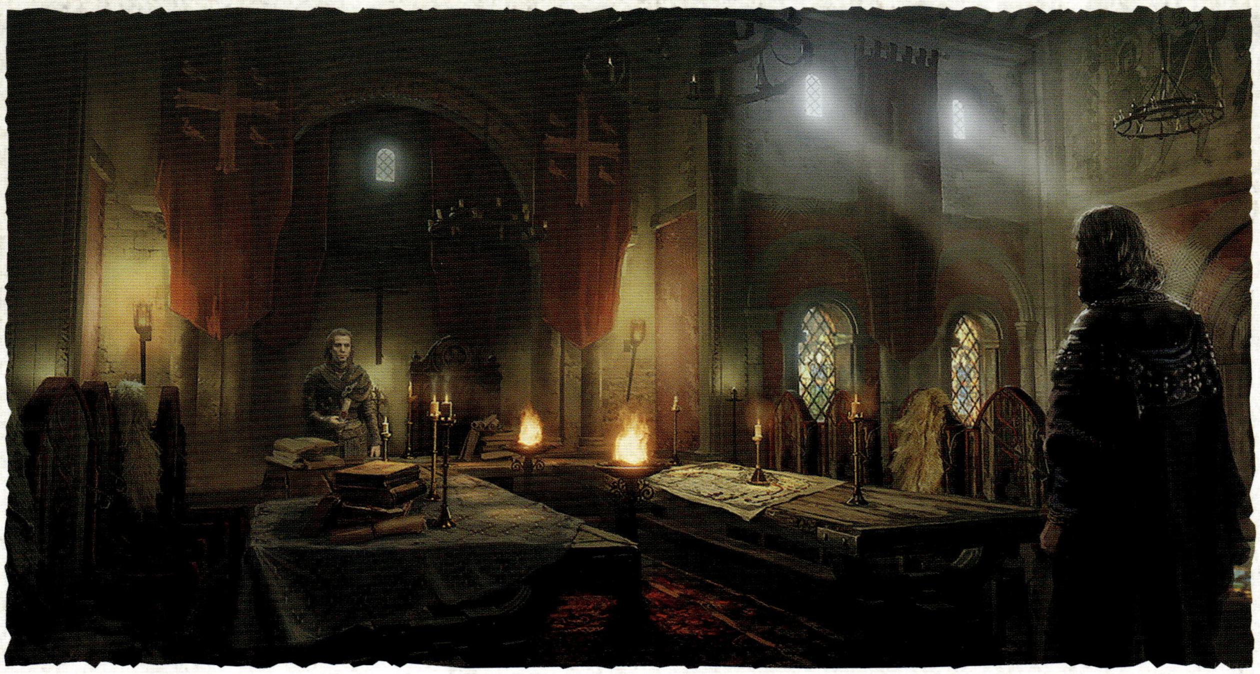

THE VIKING CONQUESTS

The Ragnarsson expedition—said to include 250 longboats carrying 10,000 warriors—landed in East Anglia in 865 CE and began to sweep shire by shire across the island. The Great Heathen Army's decentralized deployment and agile supply lines let its Viking war bands move with remarkable speed. This provided a distinct advantage over the large, slow Saxon armies that required much logistical support.

Before long, the sons of Ragnar had brought Northumbria under heel and slew their father's murderer, King Aella. By 871, their forces had also driven from Theotford in East Anglia to Reading in Mercia, where they were soon joined by the Great Summer Army—reinforcements from Norway led by the Viking jarl Guthrum. This combined force spent years consolidating control of Mercia, eventually deposing the Saxon king Burgred and establishing Danelaw across a number of shires.

By 875, the Vikings were finally ready to challenge the most powerful Saxon leader in England, King Aelfred of Wessex. From Mercia they plunged south to Werham then west across Wessex, battling Aelfred's formidable forces. (Some of these expeditions are chronicled in my journal entries in the section of this tome titled The Viking Age.) Under Guthrum's leadership, the Viking army met the West Saxons in a cataclysmic battle at Chepeham and forced Aelfred to flee for his life.

HOW VIKINGS RULE

Over my years based in Ravensthorpe, I've grown increasingly impressed by the general Viking practice of what I'd term "benevolent conquest." Make no mistake, the sheer brutality of a Viking assault is a nightmarish terror to behold. But once a targeted region submits in obeisance, these northern conquerors tend to rule with a light touch. They don't impose culture or religious beliefs on the conquered. In fact, Vikings often let local thegns oversee their old districts, a reassuring continuity that local subjects tend to appreciate.

Beyond that, Viking jarls retain power and ensure loyalty by sharing the wealth. History shows time and again that amassing great wealth while one's subjects languish is a sure prescription for insurrection. But when Norse leaders acquire loot, via trade or raid, they typically redistribute equitable portions of the take to allies and subjects. This sharing keeps the locals in line.

VIKINGS AT WAR

FIELD TACTICS

Viking raiding parties and war bands are truly terrifying to behold in battle. Their prowess is due less to superior gear or numbers than to astonishing mobility, cunning feints, brutally efficient close-quarters combat skills, and raw fury. They also rely on the elements of surprise and ambush, even in larger engagements. Employing carefully timed ruses and deception to distract and overwhelm foes, a phalanx of Viking fighters can sweep across a battlefield with shocking alacrity.

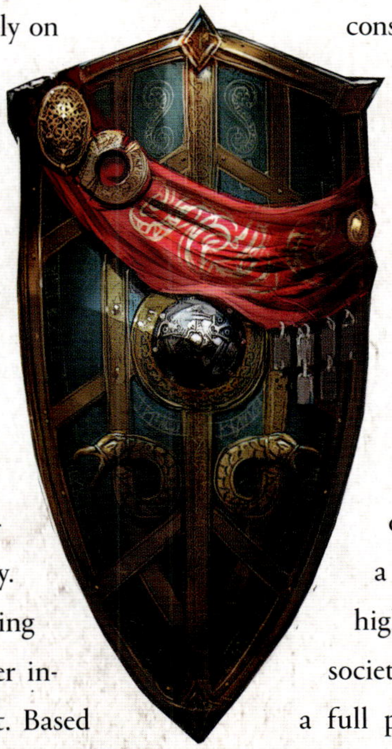

SCOUTING

Good intelligence is always the underpinning of effective military strategy. Before embarking on any expedition, Viking leaders send scouts and traders to gather information on targets they intend to hit. Based on this knowledge, they decide whether to attack an Anglo-Saxon leader or (if he's too powerful) offer their mercenary services to him.

To this point: One of my agents in Wincestre found a fascinating chronicle from 789 CE tucked in the historical records of the seminary library. The first known Viking raid on Anglo-Saxon soil took place that year, when three longships from Hordafylke landed on an isle off the southern coast of Wessex. This small raid triggered a series of reconnaissance visits; Viking scouts and merchants began to probe coastal areas, trading with locals while gaining insight into the region.

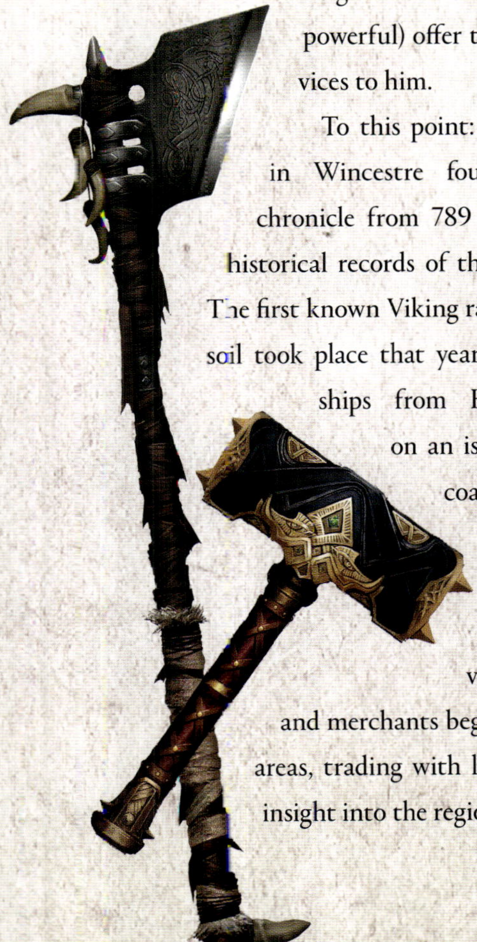

Eventually, Viking spies learned that nearby Lindisfarne Abbey was loaded with loot . . . and was lightly defended! This led to the infamous sack of the abbey in 793 CE, which many scholars consider the seminal event of the Viking Age.

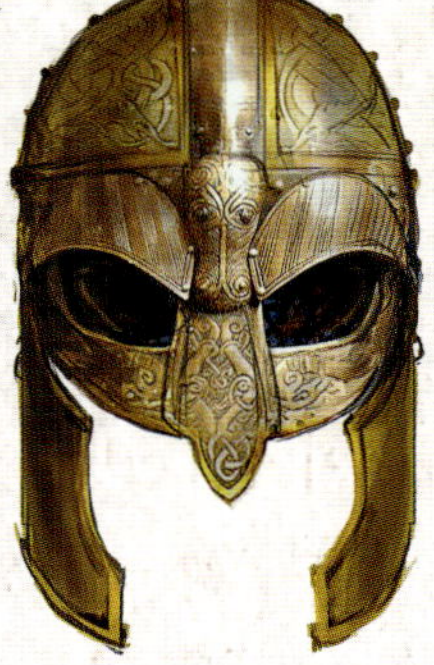

WEAPONS

Viking life is a martial culture, without a doubt. Indeed, Viking custom not only allows the owning of weapons but actually *requires* it of all free Norsemen! (Sigurd once told me this decree comes down from Odin himself.) Weapons with a fine finish and ornamental inlays are highly valued and convey status in Norse society. A wealthy Viking typically maintains a full personal armory—axe, longsword, knife, round shield, helmet, mail armor, and maybe even a bow with a quiver of finely weighted arrows.

The most common Viking weapon is the spear—even the poorest of farmers keep one on the wall. After all, the magical spear Gungnir is the primary weapon of Odin himself! Seasoned Viking warriors often pair a thrusting or throwing spear with a stout, head-splitting battle axe (often named after a she-troll for some reason). Serviceable longswords are far more difficult to smith and thus quite expensive, so they tend to be wielded only by wealthier Norsemen. (Wealthy Vikings are often buried with their prized sword.)

Viking war chiefs sometimes organize their lower-class freemen and slaves into open formations of light infantry armed with knives, cheap slings, and stones. I've also noticed that Viking settlers in England and Ireland rely on the heavy, single-edged knife blade of a seax—a cheap but effective alternative to an axe or sword.

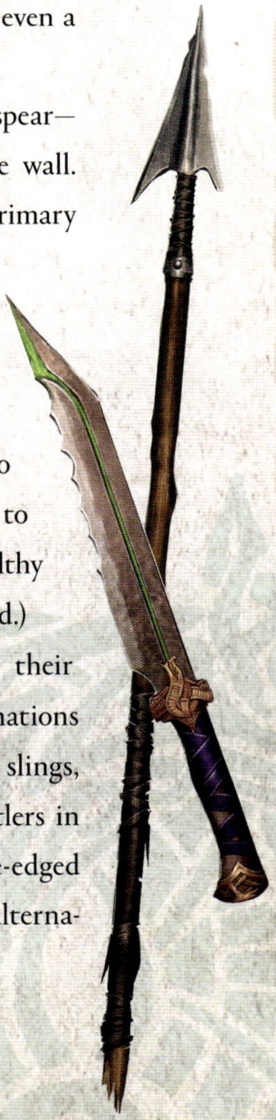

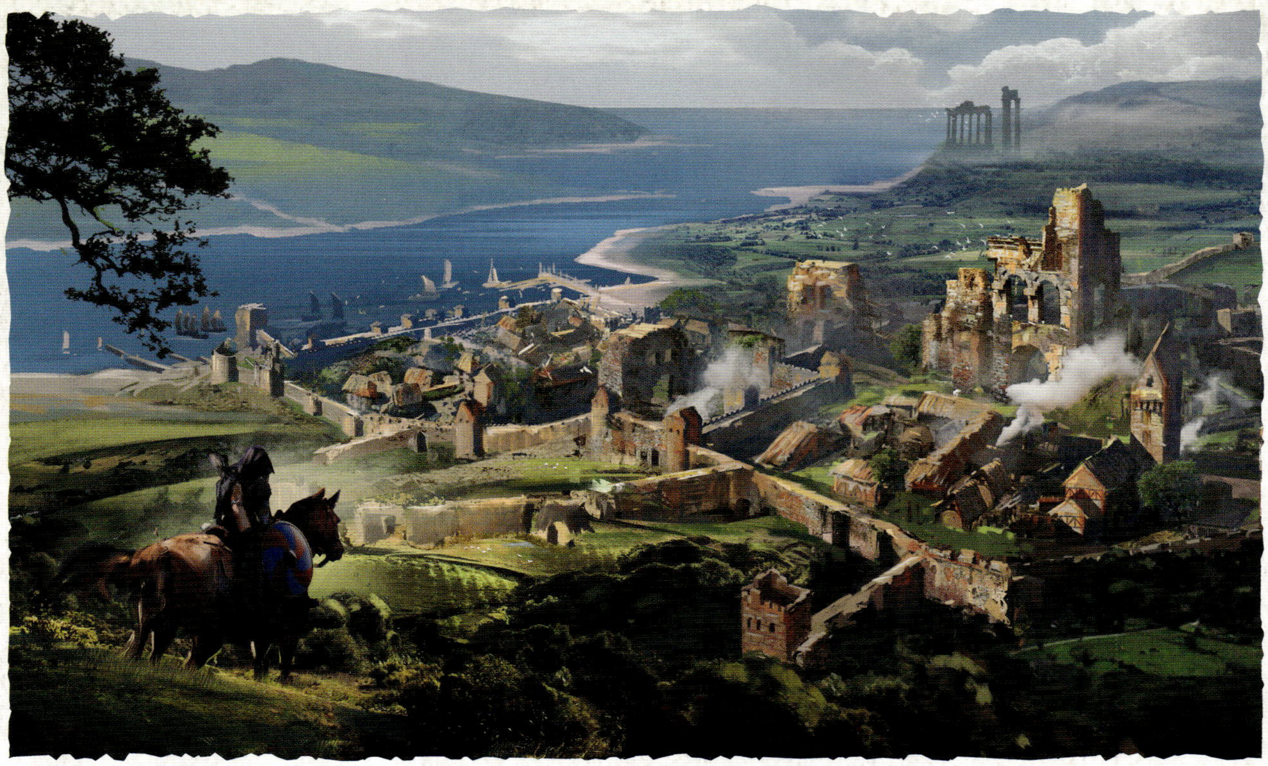

FOOT AND HORSEBACK

Vikings sometimes use horses to deploy quickly across a terrain to battle. Upon arrival, however, the combatant typically dismounts to fight. Committing to the fight on foot is seen as the mark of a true warrior—no swift retreat is possible! Eivor claims this commitment strengthens the bonds between war band brethren on the battlefield.

OVERWINTERING CAMPS

In the early days of the Viking incursions—back before Norse settlers began to make permanent homes in England and Francia—raiding parties usually carried out their forays during the summer months so they could sail back home in time for the fall harvest. Sometimes, however, circumstances forced Viking raiders to find a place to spend the winter. They would seek shelter on a small cove or river island to wait out the cold. This was called an overwintering camp.

Later, after the first conquests of Ragnar Lothbrok and the follow-up expeditions of his sons' Great Heathen Army, the large Viking forces no longer sought to return to Norway. The army still encamped for the cold months, often in villages or even major cities like Repton, Jorvik, and Lunden. Some of the temporary overwintering sites ended up as permanent settlements—like Ravensthorpe, for example, established by the Raven Clan at the camp where Halfdan's army spent the brutal winter of 871 CE.

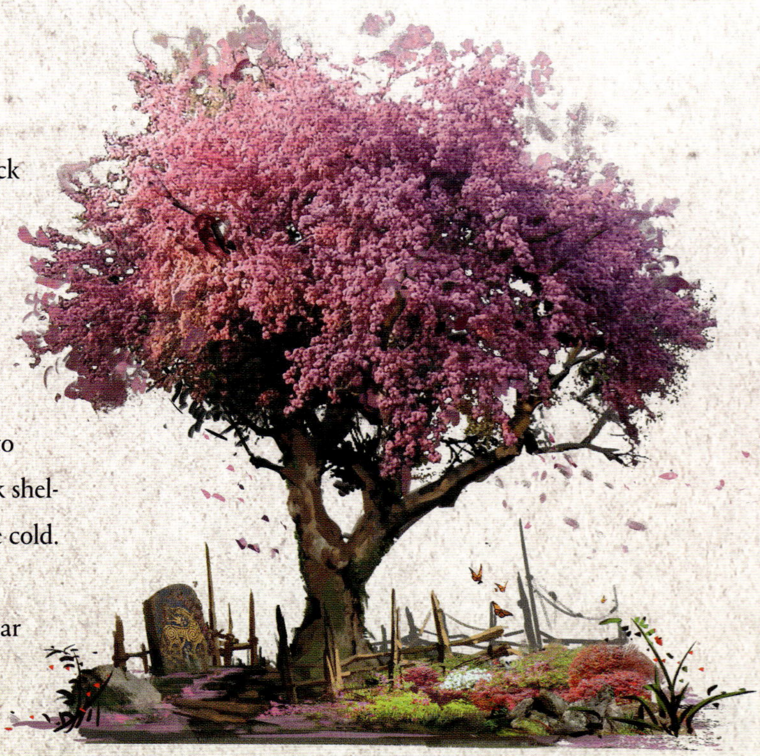

VIKING SOCIETY

Vikings are more than just savage warriors, despite what Saxon monks would have us think. As I write this in 878 CE, the relentless Viking spread across England has been ongoing for years. Norsemen are no longer strangers to this land—indeed, many call England home. In most shires, Norse and Saxon folk live peaceably side by side, farming and trading and raising families. Children of Viking settlers have spent their entire lives here, absorbing aspects of Saxon custom and religion, even speaking the local languages. And yet despite this natural assimilation, I'm impressed by the resilience of bedrock Viking values. Viking social structures are as solid and vibrant here in England as in their northern homelands.

VIKING SOCIAL STRUCTURES

FAMILY AND DESTINY: THE *HAMINGJA*

Family is indeed the cornerstone of Norse society. Blood relations are bound together by the *hamingja*, a spiritual entity that Viking lore depicts as a giant, spectral woman. This ghostly guardian of prosperity and good fortune serves as a kind of mystical heritage, the embodiment of a family's luck and destiny. Every *hamingja* demands respect and care to flourish. If a person or a family behaves badly, their luck could turn bad too. The lore also holds that a family's ancestral spirits support the *hamingja* by visiting young descendants in dreams to pass on family wisdom and values. Children learn of their inherited glory and failures.

Family is important in the Danelaw, too. Rules about landholding, inheritance, and more are all centered around the family rather than the individual. A person who does not know their lineage or ancestry is not legally recognized. To codify lineage, it is a common Viking practice to honor one's kin, living or dead, by engraving their stories and deeds on runestones.

That said, Viking communities are remarkably welcoming to strangers from outside family circles. I can certainly attest to that. As I've noted elsewhere in this compendium, my unreserved acceptance into the Raven Clan at Ravensthorpe is something I continue to find extraordinary.

THE CLAN

Several Viking households may come together to form a clan, or *ætt*. Clan bonds can be established via blood relations or marriage, or by an oath made during a legal assembly. Clansmen are bound by honor to defend or avenge one another. Each clan name is typically constructed by adding *-ung* or *-ing* to the name of a famous ancestor or god, although some use a favored animal—the Raven and Wolf Clans of Rygjafylke, for example. Clans typically have dozens or even hundreds of members.

THE *FÉLAG*

The Viking *félag* is a legal business or social partnership. Formed by two or more people, a *félag* is typically created to pool resources so its partners can fund financial ventures such as building longships or undertaking sea voyages for trade. The term *félag* can also refer to the union of a married couple, because it usually has financial implications for both families.

Indeed, forming a *félag* is often like creating an extended family for the partners. Each *félagi* (the term for a member of the fellowship) is expected to protect his fellows and their interests. If a *félagi* is killed, the *félag* partners may be expected to stage his funeral and honor his memory with a carved runestone. Depending on the circumstances—if, for example, the killing is criminal, unjust, or otherwise undeserved—the *félag* might even be obliged to avenge the deceased partner!

THE *ALTHING*

This remarkable tradition is a formal assembly of Norse freemen. Issues of trade, war, politics, alliance, honor, marriage, inheritance, and succession can be debated and settled here. The *althing* also serves as a court of law for resolving clan feuds, thus reducing social disorder. Aggrieved parties can demand justice for wrongs or slights. Rules are made, crimes judged, and punishments doled out. Interestingly, Vikings have no written legal code, but overseers called the *goði* have committed all laws to memory (more on these later).

The uncommon inclusivity of the Viking *althing* makes it an extraordinary social institution—so unlike the highly stratified systems of governance seen in most places, including my caliphate homeland. Although a king or jarl presides over the forum, all freemen are encouraged to speak openly, share opinions, and weigh in on important issues. Of course, as in all societies, the wealthiest and most powerful members tend to control the agenda and steer the decision-making process. But even so, every freeman has the right to be heard—an impressively progressive development for a people so widely portrayed in scholarly circles as a backward warrior culture obsessed with pillage and murder.

VIKING SOCIAL CASTES

BÓNDI: THE FREEMAN

The Viking freeman, or *bóndi*, forms the core unit of social organization in a Viking settlement. These hardworking farmers, craftsmen, merchants, fishermen, and traders not only drive the local economy but also play a major role in community justice and lawmaking. As mentioned above, all *boender* (the plural of *bóndi*) have the right—and indeed, the duty—to attend the freemen's assembly known as the *althing*. Any *bóndi* is eligible to serve as judge or jury during legal proceedings. Every freeman also has the right to bear arms, which is not the case for women or slaves.

THE FREEWOMAN

Freewomen in Viking settlements are revered as pillars of both family and clan. Some, like Eivor and Soma and Ljufvina, come to serve as powerful shieldmaidens—fearsome female warriors said to be infused with the spirit of Valkyrie goddesses. (Here I must note that Eivor is not particularly fond of the term *shieldmaiden*.) Among those who do not bear arms, a typical Viking freewoman

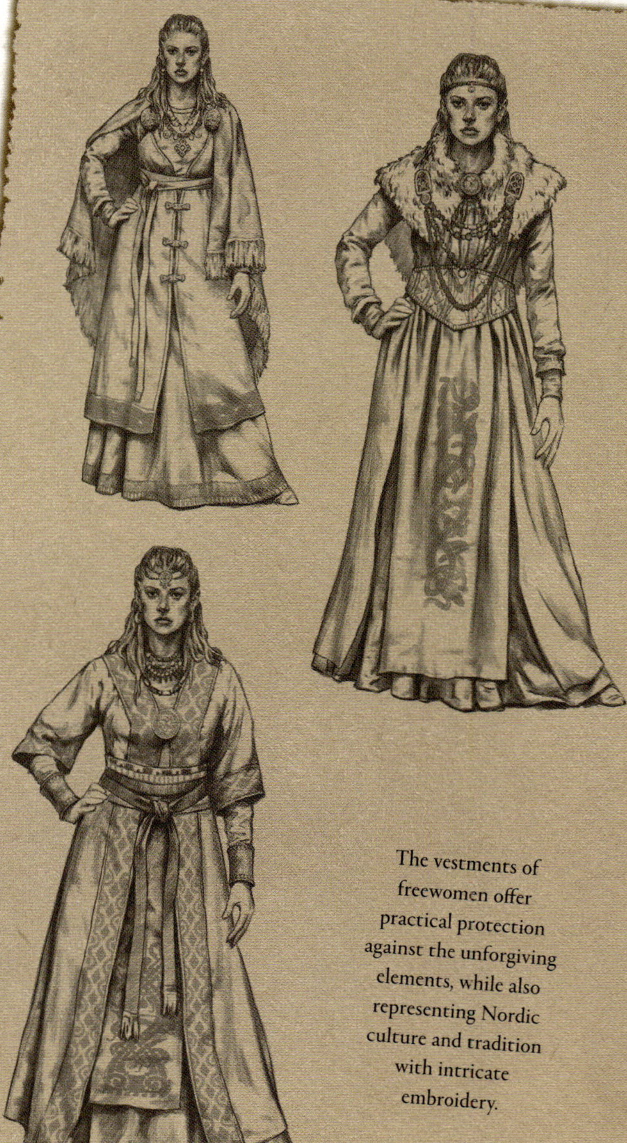

The vestments of freewomen offer practical protection against the unforgiving elements, while also representing Nordic culture and tradition with intricate embroidery.

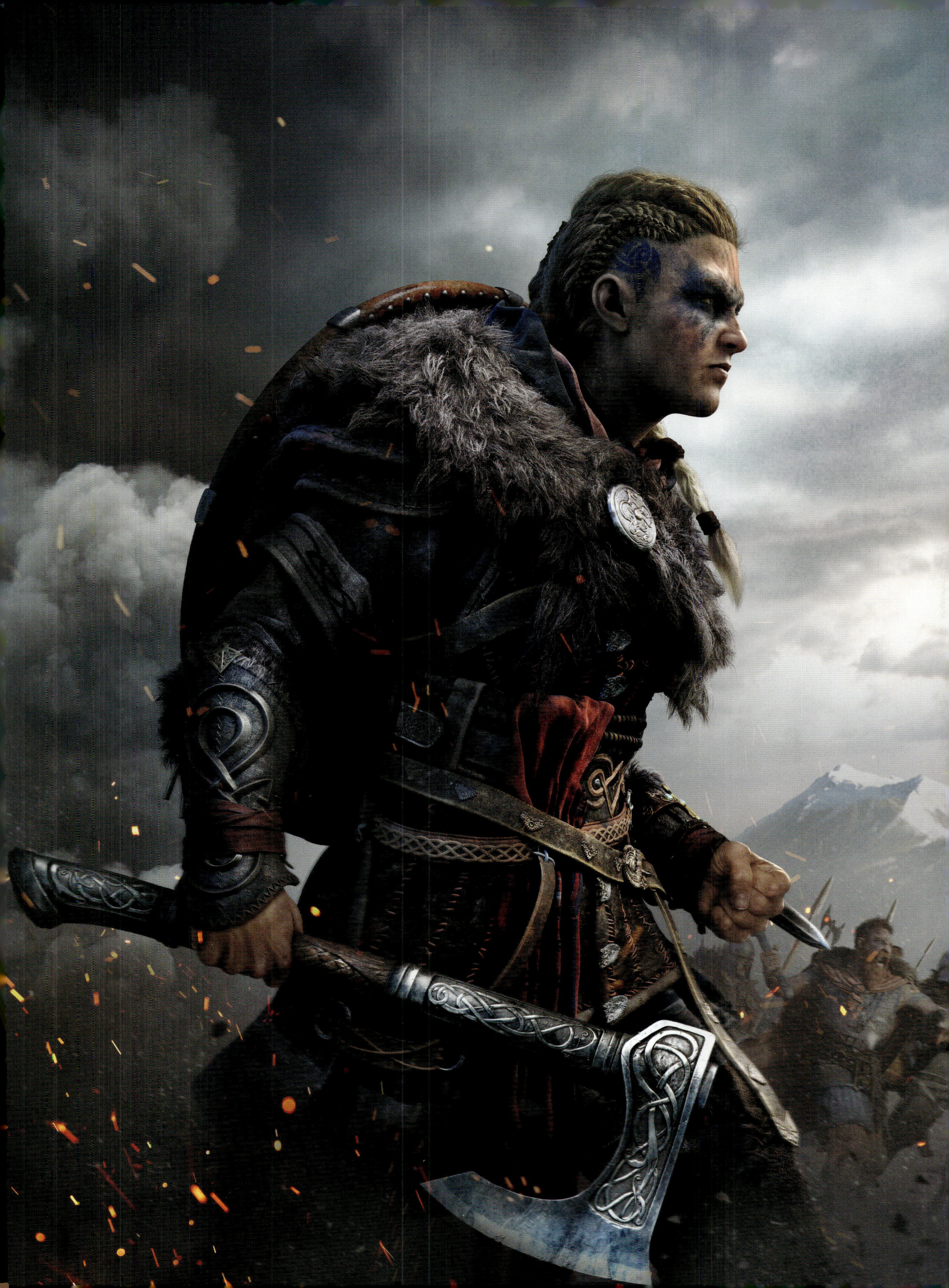

is responsible for her household's economy, including the direct care of family members young and old. Many freewomen tend to their clan's reputation and wider affairs as well.

Again, I've witnessed the formidable strength of the Viking freewoman firsthand here in Ravensthorpe. I've seen the critical role they play in Viking communities, and the tremendous respect they garner. But let me insert this observation I came upon recently, an excerpt from a private journal produced at Alcestre Monastery by the good Sister Agnes, holy abbess of the cloister. She writes:

> *In secret sojourns to local villages where Dane and Saxon mingle, I've been most impressed with the Norse freewoman. As keeper of hearth and home, she is responsible for keeping both home fires—the cooking fire, and the more fundamental flame of family and tribe—burning bright. After all, if the latter fire goes out, the harmony of clan is threatened.*
>
> *Sources tell me that for this reason, the hearth is sometimes associated with Yggdrasil, the Cosmic Tree of Norse myth and the pillar that upholds the order of the universe. If the home fires flicker too low and Yggdrasil withers, order and harmony will wither too.*

I find this a truly insightful and accurate description (especially from a Saxon nun) of the Viking freewoman's role in Fornburg, Ravensthorpe, and other Norse communities I've visited.

THE THRALL

Slavery is a stain on human history—one very consistent with the dark ethos of the Order of the Ancients. Unfortunately, the abhorrent practice has played a prominent role in the socioeconomic structure of Norse society too. Whether captured in raids or traded in markets, Viking slaves, called thralls, are hauled back in chains and used for hard labor tasks—farm work and construction projects—or sold to wealthy households as domestic help. Eivor tells me she herself and her crew were nearly shipped off in shackles by Wolf Clan captors not long before our arrival!

The Viking invasion forces brought thralls with them to England. But slavery was not new to these territories. Ironically, although Christianity opposes slavery in theory, involuntary servitude has long been common in Christian lands and in Anglo-Saxon society. Thralls have no legal rights, but some manage to save enough money to buy their freedom.

One other sad note: A Viking *bóndi* could, under extreme circumstances—crushing debt or legal jeopardy—renounce his freeman status and sell himself (and sometimes his entire family) into thralldom. Once the indebted pays back what he owes, he (and his family) could be freed once again.

VIKING LAW & JUSTICE

Social order and harmony in Norse society relies heavily on two things: the Viking concept of honor, and the community-wide assembly called the *althing* (mentioned in previous sections). Each Viking community, big or small, holds a regular *althing* to address issues of justice, law, commerce, and more.

CENTRALITY OF HONOR

Norse justice rests on the deeply cherished Viking concept of honor. Honorable behavior is simply that which is truthful and causes no harm to one's family, clan, and people. Whether individual, familial, or even ancestral, honor often determines what is considered "just" in a legal sense. Sometimes called *heiðr* (meaning "brightness"), Viking honor is seen as an observable, almost palpable, quality reflected in the gaze of others—indeed, it is often

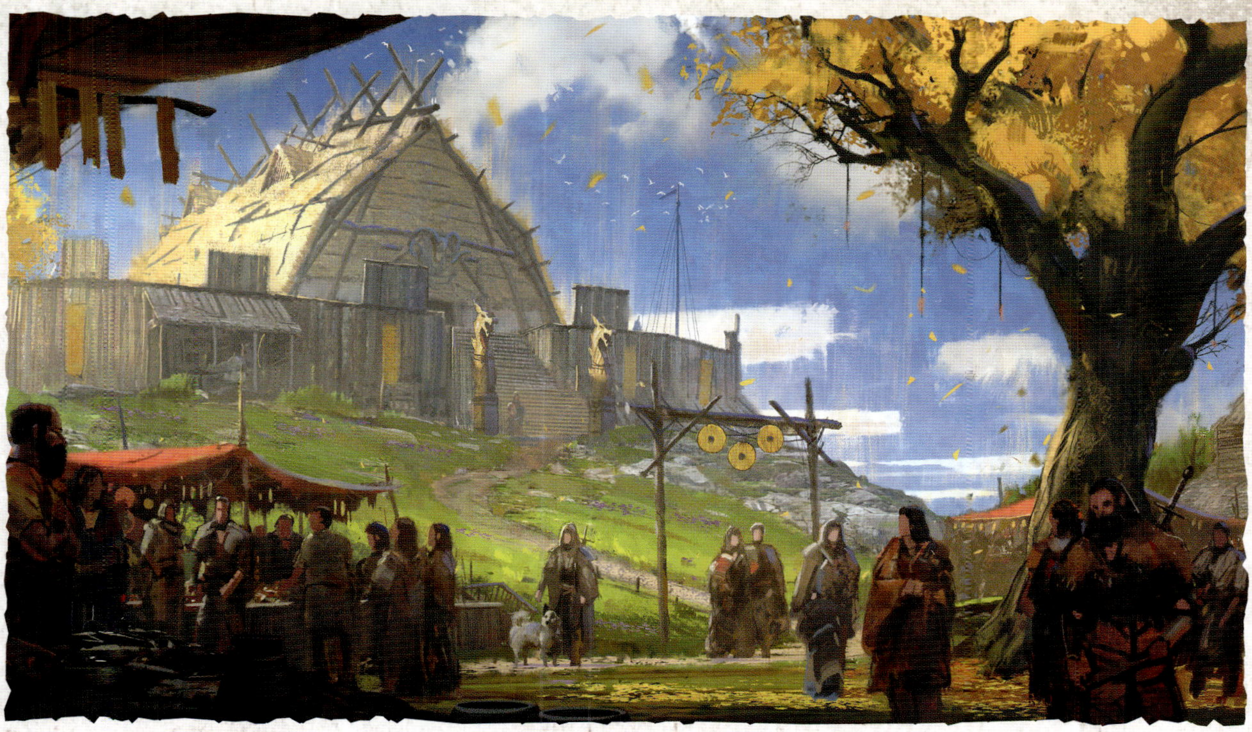

said that one's honor shines. Eivor tells me that an unfortunate offshoot of this notion is the ostentatious display of wealth as citizens seek to visibly "shine." How anyone can equate showing off to honor is beyond me.

FEUDS, VENGEANCE, AND THE *WERGILD*

In Viking society, insulting or harming an individual injures both the person and his family. Thus, a rash act of hostility against someone can bring his entire clan down on your head. For the aggrieved party, the only proper response is to seek retribution, an act seen as not only a vested right but a sacred duty. In the Viking's eyes, anyone who chooses inaction over rightful revenge risks becoming a *niðingr*—a cowardly, shameful individual.

One legal way to restore your honor (or your clan's honor) is to declare a feud. Feuds are monitored by the freemen's assembly to ensure fairness and keep the conflict from getting out of hand. Participants in a feud must pay for any damage caused, including *wergild*—literally, "man price." Each person in society, according to age, gender, and social status, is assigned a monetary value called a *wergild.* This price can be demanded as recompense for injury, loss of reputation, or loss of life. I've since learned that this practice is common among Germanic tribes; I've seen lieges listing elaborate tariffs of compensation.

Out of morbid curiosity I asked Eivor how my own *wergild* might be assessed if I were to be terminated in some illegal fashion. Grinning, she directed me to a *goði* in Repton, a serious fellow named Frode. (He's a bit dour for a Viking.) Frode asked me a few questions about my lineage and associations, consulted a set of scrolls, and then made some mysterious calculations in his head. In the end, Frode determined that my *wergild* was zero. "You have no value to others in your clan," he said.

He added that if I were at least a thrall, I'd be worth something. Eivor found my report on this quite amusing.

THE *GOÐI*, OR LAW KEEPER

Vikings don't have law libraries like those in Rome, Constantinople, or even Lunden. Instead, they have the *goði* . . . remarkable individuals who have committed

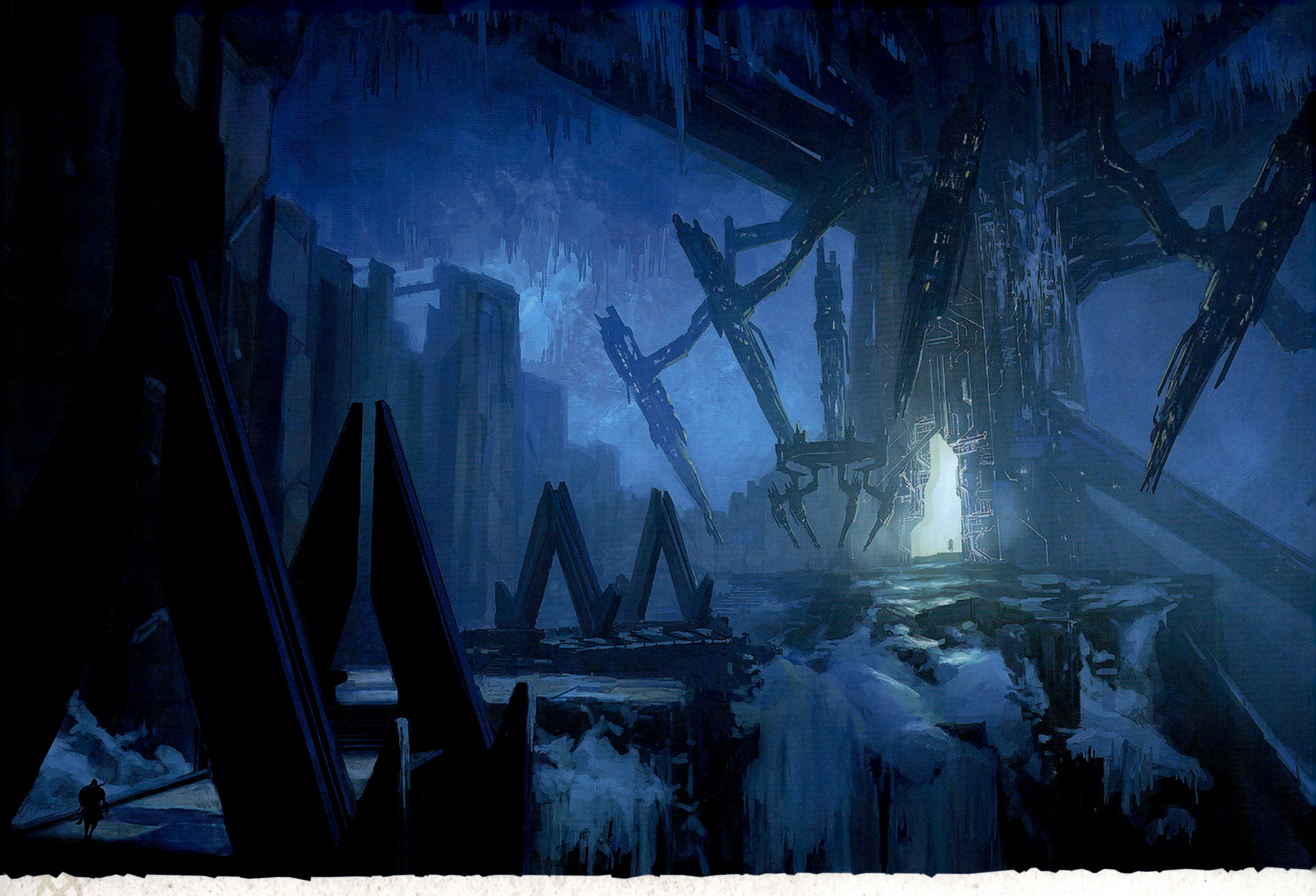

every single local Viking law to their memory. With this skill comes great social and political influence, as you might imagine. The *goði*'s unique knowledge requires that they help preside at every *althing*, the assembly where the community's freemen make decisions on trade, war, local disputes, succession, and politics.

The very title *goði*—or "god"—might imply that the law keeper also serves a religious role. While Vikings do not have clerics like Christians, they believe that the *goði* serve the gods by knowing the law. Why? Law is considered an instrument of order. Just as the gods bestowed order and harmony to the universe, so the *goði*'s knowledge of law helps to keep the peace in his community.

THE HORROR OF EXILE

Death is not the worst punishment for Vikings. Remember, Norse life is deeply family oriented and fundamentally communal. Thus, my Raven Clan friends tell me that no fate is more dire than to be judged an outlaw, or *utlagr*, and thus exiled from your community. Banishment means not only leaving the settlement but also having no further contact with family or clan . . . and Vikings believe this means separation even from your ancestors. Without land, clan, or ancestors, an outlaw is considered no more than a beast—hence, it is legal to hunt him!

VIKING BELIEFS & CUSTOMS

During my years in Ravensthorpe, I've been consistently impressed by the depth of Norse engagement with what I'll call the "mysteries of existence." Vikings are not strictly religious in the same formal sense as Christian or Muslim cultures. Although most Norse folk believe in fate and destiny, gods, spirits, realms of the dead, ancestor worship, rune

An artistic depiction of Mimisbrunnr, the mythical well in which Mimir's severed head rests. The well itself is said to be found among the roots of Yggdrasil, the World Tree.

magic, dream interpretation, and more, they have no clergy—that is, no elite cadre or institution interpreting a holy scripture or presiding over religious rituals. Some public events are led by a community's chief, or jarl. But a remarkably wide variety of citizens can officiate most Norse ceremonies.

THE VIKING "SELF": *HAMINGJA, FYLGJA, HAMR,* AND *HUGR*

Norse culture holds that spirits inhabit every person. Four different types of entities dwell within and form the Self. One is the *hamingja*, the great spirit of destiny in every family. (I mentioned this entity earlier.) Another is the *fylgja*, a sort of guardian angel who appears in dreams or trances (often as an animal) to personally guide you. Both of these totemic spirits, *hamingja* and *fylgja*, are said to pass on to your descendants.

The other two spirits belong only to you. The *hamr* is the outer Self, one's physical form—the shape or shell of a person. Basically, it's your body, the part of you perceived by others. (One Norse superstition is that "shapeshifters" can alter their *hamr* to deceive and bedevil victims.) The *hugr*, on the other hand, is the inner Self—the deep, essential nature of

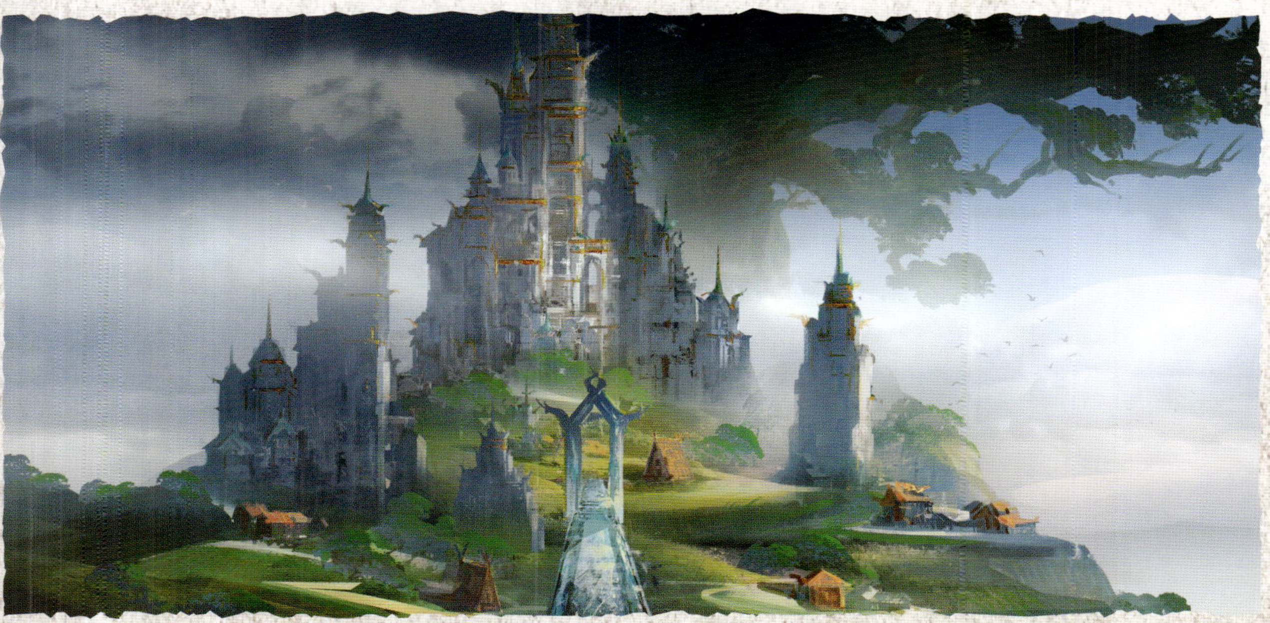

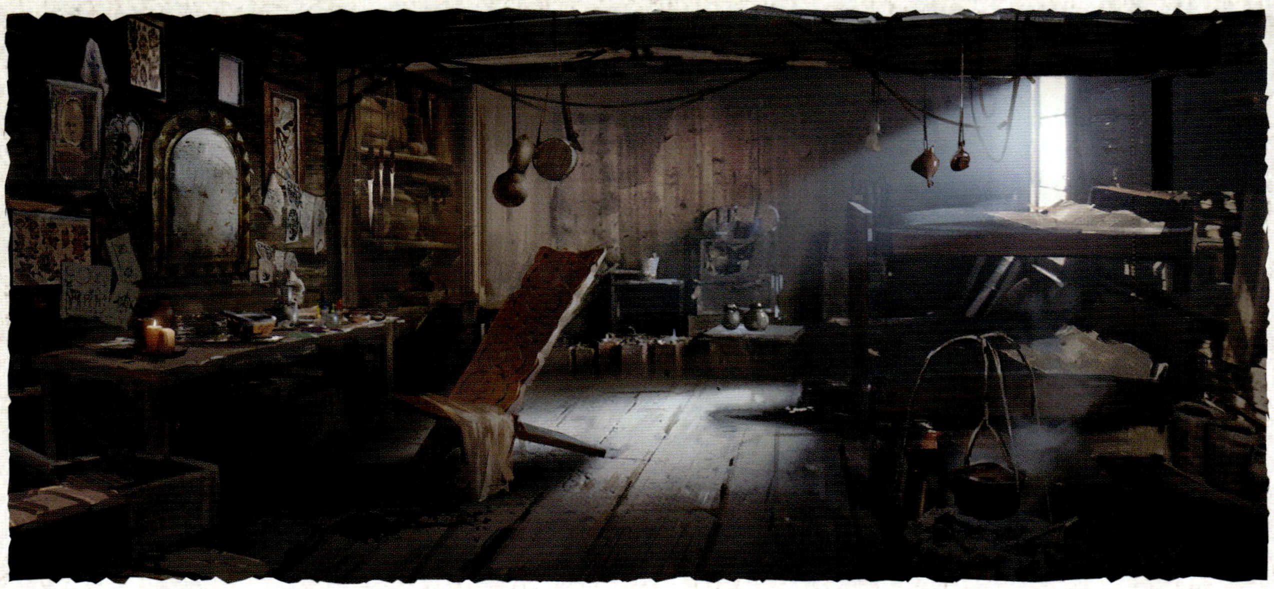

one's being. It's your personality, the way you think, your truest wishes and desires.

Authentic Vikings try to express their *hugr* via their *hamr*—that is, they seek to act and look the way they truly feel inside. This effort is why clothing, hair, body art, and other accessories carry so much import in Viking culture. They reveal one's inner spirit. Vikings want you to see who they are in a glance! An adventurous, sea-loving sailor might sport a face tattoo of the Viking runic compass, symbol of divine guidance on the waters. Or a skald might wear a cloak brooch or belt buckle engraved with Odin's three-horned triskelion, symbol of poetic inspiration.

INESCAPABLE FATE

The Norse consider fate to be the most powerful force in the cosmos. It's a magical energy flowing from Yggdrasil, the tree of life, binding all things together and propelling them unstoppably through time and space. The skalds portray fate as unyielding, uncompromising: "No man nor monster can stand against it." Not even the gods themselves can alter fate! Viking lore sees fate driving the universe toward a final, cataclysmic battle, one that will trigger the destruction of everything. This apocalypse called Ragnarök is the inescapable destiny of the Nine Realms.

RUNES AND RUNESTONES

Runes make up the futhark, the Norse runic alphabet. (Note: The word *futhark* itself comes from the sounds of the first six letters of runic script: *f, u, th, a, r,* and *k*.) In Norse culture, runes also function as symbols latent with *seiðr* magic. In fact, the Norse term *rún* means "secret or esoteric knowledge." In other words, when certain runes are engraved on a

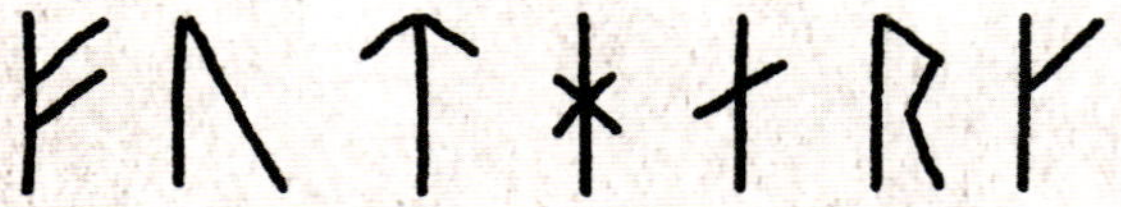

stone, you can create an object that carries special meaning and power. These runestones tell stories and honor people or events. Families commission runestones to commemorate lost loved ones. Vikings also believe that certain runestones can bestow elemental power on weapons, shields, armor, and even on warriors themselves.

THE *VÖLVA*

Special seers called *völvur*—usually women, but not always—are renowned in Viking society for their mastery of divination skills. Using oracular techniques passed down for generations, a *völva* is said to pierce the fabric of time, soothsaying the future using *seiðr* magic. She also concocts potions from

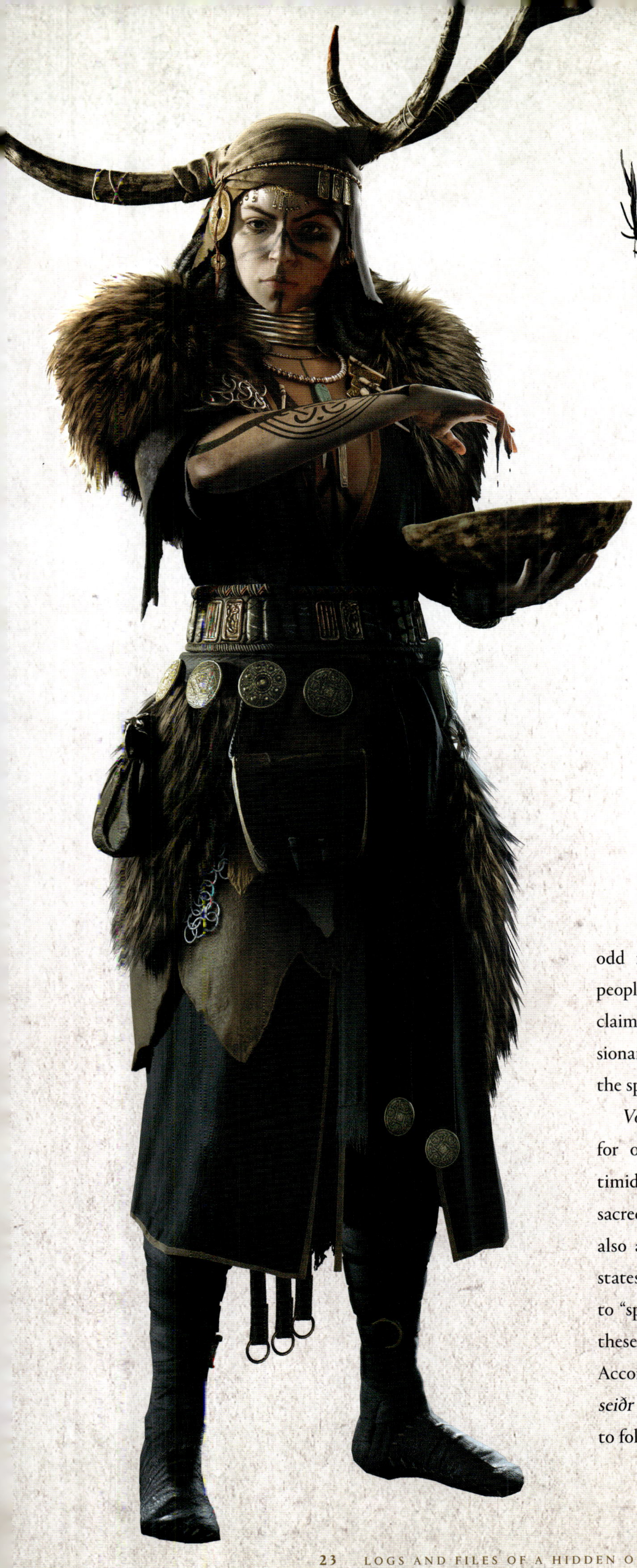

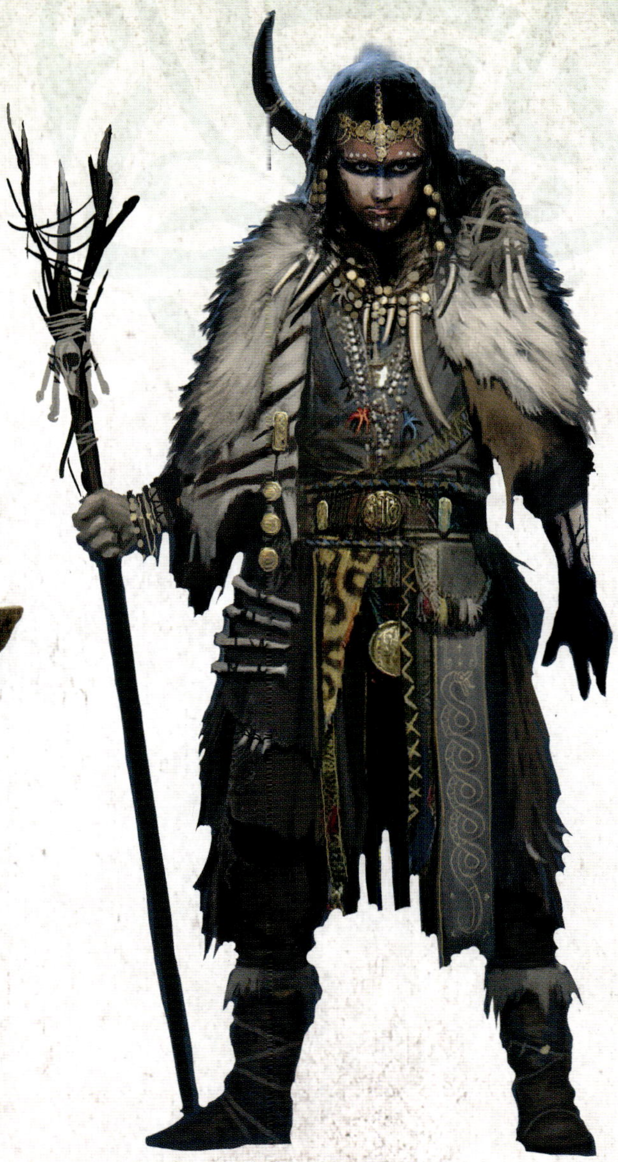

odd ingredients that, when consumed, transport people to "mystical realms." Frankly, I find these claims a bit fantastical, but Eivor swears by her visionary interactions with Valka, the *völva* serving the spiritual needs of the Raven Clan community.

Völvur typically live on the fringes of society, for obvious reasons—their powers are clearly intimidating. An experienced seer, it is said, can read sacred runes and tap their inscrutable powers. She also achieves insight by attaining ritual trancelike states. These often involve a staff used like a spindle to "spin the threads of fate." Once spun, apparently, these threads can be read and somehow understood. According to Viking lore, the first seer to practice *seiðr* was the Norse goddess Freyja. Good footsteps to follow in, if you believe in such things as gods.

The Viking Economy

FISHING

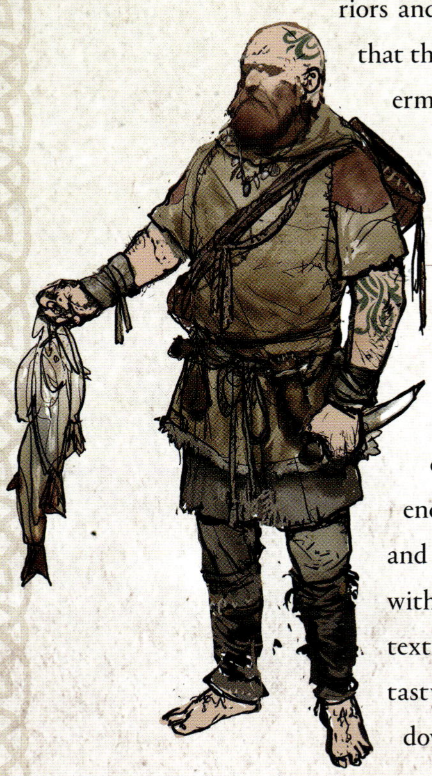

While it is true that the Norse are renowned warriors and merchants, it should be noted that they are first and foremost . . . fishermen! Indeed, most of a Viking's food comes from the sea. Dried fish is a primary staple of the Norse diet. To dry a fish, one simply attaches the catch (usually cod or haddock in the northlands) to a wooden rack. Then you let the sun and open air do their work. By the end of the week, the fish is dried and ready to eat. Usually mixed with butter for a more consumable texture, dried fish is surprisingly tasty . . . especially when washed down with a mug of mead.

FARMING

My travels in England reveal that Norse settlers are clearly flourishing here, boosted by a sharp rise in agricultural production due to the island's abundant and fertile soils. Tilling land alongside their Anglo-Saxon neighbors, Viking farmers raise livestock and cultivate cereal grains—barley for brewing beer, rye and wheat for coarse bread flours, and oats to feed their animals. Their cattle provide milk and meat, and their oxen plow the fields. Norse farms also grow legumes and herbs like dill and coriander for spice and seasoning, as well as flax and hemp to produce textiles for clothing and trading.

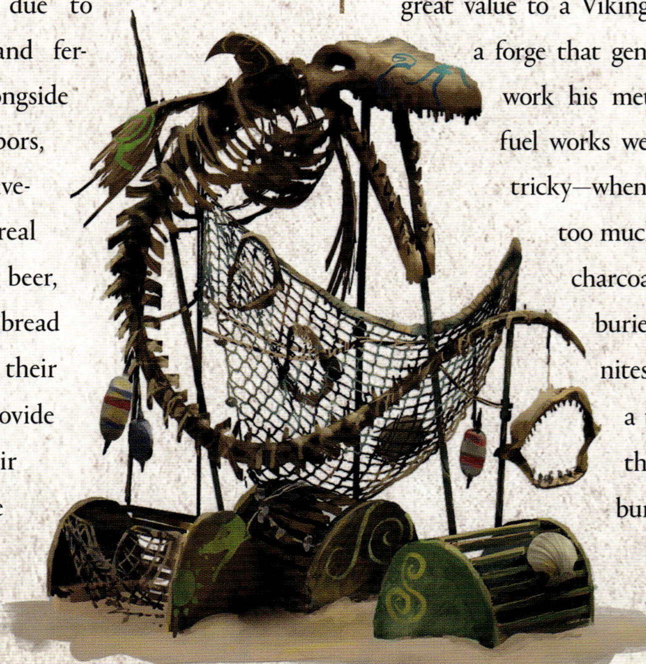

HONEY AND MEAD

Honey is valued by Norsemen as a sweetening agent in cooking and dining . . . but, more importantly, as a key ingredient in the production of mead, a drink brewed from water, honey, and yeast. Indeed, beehives are ubiquitous near Viking villages, often placed in fields of flaxseeds, poppies, and heather. Some call mead the oldest alcoholic beverage known to man, having gone by various names throughout history, such as ambrosia, nectar, and honey wine. One thing is certain: Vikings love their mead. No feast would be without it!

Here's an interesting tidbit of Viking culture—the term *honeymoon* refers to the Norse practice of giving newlyweds all the mead they want for a full moon cycle (roughly a month) after the wedding!

THE FORGE

A good blacksmith like Gunnar in Ravensthorpe brings great value to a Viking settlement. The smith needs a forge that generates extremely high heat to work his metals. Using wood charcoal as fuel works well, but prepping wood can be tricky—when burning wood is exposed to too much air, it turns to ash instead of charcoal. To prevent this, the smith buries the wood in a deep hole, ignites it, then covers his fire pit with a thick layer of turf, cutting off the air. This way, the wood can burn slowly and char for many hours before being extracted as lump charcoal and dumped in the forge.

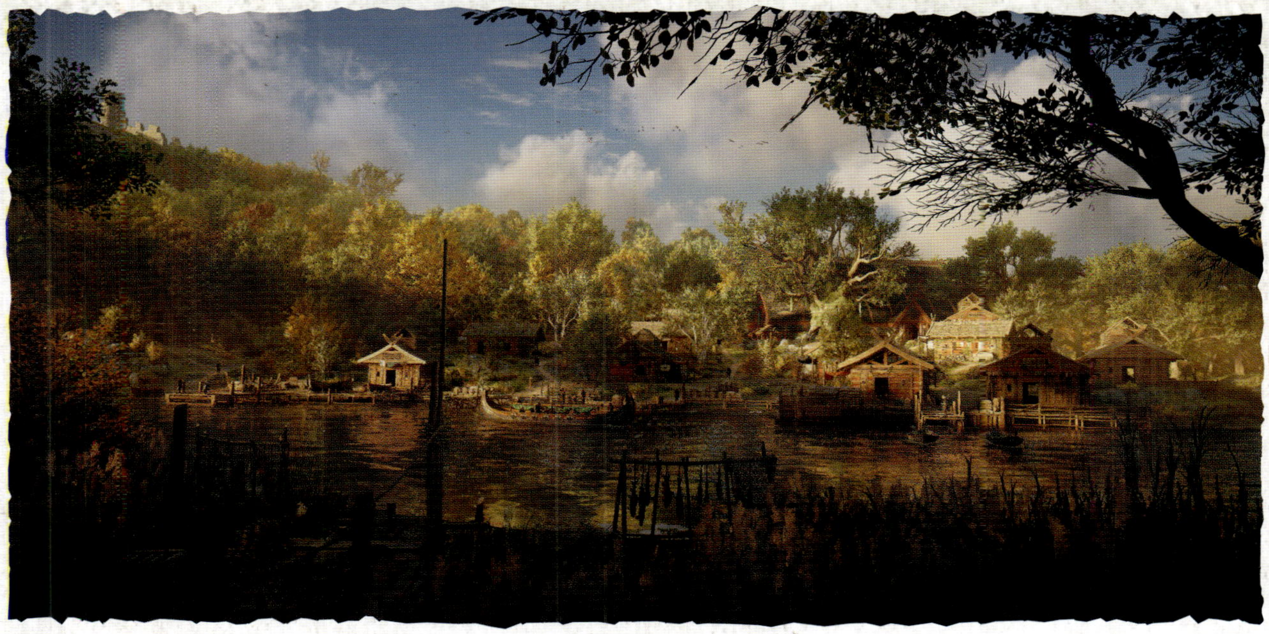

BARTER AND COINS

Bartering was the basis of the Norse exchange of goods for many generations. A trader might negotiate how many chickens is a fair trade for a bolt of wadmal wool. But as Norse traders moved further across Europe to the Middle East, coinage began to emerge as a favored tool of economic exchange. Minting precious metals into coins is a system of trade that can easily quantify the equivalent value of goods. It's also much easier to haul off a good bribe or ransom paid in coins than, say, a large herd of goats.

These days, Vikings are quite fond of their "hacksilver." When Vikings acquire silver items, they chop (hack) them up. These silver hacks are more transportable and easier to use in value-weighted transactions. Hacked-up silver can also be melted and molded into bullion, another favored currency.

THE DAILY LIFE OF A VIKING

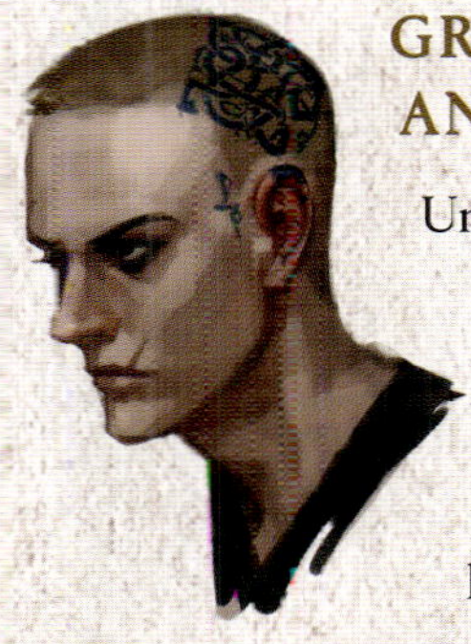

GROOMING AND HYGIENE

Unlike the hairy, wild-eyed brutes portrayed in Church chronicles, Norse men and women take great pride in their appearance, bathing regularly and anointing themselves with fragrant natural scents. Women tend carefully to their hair, braiding and intricately styling their long locks. Men trim and tidy their facial hair using truly exquisite combs, finely crafted from wood, metal, and bone. I swear these beard combs are works of art!

Sometimes, male warriors even braid their beards and adorn them with beads. After all, one's look at a feast or on a battlefield is important. As you might expect, more rigorous standards for personal grooming are favored by people of high social status with more time and coin to spend on their appearance. This social phenomenon seems consistent across every culture I've ever visited.

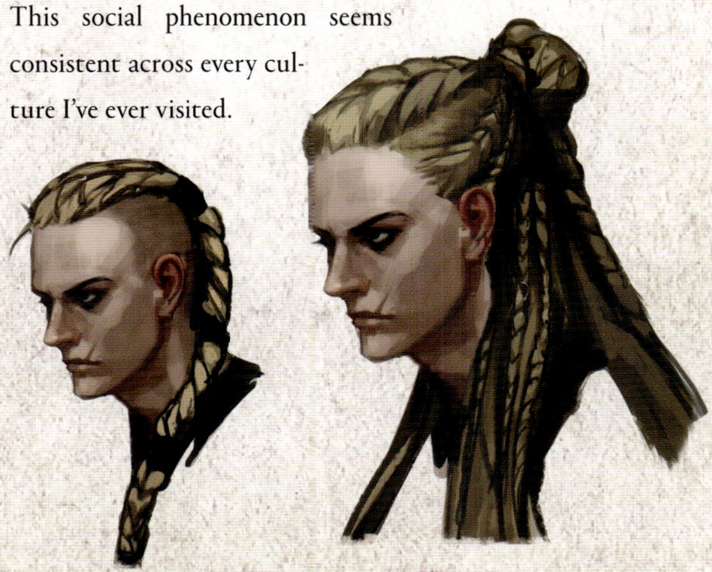

FASHION

Like personal grooming, fashion can be a way for Norse folk to showcase their wealth and social status. Deep, richly colored fabrics indicate that the material has been dyed more than once. Since dyeing is expensive, wearing such hues of clothing is a sure sign of success. (Blue fabrics are particularly painstaking and expensive to produce, and thus worn only by the very wealthy.) Jewelry is a sign of social status too. Colorful glass or stone beads are prized fashion accessories. While silver is not cheap, gold settings are far more expensive, and thus another indicator of great wealth and standing.

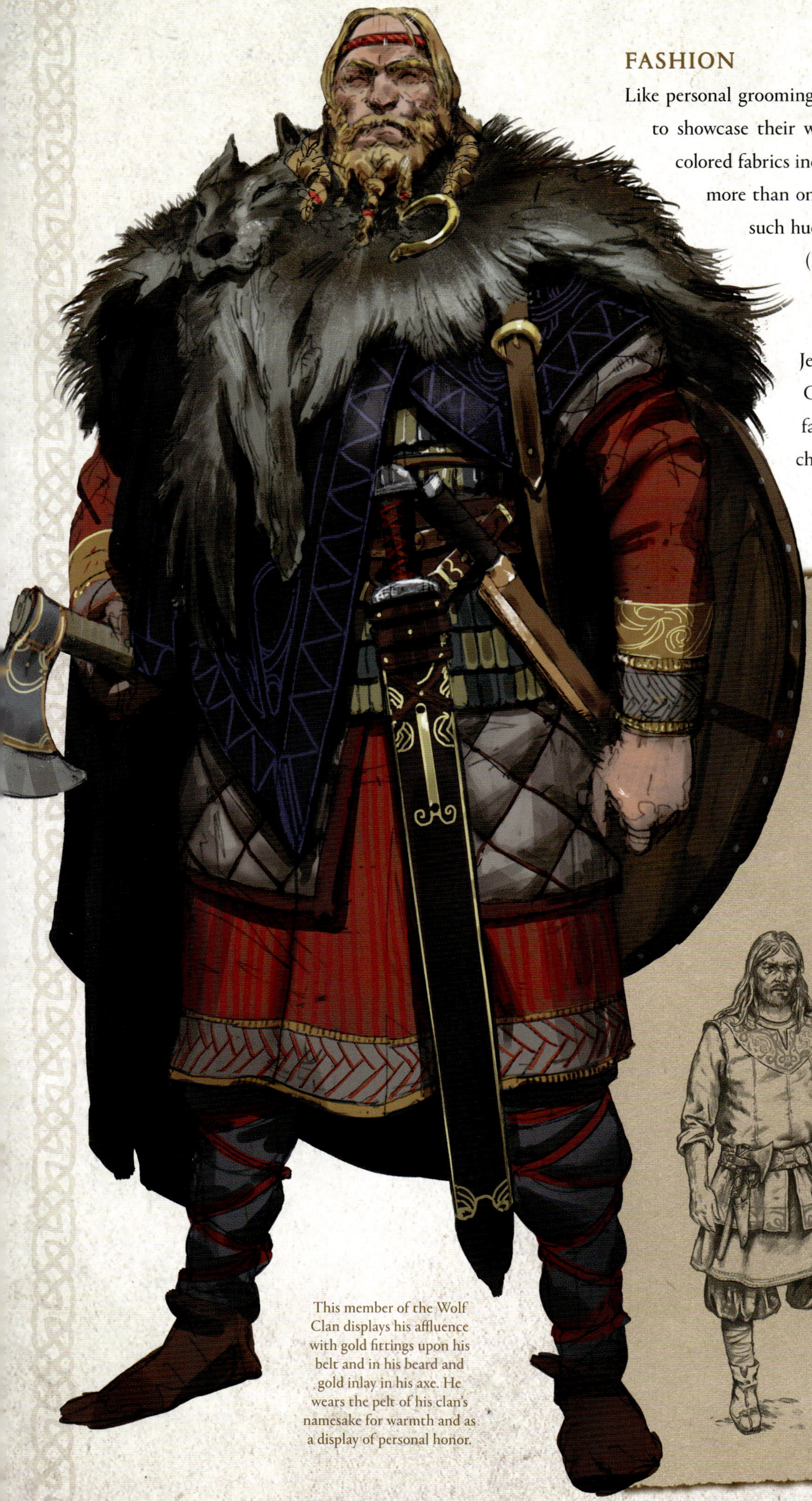

This member of the Wolf Clan displays his affluence with gold fittings upon his belt and in his beard and gold inlay in his axe. He wears the pelt of his clan's namesake for warmth and as a display of personal honor.

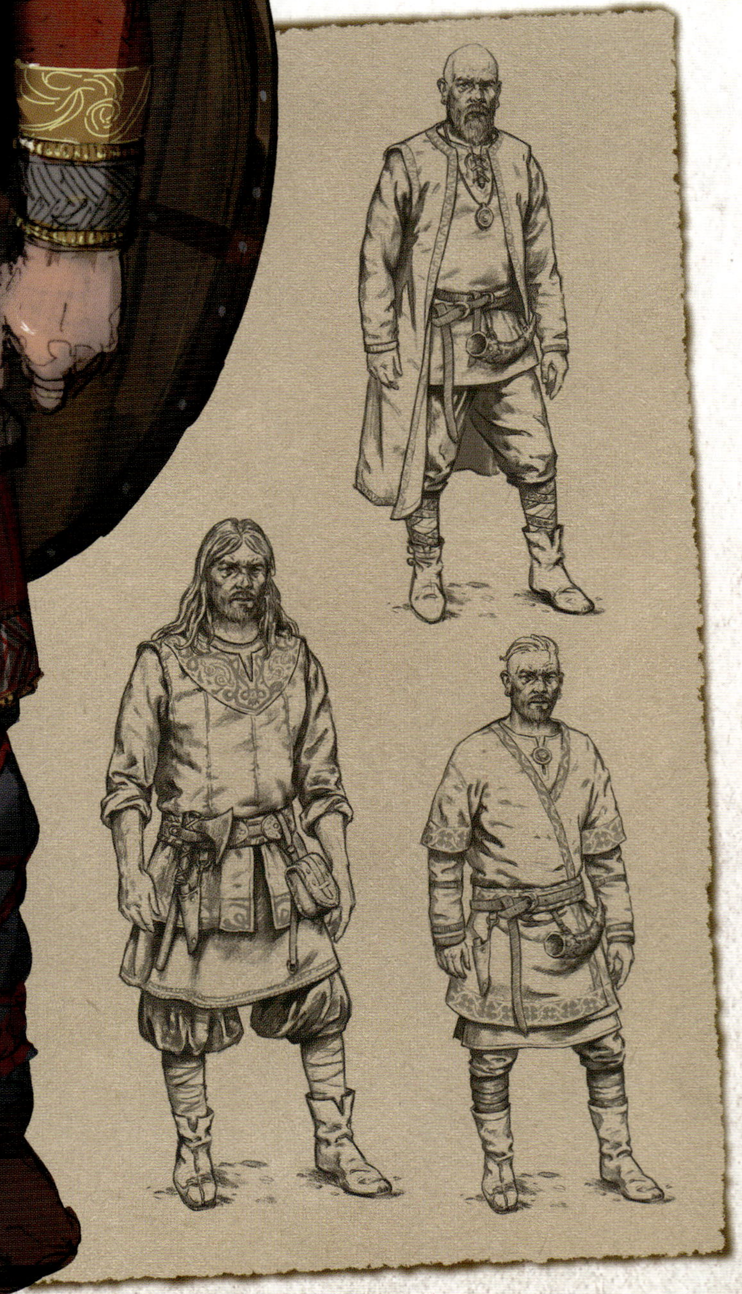

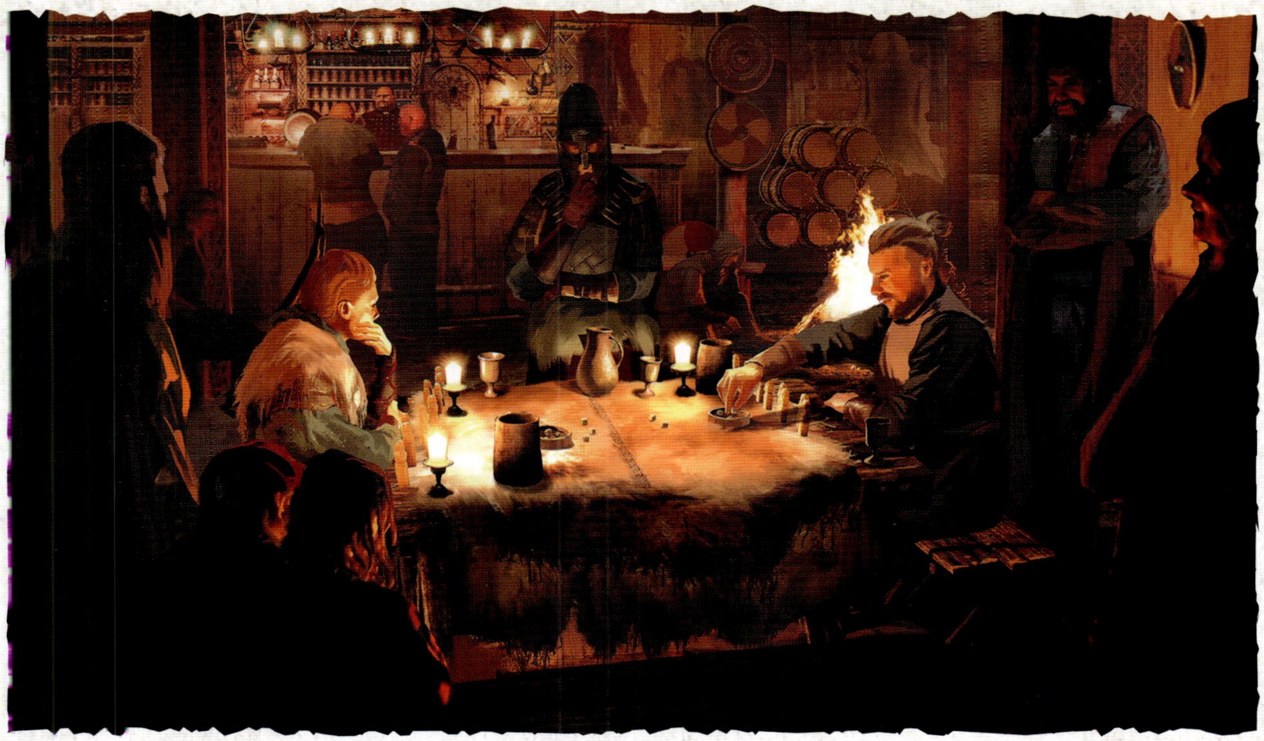

To be perfectly honest, I find much of the status-seeking behavior I encounter in the world to be superfluous and silly . . . as does Eivor, I'm happy to say. Fortunately, I've found very little of it in Ravensthorpe. The Raven Clan seems like a well-grounded tribe of kinfolk.

GAMES AND SPORT

Vikings are generally a robust, healthy people who enjoy various games and activities in their free time. I find their pastimes to be invigorating and quite challenging, both physically and mentally—a chance to hone one's tactical cunning, mental fitness, and physical strength. Ever since my grievous injury at Kjotve's hands, I've become a somewhat less vigorous participant in the athletic sports, but I continue to enjoy the games of wit and strategy.

Norse board games are often strategy contests. One called *hnefatafl* is played on a latticed 13 x 13 game board. One player controls a king and his guard detail; this group must survive the attack of the other player's pieces placed around the four sides of the board. The game pieces themselves are quite striking, made of bone or walrus ivory.

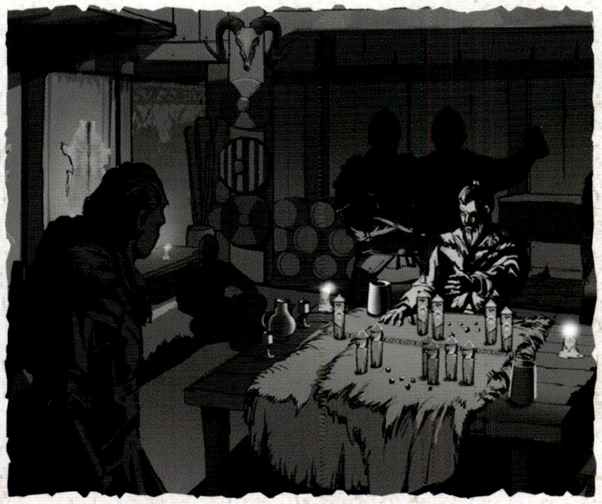

Viking outdoor sports are quite competitive and demanding, requiring strength, endurance, and agility. Back in mountainous Rygjafylke, many Norse folk would fasten long, narrow boards to their feet and race downhill in the snow—as strange a sport as I've ever seen. Another activity is a form of wrestling called *glima* where nearly any hold is legal! Both men and women participate. Each wrestler struggles to pin their opponent to the ground using sudden, unexpected moves. (*Glima* is a Norse word that means "glimpse" or "flash.") Participants take the sport very seriously, seeing it as a form of martial training for combat.

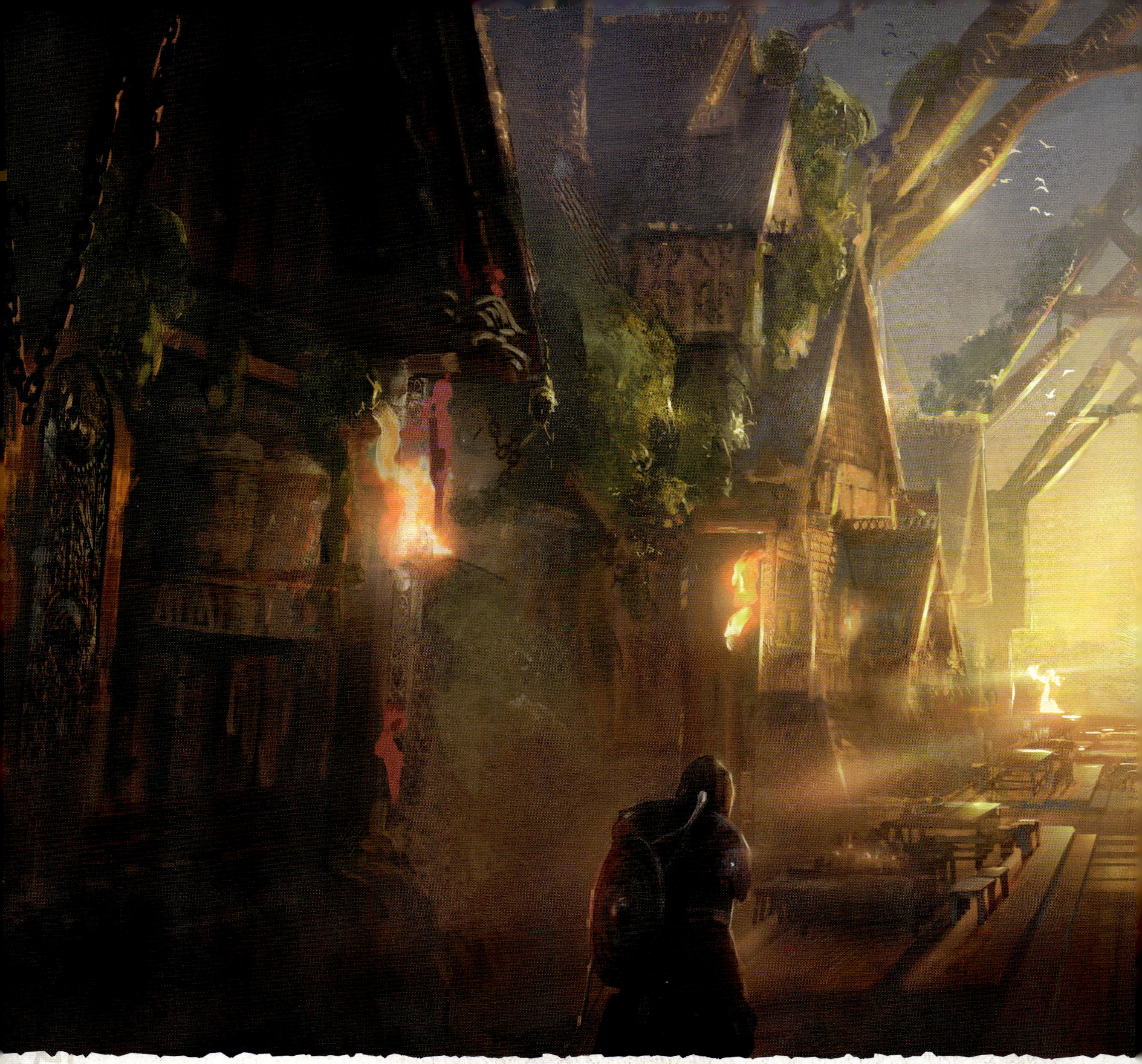

SKALDIC POETRY

I will say this about Viking sea voyages. The long hours could be filled with intolerable boredom if not for the crew's exceptional skalds. A skald is a mixture of poet, musician, teacher, and historian, all in one package. Indeed, a gifted skald is one of the most highly valued members of Viking society, a teller of tales that memorialize his clan. Skalds compose poems full of clever kenning metaphors—whale-path (sea), feather-fall (snow), spear-din or shield-thunder (battle), blood-ember (axe), ravens-meal (corpse)—that celebrate glory, mourn tragedy, and reveal deep truths about Viking values.

On our monthlong voyage from Constantinople, Skald Bragi's stories and sea chanteys were some of the most entertaining and poignant I'd ever heard. One favorite was the battle of Hǫgni and Heðinn, a tale Bragi first heard in the court of Ragnar Lothbrok. Heðinn, a Viking prince, had kidnapped the daughter of Hǫgni, a powerful Viking jarl.

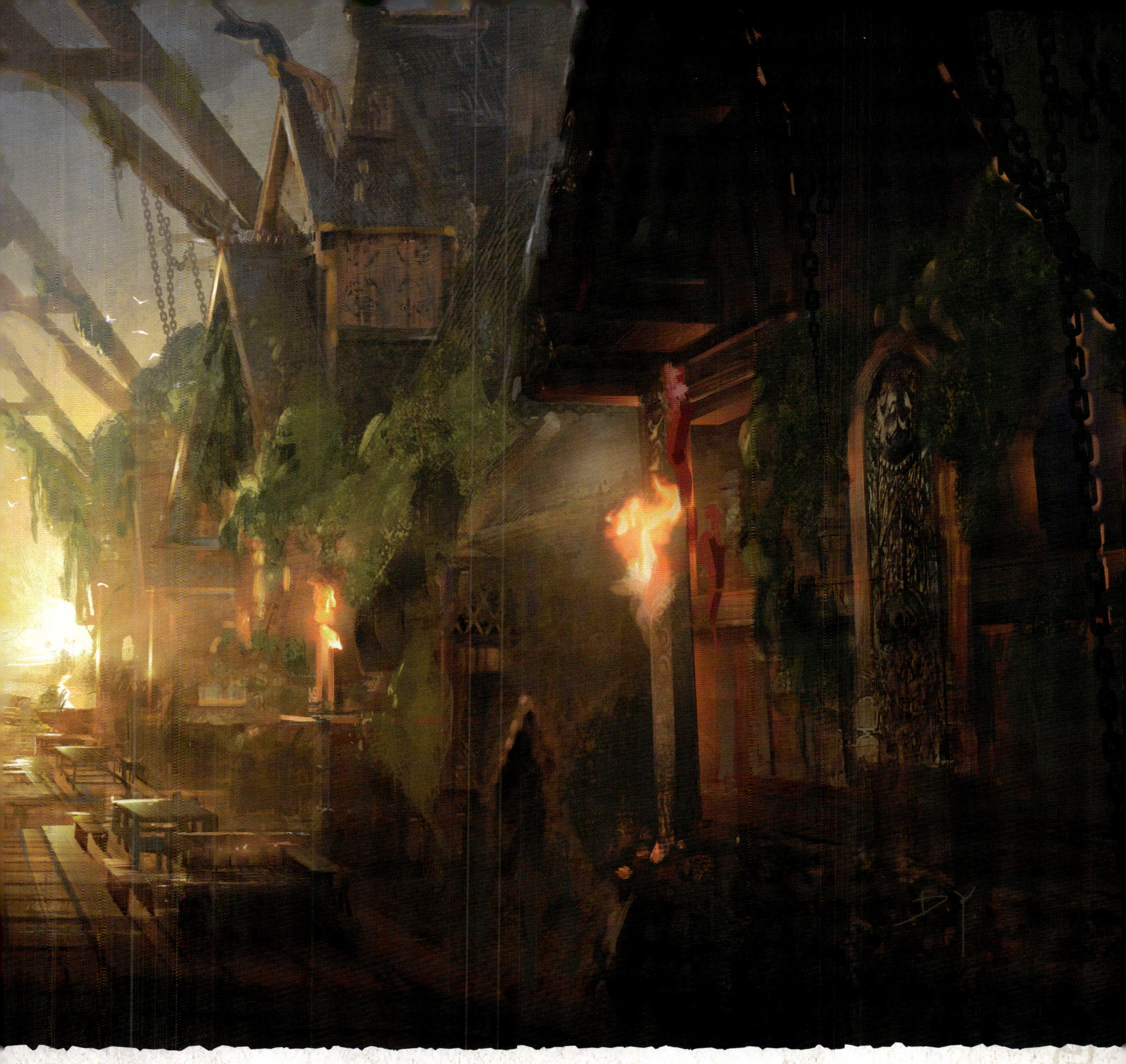

When Hǫgni tracked her down, Heðinn sent out his army to fight, and many warriors were slain on both sides. That night, Hǫgni's daughter, Hildr—who'd secretly married her captor—snuck onto the battlefield and recited *seiðr* incantations to resurrect all the fallen fighters, hoping to end the hostilities. But the next day, the warriors simply rose and fought again!

This was repeated day after day, with the bloody feud fated to replay itself until the dawn of Ragnarök.

The tale and the joyous nature of Bragi's telling reveal the Viking spirit, recalling the legend of Valhalla—a place where battles never end, where the fallen are revived again and again for the next glorious clash. I also found Bragi's kennings striking—battle is the "steel-eddy"; warriors are "battle-wolves" with "corpse-dew" dripping from "dark-hewn paths." My favorite image posited a warrior's bed during nightmares as his "floor-steed." Such a marvelous metaphor!

VIKINGS: A SEAFARING PEOPLE

Basim and I both agree that Viking culture is in a rising phase of regional dominance that may last decades, if not centuries. History shows us how maritime prowess is so often predictive of rapid economic growth and the spread of culture. In northern Europe, there is no greater sailor than the Norseman, and no trader with greater range and network than the Norse merchant. Then again, nothing is feared more than the approach of a square-sailed fleet of Viking longboats adorned with monsters on the prow.

"SEA LORE" NAVIGATION

Anyone can learn to sail a boat—indeed, in a Viking settlement, the more sailing knowledge shared by all, the better. But every Norse crew has at least one member who is particularly skilled at navigation. This person guides the expedition and ensures safe passage to the destination. The Norse term for the navigator is *leiðsögumaðr*—the human (*maðr*) gifted with knowledge of the overall route (*leiðsaga*), who knows which path (*leið*) is the fastest or least risky.

I've had the great pleasure of meeting one of these legendary seafarers. Ohthere of Hålogaland just may be the hairiest human I've ever met. According to Eivor, Ohthere's fabled knowledge of northern sea routes is locked tight inside his head . . . and he has much to teach both the Christian and Islamic worlds about navigation! Like all Norse navigators, Ohthere rarely relies on physical objects such as sunstones to plot a course. Rather, he draws on ancestral tradition and personal experience to hone his seafaring skills.

With no compasses or detailed nautical maps for guidance, a Viking navigator needs an unerring knowledge of the seascape—a knowledge referred to as "sea lore." One way to acquire such lore is a comprehensive familiarity with oral tradition. Ohthere follows sailing routes discovered decades, even centuries, ago. This sea lore is passed down by word of mouth from generation to generation, relearned and memorized and mastered via on-the-water experience. After navigating hundreds of open sea journeys, Ohthere has gained an unmatched feel for guiding a keeled boat through different currents and weather patterns, noting wind flow, the color of the sea, the shape and movement of waves. His mastery is extraordinary . . . and he's actively passing his sea lore along to eager young sailors.

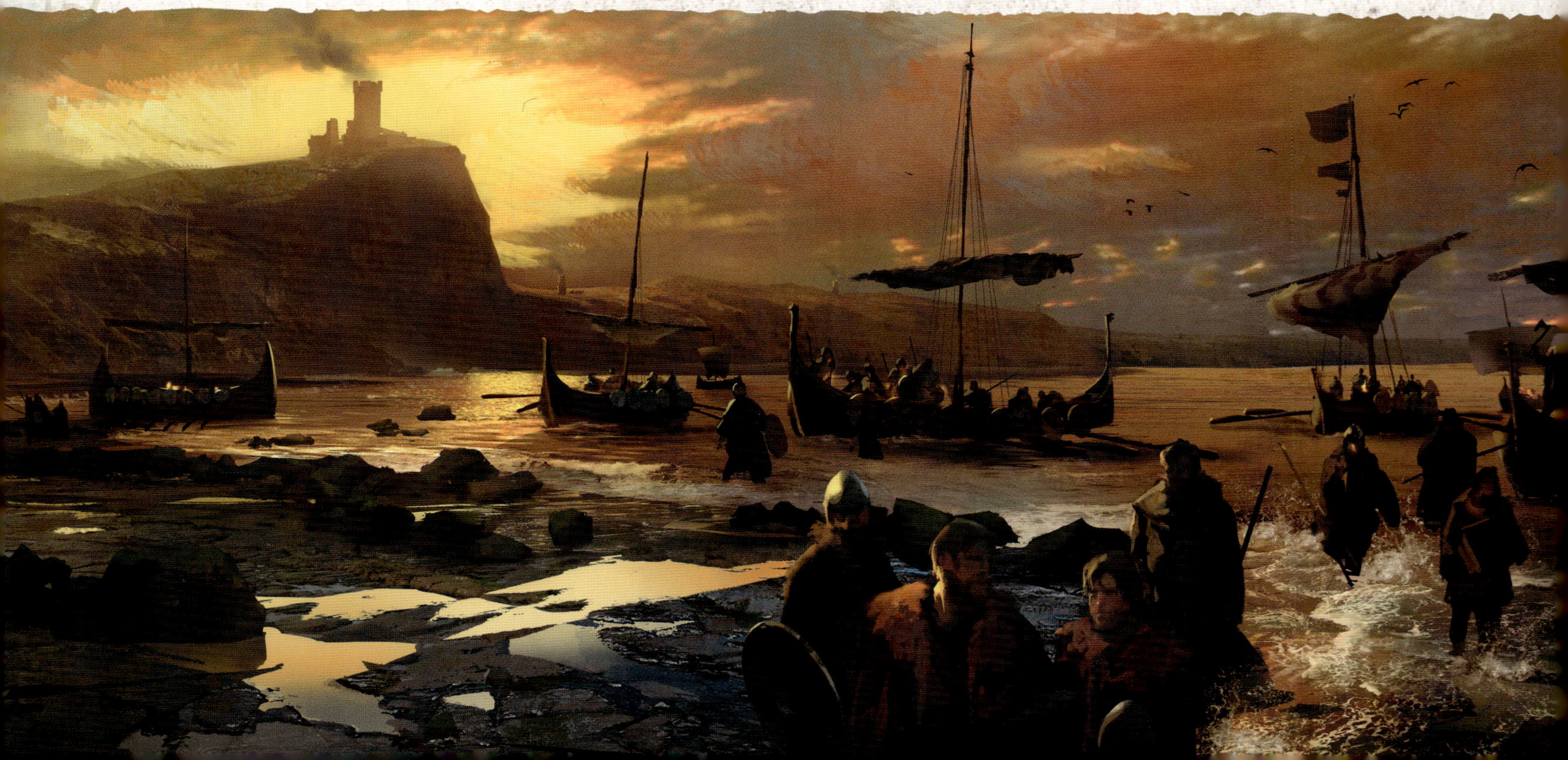

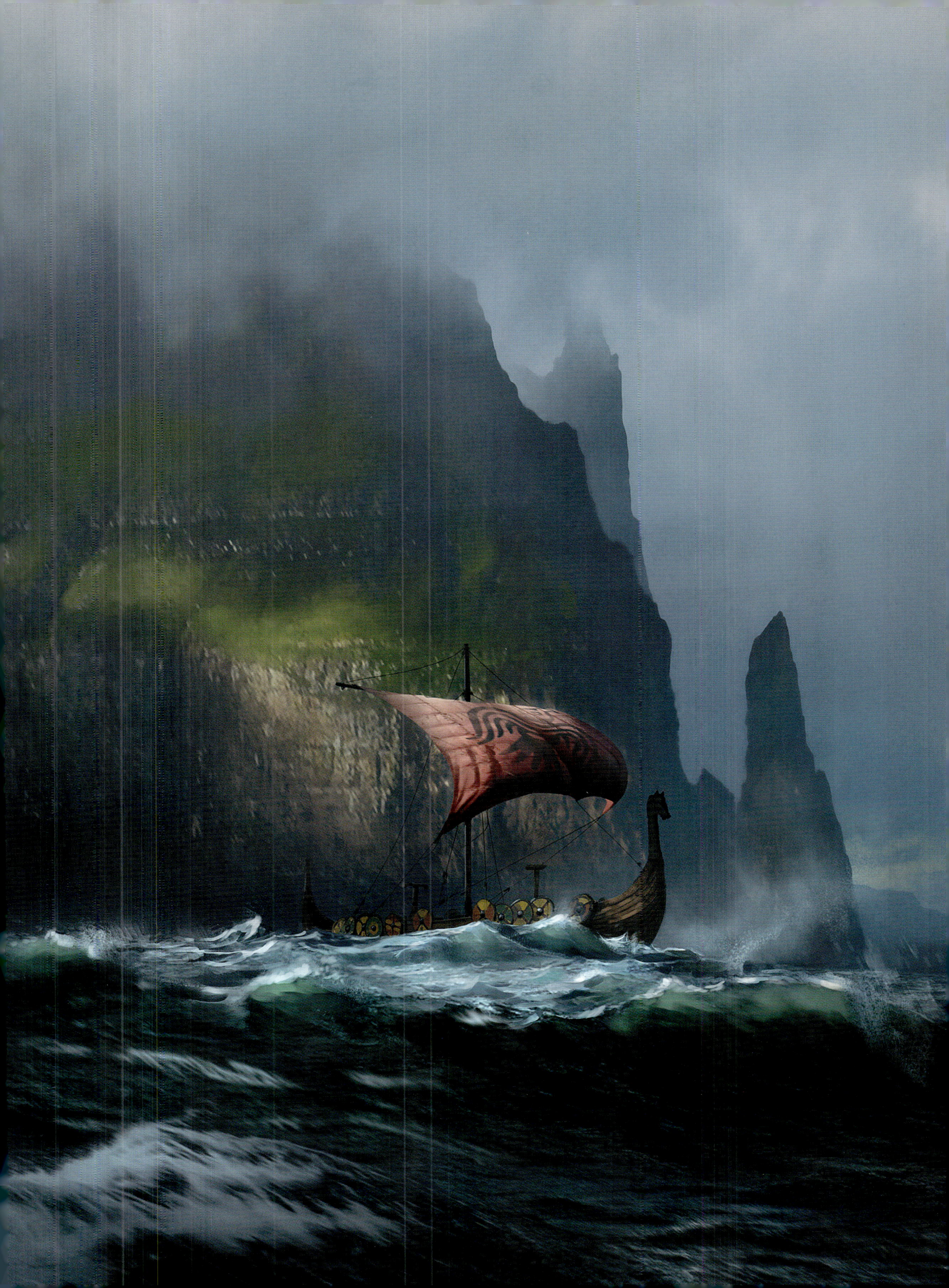

THE VIKING LONGSHIP

The fearsome Viking longship, signature vessel of the northern fleet, has served as the relentless "sea-steed" of Norse commercial expansion and social influence across Europe. Viking shipwrights, renowned for their world-class skill, combine a deep understanding of nautical design with a keen sense of craftsmanship. They typically work with a construction crew of eight to ten builders.

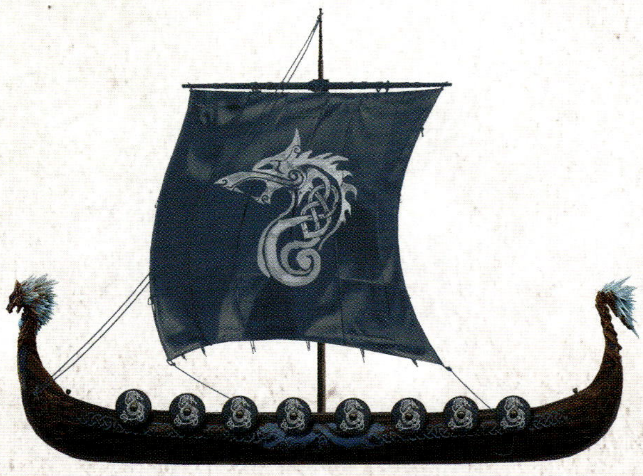

THE BOAT-BUILDING PROCESS

A true technical marvel, the Viking longship features long, narrow shallow-draft hulls that provide good speed and impressive stability in rough waters. The longship's short keel depth is well suited for upriver travel, navigating waters as shallow as one meter deep, perfect for easy beach landings. It also sports cleverly jointed mainmasts that lower to pass under bridges.

HULL AND KEEL. To build a longship, the shipwright first fashions the hull using hardwood lumber for solidity. The wood is carefully split by axe along the grain to make the boards flexible. Each hull is "clinker" built—that is, its timber planks overlap each other like fish scales. These boards are then nailed together with metal rivets and caulked with hemp and horsehair soaked in tar or tallow so water won't soak through the hull. After the hull is set, the wright adds a short keel—the backbone of the ship. A single rudder in the stern suffices for steering.

MAST. Next, the wright and his team fashion the single mast. Longship masts are made from softer wood, which allows for not only suppleness but good height too. The mast is attached to the hull using a fish-shaped piece of wood so the sail doesn't resist wind along the mast's length but rather moves with it. This flexibility, coupled with that of the ship's hull, makes the longship truly "elastic." As Gudrun, one of Ravensthorpe's master shipwrights, explained to me recently: "Rather than split the waves, my boats slither through them like an eel."

SAIL. The square felted sail is a signature feature of the Viking boat. Produced by the clan's best seamstresses, these sails are spun and sewn from a coarse, dense wool called wadmal. Wadmal sailcloth is more waterproof and resistant to tearing than other materials. Leather strips crisscrossing the sail also help it keep its shape when wet.

I'm told that felted sails are a relatively recent addition to longships; just a few generations ago, Norse sailors relied entirely on oars for maritime locomotion. Today, good oarsmen are still highly valued in a longship crew, but sails are a standard feature on every boat. One reason: As Norse land wealth has increased, bigger flocks of sheep are grazing ever larger pastures, and thus much more wadmal wool is available for sail making.

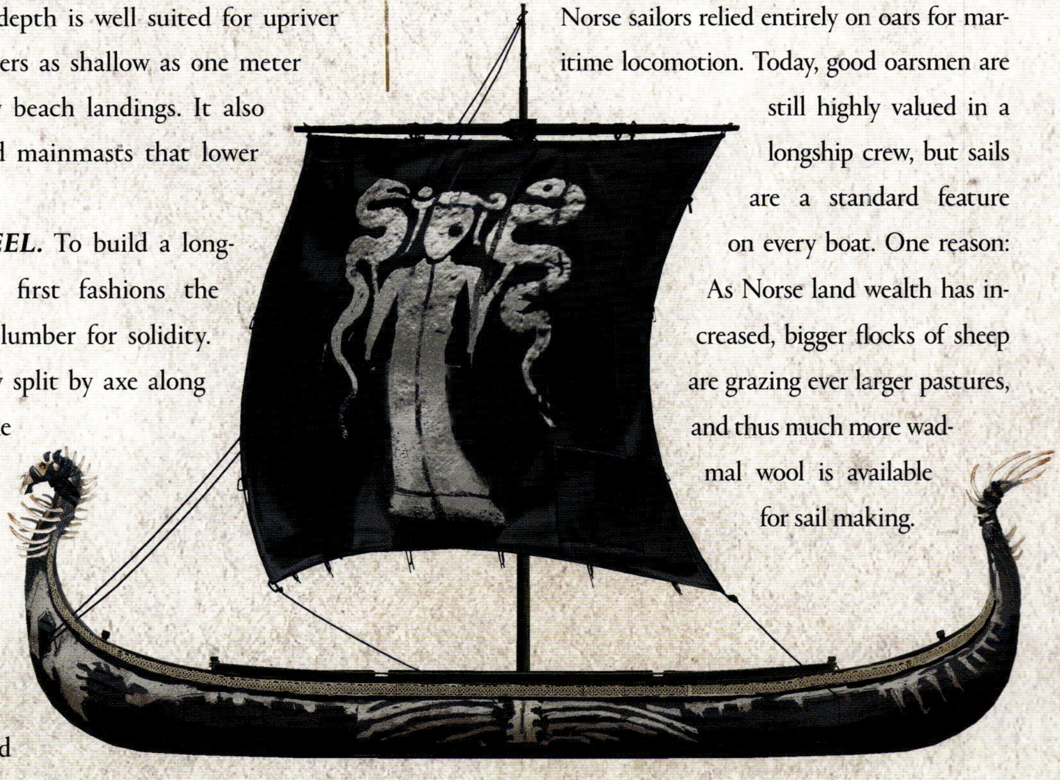

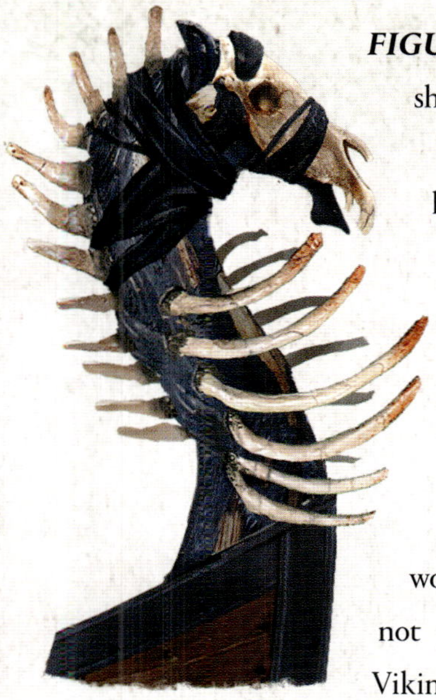

FIGUREHEAD. All Viking ships are renowned for their fearsome figureheads. Mounted at the prow, the carved heads (usually of dragons, monsters, or wild animals) are meticulously sculpted from a single piece of wood. These carvings are not just purely decorative. Vikings believe that hostile shores are guarded by protective spirits called *landvættir.* Longship mastheads are designed to intimidate or scare away such spirits. Conversely, when visiting a friendly territory, Vikings remove threatening mastheads to avoid offending or frightening their hosts!

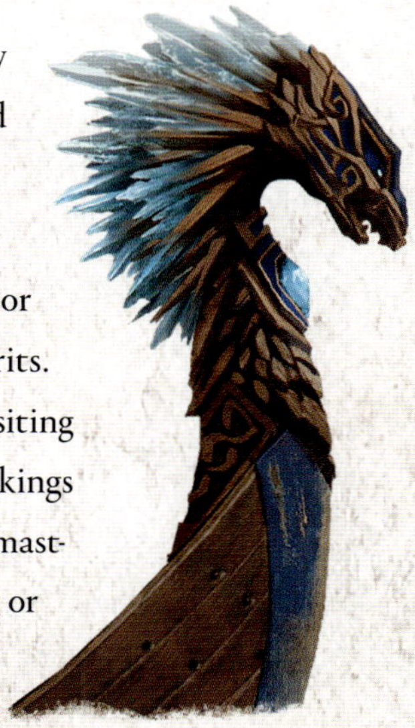

FIRST LAUNCH: "BLOODING THE KEEL"

Construction of a longship requires many months of intensive labor. Thus, the initial launch of a newly finished vessel is considered a truly special event by the community—akin to birthing a child! The "newborn" boat is ritually named and blessed; Vikings call this christening rite "blooding the keel." Again, the keel is considered the spine of the boat. Blooding the keel simply means getting the keel wet as the boat is lowered into the water for the first time.

Some monastic accounts I've read suggest that the rite's name indicates some sort of human or animal sacrifice to appease the Norse gods—literally sprinkling a gored victim's blood on the boat's keel. However, in my experience at Ravensthorpe, it seems that the term is only a metaphor . . . not unlike so many other evocative metaphors found in Norse poetry and lore.

VIKING SEA TRADE

Despite fevered portrayals of Viking blood lust by Saxon monks and displaced thegns, the bulk of Viking activity in Europe this century has been peaceful trade and commerce. From Norway, Viking

CARGO SHIP: THE *KNORR*

The Viking longship is certainly the most iconic vessel on the water today. But the seafaring Norse folk produce several types of vessels. The most common is the basic cargo hauler, an oceangoing trader called the knorr. *It has a wider, deeper hull than a longship, with planked decking only at bow and stern. As a result, the* knorr *has a more spacious cargo hold that can bear more weight than other Viking ships—up to twenty-four tons of freight, in fact!*

The knorr *may not be as swift or maneuverable as a warship, but it's the perfect vessel for commercial trade and transport, adaptable enough to navigate both deep ocean currents (the "whale-road") and shallow inland rivers (the "swan-road"). Last month, I personally witnessed one of these sturdy craft ferry a small clan of Norse settlers from Rygjafylke, including their livestock and supplies, into the Ravensthorpe port. In essence, a single* knorr *shipped in a new village for the Danelaw!*

cargo ships set out with pallets of fox, bear, otter, and beaver furs and pelts plus crates of whalebone, soapstone, walrus tusk ivory, and other highly valued northern products. They also carry amber, a fossilized resin cut and polished to make exquisite jewelry—a highly prized commodity in trading posts to the south.

In Europe and beyond, the Norse merchant fleets find plenty of eager trading partners. Before the Vikings began settling in England, they would trade wheat, wool, honey, and tin with Saxon vendors. Today, they trade for wine and salt in Francia, Arabic silver coins in the Levant, and glass in Italy. (This fine Italian glass is often reground into delicate beads for pendants and necklaces.) Finally, meeting traders from the Far East along Russian rivers, Viking traders can acquire more exotic luxuries, such as silk and spices.

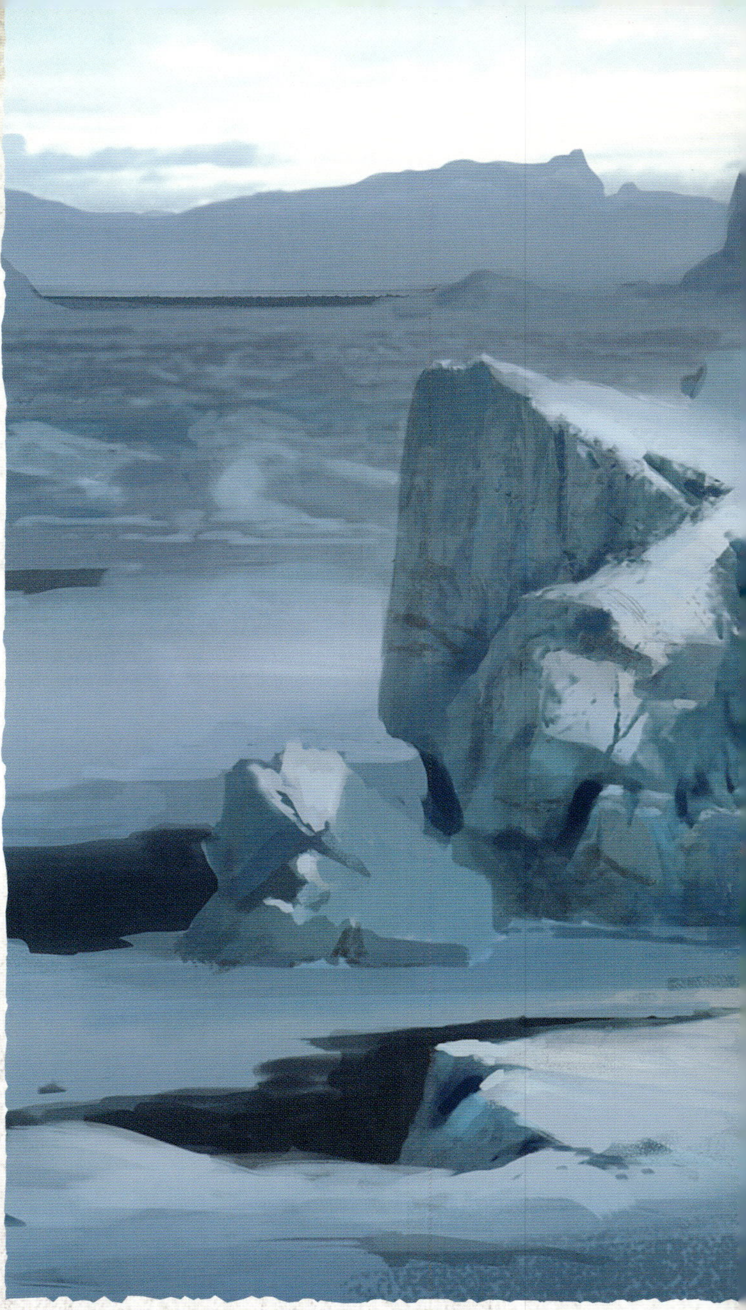

THE COASTAL TRADER

The coastal trader is exactly that—a lighter ship used primarily to haul cargo along coastlines. This practical Norse vessel is a smaller, nimbler version of the *knorr*. Easy to handle, the trader is so light

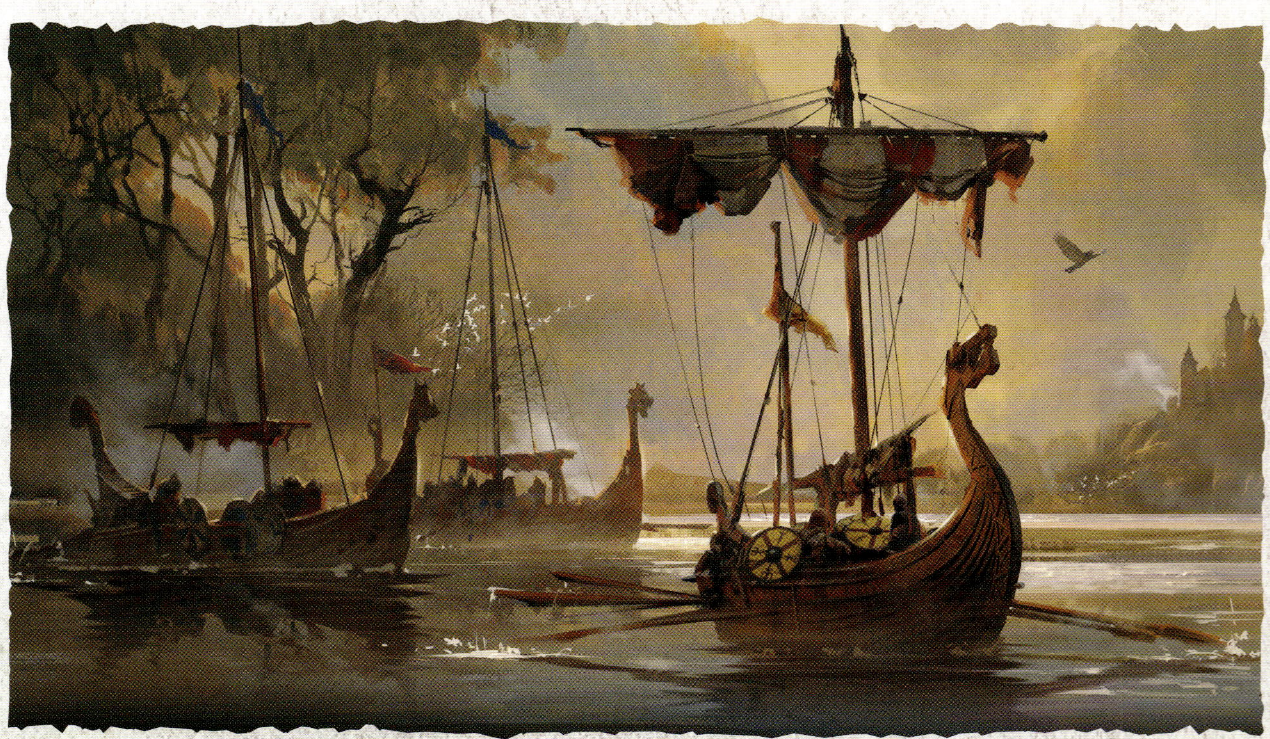

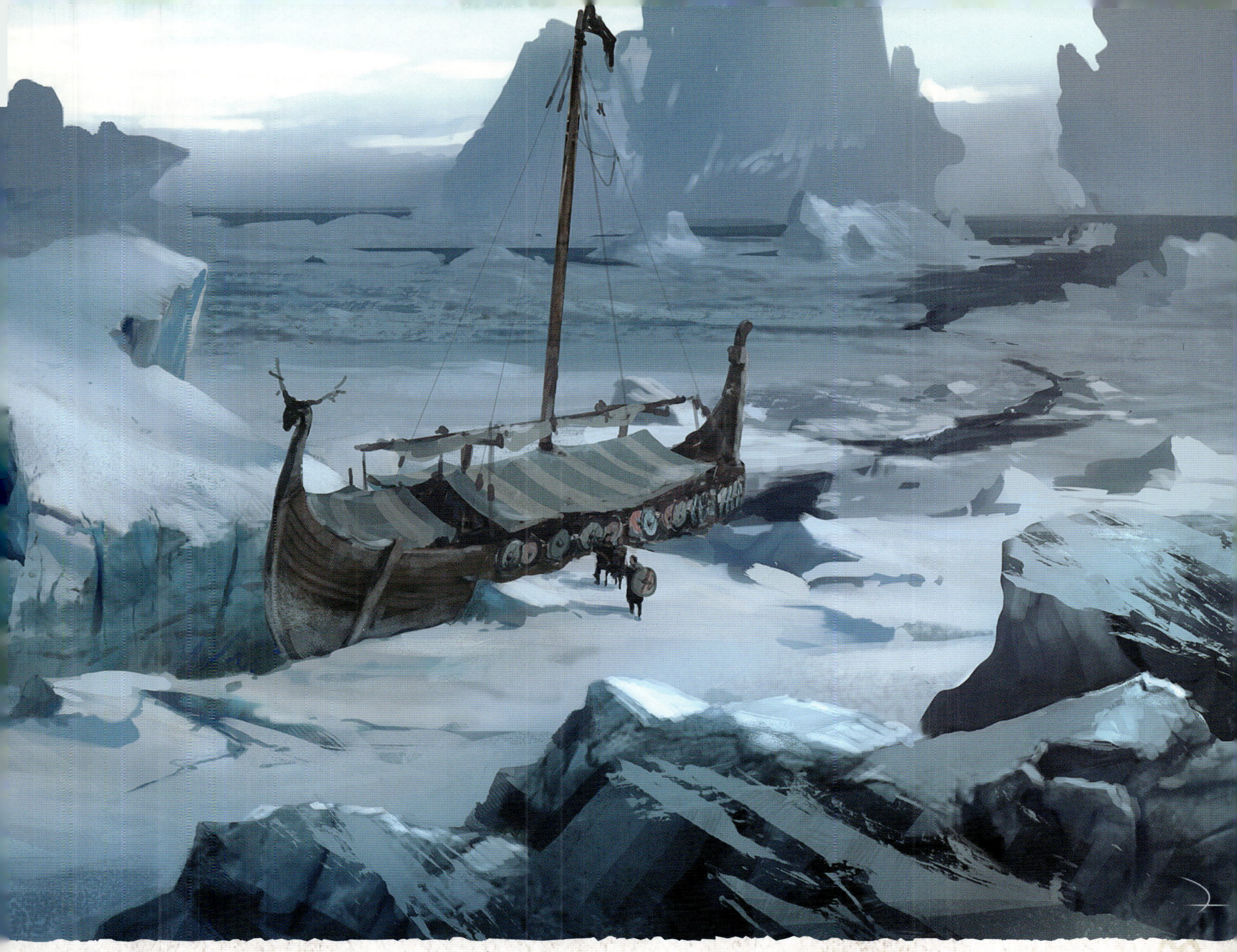

that it can be hauled overland via portage on a Viking crew's shoulders from one waterway to the next. Rounder than the *knorr*, the trader can carry no more than four to five tons of cargo. The boat can cross long stretches of open sea, if necessary, as its higher freeboard (distance from water line to upper deck) makes it more stable when buffeted by high ocean waves. But it needs a good number of working oars to navigate rivers—ten to fifteen sailors, typically.

LIFE ABOARD A LONGSHIP

Here's an aspect of Viking life that I can address from personal experience. Quarters aboard a Viking longship can be quite cramped, particularly on a longer voyage like our seemingly endless sojourn with Sigurd from Constantinople to Fornburg. The reason: Longships have an open deck—the distance between keel and deck floor is quite short, usually less than a meter—so travel supplies and equipment (oars, weapons, tools, and so on) must be stacked on deck around the crew. This leaves little room to maneuver or stretch one's legs. This can be a real problem if one is rostered on a boat full of rangy, strapping Norse sailors who enjoy referring to their new crewmate as "the Levantine bilge rat."

PROVISIONS. As you might expect, the amount and type of provisions stowed aboard a longship differ depending on where you're going—whether sailing across the open seas, skirting a

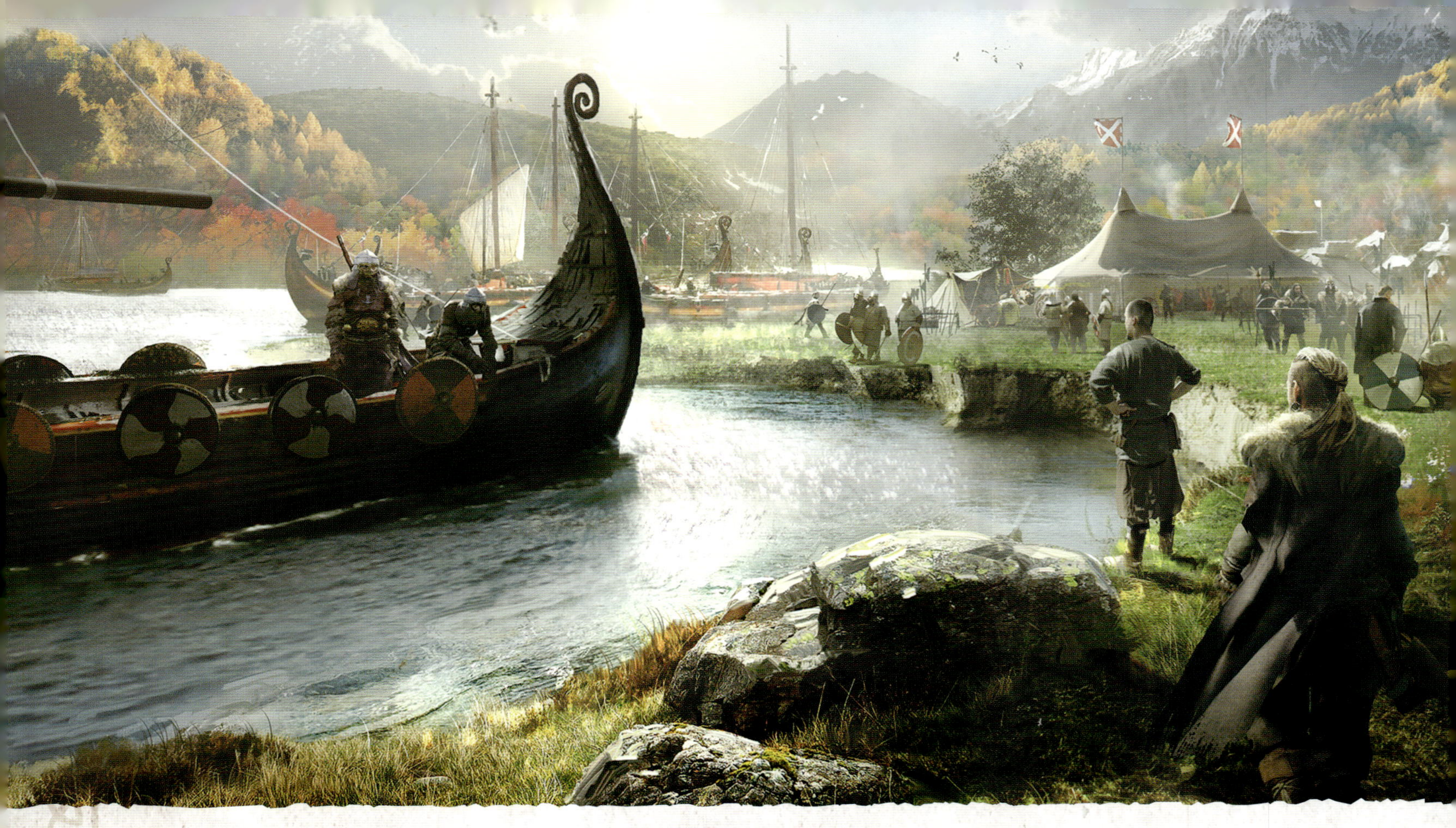

coastline, navigating a river, and so forth. Stocking a ship for a long voyage is always a challenging proposition. Fresh water is stored in casks, with foodstuffs stashed in oaken chests that each sailor-oarsman brings aboard as their personal bench. (When Eivor found I'd stashed scholarly reading materials in my own bench chest for a recent river journey, she said, "I hope these are tasty, Brother Hytham.")

Typically, the Viking sailor's maritime diet revolves around less perishable foods such as smoked meats, dried fish, and hard breads. More perishable items such as fruits or vegetables are added when possible. Since these foods spoil so quickly, the crew often seeks to replace them by foraging or "borrowing" (raiding) items from nearby settlements. Since cooking with fire is possible on land, the crew may enjoy a hot, fresh meal ashore. On the high seas, however, the cuisine is quite different. During our long tack across the Mediterranean to Jabal Ṭāriq, I consumed enough cured meat strips to last many lifetimes.

SLEEP AND REST. Basic sleeping arrangements can become an almost devilish logistic on a longship. During coastline voyages or river journeys, the crew can simply pull the boat ashore and sleep encamped on land. But for long-distance ocean crossings, crew members are forced to sleep on their bench chest or the deck floor. In cold or inclement weather, a canvas sheet is stretched over the crew, forming a rudimentary tent for protection against the elements.

DISTRIBUTION OF SPOILS. Every freeman member of a longship crew—captain, oarsman, navigator, warrior—has an equal voice in onboard decision making. But once the expedition ends, any loot accumulated from trade or raid is distributed to investors and crew according to a specified scale. The boat's owner earns the biggest share, of course. Typically, this is the captain, or *styrmaðr* (steersman), but not always. If the venture is funded by multiple partners, the wealth is distributed according to the level of their investment. The rest of the crew members usually earn smaller, equal shares, although hired *jomsviking* mercenaries might earn more.

"A VIKING'S GATEWAY"

In Viking culture, the longship is seen in almost mystical terms. Indeed, Viking sailors feel a special

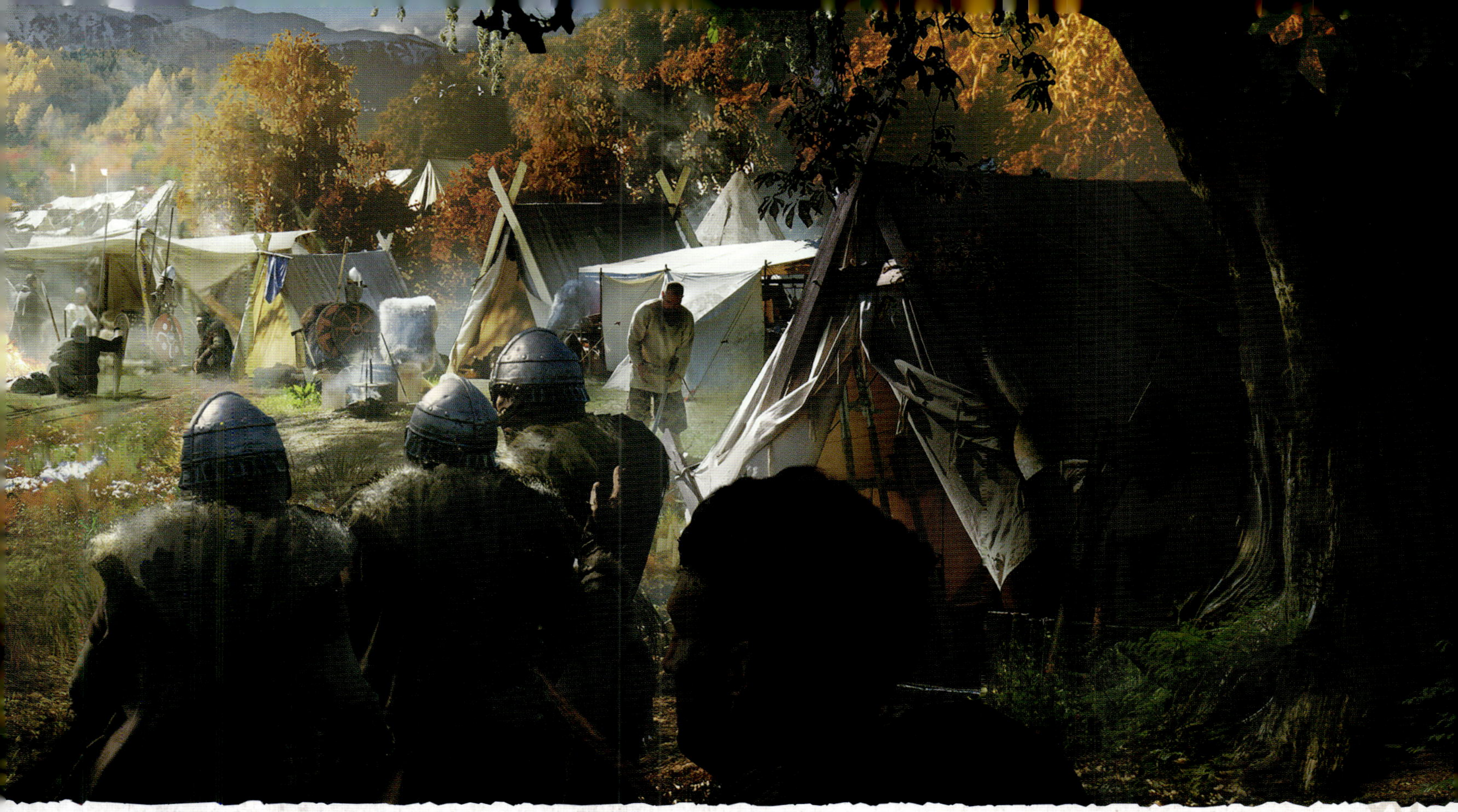

attachment to their vessel not unlike the emotional bond between a horse and rider. The boat symbolizes transition between two states. Born on land but dwelling at sea, a longship is like a creature that straddles two worlds—serving as a gateway between them. As one Frankish scholar wrote: "Symbolically then, to set sail is to dwell in a liminal space, suspended between land and sea . . . life and afterlife." This is one reason why ships figure so prominently in Viking burial rituals.

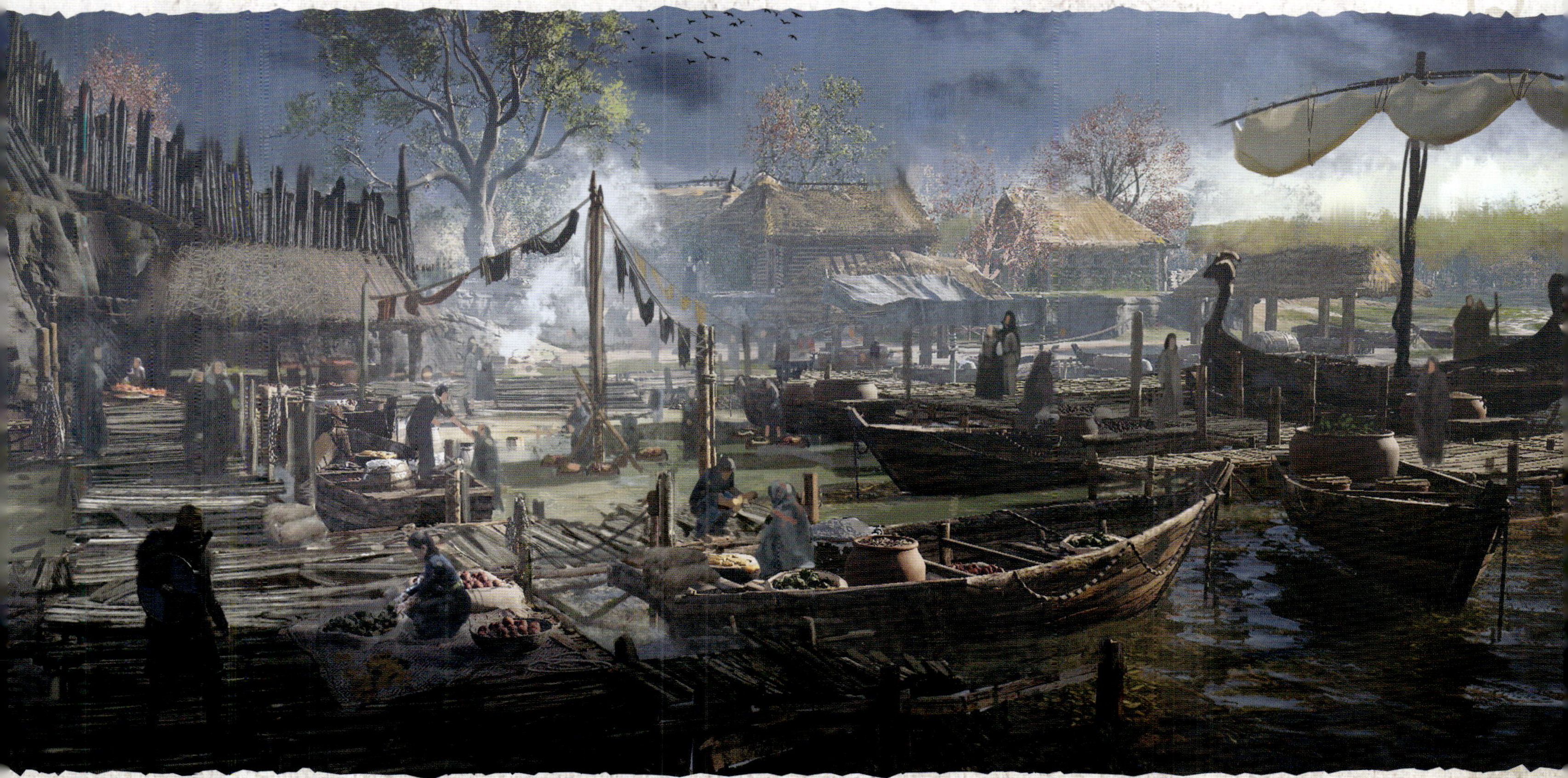

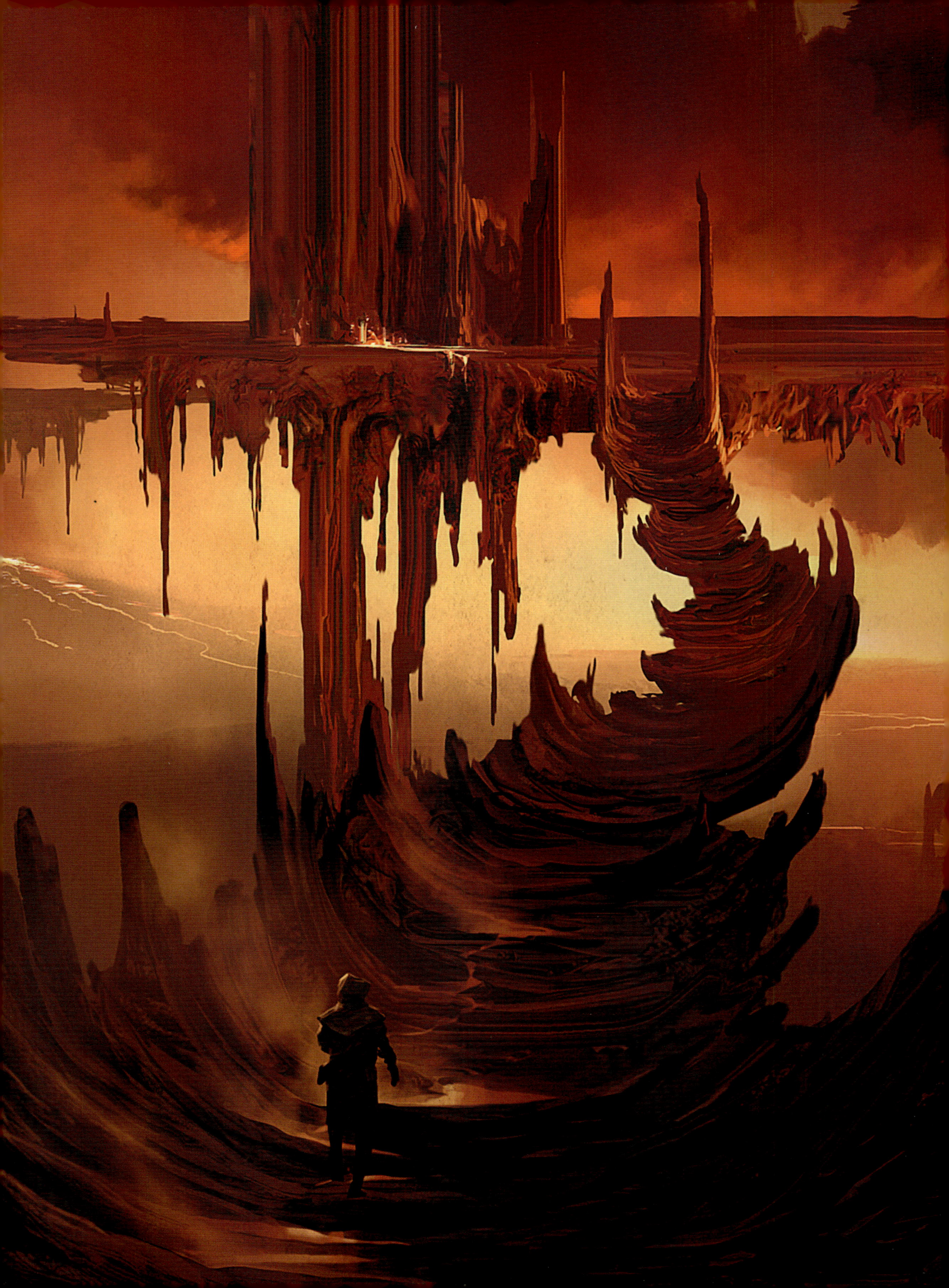

CHAPTER TWO

VIKING LORE

Norse mythology is some of the richest, most imaginative I've ever encountered in a single culture. The lore so closely reflects the Viking ethos—the adventurous spirit, the lust for life, and the unique blend of warm, communal intimacy with cold, functional brutality. Here's an overview of lore elements that, in my estimation, best reflect the way Vikings see themselves and the world. My advice: Don't try to make sense of events or chronology. After all, it's myth! Trust me, it's better to just go with the narrative flow. Another caveat: Myths and legends in any culture tend to have multiple versions. The ones presented here predominate in the 870s CE Viking communities I've explored in Norway and England.

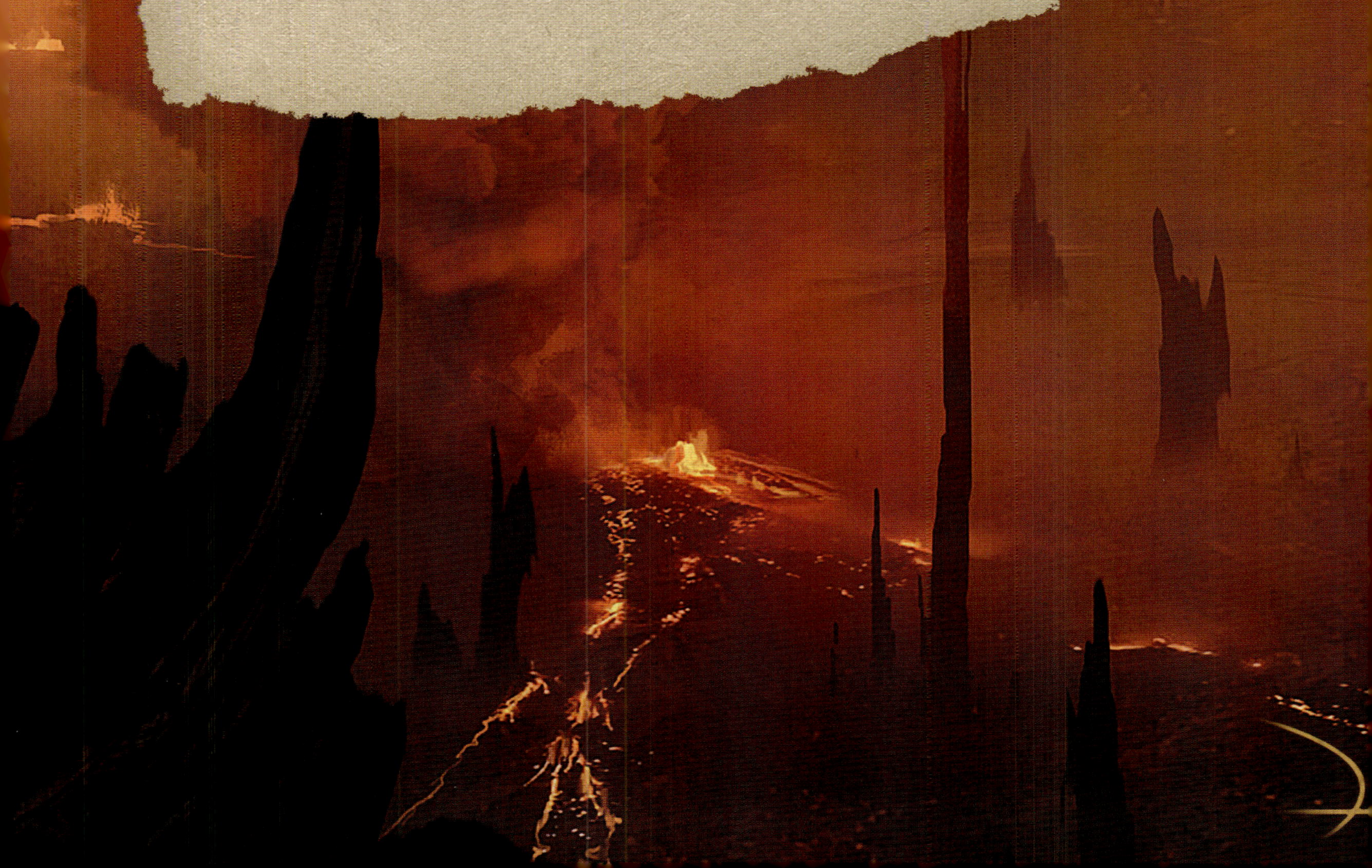

Fate and the Norns

Norse lore depicts existence as a sort of cosmic tapestry. Everything in the universe, every being, has its own "thread" of fate—a life path, immutable. These threads are woven together by three ethereal goddesses known as the Norns, the keepers of fate. Thus, everything's destiny is intertwined, knitted together into a great existential fabric.

Little is written or spoken about the Norns—I'm not certain, but Vikings may consider it bad luck to discuss them. As a result, the goddess-weavers remain shrouded in mystery. Known as Urd (past), Verdandi (present), and Skuld (future), they live in a shadowy den called the Well of Urdr (fate), tucked beneath one of Yggdrasil's great roots.

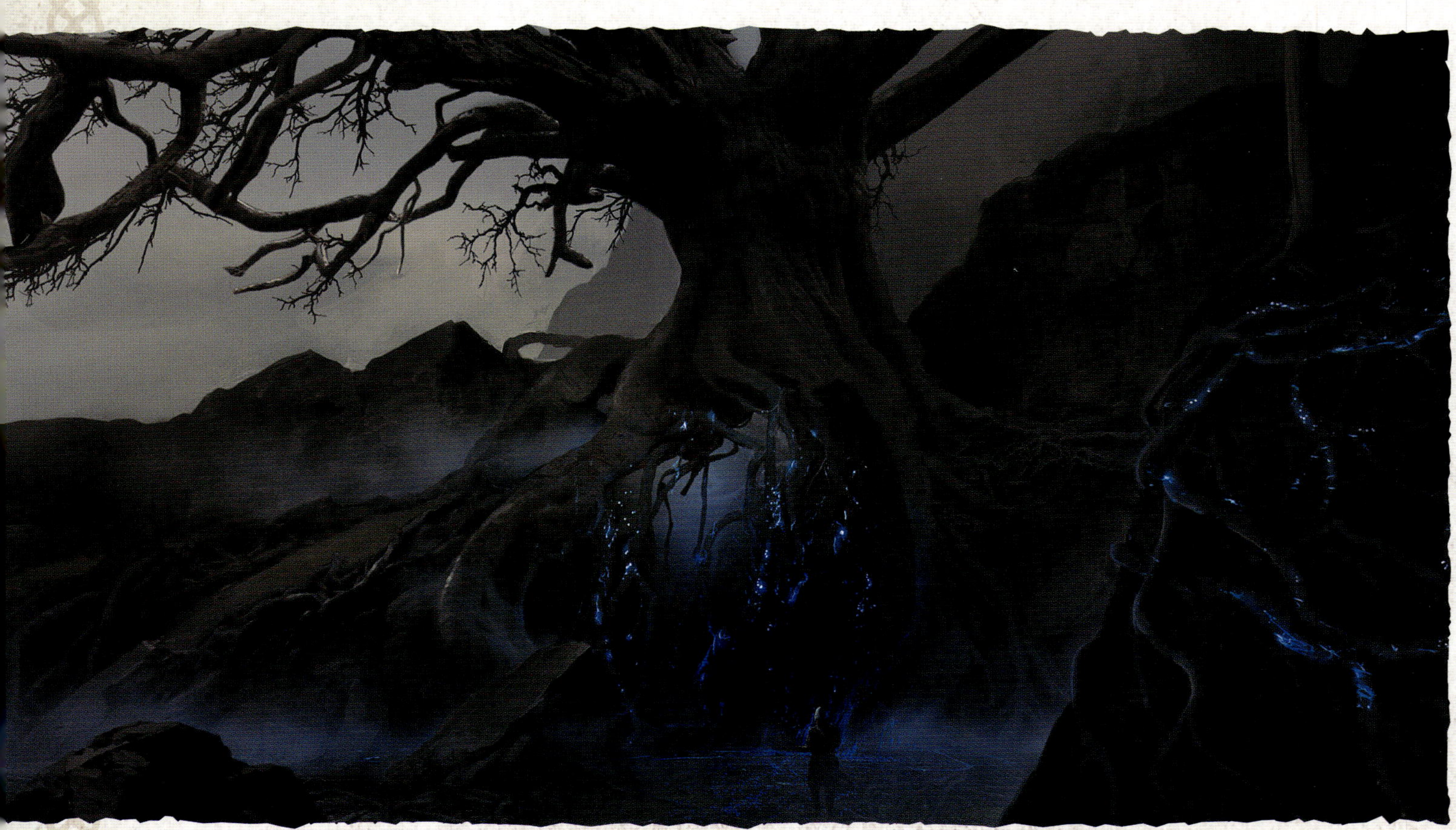

The Origin Myth: Ymir

In the beginning there was only the great void, Ginnungagap. After endless eons, a chaos of primordial forces began to swirl in the abyss. A searing hurricane of fire known as Muspelheim swirled out to one side, while the frigid ice of Niflheim churned to the other. Between them hovered silent cosmic darkness . . . until the moment they finally surged together, frost meeting fire in a storm of scalding mist.

From this mist, the great giant Ymir was born—the first being, father of the Jötnar, the race of giants born from the sweat of his axillae. Indeed, everything in existence was born of Ymir's flesh, eventually.

SURTR: THE SECOND BEING

Some legends say the second entity born from Ginnungagap, right after Ymir, was the ancient, monstrous entity known as Surtr, father of the fire giants. Emerging into the firestorm of Muspelheim with a great flaming sword, Surtr brought heat and light to the young cosmos by wielding his blade to conjure the sun.

I told you Viking myth was imaginative!

It is said that Surtr and his race are destined to be dire agents of Ragnarök, the apocalyptic final battle that topples the gods. Unfortunately, the cataclysm will leave our current cosmos a barren wasteland of ash and ruin. But another will rise in its stead—the grand cycle of death and rebirth, the world born anew.

BIRTH OF THE AESIR

According to the lore, a great cow called Audhumla appeared in the churning ice of Niflheim. As this creature licked the salt of the frozen realm, Ymir fed from her udders. This began to melt pockets of Niflheim's frozen wasteland, and a being called Buri emerged from the ice—the first Aesir god. Buri begat Bor, who married the Jötnar queen Bestla and had three sons: Vili, Vé, and Odin.

FORMATION OF THE REALMS: YGGDRASIL

The three brothers were raised in the barren wastes of Niflheim with no food other than Audhumla's milk to nourish them. Led by Odin, they grew into thugs who rebelled against their progenitors. They impaled Ymir in his sleep and began tearing his corpse to pieces. But the foul murder unleashed such a vast, roiling torrent of Ymir's blood that much of the world was swept away! The deluge flowed into a great tree of life, Yggdrasil. Other realms swirled into existence and settled along the tree's roots and branches.

Ironically, Ymir's mutilation became the essential substance of the new cosmos. His fluids became the ocean, his skin and muscles the soil, his bones the mountains, his teeth the cliffs, his hair the vegetation, his brains the clouds. Above it all, Ymir's skull became the sky, or "dome of heaven," held aloft by four primordial dwarves—Nordri, Sudri, Austri, and Vestri—who stand as the four points of the compass.

So there you have it: the physical world as we know it.

DESIGN OF MANKIND

The next step, of course, was the creation of humans. Aesir gods formed the first two people, Ask and Embla, from two trees, certainly an interesting choice—perhaps an echo of Yggdrasil and our common roots? The Norse like to say humans were created by Aesir vanity—the gods wanted inferior beings to boss around who would worship them. But the Aesir creators were kind enough to erect a great wall around Midgard, realm of the humans, to keep out giants and other hostile races This wall was built from Ymir's eyebrows, which I find quite amusing.

And against all odds, humanity thrived.

THE NINE REALMS

Again, Norse mythology posits the World Tree, Yggdrasil, as the spine of the entire cosmos, with all nine realms of existence arrayed across its roots and branches. (Some even say the ancient tree is older than Creation itself, but don't try to ponder the logic of that.) Viking skalds portray Yggdrasil as an inconceivably immense oak or ash, beautiful and symmetrical—that is, with upward branches the same length as downward roots, all curving to form a near-perfect spherical shape. The Raven Clan's seer Valka tells me this circular quality symbolizes "order and eternity."

As mentioned earlier, the two oldest realms are the icy netherworld of Niflheim and the land of primordial fire, Muspelheim. Asgard, home of the Aesir gods, is nestled in Yggdrasil's highest branches. In the middle branches sit Midgard, where mortal humans live; Vanaheim, kingdom of the Vanir gods; Alfheim, home to light elves; Svartalfheim, home of the dwarves; and Jötunheim, home of Jötunn folk, the giants. The lowest realm, tucked into Yggdrasil's roots near Niflheim, is Helheim, the realm of the dead.

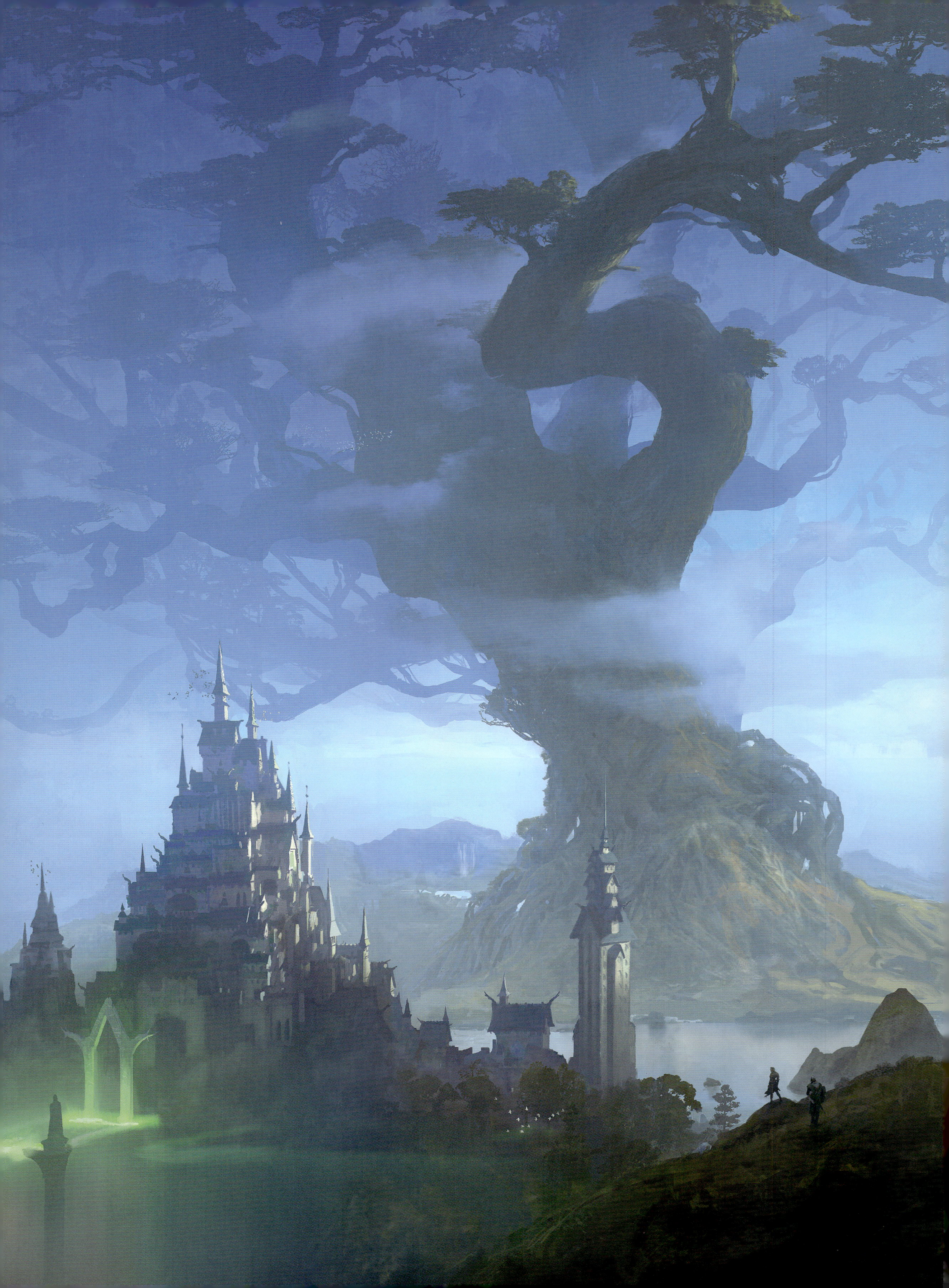

VIKING AFTERLIFE: THE LANDS OF THE DEAD

Before we explore the nine cosmic realms of Norse mythology, I want to quickly review how Norse folk view the notion of life after death. The basic belief is that the deceased are assigned specific destinations, depending on how they've lived their life on balance.

WHERE THE HONORED DEAD GO

Vikings who live an honorable life are sent to dwell in one of two different places within the walls of Asgard. Those who die bravely on the field of battle are sent to Valhalla, the great "hall of the slain"—a glorious paradise where happy warriors feast and fight forever under the grateful (and single) eye of Odin himself. The second destination for good folk is Folkvangr, the "people field." The rules and parameters for this place are somewhat nebulous. Some lore indicates that the goddess Freyja makes the selections, welcoming both men and women, often reuniting spouses or family separated by death.

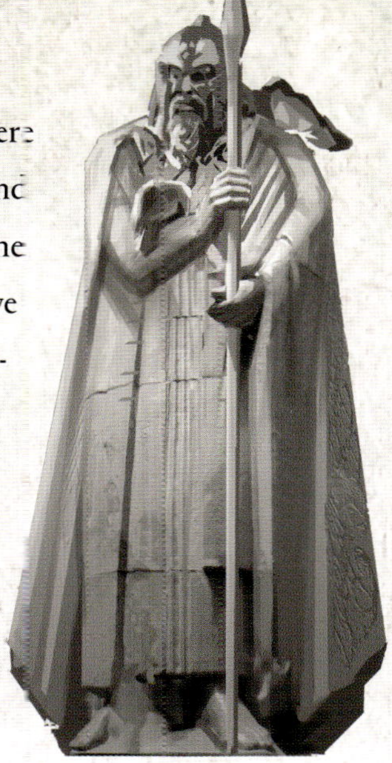

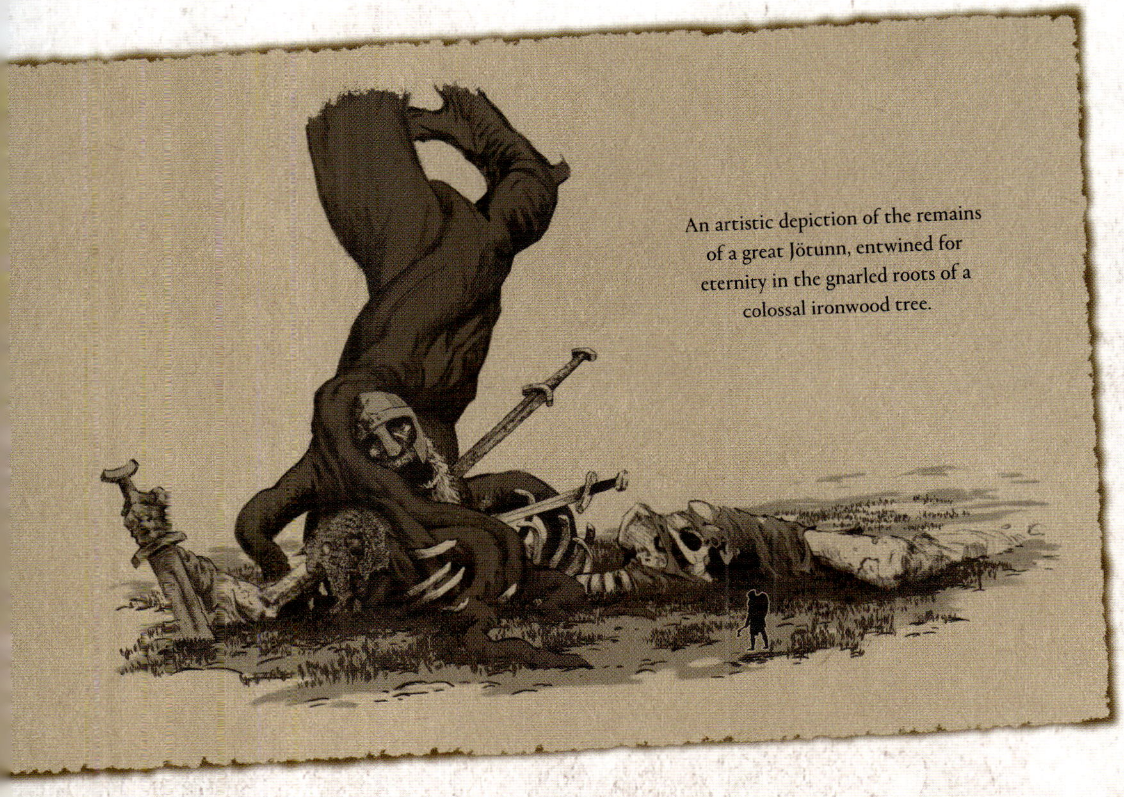

An artistic depiction of the remains of a great Jötunn, entwined for eternity in the gnarled roots of a colossal ironwood tree.

LESS GLORIOUS DESTINATIONS

Whereas Viking warriors who die bravely in battle can look forward to feasting in the hall of Valhalla, those who die of illness or old age are sent to cold, dreary Helheim. Worse, criminals and other disreputable types are punished by banishment to the frigid mist of Niflheim, a cruel and unforgiving realm.

ASGARD

REALM OF THE AESIR GODS

This towering treetop realm is the homeland of Norse lore's foremost tribe of gods, the Aesir. Said to be a fertile, verdant land riven with cerulean waterways, Asgard is ruled by Odin and his queens, Frigg and Freyja (a Vanir goddess), from their royal palace of Valaskjalf. Skaldic poets describe a resplendent kingdom, quite like classic Islamic depictions of Jannah, final abode of the righteous—a viridescent garden of bliss surrounded by bright flower-dappled meadows and rolling hills. According to Viking legend, every important Aesir god dwells in their own Asgardian citadel!

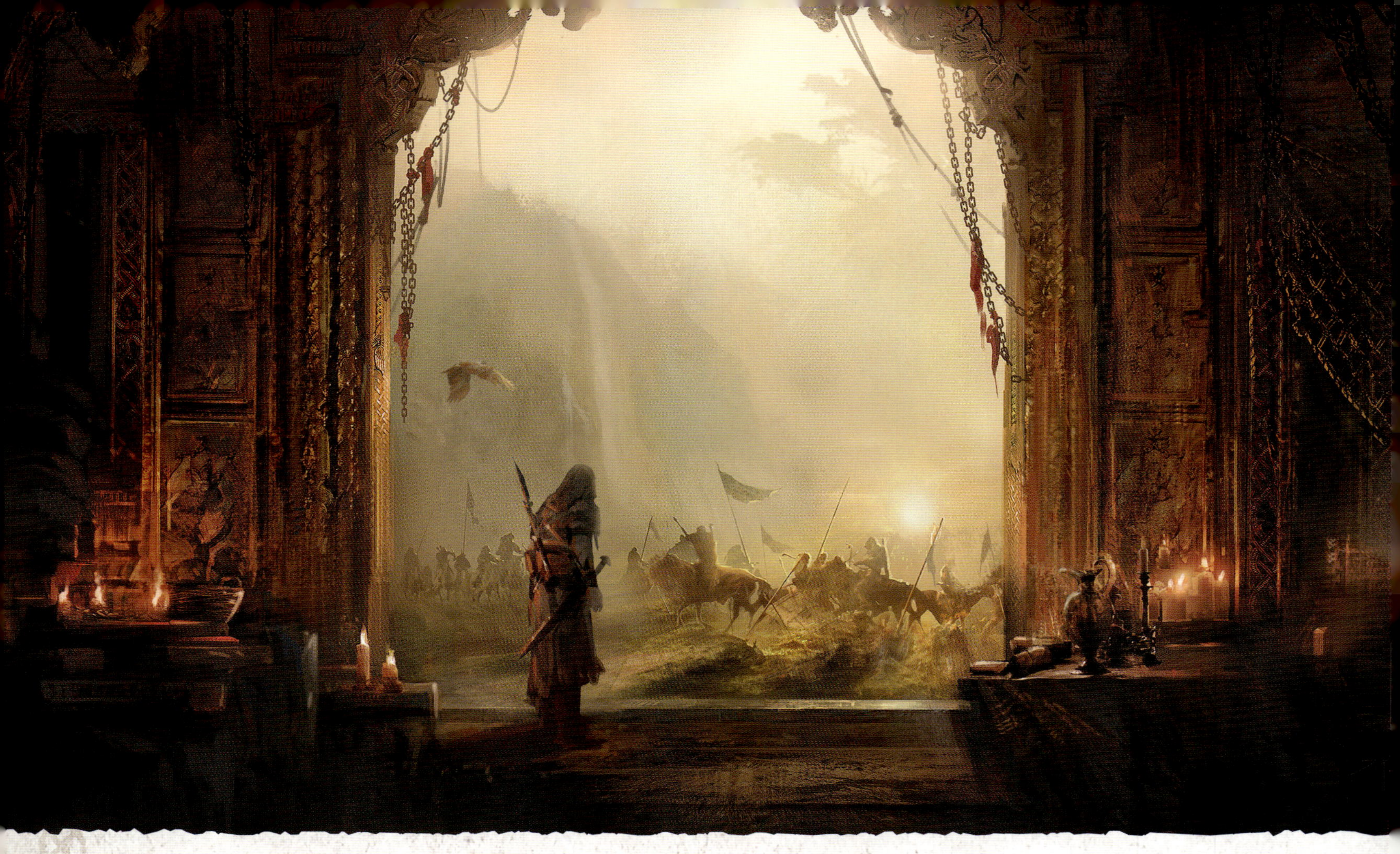

VALHALLA

Asgard houses the legendary "hall of the slain" known as Valhalla. Here are gathered all Viking warriors who've fallen bravely in battle. Called the Einherjar, these slain heroes spend their afterlife feasting and fighting joyously! It is said that such activities will continue with vigor until the dark day of Ragnarök, when all Einherjar will be called to join the gods in fending off doom . . . unsuccessfully, if the Norns' threads of fate are to be believed.

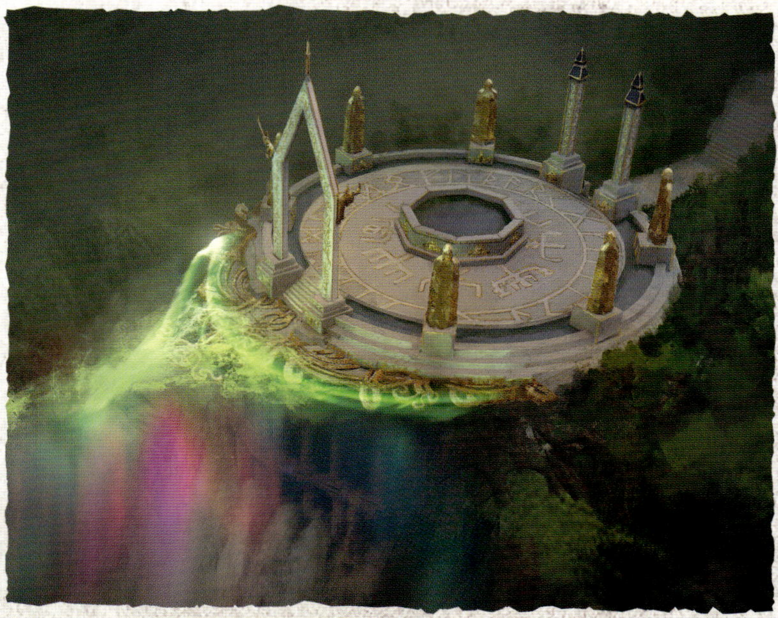

THE RAINBOW BRIDGE

In Norse lore, the only way to reach Asgard from Midgard is to cross the translucent span of the strange, mystical Bifröst. This iridescent "Rainbow Bridge" shimmers with the spectral colors, as its name suggests. A powerful god named Heimdall guards the bridge, denying access to all but Odin's chosen visitors. The Bifröst is indestructible, although legend says it will be shattered on Ragnarök, the End of Days.

ODIN ALL-FATHER: AN EYE FOR TRUTH

Much lore exists about Odin, chief of the Aesir gods. Typically portrayed as brilliant and cunning, he's said to be driven

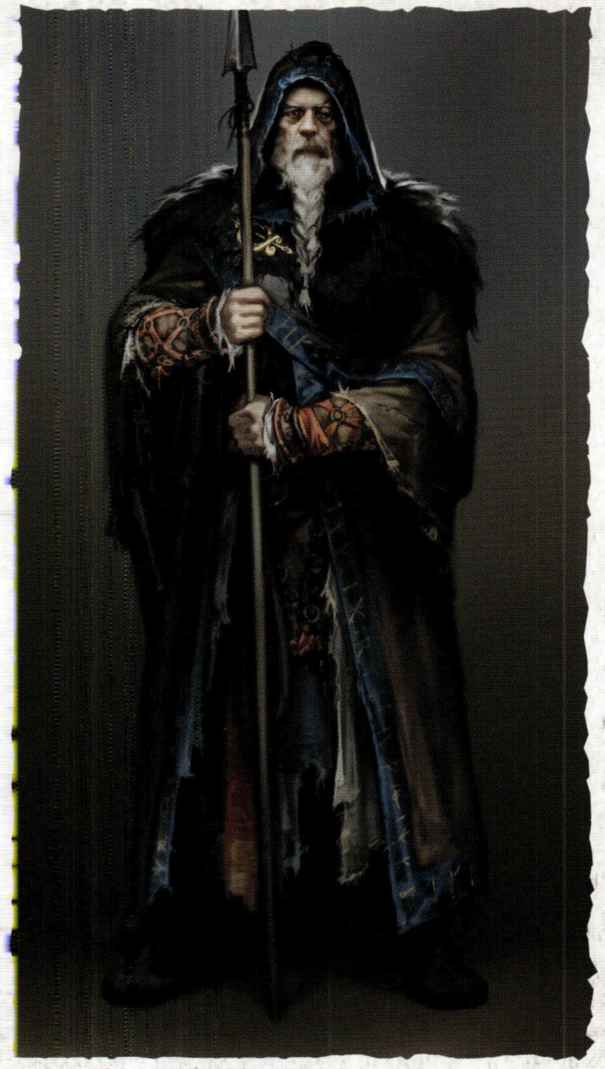

by a voracious appetite for secret truths and hidden prophecy—in particular, for unraveling the threads of his fate at Ragnarök. Perched on Hlidskjalf, his magical throne, Odin scans the realms with a supernatural gaze, obsessively seeking arcane sources of wisdom. Some say his moniker "All-father" comes from this image of the all-knowing watcher. Others say Odin gave this name to himself after he murdered Ymir, proudly claiming to be the source of all creation—even though all creation is formed of Ymir's flesh and blood.

Seeking to quench his thirst for knowledge, Odin will go anywhere and do—or give—anything for a glimpse of the future. Tales of his travels through the Nine Realms depict the All-father riding his eight-legged horse, Sleipnir, with his raven companions, Huginn and Muninn. Once, Odin went so far as to sacrifice one of his own eyes at the mystical Well of Mimir, nestled in the roots of Yggdrasil, the World Tree. What did Odin get in exchange? The lore is not entirely clear. Certainly, he sought to know what his future held. But the Norns—the keepers of fate—are loath to share such knowledge.

In any case, Odin ended up with a nasty scar across the socket where his eye used to be.

FRIGG

Odin's wife seems to play a lesser role in Norse lore than his decidedly more glamorous consort, the Vanir princess Freyja. (Some scholars suggest they're actually one and the same, but the Vikings in Ravensthorpe don't see it that way.) Goddess of

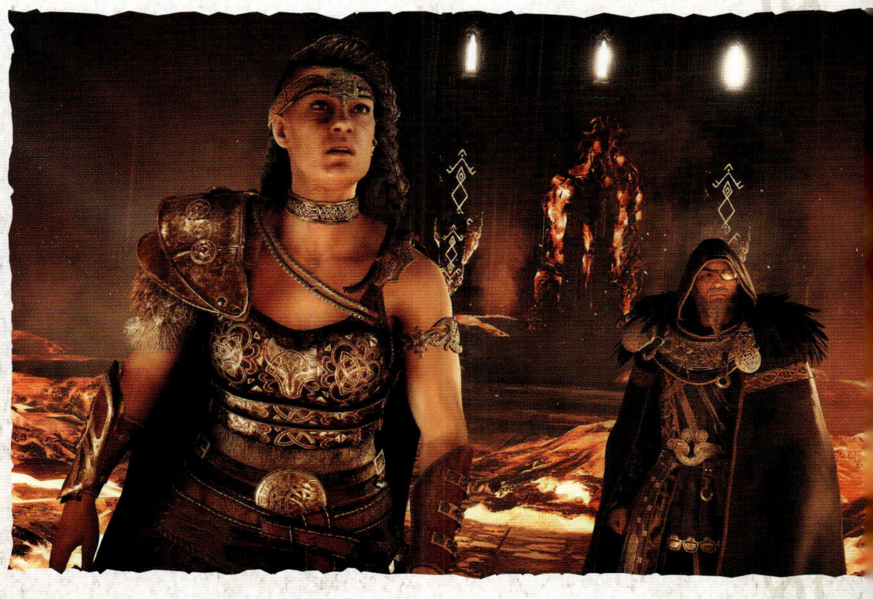

motherhood and love, Frigg bore Odin numerous offspring, including the sons Thor, Baldr, Hodr, and Hermod. Despite Freyja's arrival in Asgard and her political importance, Frigg continues to be seen as the true queen mother of the Aesir gods.

THOR, GOD OF THUNDER

Viking lore depicts Thor with great veneration. He's easily the most popular deity in the Norse pantheon. In terms of sheer power and brute strength, the Aesir god of thunder is the mightiest warrior in Asgard. Wielding Mjölnir, his brutal hammer, he can

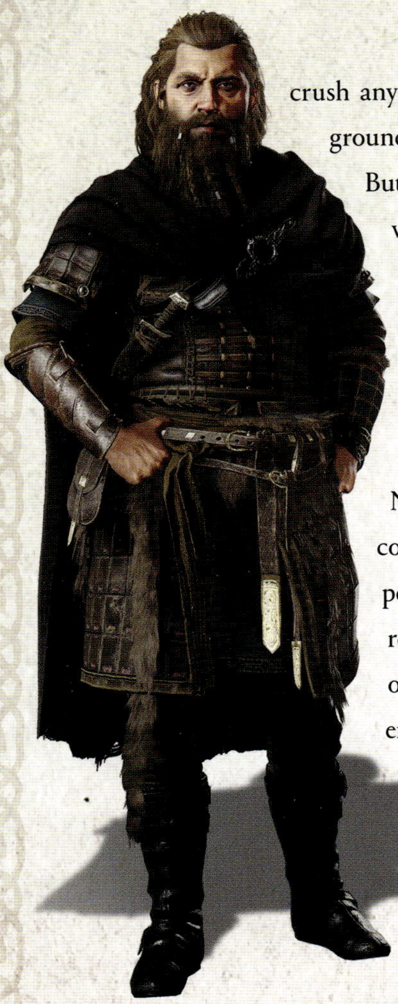

crush any foe's head in a single swing. One ground strike can unleash a temblor! But Thor's "thunder" deals out life as well as death. Crossing the sky in a flying chariot pulled by winged goats, he calls down rainstorms to fill the wells, water the fields, and boost the harvest.

Best of all, Thor is seen in Norse culture as the embodiment of courage and a protector of all Viking people—everyone in the settlement, regardless of wealth or family or list of glorious exploits. Many villagers wear Mjölnir-shaped talismans for good luck. In homage to Thor, the Viking skalds recite verses full of kennings and heiti, Norse poetic devices said to be favorites of the thunder god. His only flaw appears to be a temperamental nature that sometimes triggers blunt reactions.

THE TALE OF MIMIR'S WELL

Ages ago, the Aesir and Vanir gods clashed in a war so titanic it was said to rattle the very roots of Yggdrasil, the great World Tree. Massed armies of gods collided thunderously on the battlefield, and the toll was so terrible that the two sides finally negotiated a truce. Hostages were exchanged to ensure compliance. Thus, Odin sent his trusted counselor Mimir to Vanaheim as the Aesir's sign of good faith. In return, the Vanir leader Njörðr sent his daughter Freyja to become Odin's new queen.

In Norse lore, Mimir was considered the wisest of Odin's advisers. The exchange seemed like a smart deal at first, sure to guarantee the peace. Unfortunately for Mimir, his reputation as a cunning operative was such that the Vanir suspected him of being more a spy than a hostage. When Njörðr noticed Mimir listening at a Vanir tribal council, he impetuously lopped off the adviser's head and sent it back to Asgard, embalmed in herbs.

Now, Odin had been learning *seiðr* magic from his new queen, and he found a spell to keep Mimir's head alive. The All-father placed the head by a mystical well at the very bottom of Yggdrasil's roots. Its water is said to be magical, bestowing great wisdom on anyone who drinks it . . . but only in exchange for a terrible price. Indeed, legends say Odin himself paid this price, offering his own left eye as a sacrifice to the well. Mimir's assigned task is to make sure no one drinks without paying as dear a price. This secret place is known as the Well of Mimir, or Mímisbrunnr.

HEIMDALL, THE BRIDGE SENTRY

Descriptions of Heimdall, the sentinel guarding the aforementioned Rainbow Bridge, portray quite a

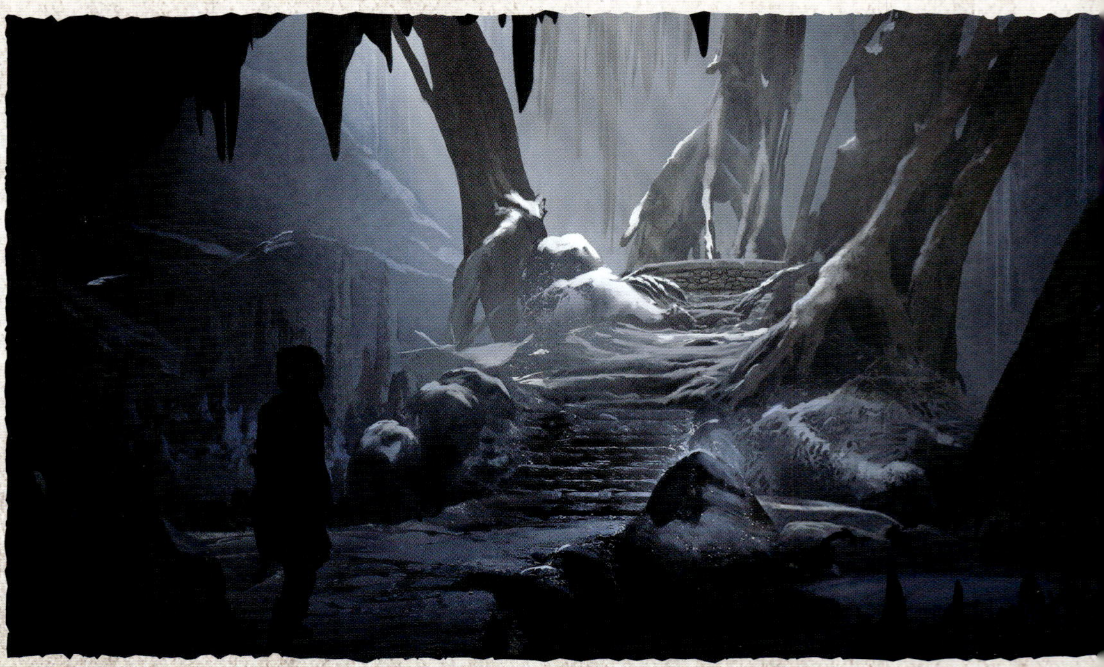

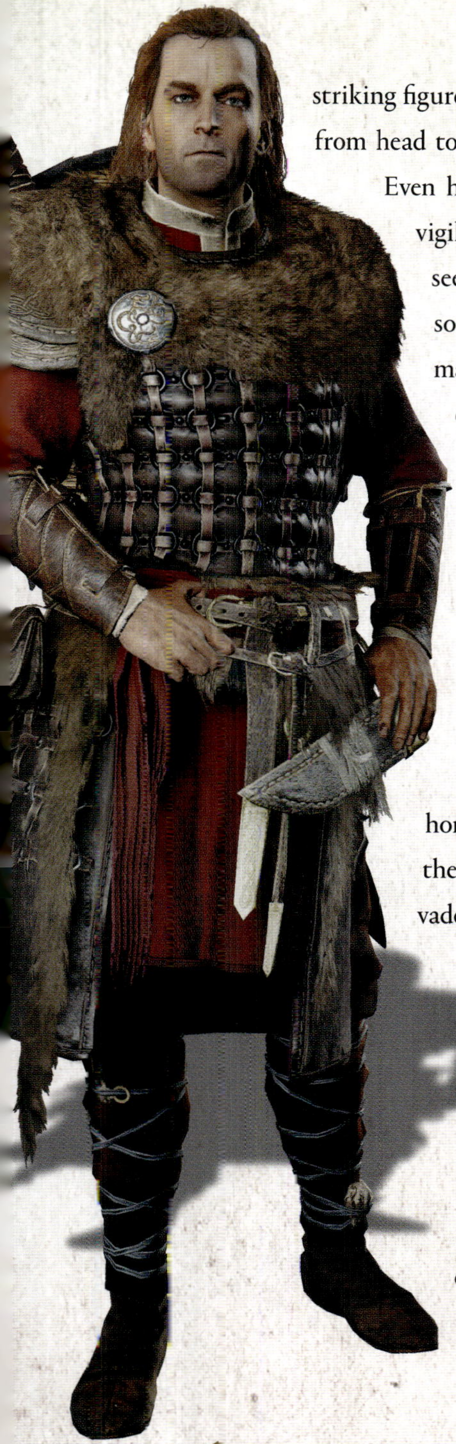

striking figure. He shines like an oil torch from head to toe, gleaming like the sun. Even his teeth are solid gold! His vigilance is unmatched—he can see for miles and hear every sound, making him the ultimate watchman of Asgard. All day and all night, Heimdall scans beyond the horizon for threats.

One day in the future, according to legend, Heimdall's sentry watch will end when he spots Surtr leading a swarm of fire giants and countless hordes of Hel's denizens across the Rainbow Bridge. As the invaders storm Asgard, Heimdall will raise Gjallarhorn, the great trumpet whose blast can be heard in all realms. His warning will summon gods, men, dwarves, and elves to stave off the doom of Ragnarök.

TÝR, GOD OF WAR AND JUSTICE

Odin appointed this esteemed adviser to his inner circle long ago. Technically serving as the Aesir tribe's war god, Týr is better known in Norse lore as an arbiter of justice and cosmic order and a skilled diplomatic emissary. Indeed, this so-called war god was a primary architect of the clever truce and hostage exchange that ended the brutal Aesir-Vanir conflict.

Perhaps the best-known Týr tale depicts his selfless sacrifice so Odin could imprison the great wolf Fenrir. The All-father tried to trick the lupine beast into a "test of strength"—the gods would bind Fenrir with a golden rope and watch him escape with ease, or so he said. But Fenrir was suspicious, and rightfully so. In truth, the rope was unbreakable, woven by the great dwarf craftsman Ivaldi. Fenrir would not submit to the binding unless a god first placed a hand in the wolf's mouth.

Knowing his forearm would be lost, Týr volunteered. Odin bound the monster . . . and Fenrir bit down hard.

LOKI THE TRICKSTER

Loki is a complicated figure in Norse mythology. Although one or perhaps both of his parents were giants, Loki was raised in Asgard and is considered a member of the Aesir tribe. However, his oft-troubling exploits violate every traditional Viking value. He's portrayed as a wily, unpredictable shapeshifter with potent magical powers and a penchant for trickery and betrayal. Things like truth, honor, and loyalty clearly mean very little to him. Several Viking lore keepers I've consulted hold conflicting views on whether Loki is a giant, a god, or something else entirely!

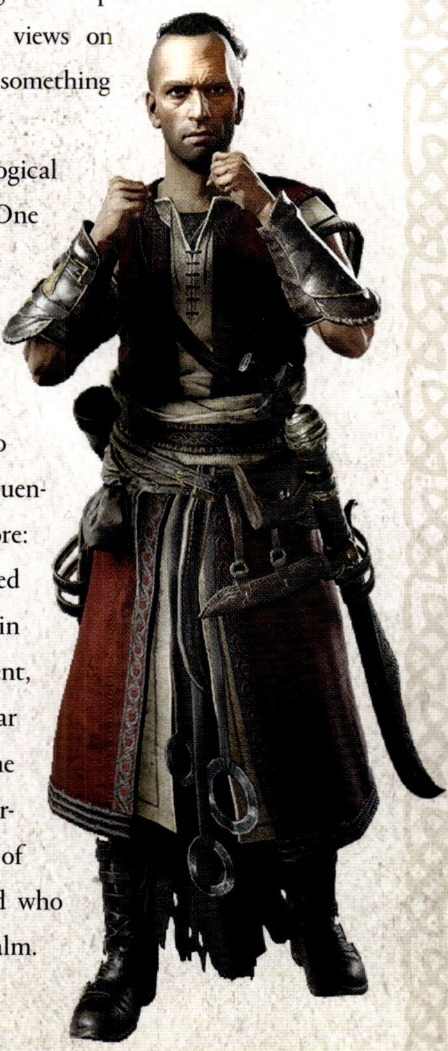

Loki's influence in mythological events is certainly far reaching. One of Loki's most infamous betrayals resulted in the loss of the beloved Aesir god Baldr, son of Odin and Frigg. (See the following entry for more.) He also sired some of the most consequential monstrosities in Norse lore: the great wolf Fenrir, destined for mortal combat with Odin at Ragnarök; the World Serpent, Jörmungandr, fated to a similar struggle with Thor on that same apocalyptic day; and Hel, the terrifying queen of Helheim, ruler of the teeming hordes of the dead who populate her cold underworld realm.

THE DEATH OF BALDR

Baldr is one of the most beloved gods in the Norse pantheon, and this tale is one of the best-known myths in Norse society. When Baldr was born, his mother, Frigg, a noted seeress, had a dream that foretold his violent death. Shaken by this prophecy, she canvassed all of creation in a motherly frenzy—every creature and plant, fire and water, metal and stone—extracting oaths of protection for her newborn son. Incredibly, she succeeded—every single entity in the cosmos, living or inert, swore to leave her son unscathed. Well, except for one thing: mistletoe. But Frigg felt no threat from such a soft, gentle, innocent plant.

Baldr grew up to be quite a shining star. (Indeed, some translate his name as "shiny one.") Portrayed as a charming, generous, and just spirit, the son of Odin and Frigg was particularly adept at settling disputes and quickly became a favorite among all his fellow Aesir. And nothing could hurt him! Weapons bounced harmlessly off his skin, leaving him unscathed. All this irritated Loki, who began to scheme ways to undermine Baldr's popularity.

The sly shapeshifter took the form of an old woman, befriended Frigg, and learned about mistletoe's omission from her protection list. Then he gleefully fashioned a sharp spear tipped with a humble sprig of that plant. Baldr's blind brother, Hodr, took the spear and hurled it as Loki directed—targeting a rabbit, he thought. But instead, he pierced Baldr's chest, killing him! Baldr's spirit was swiftly escorted down to Helheim, where he sits, pale and forlorn, at Hel's table in her palace hall.

THE FINAL BETRAYAL

The story of Baldr ends with one more stunning example of Loki's treachery. Shattered by grief, Frigg asked her son Hermod to mount his father's magical steed, Sleipnir, and ride to Helheim itself to bring Baldr back. After nine exhausting days and nights traveling down Yggdrasil's roots, Hermod reached Hel's halls and made a convincing case for his brother's release. Helheim's queen agreed, but on one condition: "If Baldr is so universally beloved, let me first see all things weep for him."

Helmod returned with the news, and the Aesir immediately sent envoys to everything in creation, living and inanimate. And every entity, including mistletoe, wept for Baldr—all except one creature. A haggard old cave-dwelling giantess named Thökk refused to shed even one tear. As a result, Hel's condition was not met, and she refused to release Baldr's spirit back into the living world from her joyless realm.

Thökk, as you might have suspected, was the shapeshifter Loki in disguise!

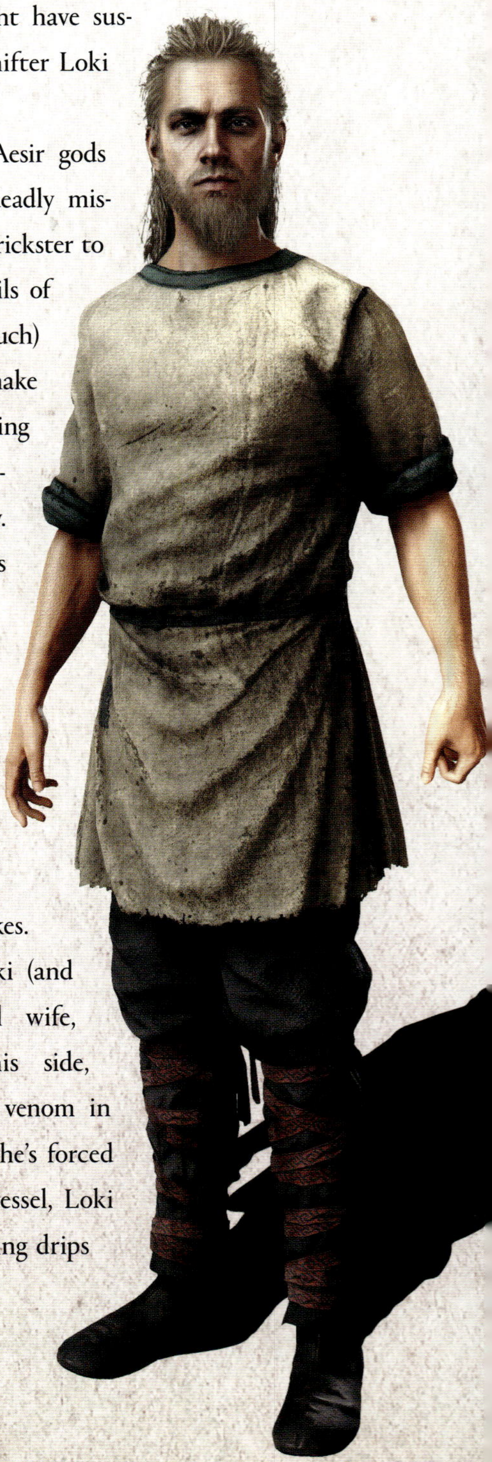

It didn't take the Aesir gods long to unveil Loki's deadly mischief. They bound the trickster to a rock (using the entrails of his son Nari, a nasty touch) and set a poisonous snake above him, venom dripping from its fangs. Loki remains there to this day. Every drip that strikes him triggers paroxysms of burning pain. Indeed, his agony is so great that it shakes the very earth with terrible spasms. From this comes the Viking origin story of earthquakes.

Fortunately for Loki (and our world), his loyal wife, Sigyn, remains at his side, catching the dripping venom in a bowl. But whenever she's forced to go and empty the vessel, Loki catches a few excruciating drips in the face!

ALFHEIM

Realm of the Elves

This homeland of the light elves, draped in mystery, is said to be tucked into the upper branches of Yggdrasil along with the two godly realms, Asgard and Vanaheim. Light elves are typically portrayed as radiant, demigod-like beings—"luminous and fair as the sun to behold"—with mystical qualities and powers. A couple of Viking seers I've consulted tell me their visions reveal Alfheim as a verdant, bright, and peaceful world.

But very little elven activity is described in the rare scholarly surveys of Norse mythology I've found, nor is there much oral tradition passed down—not even a basic description of the realm itself! A few old tales suggest that the Vanir god Freyr, brother of Freyja and son of Njörðr, is a great friend of the light elves. In fact, some lore suggests Freyr built his palace in Alfheim with elven help . . . and he may even be their ruler.

VANAHEIM

Realm of the Vanir Gods

This homeland of the Vanir tribe of gods, much like Alfheim, is enshrouded in mystery. I've heard Viking storytellers call it a "realm of harmony" and describe an almost primal wilderness. In old Norse sagas, the Vanir gods share a close bond with both the natural and spirit worlds, befriending wild creatures and wielding magic to grow gardens and shape forests. Vanir seers also practice the dark art of *seiðr* to conjure visionary trances for purposes of prophecy and divination.

THE LONG WAR

As mentioned earlier, Norse lore speaks of a lengthy, bloody conflict between Asgard and Vanaheim. It dragged on for so many years it was called the Long War. Odin's Aesir army, wielding conventional physical weapons—blade and arrow and hammer—would march on Vanaheim and launch fierce frontal assaults, raging across the battlefield in a very Viking-like frenzy of blood lust. But the Vanir, masters of dark magics, would counter with terrible spells and incantations. Towering tidal waves would sweep Aesir soldiers to their doom. The sides were so evenly matched that neither could gain the upper hand.

War weariness finally ended the hostilities, with a political exchange of hostages to guarantee the truce. As part of this exchange, the Vanir princess Freyja went to Asgard to become Odin's new consort. In return, Odin's closest adviser, Mimir, was sent to Vanaheim to serve in Njörðr's court. The tale illustrates what the squabbling gods have slowly come to realize—that Aesir and Vanir must together brace against the coming firestorm of Ragnarök.

NJÖRÐR

Leader of the Vanir tribe, Njörðr also looked after the sea, the wind, and fishermen. His role in Norse lore is slim in the sagas I've seen and heard; few tales are told of his exploits. In fact, he is probably best known as the father of the twins Freyja and Freyr, two Vanir gods who played much larger parts in the mythology.

FREYJA

Freyja cuts quite a figure in Norse lore. Known as a striking beauty, she's the goddess of fertility and caretaker of childbirth. Yet she's also the most feared

Vanir warrior on the battlefield, conjuring fierce and powerful spells that can lay waste to entire legions of foes. Master of many forms of magic, Freyja is particularly gifted at *seiðr*—the dark, ancient art of divination. The *seiðr* trance is said to lift one above the flow of time, spying ahead to where fate's threads go. All legends agree that Freyja taught *seiðr* and other magics to Odin, giving him some unsettling glimpses of the future.

Side note: Legend also has it that Freyja was quite a cat lover. It is said that her palace chambers in Asgard were crawling with feline residents. Even Freyja's chariot was pulled not by horses but colossal gray-and-blue forest cats, gifts from Odin's son Thor. She also considered pigs and boars to be sacred creatures.

FREYR

Twin brother of Freyja, this god is typically seen as the spirit of fall's harvest. Some skaldic tales suggest that Freyr's rough treatment at the hands of the Aesir during a diplomatic mission to Asgard may have triggered the Long War between the tribes. Norse lore also indicates that Freyr reigns over the elves in Alfheim . . . and seems destined for a momentous clash with the fire giant Surtr at the dawn of Ragnarök.

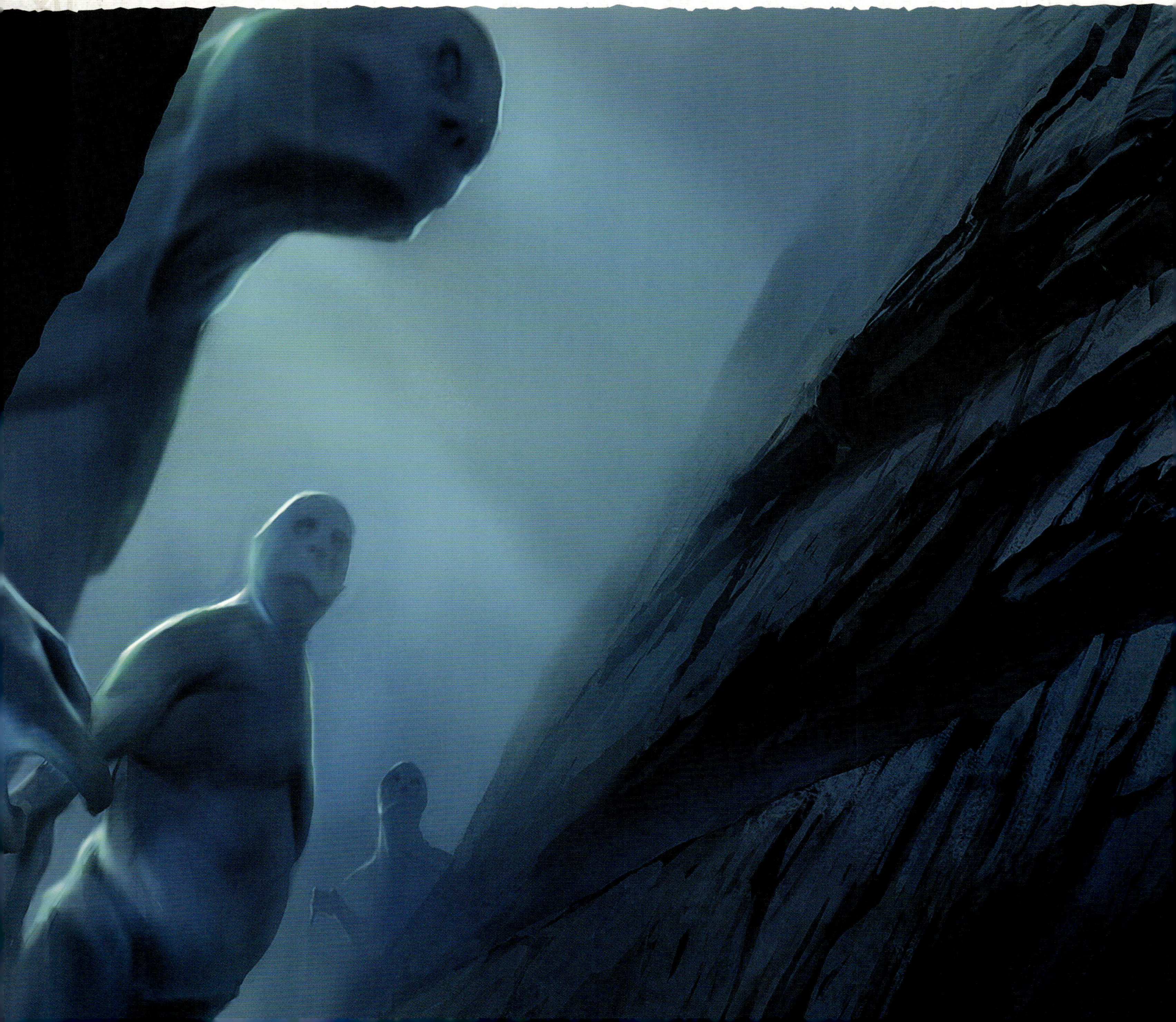

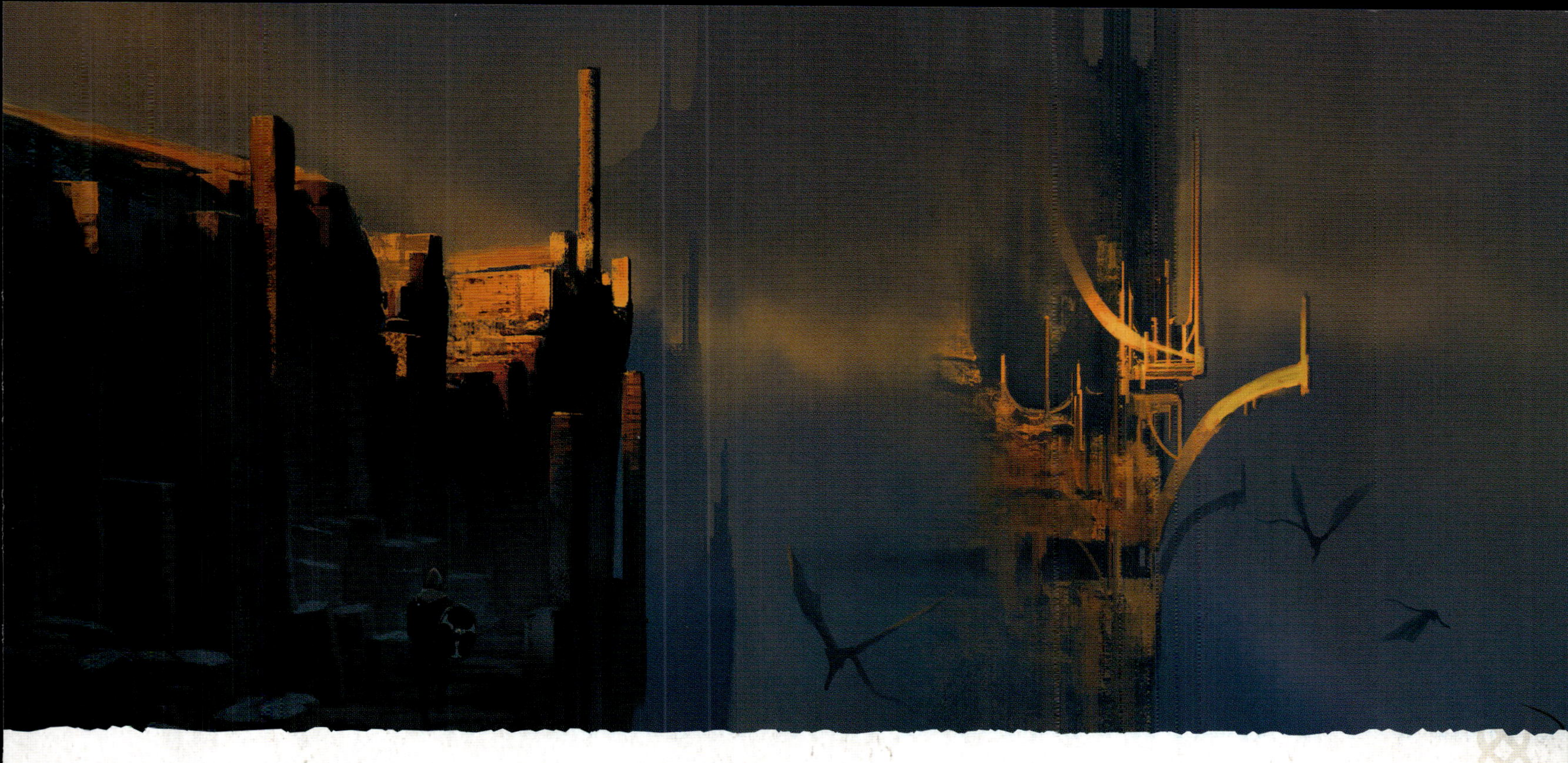

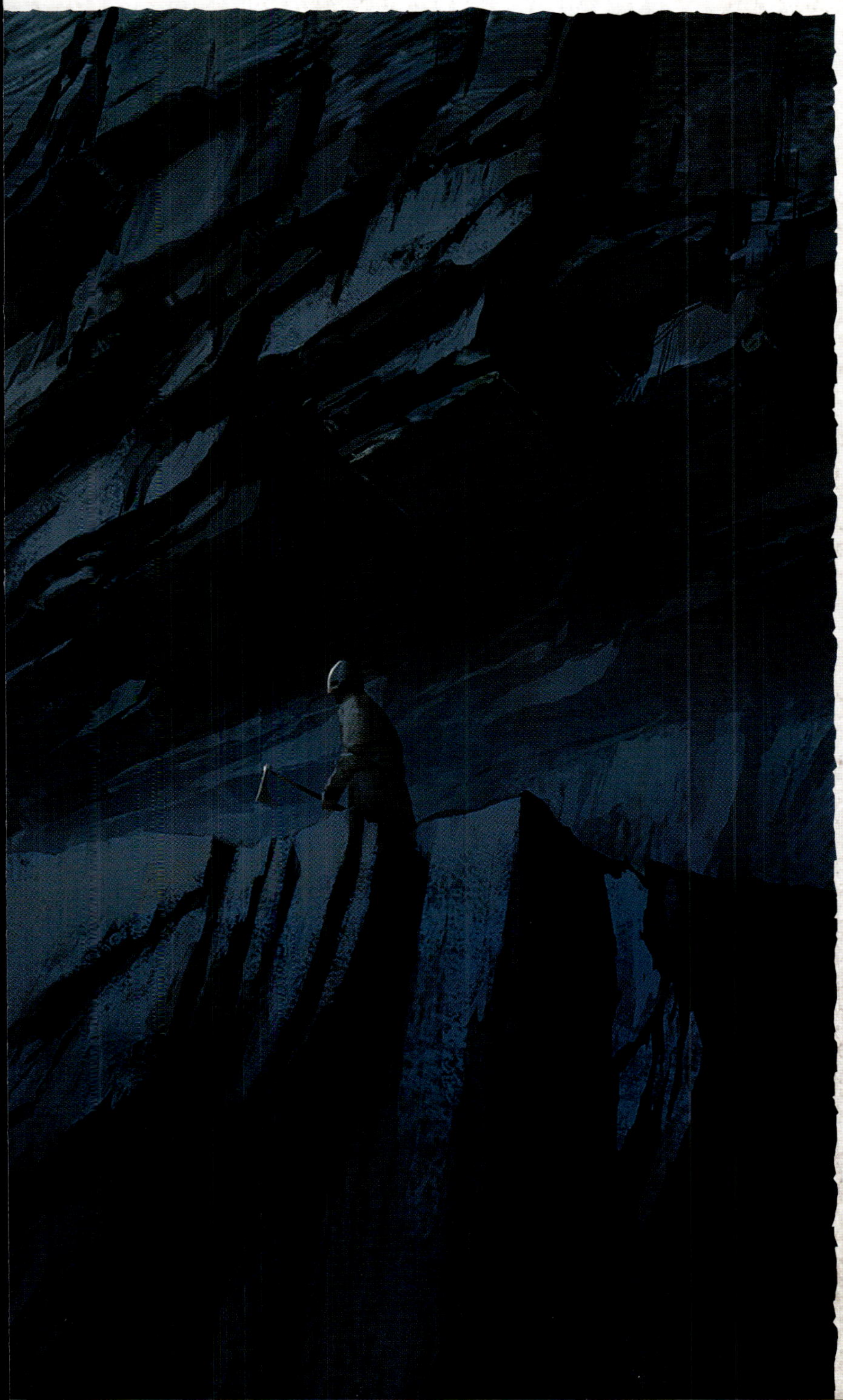

JÖTUNHEIM

REALM OF THE FROST GIANTS

Jötunheim is the land of the Jötnar, the great frost giants of Nordic myth. In Viking lore, the Jötnar dwell in a snowbound, mountainous wilderness full of dark boreal forests and frozen lakes. (Interesting that Jötunheim is a lot like Norway in winter.) The realm's capital is Útgarðar, constructed in terraces up the side of a great peak. The countryside is said to be full of dark magic, illusion, and elements of chaos. Denizens of Jötunheim are known to be great masons and builders, aided in these endeavors by their tremendous size and strength.

Since time immemorial, the Jötnar and the Aesir have been unfriendly rivals, fighting numerous skirmishes with occasional flare-ups of all-out war. Asgard has long kept the giants out of Midgard, but not necessarily due to a godly love for humans—the truth is, the gods don't want the giants (who dislike the gods) to be a bad influence on humans.

Of course, even though Jötunheim and Asgard are often at odds in Norse mythology, we see a lot of intermingling of the races—a significant number of gods have Jötunn blood in

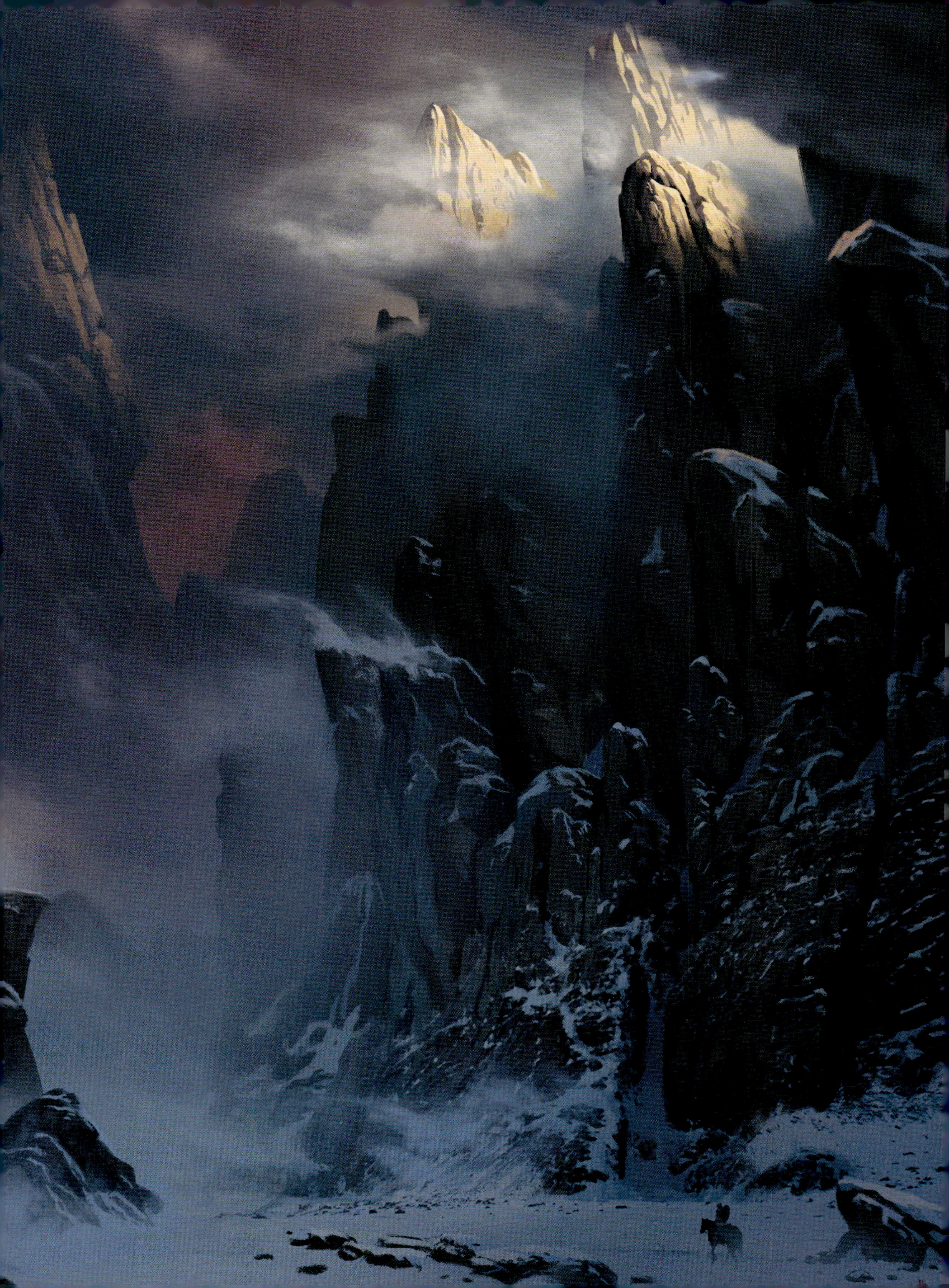

their ancestry, and vice versa. Thor is the son of Odin and the giantess Jörd, for example. Odin himself is a descendant of Ymir, the first giant. Of course, this didn't stop Odin from slaughtering his ancestor. To escape Odin's wrath, the other giants rode the cascading waves of Ymir's blood until they washed ashore in a new world—Jötunheim.

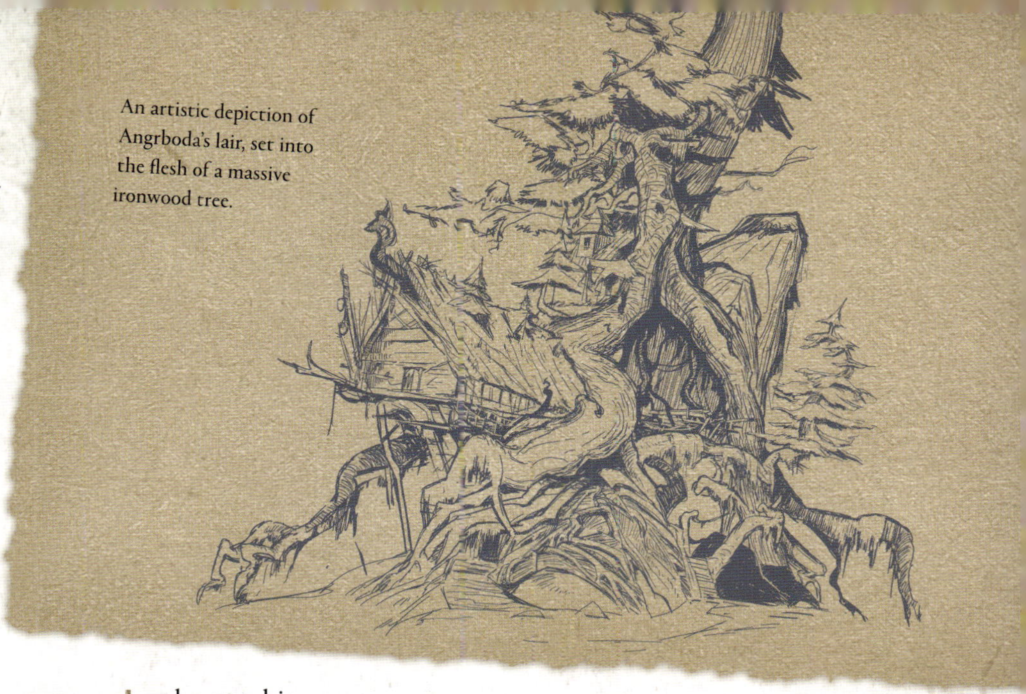

An artistic depiction of Angrboda's lair, set into the flesh of a massive ironwood tree.

ANGRBODA, MOTHER OF MONSTERS

This skilled Jötunn necromancer is said to conjure fear and illusion from her lair in Jötunheim's Iron Wood. In Norse, her name translates as "grief bringer" or "she who bodes sorrow." (What were her parents thinking?) In Norse lore, the giantess becomes the consort of Loki, and their unholy union produces the enormous wolf Fenrir, a creature supposedly destined to kill Odin at Ragnarök. Her other children include Hel, daunting ruler of the dead in Helheim, and Jörmungandr, the massive serpent draped across Midgard. What a brood! No wonder the Vikings call her "mother of monsters."

THRYM, THE TOO CUNNING

The story of this one-time king of the Jötunn people is a favorite with Norse storytellers. Thrym, as his nickname suggests, was a clever ruler—but alas, he met his match in the craftiest king of all. One day during a visit to Midgard, Thrym found Thor sleeping in a glade. The Jötunn lord quietly slid Thor's hammer, Mjölnir, from its sling and promptly snuck back to Jötunheim with the pilfered prize.

Instead of stashing the lethal weapon (often referred to as "Giant Slayer") in a safe place, Thrym offered to deliver Mjölnir back to Asgard in exchange for Freyja's hand in marriage. Sly Odin, master of the art of subterfuge, agreed to the terms. But the Aesir king disguised Thor in Freyja's veiled bridal circlet and sent the wedding entourage to Jötunheim. When it arrived at Thrym's palace, Thor leapt out, grabbed his hammer, and slaughtered the entire court. While Vikings certainly appreciate a shrewd ploy, they tend to favor direct and forceful action at the decisive moment!

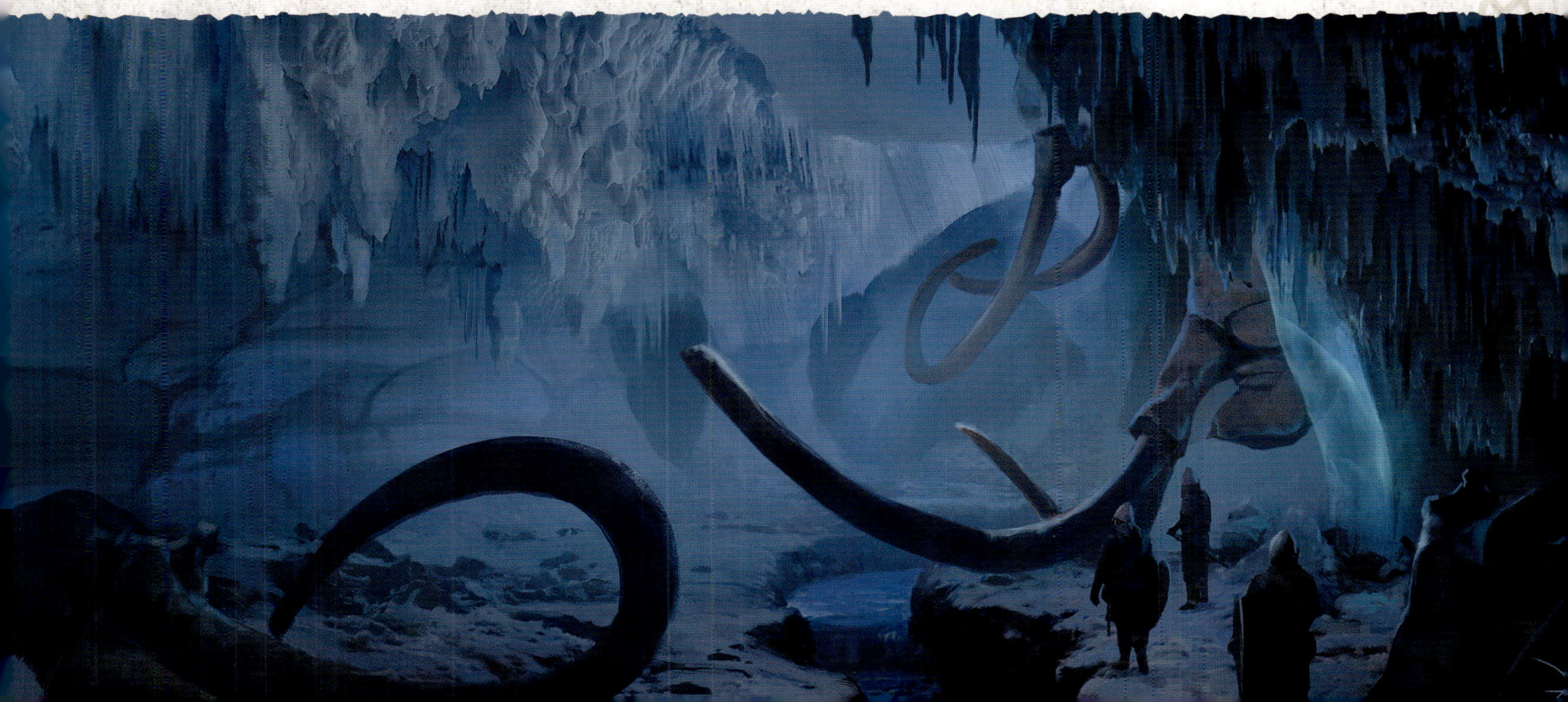

HRIMTHUR, THE BUILDER

This tale of a giant who outsmarted himself illustrates how Vikings see the capricious nature of power in the cosmos. Norse lore suggests that while Aesir gods are nonpareil warriors, their construction skills are mediocre at best. So when Odin—increasingly paranoid about Ragnarök prophecies (howling fire giants storming the Rainbow Bridge, etc.)—began to survey Asgard's security features, the potentate found his city walls deplorably subpar. As if by magic, a traveling mason arrived at Odin's court with an offer: he would build impregnable fortifications around Asgard in exchange for Freyja's hand in marriage. The Aesir did not realize that this mason was the wily giant Hrimthur in the guise of an ordinary mortal.

(Does this offer sound familiar? It seems that Norse lore spinners enjoy dangling Freyja's hand in marriage as part of sly negotiations!)

The ever-crafty Odin accepted the deal but added a caveat: the builder had to finish the job in one season, and he could not hire anybody to help. If he didn't meet the deadline, his "payment" was forfeit. Hrimthur agreed but asked if he could use his horse for labor. Odin said yes, and the project began. It turned out that this horse, a stallion named Svaðilfari, was stronger than twenty gods and could haul great stones with ease. With Svaðilfari's help, the Jötunn stonemason finished the fortification before the deadline—but then rather foolishly revealed himself to be a giant from Jötunheim.

Well, just as in our previous tale of Thrym, Odin relied on the brute savagery of his son Thor to salvage the situation. At his father's behest, Thor hammered Hrimthur's skull into shards and pulp, and that was that. Apparently, hiding one's true nature is a capital offense . . . even if you complete your end of the bargain!

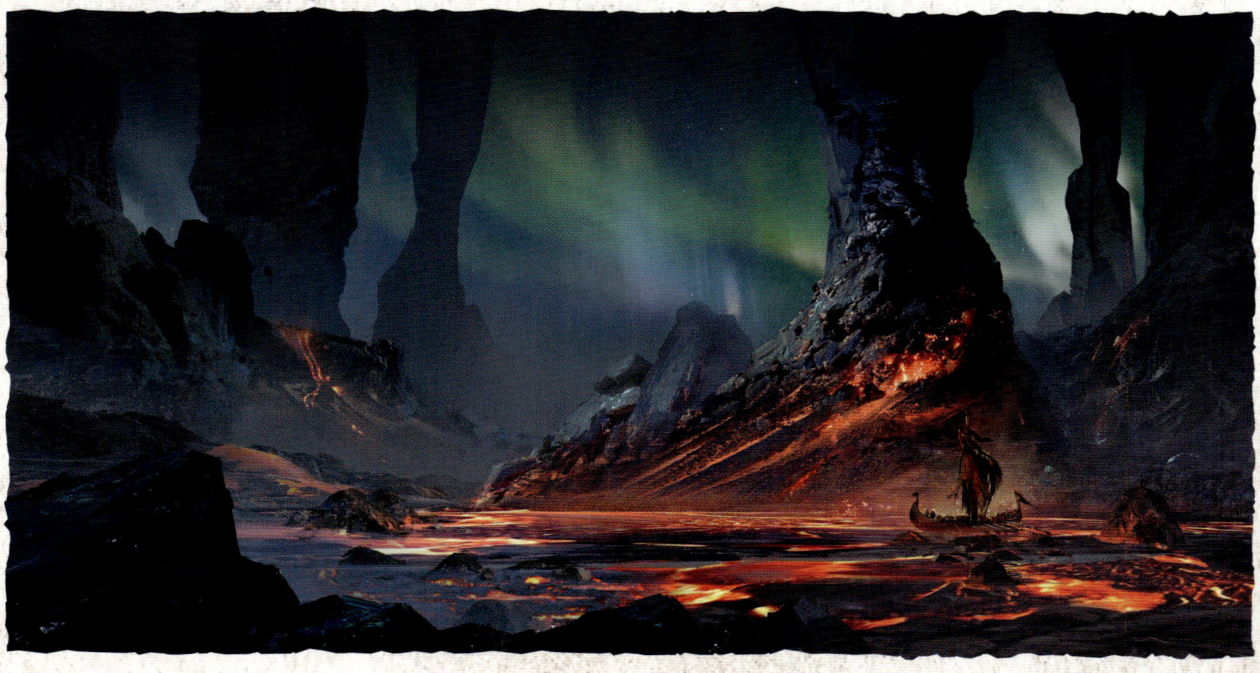

MUSPELHEIM

Realm of the Fire Giants

This surreal realm of flame, smoke, and brimstone is said to be the primordial source of all fire and light itself, the origin of sun and stars and all that is bright and burning. Muspelheim is also home to the fire giants and their dread leader, Surtr. This legion of terrifying warriors, called Muspels, are said to have reddish skin and wield flame and blistering embers as weapons. Like their bluish, frosty cousins the Jötnar, the Muspels are direct descendants of the primal giants who emerged from Ginnungagap.

SURTR

In Viking lore, no sources I've found indicate any direct encounter with the lord of Muspelheim or his legendary flaming sword, said to be "more dazzling than the sun." Fated to lead his tribe of fire giants into a cataclysmic battle with the gods on Ragnarök, Surtr has spent countless eons in his ember-seared lair, lurking and waiting for his destiny to unfold.

SVARTALFHEIM

REALM OF THE DWARVES

Realm of the dwarven race, Svartalfheim is depicted in Viking tales as a landscape of mineral-rich mountains surrounding wild forests and raging rivers. Dwarves appear in the lore as hardy miners and builders as well as inimitably skilled craftsmen. They extract their realm's abundant natural resources to erect mountaintop citadels and frame vast underground halls. Dwarves are also known for their exquisite weaponry and artifacts. One notable example: Mjölnir, Thor's brutal and all-powerful hammer, is said to have been crafted in Svartalfheim by the dwarven blacksmith brothers Sindri and Brokkr.

IVALDI AND SONS

Ivaldi is the legendary dwarf craftsman and smith who owed Odin a great debt after the god saved his life. Ivaldi's skill at the forge fire was unmatched, and he is perhaps best known for fashioning Gleipnir, an unbreakable golden rope; Odin used Gleipnir to bind the great wolf Fenrir. In the lore, Ivaldi's sons eventually surpass him in talent and production, famously crafting some of the most renowned artifacts in Norse mythology. One is Odin's legendary Gungnir, the spear that never misses its target. Another is *Skidbladnir*, the Vanir god Freyr's longship, considered the greatest seafaring vessel ever built.

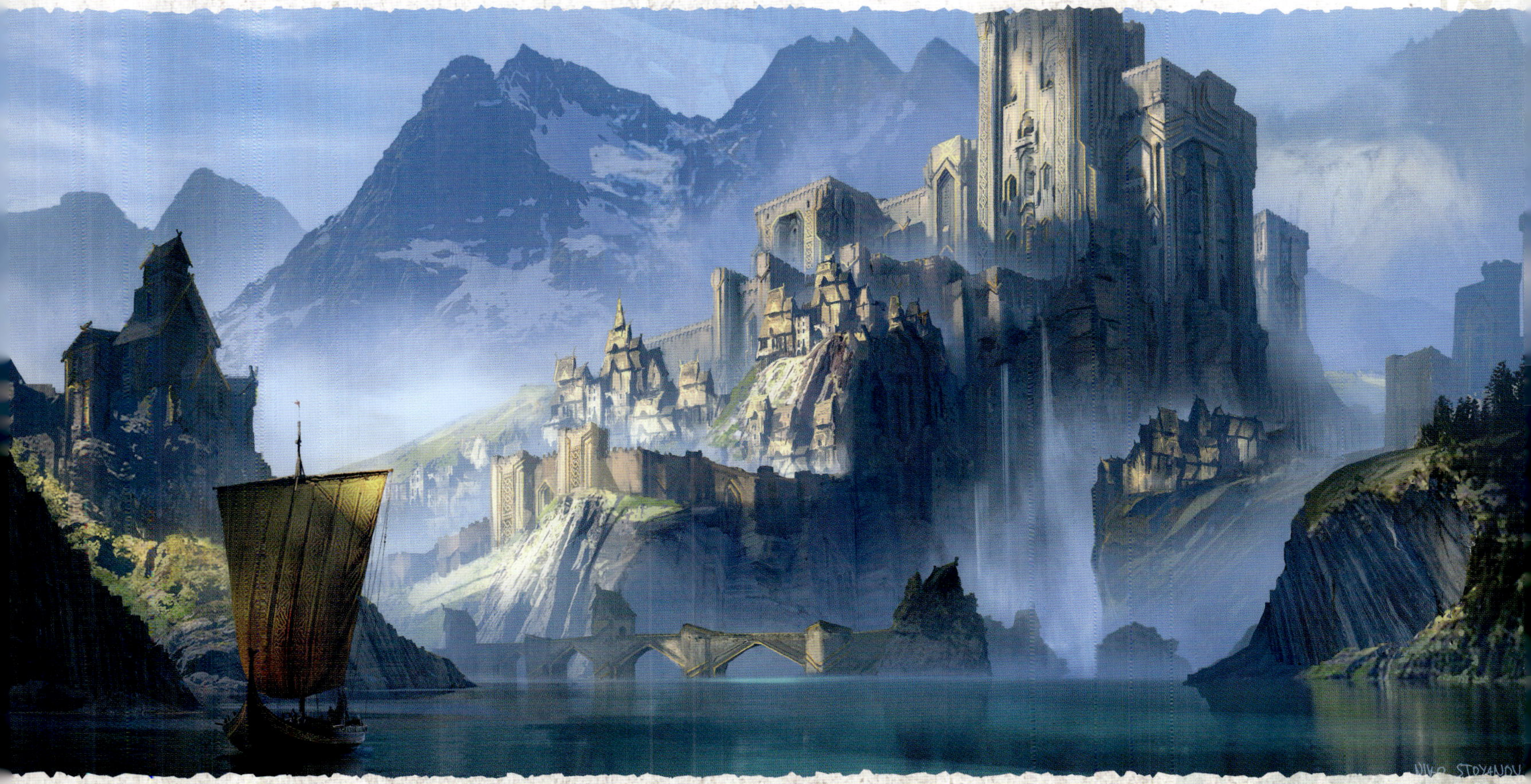

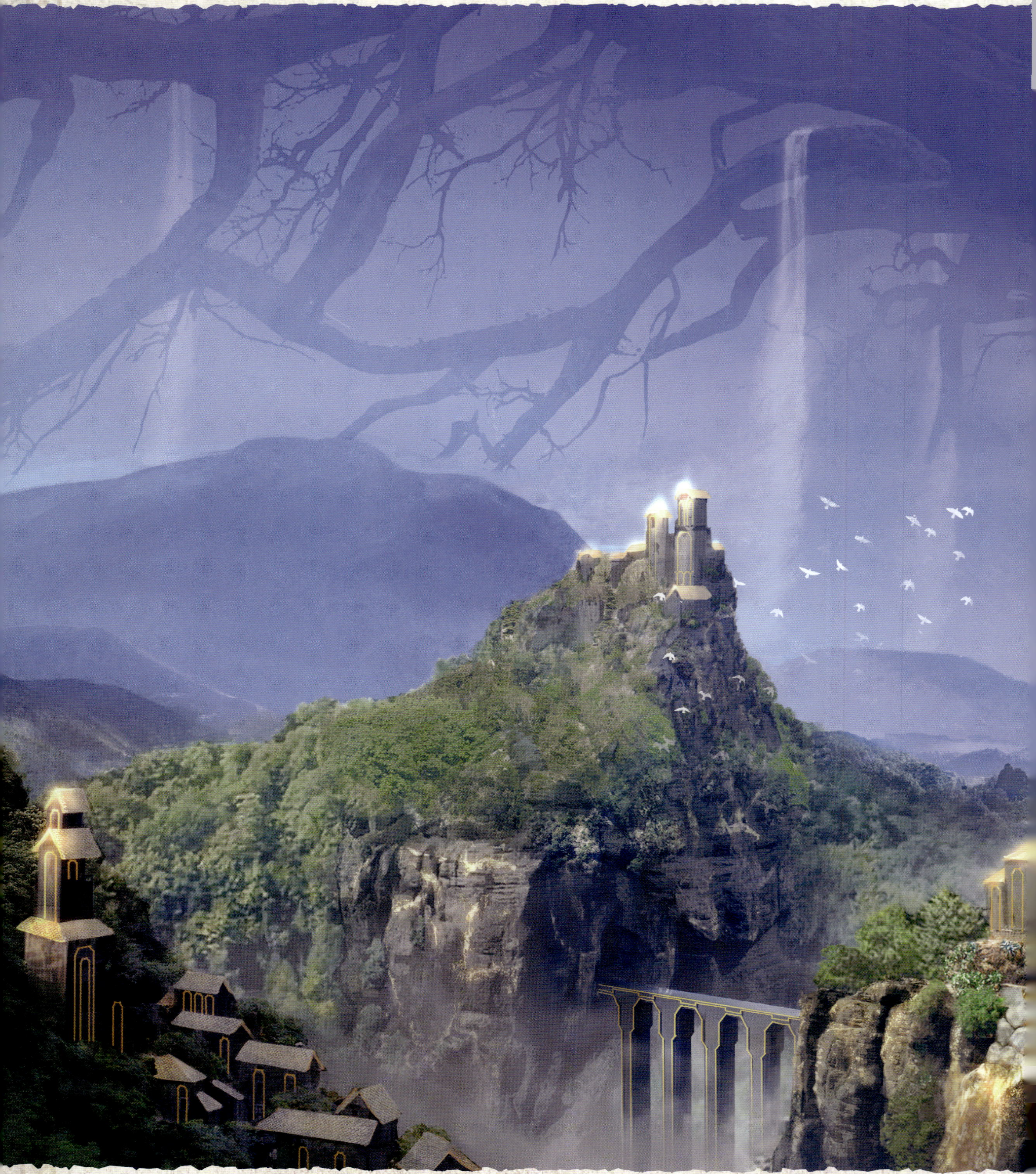

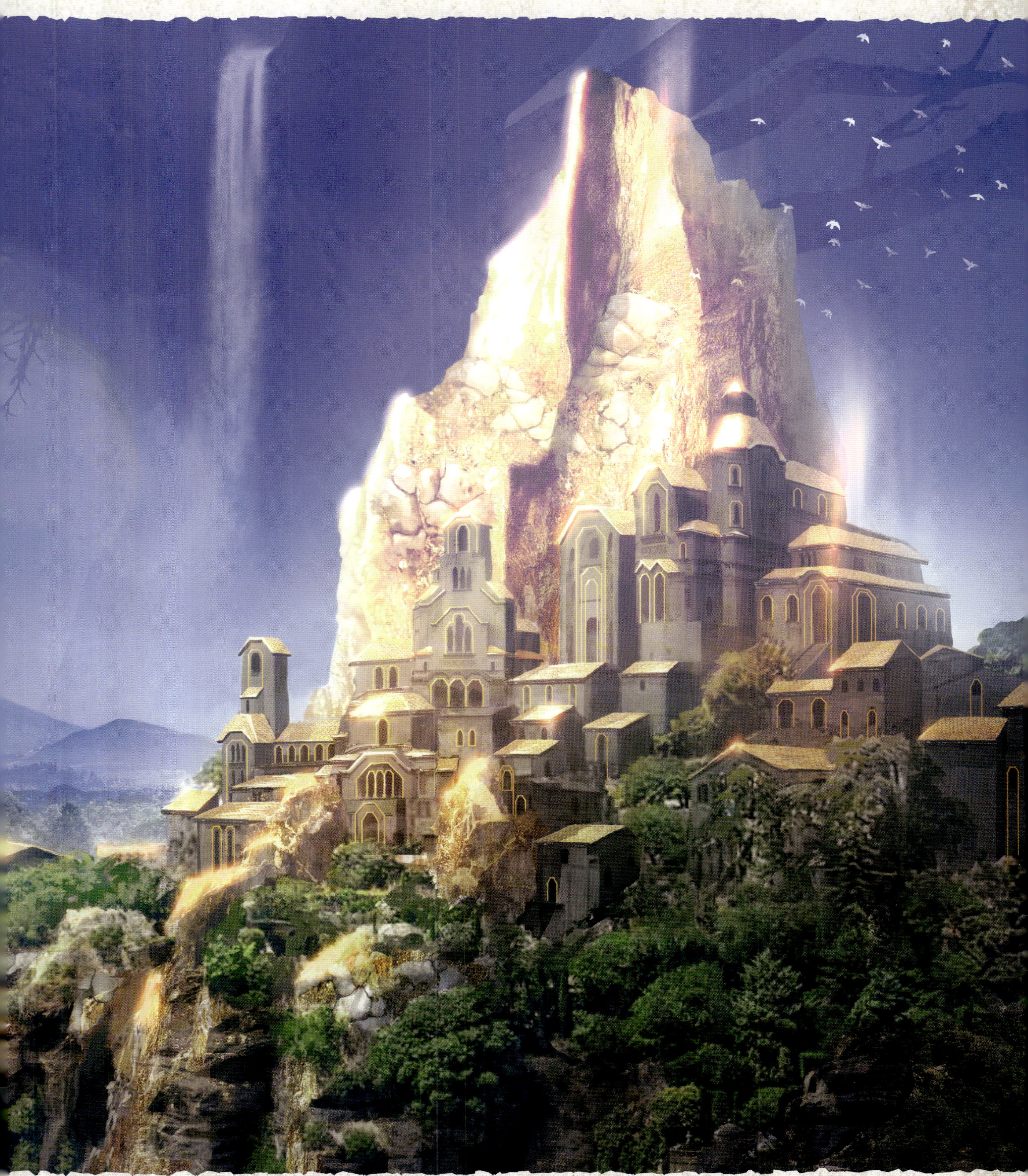

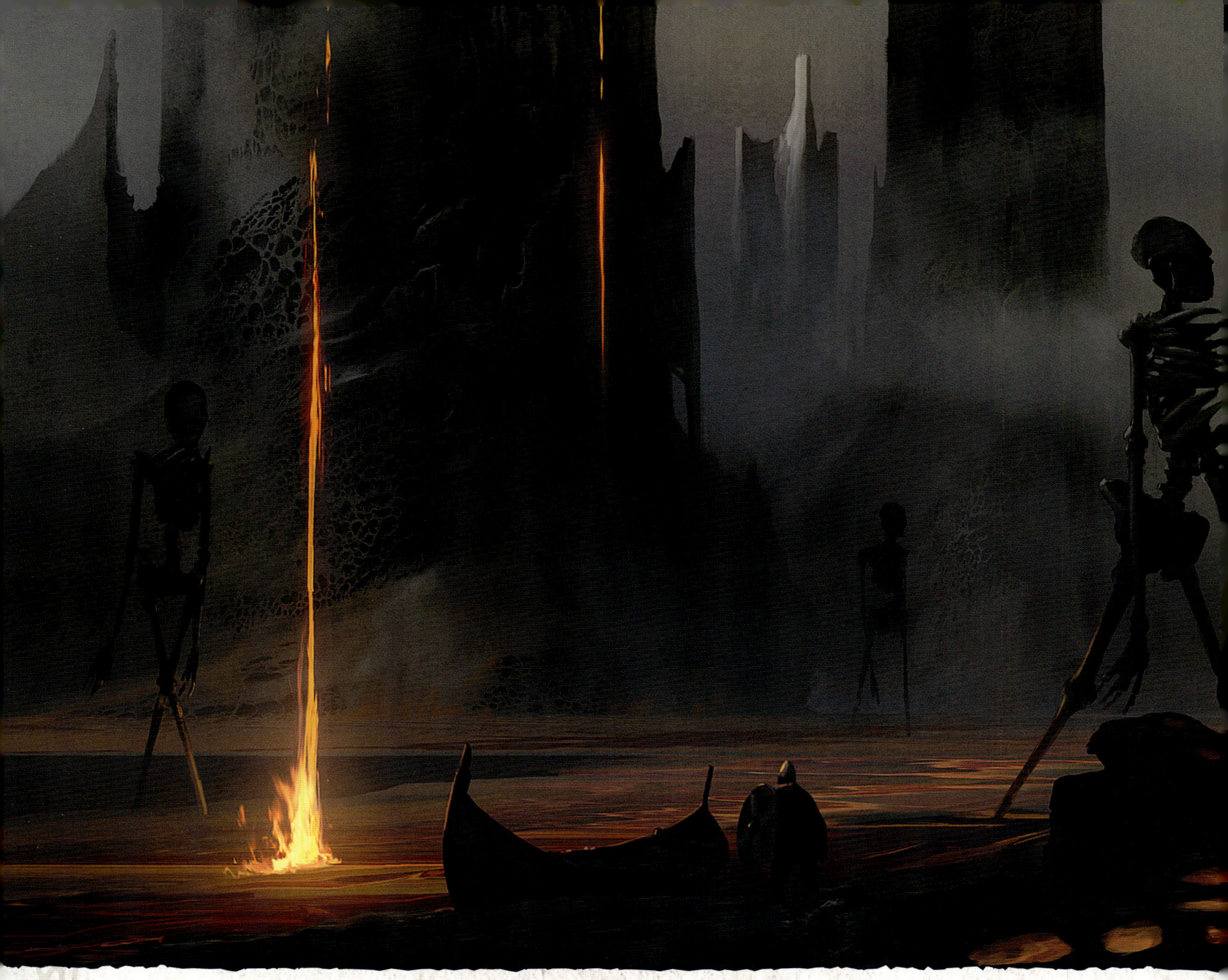

HELHEIM

Realm of the Dead

Helheim is the Norse afterlife destination for people who die of illness, accident, or old age. In other words, if your passing is merely ordinary—i.e., not a glorious death in battle—you are shuttled here instead of escorted by Valkyries to Valhalla's banquet hall. Governed by the imposing goddess Hel, this realm is not the ghastly pit of damnation one sees depicted in Christianity's concept of hell. But the lore suggests it's not exactly a pleasant place, either. Detailed descriptions are hard to come by, but the few passages I've read suggest a cold, dim, dreary world full of mundane activity.

HEL

This daughter of Loki and Angrboda is widely described in Viking lore as "monstrous" . . . and yet her role as queen of Helheim doesn't appear to be particularly punitive. In fact, some lore suggests that her primary role is to greet the dead. Legend places Hel's palace hall just inside the massive gate at the realm's lone entrance.

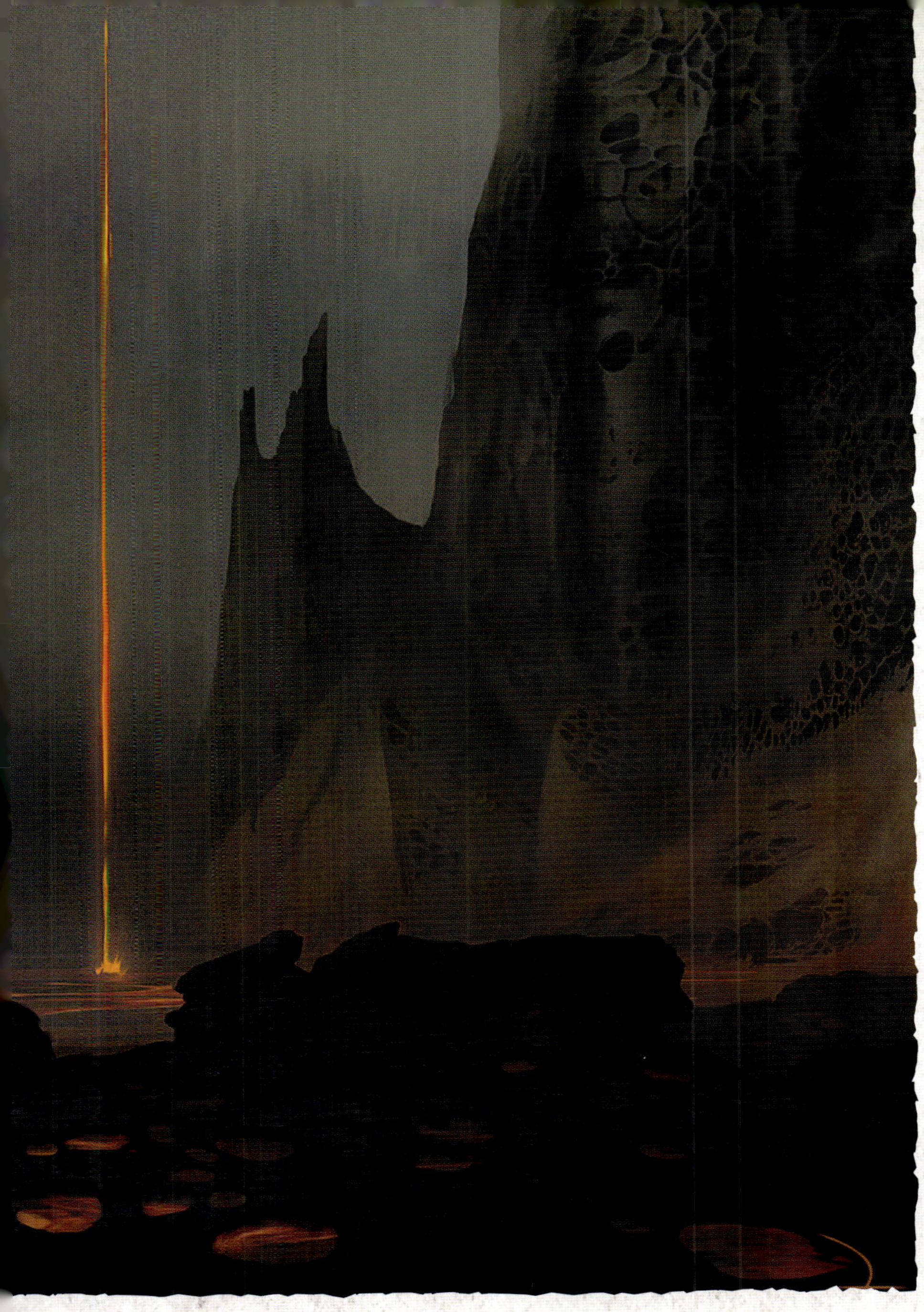

GARM

Ingress to Helheim is via a dark cave guarded by this massive, vicious hound said to be "befouled by blood." Legend says Garm is destined to battle the Aesir god Týr at Ragnarök, with each simultaneously causing the other's demise. Beyond Garm's cave, the river Gjöll (a name that translates to "howl") flows from a black spring and surrounds Helheim with impassable waters.

MODGUD

Legend posits that only one bridge spans the treacherous waters encircling Helheim. Called Gjallarbrú, it leads to Helheim's entrance, Hel Gate. There, the mighty giantess Modgud stands as sentry to make sure only those who belong may cross. Sources suggest that Modgud is essentially invincible. Once dark souls enter Helheim, she makes sure that none escape—not even gods!

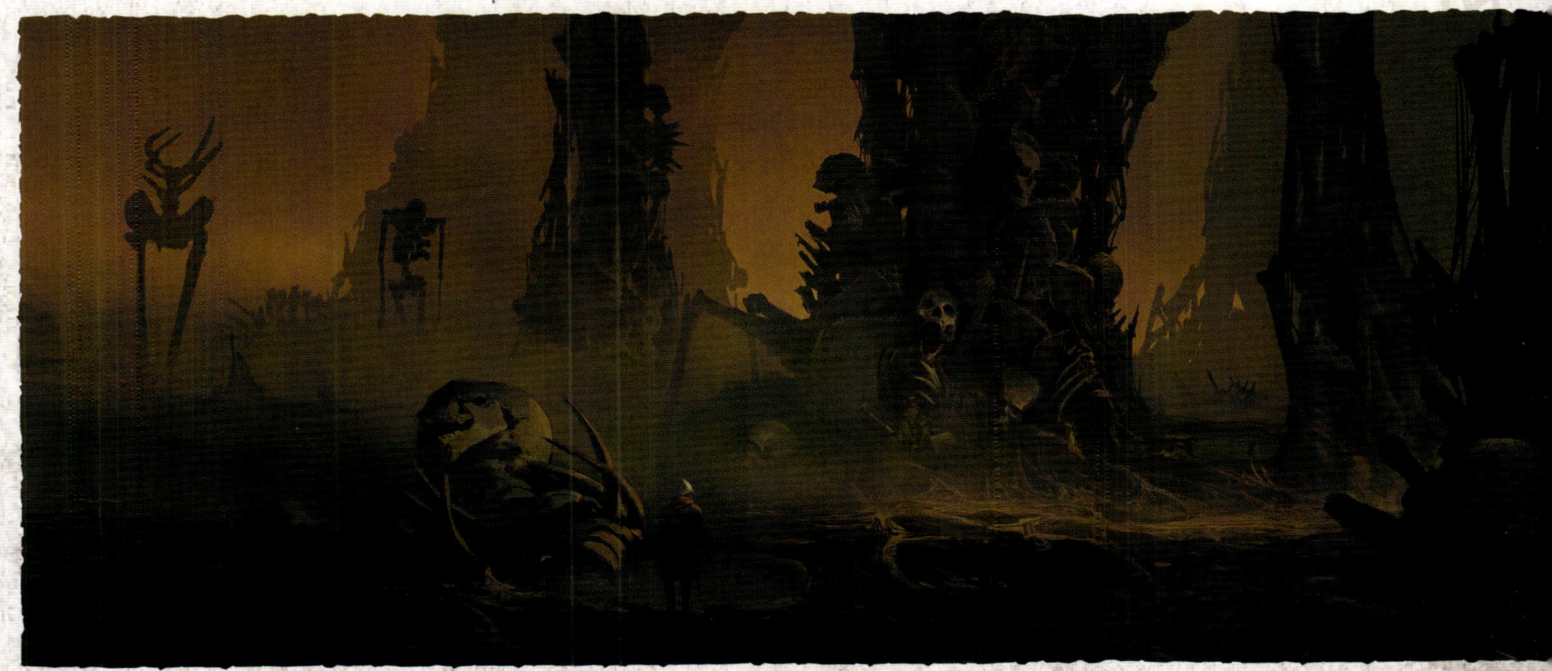

NIFLHEIM

Realm of Frozen Mist

I've read and heard much conflicting Viking lore about the composition and placement of the realms among Yggdrasil's lower roots. But one thing seems consistently clear: Niflheim makes Helheim's bleakness seem like a tropical paradise in comparison. In Norse mythology, this primordial wasteland of ice and frozen mist was one of the first two realms (along with fiery Muspelheim) to emerge from the great void of Ginnungagap. The ensuing clash of fire and ice created an explosion of life steam that became Ymir, the first being and source of all things in creation.

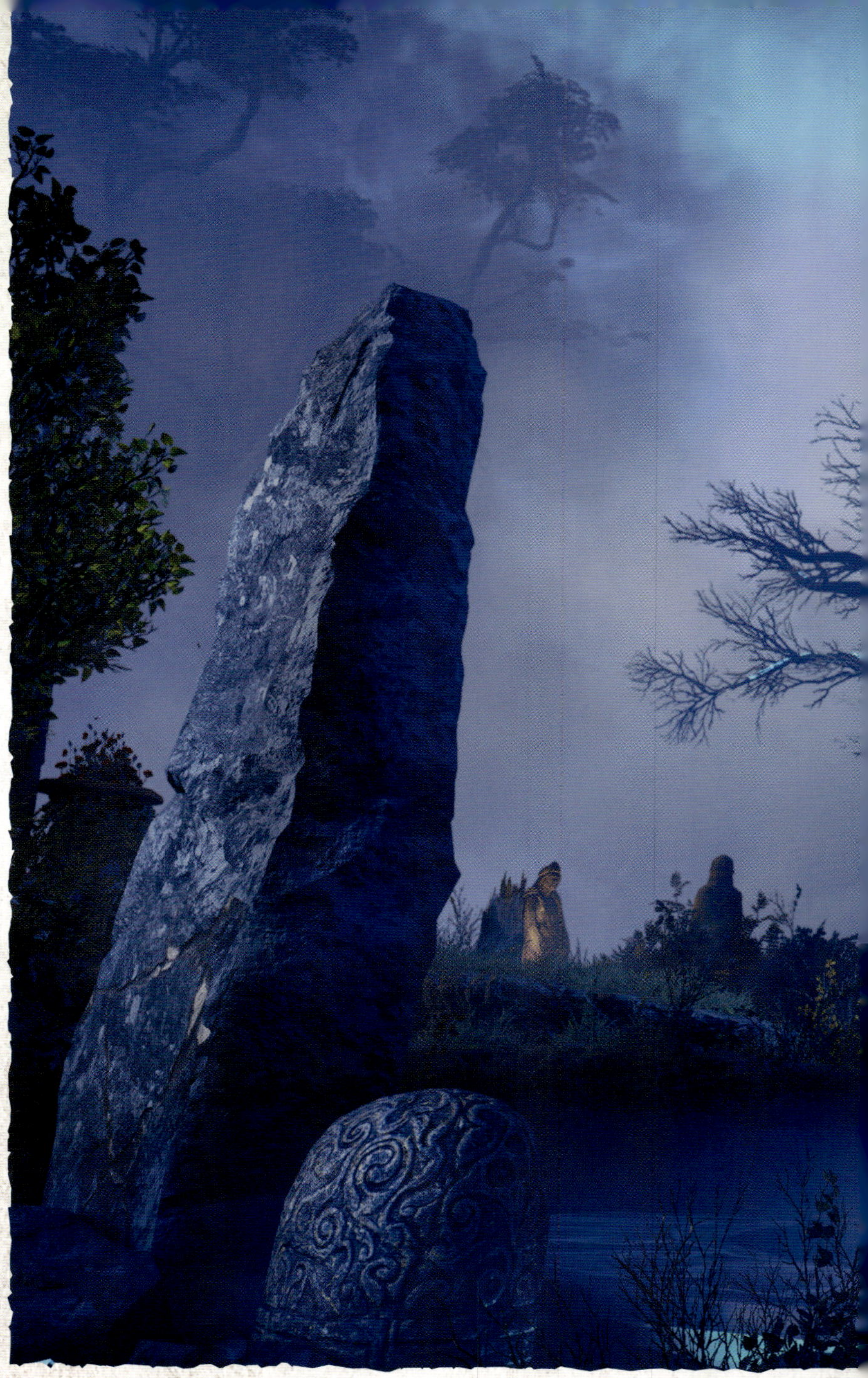

NIDHOGG

As mentioned earlier, Niflheim is the afterlife destination for truly terrible people. Legend also speaks of a great slithering snake called Nidhogg caught gnawing at Yggdrasil's roots and banished to Niflheim. As a result, the murderers, rapists, traitors, thieves, oath breakers, and other dishonored dead sent to Niflheim suffer in eternal agony as Nidhogg feasts on their still-sensate corpses.

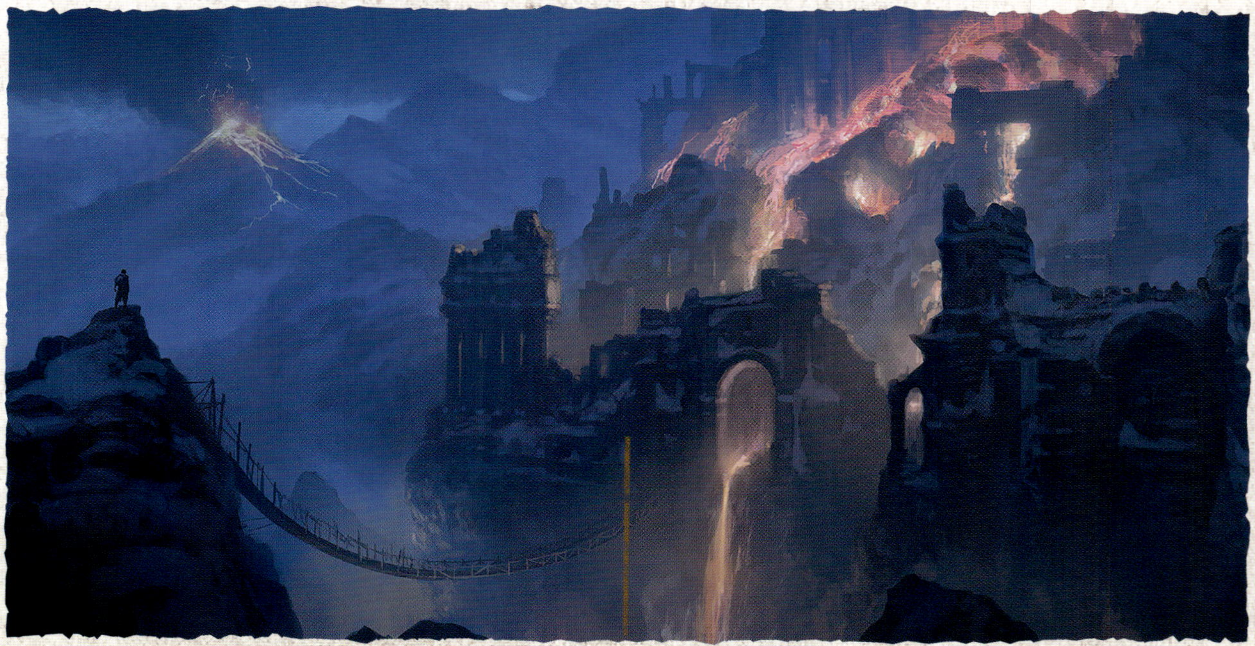

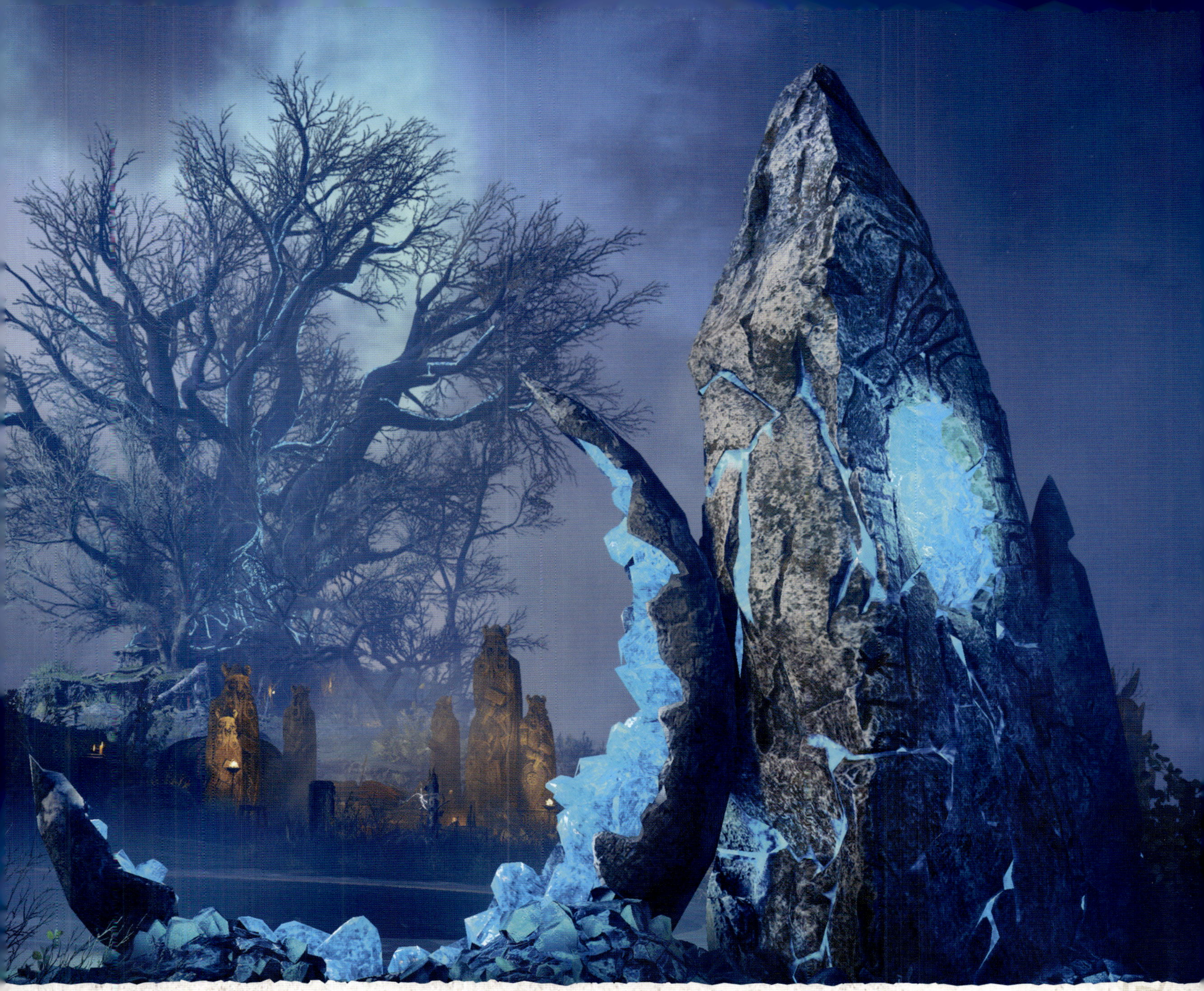

MIDGARD
Realm of Mortal Humans

Vikings call the earth as we know it Midgard. This is the realm bequeathed to the race of humans. The lore places it at the midpoint of the great World Tree, Yggdrasil—hence its name, which means "Middle Earth." The Norse tales seem to suggest that Midgard is exponentially bigger than any of the other realms. It is seen as the breadbasket of the cosmos, with fertile soil, abundant game, and (for Vikings in particular) a vast bounty of fish in its waters.

I'm particularly fascinated by the myth of Jörmungandr, the giant World Serpent wrapped around Midgard. It is said this colossal creature will rise on Ragnarök, waking from eons of slumber to spew deadly poisons across the land and sea. The lashing of his massive serpentine tail will heave the oceans ashore in mountainous waves, inundating the land as he lends his efforts to Midgard's destruction.

I certainly hope I'm not around to witness such things.

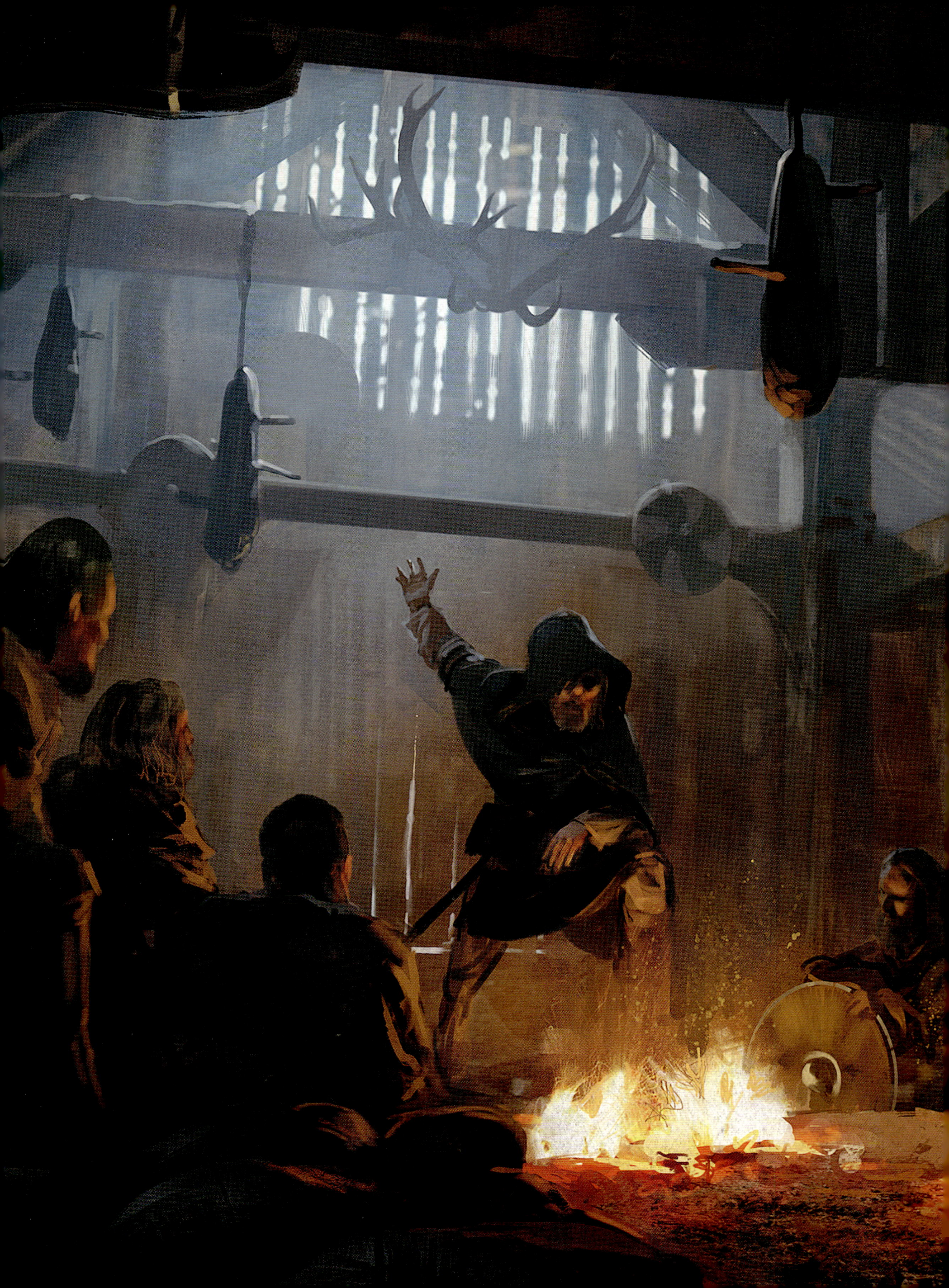

CHAPTER THREE

THE VIKING SETTLEMENT

Aside from going a-*vikingr* (raiding), nothing is more definitively Viking than the communal experience of village life. Picture the prototypical longhouse on a hilltop, overlooking a waterfront bustling with commercial activity! Indeed, there is no overstating the centrality of the clan-based settlement as the organizing principle of Viking society. Each town is a self-sustaining community, with farmers and fishermen and hunters and herders, plus a full array of specialized craftspeople, including blacksmiths, shipwrights, woodworkers, brewers, bakers, and weavers. All gather regularly for purposes of government—to set rules, apportion lands and inheritance, settle disputes, appoint "law-speaker" judges or other functionaries to administer tasks, and when necessary, choose new leaders or war chiefs.

Allow me to preface my overview of a particular Viking settlement, Ravensthorpe, with an observation. I hope I don't sound smug or chauvinistic when I posit that the geographic region from which I hail—the Levant and the Byzantine sphere—constitutes the apex of human civilization. Indeed, Baghdad and Constantinople are easily the most affluent and cosmopolitan cities in history! Most of my Levantine brethren see northern Europe as a barbarian hinterland full of foul weather and fouler people.

But my response is this: I see in these Norse folk a crude but powerful nobility, a remarkable strength of character, and great economic and cultural potential. I would also point out that I now gladly consider this community my home.

RAVENSTHORPE: A TOWN TOUR

I remember our arrival in England as if it were yesterday. The winds were light as we tacked southwest into the mouth of a great waterway—the Nene River, Sigurd called it. (Years earlier, the Raven prince had spent a season bivouacked here with the Ragnarssons' army, a stopover on his long sojourn to Constantinople.) Just upriver, not

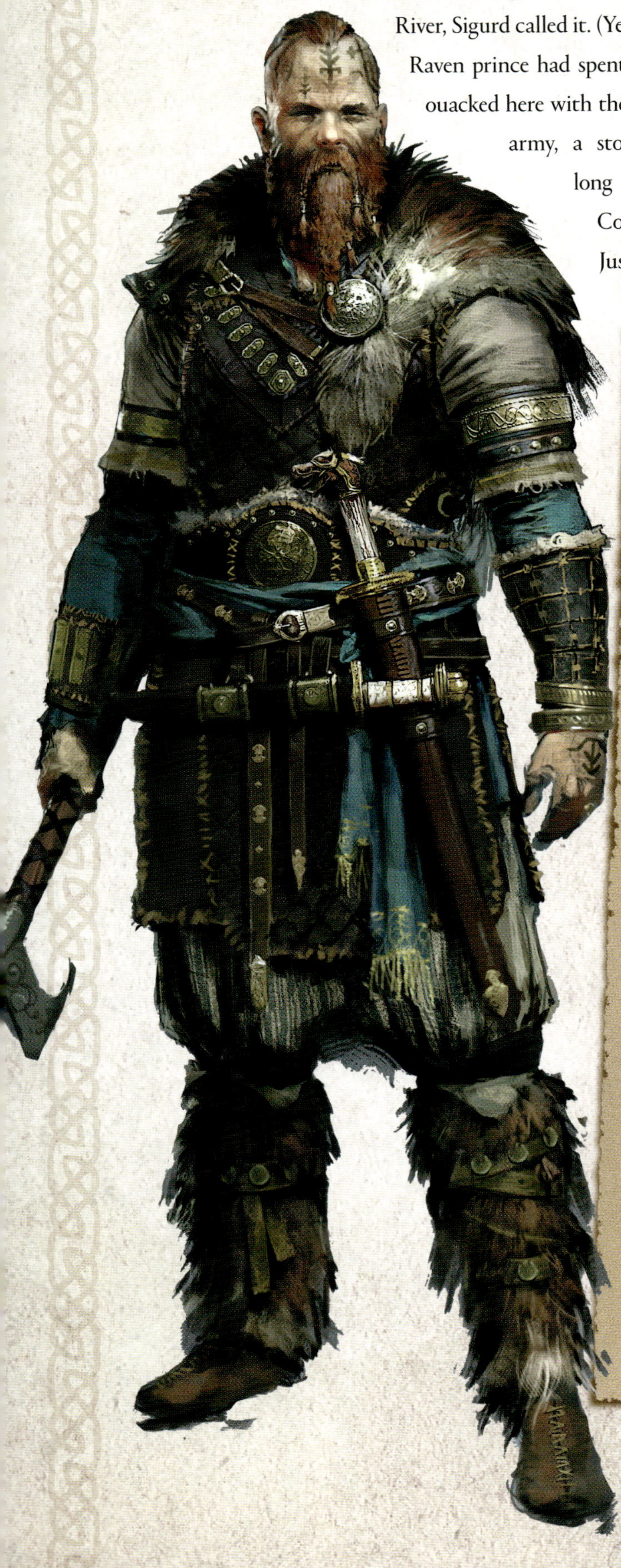

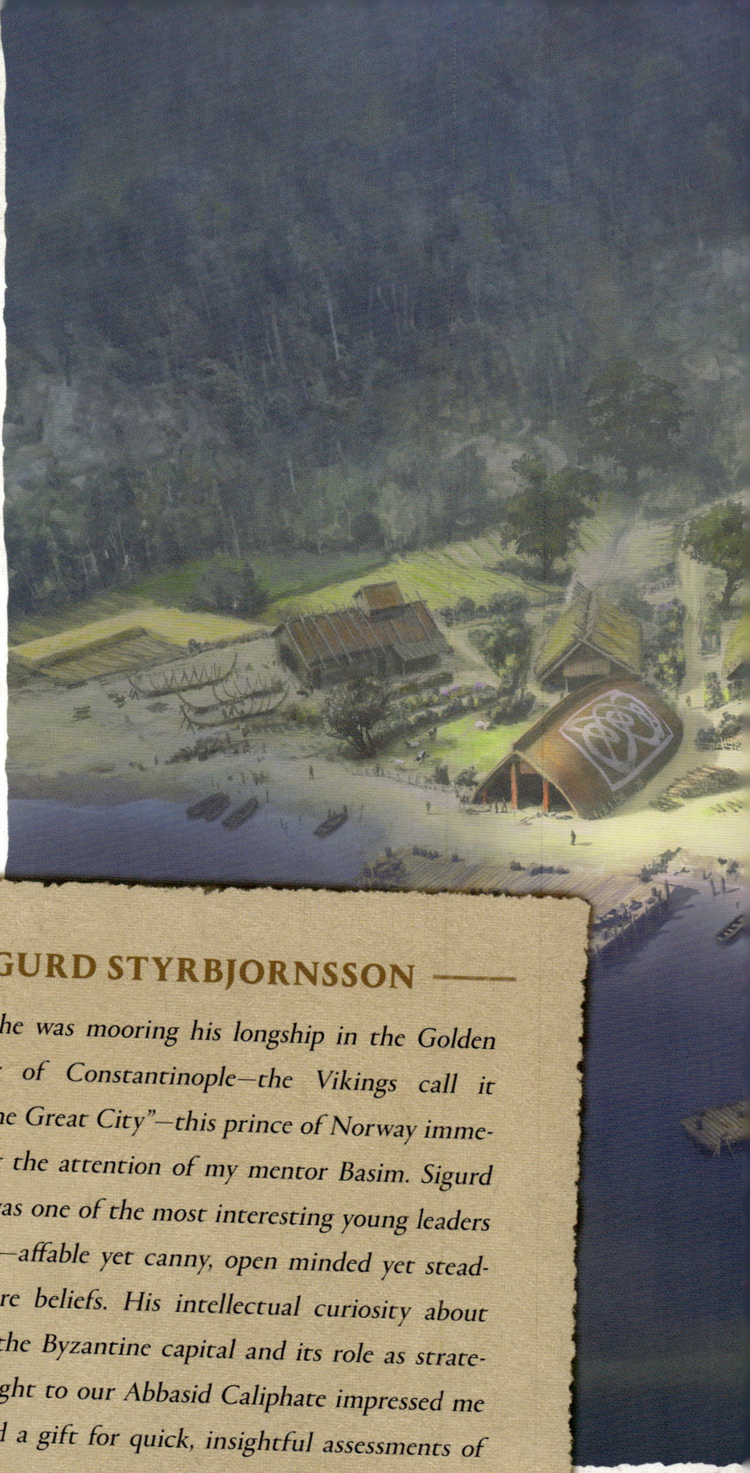

SIGURD STYRBJORNSSON

First met as he was mooring his longship in the Golden Horn harbor of Constantinople—the Vikings call it Miklagard, "the Great City"—this prince of Norway immediately caught the attention of my mentor Basim. Sigurd of Fornburg was one of the most interesting young leaders we'd ever met—affable yet canny, open minded yet steadfast in his core beliefs. His intellectual curiosity about all aspects of the Byzantine capital and its role as strategic counterweight to our Abbasid Caliphate impressed me greatly. He had a gift for quick, insightful assessments of what is important.

Sigurd's general enthusiasm reminded me of a favorite aphorism by the Greek sage Heraclitus: "Man is most nearly himself when he achieves the seriousness of a child at play." Indeed, such a temperament seems essentially Viking in nature. The almost childlike joy with which Norsemen engage in everything from dining and craftwork to hunting and warfighting is wondrous to behold.

In any case, I saw Sigurd as a natural ally against our foes in the Order of the Ancients. But Basim saw something more . . . something inherent in Sigurd's very being. Something very nearly spiritual, it seems.

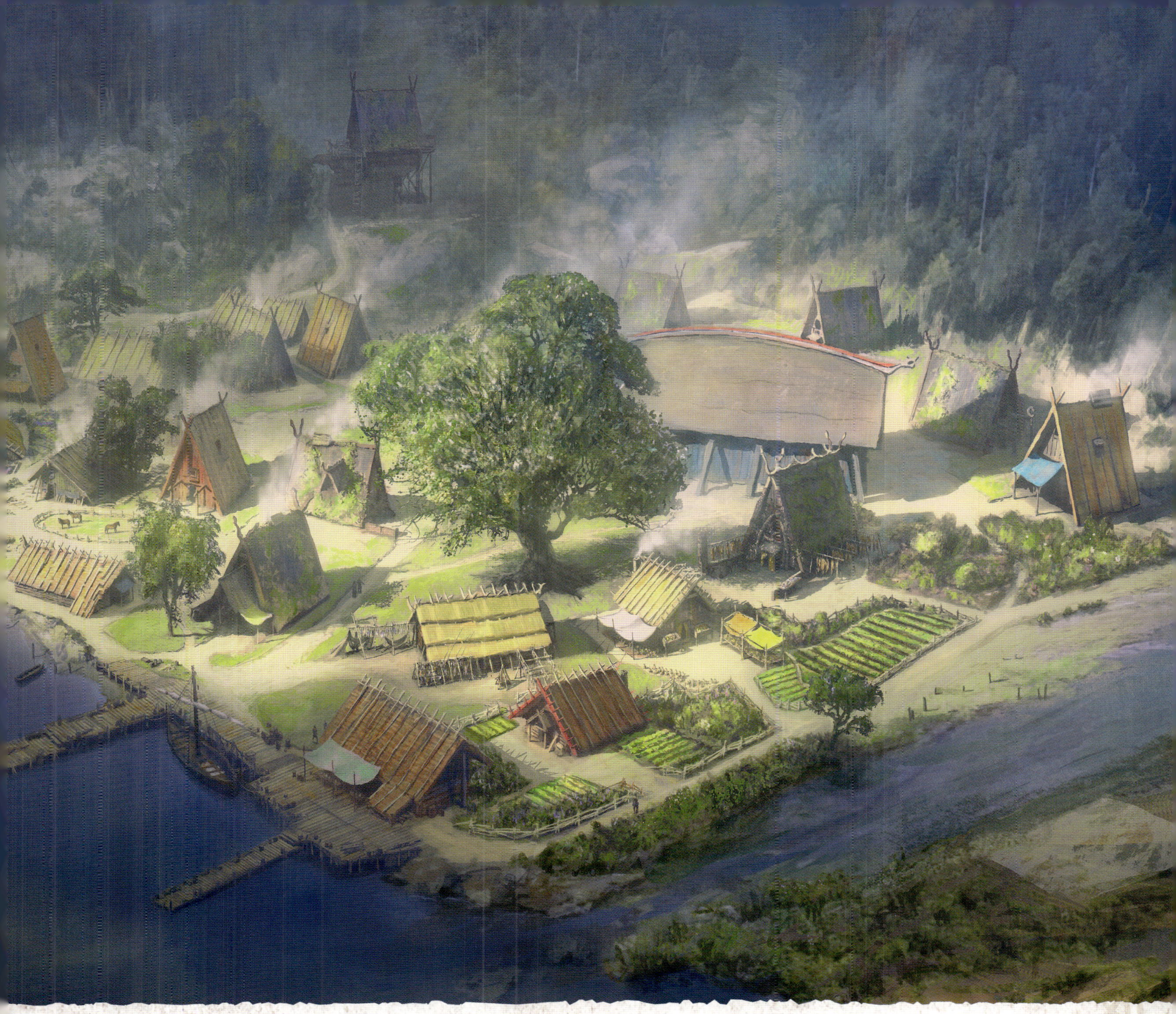

far past the spire of Medeshamstede Abbey, we found Halfdan Jarl's abandoned overwintering camp on the north bank, nestled in a copse of trees.

This became the site of Ravensthorpe, home of the Raven Clan. On that founding day, Sigurd delivered perhaps the best expression of the Viking communal spirit I've ever heard. After inviting two newcomers—the Eastern merchant Yanli and the Saxon stableman Rowan—to join our fledgling community, Sigurd turned to the rest of us and said: "From strangers into friends into family. In all that we do here, let us lead with hands extended before we raise our axes."

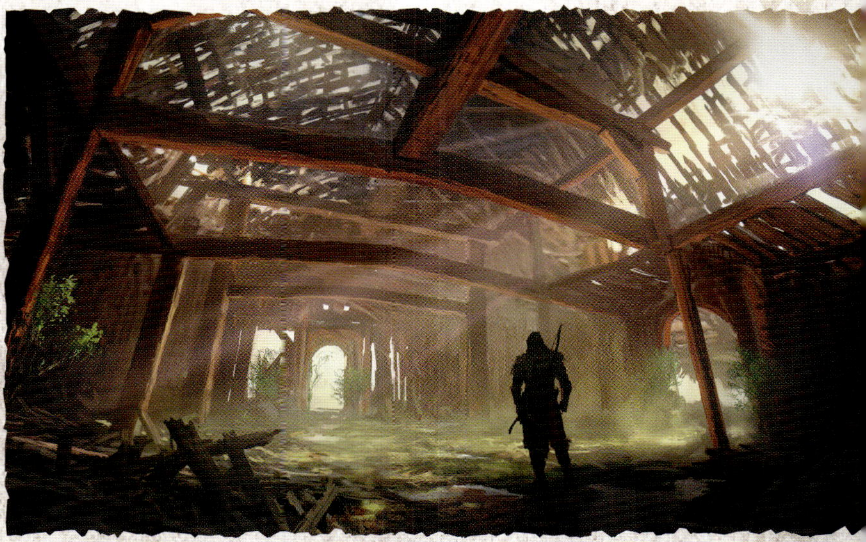

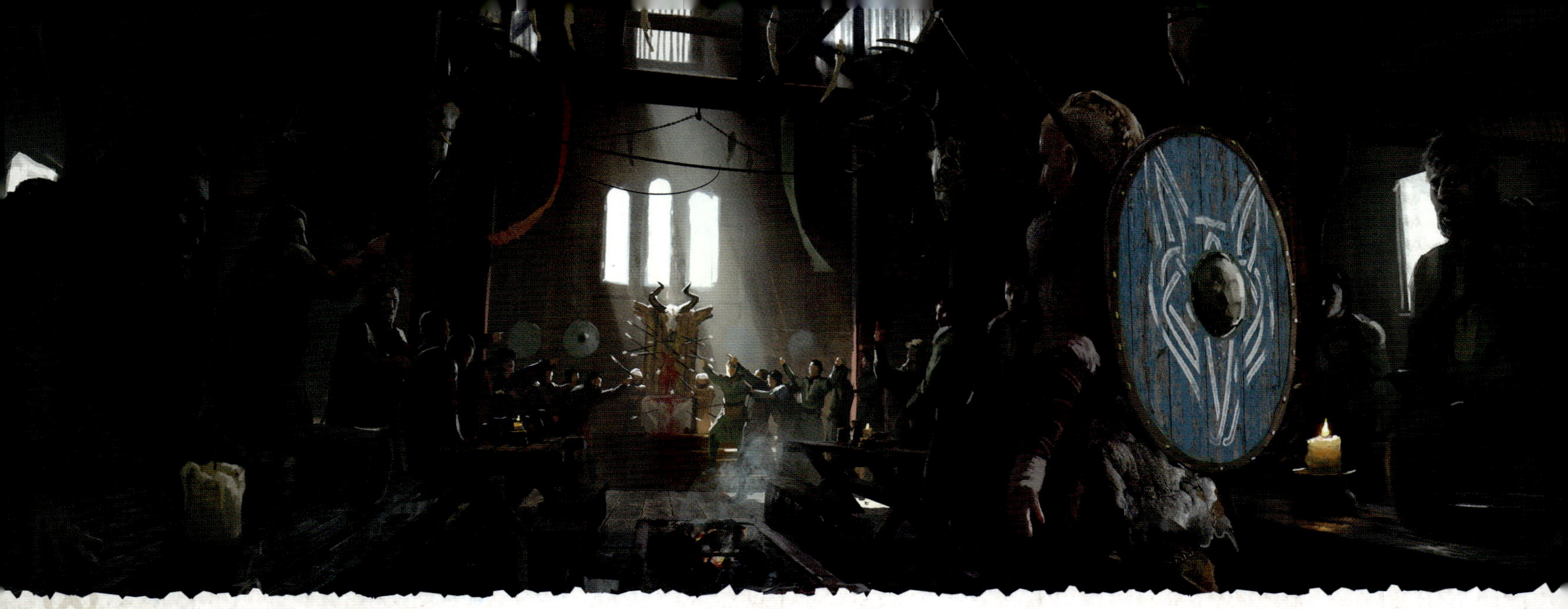

COMMON AREAS

LONGHOUSE AND GREAT HALL

The longhouse is the community center of the Viking settlement. Built from large timber beams and sometimes decorated with ship parts, this long rectangular building typically features an open central space called the great hall that serves many roles. It can host clan gatherings and feasts, leadership meetings, and military planning sessions. It also functions as a secure storage facility for critical village supplies, crops, and tools, and as a sturdy stronghold in case of attack. Each longhouse's signature architectural design and decorative elements—colors, banners, engravings, frescoes, wood carvings, etc.—also express the settlement's sense of a distinct identity.

DOCKS

The Norse economy is so dependent on fishing, sea trade, raiding, and other maritime activity that you'll find most thriving Viking settlements built right on the water, whether seacoast or riverbank. Viking ships have shallow hulls, so they can be hauled ashore relatively easily. But most port towns like Ravensthorpe construct sturdy fixed waterfront docks to facilitate easy cargo loading and unloading. Builders sink heavy pilings deep into the riverbed, tie them together with a network of struts, and then nail a platform of wood planks on top to provide a walkway with remarkable stability.

Vikings are such fearless seafaring traders that their fleets provide most of the actual transit of goods in mercantile exchanges with Eastern merchants. Vikings load their boats at docks like these with local exports—furs, tusks, amber, and the like—for transport to Eastern markets, where the actual trading occurs. Then the Viking traders bring home their haul of Levantine and Far Eastern imports—silk, spices, silver coins, gems, and jewelry.

As a result of this Viking-initiated trade flow, Eastern merchants have no need to explore northern European trade routes themselves. And why visit otherwise? It's too cold and barbaric up here! (At least that's what we've been told for decades.) This explains why Yanli and I are the only two "exotic" townsfolk in Ravensthorpe.

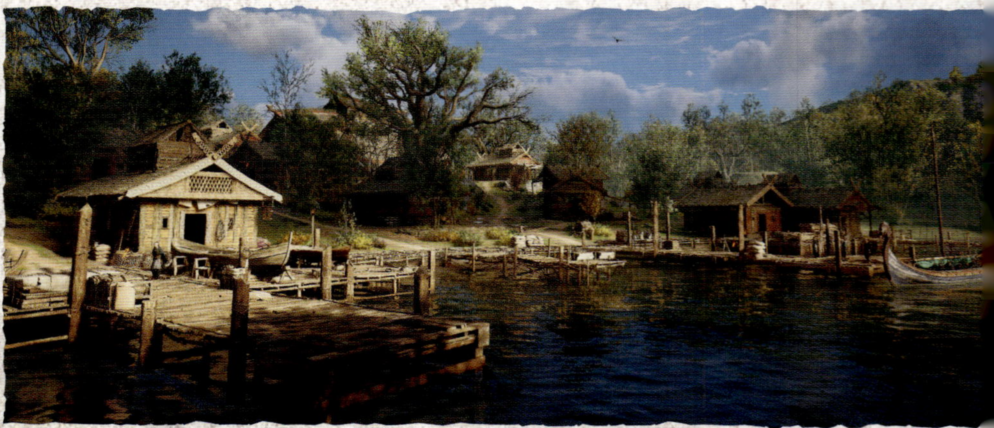

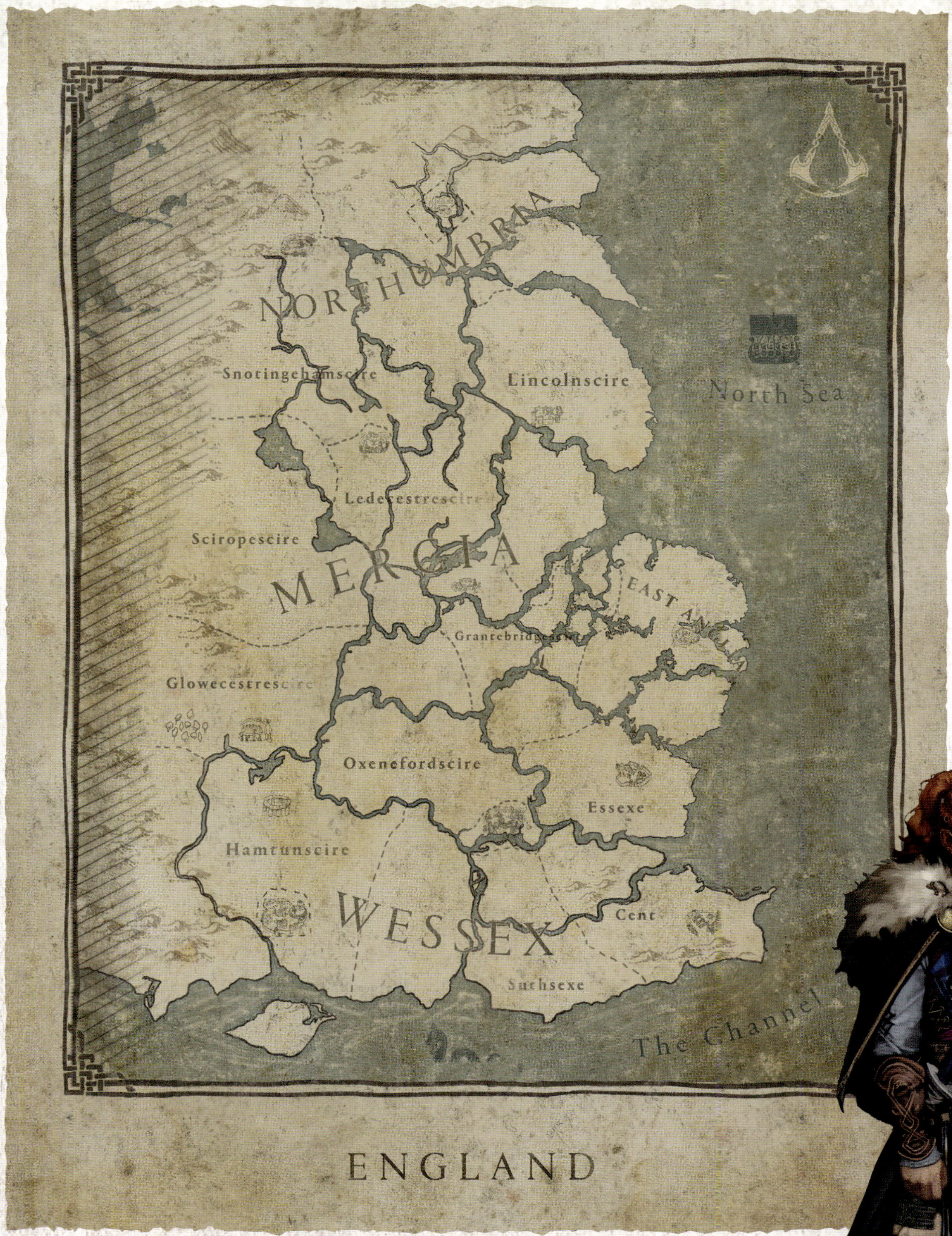

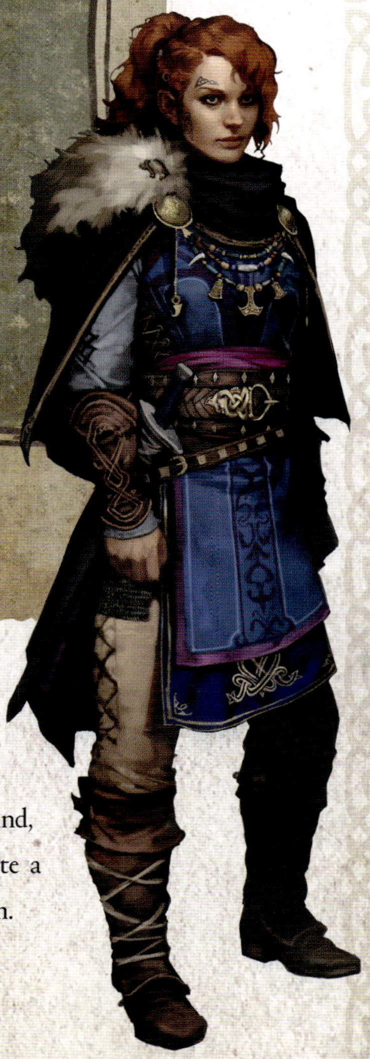

RANDVI

Randvi, wife of Sigurd, is the formidable Raven Clan chief who keeps track of the strategic situation on her Alliance Board in the Ravensthorpe longhouse. Her network of scouts, led by Sunniva and Norvid, keep tabs on regional political and social developments in every shire across England's four kingdoms. Indeed, Randvi's strategic savvy is truly invaluable! Her abiding respect and fondness for Eivor, reciprocated in kind, has bonded the two together into quite a charismatic and effective leadership team.

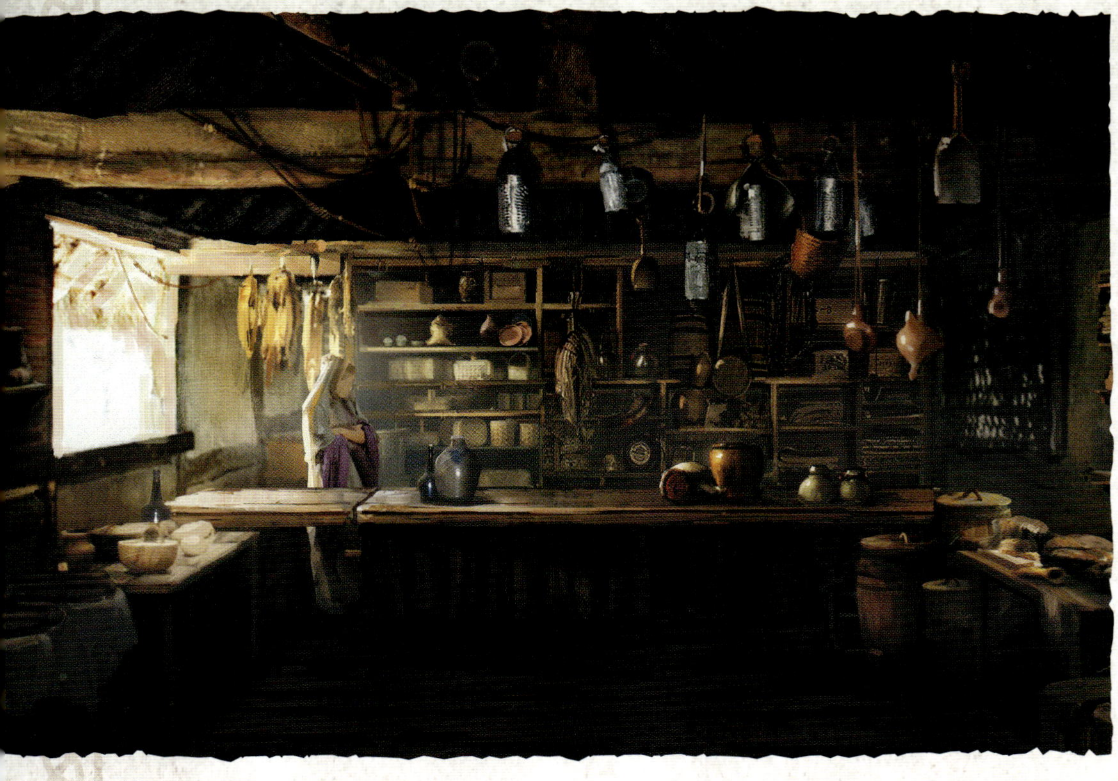

SHOPS

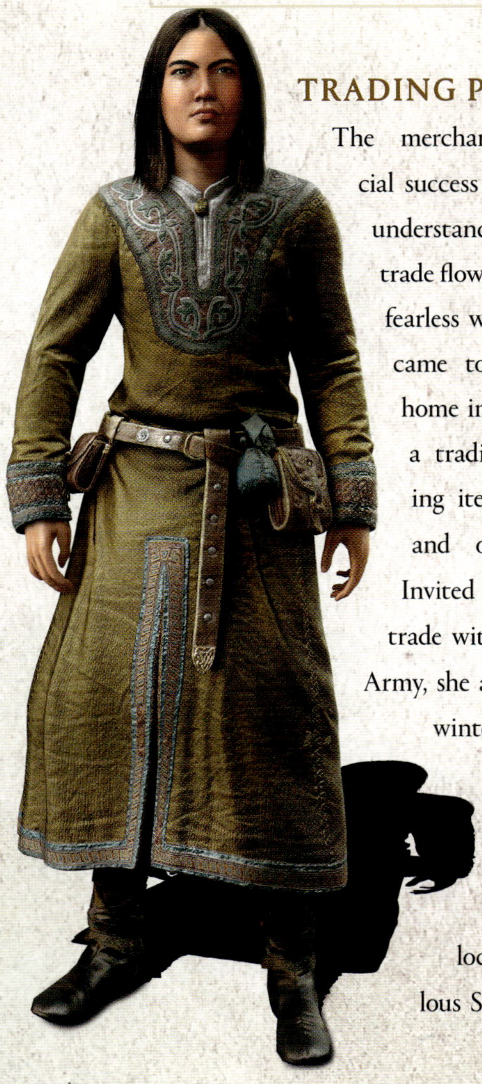

TRADING POST

The merchant Yanli's commercial success arises from her keen understanding of the regional trade flow, as described above. A fearless world traveler, she first came to England from her home in Zhongzhou to build a trading network, importing items from the Orient and other exotic places. Invited by Halfdan Jarl to trade with his Great Heathen Army, she arrived too late at his winter camp—the Vikings had already moved north, leaving an abandoned outpost overrun by ragtag local gangs. The scurrilous Saxon brigands robbed Yanli of her goods and planned to sell her as a slave. But our fortuitous arrival rescued her from that fate; Sigurd invited her to establish a trading post in his newly founded settlement.

The shrewd woman buys and sells many common (and uncommon) goods in her well-stocked depot: gear, rations, leather, ores and ingots, personal cosmetics (including hair dyes and some rather unsettling tattoo designs), arrows for one's quiver, and an assortment of runes said to add efficacy to weapons and armor. Yanli also sells schematics for the clan's longships or distinctive additions to the settlement grounds—things like sculptures, tombstones, and wells. My favorite items are her scrolls listing "Fantastic Fishes and Where to Find Them." If you have a hunger for brown trout or shad or eel, these documents show where best to fish for them!

FISHING HUT

Arth and his grandfather Merton (a man of few words . . . nay, of *no* words) operate the village fishery. Bring them fish, and they'll pay you fairly! Young Arth is a precocious and sociable child, and even Merton admits that his grandson is "more of a people person" than is the old man. Arth maintains a special fondness for Eivor and enjoys her regular patronage, abetted by Merton's gift of a fishing rope to the Viking leader.

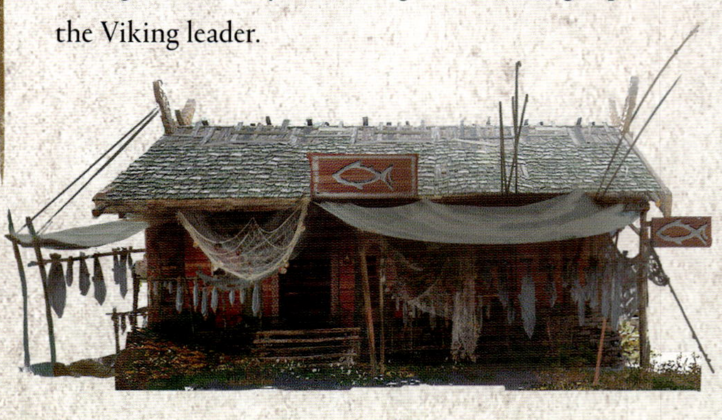

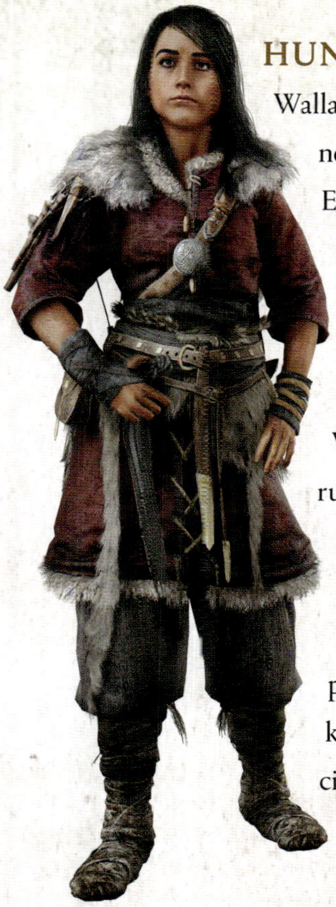

HUNTER'S HUT

Wallace is said to be the finest tanner and taxidermist in all of England, while Petra is a highly skilled hunter with an eye for trophy kills. If you're capable enough, Petra may bid you join her on elite hunts! Wallace trades rewards, such as runes or ingots, for delivery of special items, like reindeer antlers, wolf claws, boar tusks, or deer hooves. He also seeks the pelts of legendary animals. He keeps a careful log of these special creatures; if you can bag one, Wallace mounts it as a keepsake trophy for the longhouse.

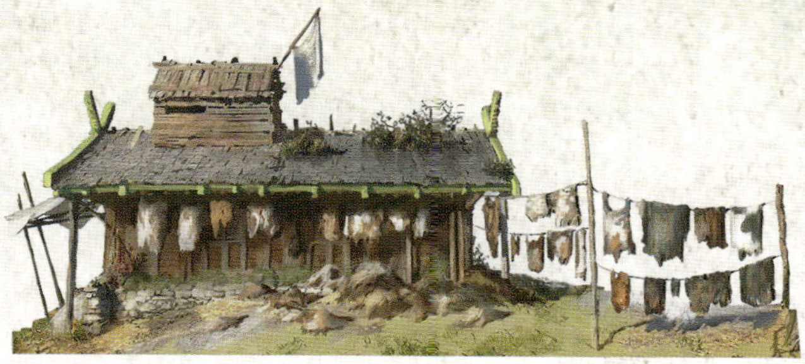

GRAIN FARM

I must admit, after growing up in the fertile crescent of my Mesopotamian homeland—the abundance produced by the Tigris-Euphrates river system is legendary—I fully expected to be unimpressed by the agriculture of these northern climes. But farming across the British Isles is surprisingly robust and productive! This farmstead is where the hardworking Viggo, his wife Runa, and their children Silvi and Knud grow and harvest all of Ravensthorpe's barley, oats, and rye. As long as Gunnar keeps their plow blade sharp, the farm's yields are plentiful. Its high-quality grains help make Tekla's fermented brews the best in Mercia.

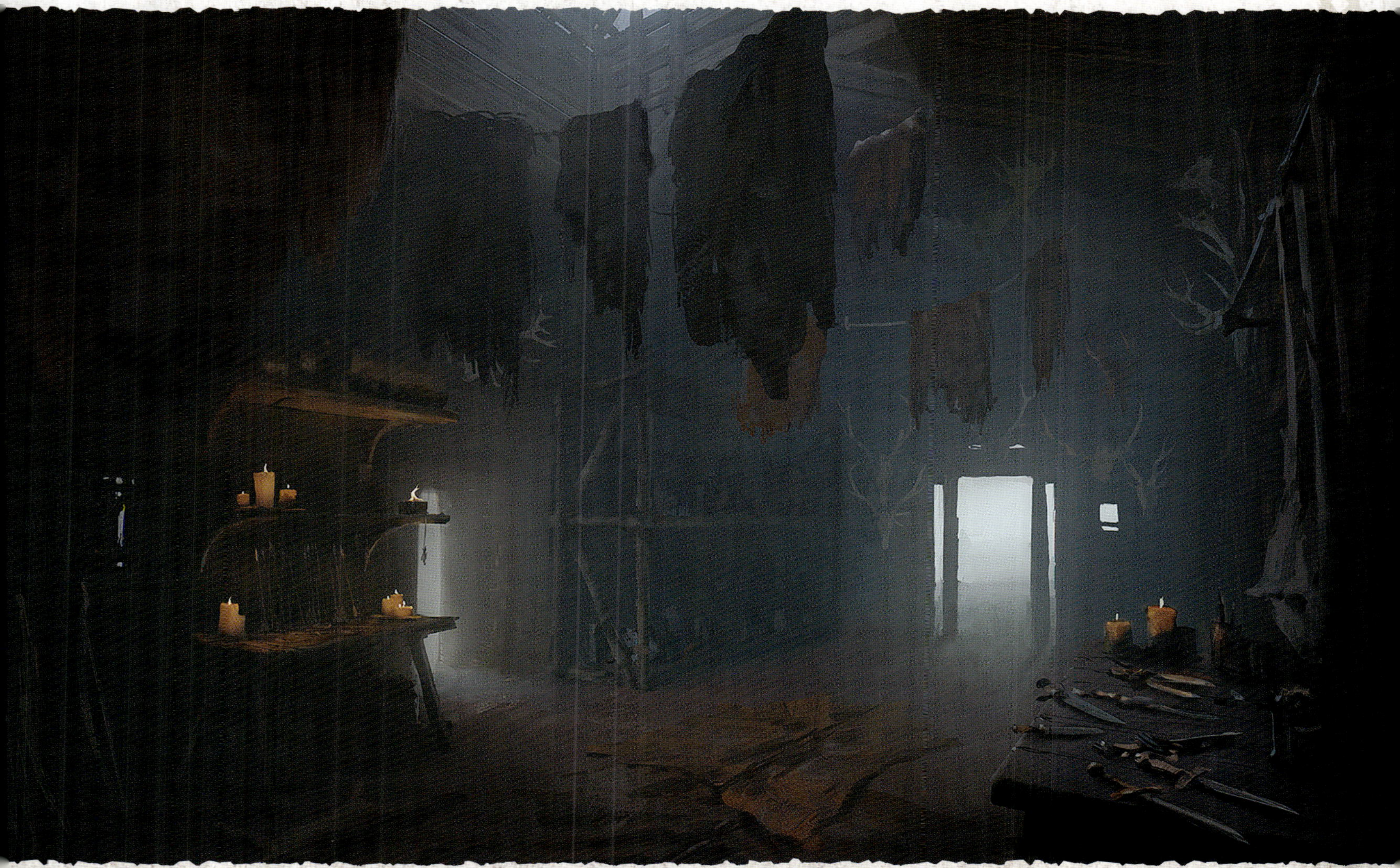

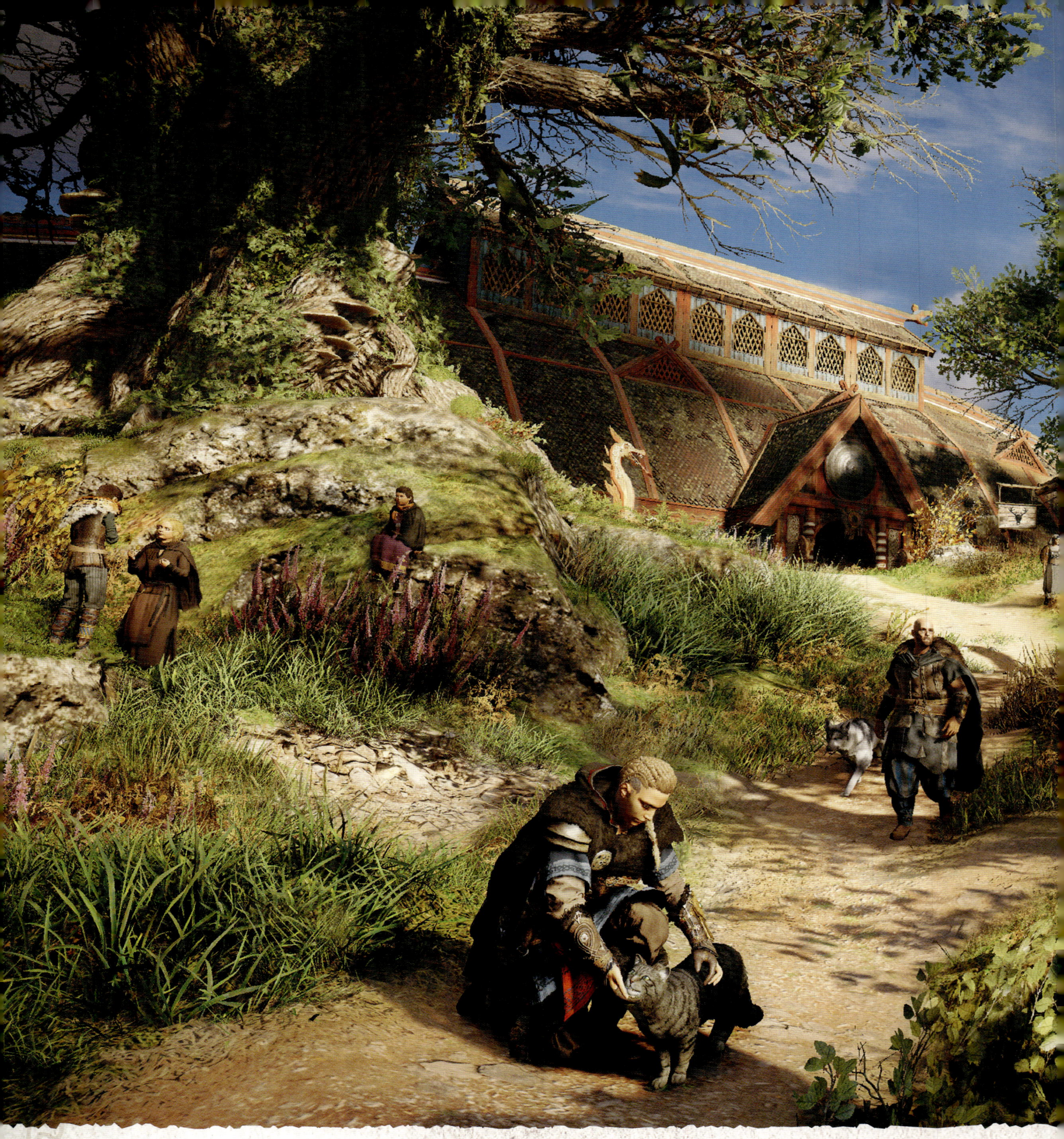

Let me add that I find Viking farmers to be such generous, humble, and agreeable folk. Sometimes, I help Viggo and Runa work their fields—good, bracing labor that helps rebuild the strength I lost in my ill-fated encounter years ago with Kjotve the Cruel. Few things are better for the soul than hard work with good people! Afterward, Runa always serves up a bounteous feast that we enjoy over simple talk of the weather and other topics of satisfyingly primal substance.

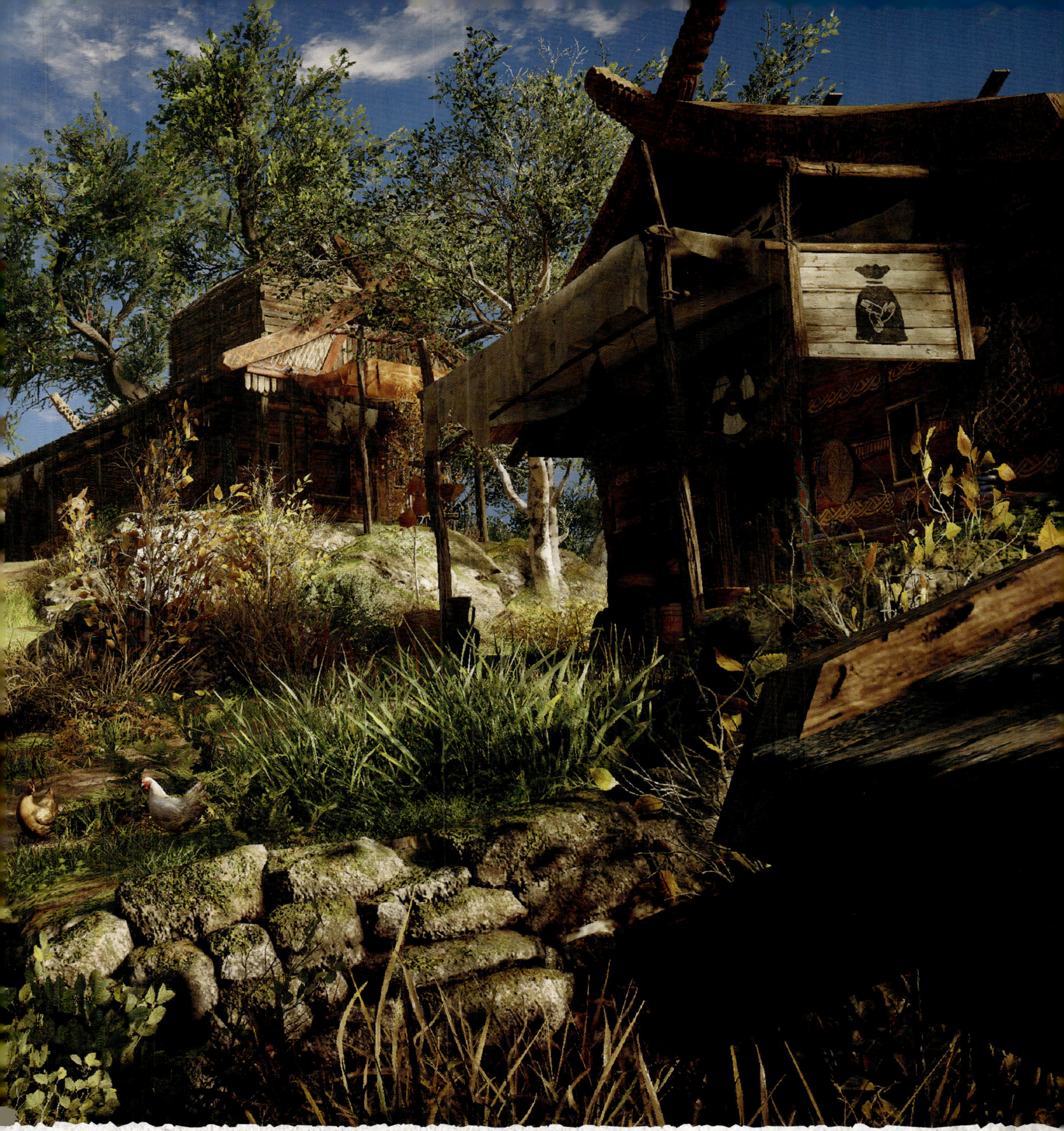

CATTLE FARM

This enclosure is where the Saxon family of Leofric, his wife Winfrith, and their son Bertham raise cattle for beef and dairy products. A productive cattle farm certainly adds to the bounty of any settlement feast!

Not long ago, a bit of local romantic intrigue arose when young Bertham began sneaking out for secret trysts with his lover Mayda, a fellow farmer who tended Ravensthorpe's chicken farm. I'm told Mayda refers to him as "Bertie Bee, sweet as honey!"

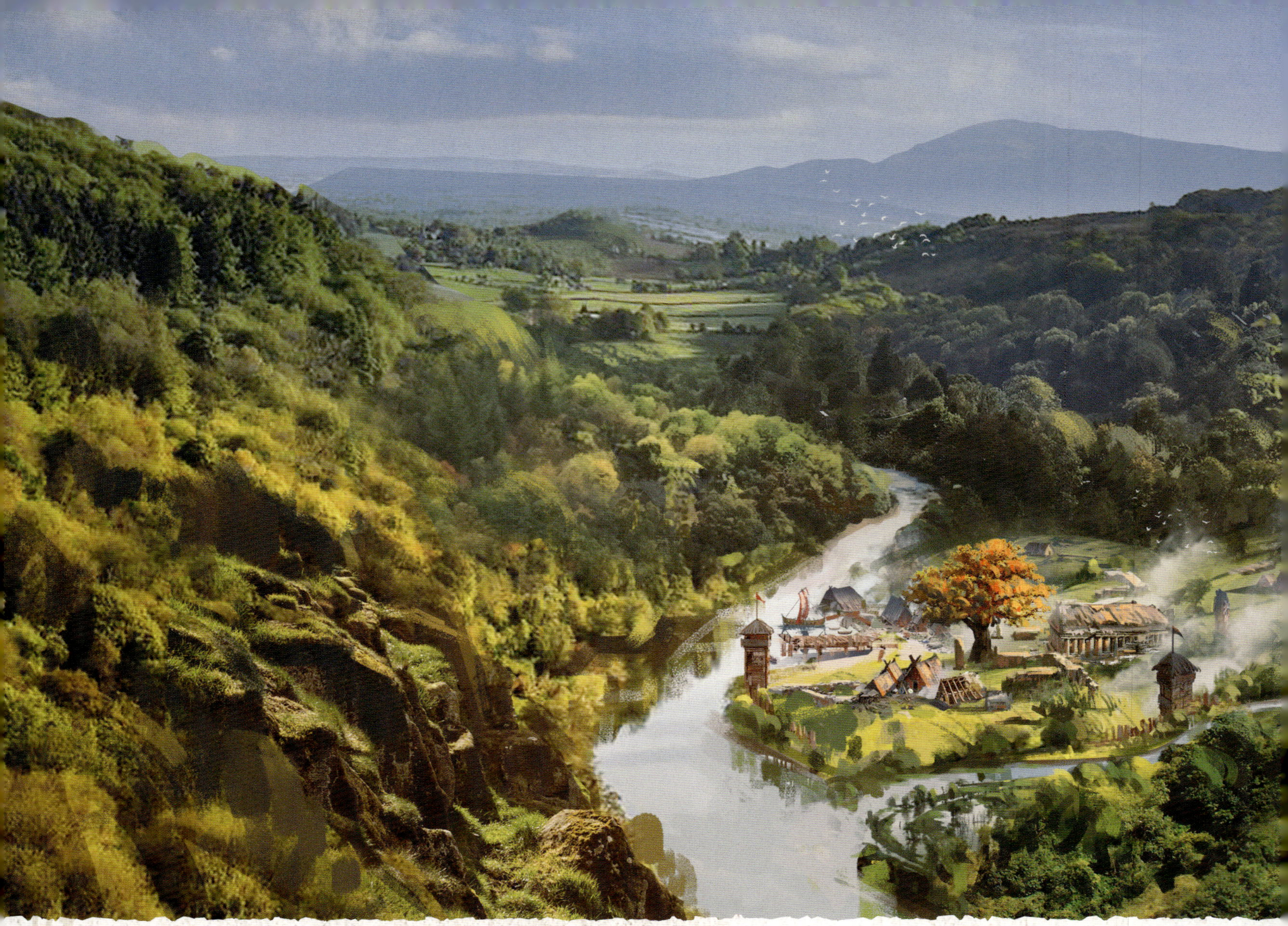

FOWL FARM

This small spread is where the Saxon farmer Bronson raises chickens and gathers eggs for the Raven Clan. At first, he worked with his daughter Mayda, but she left the farm to start her own craft shop (see Mayda's House below) . . . and to be with her lover Bertham, the cattle herder. Eivor told me of a letter to Mayda from Bertham containing one of the most amusing proclamations of love I've ever heard: "Every time I see you in town, it feels like there are frogs swimming around in my stomach, but in a good way."

MAYDA'S HOUSE (WEAVER)

After Mayda's relationship with Bertham drove her away from her overprotective father's chicken farm, she sought Eivor's help to build a cozy home directly across the road from her lover Bertham's cattle farm. There she took up dyeing woolen yarn in vats and weaving tapestries of intricate design. I make it a habit to stop by and preview the brilliant patterns Mayda is stringing through her warp-weighted looms!

BREWERY

Here, brewmaster Tekla brews the finest ales in England—this according to her own assessment, though I'm inclined to believe it. I am not much of a drinker myself, but these Vikings do love their ales and meads. Tekla's renowned Winter Brew is a staple at many a cold season's feast in these parts—her secret ingredients are apples, lavender, sage, and pine tar. But her Summer Brew, with hints of wildflower and new honey, is every bit its equal in my estimation.

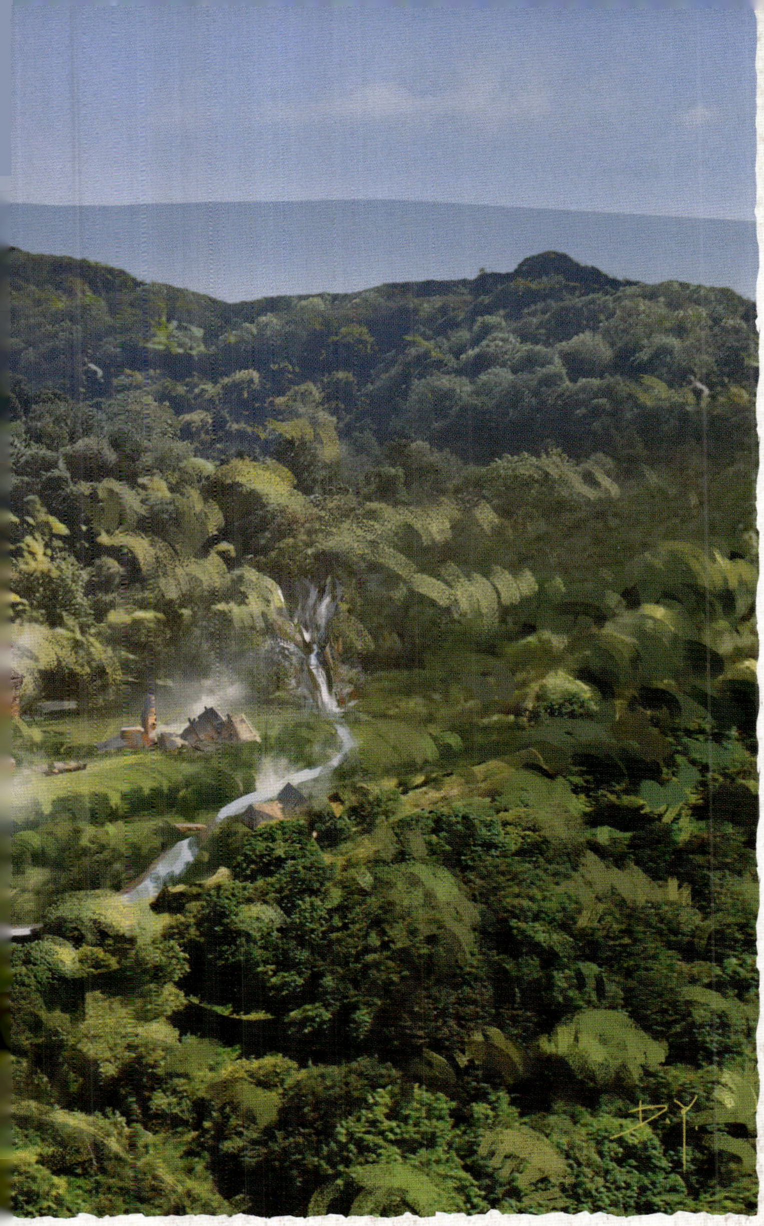

Back in my caliphate, drinking fermented beverages is a strictly private affair—one does not drink in public. In fact, one does not even appear intoxicated in public! Thus, I've found it endlessly fascinating that Vikings see the consumption of ale and mead as such a loud, uninhibited, joyous, and decidedly boastful communal activity. Public feasting without brew here is like bathing without water, it seems!

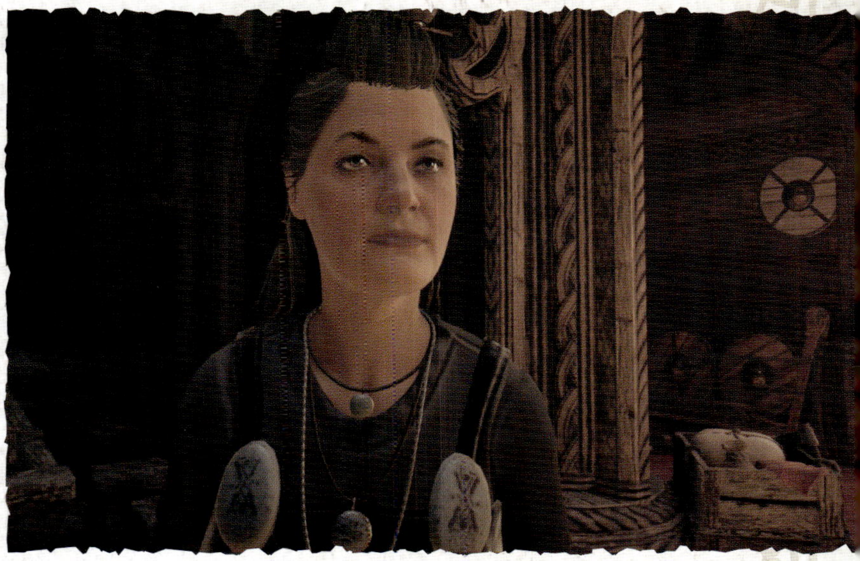

BAKERY

Basim once told me that Ravensthorpe's bread master, Tarben, bakes some of the tastiest bread he's ever sampled . . . and my mentor is quite the seasoned world traveler. Tarben buys the finest assorted grains from Viggo and Runa's farm as well as milled winter wheat from Saxon merchants along the river. Then he bakes it into mouthwatering works of art.

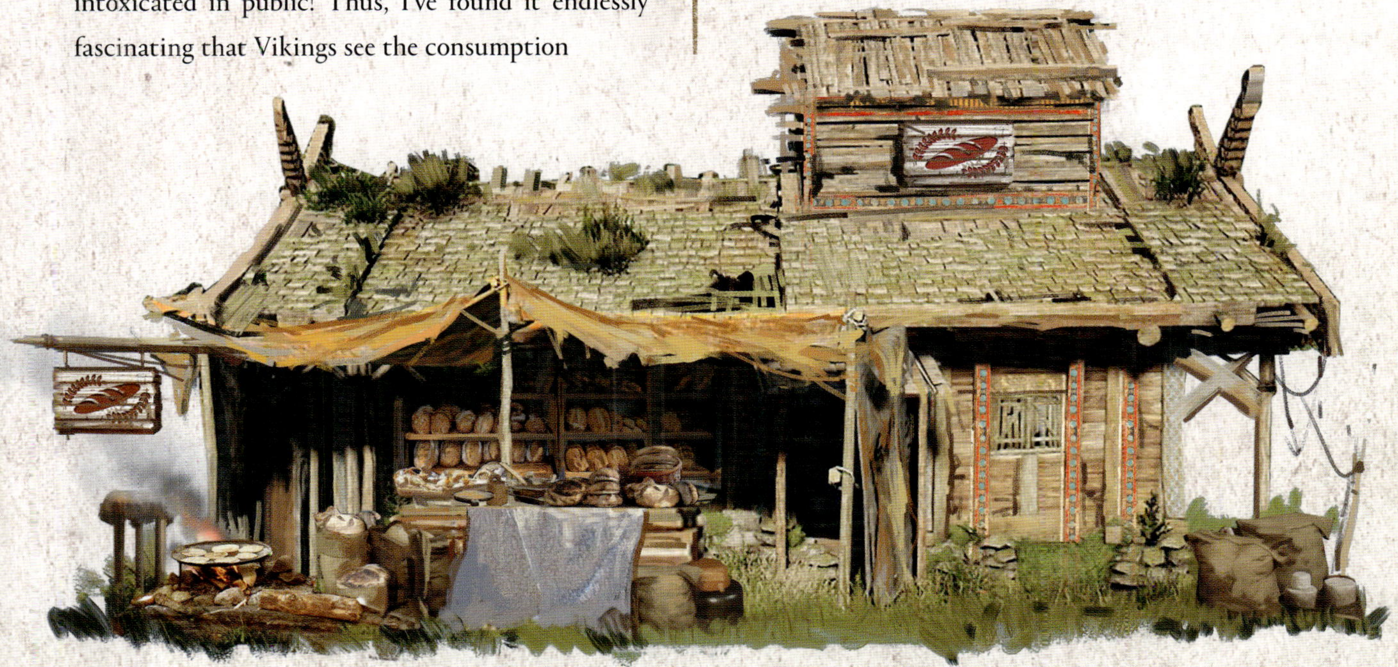

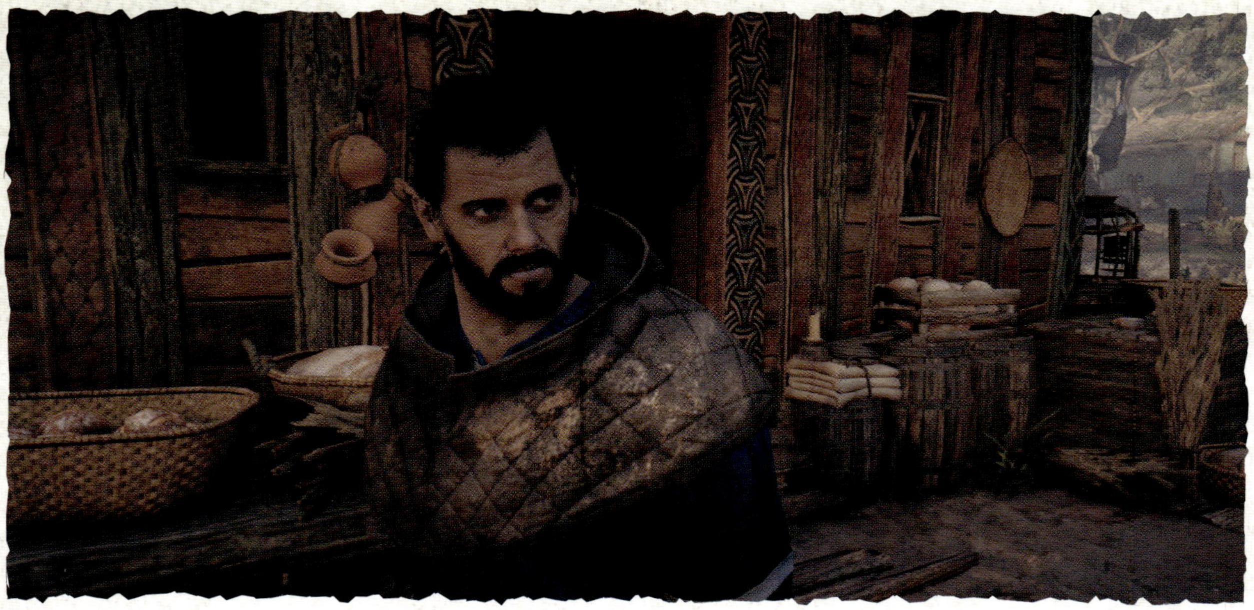

Tarben himself has something of a shadowy past—darker than his rye loaf, I'm told. When Eivor first met Tarben in the village, she remarked that "he has the look of one who swings an axe." Later, she learned that Tarben once operated as a Saxon bandit named Guthban, member of a cutthroat gang in Lincolnscire. In fact, Tarben's own mother was a murdering brigand, known to many as "the Merciless." To Tarben's great credit, he put this cruel past behind him, changed his name, and sought a fresh start in Ravensthorpe.

KARI'S HOUSE (WOODSHOP)

This woodshop down on the riverfront near the shipyard is a source of rough-sawn lumber and

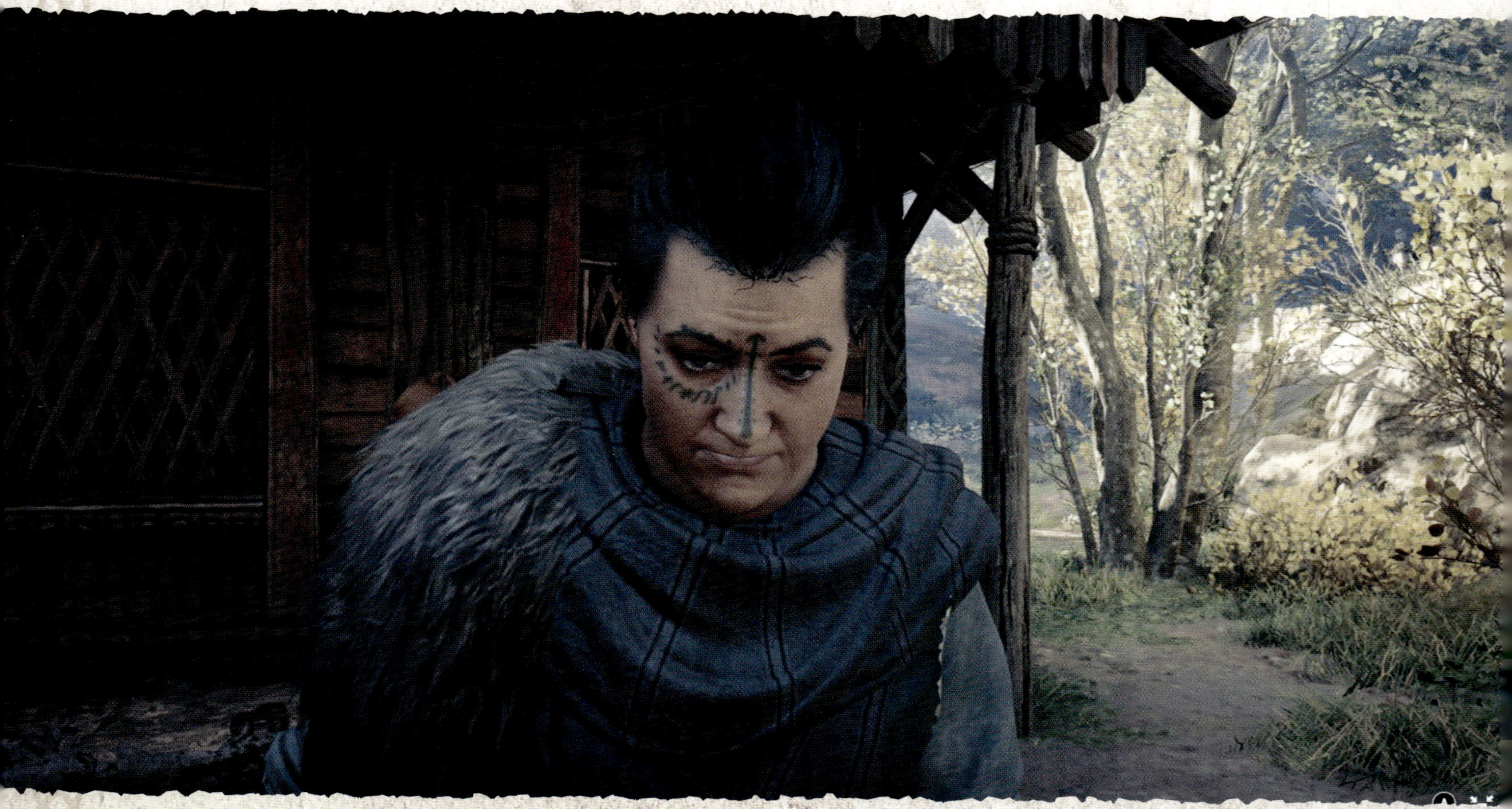

surfaced wooden materials for construction of buildings and important fortifications in the settlement. The resident Saxon carpenter, Kari, is a first-rate craftswoman. Eivor notes that her separation from her husband, a noted philanderer, has made her an even stronger and more self-assured woman.

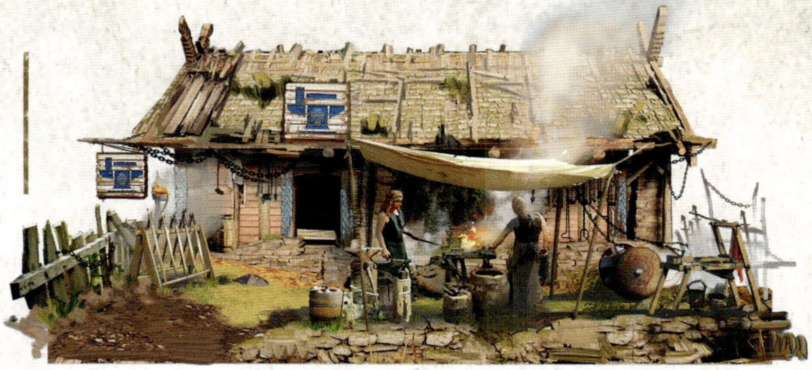

SPECIAL SERVICES

BLACKSMITH

A skilled blacksmith offers critically important services to any Viking community. Aside from the obvious importance of crafting dependable weapons and combat gear, a good smith can enhance gear quality using exotic resources like ingots of carbon, nickel, or tungsten. He may also adorn items with additional rune slots, so runes can be inserted for added efficacy. The smith also crafts the basic metal tools—hammers, awls, scythes, plow blades, utensils, and so forth—necessary for everyday economic life.

For these reasons, Gunnar—the only skilled blacksmith in Ravensthorpe—got considerable support from the Raven Clan leadership in the village's early days. Sigurd and Randvi both tasked Eivor with helping Gunnar get his forge up and running quickly for the villagers. Supplies and raw materials pillaged from nearby Saxon "monk huts" like Alcestre Monastery and Medeshamstede Abbey served in this regard. Soon Gunnar had a forge bigger and hotter than his old one back in Norway!

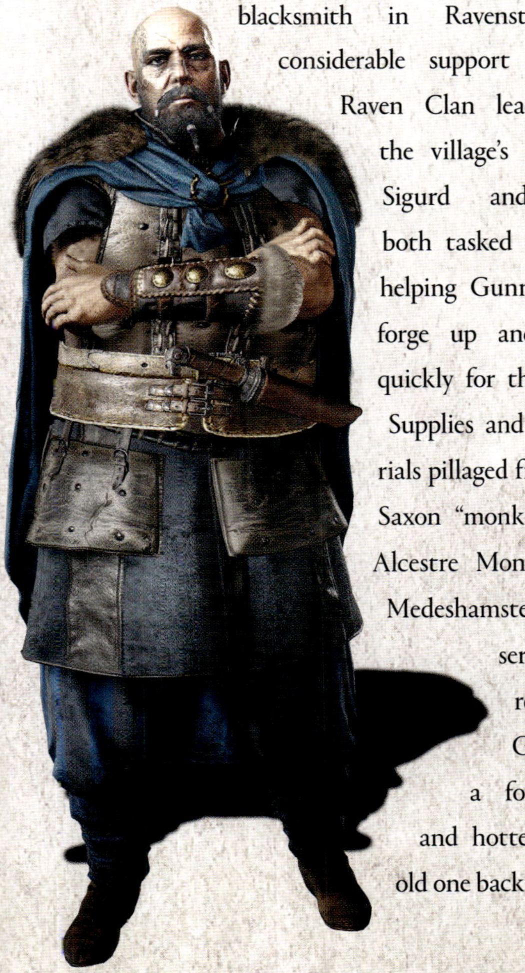

STABLE AND AVIARY

A well-tended stable is a great boon to any village. In Ravensthorpe, Rowan is the town's Saxon stablehand and gamekeeper. He followed the Sons of Ragnar across England, selling and training quality mounts for the Viking jarls and their war bands. As he told me: "Sold many a mare and stallion to the brothers—good men, always paid me fair." Rowan handles horses with a preternatural ability to understand their needs and is masterful at training mounts for endurance, strength, and swimming.

Rowan admits he grew up a sickly boy with a stammer whose best friends, he says, were the town horses—"the only ones who never teased me." He claims to understand horses when they "speak" in the same way he does people. Rowan has just as deft a touch raising ravens, falcons, eagles, and other majestic birds of prey. His aviary is small but well tended, and he provides expert care for Eivor's remarkable bird Sýnin. His advice: "Talk to your raven regularly. They like that!"

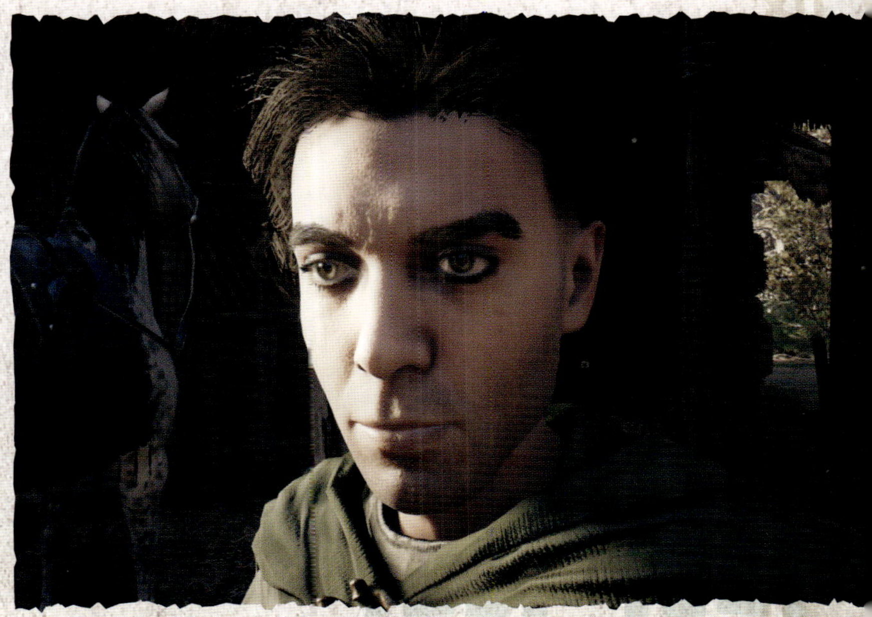

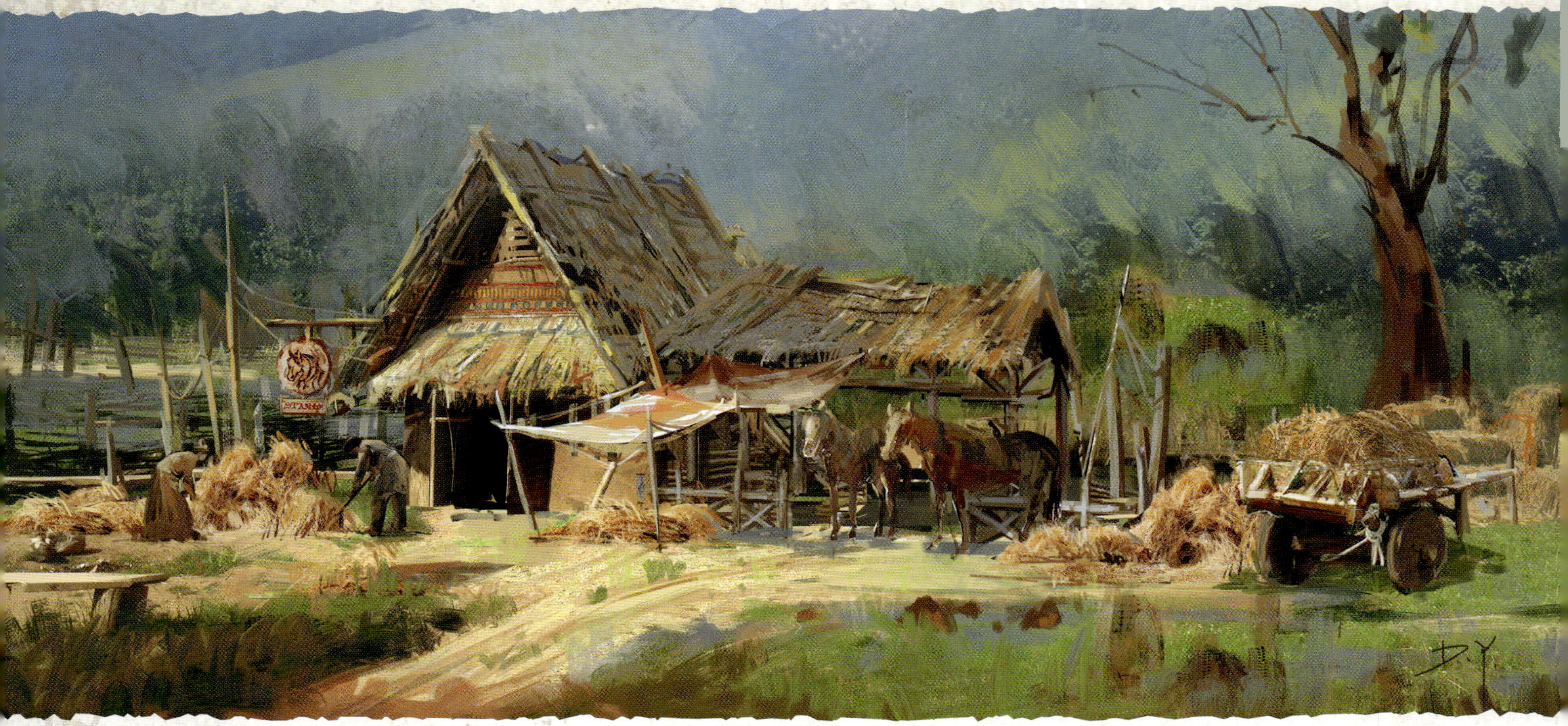

SHIPYARD

Gudrun and her husband Gudmund are brilliant shipwrights with great skill in designing and customizing Viking longships. They make a perfect team: Gudrun's focus is on the core construction of the vessel, and she's obsessed with crafting an efficient, functional boat. But her spouse is more of an artist with a flair for design who gives each boat a distinctive personality. Indeed, Gudmund often tells his wife that the "face" of a longship conveys an essential message to all who view its arrival!

Their young daughter Eira is one of the sprightly children who scamper daily through the township. Along with her friends Knud and his sister Silvi—children of Viggo and Runa, the grain farmers—Eira keeps things quite lively. The trio once caught a passel of squirrels and let them loose in the shipyard! (I found it quite amusing,

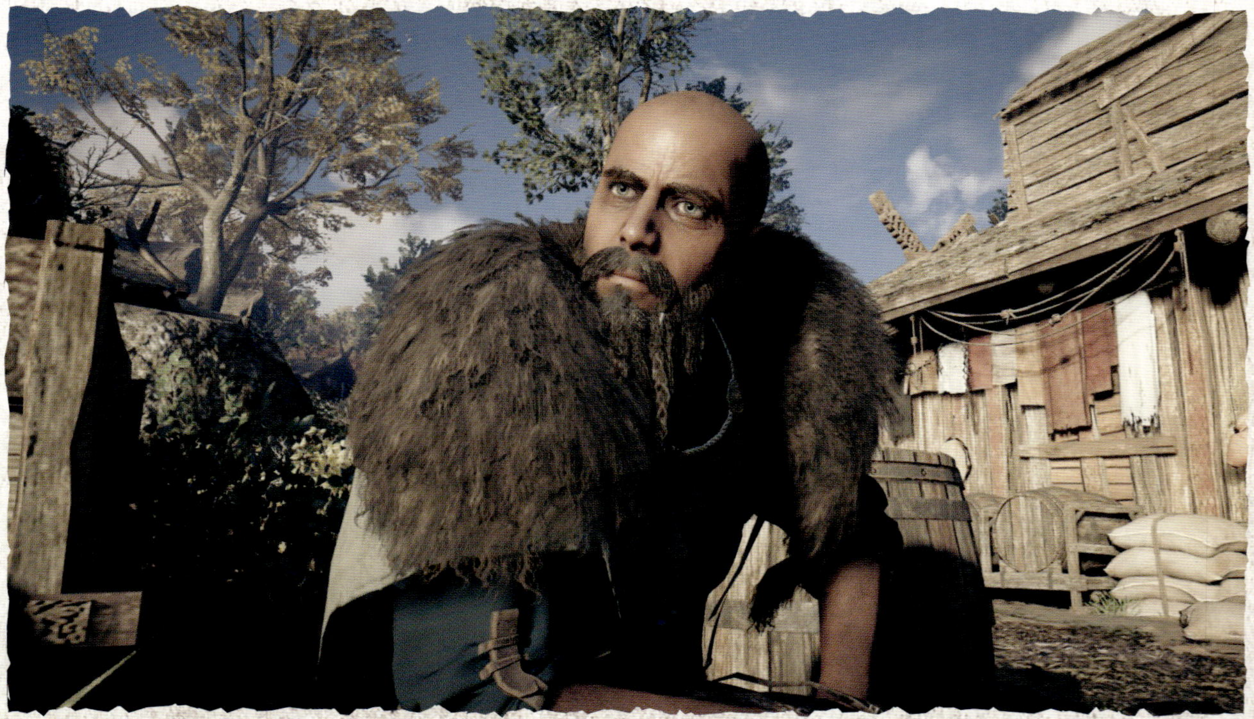

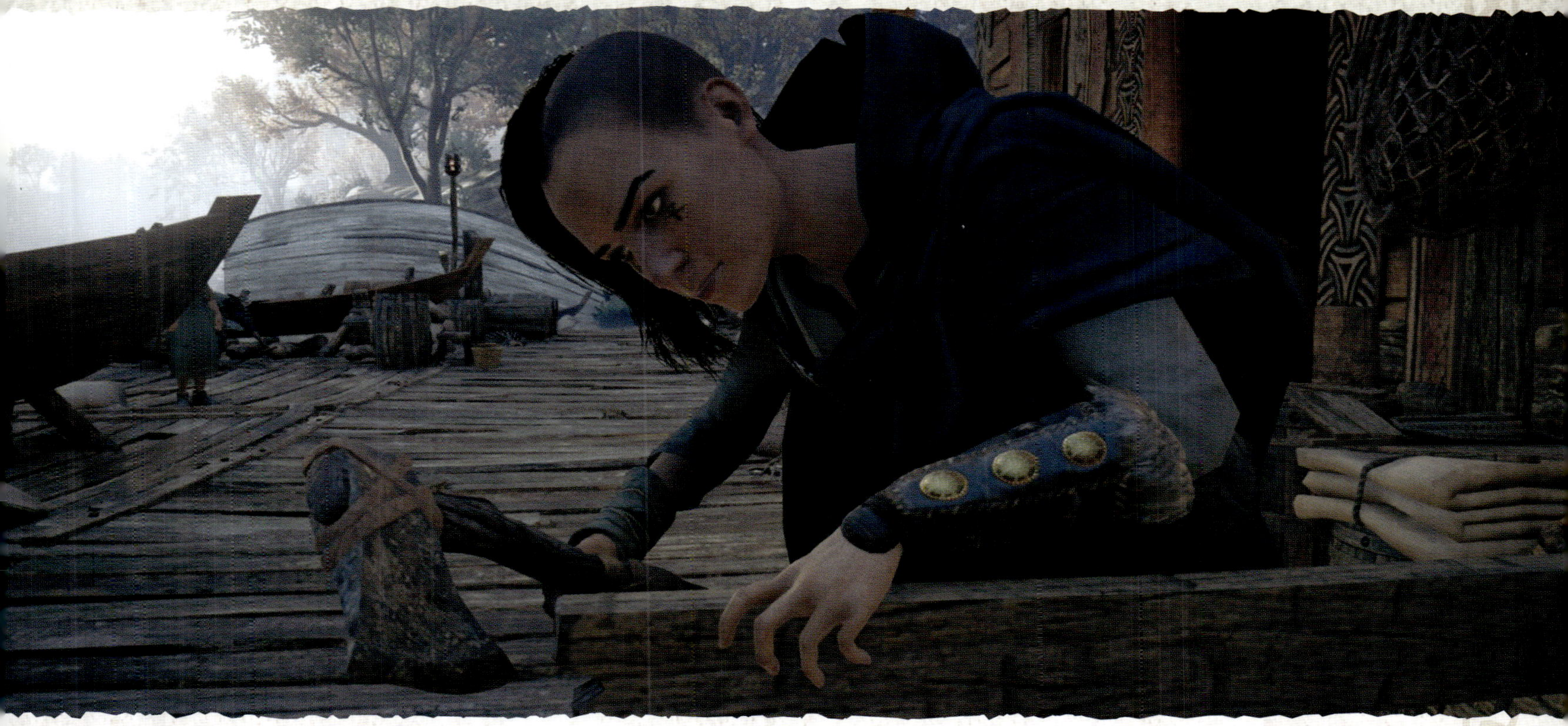

although Gudrun most certainly did not.) In my travels, I've always felt most natural and content in townships with happy, free-spirited youths roaming the community.

BARRACKS

This facility is built for housing, training, and managing a ready militia of Viking raiders known as Jomsvikings. The barracks master, Eydis, is a superb instructor and tactician who keeps Eivor's warriors in excellent fighting condition. Her goal: "Build the most vicious crew ever to sail the rivers of England!" A note on Jomsvikings: These skilled and honorable fighters follow a strict code of conduct and dedicate their lives to battle. If you can afford their services, you'll find no better or more loyal warriors for your longship crew.

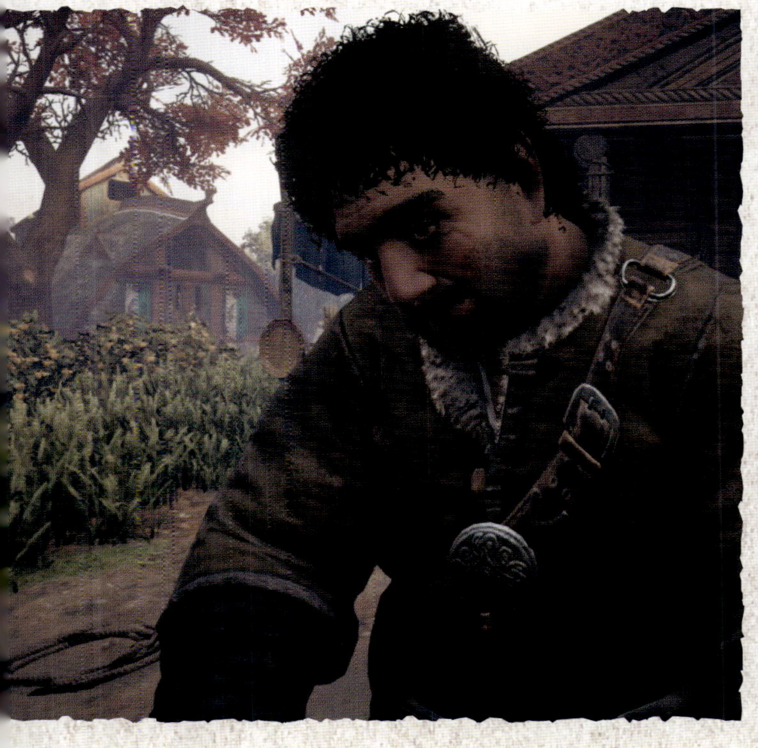

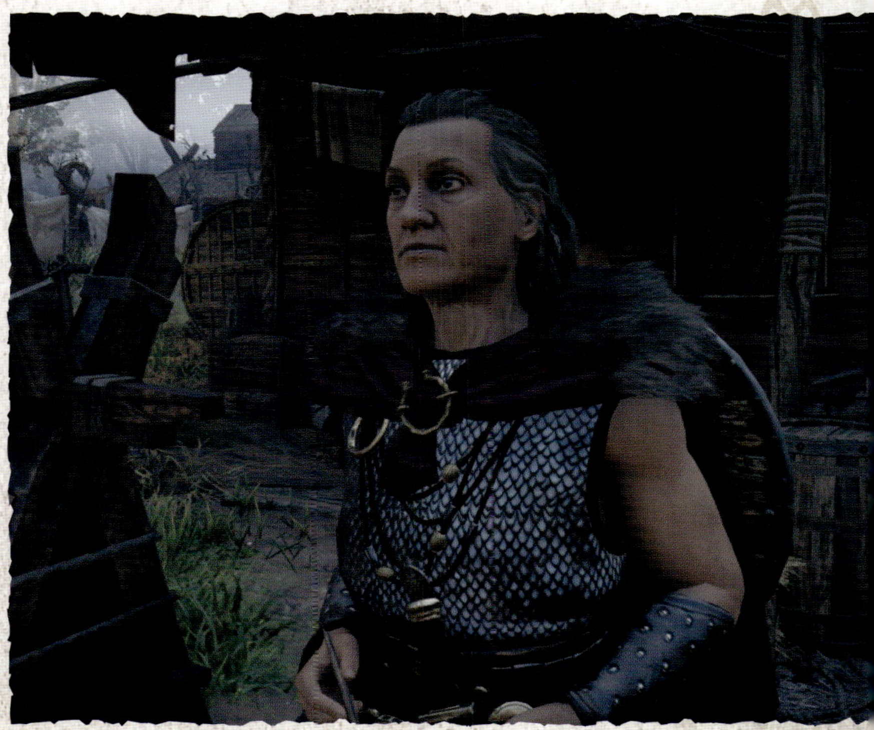

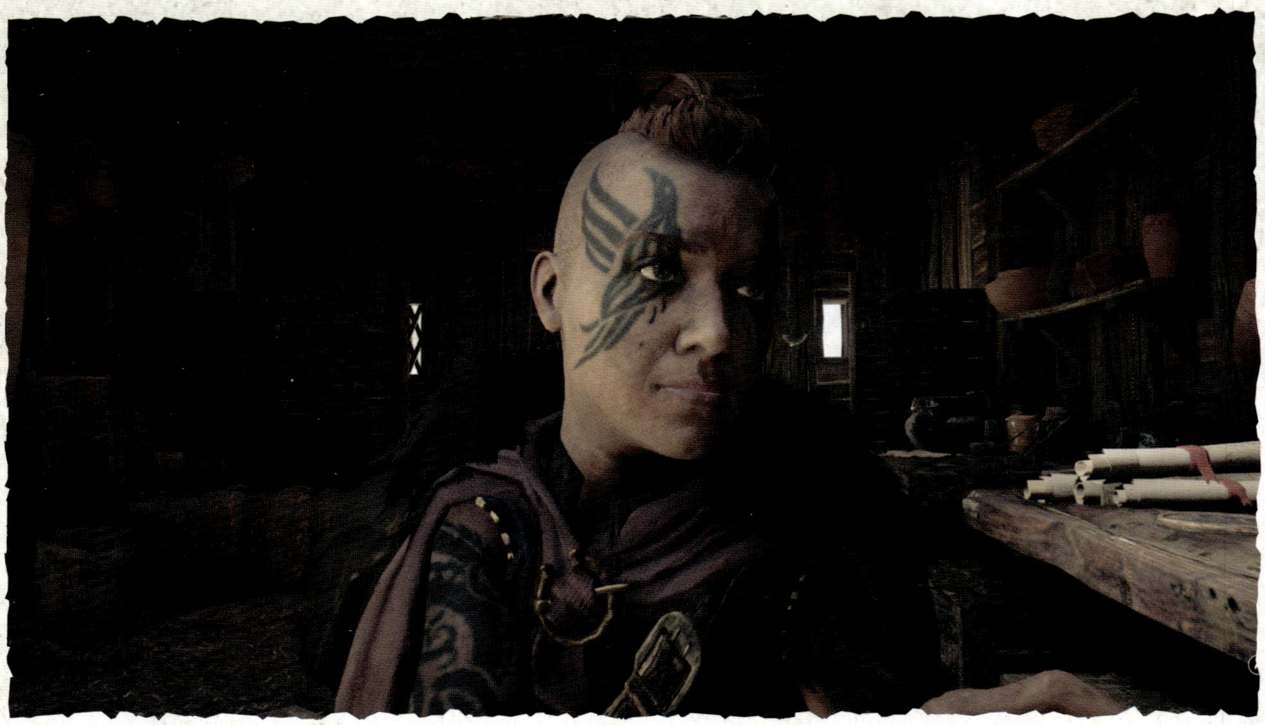

TATTOO SHOP

Svend and his apprentice Tove founded this service shop in Ravensthorpe's earliest days. Svend was a true artist . . . well, if you think of human skin as a canvas. Indeed, Vikings believe that body art not only expresses one's inner self (referred to as one's *hugr*) but also enhances one's physical and mental skills in battle. Svend could execute any tattoo design, it seemed. He was also an accomplished barber, quite skilled with haircuts.

The old man formed a fatherly bond with Tove, and he mentored her until she too became a highly skilled tattooist and barber. Unfortunately, not long after the Raven Clan's successful outreach into East Anglia in 873 CE, Svend died in his sleep. Tove found it difficult at first to accept her mentor's passing, but with Eivor's encouragement she took over Svend's role in the community.

CARTOGRAPHER

Here's a workshop unique among Viking settlements, I'm told—one that brings significant value to Ravensthorpe. Its young proprietor, a Norseman named Olsen, has traveled extensively across these British Isles and mapped everywhere he's been. Indeed, Olsen's amazing maps can help any traveler identify points of interest,

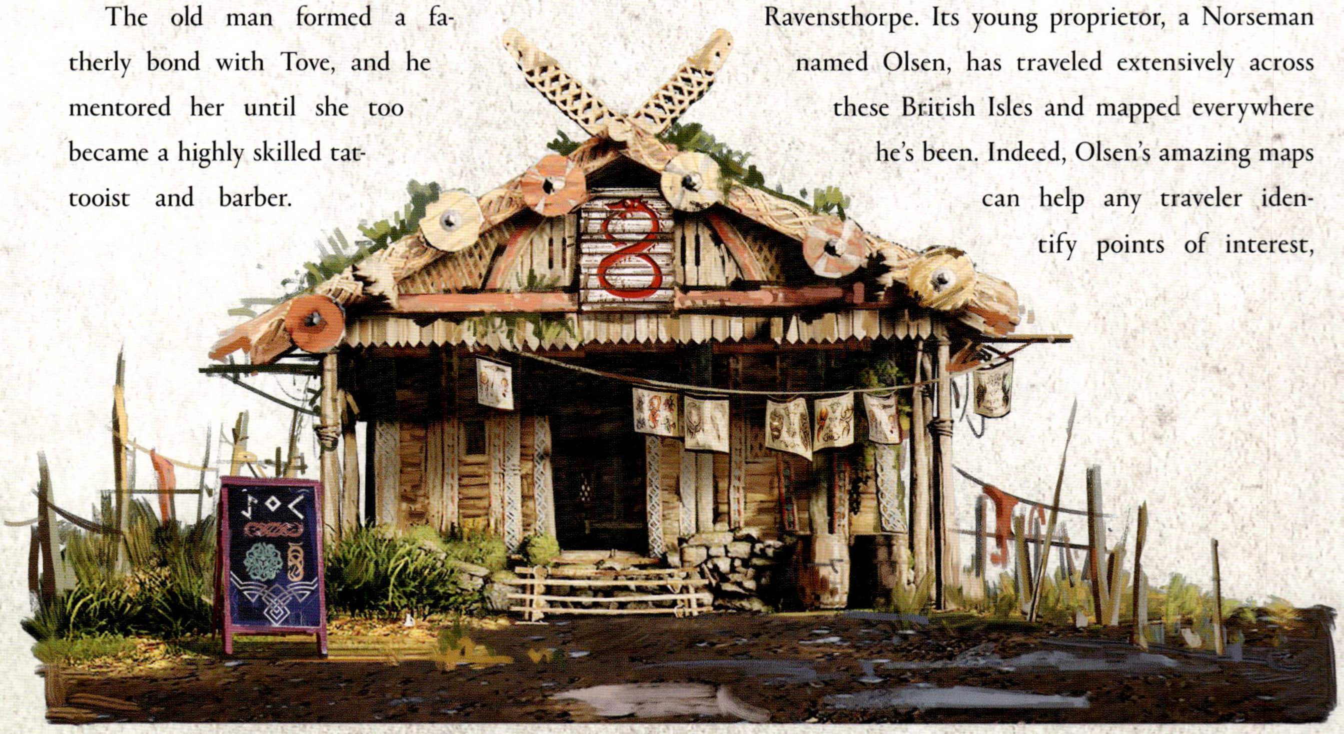

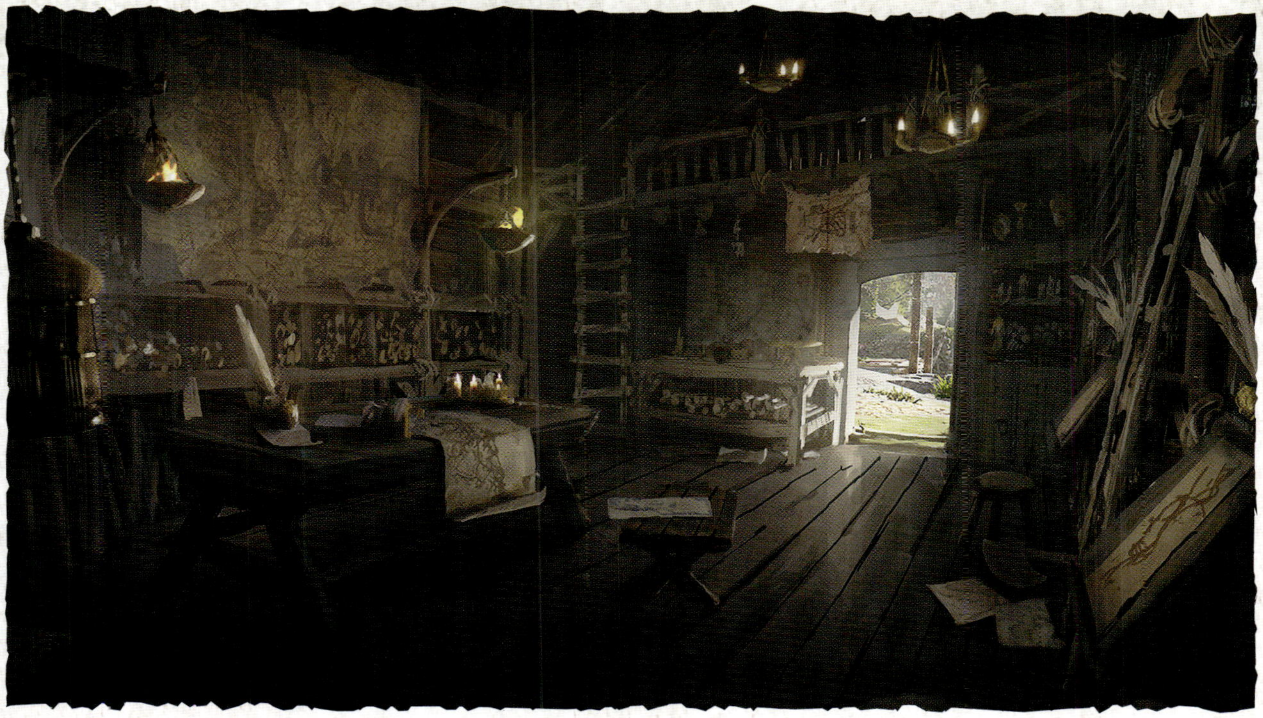

including valuable items and resources, in territories all over England.

I must say, Olsen is a truly remarkable cartographer for a fellow with no formal training whatsoever. Back in the Levant, mapmaking is a highly intricate and complicated craft, requiring many years of apprenticeship and guidance. But Olsen seems to have an innate spatial awareness that imprints geography upon his mind and then translates it almost effortlessly onto parchment!

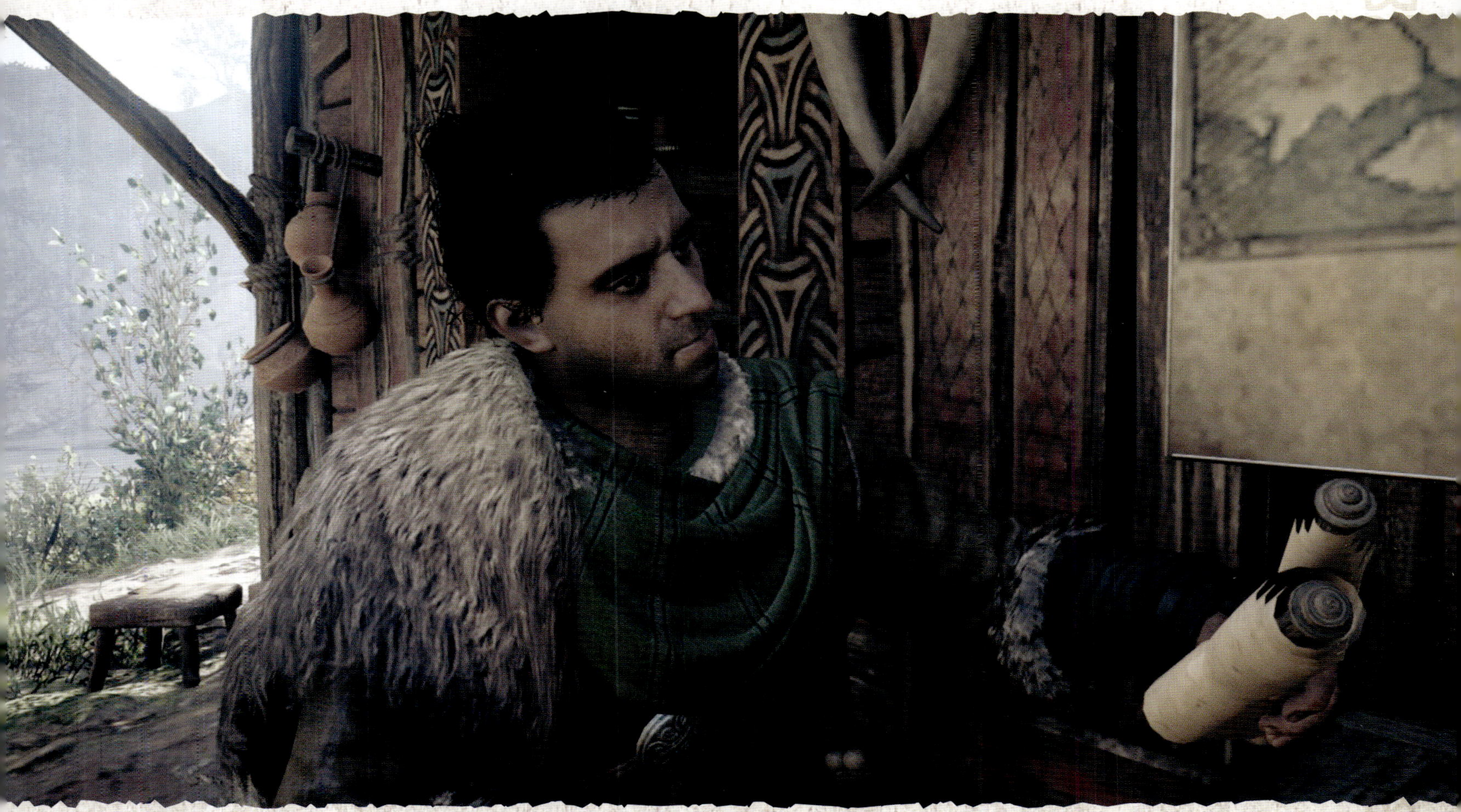

SEER'S HUT

Back in Norway, the mysterious and gifted seer Valka helped Eivor come to grips with her early visions of Odin, the All-father. When the Raven Clan made its move to England, Valka stayed behind in her hut outside Fornburg, caring for her ailing mother, Svala. But when Svala passed on, Valka made passage—"We flew like seabirds," she said—to Ravensthorpe. Eivor helped Valka build a suitable hut in the settlement.

As Ravensthorpe's *völva*, Valka serves the entire community's spiritual needs. But here, she's been particularly devoted to Eivor, who Valka claims is "touched"—i.e., a conduit for godly tidings. Always seeking ingredients—common ones, like juniper berries and red clay, or exotic ones, like white pigeon talons or perch gills—Valka uses them to mix special elixirs that have inspired Eivor to explore her odd visions and dreams.

A side note: Valka's importance to the settlement—and the high status of leaders like Eivor and Randvi—contrasts with the station of women in my own homeland. In Viking villages, women regularly fill leadership roles and serve important functions in the local economy. Yanli's trading post, Tekla's brewery, Kari's woodshop, Gudrun's shipyard, Tove's tattoo parlor—the list of establishments run by the strong and talented women of Ravensthorpe is long! Even the town's deadly Jomsviking initiates train with Eydis, a woman with a frighteningly thorough knowledge of martial skills.

Back in my Abbasid Caliphate . . . well, women are certainly a powerful social force, but they cannot serve important political or economic roles. Indeed, no public life is possible for

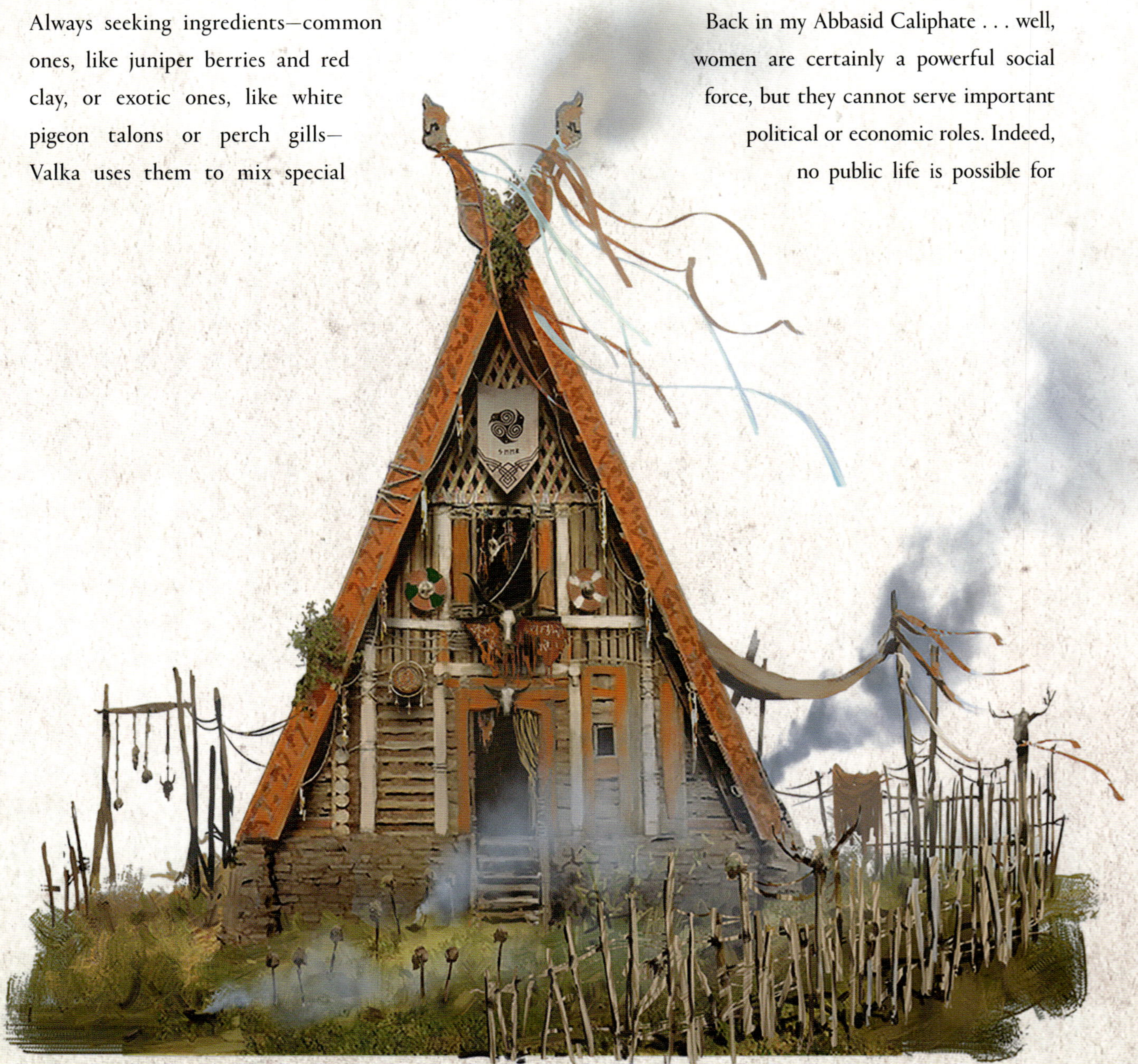

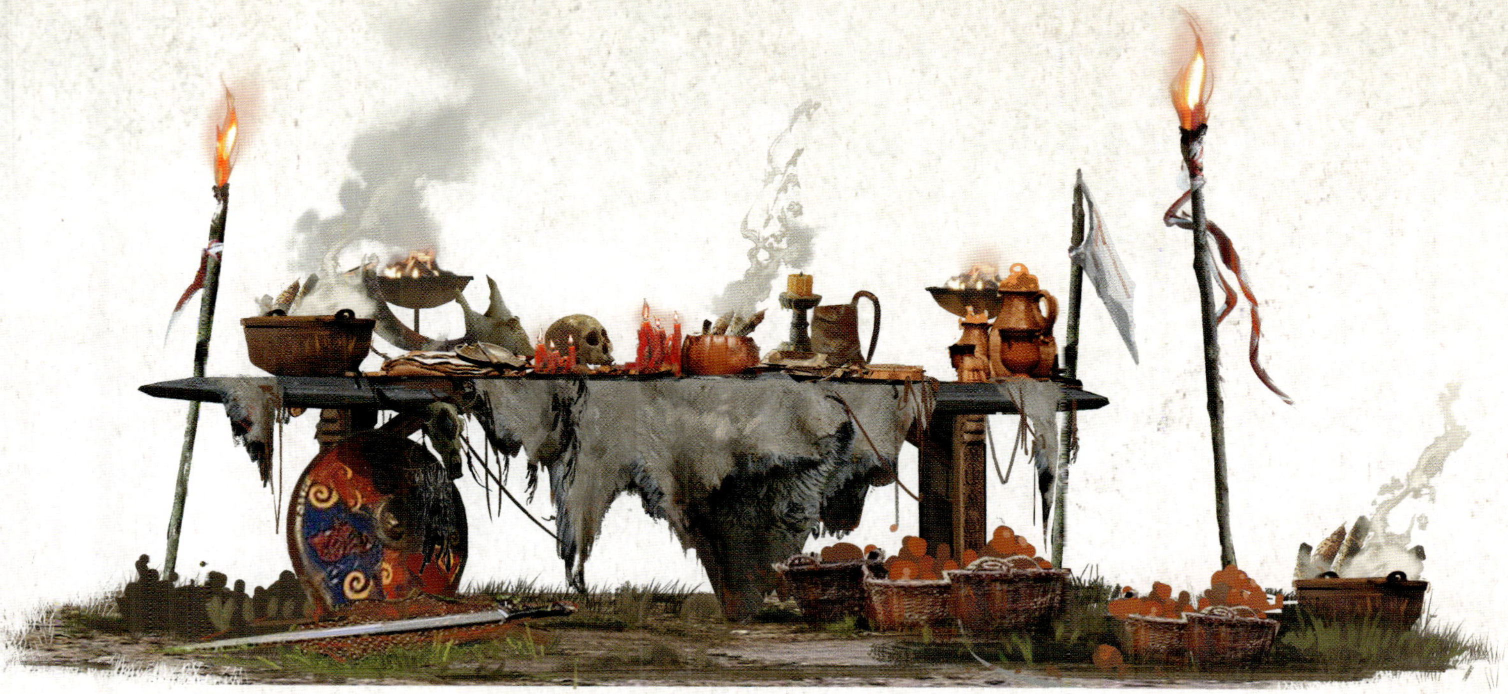

women today in the ninth century CE. Truly, this seems a terrible waste of talent. Here, Viking women can even divorce their husbands! Such a thing would be unthinkable back home.

THE THOUSAND EYES

This establishment is not common to all Viking settlements but valuable in a place like Ravensthorpe with broad regional ambitions. The Thousand Eyes is a trading guild comprising vendors of exotic goods and treasures from all corners of the known world. The guild bills itself as an agency that can connect interested traders to a sprawling shadow market that stretches "from the dunes of Egypt to the moors of England." All prices in this market must be paid in opal only!

The master of the Thousand Eyes guild is a fascinating young lad named Reda. Tekla calls him an old soul in a new body. Reda was first introduced to

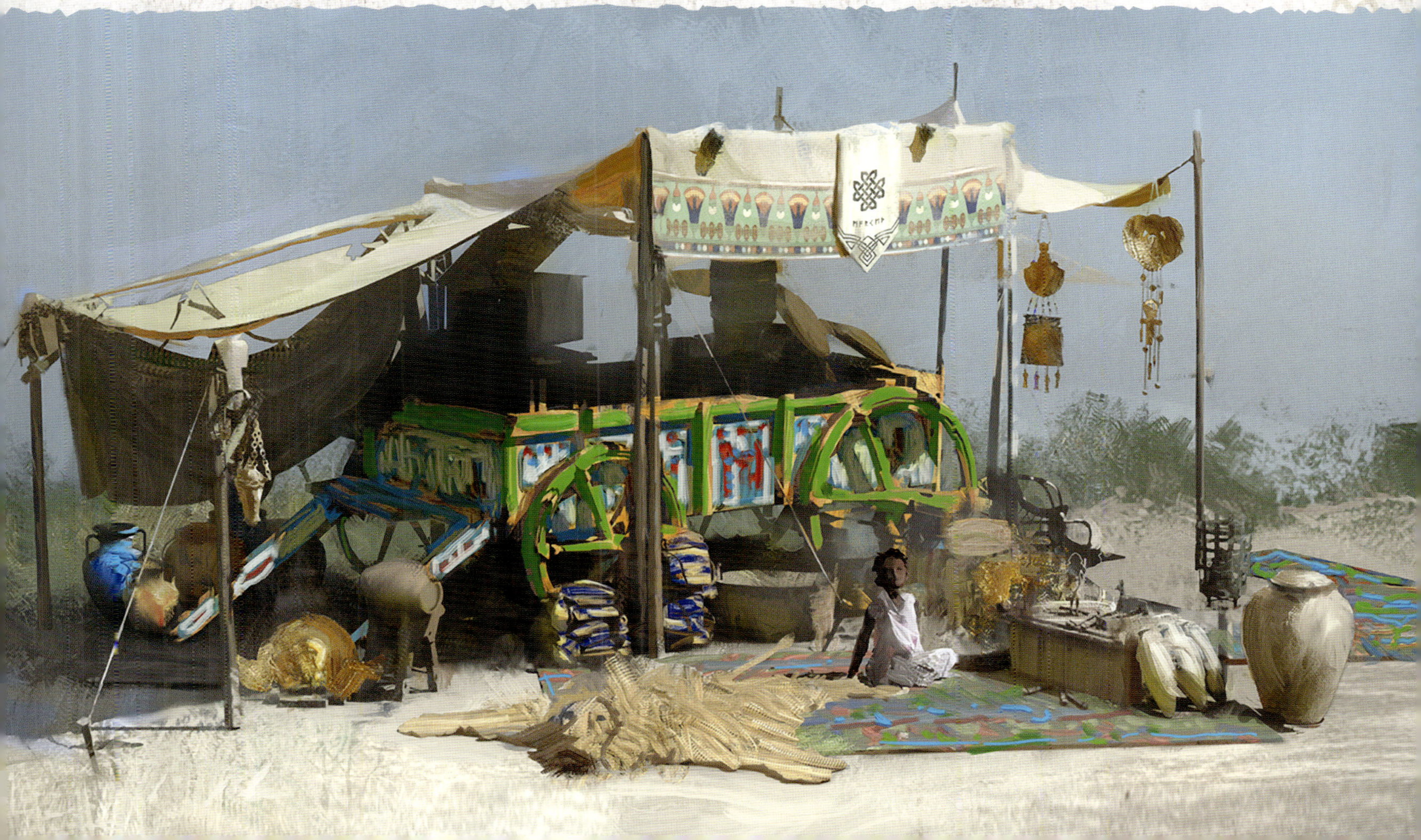

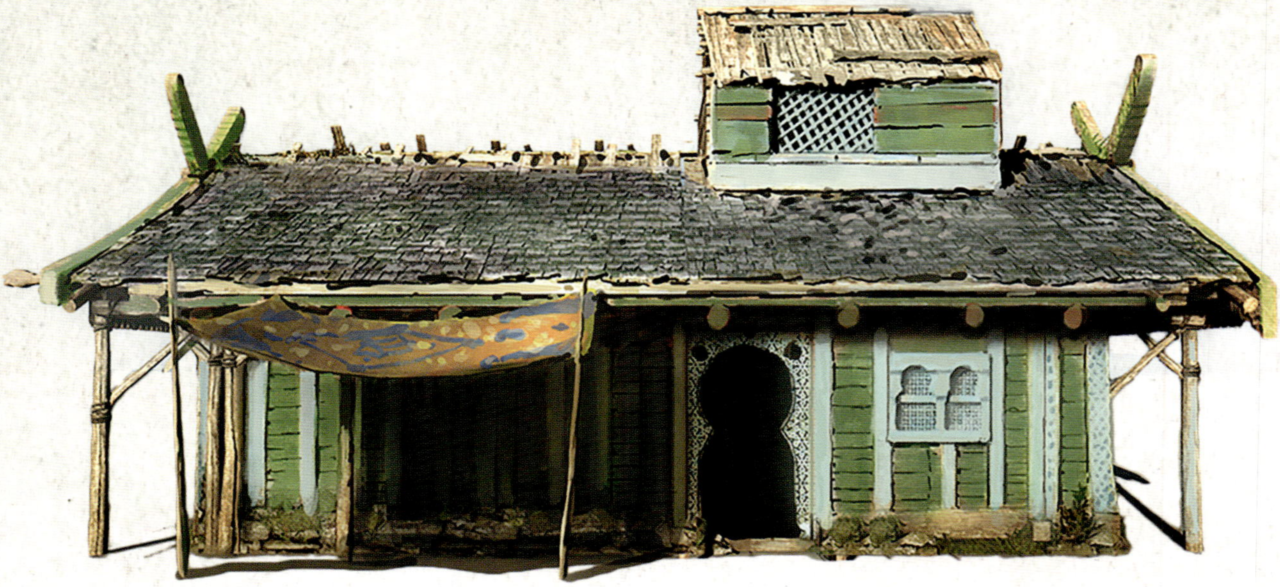

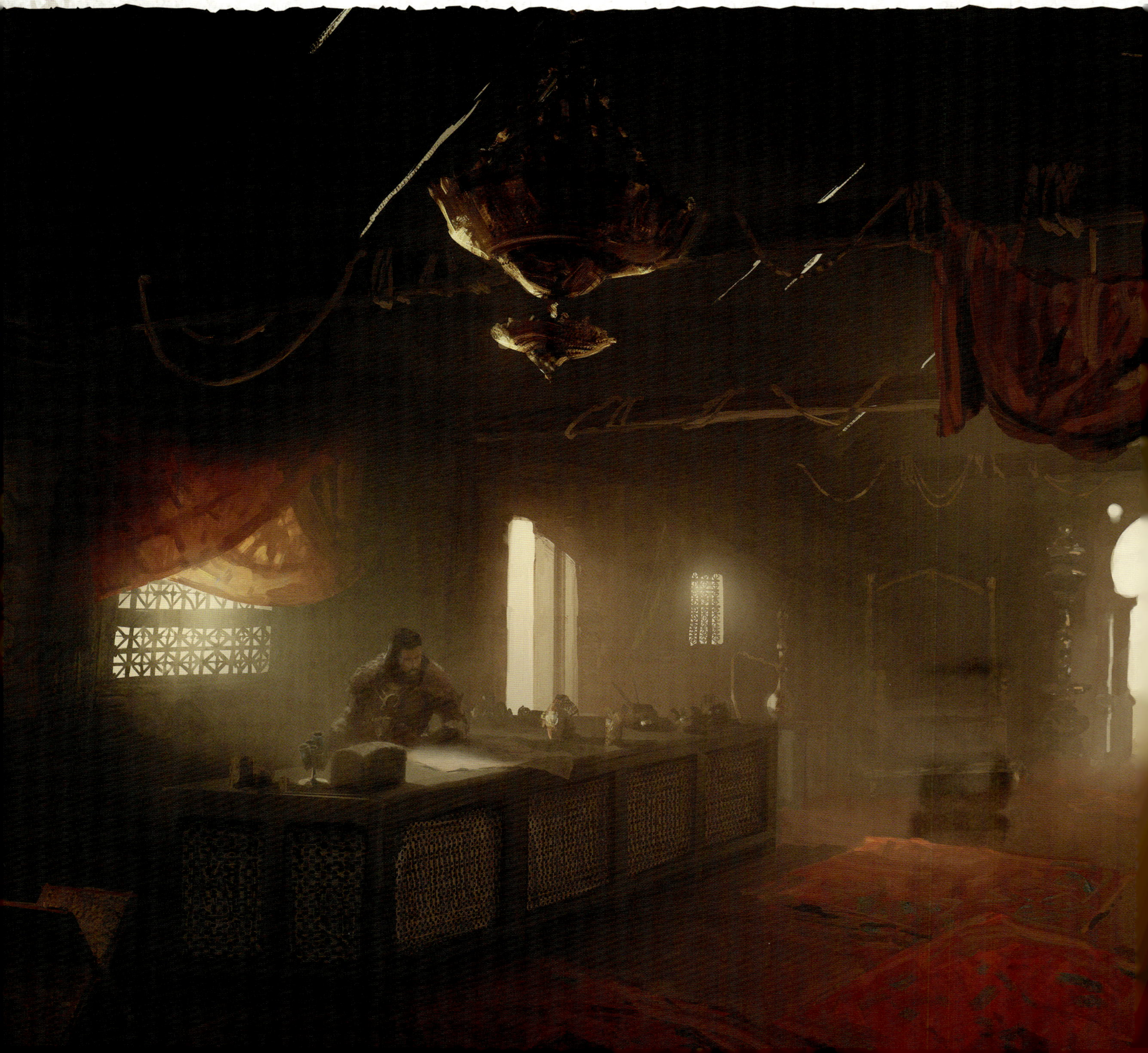

me as "a legend, a hero of the people, and the richest merchant west of the Indus!" He claims to sell the finest and rarest items in the world and boasts a network of associates in England—so-called "Eyes"—all clad in attire similar to Reda's vestments, all seeking trade or special contracts.

HIDDEN ONES BUREAU

Upon our initial arrival at the outpost that would become Ravensthorpe, my master Basim requested help in establishing a Hidden Ones bureau. This post would serve not only as our housing but also as our brotherhood's headquarters in England—a home base for our mission to eradicate the Order of the Ancients from these lands. Basim assigned oversight of its construction to me, and I gladly accepted. With Eivor's generous help, it has become a fine space for my work.

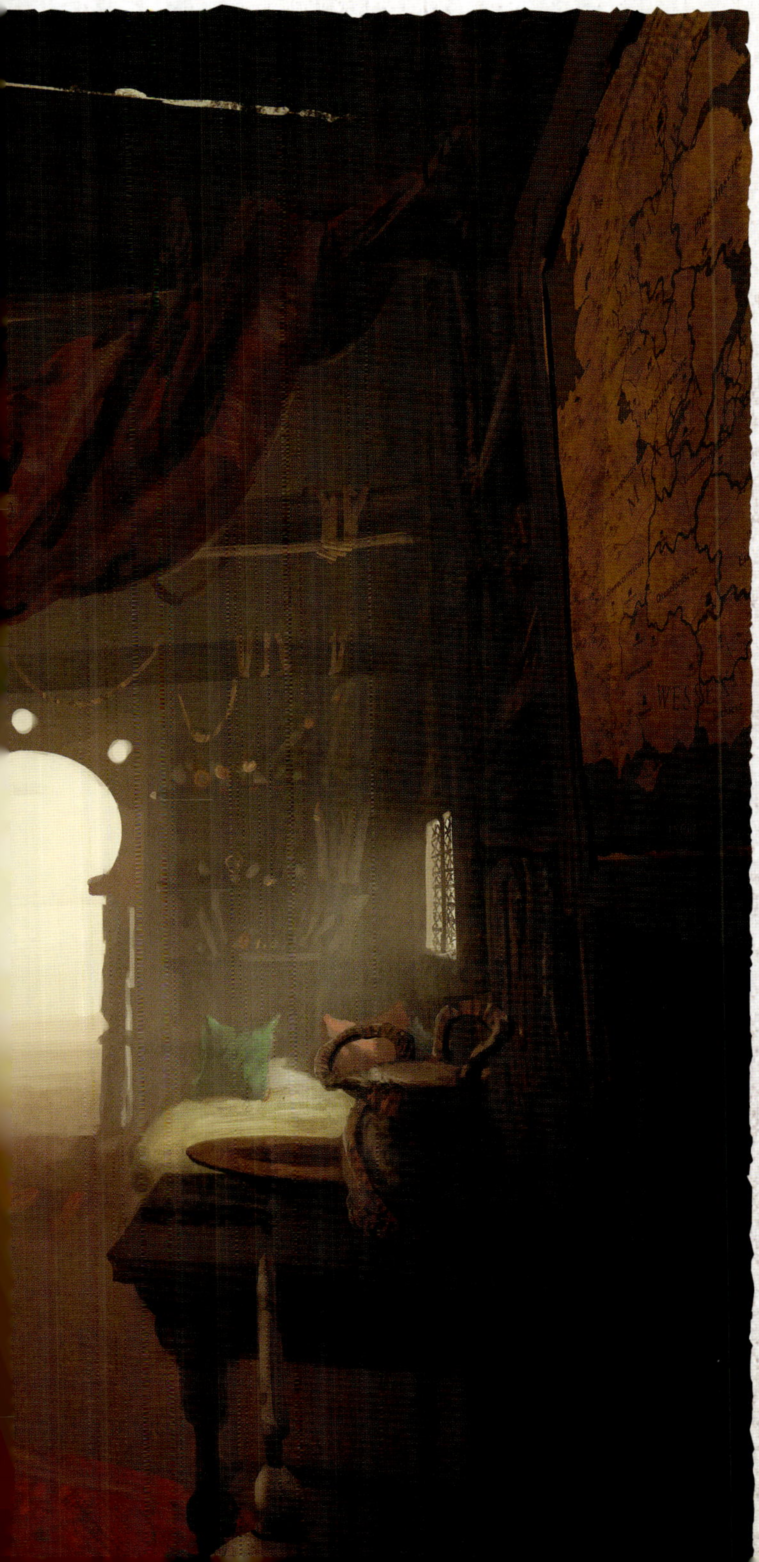

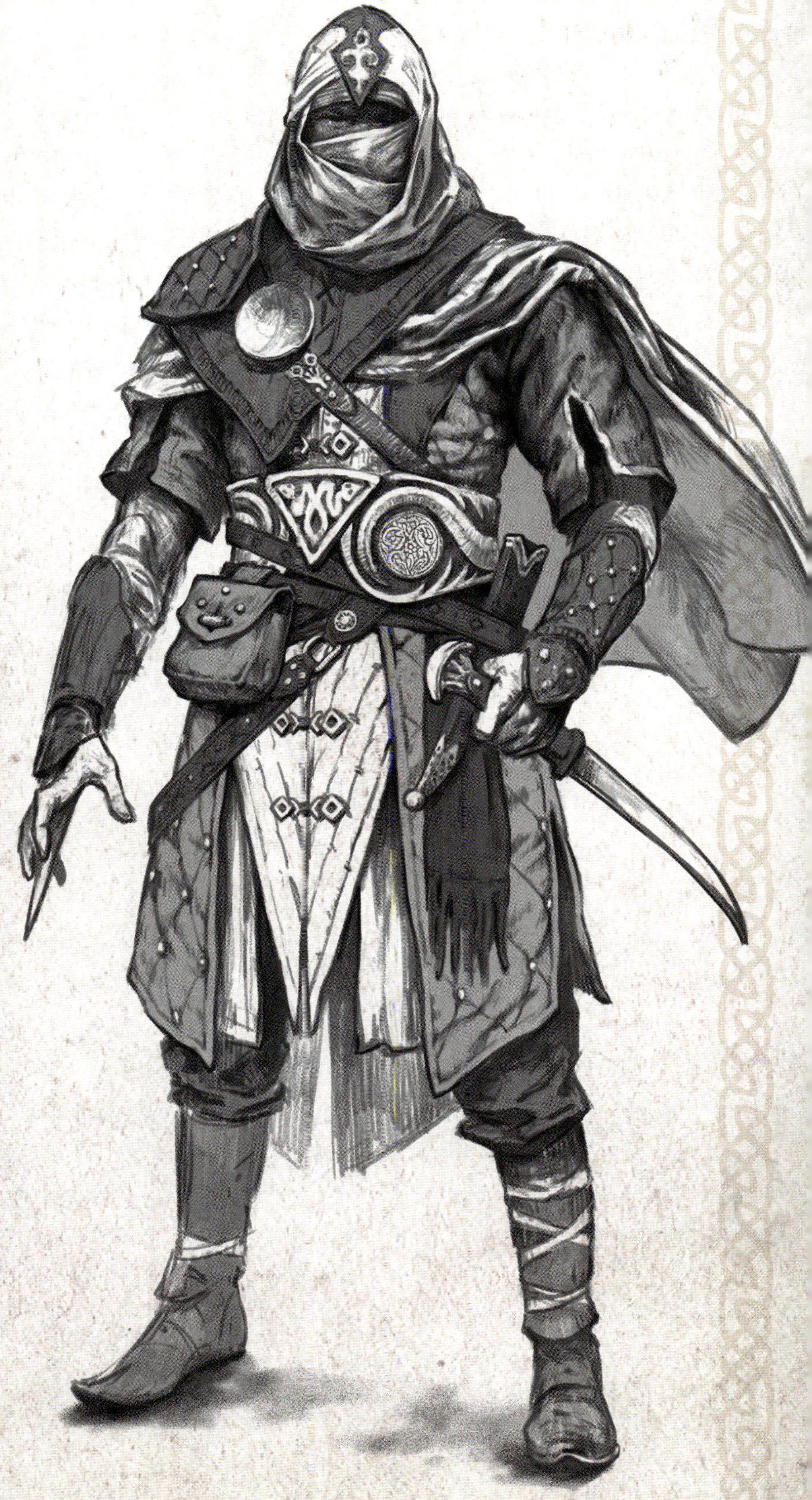

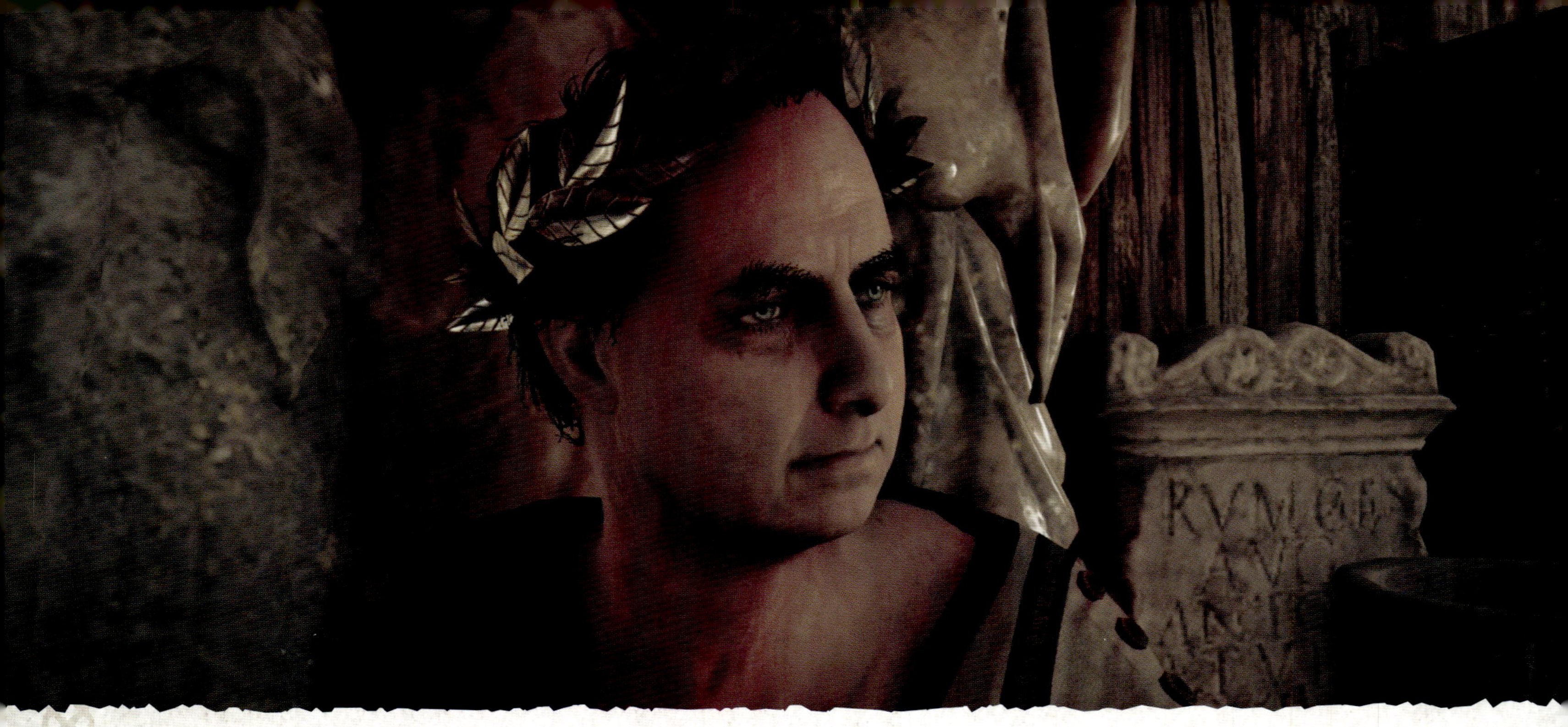

OTHER TOWN ACTIVITIES & POINTS OF INTEREST

MUSEUM

Stop by this gallery of Roman relics and say "*Salve!*" (hello). The proprietor, who goes by the almost comically ostentatious moniker of Octavian Claudius Britannicus, is in fact a Saxon named Osbert, an avid collector of Roman antiquities. He's accumulated an impressive treasure trove of statuary and other stuff dating back to the days of imperial rule. Indeed, many such ancient artifacts can be found scattered in Roman ruins across Britain's kingdoms. Bring them to Octavian, and he'll appraise and purchase them for a good price.

FLYTING

The venerable practice of flyting—a ritual battle of wits that features a poetic, stylized trading of insults—has been a part of Viking tradition for centuries. In Ravensthorpe, winners gain prestige, prizes, and plenty of free mead. The settlement's resident master of wordplay is a clever fellow named Alvis, who tells me that flyting traces back to the very gods themselves. Apparently, Loki was quite good at humiliating his fellow Aesir!

ORLOG

I'm none too keen on the dice game known as orlog. I'm not much of a gamesman, and I always seem to lose. I'm not saying that Mundi cheats, but he certainly seems to win more than his share of rounds, more than seems warranted by random dice throws. But I've seen

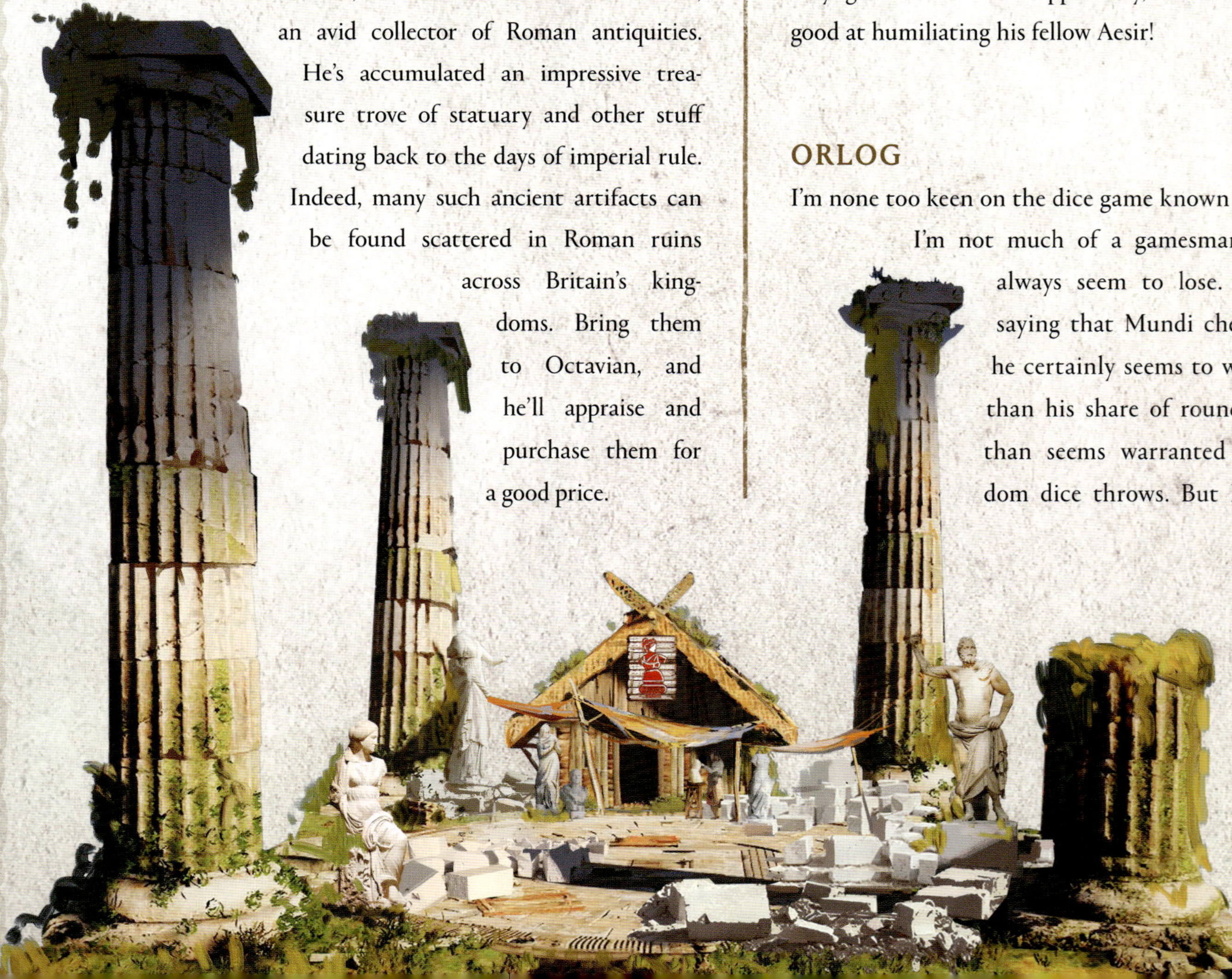

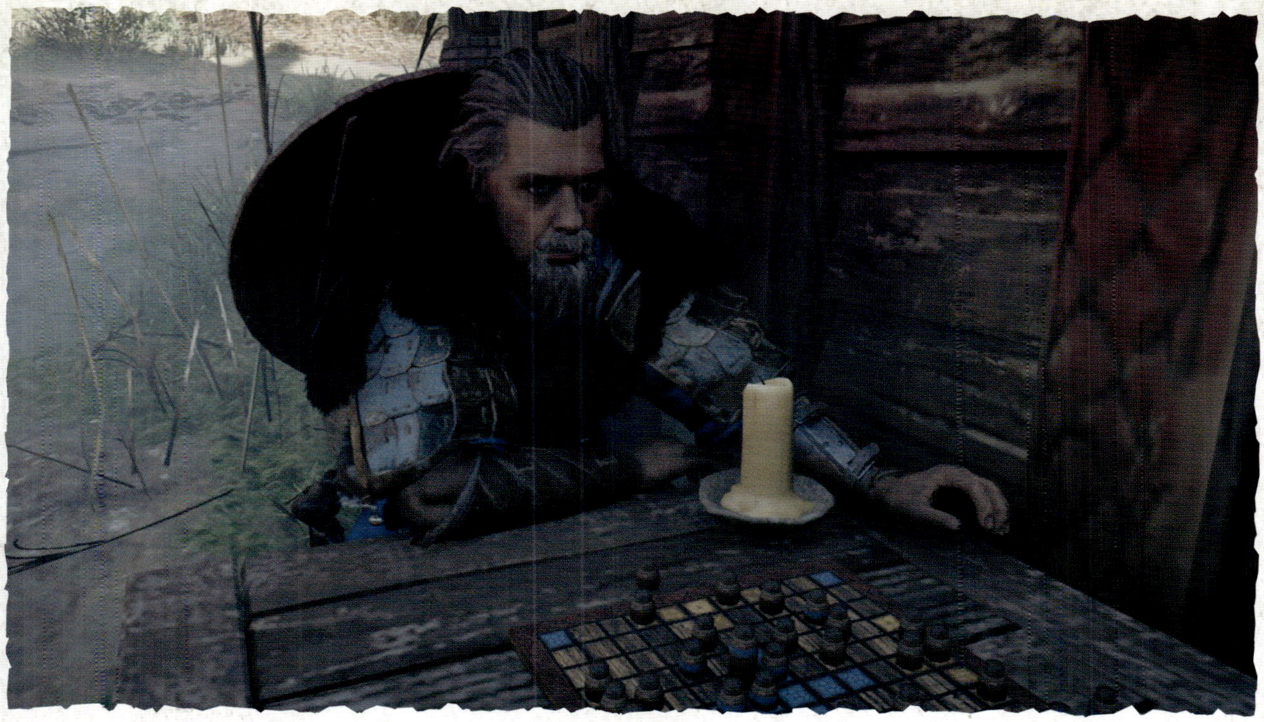

Eivor score plenty of orlog wins, so perhaps there is an element of skill involved that I'm not mastering or even seeing.

ALVIS AND HOLGER'S HOUSE

Eivor helped these artistic siblings build a sturdy home tucked between Ravensthorpe's great longhouse and the crumbling Roman columns just beyond. Destined to be a haven for "art and arguments"—that is, for Holger's unique canvases and epic sagas as well as Alvis's skaldic rhymes and flyting wordplay—the house has seen its share of drama. Holger has a penchant for "borrowing" inappropriate art supplies, like Gudrun's sailcloth or the tail hair of Rowan's horses. This often leads to disputes that must be adjudicated before the jarl's seat in the longhouse.

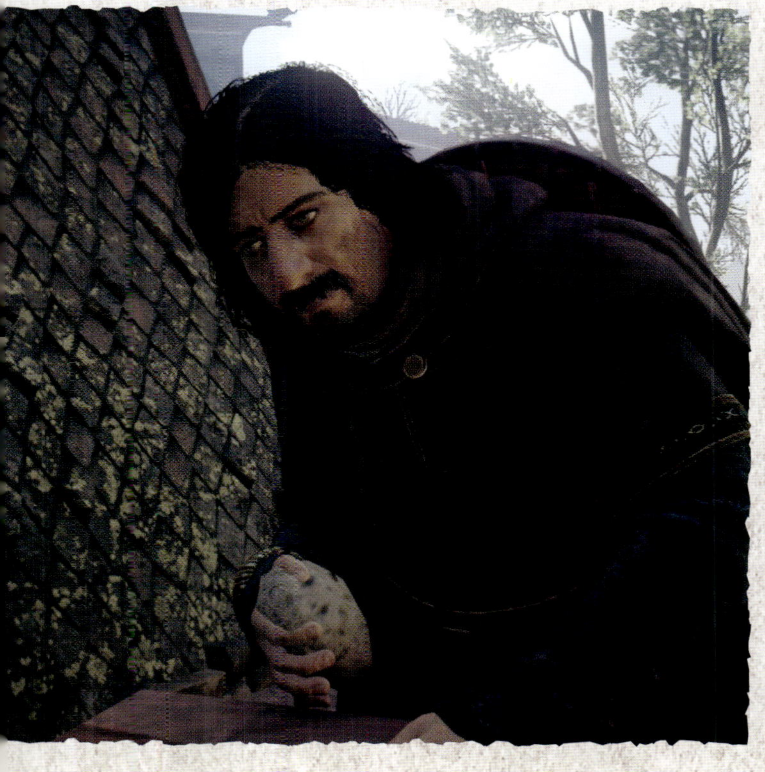

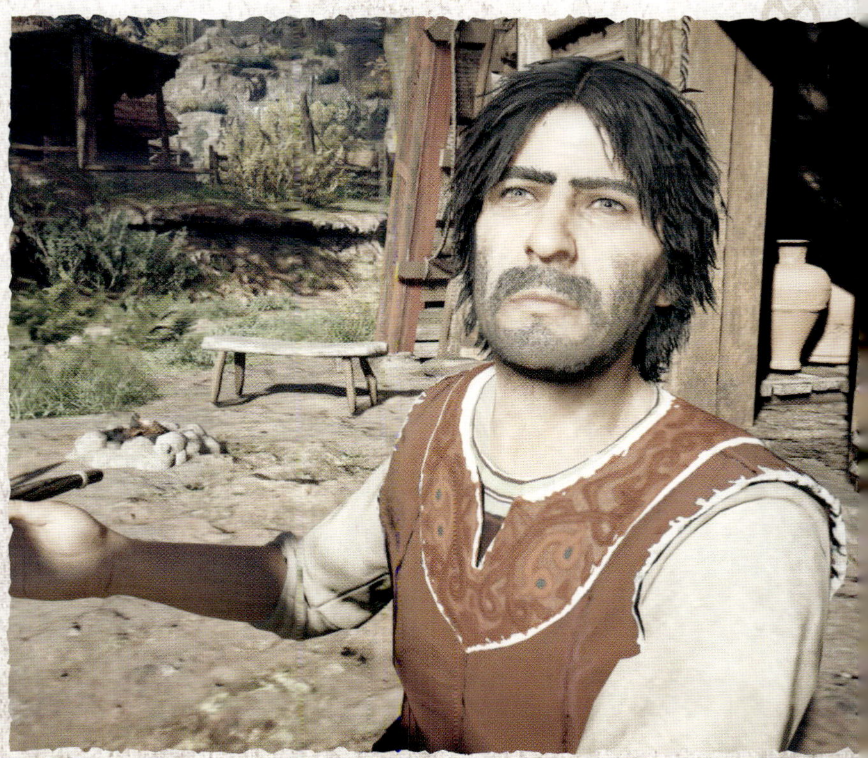

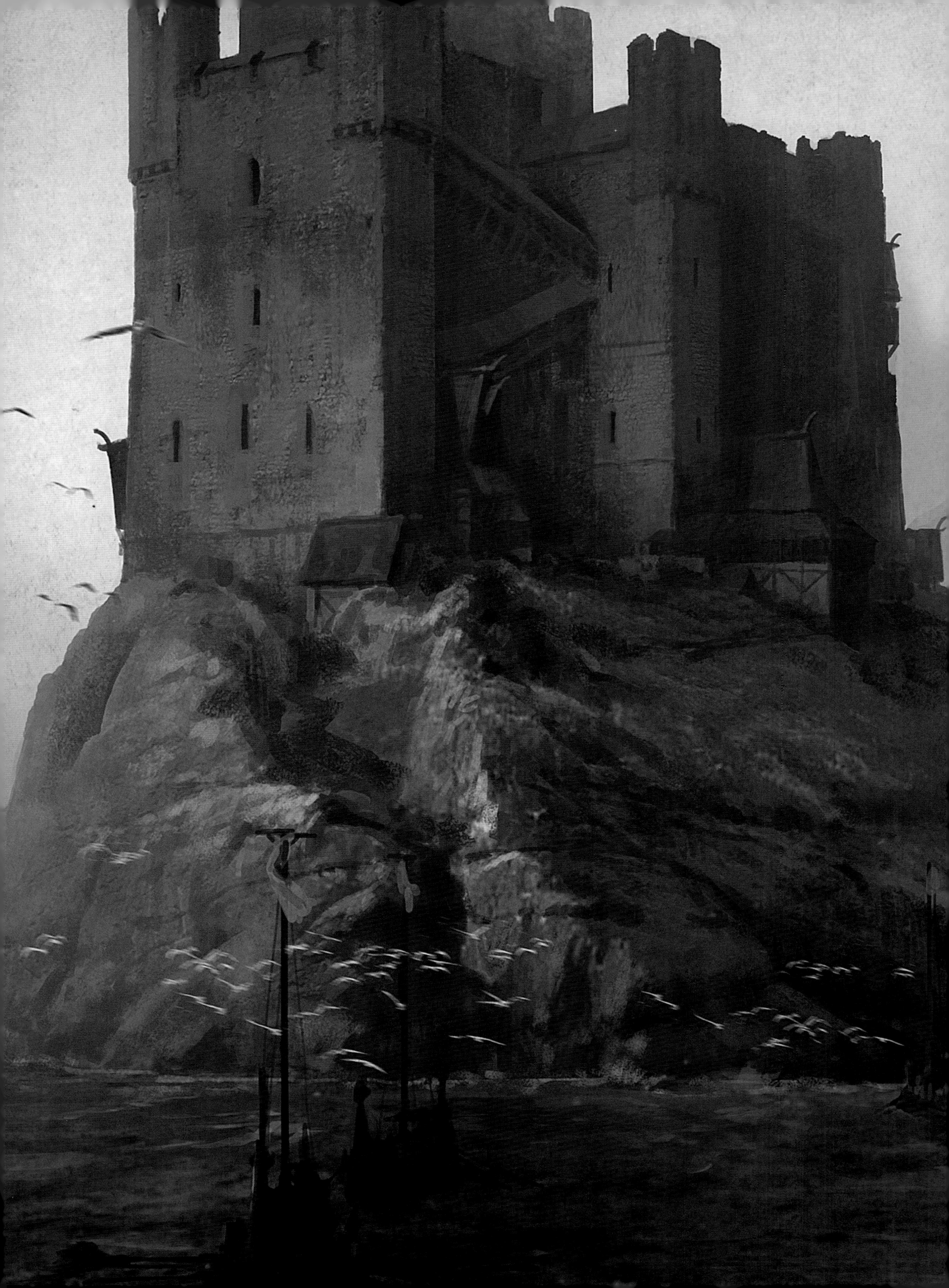

CHAPTER FOUR

THE VIKING AGE

Cynics see "history" as the propaganda of conquerors. But for centuries, Hidden Ones lurking in civilization's shadows have produced unfiltered accounts of human events. Recently, we've begun to classify the remarkable southward surge of raiders, tradesmen, and settlers from Norway as a distinct new era. Many church-based scholars disagree, of course. But clear-eyed observers from England, Francia, the Papal States, and all the way to Constantinople now identify the terrifying sack of Lindisfarne Abbey in Northumbria on June 8, 793, as the beginning of a new "Viking Age." Since that date, seafaring Norse folk have become a historical force in Europe.

My own firsthand observations align with this assessment. When Basim and I first arrived at Fornburg in Norway, I admit I was surprised by the level of cultural and technical sophistication I encountered. Most accounts I'd read of Vikings depicted barbaric heathens. I should have known better. Such chronicles were largely produced by Christian clergy and others whose economic control of northern Europe was threatened by Viking incursion. Demonizing one's enemy as "savage" is an age-old tactic, one that even cloistered monastic scholars will employ when it suits their purposes.

Thus, in service to truth, I present the following chronicle of recent events, distilled from the journals I've kept during my assignment in the Ravensthorpe bureau. Where necessary for accuracy or clarity I've added notes, dossiers, and other editorial revisions. But the bulk of this document is a contemporaneous account of events as they happened.

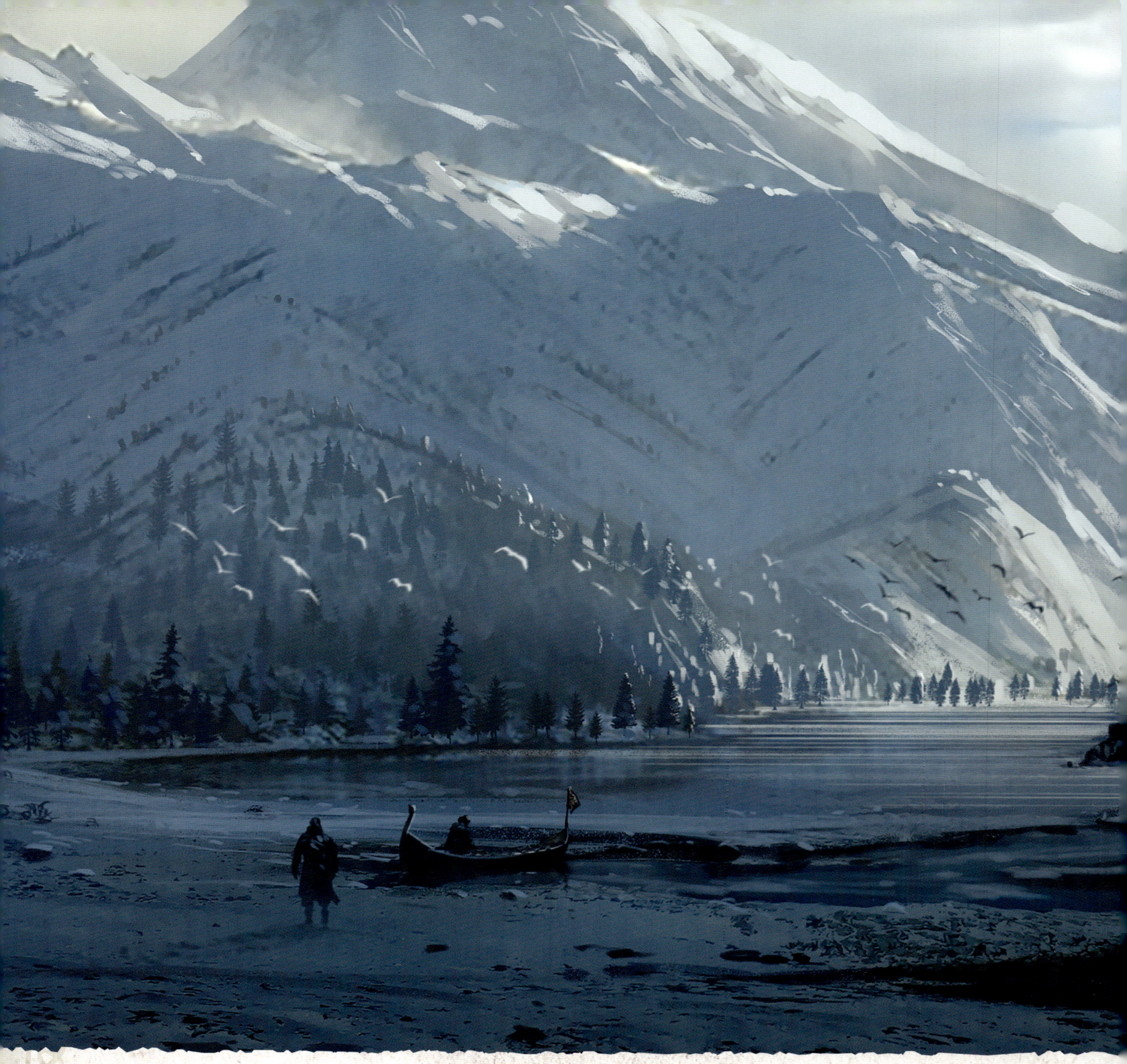

Norway

During the interminable sea journey from Constantinople to Fornburg, Basim engaged Sigurd in many discussions that touched on our true purpose in visiting Norway. Hidden Ones bureaus in Europe had uncovered correspondence that suggested the Order of the Ancients was making aggressive moves into northern lands. We'd learned that Kjotve the Cruel, a Viking clan leader based in Rygjafylke, was a recently recruited palatinus tasked with consolidating the order's control of the region. Kjotve's Wolf Clan, it turned out, was a longtime nemesis of Sigurd's Raven Clan. Thus, we hoped to exploit the natural enmity and conscript the Raven prince and his kinfolk into our counteractive efforts.

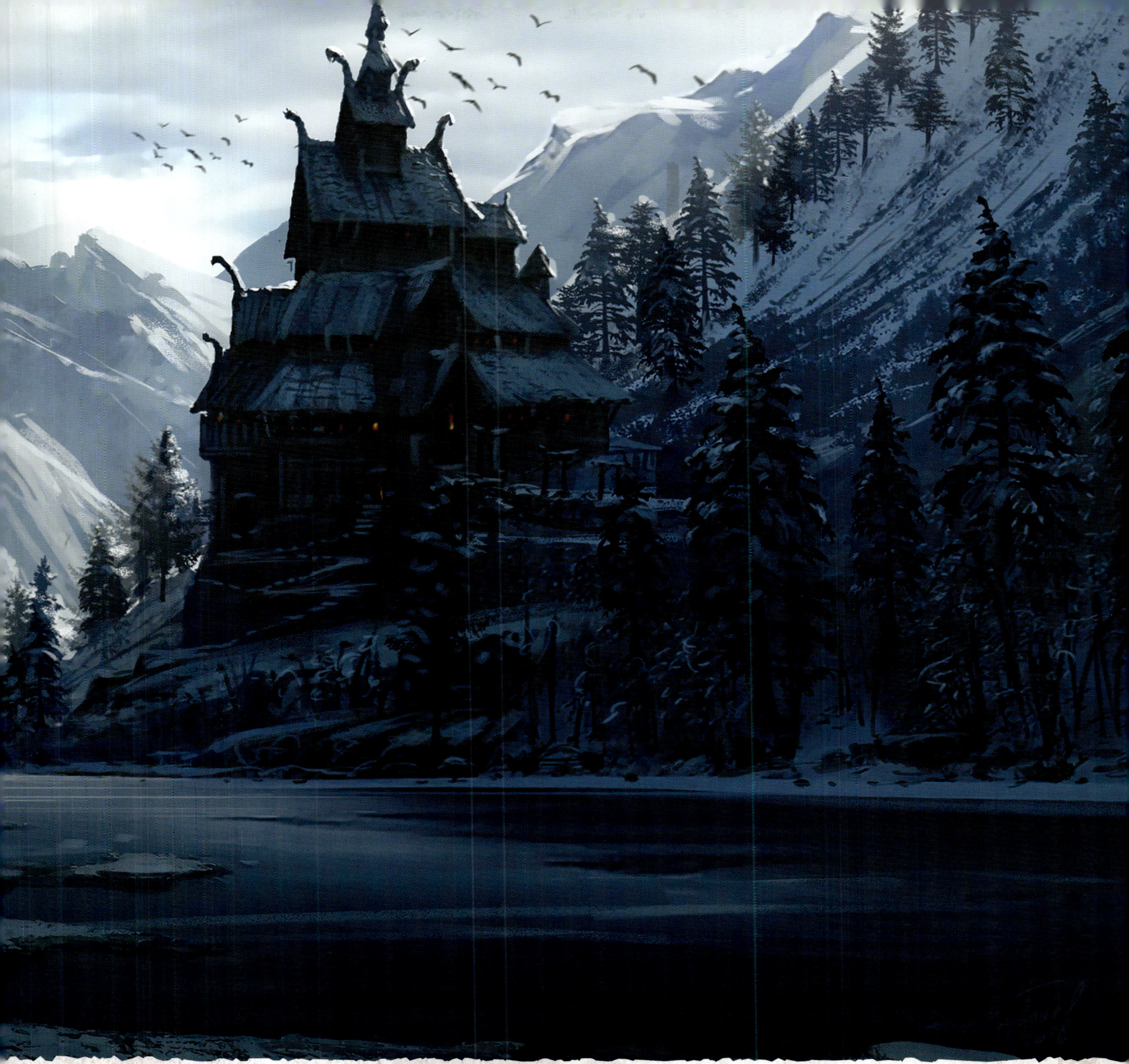

MAJOR FACTIONS & SECTS

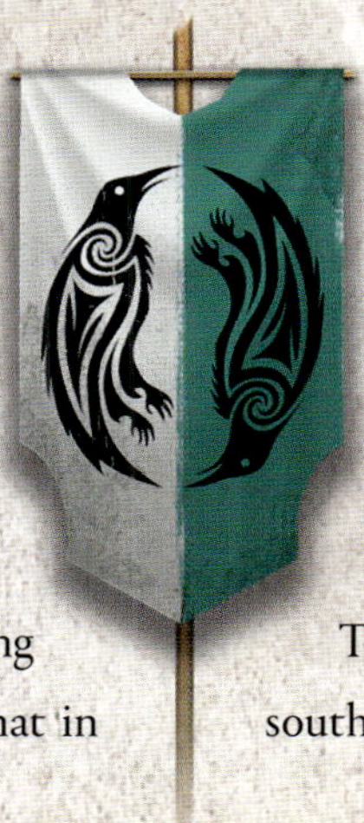

RAVEN CLAN

I've spoken at length about this remarkable Viking enclave elsewhere in this journal. (For Raven Clan dossiers, see Chapter 3: The Viking Settlement.) But it's worth mentioning again that in my extensive travels with Basim I've encountered few, if any, communities that I hold in such esteem. The clan's open embrace of outsiders like me is a thing of wonder.

WOLF CLAN

This coarse tribe of Norsemen was based in southern Norway and led by a palatinus of the order

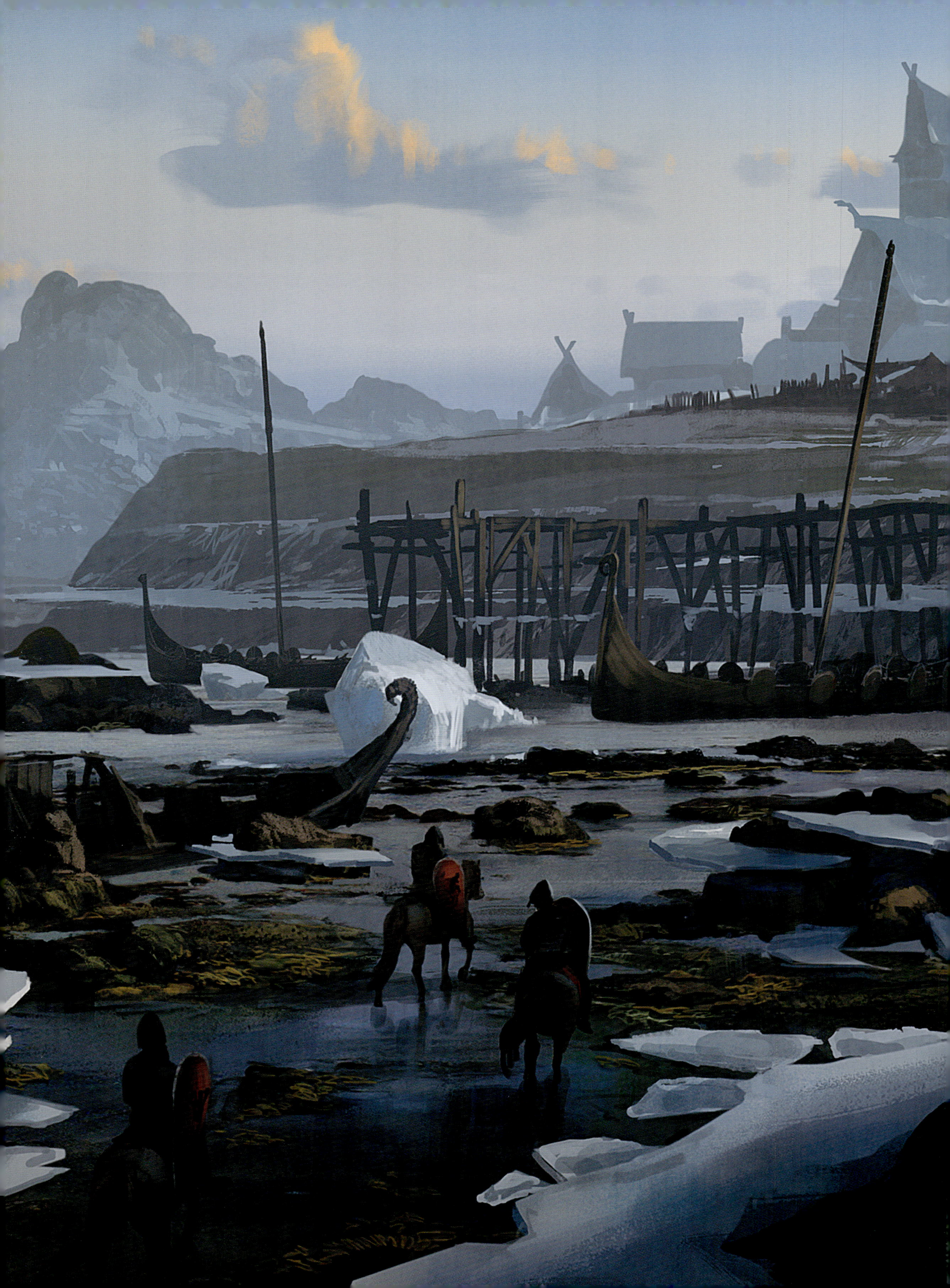

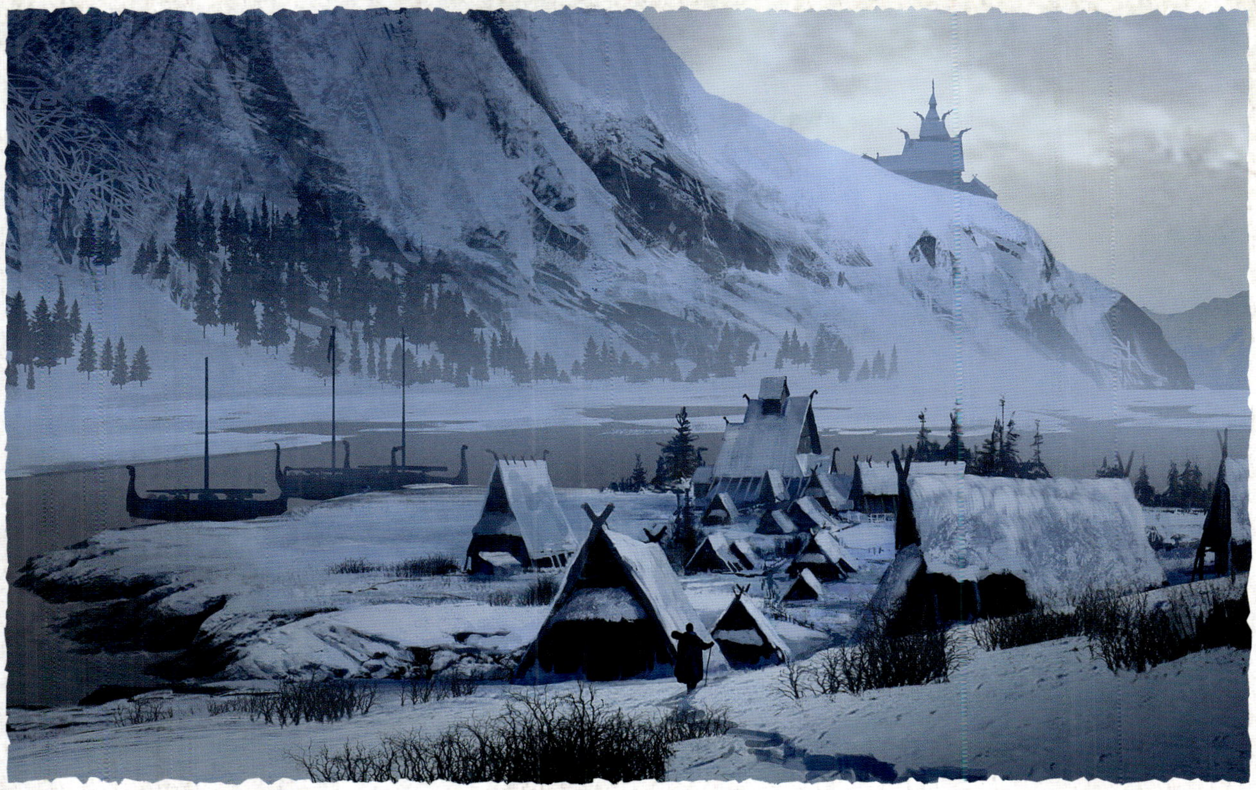

known as Kjotve the Cruel. His methods reflected his name—indeed, the sheer brutality of Kjotve's ways likely drew the attention of the order's hierarchy, who saw him as a suitable instrument of their plans to subjugate the northern latitudes of Europe.

KING HARALD'S CONFEDERATION

Harald Fairhair's call for Norse clans to band together under the banner of a united Norway continues to gain momentum. Based in Alrekstad, this collective of northland tribes will soon prove a formidable political entity. The effort has most certainly boosted King Harald's profile in the region. Ironically, his ambition is pushing the stronger, more independent Viking clans out of Norway.

MISCELLANEOUS NORSE BRIGANDS AND BANDITS

Various bandit gangs still operate with impunity in Rygjafylke's high country and back roads. Some have gathered in encampments, ready to descend on any foolish passersby. The highwaymen of Norway fight hard, swing crude clubs and axes, and sometimes sling rocks and arrows.

RYGJAFYLKE

BATTLE FOR THE NORTHERN WAY

Sigurd had already impressed us with his restless intelligence and his curiosity about the wider world beyond Norway. But I saw something truly formidable—and, to be honest, a bit intimidating—in his adopted sibling, Eivor. I'll admit that I didn't fully trust her at first . . . and as I mentioned earlier, I was shocked when Basim entrusted her with our assassin's wrist blade so quickly. But over time, I grew to recognize extraordinary qualities in Eivor that my savvy mentor had identified almost immediately. Indeed, Eivor quickly became a primary agent of our plan to counter Kjotve, the order's northernmost instrument.

KEY EVENTS

With our vigorous encouragement, Eivor ruthlessly scoured the Fornburg area for Kjotve's spies, then led a lightning strike on his supply stores at Nottfall. As preparations commenced for an assault on Kjotve's fortress, the Raven Clan gained a formidable new ally in King Harald Fairhair of Hordafylke. With his support, the storming of the Wolf Clan stronghold was a resounding success.

Unfortunately, my personal experience of the battle was considerably less triumphant. Basim had painstakingly trained me for the task of confronting the order's highest ranks, but Eivor insisted on facing Kjotve herself—a matter of family honor, she said, as Kjotve had murdered her father in a most despicable manner. Seeing the almost feral look in her eyes, I agreed. No matter who killed Kjotve, the Hidden Ones would benefit.

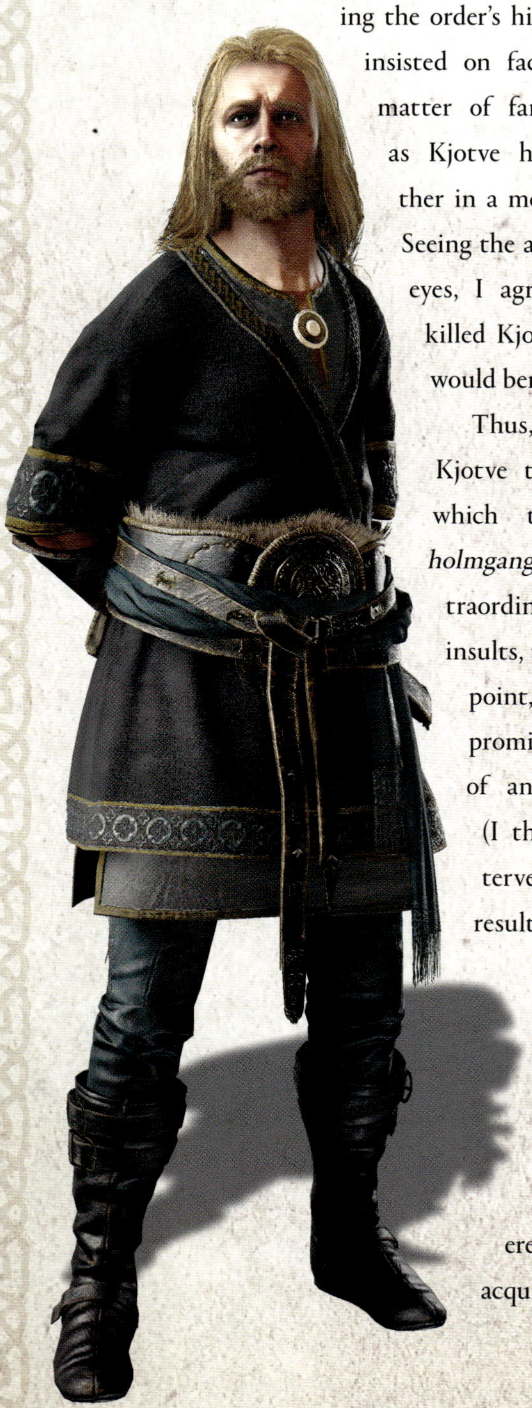

Thus, Eivor summoned Kjotve to a one-on-one duel, which the Vikings call a *holmgang*. After a rather extraordinary exchange of grim insults, the fight began. At one point, Eivor seemed compromised and on the verge of annihilation. Heroically (I thought), I tried to intervene, to disastrous results—I far underestimated Kjotve's brute strength, and his crippling parry of my attack left me badly injured.

But Eivor recovered, killed Kjotve, and acquired his Order of the Ancients medallion, an artifact signifying the bearer's allegiance to the foul brotherhood. An image of the great World Tree, Yggdrasil, is embossed upon it—the mythical ash tree that connects the Nine Realms. Eivor gave this sigil to Basim. Then she led the final surge through Kjotve's fortress and chased off his sniveling son Gorm.

ALTHING IN ALREKSTAD

Soon after Kjotve's demise, King Harald called for an *althing* (a Norse term for an assembly of freemen) in his home settlement of Alrekstad, located in the Hordafylke region north of Rygjafylke. My grave injuries left me unable to attend, but Basim escorted the Raven Clan leadership. At the *althing*, Harald called for unity of all clans under his kingship. Kjotve's son Gorm emerged from hiding and offered Harald his oath and axe, but Harald banished him from Norway, renaming him "Worm."

Then Styrbjorn, war weary and seeking a lasting peace, shocked both Sigurd and Eivor, his heirs, by bending his knee in fealty to Harald, placing Raven Clan and its lands under the rule of the fair-haired king. Sigurd spoke out harshly—the clan's kingship was his by right—and stormed off. But Styrbjorn

HARALD, KING OF NORWAY

Known as Harald Fairhair due to his flowing blond locks, this son of Halfdan the Black believed his destiny was to unite disparate Norse clans into a single unified kingdom of Norway under his personal rule. Although fair of mind as well as hair, Harald was not above placing a ruthless boot on the throat of dissenters.

KJOTVE THE CRUEL

Brutal head of the Wolf Clan in Rygjafylke, Kjotve employed such vicious methods of conquest that it was inevitable he'd catch the order's admiring eye. His son Gorm rode the tails of his father's cloak as Kjotve spread the order's code of control across the northlands.

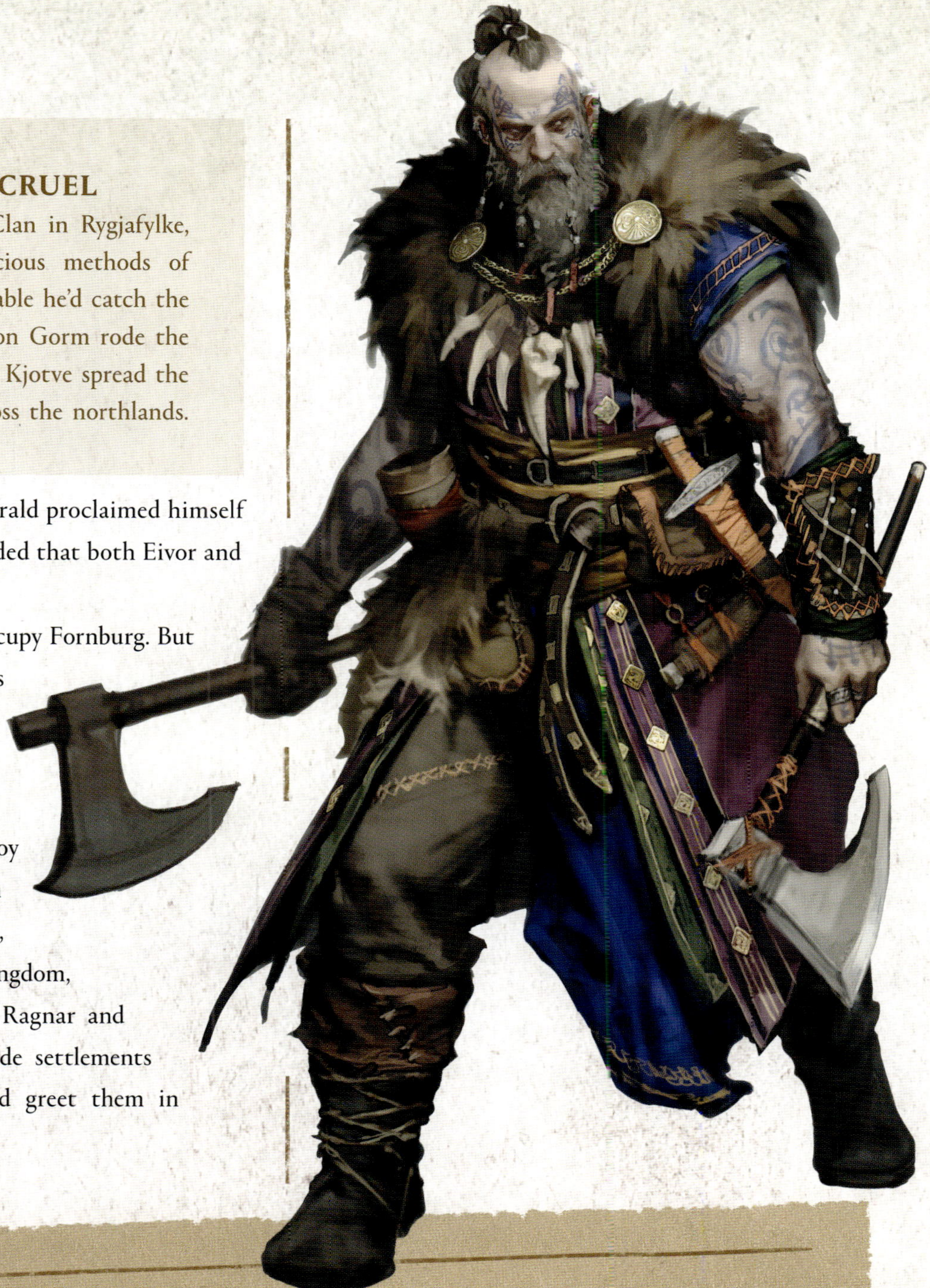

would not be dissuaded. Harald proclaimed himself king of Norway and demanded that both Eivor and Sigurd serve under him.

Harald sent troops to occupy Fornburg. But the Raven Clan, with Basim's blessing, did not plan to submit. As Sigurd proclaimed, "We are not the heel-trodden subjects of a boy king." He called for his kin to leave Norway for England, there to make their own kingdom, a new home. The Sons of Ragnar and their clans had already made settlements there, so Viking kin would greet them in the new land.

A side note: I told my mentor Basim how I felt I'd found long-lost family in the Raven Clan, even before we set sail from Rygjafylke. Eivor, Sigurd, Randvi, and the others seemed to regard me as kin. Truth be told, I'd begun to feel more at home in Fornburg than in my own Levantine village of origin. The feasts in particular were truly remarkable communal experiences.

Thus, I found the clan's abrupt decision to exit Norway somewhat disconcerting. Certainly, I understood the reason—none would bend a knee to King Harald. As Eivor put it, "I will not be captive to another man's gaudy design. My destiny is my own to weave." But once the decision was made, I was stunned by the almost gleeful abandon with which the clan packed its essential belongings into three longships in a single day. As we set out across the North Sea, Sigurd's parting words betrayed not even a hint of nostalgia: "The further I sail from this place, the louder I will sing!"

I must say . . . as much as Norse folk love their settled communities, they are most truly alive in transit, sailing to destinations unknown, seeking adventure and glory. Exhilarated, fearless, unbothered by uprooting or the unknown. Indeed, Vikings on the move seem positively aglow. I believe it's the clearest expression of their essence as a people.

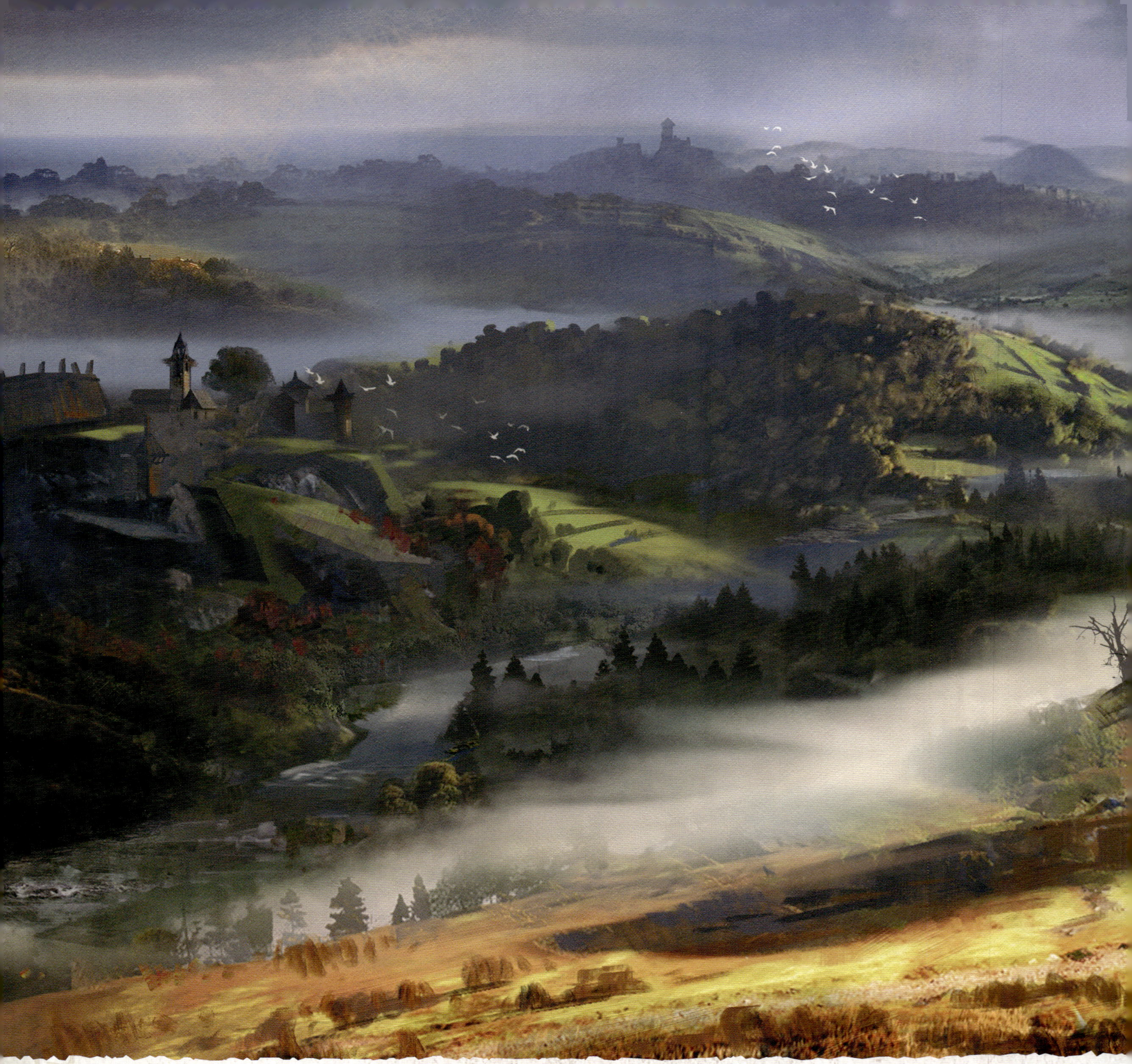

ENGLAND

First, a bit of history. Today, England comprises four kingdoms: Mercia, Wessex, East Anglia, and Northumbria. Some years ago—the exact date is hard to pin down—the Norse king Ragnar Lothbrok led a fearsome assemblage of Viking raiders south from Norway to a series of conquests across the British Isles. But in 865 CE, Ragnar was defeated and captured in Northumbria. There, King Aella tossed the Viking leader into a pit of poisonous snakes and left him to die in agony.

This petty Saxon brutality triggered a fateful landslide of events. Later that year, Ragnar's vengeful son Halfdan Ragnarsson and his brothers Ivarr and Ubba mustered and led the so-called Great

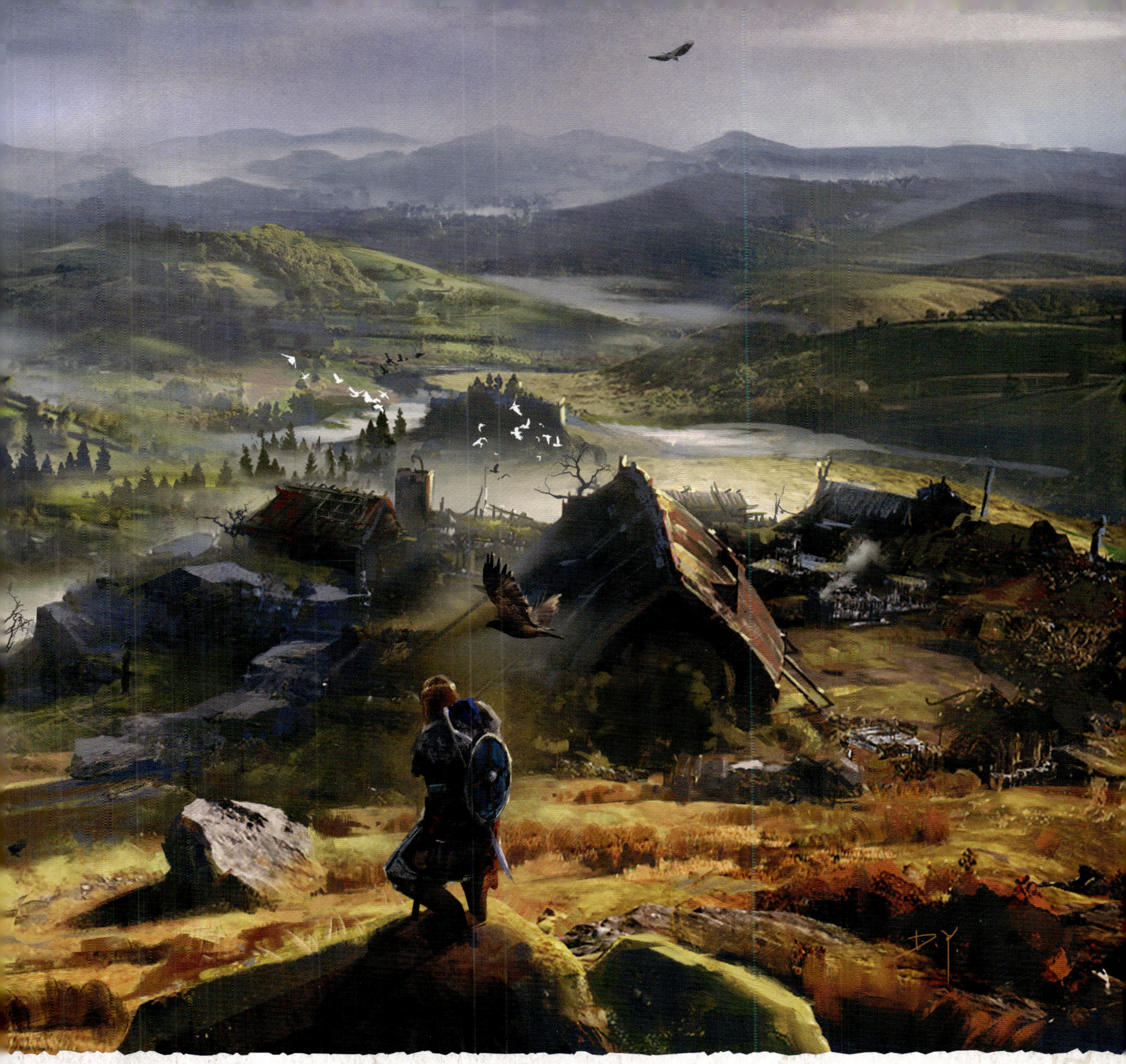

Heathen Army of Viking warriors into England seeking retribution and, of course, plunder. In 871 CE, a second Viking surge called the Great Summer Army led by Guthrum landed in Reading to reinforce Halfdan's legion.

After eight years of glorious but chaotic conquests and shifting alliances, the combined Viking force lay scattered across England's shires in a somewhat decentralized jumble. This fragmented situation is what Sigurd, Eivor, and the Raven Clan encountered on their arrival from Norway. Below, I've transcribed my journal of our activities in these lands—again, a contemporary account augmented by notes added later.

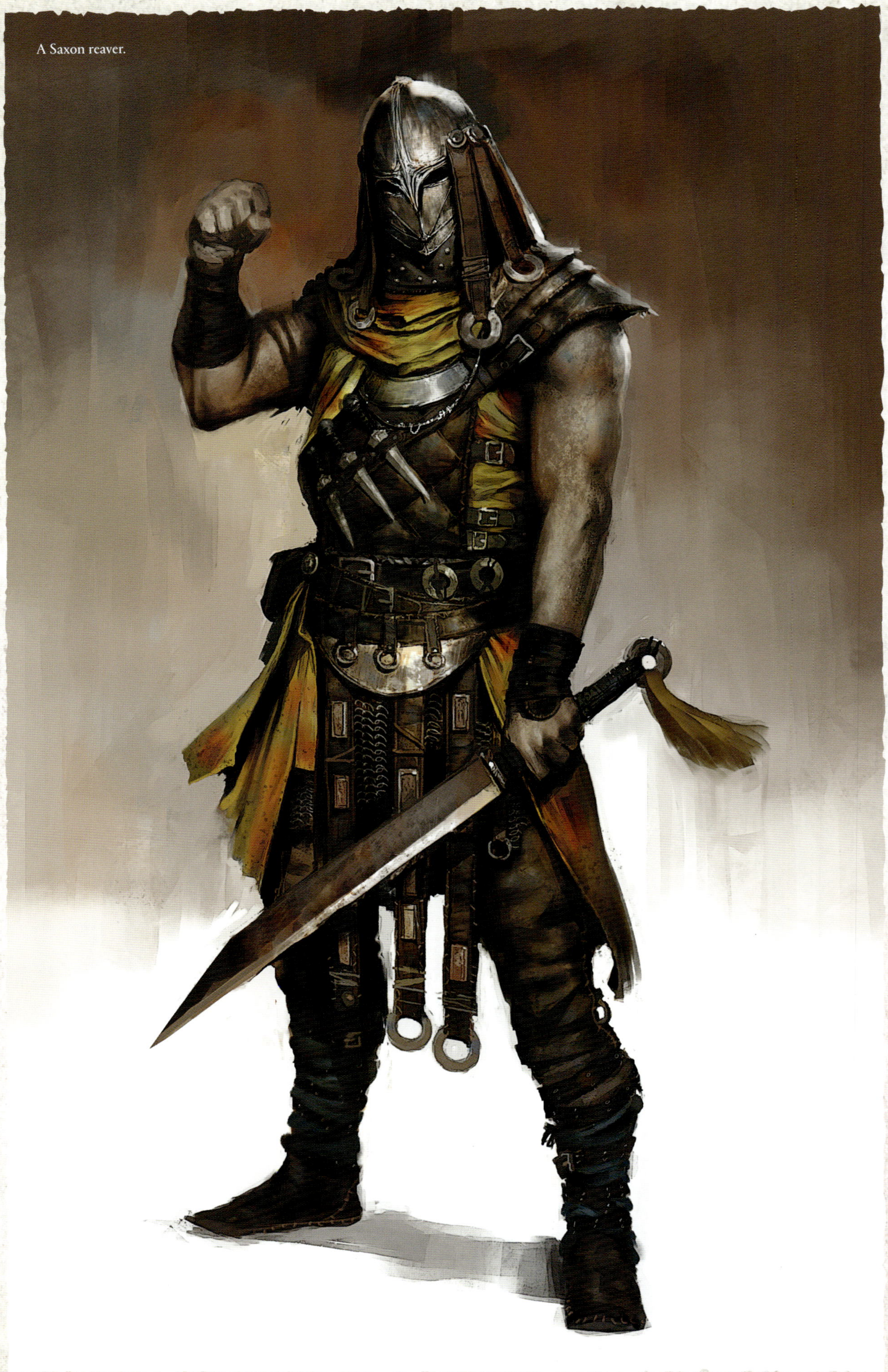

A Saxon reaver.

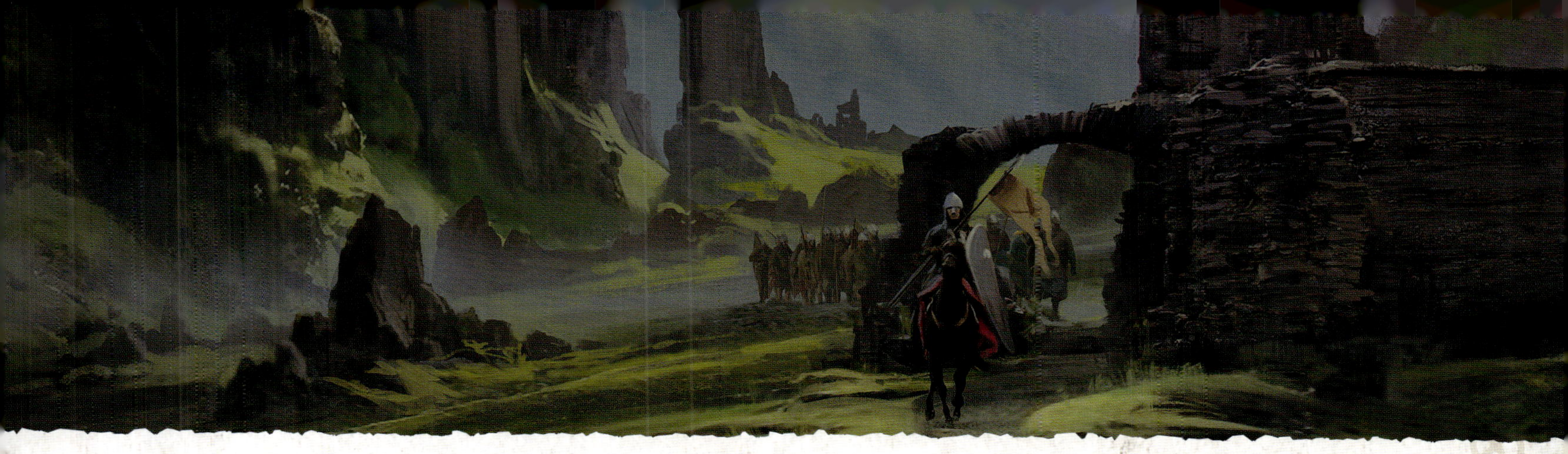

MAJOR FACTIONS & SECTS

SAXONS

After harassing Britain's coastal settlements for generations, this collection of Germanic tribes began to flow across the sea in conquering waves in the fifth century CE, filling the power void left by the collapse of the Western Roman Empire. Like the Vikings who would follow four hundred years later, the first Saxons arrived as seafaring raiders who quickly established coastal enclaves, then pushed inland up England's waterways.

Contemporaneous writings note that by 442 CE, Saxon rule had been established across most of the island. Multiple Saxon provinces were established, but over time, these evolved into today's four Anglo-Saxon kingdoms of Mercia, East Anglia, Northumbria, and Wessex. By the late 700s, most inhabitants had also converted to Christianity.

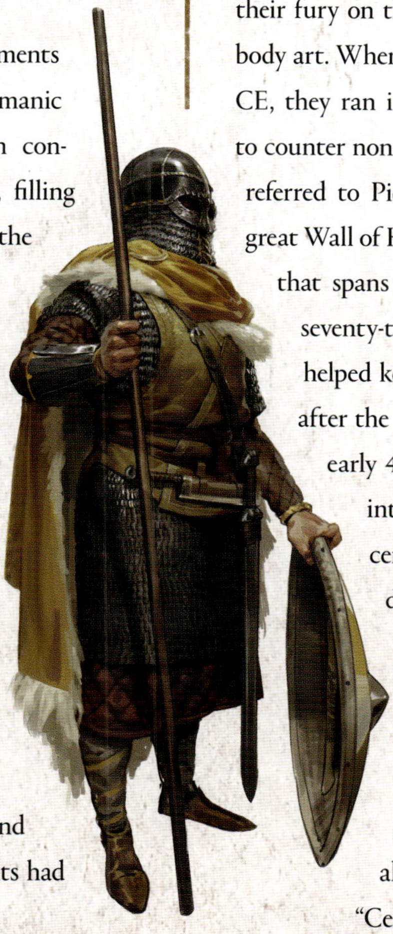

Saxon armies were composed largely of ceorls—i.e., freemen of the lowest rank, mostly farmers or craftsmen with rudimentary combat training. But elite Saxon soldiers were fierce warriors with skills and tactics drawn from many years of fighting not only *against* Roman legions in England but also *with* them—Saxon tribesmen were often recruited by Roman overseers and trained to serve as auxiliary units.

PICTS

The Picts are a proud, tough, and aggressive clan from the northern hills of Britain. Little is known about this insular tribe of Christianized Celtic peoples other than their fury on the battlefield and the intricacy of their body art. When the Romans first invaded Britain in 43 CE, they ran into furious Pict resistance. Eventually, to counter nonstop Pict harassment, the Romans (who referred to Picts as "troublesome savages") built the great Wall of Hadrian, an impressive architectural feat that spans the entire northern neck of Britain—seventy-three miles from coast to coast! This helped keep Pict tribes at bay for centuries. But after the Romans withdrew from England in the early 400s, the Picts flowed southward again into what is now Northumbria. In recent years, both Saxons and Vikings have driven Pict tribes back north . . . but often at great cost.

BRITONS

Some have called this cluster of tribes along England's western border the "Celtic Britons" because of a shared Celtic heritage with Picts and other northwestern peoples. Hostile to Roman and then Saxon invaders for centuries, and now to the Norse newcomers, the Britons have frequently clashed with the kingdoms of Mercia and Wessex. Today, a powerful and clever warlord named Rhodri ap Merfyn has consolidated power over a number of Briton-dominated territories, forming a united kingdom of Briton. Indeed, some are calling him the first king of the Britons!

LEDECESTRESCIRE, MERCIA

THE KINGMAKER'S SAGA

The Raven Clan arrived from Norway in the central Mercian shire of Ledecestrescire to settle and launch its first forays into regional affairs. Traditionally, the shire's municipality of Repton had been home to the Mercian king's throne. But after the Norse invasion, Ledecestrescire devolved into a patchwork of warring camps, with the Sons of Ragnar occupying Repton and the embattled King Burgred (the Mercian monarch since 852 CE) holed up in Tamworth Fortress, a well-fortified haven for his loyalists. The following journal entries chronicle how the Raven Clan established its home settlement on Ledecestrescire's southern border and began a quest for regional influence.

KEY EVENTS

After a week of tacking across the swan-road—another clever Norse kenning, this one referring to a sea or waterway—our little fleet glided into the mouth of the Nene River, snaking into the heart of England's midsection. Not far upstream we found a Viking wintering camp abandoned by the Great Heathen Army. Halfdan's old quarters featured a sturdy, serviceable longhouse—a good start for any settlement with aspirations of greatness. At Eivor's suggestion, the outpost was named "Ravensthorpe"—the village of ravens! Perfect, I must say.

As the settlement steadily expanded, Raven scouts began to probe the area and make daily reports to

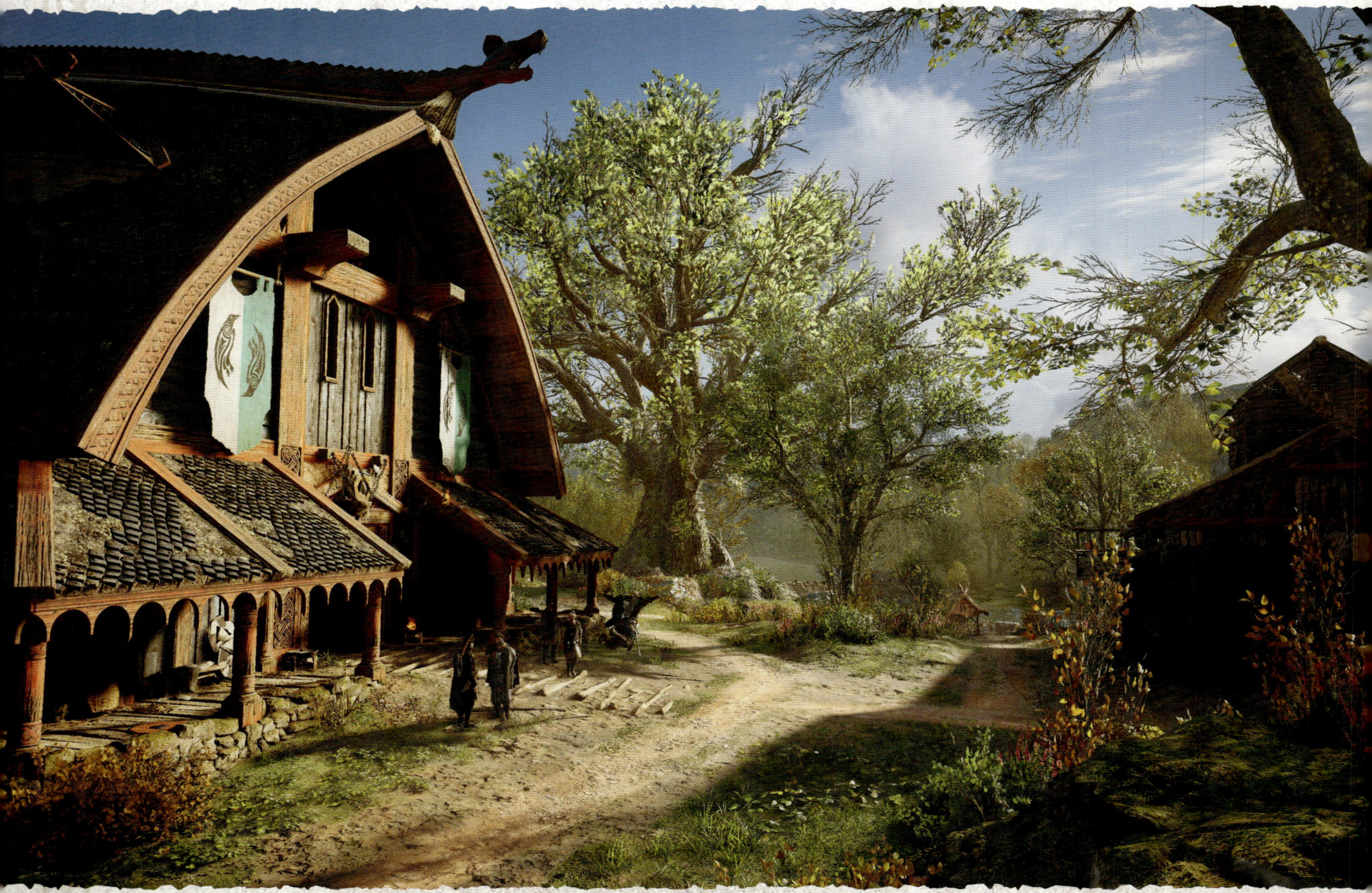

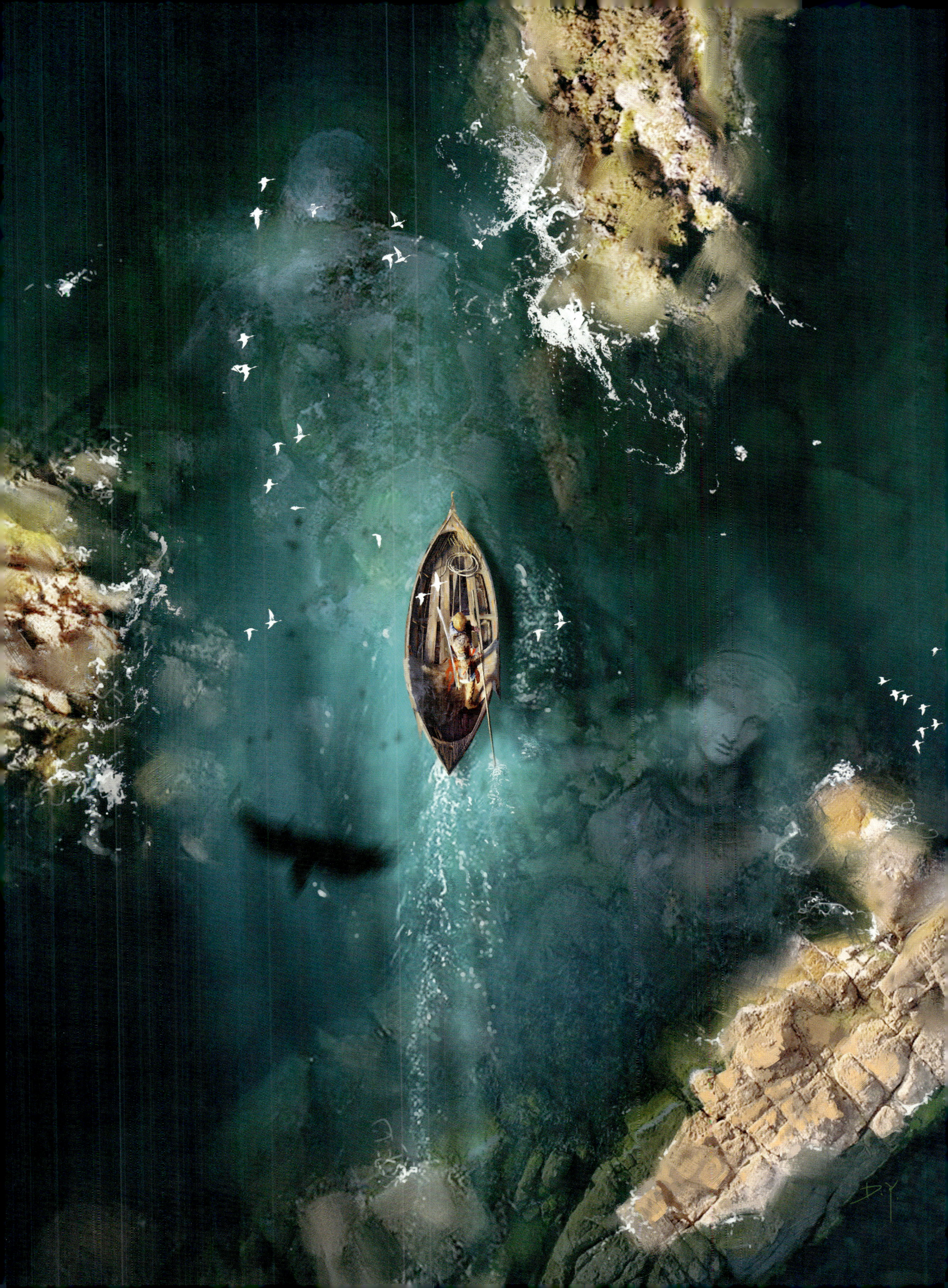

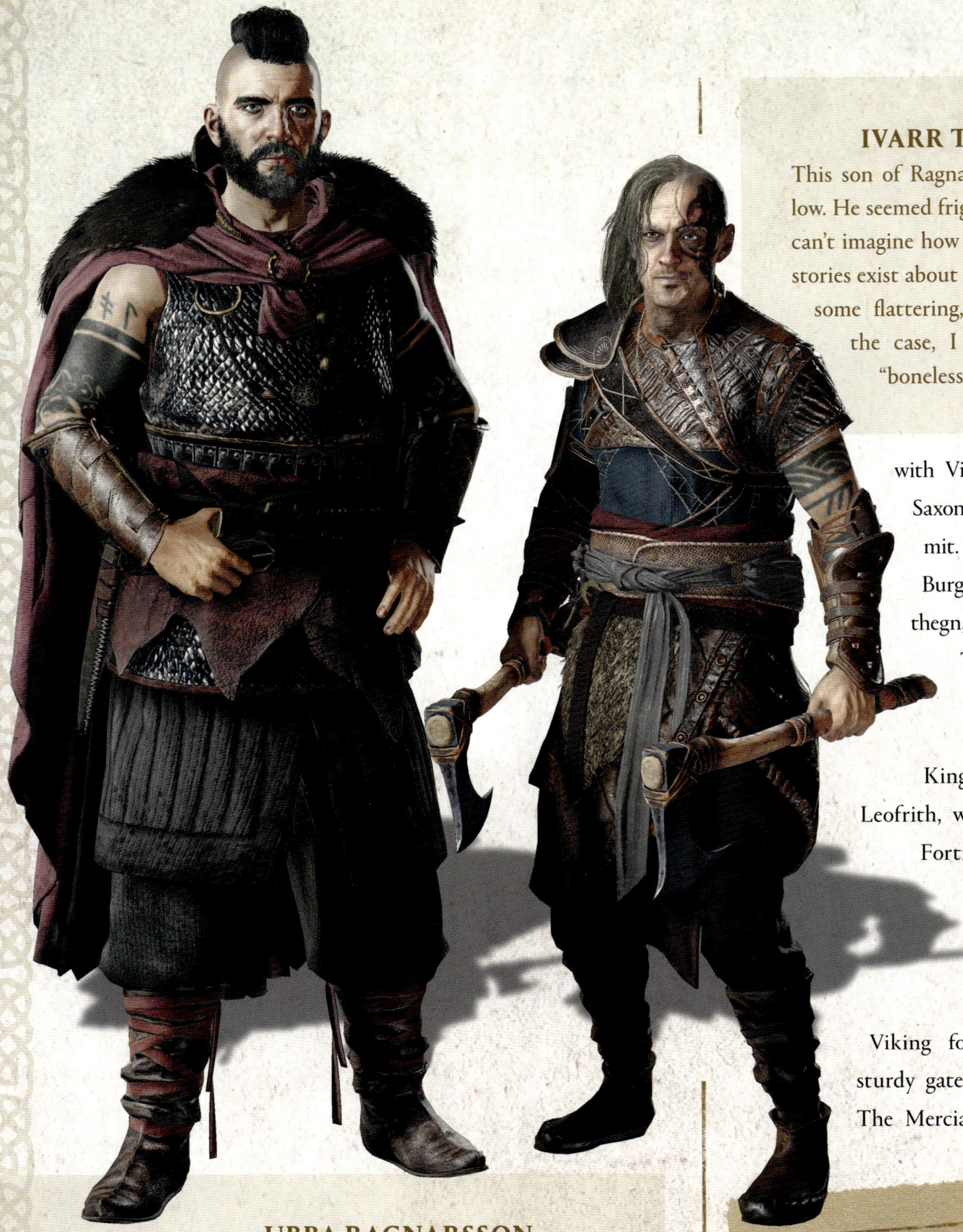

IVARR THE BONELESS

This son of Ragnar was an intense, cruel fellow. He seemed frightening enough as an ally; I can't imagine how he'd be as a foe. Conflicting stories exist about the origin of his nickname—some flattering, some mocking. Whatever the case, I suspect nobody calls him "boneless" to his grimly scarred face.

UBBA RAGNARSSON

Eivor calls Ubba the "sane brother." His easy camaraderie with Sigurd has helped the Raven Clan find a ready ally—and an important connection to the already established Danish presence in Mercia.

Randvi in the longhouse meeting room, where she tracked their findings on a map. Meanwhile, Sigurd and Eivor joined the sons of Ragnar—Ivarr and Ubba Ragnarsson—in Repton, a busy municipality on the Trent River and the traditional center of power for the Mercian royal family. Local jarls were falling in line with Viking rule, but the stubborn Saxon king Burgred refused to submit. The Ragnarssons' plan: oust Burgred and install a friendly local thegn, Ceowulf II, on the throne. The new king would administer a new Mercia, uniting Saxon and Dane.

King Burgred and his war thegn, Leofrith, were holed up in Tamworth Fortress with a garrison of troops, doggedly weathering a Viking siege. With Eivor leading the way, the combined Viking forces breached Tamworth's sturdy gates and stormed the fortress. The Mercian monarch fled, but Eivor

A quick side note: I must say, I've been impressed by the general Viking practice of what I'd term "benevolent conquest." Make no mistake, the sheer brutality of a Viking assault is a nightmarish terror to behold. But once a targeted region submits in obeisance, these northern conquerors typically rule with a light touch. They don't impose their culture or religious beliefs on the conquered. In fact, Vikings often let local thegns oversee their old districts, a reassuring continuity that local residents tend to appreciate.

tracked down his secret havens. She found Burgred's queen, Lady Aethelswith, sequestered in one . . . and after some persuasion (handled expertly by Eivor), the lady revealed her husband's location in another.

After Burgred's capture, a witan—a gathering of Mercian lords—officially decreed him unfit to rule and initiated the coronation of Ceowulf II. Burgred formally abdicated and handed over the Mercian crown . . . but not before uttering a chilling curse, declaring that he'd summoned zealots of the order to hunt down and kill Eivor!

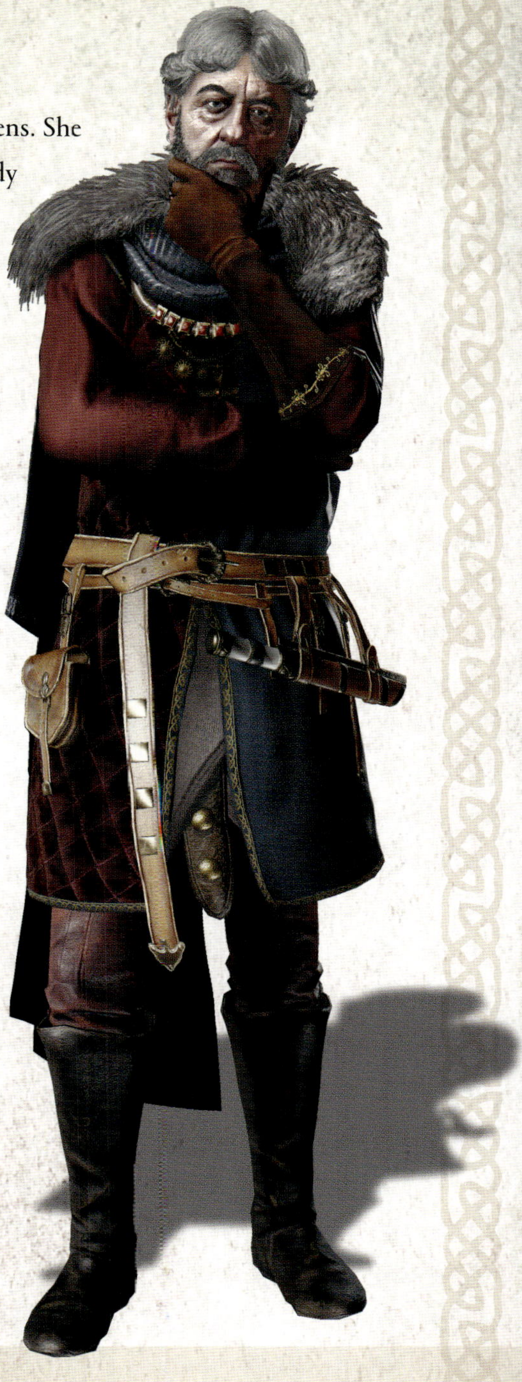

CEOWULF II

This savvy Saxon nobleman served in King Burgred's Mercian court during the Viking invasion. A practical man, Ceowulf quickly assessed the situation, jumped ship to join the invaders, and agreed to assume the Mercian throne as a Ragnarsson figurehead once Burgred was removed. This pact may seem disloyal or self-serving, but Ceowulf clearly had the best interests of his people in mind and hoped to spare them from the bloody berserker fury of the Norsemen he'd witnessed on the battlefield.

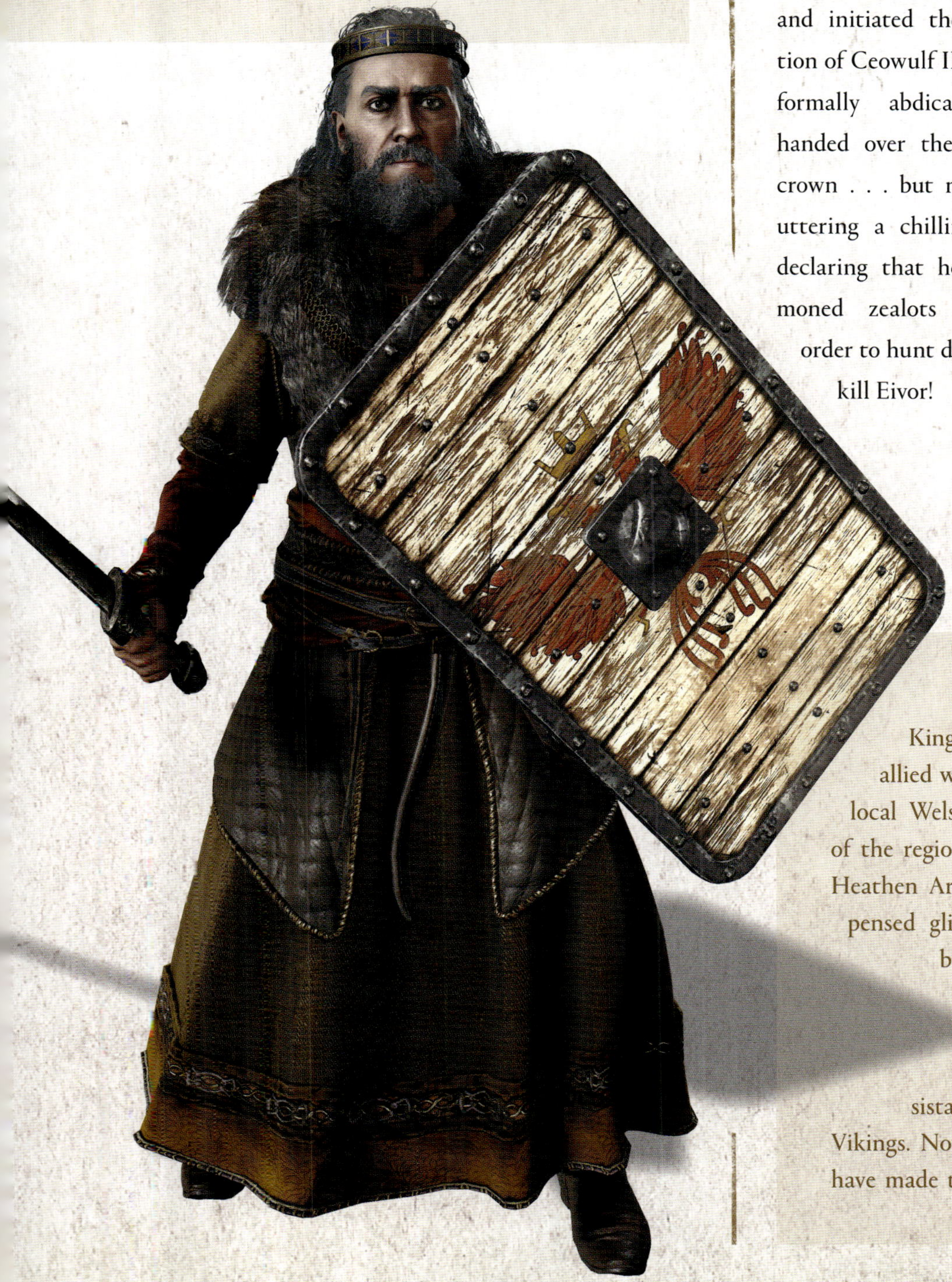

KING BURGRED

King of Mercia since 852 CE, Burgred allied with the West Saxons to defeat the local Welsh tribes and consolidate control of the region. Thirteen years later, the Great Heathen Army arrived. At first, Burgred dispensed glittering mounds of hacksilver to bribe the northern invaders for peace . . . while he surreptitiously rallied local thegns to form a united resistance. But nobody wants to fight Vikings. Now, in 874 CE, the sons of Ragnar have made their play for the Mercian throne.

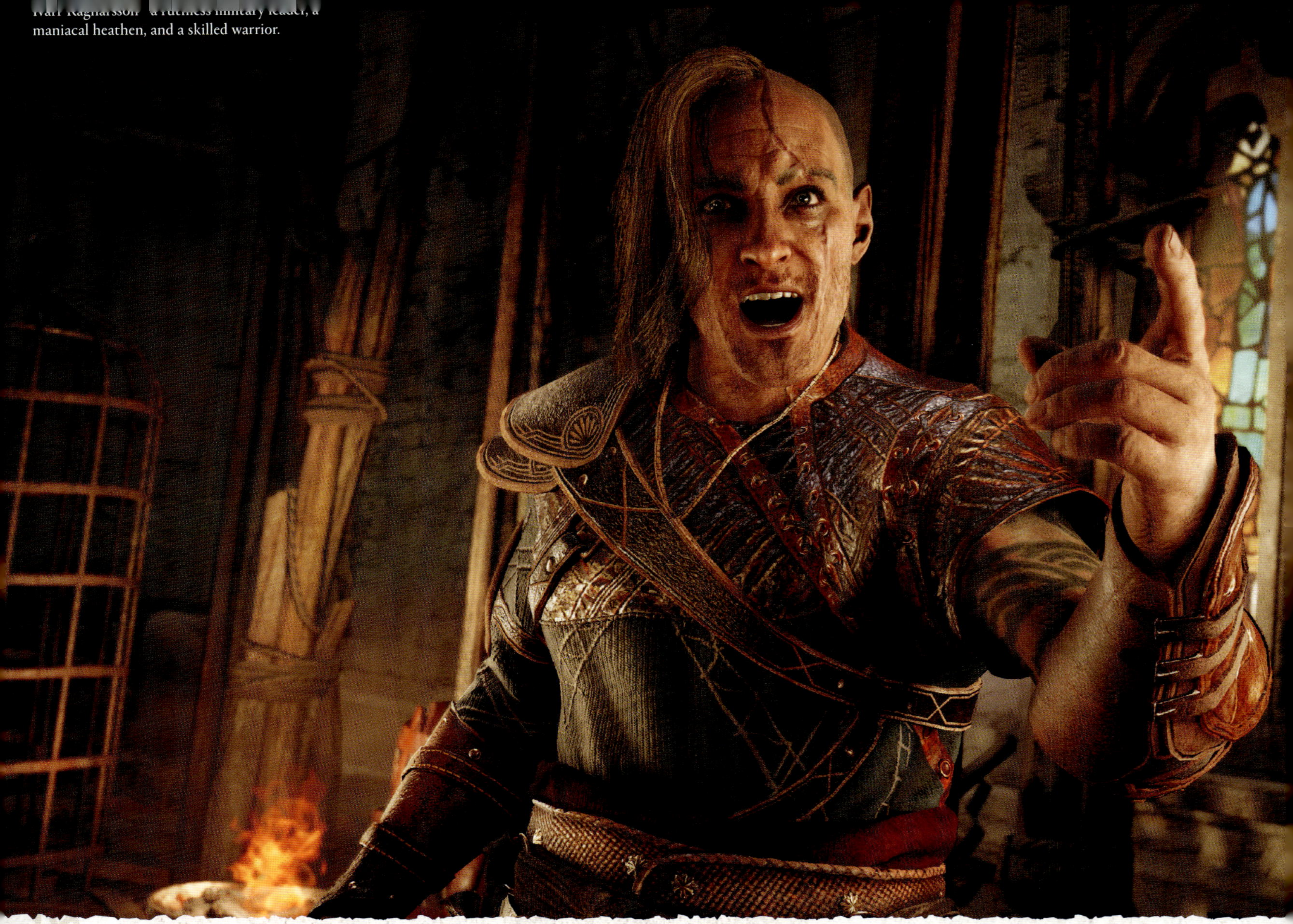

Ivarr Ragnarsson—a ruthless military leader, a maniacal heathen, and a skilled warrior.

After Ceowulf's coronation, the new king banished Burgred and Aethelswith to Rome, never to return. But sudden word of Mercian troops led by Leofrith assaulting Repton sent the Vikings rushing off to repel the counterattack . . . and to protect Ceolbert, the new king's son and heir. As intense fighting roiled Repton's streets, Eivor tracked them and defeated the great Saxon general.

ZEALOTS

Zealots may be disguised as holy ones, but they execute a distinctly unholy plan. These fierce foot soldiers of the Order of the Ancients wander the earth, brutally enforcing the dictates of their sect. Each one has a unique set of skills and proclivities, a "warrior code" developed in secret training within Saxon, Anglian, or Brittonic martial traditions.

LADY AETHELSWITH

This daughter of Aethelwulf, the late king of Wessex, married Burgred to become queen of Mercia. A proud but pragmatic woman, Aethelswith had deep affection for not only her personal entourage but all her Mercian subjects. Rumors persist that her father had favored the precepts of our order's enemies, but the lady didn't appear to share this inclination.

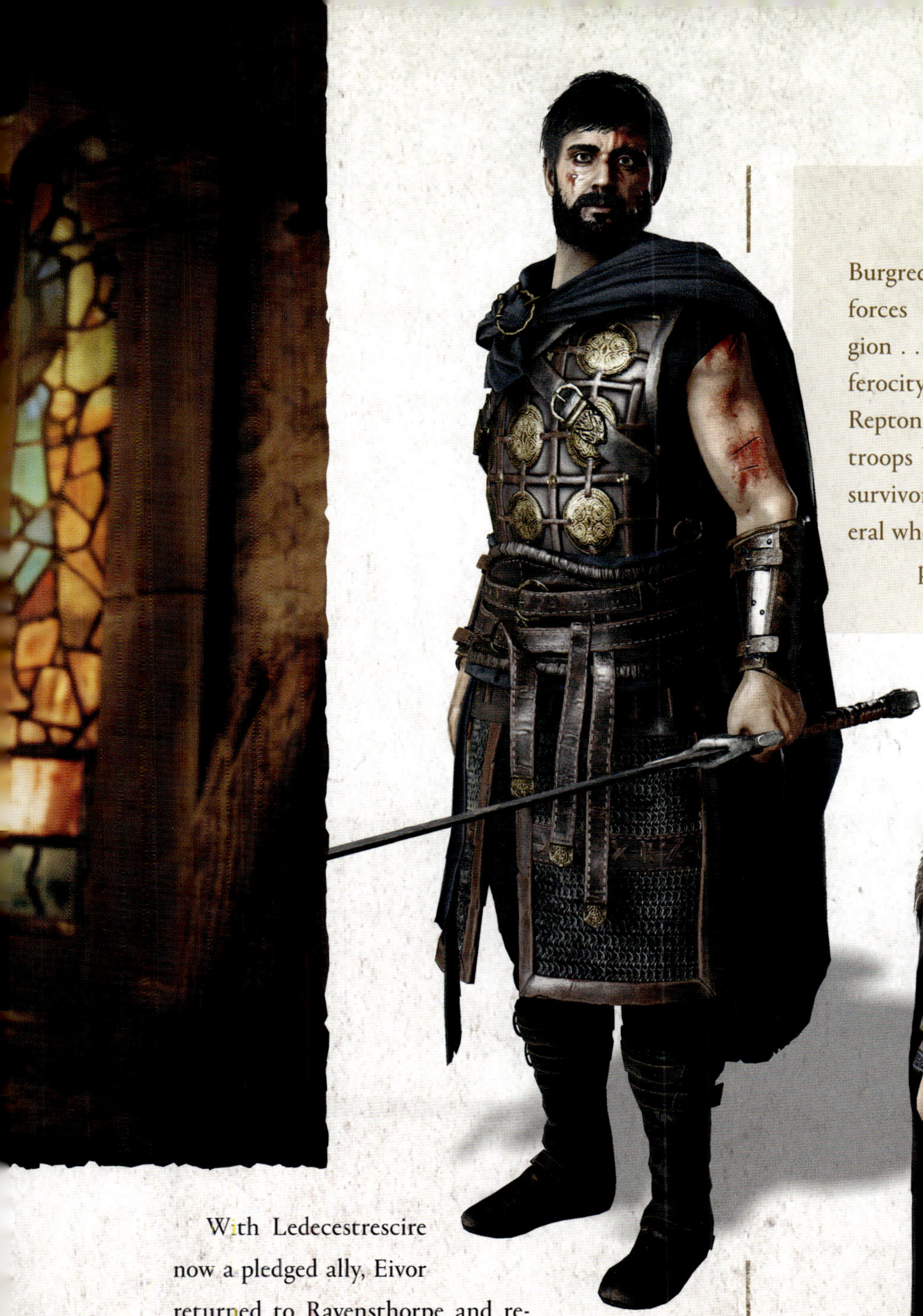

LEOFRITH

Burgred's war thegn, Leofrith, guided Mercian forces to victory after victory in the region . . . until he encountered the unmatched ferocity of the Great Heathen Army. After Repton fell to the Vikings, Leofrith pulled his troops back into Tamworth Fortress. Mercian survivors describe him as a clear-thinking general who realized that only a shrewd deal could protect his people from massacre.

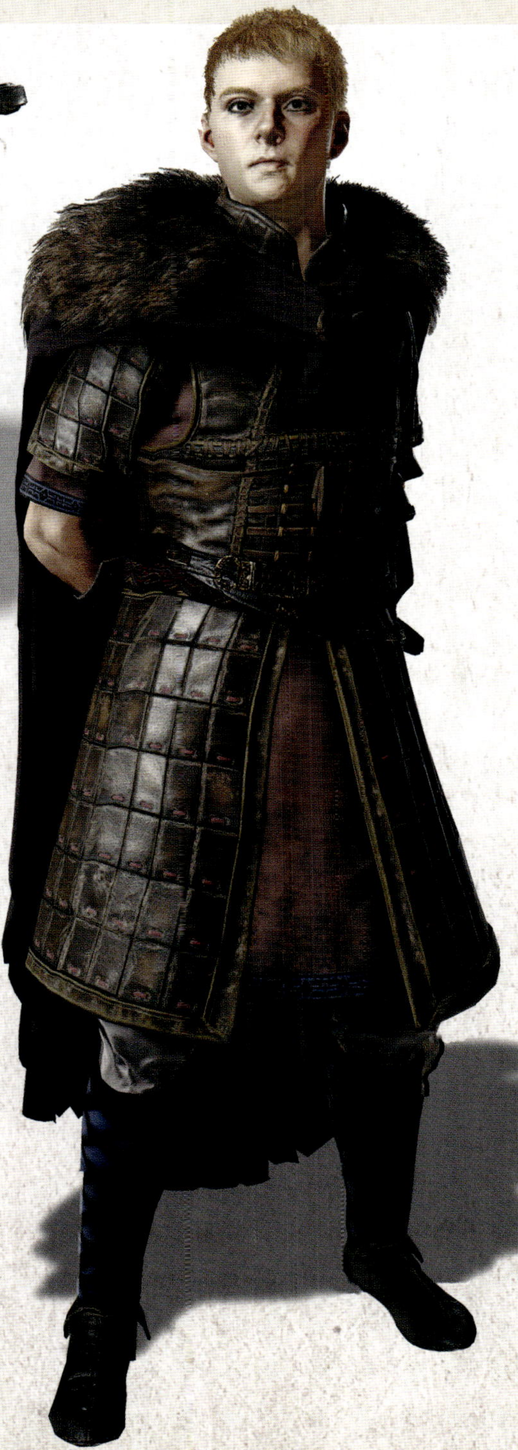

With Ledecestrescire now a pledged ally, Eivor returned to Ravensthorpe and reported the news to Randvi. Together, they selected the next alliance target: Grantebridgescire and the Summer Army of the Danes. Eivor also made a full report to me at my bureau.

CEOLBERT

Son of Ceowulf II, this unfortunate lad was conscripted into the machinations of power politics when his father became the puppet king of Mercia. Eivor invested considerable effort in mentoring the young fellow in the ways of war and leadership. Unfortunately, so did Ivarr Ragnarsson.

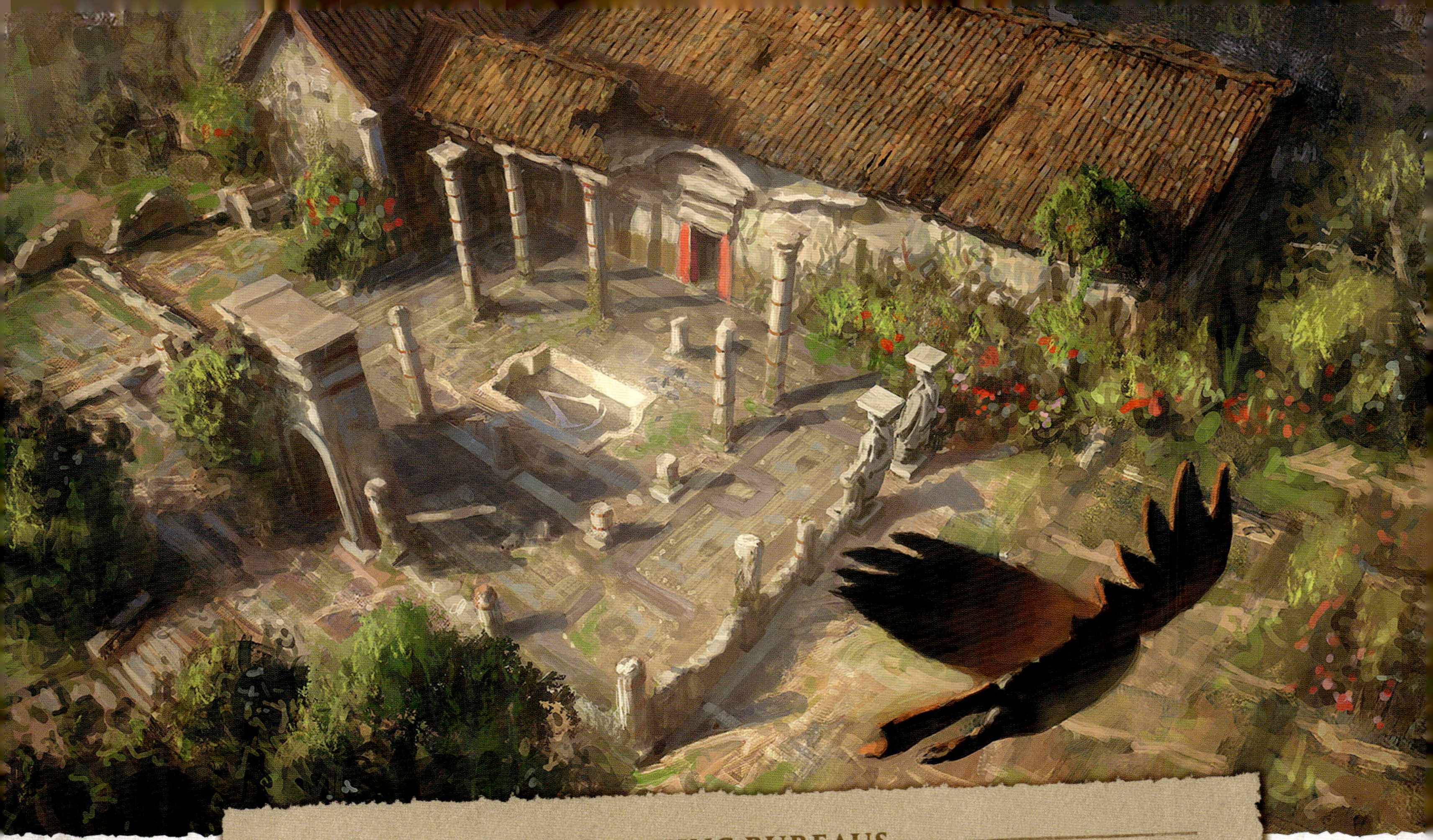

SEEKING BUREAUS

Just a few decades after Emperor Claudius conquered Britannia in 41 CE to make it a Roman province, my Hidden Ones predecessors began establishing bureaus on this island. By the time of the final Roman withdrawal from England in about 410 CE, six bureaus were fully operational here. Ultimately, they had to be shut down. I urged Eivor to keep a sharp eye out for these abandoned offices, hoping to find long-lost codex pages that could shed light on our history in the region. She discovered the old Ratae bureau in the eastern outskirts of the city of Ledecestre.

GRANTEBRIDGESCIRE, MERCIA

THE SONG OF SOMA

The so-called Great Summer Army of Danes led by Guthrum had joined the original Viking invasion force (the Great Heathen Army) in pacifying Mercia and Northumbria, then moved south to establish control of Grantebridgescire. From there, Guthrum headed into Wessex but left the skilled warrior Soma in charge of Grantebridge, a bustling hub of trade; her charisma and impressive mastery of trade logistics made Soma the perfect jarlskona. But when Eivor rode south from Ravensthorpe to seek alliance, she found that a Saxon force had driven Soma's Danes from Grantebridge.

KEY EVENTS

The Saxon assault, led by a palatinus of the order named Wigmund, had driven Soma's fighters across the Great Ouse River and scattered them through

SOMA

A fierce fighter of Sámi origin, Soma left the northernmost realms of Norway—a region some refer to as Lappland—to join the Viking invasion of England. Both Ubba and Guthrum recognized her natural qualities of leadership, so they put her in charge at Grantebridge, a key trade center with military significance.

the fenlands northeast of town. Soma asked Eivor to rescue a trio of her trusted advisers scattered in the foggy marshes. After rounding them up, Eivor helped Soma's reassembled force counterattack and retake their post in Grantebridge. In gratitude, Soma let Eivor sound the victory horn!

But Soma feared that one of her three lieutenants had betrayed her by revealing the existence of a secret tunnel system excavated under the town. Eivor helped her smoke out the culprit, and then assassinated Wigmund in a nearby monastery, acquiring his order medallion for me. This not only eliminated Soma's primary Saxon nemesis in Grantebridgescire but also shattered the order's organization in the shire. In the end, Eivor's Raven Clan gained a great ally in Soma Jarlskona and the Danes of Grantebridge.

After Eivor reported to Randvi on the successful alliance with Soma, a wave of vicious Norse bandits suddenly rolled through Ravensthorpe. Fortunately, the attack was thwarted. A lone enemy survivor admitted that his crew came by way of East Anglia, where chaos had filled the void left by the Viking army's focus on Mercia.

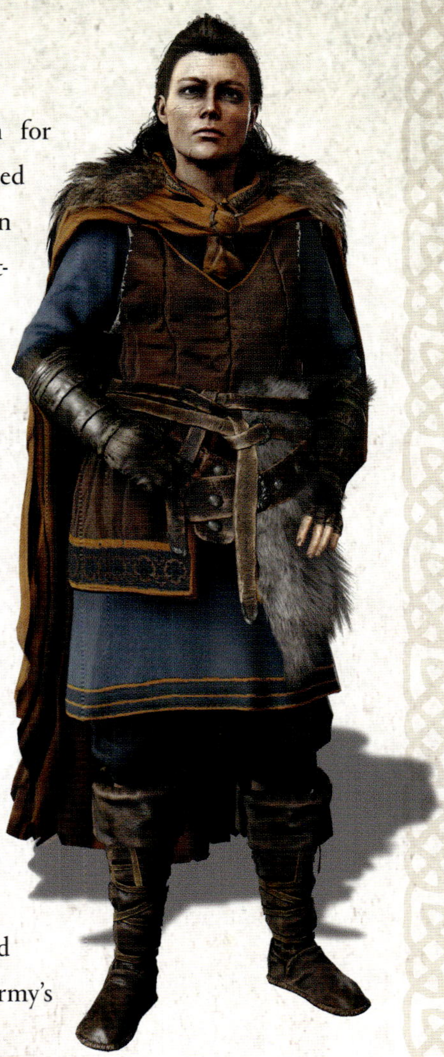

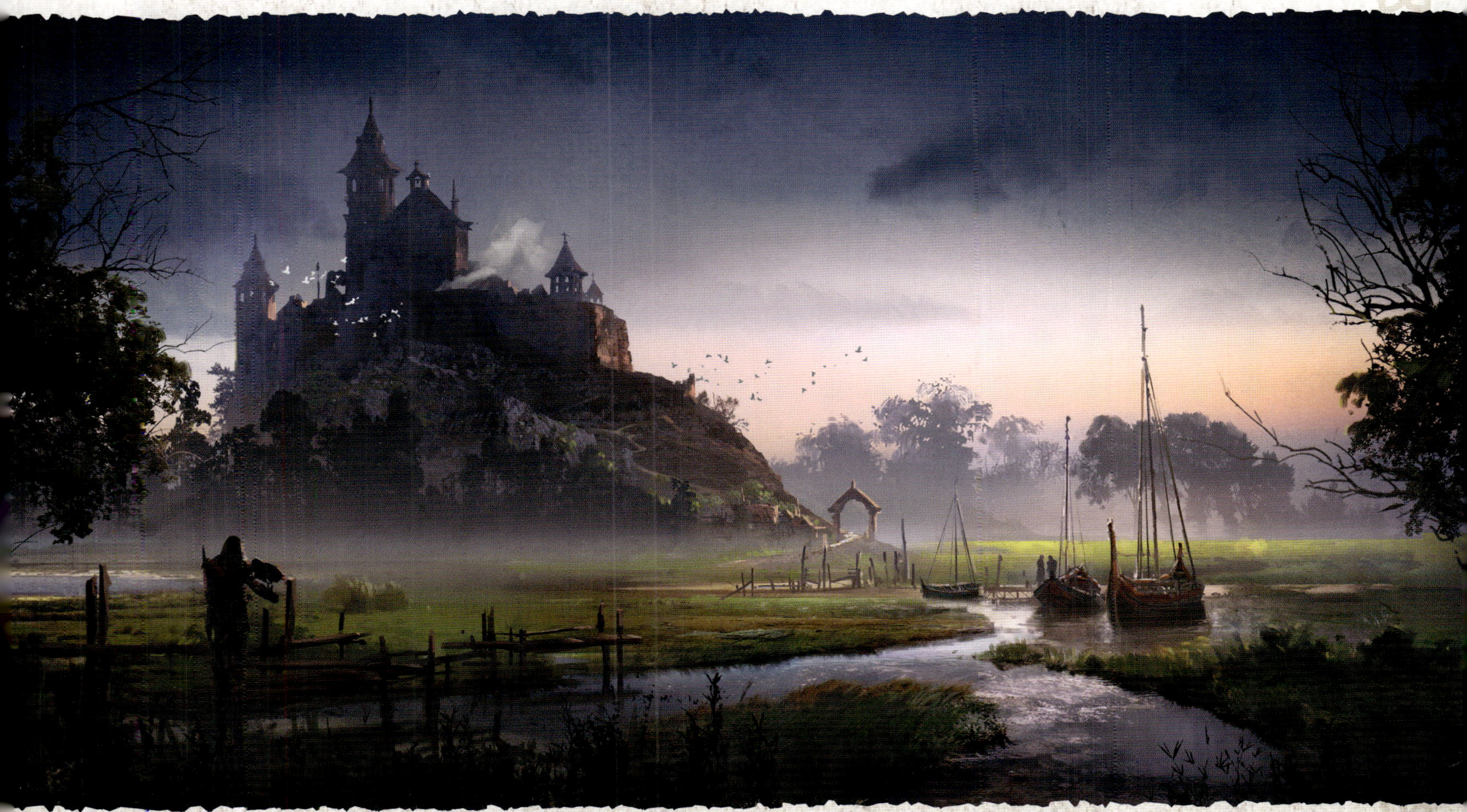

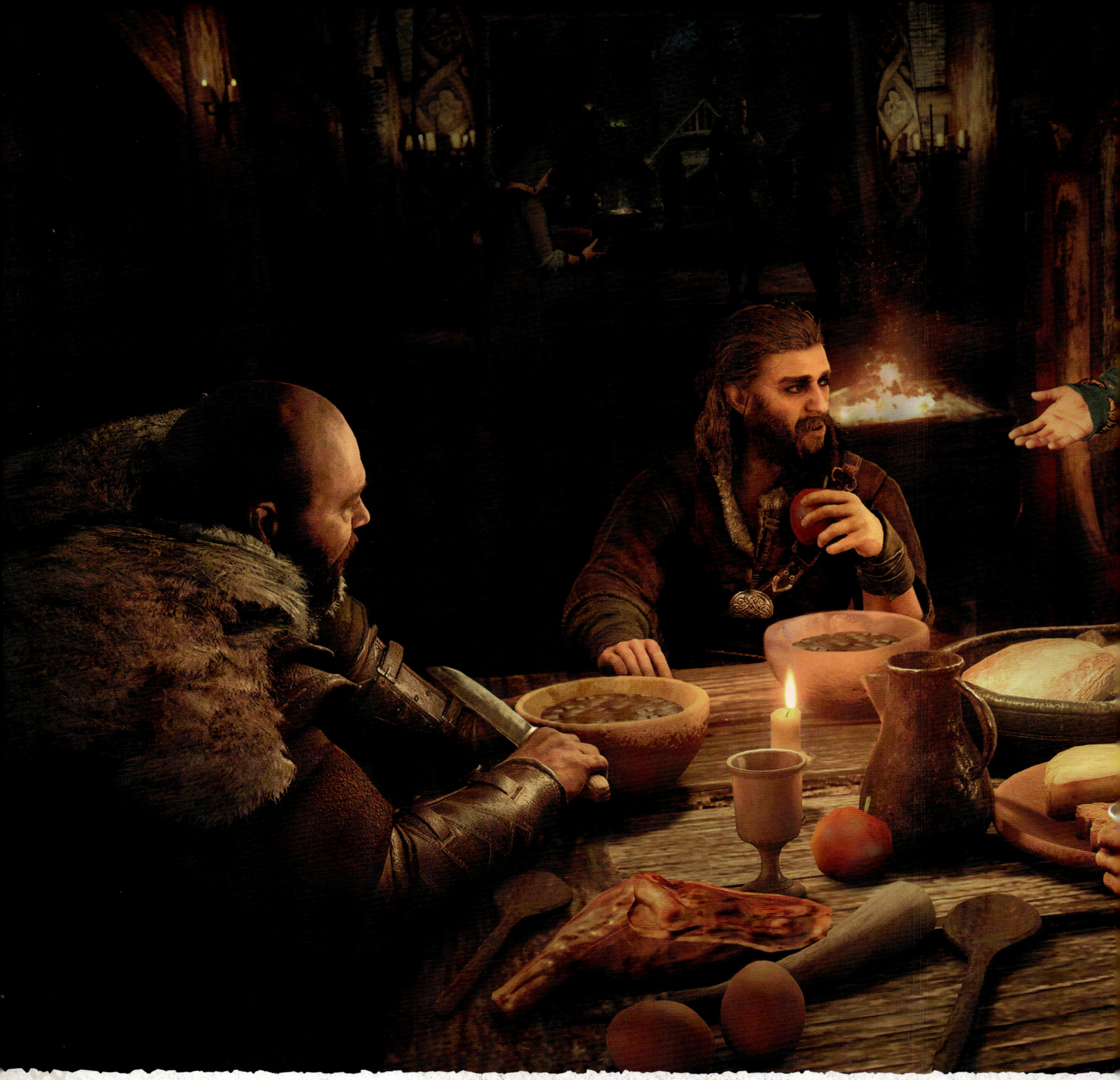

East Anglia

THE TALE OF THEGN OSWALD

The Danish bandits who attacked Ravensthorpe served a clan leader named Rued, a murderous brigand based in East Anglia. After conquering that kingdom, Halfdan Jarl had assigned a fellow Dane named Finnr as steward. Finnr's job was to appoint a local thegn to rule as a client king, much like Ceowulf II in Mercia. Halfdan demanded the candidate be Saxon but married to a Dane as a display of unity.

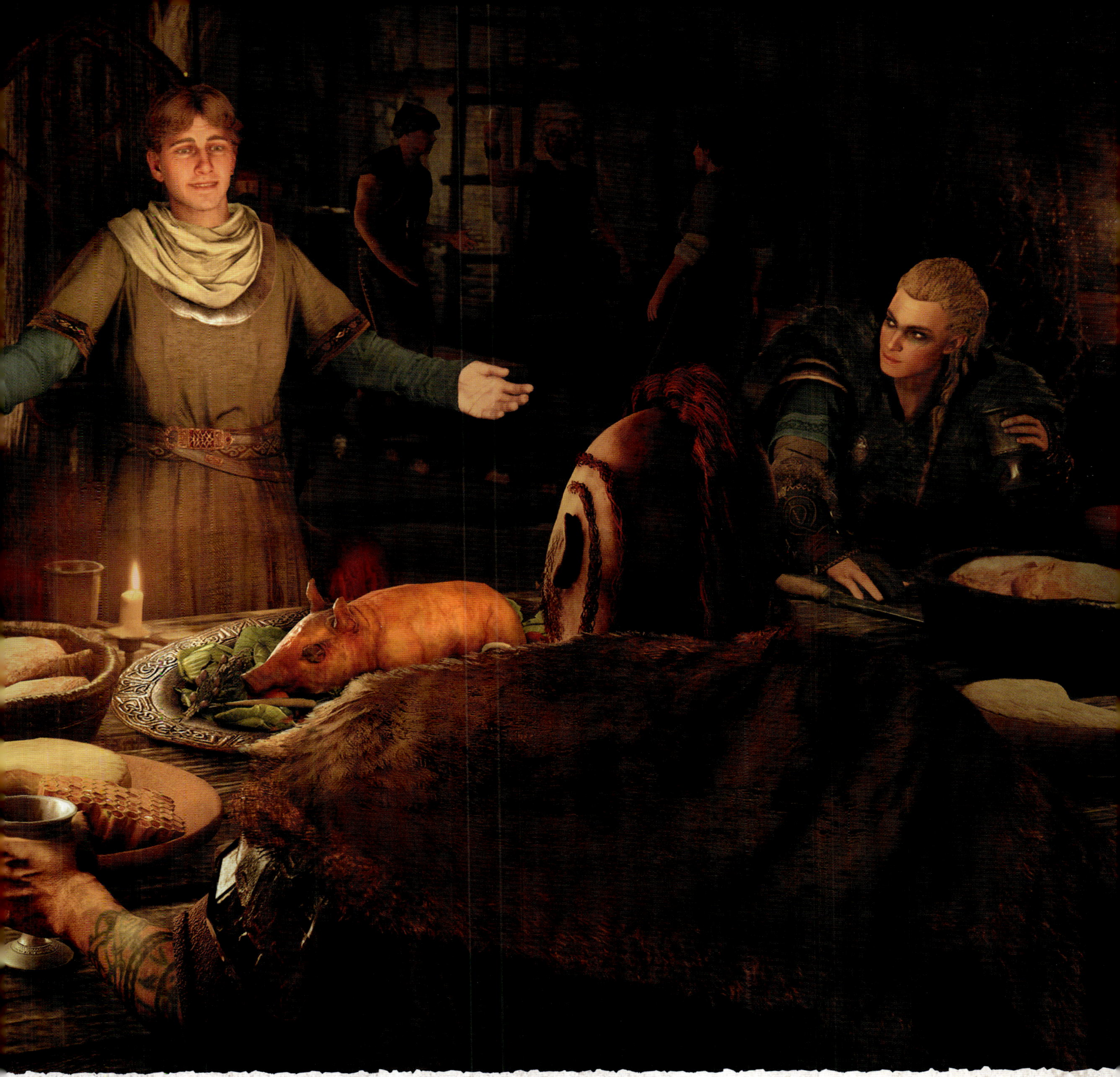

But years later, no king had yet been anointed. Meanwhile, East Anglia's boggy countryside had descended into lawless chaos—a chaos now threatening to spread to other territories. Reports from Randvi's scouts referred to East Anglia's patchwork of swamps as "a sinkhole of blood and misery" after years of war and attrition. Rued's brutal clan continued to plunder its way across the kingdom.

KEY EVENTS

Eivor traveled to East Anglia's ruling seat, Northwic, to meet Halfdan's steward. His first attempt to crown a Saxon puppet had ended when Rued's clan perforated the unfortunate lord with a deadly flight of hunter's arrows. Finnr told Eivor that his new candidate, an ealdorman named Oswald of Elmenham,

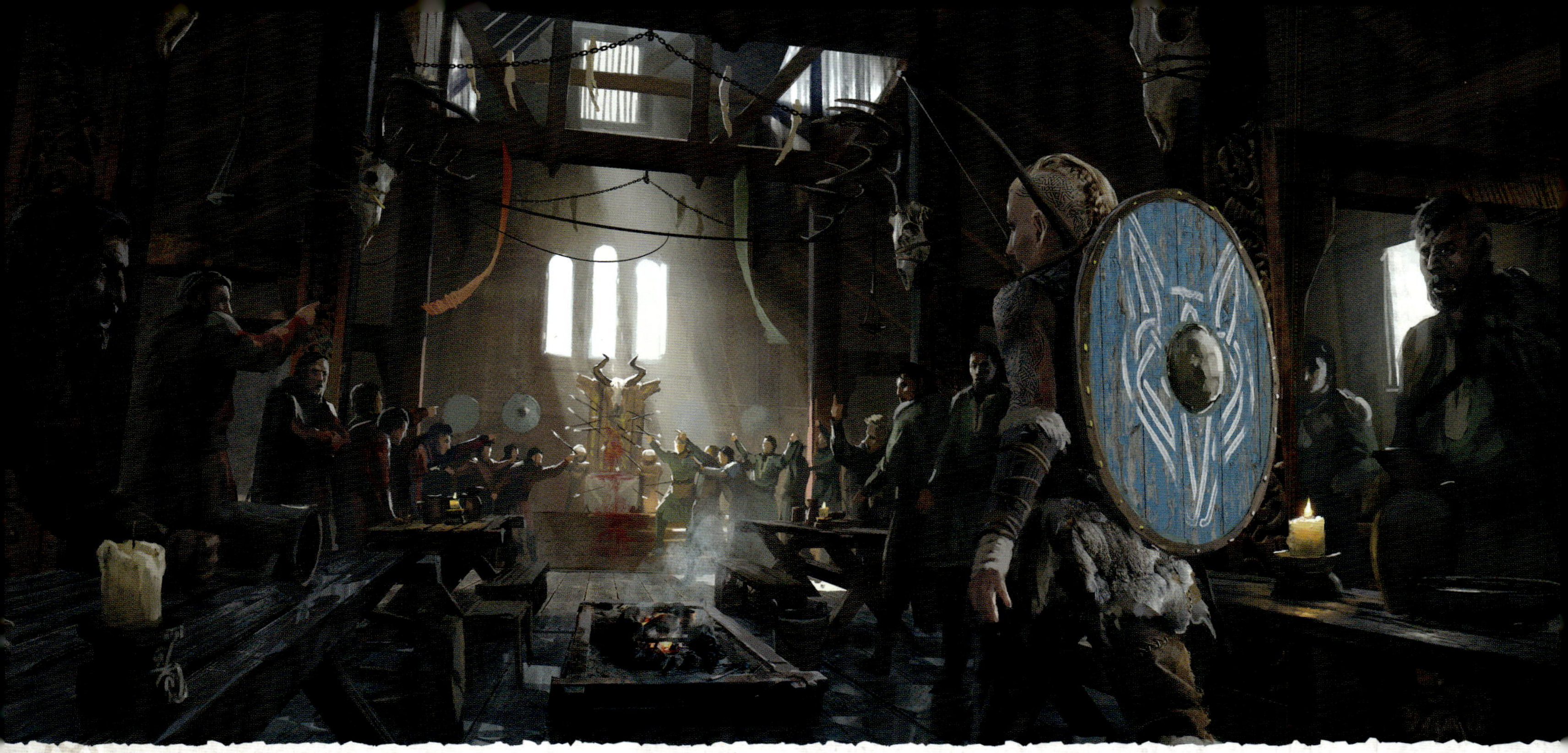

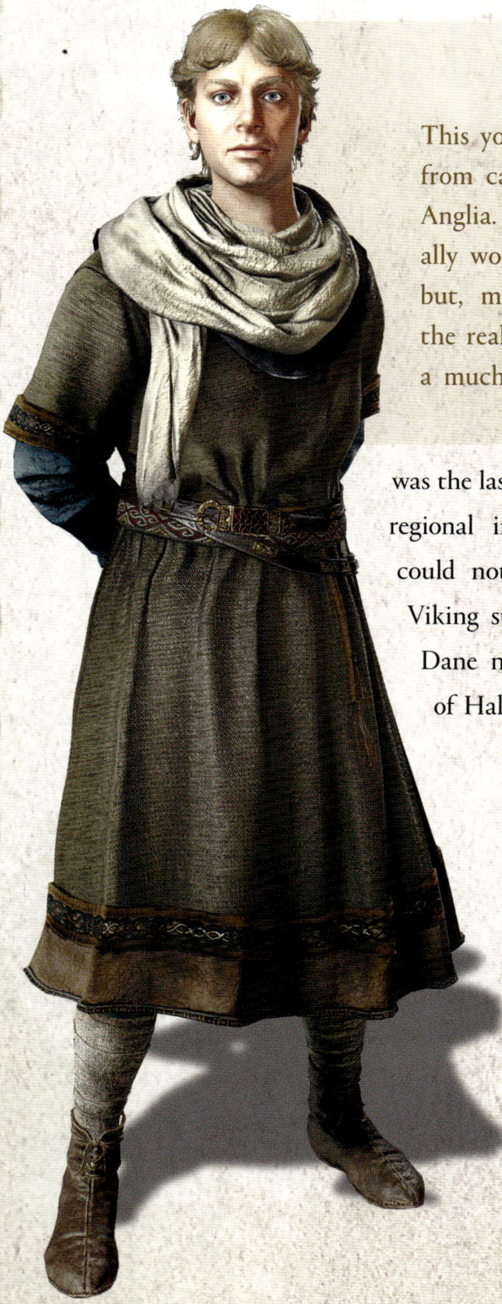

OSWALD

This young thegn of Norfulc seemed far from capable of serving as king of East Anglia. But his earnest nature eventually won over not only Eivor and Finnr but, more importantly, his subjects of the realm. The people's respect made for a much more potent and dynamic fyrd!

was the last Saxon noble with any regional influence. But Oswald could not rule without strong Viking support. By marrying a Dane named Valdis, a cousin of Halfdan, Oswald hoped to gain the allegiance of her powerful family. But Valdis's brothers would not approve, seeing Oswald as soft and unworthy.

With Eivor's help, Oswald slowly began to earn the Vikings' respect. Eventually, he led a crew (including Valdis and her brothers) to Rued's hideout, a fort in Dunwic. There, Oswald challenged Rued to a *holmgang*, the renowned Viking duel. Locked in a desperate death grip, both combatants fell off a high tower…and both were presumed deceased.

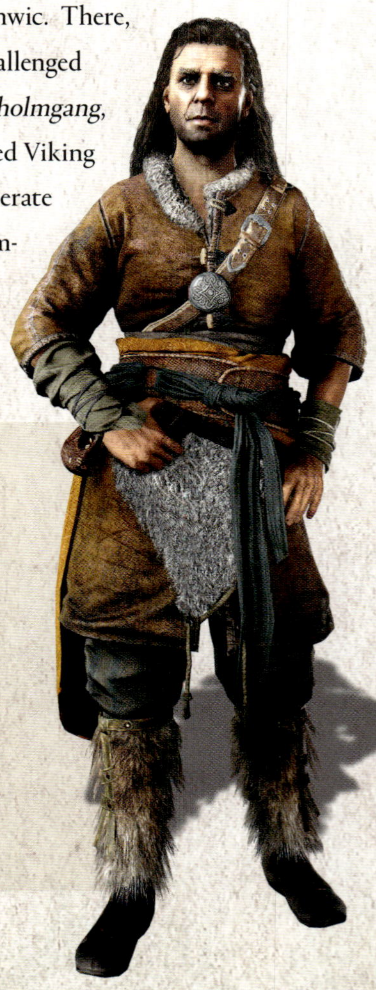

FINNR

As Halfdan's long-suffering steward of East Anglia, Finnr despaired of finding any Saxon candidate suitable to ascend the kingdom's throne. Drink and cynicism had dulled his edge, but Eivor's intervention gave Finnr new hope. He was destined to become a stalwart ally of the Raven Clan.

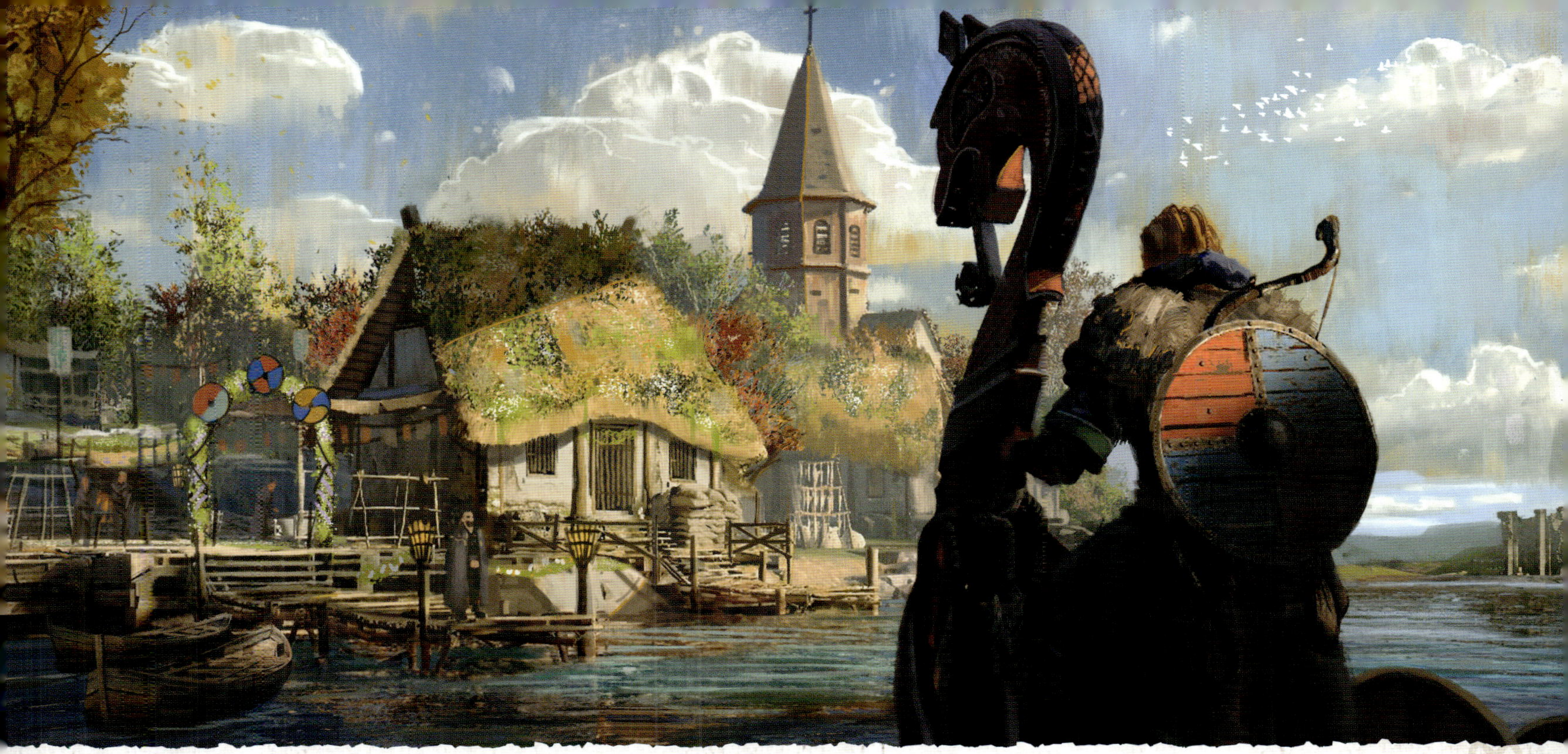

Brave Oswald's apparent demise inspired his Saxon kinfolk to rise up and form a fyrd—an army of peasants and farmers—to join Eivor, Valdis, and the Danes in an assault on the remaining outlaws holed up in Rued's stronghold, the imposing Burgh Castle on East Anglia's coast. First, Viking longships launched a daring seaborne attack. Then Eivor and her Viking warriors breached the gates and infiltrated the castle . . . where they found that both Oswald and Rued had somehow survived the fall at Dunwic!

Eivor defeated Rued, and the castle fell. In short order the newly crowned King Oswald of East Anglia wed Valdis—the queen Finnr called "soul, fist, and beauty of this land." And with Oswald's grateful pledge of alliance in hand, Eivor returned to Ravensthorpe to drop a raven marker atop East Anglia on Randvi's map.

RUED

This cruel head of a Dane raiding clan terrorized East Anglia for years. His followers laid gleeful waste to entire townships as they pillaged across the eastland marshes.

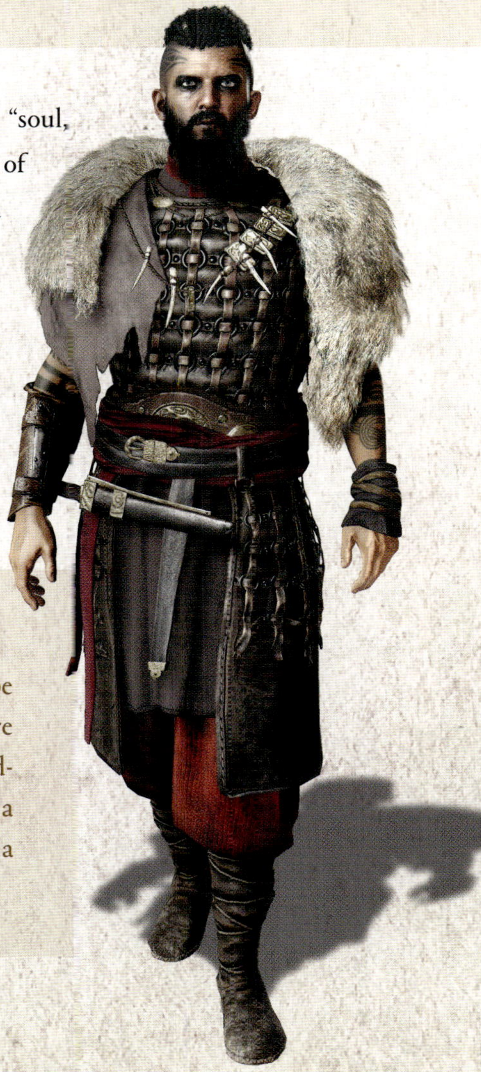

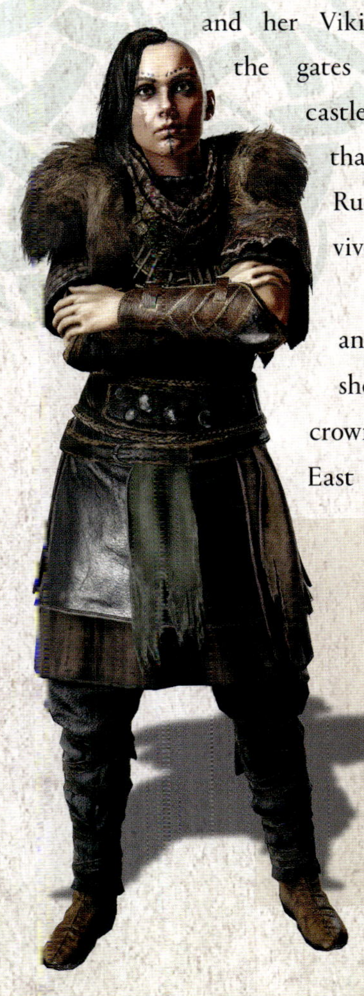

VALDIS

Betrothed to Oswald, Valdis was slated to be queen of East Anglia. But Valdis was more than just a nuptial bargaining chip in the melding of kingdoms. A stalwart clan leader and a Viking warrior of great prowess, she would be a powerful ally for Ravensthorpe.

OXENEFORDSCIRE, MERCIA

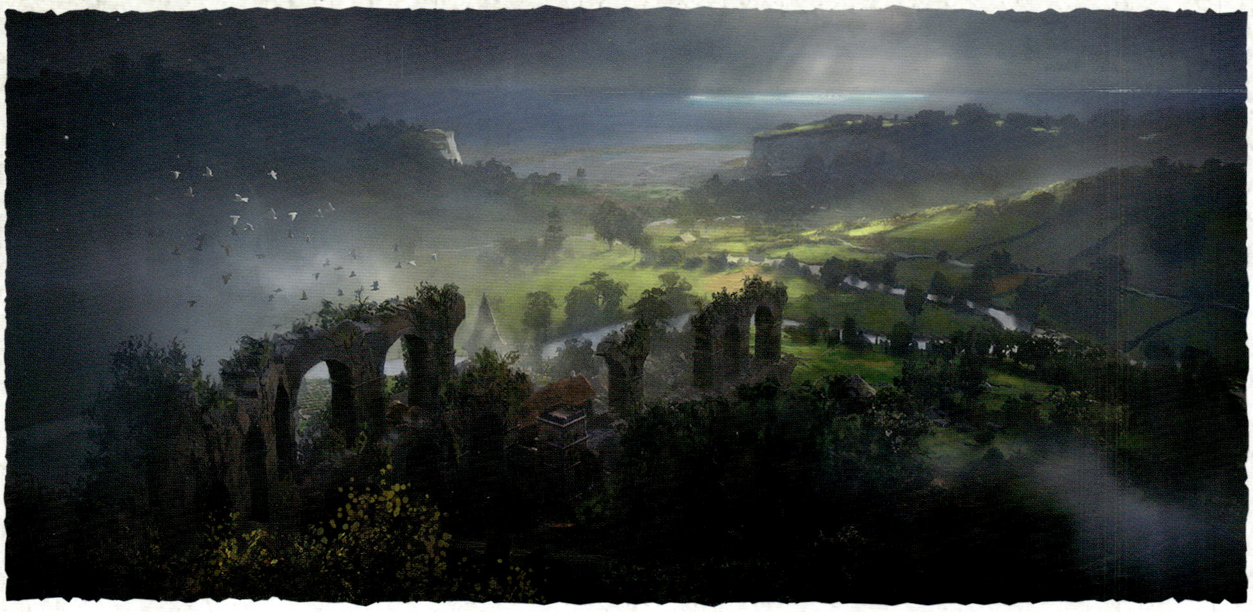

THE PALADIN'S STONE

Eivor traveled south to the township of Buckingham in Oxenefordscire to rendezvous with Sigurd and Basim. There, they would meet Geadric, a Saxon thegn they hoped to install as the shire's new ealdorman. Geadric led a group of local lords locked in a grim power struggle with Lady Eadwyn, widow of the previous ealdorman, Theodric. Randvi's scouts had filed reports on Eadwyn's relentless efforts to seek Saxon allies . . . including outreach to the avowed Viking foe Aelfred of Wessex. Indeed, Buckingham was growing ever more hostile to Norsemen and other outsiders.

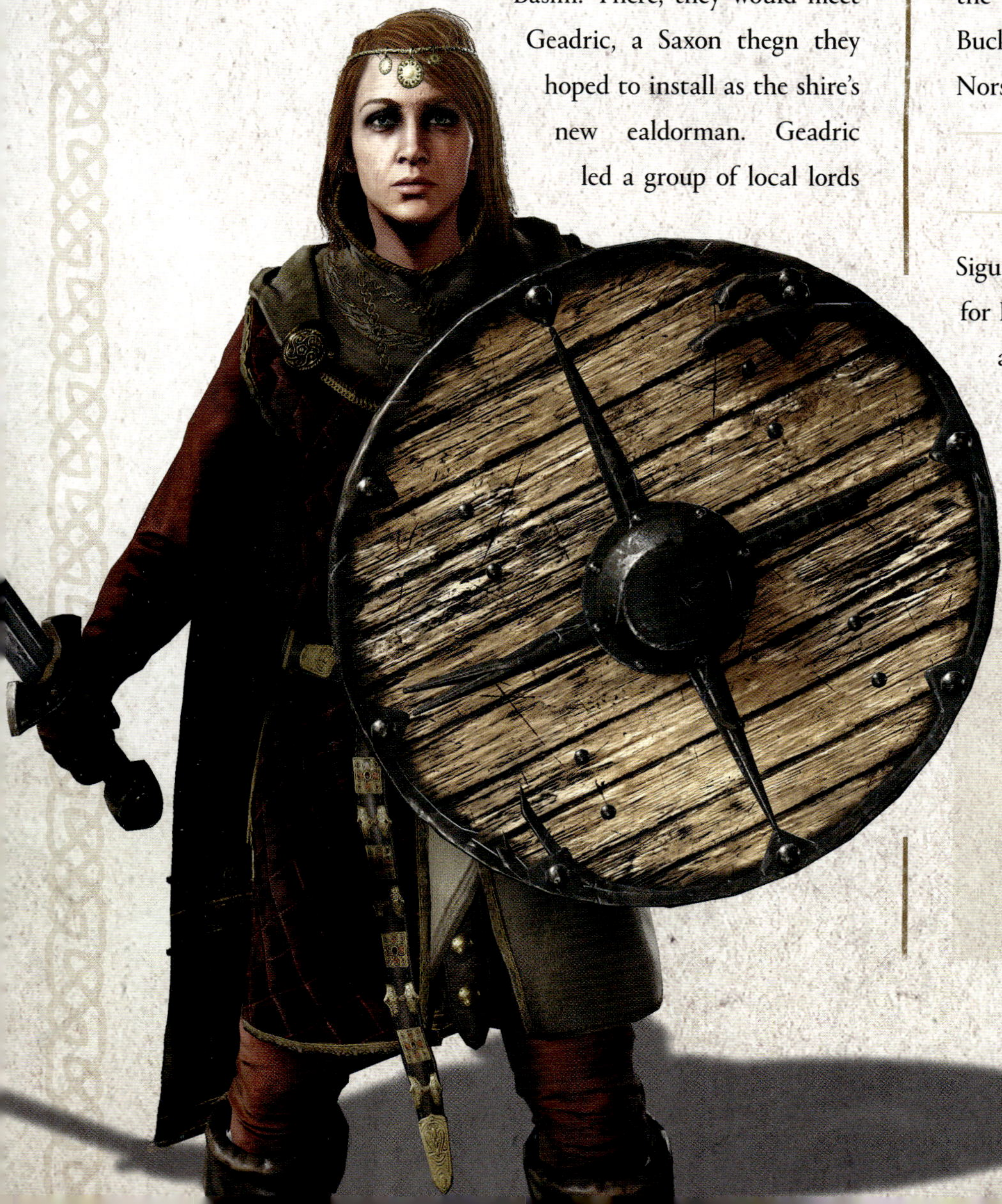

KEY EVENTS

Sigurd called Aelfred "a fearsome king" whose support for Eadwyn would likely eliminate Oxenefordscire as a possible ally of the Raven Clan. The lady's initial plan was to simply behead any thegn in the shire who opposed her rule. But Eivor, Sigurd, and Basim managed to avert a planned mass

LADY EADWYN

This lady was tough as boiled leather, by all accounts, and hated Danes—she bore a nasty grudge against them, as her husband was killed in a raid by Guthrum's army. Thus, she conspired with the Saxon lord Aelfred of Wessex to keep the shire's ruling rank in her family . . . and to keep Oxenefordscire free of Viking influence.

GEADRIC

He may be a thegn, but nobility's not his cast. A dogged, determined man who fights the way he talks—blunt and to the point—Geadric earned his rank and land from Theodric, the shire's late ealdorman. His rough-hewn style and unwavering loyalty have earned him a loyal following of fellow thegns.

execution of Geadric's followers. These newly liberated thegns then raised a fyrd of fighters to back Geadric in his looming civil war against Eadwyn and her Wessex allies.

But Eivor reported that Basim and Sigurd seemed far more interested in the fate of a so-called holy woman named Fulke, imprisoned by Eadwyn in the abbey dungeon at Saint Albanes. One disdainful thegn called Fulke "a sower of poisoned knowledge and an enemy of the church"—a madwoman *and* a heretic! But both Sigurd and Basim claimed that Fulke harbored some sort of secret that could change everything.

With Eivor's help, they sprung the woman from Saint Albanes and queried her about a particular monolith carved with ancient runes—she knew it and called it the Saga Stone. As it turned out, Lady Eadwyn had hauled off the artifact to her stronghold in Cyne Belle Castle. Storming the castle with Geadric and his fyrd fighters, the Vikings defeated Eadwyn and her troops. Eivor gained Geadric's pledge of alliance between Oxenefordscire and the Raven Clan. And the Saga Stone was recovered.

But when King Aelfred suddenly arrived with a large

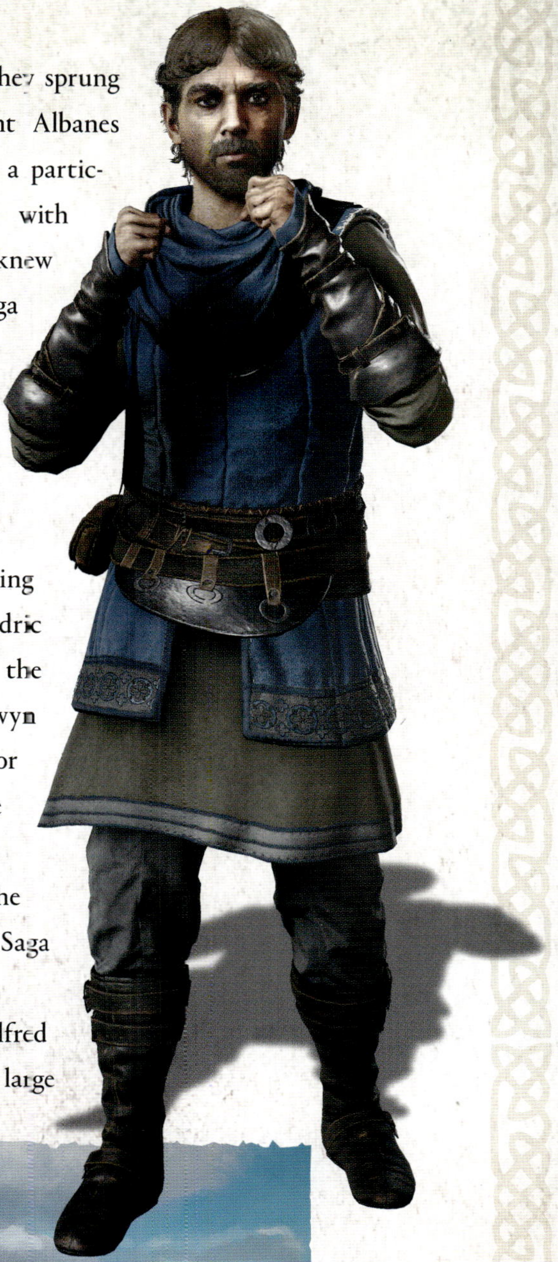

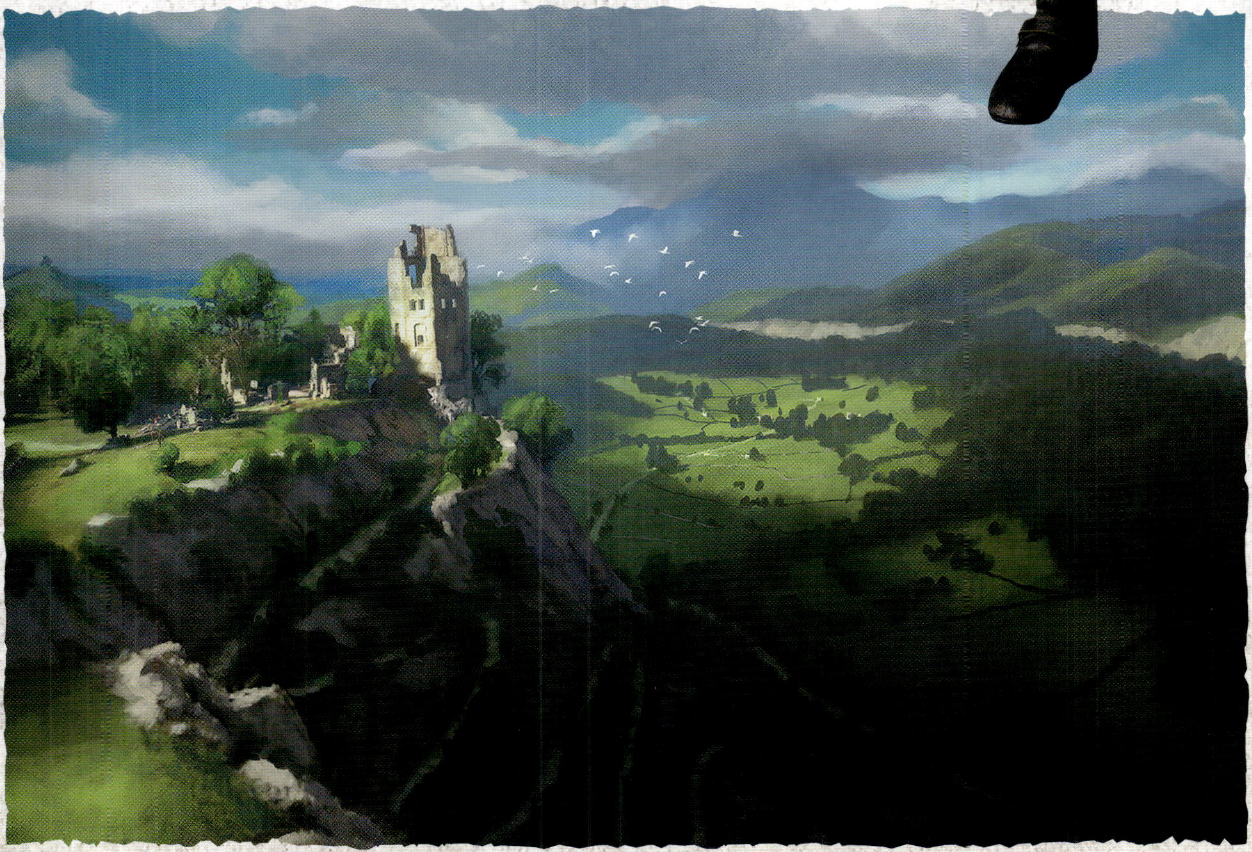

Wessex army, Sigurd called for a parley with the Saxon leader. Aelfred agreed to turn back in exchange for a Danish withdrawal north across the Great Ouse River. The negotiation included an exchange of warriors—Sigurd for Aelfred's war thegn, Wolfrich—to solidify the truce. But Eivor was disturbed when Fulke took charge of Sigurd. I was relieved to learn that Basim moved to shadow them and monitor Sigurd's safety.

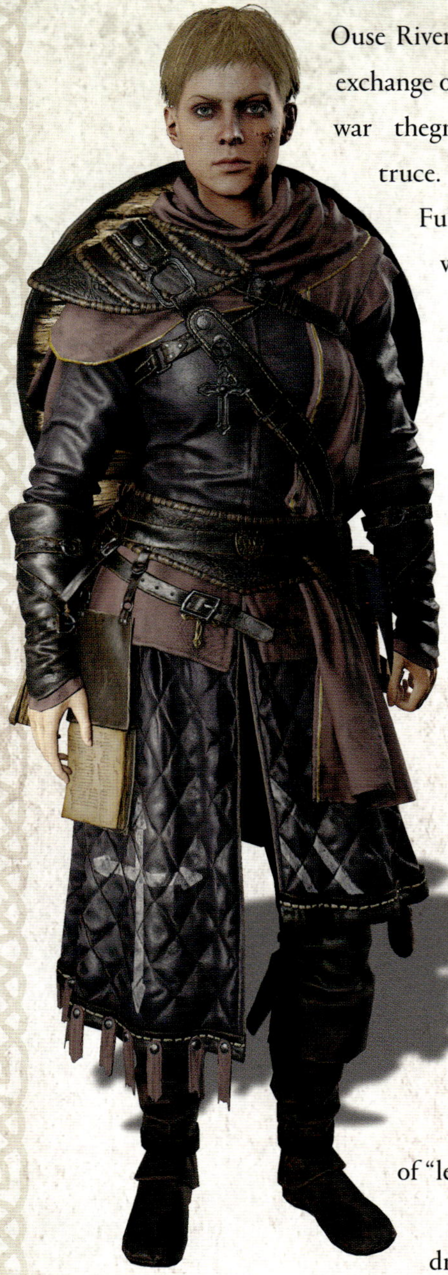

One final note: In her report to me, Eivor spoke of an odd, secretive sort of partnership emerging between Sigurd and Basim. She claimed that Basim had blinded her brother with grandiose ideas, such as Sigurd proclaiming himself a god. I found myself sharing Eivor's skeptical appraisal of the entire situation—this mysterious Saga Stone and Fulke's fantasies of a demiurge she called Saklas from an ancient race of "lesser gods."

But what of Sigurd's strange dreams and prophecies?

FULKE

This charismatic Flemish woman has dabbled in gnostic mysticism, adding strange dark twists to Christian dogma. Her fascination with Sigurd was most disturbing. She claimed to see him as a deific figure—a characterization with which both my mentor Basim and Sigurd himself seemed to concur!

Eivor admitted to me that she is familiar with such visions and forebodings. I find all of this most perplexing and disturbing.

AELFRED, KING OF WESSEX

This scholarly Christian monarch attained the throne of Wessex in 871 when his brother King Aethelred succumbed to battle wounds fighting Halfdan's Great Heathen Army at Marton. Despite his bookish demeanor, Aelfred is an accomplished military strategist and field general. His boyhood pilgrimage to visit Pope Leo IV in Rome—a meeting filled with Leo's blustery tales of fighting Saracen heathens at Ostia—made a lasting impression on the lad.

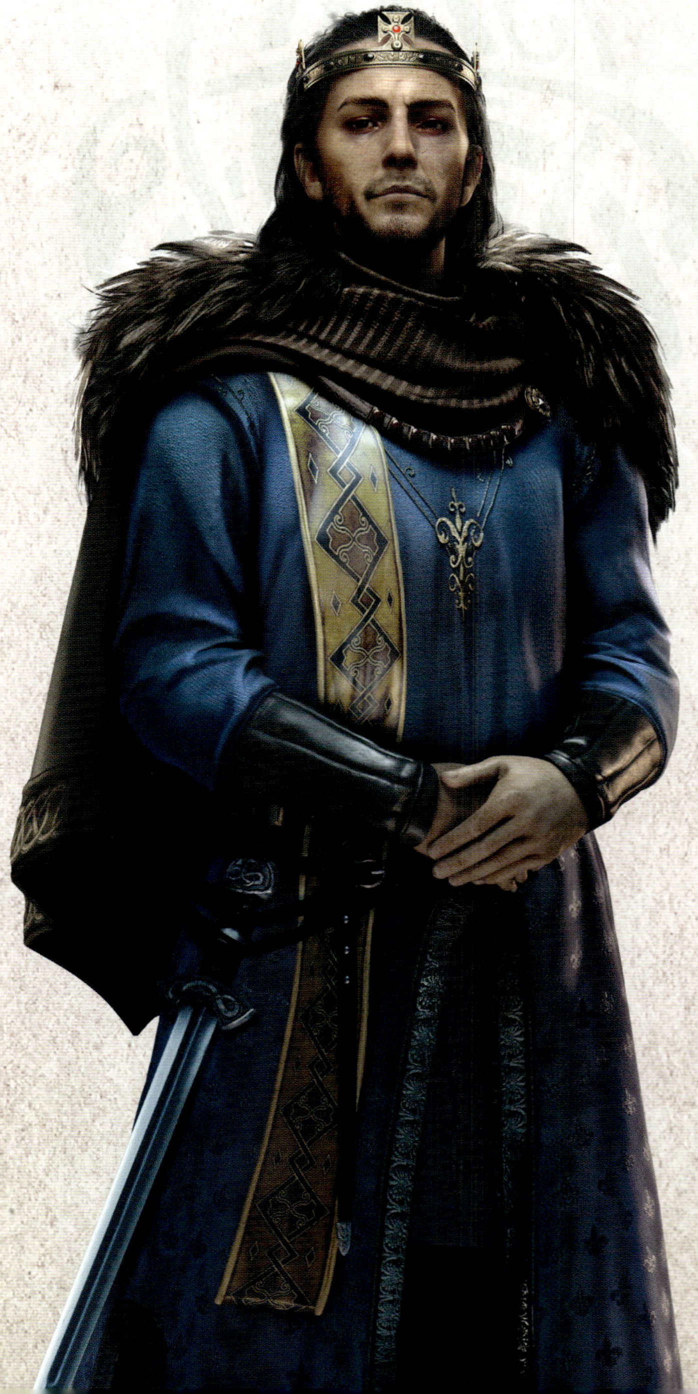

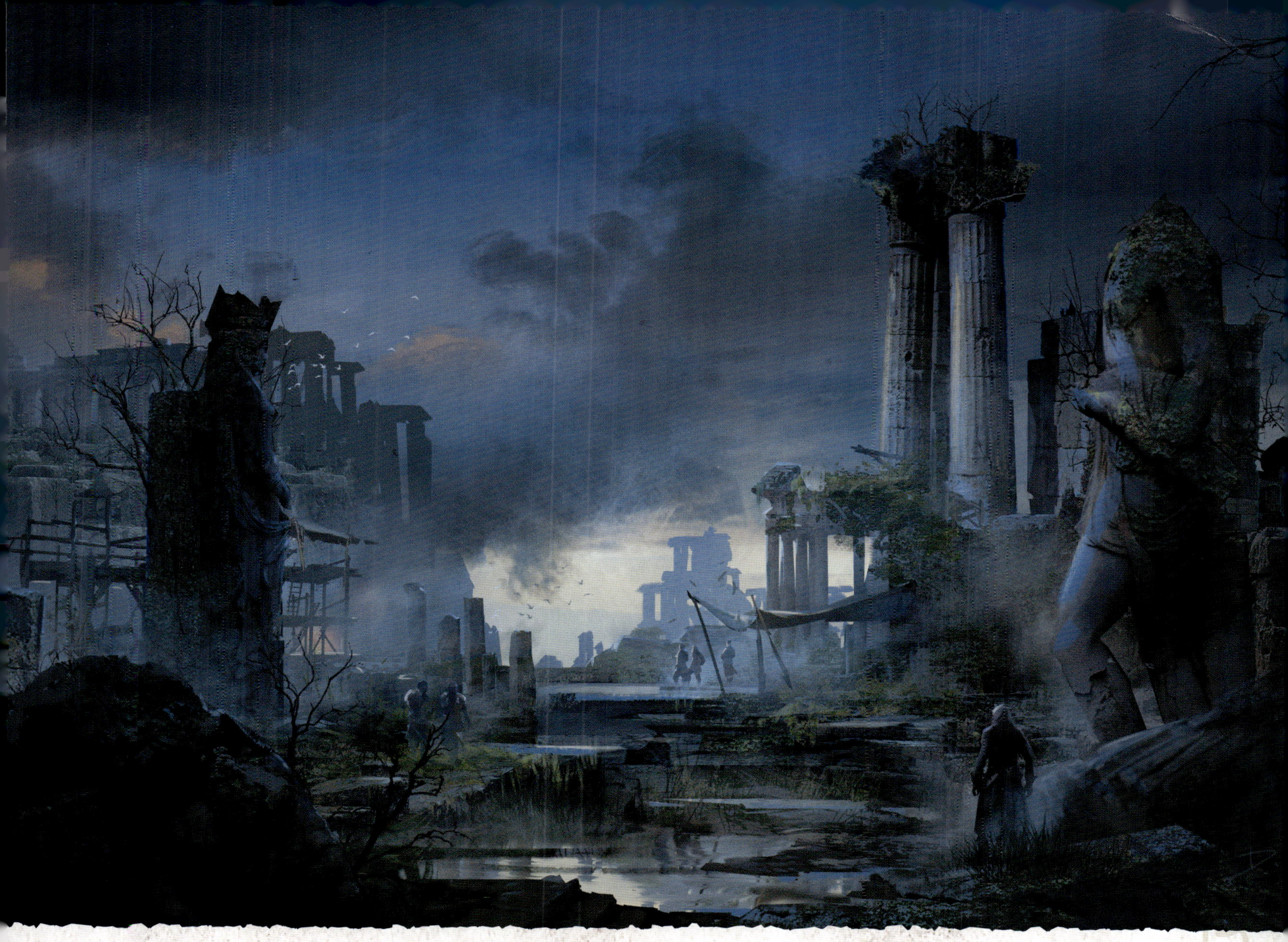

Lunden

THE CITY OF WAR

Wild, decadent Lunden was a war zone, torn by years of fighting between Wessexians, Mercians, and Danes. Now the Order of the Ancients was using this chaos to recruit soldiers and extend its grip over England. I was most grateful when Eivor agreed to investigate the city where the order had dug in its claws. Lunden had long resisted attempts to tamp down its turmoil, fending off even the Ragnarssons and the Summer Army when they occupied the site as a winter bivouac.

Randvi sent Eivor to the city's north gate—known as Crepelgate—to seek entrance and assess the situation. There she met Stowe, the shire-reeve of Lunden's western half—the king's representative, tasked with enforcing laws and collecting taxes in that district. But when Stowe escorted Eivor to the governor's villa to discuss terms of a possible alliance with the Raven Clan, they arrived to the gruesome aftermath of a terrible murder.

KEY EVENTS

Eivor investigated the bloody scene of Governor Tryggr's murder. A note there written by the same Poor Fellow-Soldier of Christ we'd seen before spoke of three heathens from an "order of heretics" (clearly the Order of the Ancients) and listed them as the Arrow, the Leech, and the Compass. Eivor concluded that these were Tryggr's murderers. With help from

Stowe and his fellow reeve Erke, she managed to eliminate the first two operatives and then lure their leader, the Compass, to a final reckoning.

Eivor delivered the order medallions she'd gathered to my bureau in Ravensthorpe and reported her success in purging Lunden of the order's scourge. It was

STOWE AND ERKE: THE REEVES OF LUNDEN

A native son of Lunden, the Saxon Stowe partnered with his "imported Dane" counterpart, Erke, to serve as the two shire-reeves of the city. Overseeing Lunden's western half, Stowe was a fair, honest man of humble origins and quiet strength. Erke, a soldier who rose to the position of reeve via somewhat shadier dealings, administered Lunden's east borough. Despite their differences, the two remained loyal friends. In Eivor's eyes, the pair seemed well capable of keeping an equitable peace in Lunden.

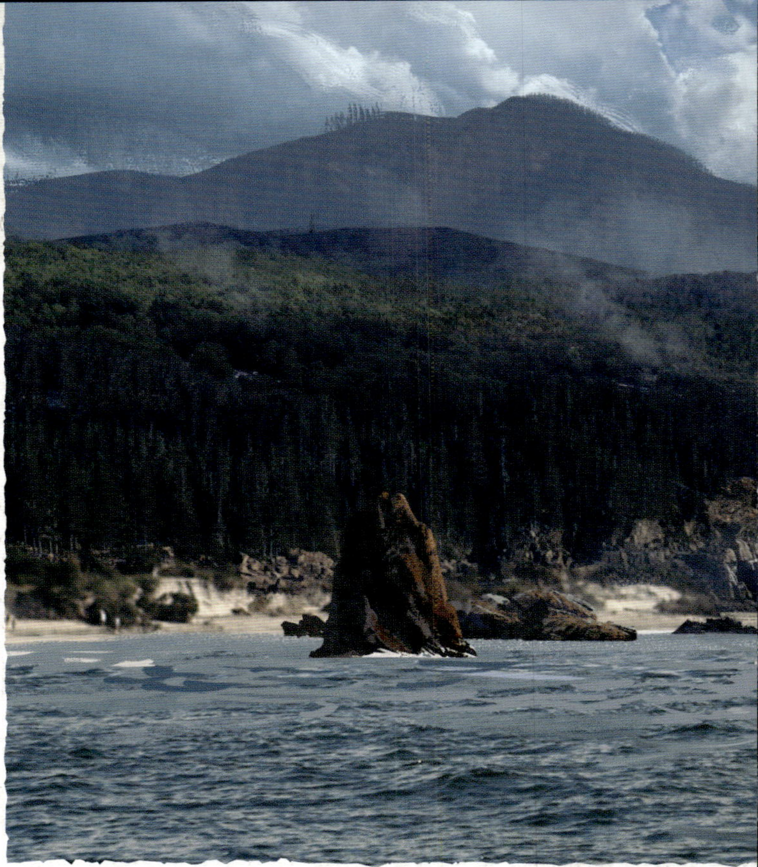

certainly good news, but tempered by the latest intelligence from my own Hidden Ones network: it seemed Jorvik, the capital of the kingdom of Northumbria, was suffering the same blight. The order was moving swiftly through that city's veins, like an evil humor.

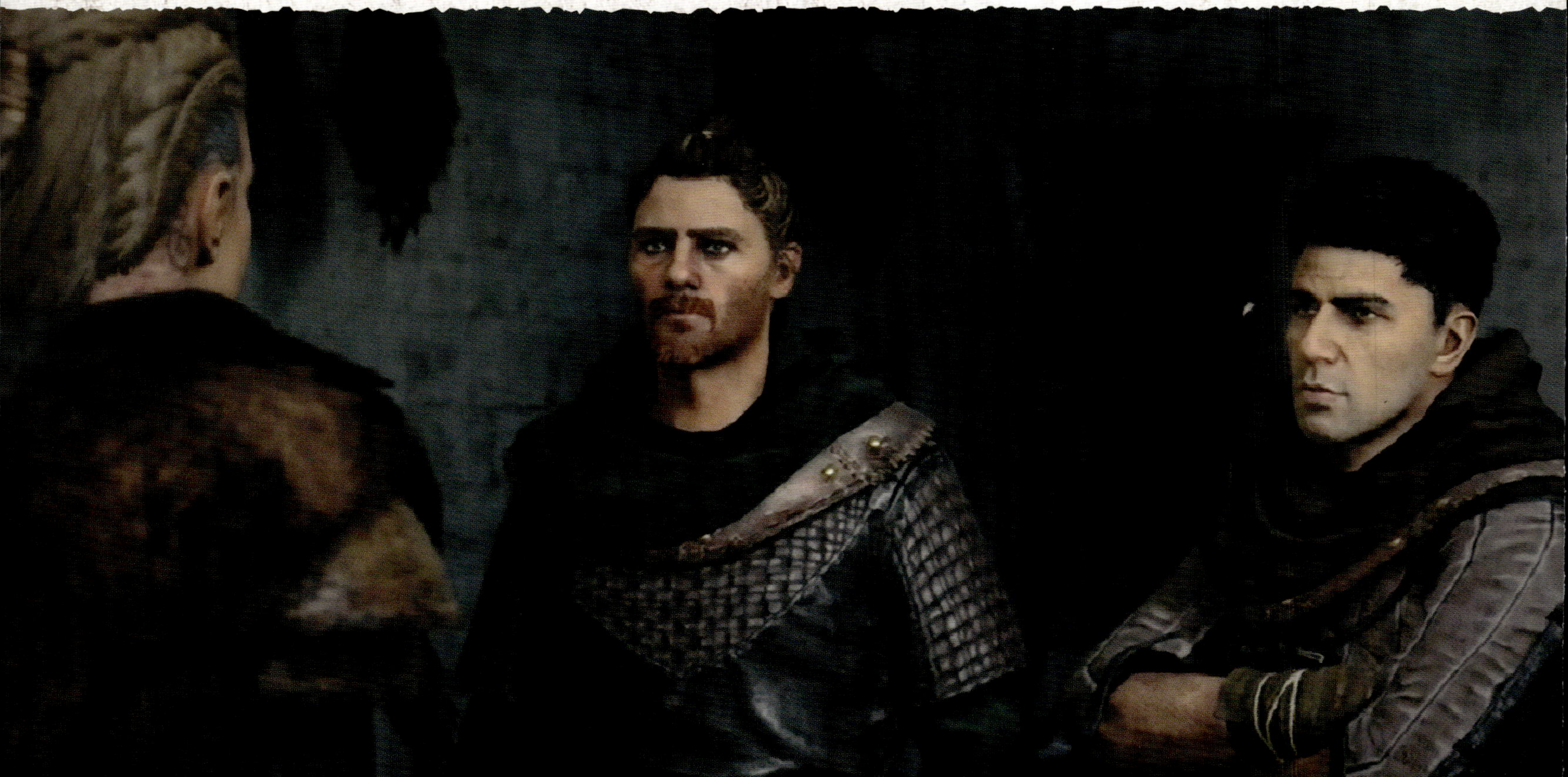

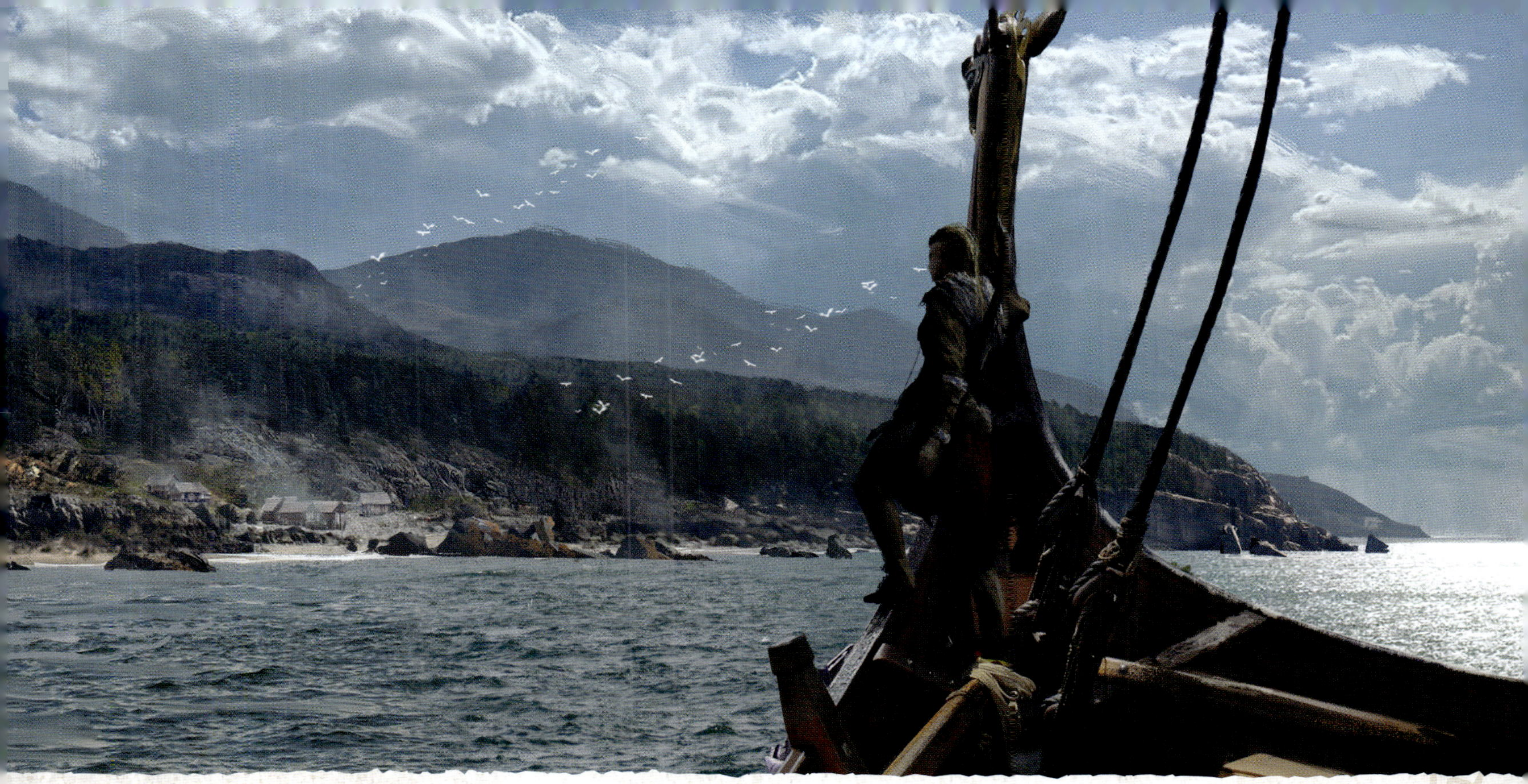

Vinland

IN A STRANGE LAND

Eivor's first encounter with a high-ranking member of the order was her dispatch of Kjotve (the Axe) in Norway. Next, in the course of establishing early alliances in England, Eivor eliminated two key palatinus figures, Hunta (the Baldric) in Ledecestrescire, and Leofgifu (the Scabbard) in Grantebridgescire. Notes found on these targets and the three order members recently assassinated in Lunden helped us reveal the identity of a high-ranking maegester known as the Keel. This snake turned out to be none other than Eivor's old Wolf Clan nemesis, Gorm Kjotvesson!

Gorm was not easy to reach, however. My contacts reported he'd taken his father Kjotve's place in the order hierarchy and traveled to a new shore—a mysterious land called Vinland, far west of England, said to be discovered centuries ago by an Irish sailor named Brendan. Seeing the order's dark ambitions seeping westward as a direct threat to her own campaign to secure alliances in Britain, Eivor agreed to undertake the hazardous sea journey to Vinland and hunt down the Keel.

KEY EVENTS

Randvi provided Eivor the disguise of a common sailor's clothing and sent her to a merchant named Nessa to navigate the voyage to Vinland. After tacking west for three arduous weeks on the whale-road (as the Vikings call the sea), the longship arrived in what Nessa called "Saint Brendan's land." Unfortunately, Eivor's disguise precluded the transport of her formidable store of weapons and gear. However, after arrival in Vinland, she found a way to hunt and trade goods for better equipment.

GORM KJOTVESSON, MAEGESTER OF THE ORDER

Exiled from his homeland and given the moniker "Worm" by King Harald of Norway, this sour son of Kjotve the Cruel was an easy mark for the order, an organization that preys on discontent. Indeed, Gorm's bitterness fueled a rapid rise through the ranks. His deployment to Vinland suggested a troubling new focus for the order's expansion plans.

Once Eivor was properly equipped, she tracked Gorm to one of his camps in the wilderness and assassinated him. She said he fell fast and dropped an odd artifact—a crystal ball, humming with strange, unearthly power. Eivor left the glowing item with local leaders, telling them, "This seems to belong to your land." They thanked her, calling her "Kenhnarà:ken." Then Eivor embarked on the long, cold journey home to Ravensthorpe.

When Eivor reported this, I told her, "Another master of the order, hewn from the trunk of their dying tree! We are getting closer to the roots."

SCIROPESCIRE, MERCIA

THE BOOK OF DRAGONS

Randvi informed Eivor that Ceowulf II's son Ceolbert was in a tight spot in Sciropescire, a place mired in a long, bitter war of attrition against the Britons to the west. Ceolbert had hoped to negotiate a truce with the Briton King Rhodri—both sides were war weary—but Randvi feared the young prince wasn't fully up to the task just yet. Thus, Eivor set out to supervise the talks, arriving in the township of Quatford on the Afon Hafren River to find Ceolbert sparring with Ivarr Ragnarsson in the longhouse—Ivarr's way of showing affection for the lad, apparently. Rhodri and his queen, Angharad, waited nearby, and a bishop named Deorlaf was standing in as temporary ealdorman.

KEY EVENTS

Unfortunately, Ivarr's reckless brutality shattered the parley for peace. (Ivarr bore a wicked grudge against Rhodri, who had inflicted the nasty scar on Ivarr's face.) Rhodri, Angharad, and their war thegn, Ynyr, escaped as Quatford's streets turned into a wild melee. After the Danes cleared the Briton troops from the township, Eivor went on a raiding mission, decimating Rhodri's supply lines while recruiting a fyrd of locals for the upcoming battle. Finally, Eivor met Ivarr and Ceolbert in Wesberie and torched the town. This lured Ynyr into a fight, and Eivor slew him in a battle of titans!

Afterward, Bishop Deorlaf invited Rhodri to another meeting, seeking

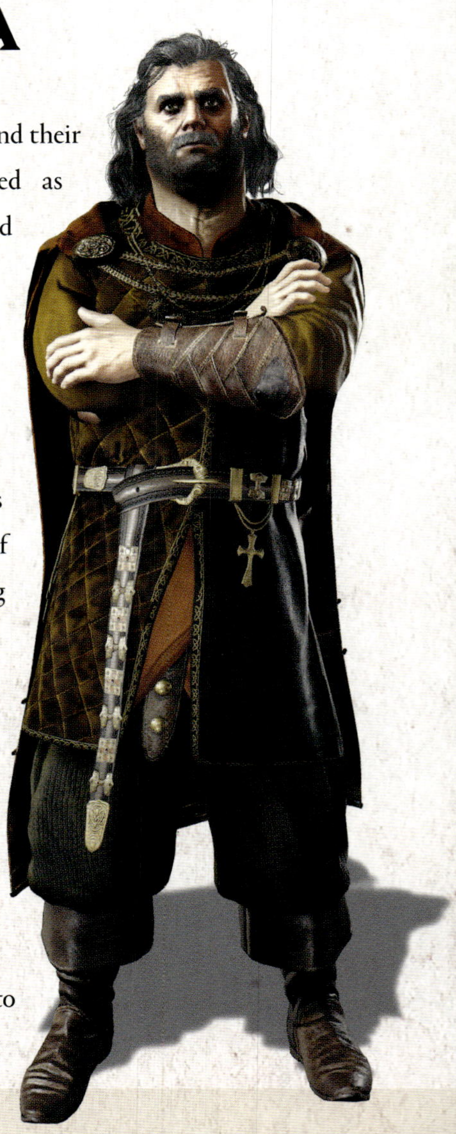

BISHOP DEORLAF

Serving as interim ealdorman until young Ceolbert could take the mantle, the bishop of Quatford was an almost preternaturally calm man. Is such a trait reassuring or unnerving? I found it interesting that an aggressive leader like Eivor regarded Bishop Deorlaf's cautious counsel as well measured, even wise.

RHODRI, KING OF THE BRITONS

A strong and somewhat impetuous man, Rhodri was king of the Britons west of Mercia for nearly four decades. For years, he clashed with both Saxons and Vikings—even faced down the vaunted "king killer," Ivarr Ragnarsson, leaving a scar on his face. Rhodri would not be bullied at the Quatford parley for peace.

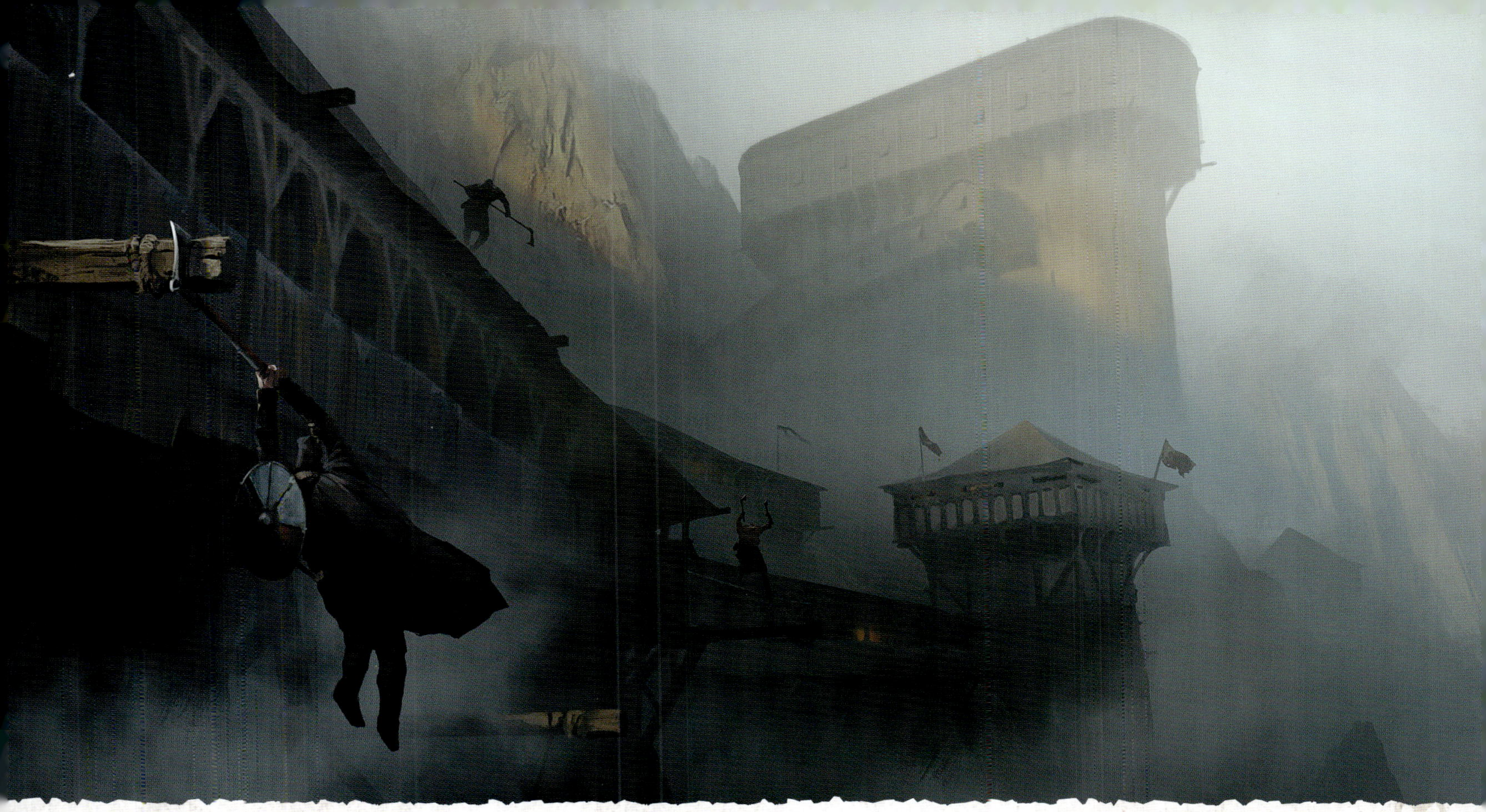

ANGHARAD, LADY OF THE BRITONS

Lady Angharad of Seisyllwg brought an entire western kingdom to her marriage with Rhodri. A well-educated woman, she also brought a measure of clearheaded sight—the perfect partner for her occasionally hotheaded husband.

to lock in a lasting accord between Britons and the Mercian shire. Lady Angharad handled the negotiations for her side—the hot-blooded rivals Ivarr and Rhodri were kept away, as was the ealdorman in waiting, Ceolbert, who was out boar hunting. With cooler heads conducting the parley, a truce was finally declared. But alas, when Eivor sought Ceolbert to relate the good news, she found him in a cave, a victim of murder! The dagger lodged in his chest was of Briton design, and the angry Danes swore to exact vengeance.

Ivarr led a ferocious assault on Rhodri's stronghold at Caustow Castle, and in the end the Britons were defeated and Rhodri hauled up to Manstone Rock to suffer the gruesome Viking torture known as the blood eagle—a truly sadistic ritual and a low mark of Norse culture, in my estimation. But then came an unexpected twist of the knife: Ivarr, in a fit of crazed megalomania, admitted to Eivor it was he who killed Ceolbert to spark a war, and he challenged Eivor to a death duel. And thus did Ivarr the Boneless, "king killer," meet his doom.

Back in Quatford, the good bishop Deorlaf was named ealdorman of the shire and pledged alliance to Ravensthorpe. Lady Angharad swore peace, and the long years of bloodshed between Britons and the Saxons of Sciropescire was ended.

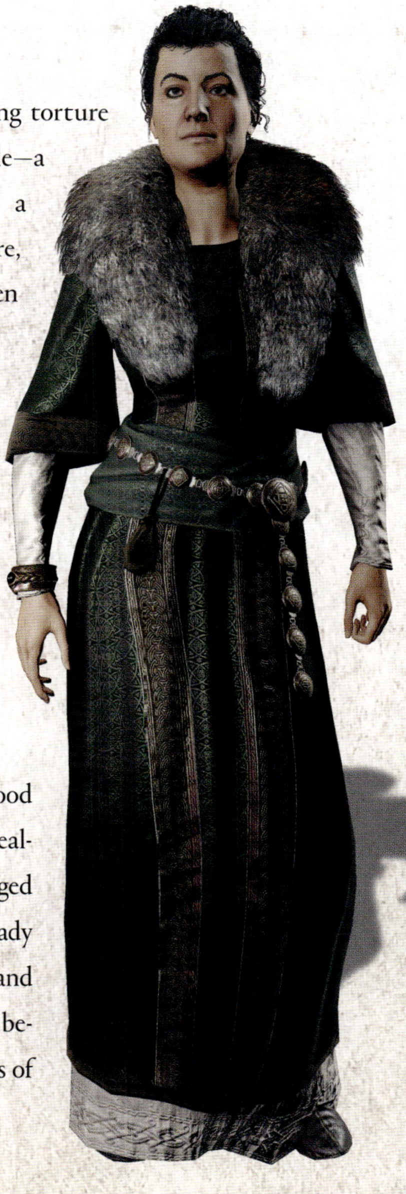

CENT, WESSEX

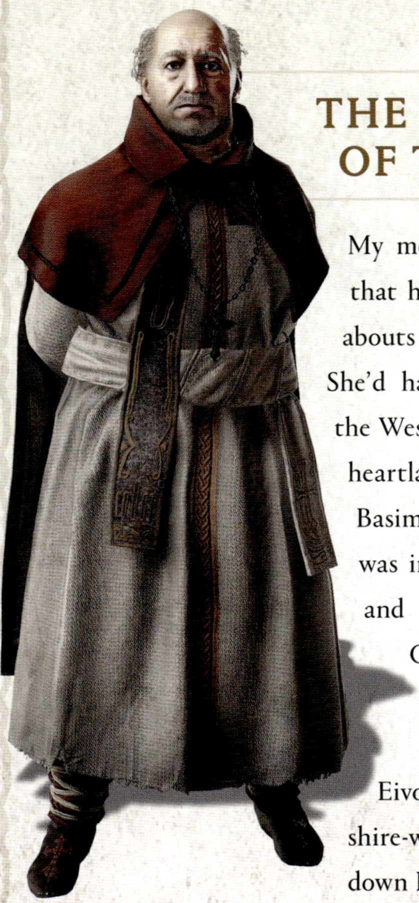

THE INSTRUMENT OF THE ANCIENTS

My mentor Basim informed Randvi that he'd located the general whereabouts of the madwoman Fulke. She'd hauled her hostage, Sigurd, to the Wessex shire of Cent, the religious heartland of England. Eivor met Basim at Saint Hadrian's Priory and was introduced to a well-connected and power-hungry abbot named Cynebert. In exchange for helping the ambitious monk plot his rise to ealdorman of Cent, Eivor and Basim planned to use his shire-wide network of spies to track down Fulke and liberate Sigurd.

KEY EVENTS

Once Eivor learned who King Aelfred of Wessex planned to appoint as ealdorman of Cent—a thegn named Tedmund—Cynebert concocted a scheme to acquire influence with this new leader. The sneaky abbot conscripted Eivor and Basim to conduct a full-scale assault on Tedmund's stronghold at Rouecistre

ABBOT CYNEBERT

Sitting atop Cent's religious hierarchy, the abbot was a classic power broker whose secret agenda was leveraging the power he brokered for his own purposes. With eyes and ears everywhere in the shire, Cynebert promised to find where Fulke incarcerated Sigurd—for a price.

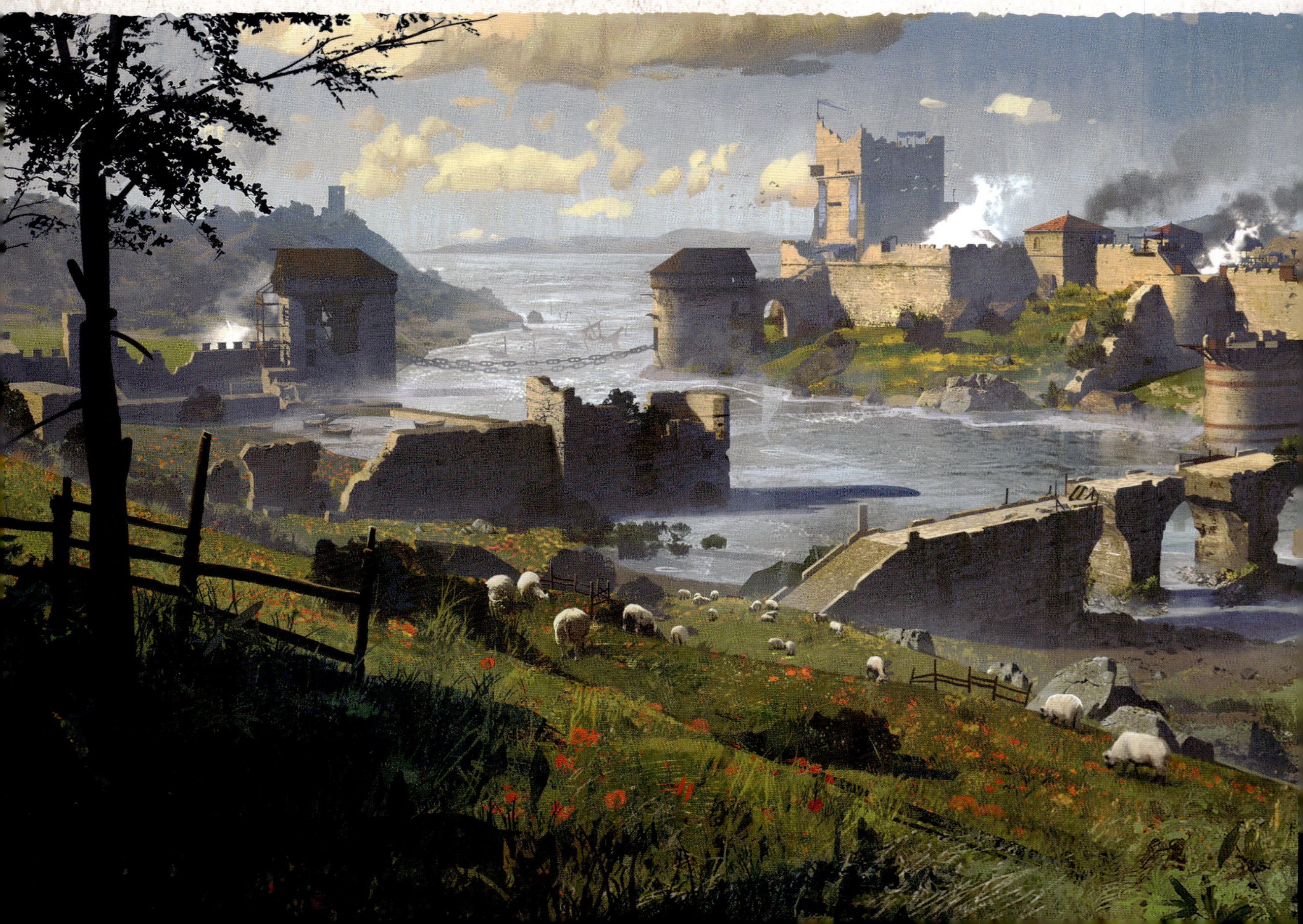

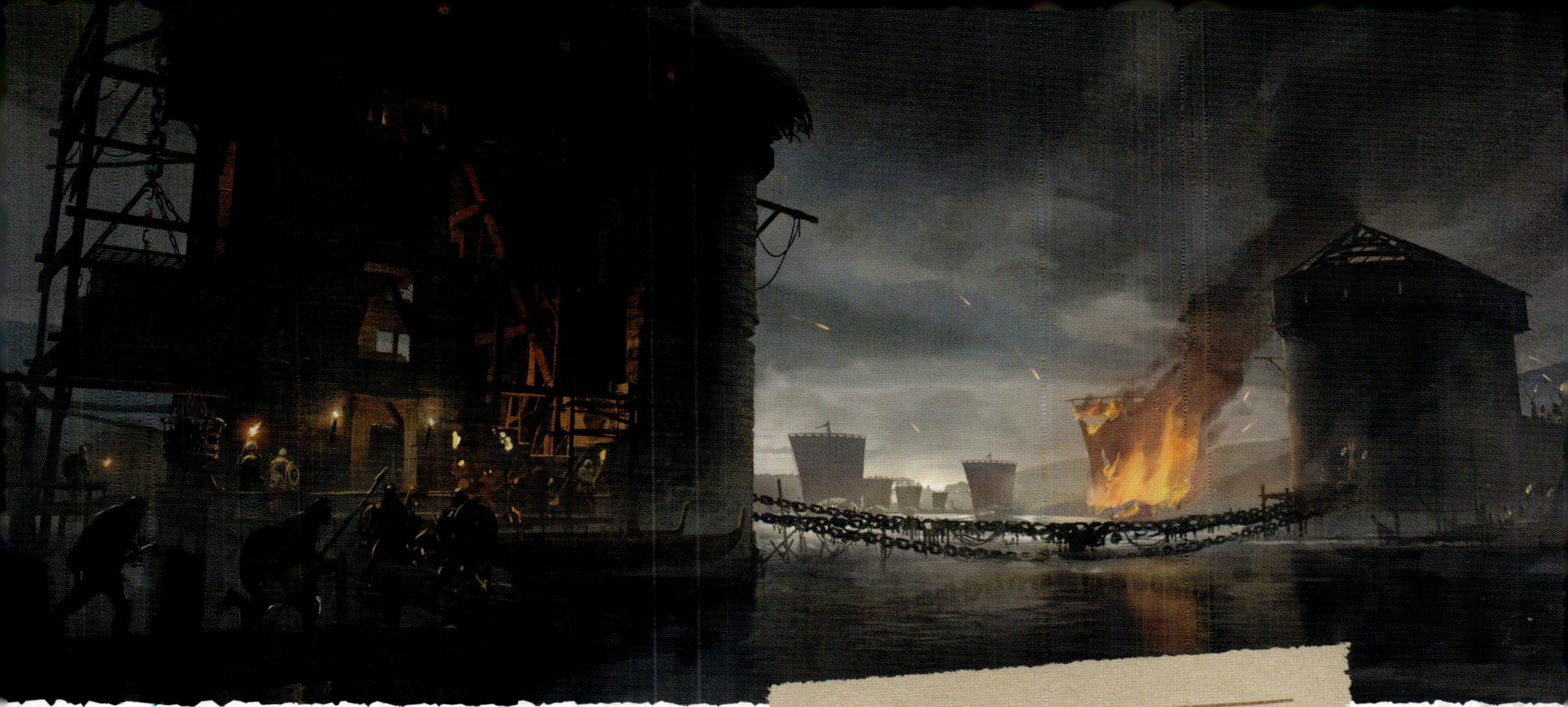

Fortress on the Medeuuage River, after which the good abbot would swoop in to rescue Tedmund via ransom. Reinforced with fyrd warriors led by Geadric from Oxenefordscire, Eivor's Vikings routed the Wessexian defenders and captured Tedmund. But before Eivor and Basim could arrange the sham ransom exchange with Abbot Cynebert, Tedmund dropped dead—a victim of poison!

One sad postscript: When Eivor returned to Ravensthorpe to make her report to Randvi, one of Sigurd's fiercest allies, Dag, openly challenged Eivor's position as interim clan leader. Eivor was forced to duel her lifelong clan mate to the death—his death, of course.

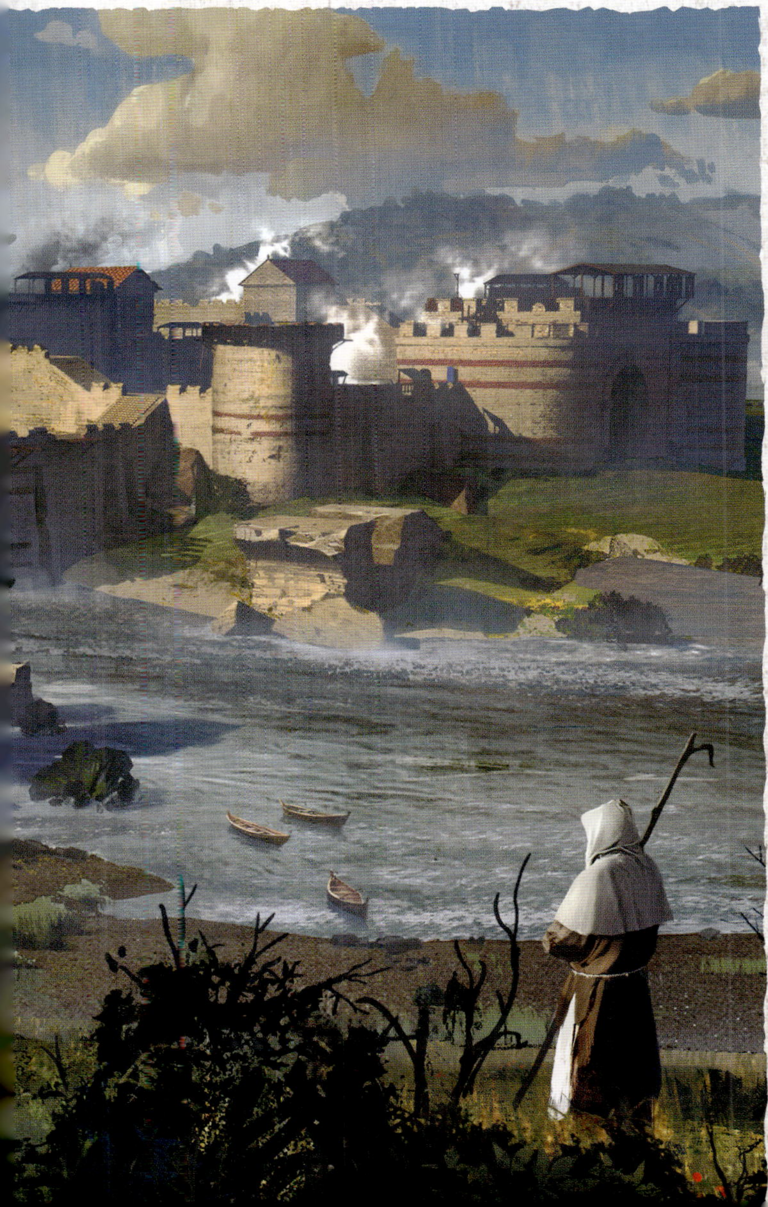

Soon after, Eivor and Basim tried to reconvene with the clergyman . . . only to find him assassinated by none other than Fulke herself! Fulke delivered a strange soliloquy about Sigurd's godhood, then fled. Eivor and Basim tracked her to an Order of the Ancients sanctum beneath the famed cathedral in Canterbury. There they discovered a trove of order documents . . . some of which revealed Fulke's high rank in that foul hierarchy!

Unfortunately, Fulke and Sigurd were already gone. Left behind—a small box holding the grisly remains of Sigurd's right forearm plus a cryptic, half-burned scrap of scroll with details of Portcestre Castle in Suthsexe, a seemingly impregnable bastion where the order trained its soldiers. Could Fulke have taken Sigurd there? Basim also recovered a number of other confidential order documents, earmarked for my own study.

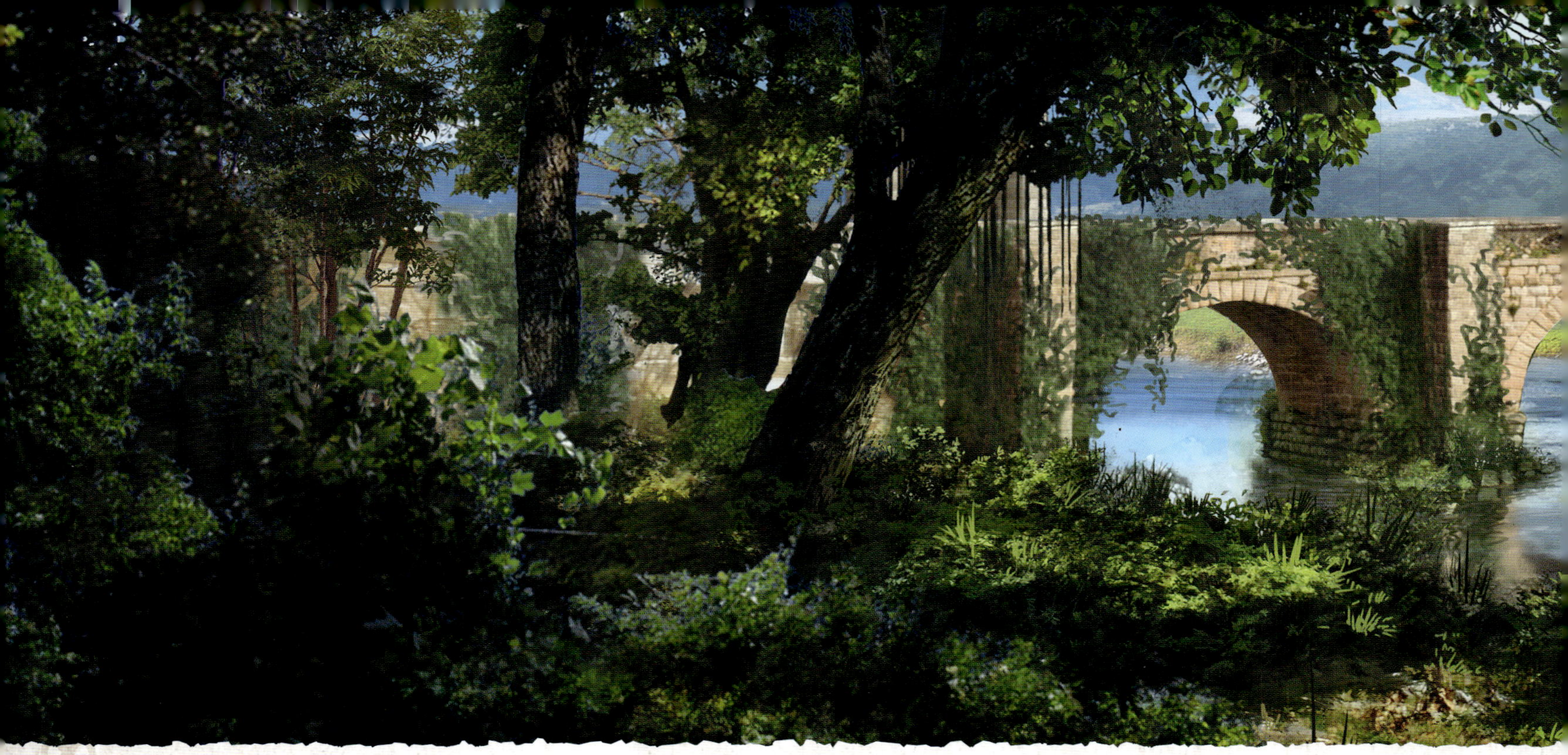

Essexe, Wessex

A BREVIARY OF BROKEN HEARTS

Randvi received a summons from Birstan, ealdorman of Essexe, and Lady Estrid, requesting help in "a matter of great secrecy." Birstan's leadership qualities had long been in question. His thegns saw him as too self-indulgent to govern the shire responsibly, and they were growing rebellious. Randvi hoped Eivor's intercession might bring stability to Essexe plus an invaluable pledge of alliance in return. But when Eivor journeyed to the county seat of Colcestre, she found the ruling couple's proposition to be particularly personal . . . and slightly bizarre!

ESTRID, LADY OF ESSEXE

This Frankish noblewoman's arranged marriage to Ealdorman Birstan brought great political benefit to Essexe but only misery to her. Estrid's great beauty and parlor wit were lost on her hunting-obsessed husband, and she missed her continental homeland terribly.

BIRSTAN, EALDORMAN OF ESSEXE

More an outdoorsman than a ruler, Birstan ignored his sophisticated wife and pined for his childhood love, Alfida. Eivor reported that after she rescued Birstan from a hunting catastrophe, he thanked her and exclaimed: "We Saxons hear only that Danes and Norse are ferocious barbarians, all teeth and claws, with little subtlety or wit." Alas, this unfortunate misreading of Viking culture remains widespread in Anglo-Saxon circles.

KEY EVENTS

Birstan and Estrid, it turned out, were extremely unhappy in their marriage—a union of political necessity, not love. Estrid, a Frankish princess who loathed Essexe, wanted only to return to Francia. Meanwhile, Birstan pined for his true love, a Saxon woman named Alfida. The Essexian couple called their plot to rectify the situation "a woman lost and a woman found"—first, fake Estrid's kidnapping and ferry her back to her homeland, and then track

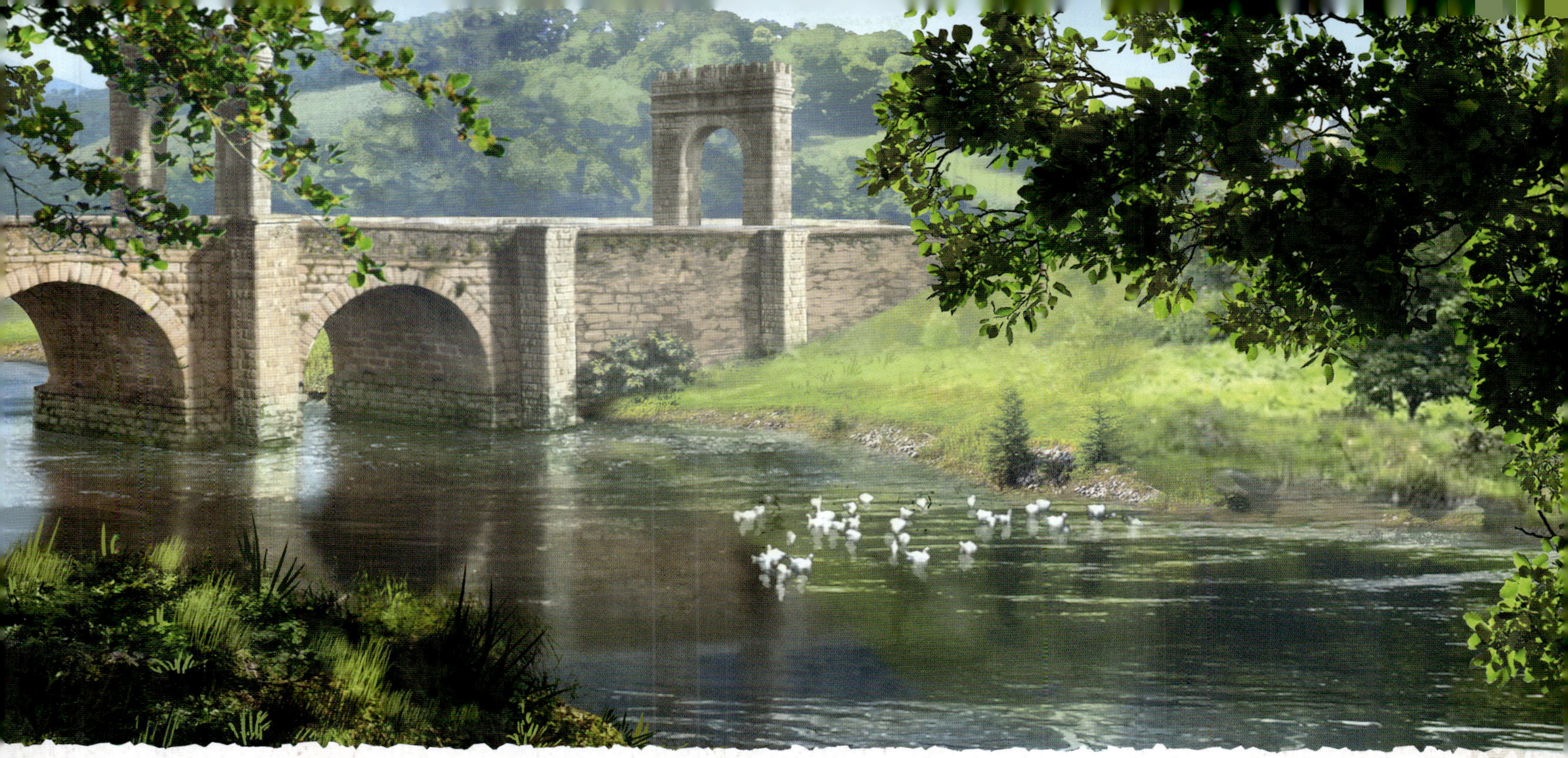

down Alfida for Birstan and bring her to the ealdorman's house. Since the payoff would be a valuable strategic alliance for Raven Clan, Eivor agreed to facilitate this convoluted plan.

Finding Alfida was easy enough—a poor peasant woman now, she lived a simple life in the town of Maeldun with her younger brother, Eluric. But engineering Estrid's fake kidnapping was trickier. First, Eivor had to contact the fellow originally hired to carry out the abduction, a strapping young Dane named Rollo. After liberating Rollo's band of fighters in Port Walton, Eivor sent them to Colcestre for the Lammas Festival, per Estrid's instructions. Using the festival commotion as cover, Rollo and his crew slipped into town to create a showy diversion so Eivor could "kidnap" Estrid and sneak her off to the coast.

ROLLO

This fiery young Viking from Norway has displayed a robust ambition since arriving in England as a warrior of note with Guthrum's Great Summer Army. Eivor believes this strapping lad is destined for greatness. I'm not sure I see it in him myself, but I've grown to trust Eivor's judgment in such matters.

Setbacks nearly derailed the plot. But in the end, Rollo's sea-steed whisked Estrid across the channel to Francia, and a happy Birstan heartily pledged the alliance of Essexe to Ravensthorpe. The ealdorman even picked up an heir in the overall transaction when he learned that Alfida's "brother" Eluric was actually her son . . . by Birstan!

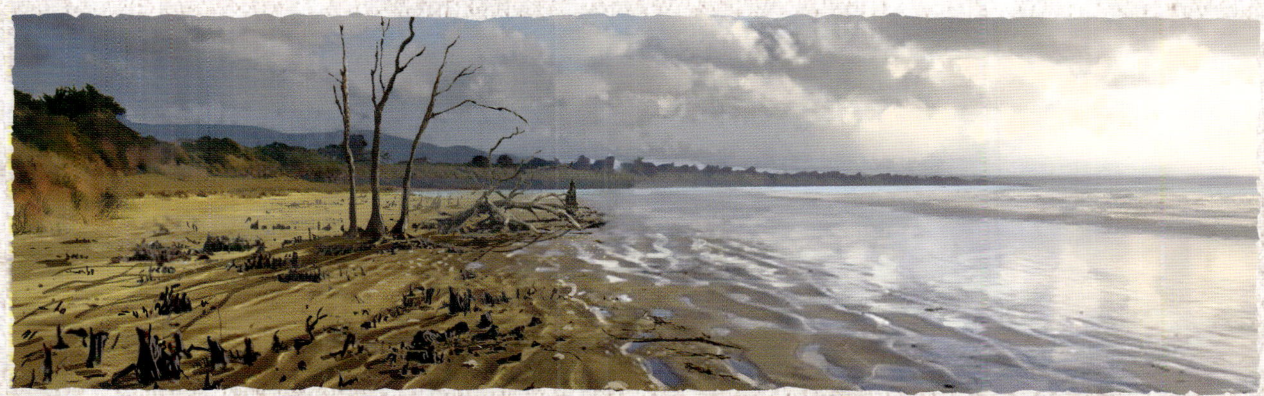

LINCOLNSCIRE, MERCIA

THE LAY OF HUNWALD

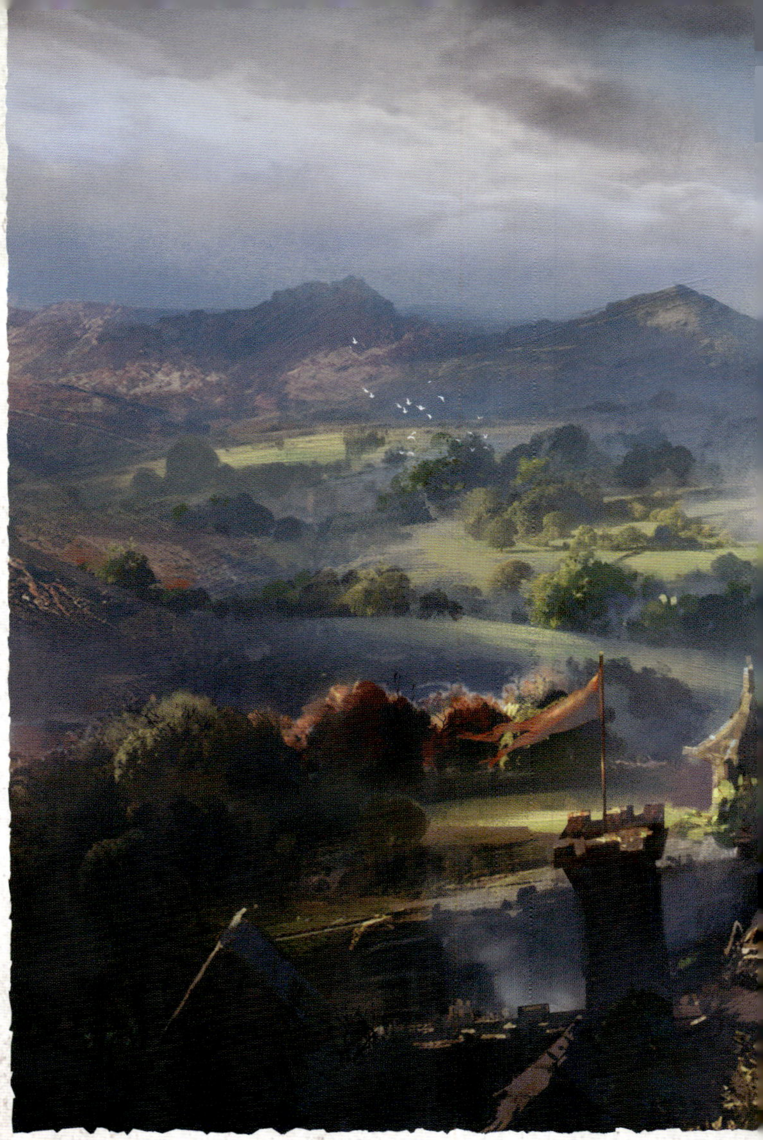

In Ravensthorpe, we met a gregarious young nobleman named Hunwald, son of Lincolnscire's ailing ealdorman. The young lord was banished from his shire by a cadre of unscrupulous thegns and clergy seeking to keep him from succeeding his father. Hired assassins seemed to be stalking him as well. Hunwald believed himself the successor to a long line of Anglian kings, heirs to the legendary kingdom of Lindsey. He promised Eivor a steadfast alliance with Lincolnscire in exchange for help regaining his place at his father's side. But when Eivor escorted Hunwald back to

HUNWALD

Self-proclaimed prince of Lindsey and son of Lincolnscire's ealdorman, Hundbeorht, this sincere lad sought to protect his ailing, delirious father from the greedy thegns and clergy trying to control the old man. Eivor believed that despite his naivety and gregarious bluster, Hunwald's earnest heart gave him the primary quality of a good and fair ruler.

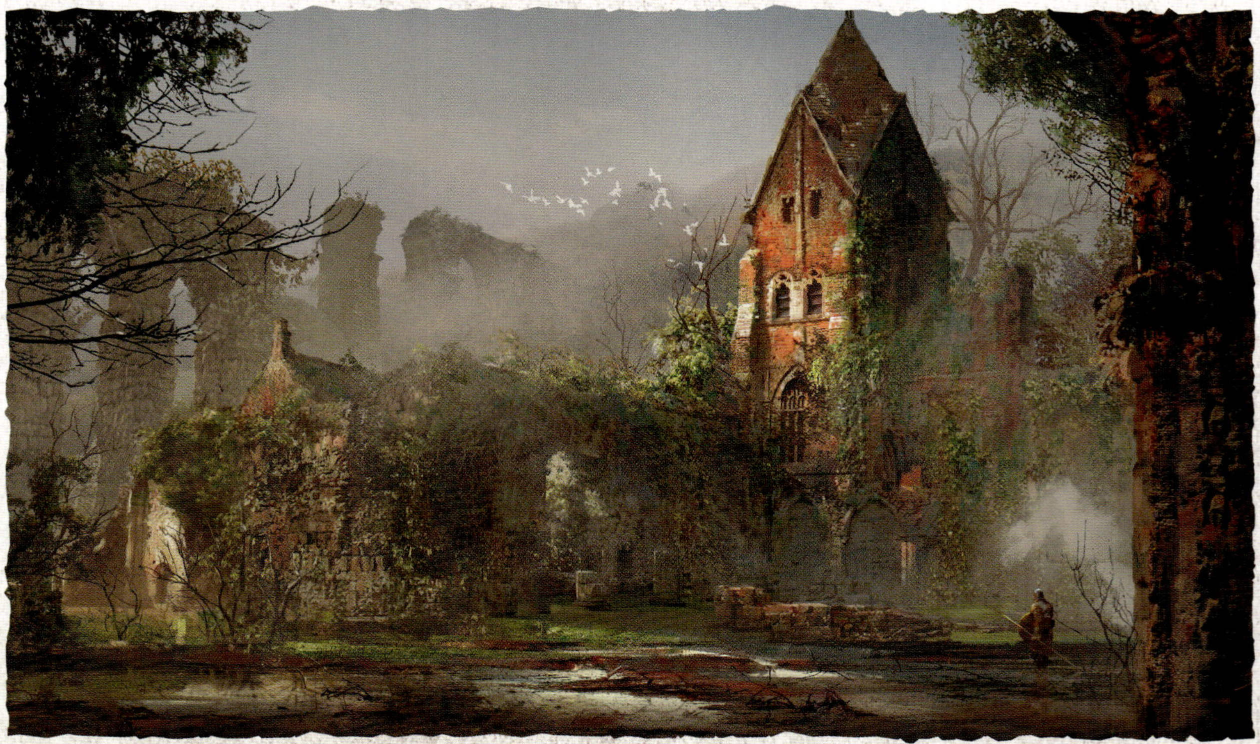

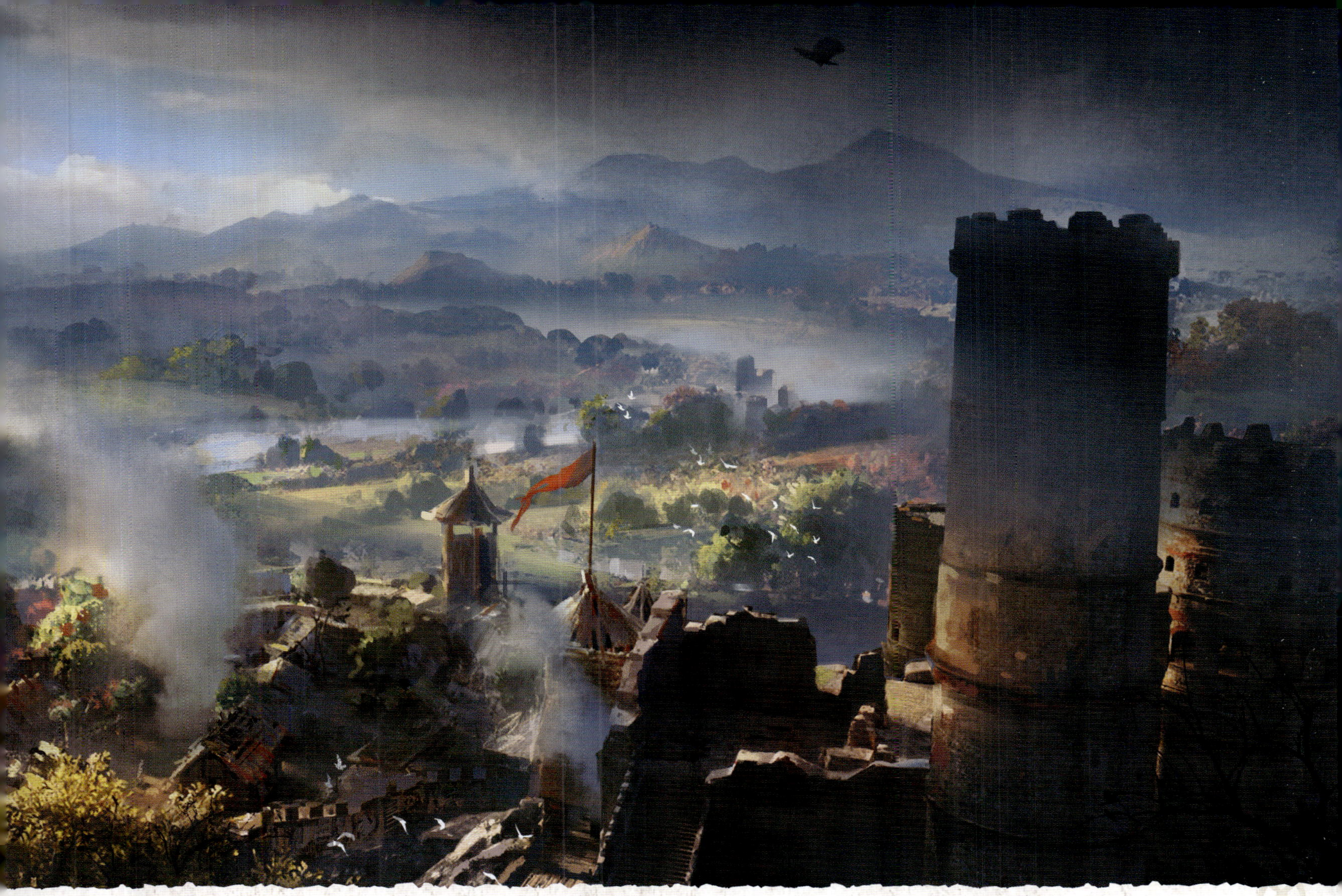

Lincoln—the lad called the city "a hornet's nest"—they learned that his ealdorman father, Hundbeorht, had been summarily removed to some undisclosed location.

KEY EVENTS

After quite a bit of effort and investigation, Eivor finally tracked down Hunwald's father to Bolingbroc Castle. Unfortunately, the ealdorman's health had deteriorated too much—and by the time Eivor reached Hundbeorht, the lord of Lincolnscire was dead. Back in Lincoln, the sad news prompted the bishop Herefrith to call for a shiremoot—an assembly of the ruling class, much like a witan or a Viking *althing*—to select a new ealdorman.

In the end, Eivor attended the shiremoot in Lincoln and supported Hunwald's candidacy for ealdorman over the other contenders, including Bishop Herefrith. This proved a good choice—the cleric turned out to be none other than the Crozier, a preost of the Order of the Ancients that my own investigation had revealed to be lurking in Lincolnscire! His perfidy was terrible, but Eivor's justice was equally so.

After leading Hunwald's fyrd in a fierce assault on the fortress of Anecastre, Herefrith's stronghold, Eivor acquired yet another order medallion for my collection.

HEREFRITH, BISHOP OF LINCOLN

The bishop spent many years "serving" his parishioners and, more importantly, the ruling class of Lincolnscire, including Ealdorman Hundbeorht and his son Hunwald. What nobody knew is that Herefrith was secretly a preost of the Order, operating under the code name "the Crozier." The foul cleric used his post to indoctrinate his flock and manipulate the shire's political hierarchy.

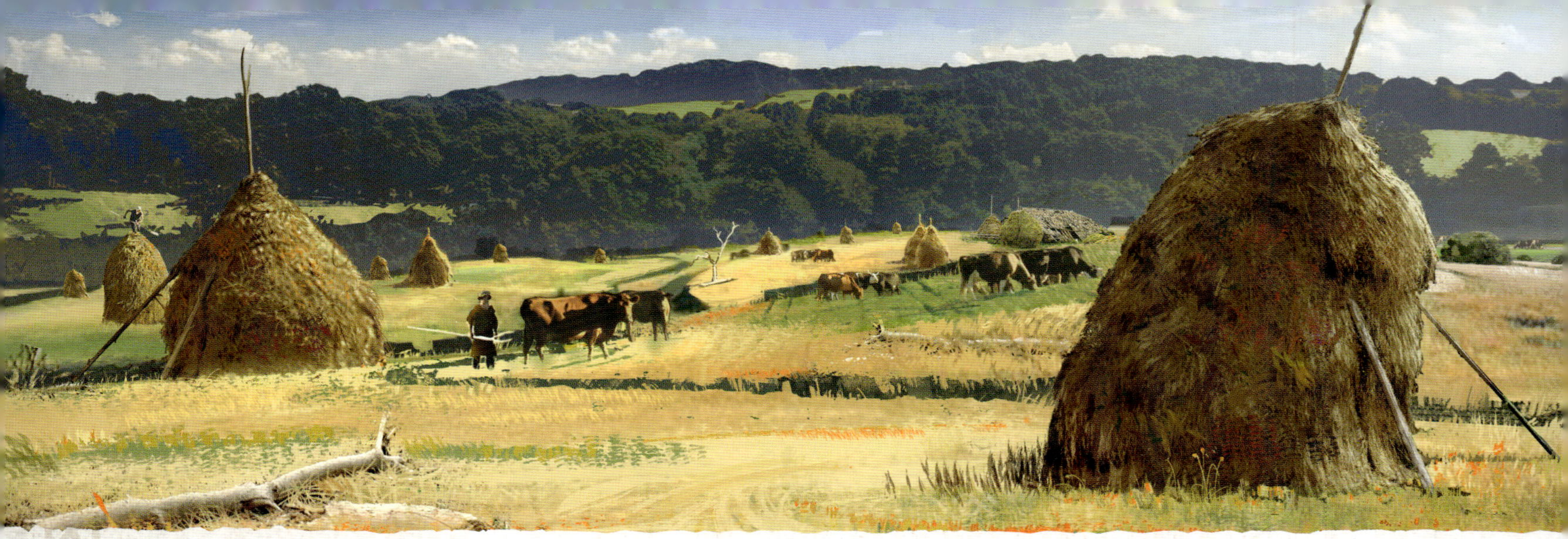

SUTHSEXE, WESSEX

THE SIEGE OF PORTCESTRE

Eivor soon tired of waiting for word from Basim—Sigurd had been in Fulke's "care" long enough. After consulting with Randvi, Eivor decided to call in favors from the Raven Clan's carefully cultivated alliances. Her plan: Launch a full-scale invasion of Suthsexe and lay siege to the supposedly impenetrable fortress of Portcestre, where a maimed Sigurd languished in captivity. As her army gathered piecemeal in a staging area at Croindene, Eivor met Basim and the legendary Guthrum, the "Reaver of the South" who'd led the Great Summer Army as it stormed through Mercia and Northumbria. The fearsome Viking jarl now had his eyes set on Wessex, looking to rout his nemesis, King Aelfred.

KEY EVENTS

Eivor's allies began to rally in Suthsexe to support her expedition: Stowe and Erke, the reeves of Lunden; Brother and Broder, brothers of the East Anglian queen; the Viking leaders Ubba Ragnarsson and Soma Jarlskona from Grantebridge; and others pledged to an alliance with Raven Clan. After defeating a regiment of Wessex fighters in the hills south of Cicestre Abbey, Eivor and her allies cut off multiple supply lines to Portcestre and sabotaged Saxon garrisons, hoping to weaken Fulke before her forces could settle in and fortify their citadel. As Eivor's invasion force continued to assemble in their forward camp for the Portcestre assault, new arrivals included Hunwald and his archers of Lincolnscire and Birstan delivering a brutal battering ram from Essexe.

Even Bishop Deorlaf arrived to lend his support. His aid proved invaluable when his men of Sciropescire launched diversionary strikes on a large column of King Aelfred's West Saxon troops marching from Wincestre to reinforce Fulke's garrison. Meanwhile, a wild, chaotic frontal assault breached the Portcestre gates, Eivor and Basim tracked down Sigurd, and the livid Viking terminated the insidious influence of Fulke in a final duel.

Sigurd returned to Ravensthorpe a dark, melancholy shadow of the man he once was, believing himself to be an actual god reborn. Both Eivor and I found this most disturbing.

GUTHRUM

The imposing Viking jarl landed his Great Summer Army at Reading in 871 and marched to join forces with Halfdan's Great Heathen Army. After a series of victories in the north, Guthrum led a sizable contingent south into Wessex, where he launched a bloody campaign against King Aelfred's Saxon forces.

Jorvik

THE CITY OF GREED

Over the past decade, Jorvik has grown to rival Lunden not only as a center of commerce but also as a hotbed of the order's corruption of England. Recent surveillance by Hidden Ones agents revealed three more high-ranking order members recruiting and spreading their poisonous tenets across the city. I passed this intelligence to Eivor and strongly encouraged her to impede the trio's efforts. Randvi suggested she start by consulting a pair of old Norseland friends, Hjorr and Ljufvina, who'd spent recent years helping to develop Jorvik into a thriving center of international trade.

HJORR HALFSSON

Years of experience in Norway's royal courts prepared Hjorr for a leadership role in Jorvik, where he sat on King Ricsige's council of advisers. His knack for commerce made him an important voice for the city's merchant class. With his wife, Ljufvina, he became a stalwart ally of the Raven Clan.

KEY EVENTS

When Eivor arrived in Jorvik, the order—operating under the name "the Red Hand"—had already sent thugs to raid Ljufvina's home. (Ljufvina tore them to shreds.) A letter delivered from the mysterious Poor Fellow-Soldier of Christ revealed code designations of the group's ranking members: the Needle, the Firebrand, and the Vault. Eivor and Hjorr met with the king of Northumbria, Ricsige, and agreed to target the criminal group.

LJUFVINA BJARMARSDOTTIR

A fearsome warrior, Ljufvina did not share her husband Hjorr's affinity for political maneuvering and the accumulation of personal wealth. She once told Eivor: "Politics. It takes the Norse out of a Norse'—an essentially Viking sentiment, I must say. Ljufvina originally hails from Bjarmeland, a territory well northeast of Norway, where some say she was a restless, adventure-seeking princess.

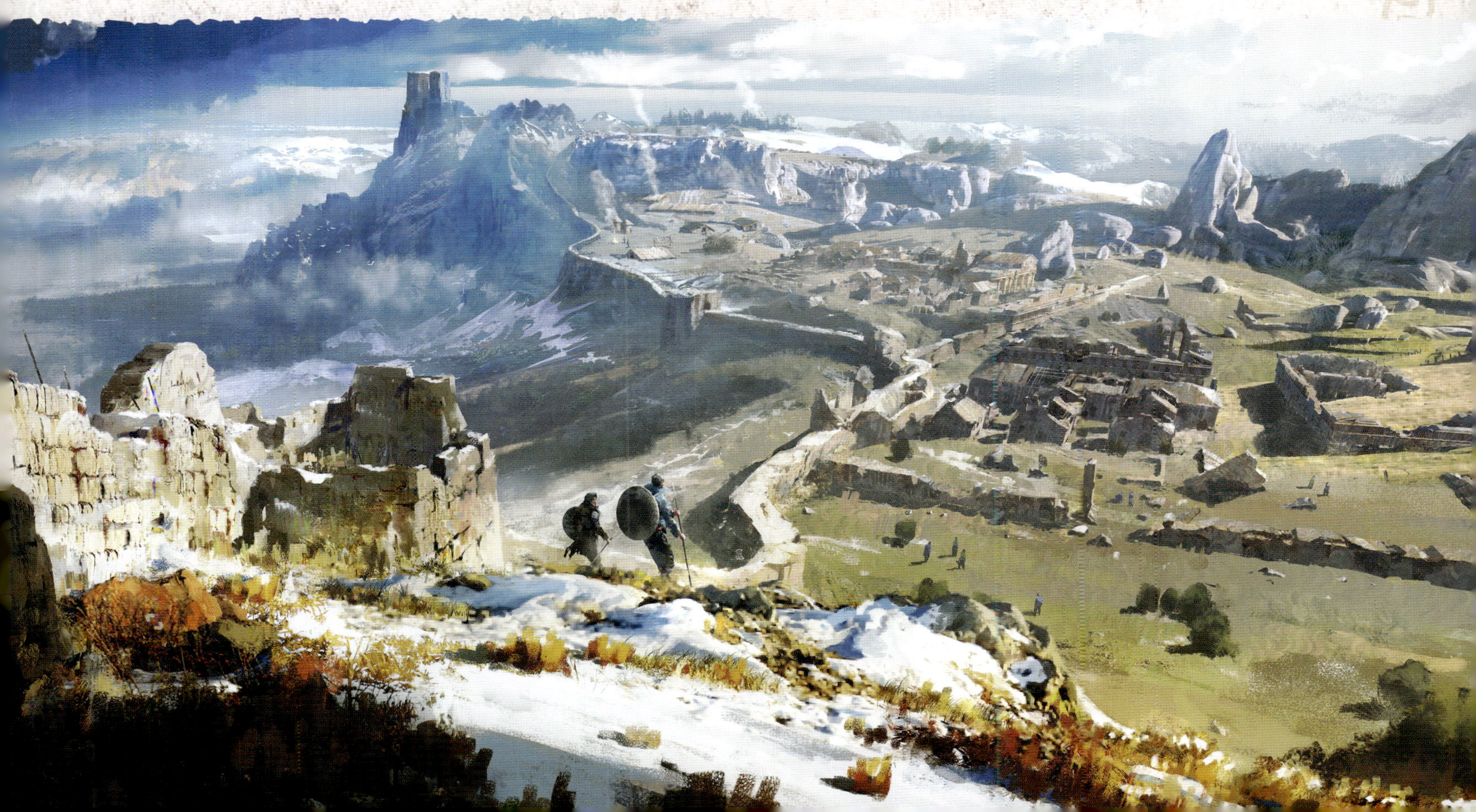

Investigations revealed that the order was collecting Christian texts in order to destroy them. First, Eivor tracked down and killed the Firebrand, who turned out to be the abbess Ingeborg, a woman plucked from the church by the order, lured by the belief that common folk cannot be trusted to interpret truth for themselves. The order offered one truth, and only one. As the abbess told Eivor: "Knowledge must be controlled."

Next, Eivor ended the suffering wrought on city merchants by the Needle, who turned out to be the Jorvik dockmaster, Grigorii. Finally, Eivor hunted down the ringleader, the Vault—none other than the councilman Audun, high-reeve of Jorvik and one of Halfdan's favored thegns, who had secretly succumbed to the lure of power and riches woven into the order's cloth of treachery.

When Eivor returned from Jorvik to Ravensthorpe after her successful purge, she brought far more than just another pledge of alliance. Checking in at my bureau, she displayed an even deeper desire to combat the order's plague.

RICSIGE, KING OF NORTHUMBRIA

Overseeing England's northern kingdom as Halfdan's puppet king in Jorvik, Ricsige was a cynical and cunning monarch. He knew his place, but he did not like it. The city's corrupt mercenary milieu suited him well, but he welcomed Eivor's intercession with the deadly Red Hand syndicate . . . a front organization for the Order of the Ancients.

EURVICSCIRE, NORTHUMBRIA

THE SAYINGS OF HALFDAN

Randvi reported that Halfdan Ragnarsson, Conqueror of the North, had sent an intriguing summons to Eivor Wolf-kissed. After hearing of her exploits, the legendary Viking leader invited the "Hero of Jorvik" to his war camp in the Northumbrian shire of Eurvicscire. For years, Halfdan Jarl had ruled the northern territories with a sense of common purpose—Norse and Saxon alike respected and followed him. But lately, sapped by constant vigilance, working nonstop to secure his northern border from incessant Pict raids, the great warrior was beset by weariness . . . and worse, by paranoia. Halfdan feared that members of his own inner circle were seeking to usurp him, including perhaps the Saxon puppet he'd installed as king of Northumbria, Ricsige.

HALFDAN RAGNARSSON

His brothers Ubba and Ivarr were certainly formidable fighters and leaders, but Halfdan was most perfectly his father's son—powerful, charismatic, an inspiration to the warriors who served under him. His Great Heathen Army rampaged through city and shire, crushing foes like the terrifying hammer he wielded. Unfortunately, Halfdan's distrust of his own leadership team was driving him to roiling fits of suspicion.

KEY EVENTS

Halfdan suspected his longtime war chief and friend, Faravid, of plotting treason against him and asked Eivor to investigate. Eivor joined Faravid's war party in an attack on a Pict war band in Stenwege Camp. There, she learned that Faravid was also planning an assault on a major Pict stronghold, Magnis Fortress . . . but without Halfdan's consent. Eivor took a calculated risk by employing Hjorr in Jorvik to falsify orders from Halfdan to King Ricsige in order to procure the support of his Saxon fyrd for the attack on Magnis.

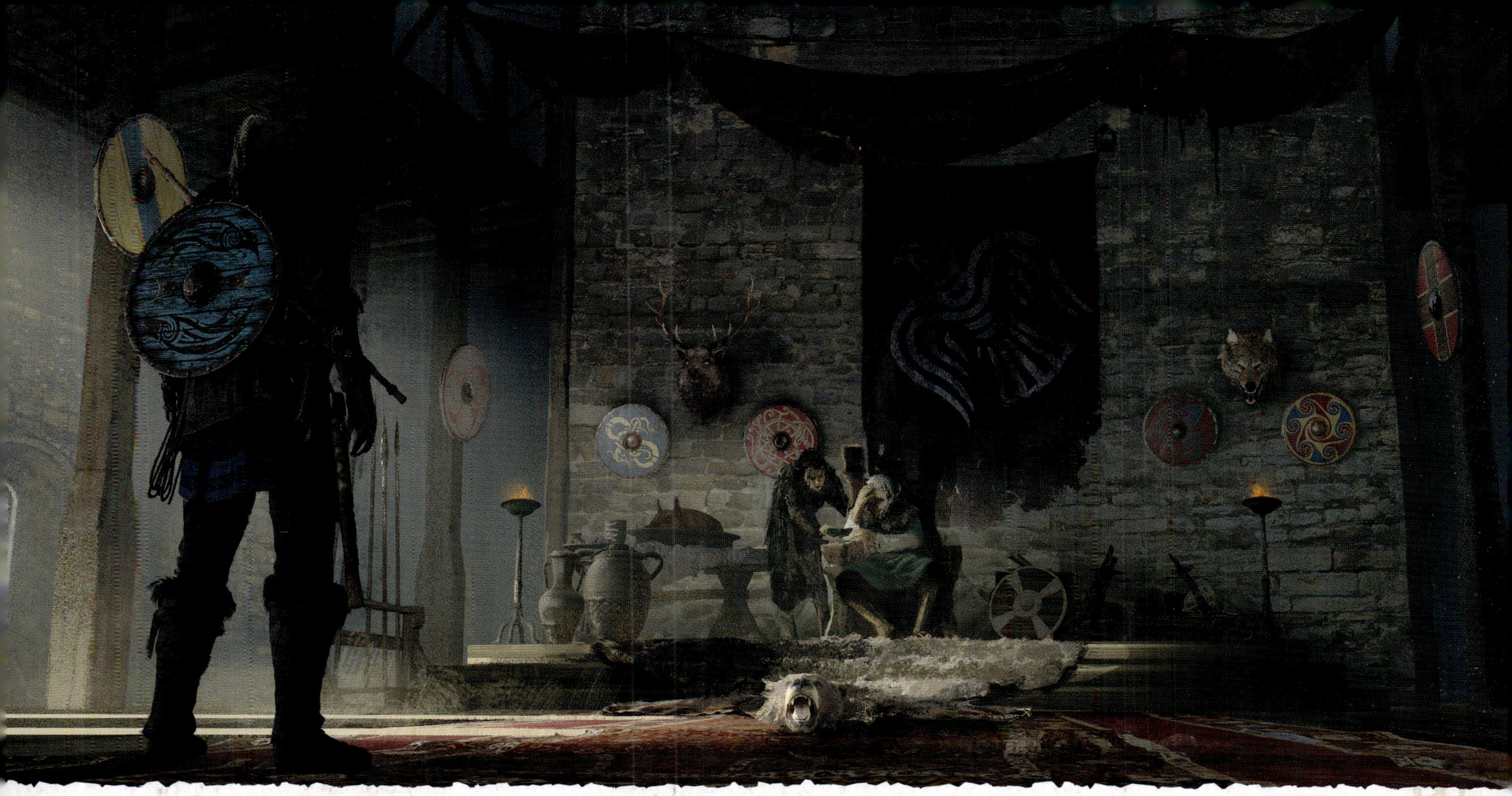

The traitorous Ricsige and his Saxons secretly slipped off to ally with the Picts. Viking forces led by Halfdan and his lieutenants Eivor, Ljufvina, and Faravid secured Magnis Fortress, but suddenly Ricsige and his fyrd descended on the stronghold from the north! In the ensuing slaughter, Halfdan's warriors repelled the united Picts and Saxons. Then Eivor hunted down Ricsige, ending his treason with her blade. Afterward, back in Jorvik's Royal Hall, a final scene played out—Halfdan had decided to forgo any future puppet kings and chose to assume the throne (and its great burdens) himself.

But as the coronation unfolded, another treachery was revealed. For years, Faravid had been gifting Halfdan Jarl with drinking cups made of lead! The poison had slowly debilitated the great leader. Eivor's desire to secure an alliance with Eurvicscire led her to back Halfdan and, sadly, to serve as Halfdan's champion in a duel with Faravid. After Eivor defeated the unrepentant war chief, Halfdan administered bloody justice.

During this time, I received a strange letter, another missive from the one calling himself "A Poor Fellow-Soldier of Christ"—the same correspondent who had guided Eivor to several order members earlier. This note pointed to a "man in white at the house of God in Wincestre."

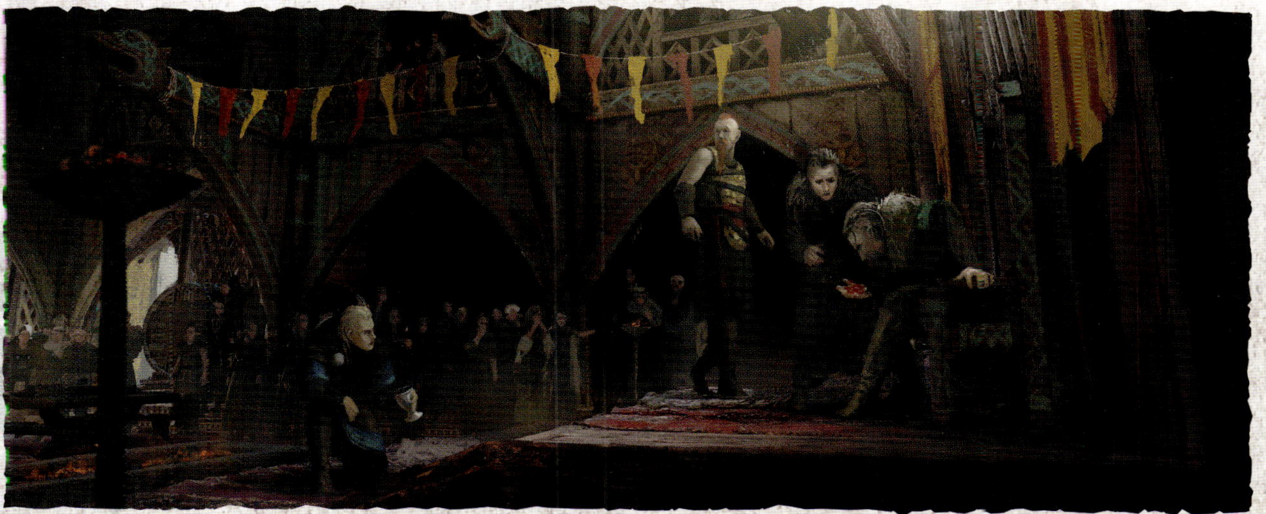

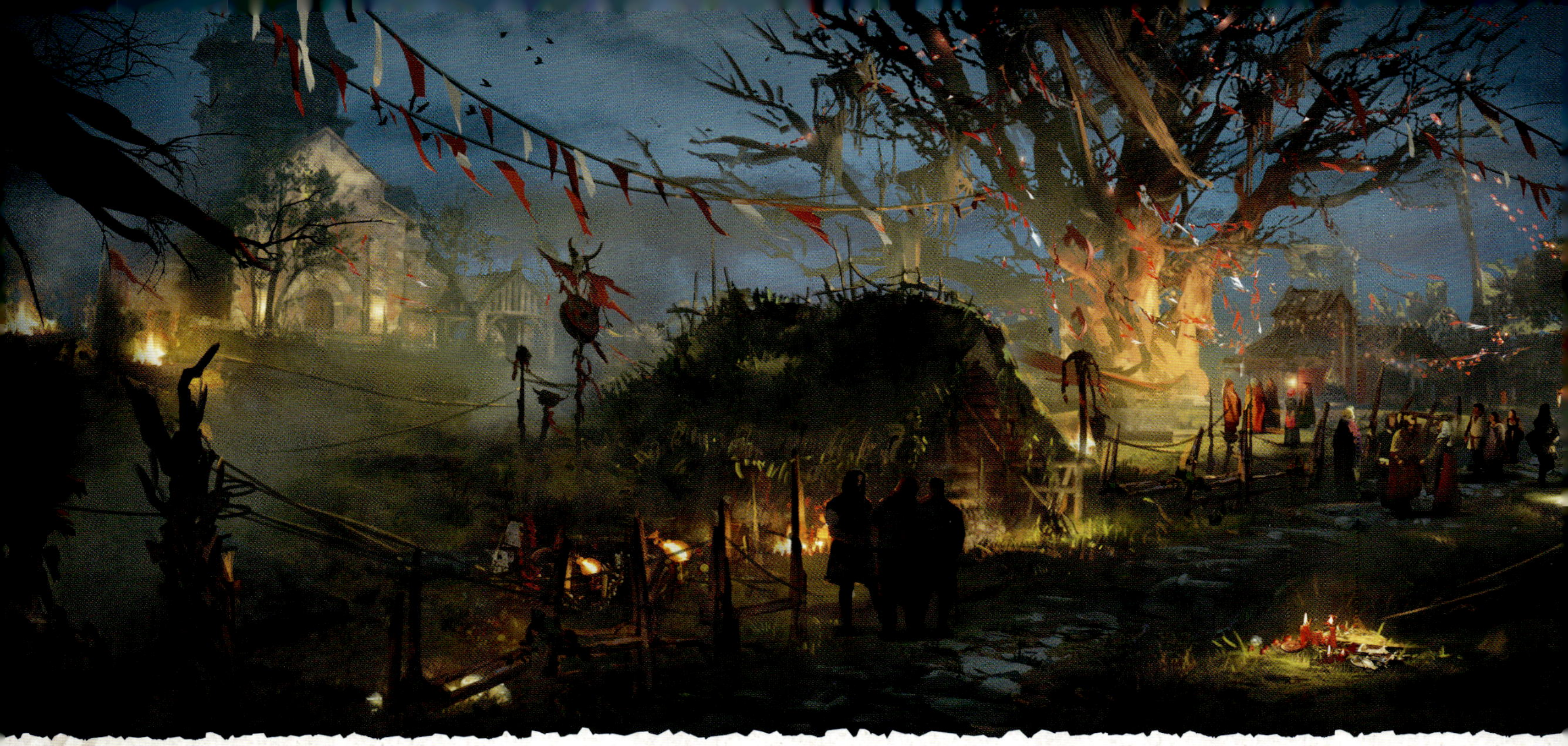

GLOWECESTRESCIRE, MERCIA

A TALE OF WICKER-FIRE

Eivor went to Glowecestrescire seeking alliance, of course, but also to stand with Gunnar, the Raven Clan's beloved but chronically lovelorn blacksmith. Gunnar had fallen for a woman named Brigid—a lovely girl with a truly vexing accent—and traveled to Glowecestre in western Mercia to marry her. Unfortunately, Eivor's journey of personal support soon turned into something else entirely. She arrived during the shire's annual harvest festival, known as Samhain—an oddly pagan rite for a town full of Christians! Samhain revelers dressed like spirits and monsters, paid tribute to souls of the dead, and the whole thing culminated in the burning of a giant wooden effigy called the Wicker Man.

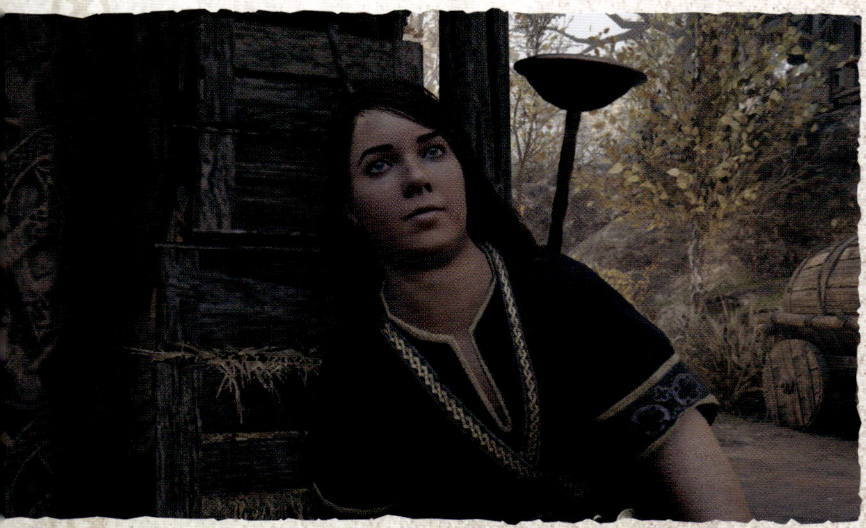

KEY EVENTS

Eivor was shocked that this year's Samhain celebration would include the ritual sacrifice of the shire's ealdorman, a strangely good-natured fellow named Cynon. The man would be caged inside the Wicker Man and burned alive! Eivor found Cynon's willingness to

BRIGID

Those of us who are fond of our Ravensthorpe blacksmith, Gunnar—and that includes almost everyone in the settlement—were delighted to hear that he'd finally found love in Glowecestre. I've heard many odd dialects in my travels with Basim, but this woman Brigid speaks with the most convoluted twisting of tongue, palate, and larynx I've ever heard. Thank the gods that Gunnar seems to understand her.

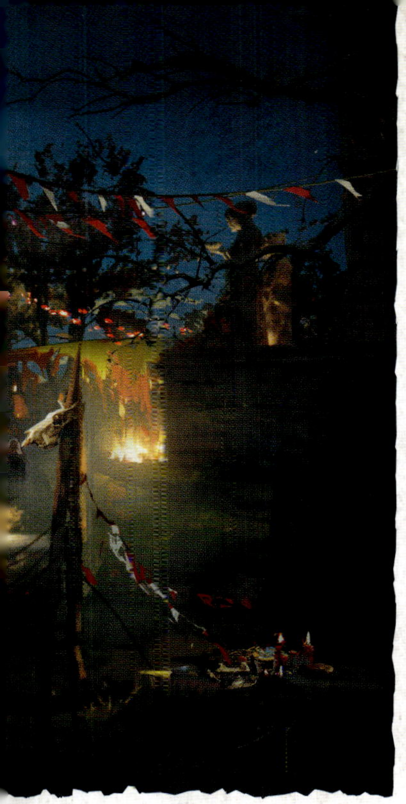

submit to this macabre practice quite unsettling. After Gunnar introduced Brigid, his betrothed, Eivor met Cynon's designated successor, Tewdwr—a young man with a wary distrust of pagans (i.e., Norse). Ironic that any participant in this bizarre Samhain festival could look askance at anyone else for their so-called paganism. Regardless, Eivor decided to embrace the Samhain spirits (literally). As she swilled ale with Tewdwr, the two descended into quite a bout of drunken carousing.

Eivor awoke in Tewdwr's hut the next morning surrounded by the aftermath of a shocking massacre—dead bodyguards, shattered furniture, blood spattered everywhere . . . and her drinking partner missing! Cynon appeared with guards and accused Eivor of murdering Tewdwr. But she escaped and, with the help of a local pagan witch named Modron, found clues in the Celtic hinterland that led her to Tewdwr. He'd been attacked by outlaws hired by Cynon to kill him. But the killers double-crossed the ealdorman by kidnapping Tewdwr instead, hoping that by keeping him alive they could extort more

CYNON

Twenty years he directed Glowecestrescire as ealdorman. Now Cynon planned to pass on the torch of leadership to his chosen successor, Tewdwr. Interestingly, this torch passing included actual torch work—the transition of power would be consummated by Cynon's ritual immolation inside a wooden effigy called the Wicker Man. I never cease to be amazed by these Saxon Christians and their odd blend of enlightened goodwill and barbarous cruelty.

money. Eivor freed Tewdwr, left him with Modron for safekeeping, and then tracked down Cynon and his entourage.

Eivor eventually discovered that the plot was the result of both personal and political complications: years ago, Modron and Cynon had an illicit union

TEWDWR

At first, this devout Christian pilgrim deplored any hint of paganism—for example, Eivor's Norseness and the healer Modron and her Celtic rites. But eventually, his initial aversion to Eivor eroded in the face of their growing camaraderie and understanding. I expect Tewdwr's ascension to ealdorman of Glowecestrescire will be good for our relations with that shire going forward.

that produced a child. Modron feared the designation of a fervent, militant Christian like Tewdwr as ealdorman. Thus, she threatened to expose Cynon's mortal sin—laying with a pagan witch, a true abomination in a Christian shire—unless he helped her arrange Tewdwr's assassination. Fortunately, Eivor intervened to save Tewdwr's life.

In the end, both Cynon and Modron faced a justice administered by the Wolf-kissed one . . . and a strong bond of alliance was built with the new ealdorman of Glowecestrescire.

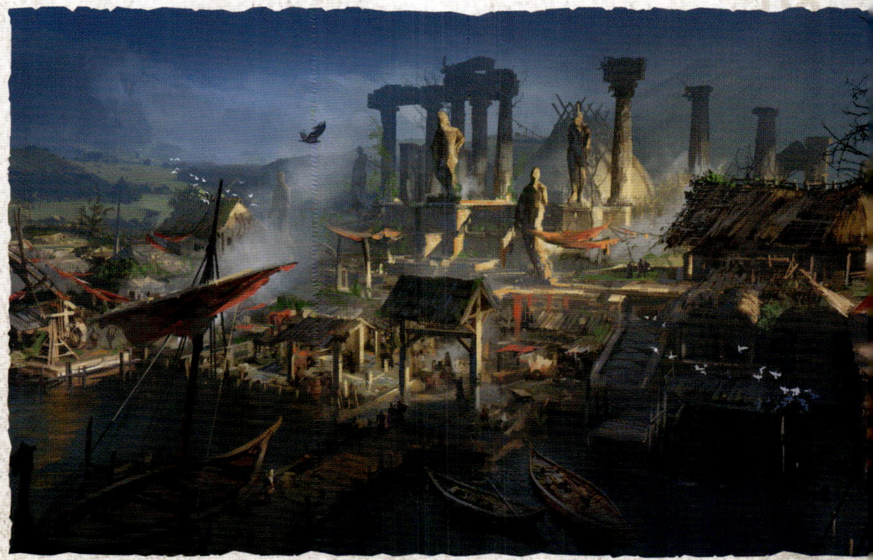

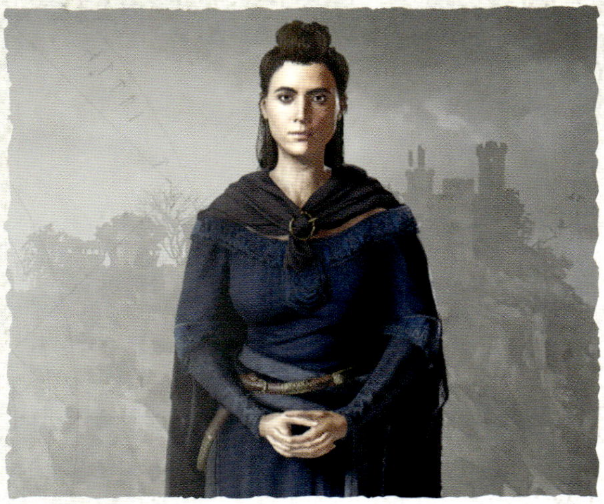

MODRON

The so-called witch of Glowecestre carried on certain Celtic traditions and rituals embedded in the region by its pagan history and Arthurian legend. Modron was also a powerful healer—some said she was imbued with the gift of prophecy, as well. One thing was sure: she despised Tewdwr's Christian sanctimony so much that she concocted a grim plot against his life!

SNOTINGHAMSCIRE, NORTHUMBRIA

THE TALE OF TWO JARLS

Eivor received a summons from her childhood friend Vili in Snotinghamscire, asking her to attend a great feast celebrating his father Hemming, the shire's jarl. Under Hemming's wise reign, the ruling seat of Snotingham had become well known as a place where Saxon and Dane folk dwelled together peacefully. A pledge of alliance from Hemming Jarl would add a truly formidable partner to Randvi's strategic map. When Eivor arrived in Snotingham, she met another old comrade, Trygve, who reported that Vili and his father were out staving off another Pict invasion, an omnipresent threat in the northland.

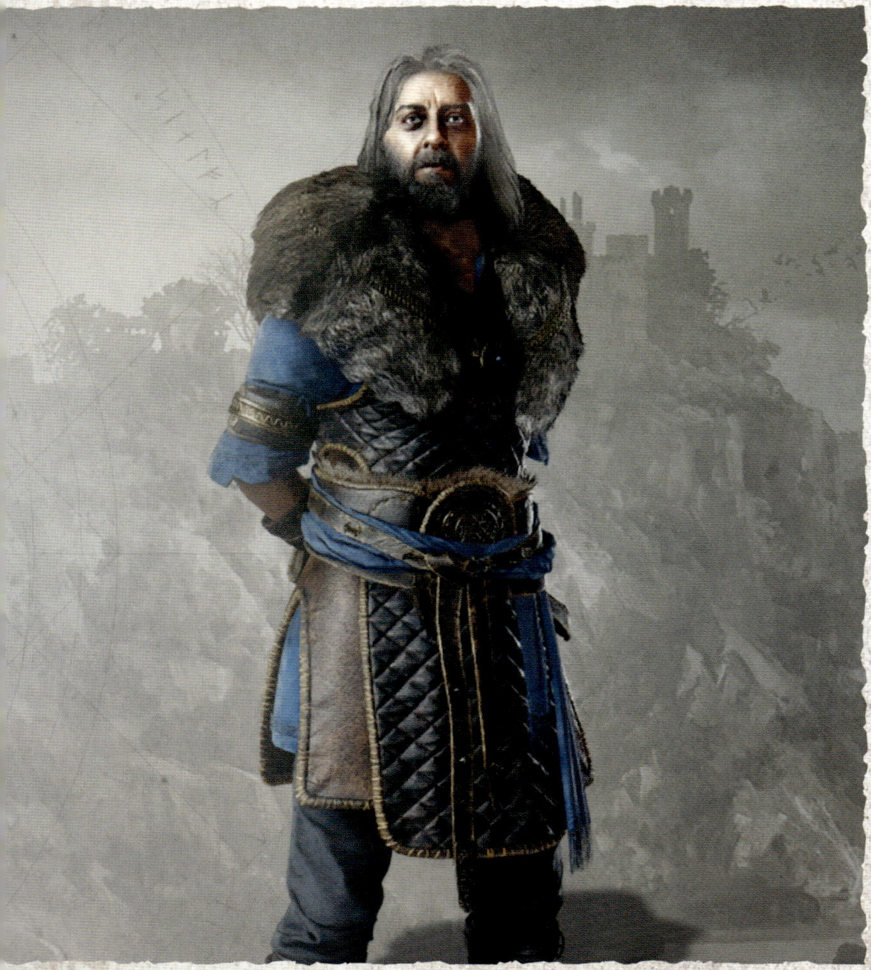

HEMMING JARL

One of Halfdan's most trusted generals, Hemming had long been the tip of the Viking spear against the Picts massing north of Hadrian's Wall. His reign in Snotinghamscire was notable for his ability to bring Danes and Saxons together as fellow shire-folk. Unfortunately, his health was failing, and a new jarl needed to be chosen. Who could follow in such footsteps?

KEY EVENTS

To support Hemming and Vili, Eivor escorted Trygve's convoy of supply-laden "sail-steeds" up a hostile stretch of the Dubras River to the Viking encampment outside Ulkerthorpe Fort, the Pict citadel. After successfully storming the stronghold and routing his foes, Hemming confided to Eivor that he was gravely ill and ready to step down. Sadly, it wasn't long before the great jarl passed into shadow. After the funeral, an *althing* was called, bringing nobles and thegns from across the shire to choose a successor.

Hemming Jarl's longtime wish, of course, had been to see his son take his place . . . and Vili was indeed the obvious candidate. But Vili did not want the full weight of the clan on his back—instead, he yearned for freedom. He told Eivor: "I only want sun on my skin and an axe in my hand. Ale and adventure! Not the staid life of a jarl." Nor did loyal Trygve, the other clear candidate, wish to step ahead of the young Hemmingson he'd helped raise and train. But Eivor helped broker a suitable final decision at the *althing* . . . and the Raven Clan gained as strong an ally in Snotinghamscire as any on the island.

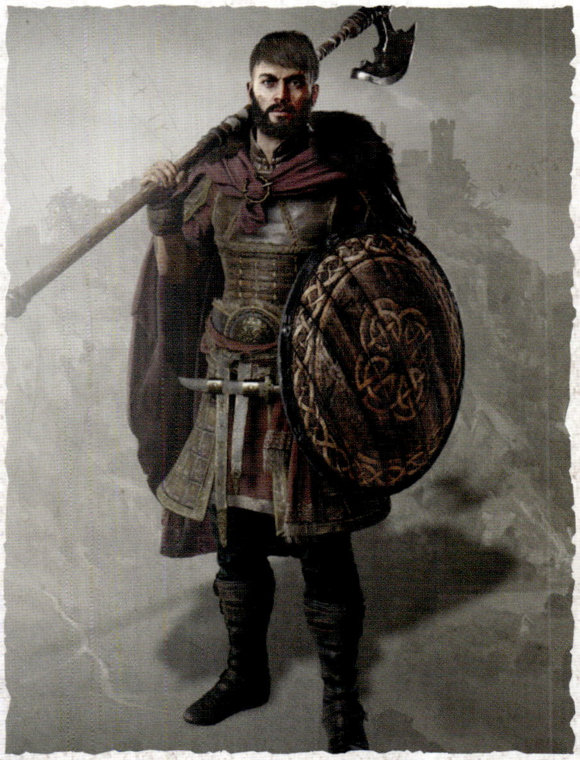

VILI

Eivor's dearest childhood friend, Vili Hemmingson was a great warrior and a natural leader—a fitting offspring of his father, Hemming. But Vili's free spirit warred against his sense of filial responsibility. Was he ready to inherit the role of jarl to his people? Or would it be too great a burden to bear?

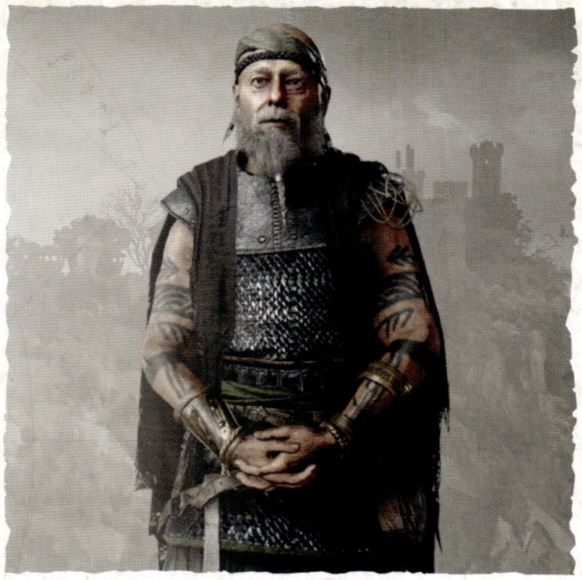

TRYGVE

This loyal warhorse was Hemming's capable steward . . . and he loved Vili like a son, too. Eivor felt Trygve could be an excellent jarl. But would he be more valuable as a trusted adviser in the court of young Vili?

Side note: I've spoken with both Eivor and Basim about the changes we've noted in Sigurd since his rescue from the order's cruel witch-woman Fulke. Interestingly, we all see him differently. Basim sees only a more introspective and thoughtful man. But Eivor senses a fundamental alteration of Sigurd's personality—a loss of feeling, all happiness leached from his demeanor. To be honest, I tend to agree with Eivor—Sigurd now speaks as if strange gods whisper in his ears.

Wincestre

THE CITY OF FAITH

Eivor was ready at last to infiltrate the Wessex capital city of Wincestre. Following up on a tip from our shadowy source, the Poor Fellow-Soldier of Christ, Eivor found a very high-level contact in the Old Minster church—none other than King Aelfred himself! The Wessex monarch spoke of an order-instigated assassination plot against him by three powerful order acolytes. Aelfred called the Order of the Ancients a terrible cancer and asked Eivor to help him surgically remove it from the English body politic. She agreed, and the deal was made.

KEY EVENTS

With investigative help from Aelfred's loyal factotum, Reeve Goodwin, Eivor was able to root out and terminate the order operatives: the Gallows, a corrupt reeve of Wincestre named Selwyn who used public executions as a fear tactic; the Quill, an antieducation zealot named Hilda who employed orphaned children to spy and steal and target foes; and the Seax, the fallen bishop Ealhferth, who went so far as to fake his own death so he could sneak up on Aelfred in disguise and assassinate the Wessex king.

GOODWIN, REEVE OF WINCESTRE

Lord Aelfred's right-hand man is a gifted administrator, having helped his king implement progressive reforms in Wincestre and all across Wessex. But Goodwin is also a surprisingly adept swordsman and fighter. His ironclad loyalty to Aelfred includes protection and enforcement.

In the course of Eivor's investigation, she managed to infiltrate the order's inner sanctum in Wincestre, called the Temple of Mithras. There she recovered documents filled with information about the order's methods—critical intelligence that she eventually passed on to me. By crippling the order's operations in Wincestre, Eivor helped us put the vile organization on the run in England! Only Hamtunscire remained as a shire where we Hidden Ones did not yet have the upper hand.

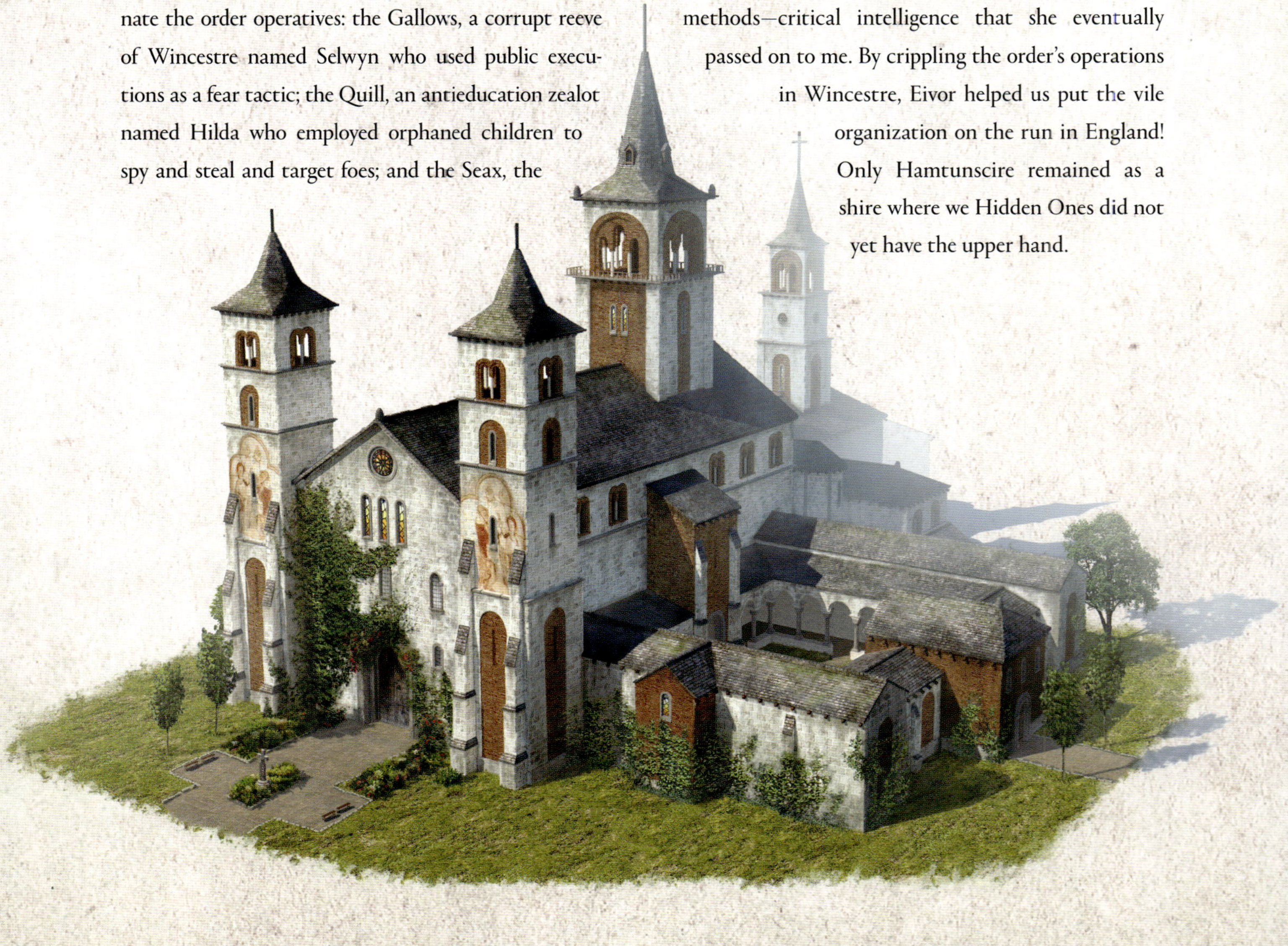

HORDAFYLKE

IN THE HALL OF THE SLAIN

Here, I must insert Eivor's account of an excursion whose details I find not only unsettling but also, frankly, hard to believe. Having observed Sigurd almost daily here in Ravensthorpe since his return from captivity, I was well aware of the young jarl's moody and erratic behavior. But a few weeks ago, Eivor visited my bureau to report that Sigurd, gripped in a fit of sparkle-eyed mania, had convinced her to ferry him back to Norway. Sigurd insisted he had something magnificent to show his adoptive sibling—a path to Valhalla, he claimed! Soon after they departed, my mentor Basim learned of the trip and rushed off to join them in Norway. I was happy to hear he would be there to oversee this expedition.

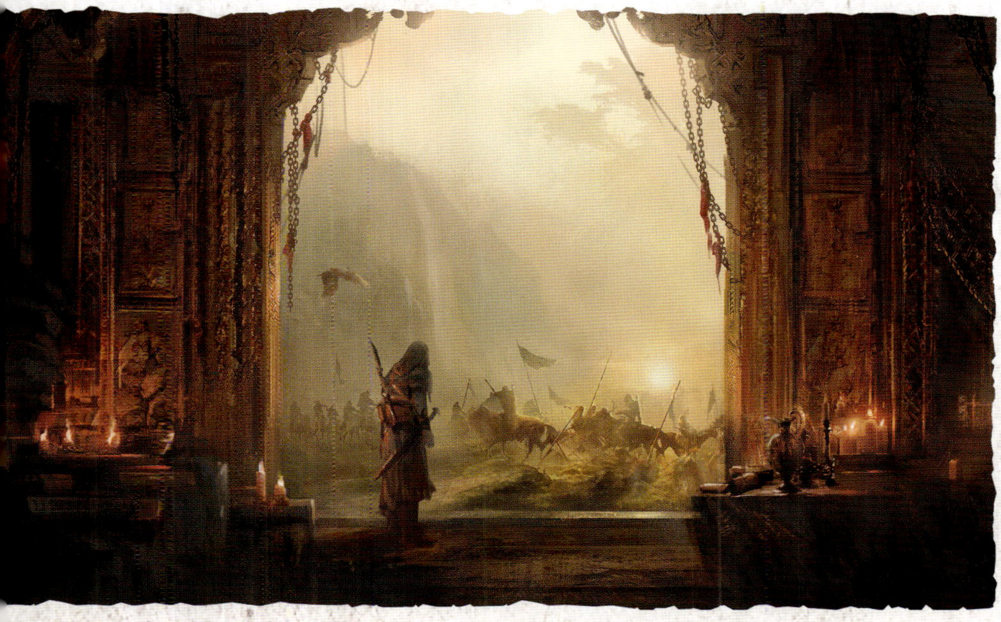

KEY EVENTS

Here, unredacted, is what Eivor reported on her return: Upon arriving in Alrekstad, Sigurd and Eivor paid a perfunctory visit to their father Styrbjorn in a local pub. Then came a frigid sail up Hordafylke's icy northeast fjord. Led by Sigurd's memory of his visions, the two trekked up a perilous mountain path to a cavern known as Goinnhellir. The cave's passage led to a massive stone gate of unknown origin that, according to Eivor—and I have no reason to doubt her—opened to a spoken password! Inside they found some sort of towering, tree-like mechanism that seized them both, rendering them unconscious.

This is where the story gets truly fantastical.

Eivor claims she woke in Valhalla—a vast hall with rolling battlefields beyond, filled with Viking warriors. These were the legendary Einherjar, great champions killed in battle, then escorted by Valkyries to Asgard's hall of the slain to commune with the gods in an exhilarating and endless cycle of feasting and fighting. In Viking lore, it is said this mystical existence continues until all are called to fight in the apocalyptic final battle known as Ragnarök.

But Eivor soon tired of this repetitive dream world, finding it surreal and filled with unsettling contradictions. She convinced Sigurd to escape with her. But her exit was blocked by the All-father himself, Odin, angry king of the Norse pantheon. Eivor claims Odin attacked her in a dark arena . . . and she escaped Odin's wrath only to find their exit blocked by none other than Basim, who had tracked them into the cavern.

For all the insanity of Eivor's tale, this is the part I find most shocking. She insists that Basim threatened Sigurd's life, blade to throat. She said my master was cruel, brutal, even maniacal, spouting nonsense like an alehouse drunk . . . all the while raving about seeking vengeance for his son. In the end, Eivor defeated Basim, tethered him to the machine tree, and left him behind.

Son? I knew nothing of this. In all our many years together, Basim never spoke of such a thing!

Hamtunscire, Wessex

THE PROPHECIES OF THE KING

Guthrum Jarl and his war bands descended on Hamtunscire to seize the last shire in Anglo-Saxon England not under Viking control . . . and thus squeeze King Aelfred of Wessex from the regional picture. War seemed imminent, but Guthrum called a parley with Aelfred in Werham—a last attempt to hammer out an acceptable accord. Aelfred had offered a Danegeld (a hefty ransom of silver) to Guthrum to leave Werham, and the Dane accepted. But as Aelfred exited the hall, he reported—in a mocking tone, according to those present—that Ubba Ragnarsson had been killed by West Saxon forces in north Hamtunscire. Enraged by this news, Guthrum's troops went on a rampage, pillaging Werham as Aelfred and his entourage escaped to his stronghold in Chepeham.

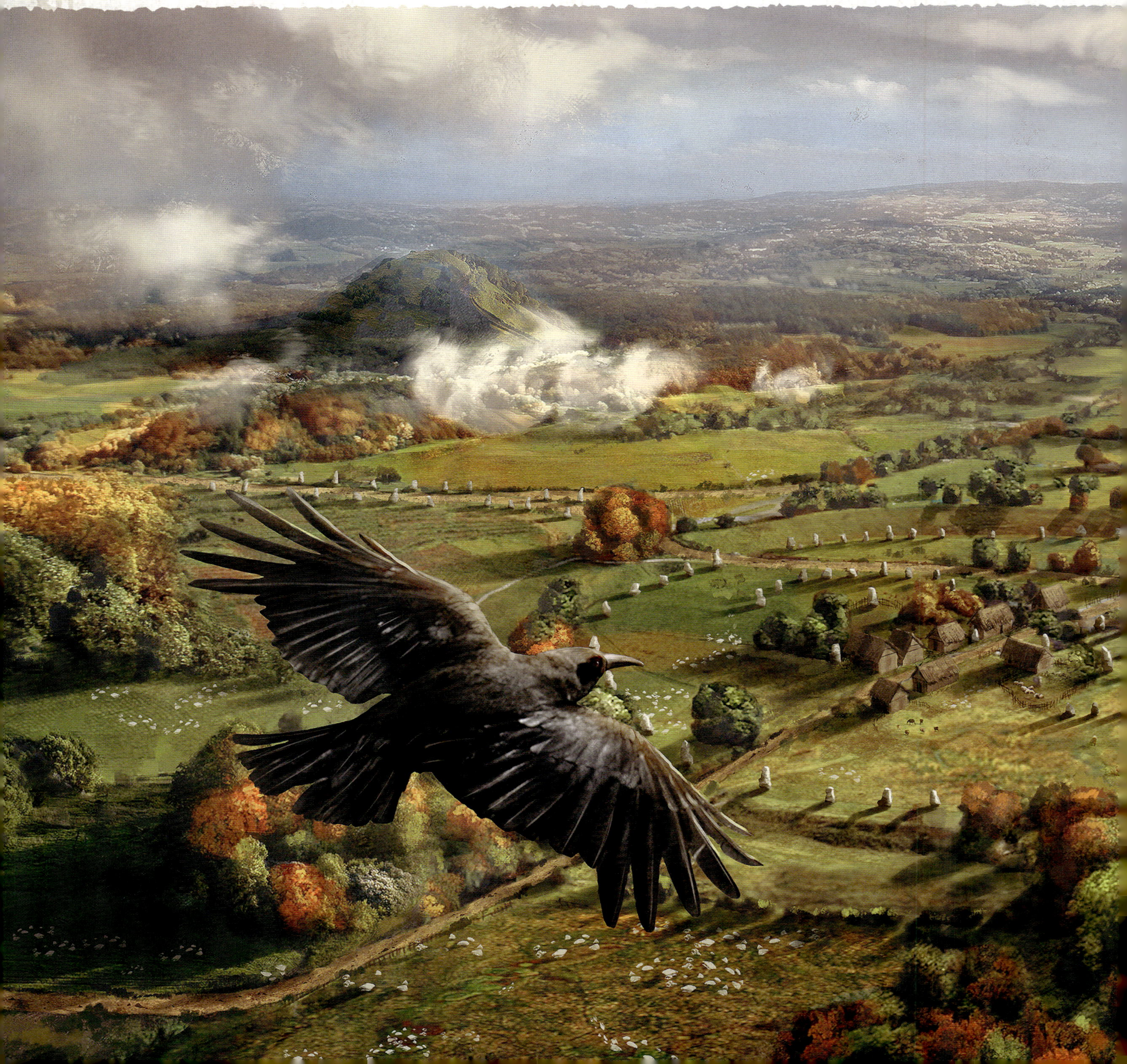

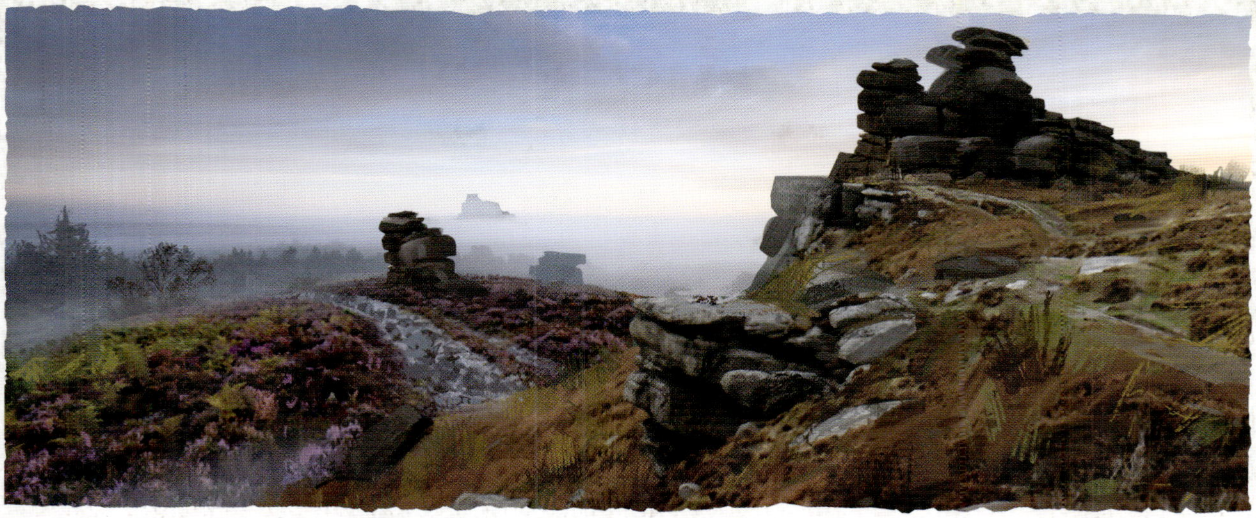

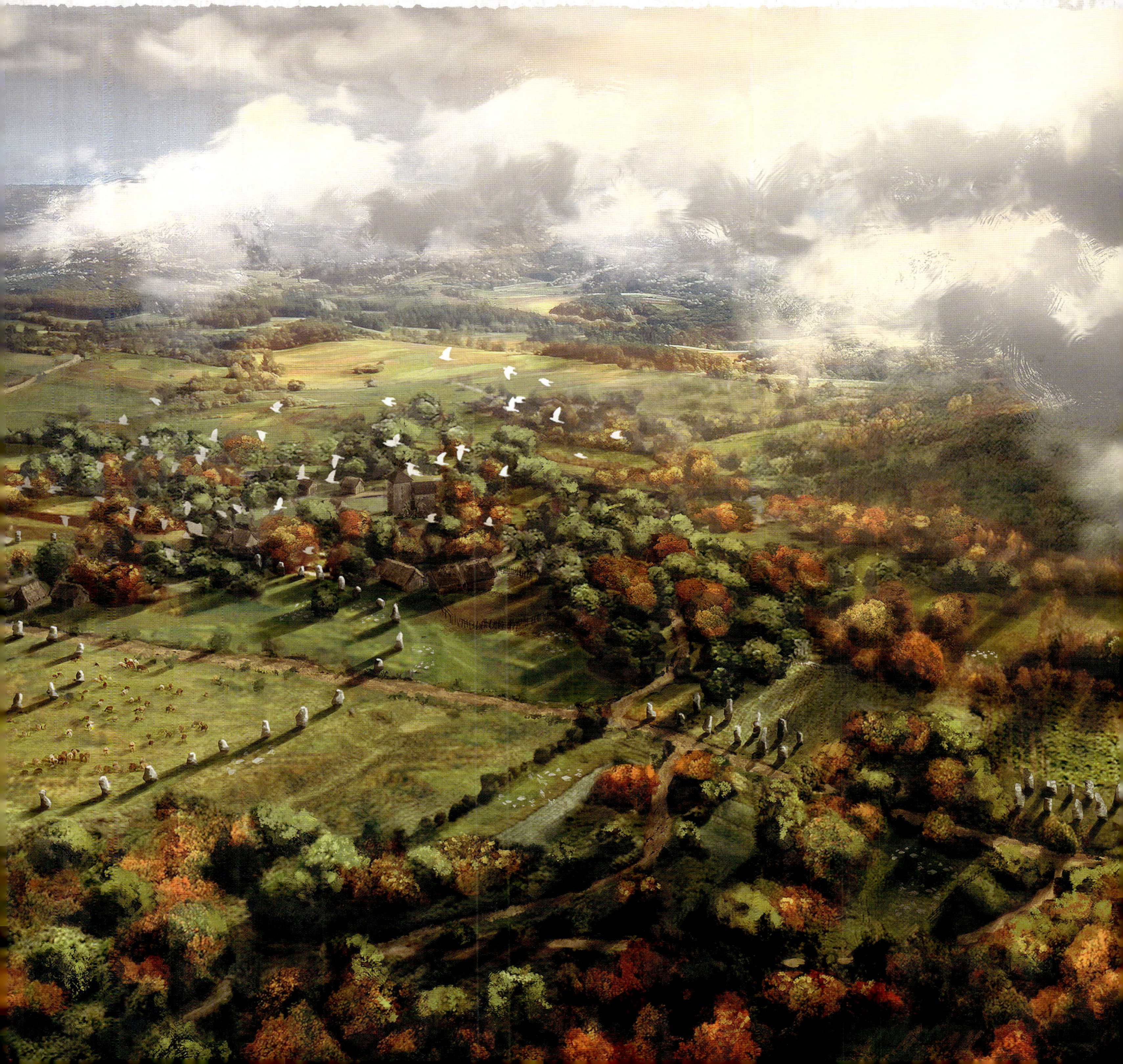

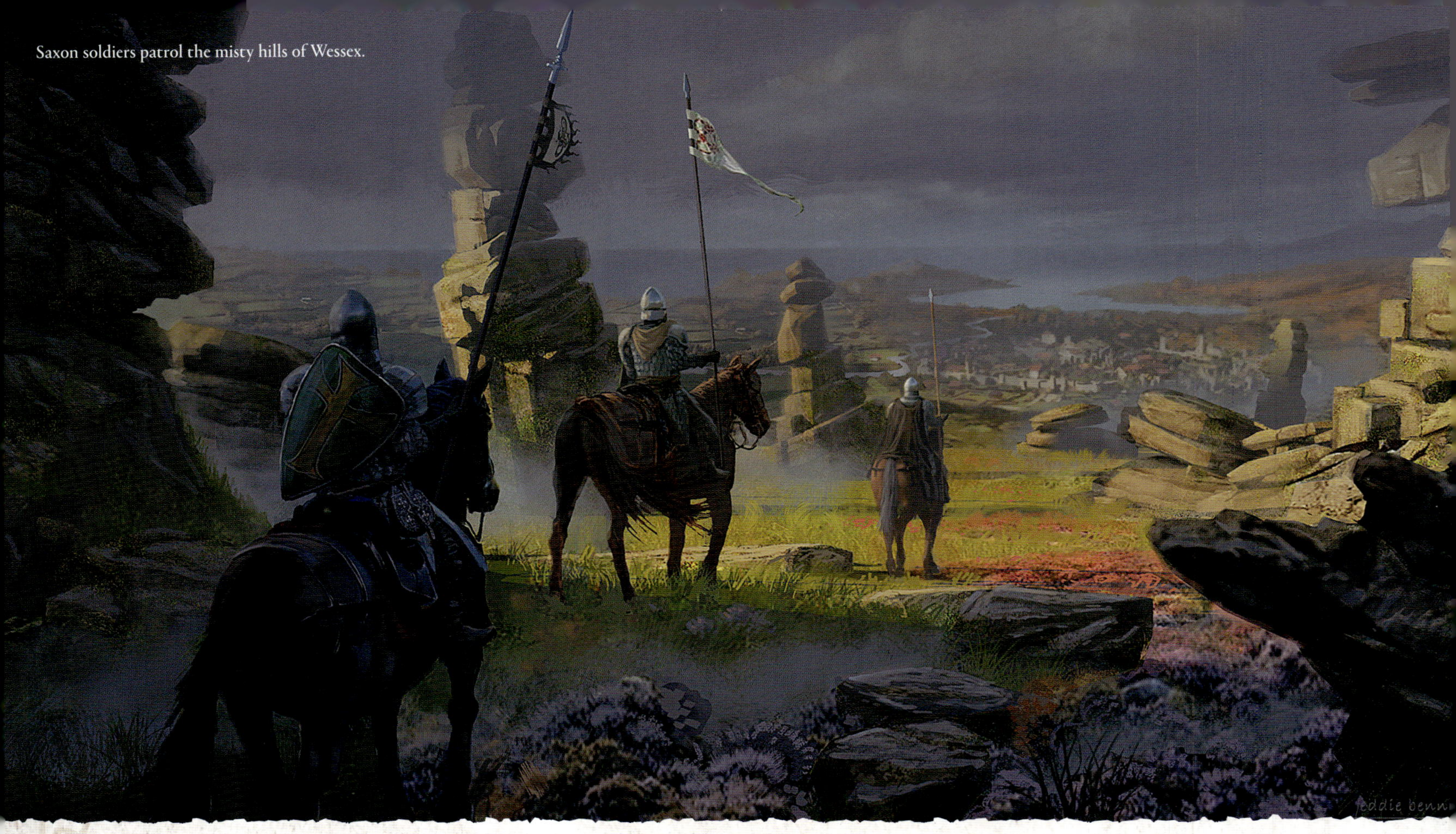

Saxon soldiers patrol the misty hills of Wessex.

KEY EVENTS

While Guthrum mustered his fighters at the river outside Chepeham, Eivor called in favors from across the kingdoms of England, bringing in fighters both Dane and Saxon alike. Then she joined Guthrum in leading a mighty assault on the West Saxon township. It was a terrible battle—Eivor lost good allies and friends, including Hjorr, young Hunwald, and the great warrior Soma Jarlskona. But Guthrum emerged victorious in the end, and a new rule came to Wessex.

Aelfred, however, managed to slink away—a king without a kingdom, or so it seemed.

AN EPILOGUE IN AETHELNAY

The battle of Chepeham in January 878 CE did not end Eivor's work in England. Her clan's political and military influence was now profound; Raven allies ruled every shire in all four Anglo-Saxon kingdoms. Yet ongoing was Eivor's profound commitment to the task of purging the Order of the Ancients and lending support to our creed—this despite Basim's apparent betrayal in Norway.

After Chepeham, Eivor took up the task of hunting down the remaining members of the order—every zealot, preost, palatinus, and maegester known to be operating in England. Eventually, our trove of accumulated clues led Eivor to the very top of the order's

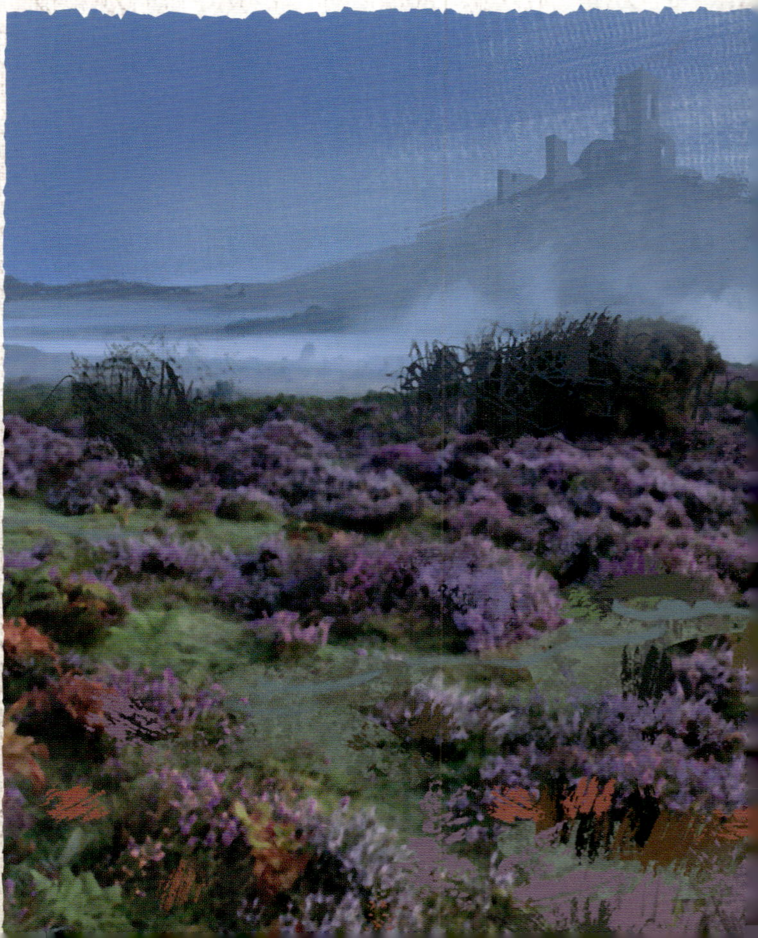

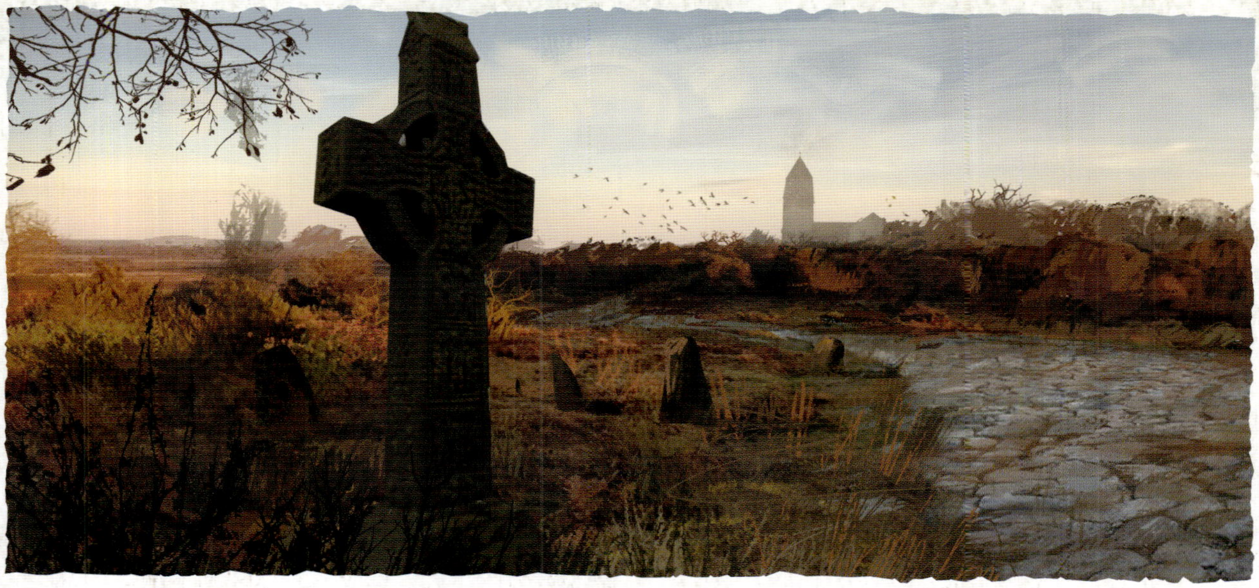

hierarchy, the man who directed the order's operations in Britain: the Father.

She found him in Aethelnay, a sleepy West Saxon town nestled in the boggy fenlands of western Hamtunscire. The grand maegester of the Order of the Ancients was none other than Aelfred of Wessex himself! Living now in exile as a commoner, Aelfred offered Eivor another shocking revelation—he was also our Poor Fellow-Soldier of Christ, the cryptic correspondent whose clues had helped us eliminate the order's entire hierarchy. Repelled by the order's godless views—he called them "defilers of God's majesty and grandeur"—Aelfred had long worked to destroy the heresy from the inside, hoping to construct a new "God-fearing" organization in its place.

As Aelfred handed Eivor his order medallion, he described the envisioned replacement: "A greater idea, a universal, divine order, insp red by God for the betterment of man." Then he gave Eivor the key to his study in Wincestre, a place he insinuated might be laden with secrets interesting to those of us who've fought tooth and nail against the Order of the Ancients for so long.

Lord Aelfred's final message was one of warning: "The wars have not ended, Eivor. You have simply stopped fighting. But men are brewing plots, in mead halls and bedrooms. You wi l see."

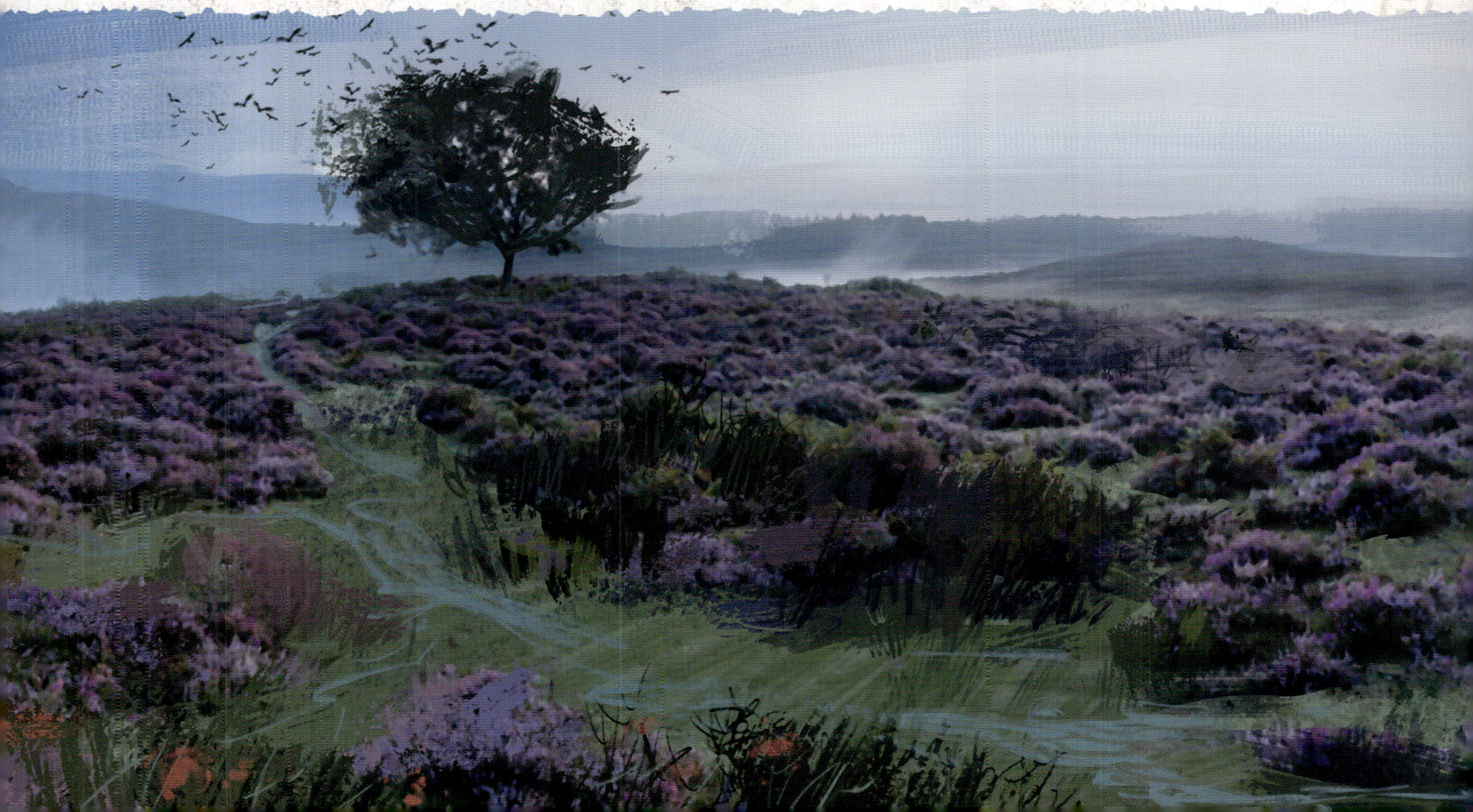

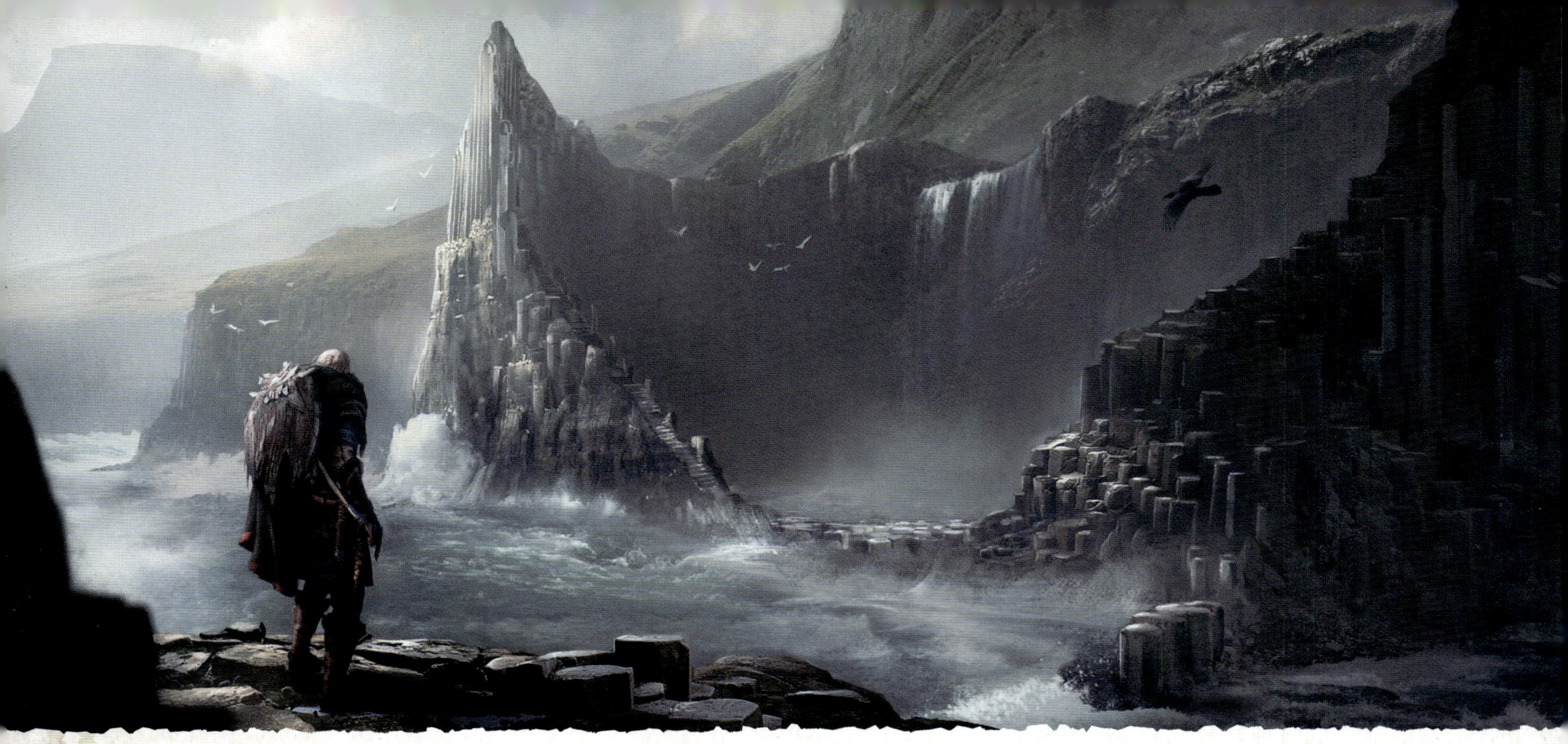

Ireland

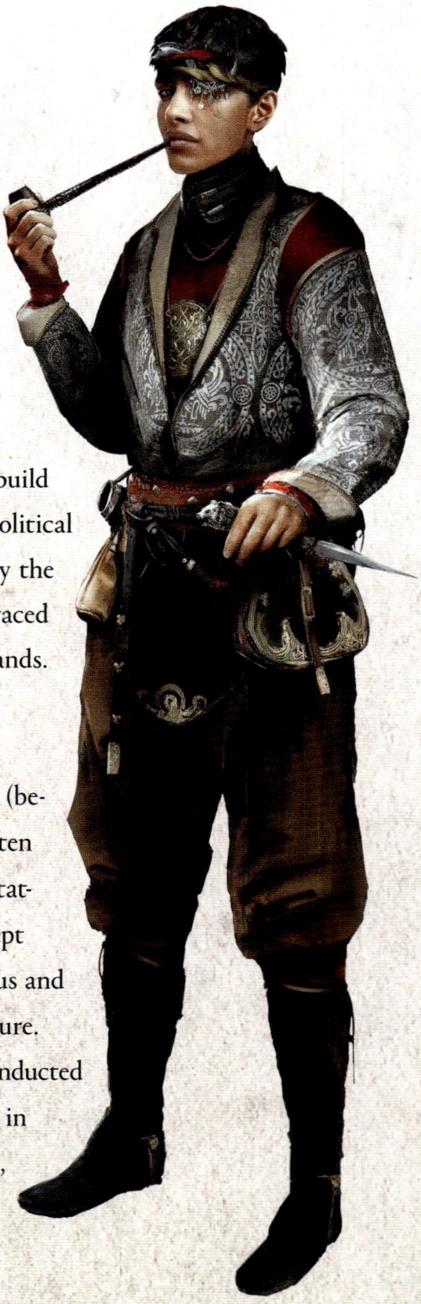

During my stay at Ravensthorpe, I met a savvy Persian merchant named Azar. Like me, Azar had left the Abbasid Caliphate for Europe. Her own travels led to Ireland, where she ended up a trusted trade emissary for the king of Dublin, Bárid mac Ímair. The two shared a passion for mercantile pursuits, and together they sought to develop Dublin into a regional trading hub. As it turned out, King Bárid was also a long-lost Norse cousin of Eivor Wolf-kissed! After Eivor helped Azar erect a trading post for Irish goods in Ravensthorpe, the two sailed across the Irish Sea to meet Bárid in Dublin.

Eivor's overall challenge in Ireland proved to be twofold: help Bárid and Azar build a booming Dublin-centered trade network while also navigating Ireland's tricky political maze of jealous kings, north and south. These tasks were further complicated by the insurgent menace of the Children of Danu, a cult of radicalized zealots who embraced their native druidic roots that had otherwise long since been abandoned in Irish lands.

MAJOR FACTIONS & SECTS

THE IRISH

For many years, the northern and southern branches of Ireland's dominant Uí Néill dynasty shared the Irish high kingship, trading it back and forth. Whenever in power, the northern Uí Néill ruled out of Ulster, and the southern Uí Néill ruled from Meath. Eventually (because power so often corrupts), this "rotating throne" concept became contentious and even bloody in nature.

Vikings had conducted hit-and-run raids in Ireland for decades, but eventually larger war bands arrived looking to conquer territory. As a result, the feuding Irish factions temporarily allied under a high king named Áed Findliath to fend off the Norse invaders. Once the pagans were stalemated—the Vikings in Ireland were not as well organized as those in England, and the Irish are fierce fighters in their own right—the north-south struggle for the high throne resumed.

The current high king of Ireland is Flann Sinna of the southern Uí Néill. He has forged a fearsome army from a unique mix of Irish natives and warriors from local Viking clans.

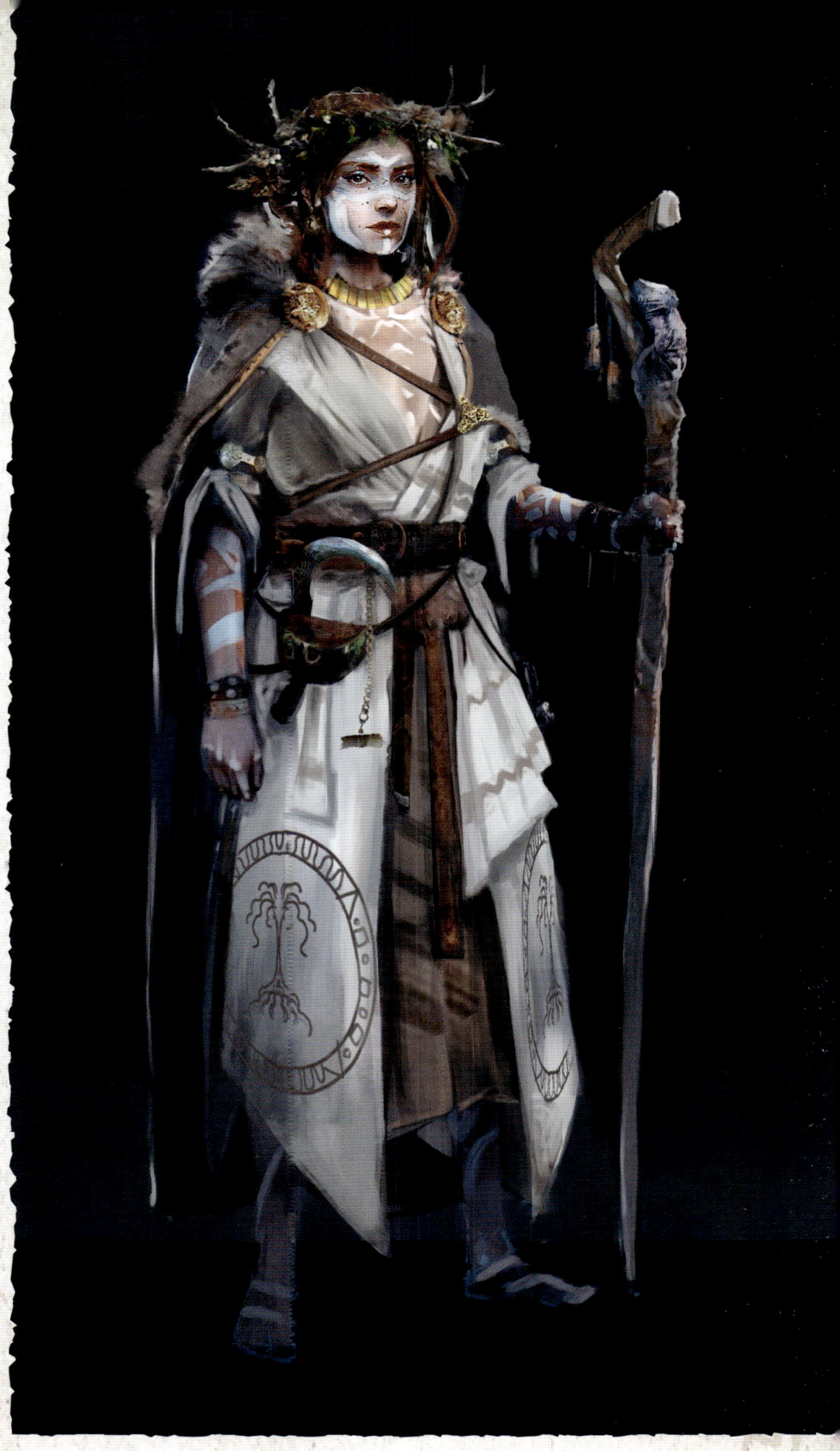

CHILDREN OF DANU

This fanatical death cult is hell bent on scrubbing Christianity from Ireland and restoring the druidic traditions of their Gaelic ancestors. They worship the Irish goddess Danu of the Tuatha Dé Danann, a pre-Christian pantheon of Gaelic deities associated with burial sites like the Boyne tombs. Seemingly infused with a strange, often toxic brew of Ireland's fogs and fen mists, the Danu cult has immersed itself in the darker aspects of Gaelic paganism—torture, human sacrifice, necromancy, and the summoning of murderous spirits. Eivor has made it a primary mission to track and assassinate every one of these twisted cultists—not unlike her vendetta against the Order of the Ancients!

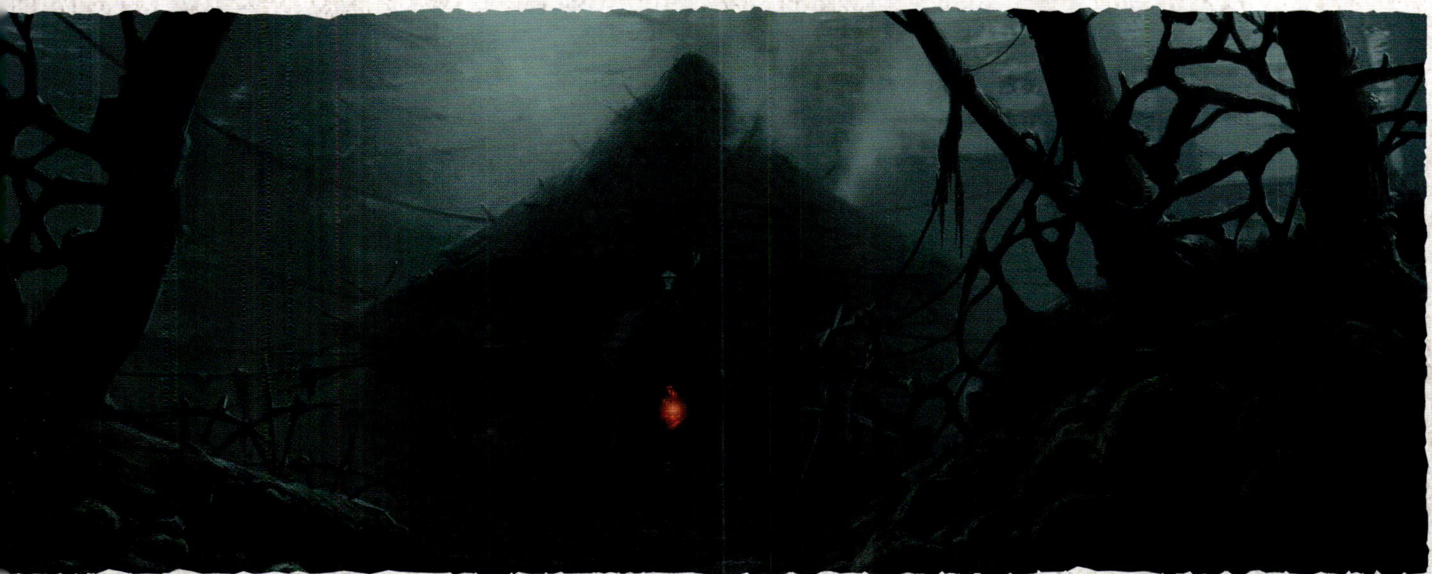

DUBLIN

In Dublin, Eivor discovered that her cousin Bárid had big plans indeed. His ambition was to impress Ireland's preeminent leader, Flann Sinna, who would soon be crowned high king—a man who, unfortunately, distrusted Vikings. Bárid hoped to secure his own tenuous kingship in Dublin by tethering his growing trade network to the high king's economic interests. As he told Eivor: "Flann will see that the strength of Dublin's ports is the strength of Ireland." It was a sound scheme, certainly. But it would require some aggressive commercial expansion and a bit of muscle. This Eivor would provide.

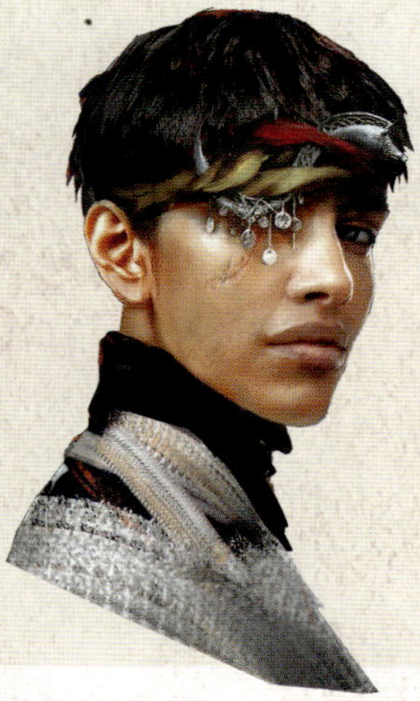

AZAR

Scion of a wealthy family of Persian merchants, Azar developed a remarkable acumen for matters of trade. Seeking to blaze her own trail of success, she set out for Europe. In Ireland, Azar found a kindred spirit in King Bárid and helped build Dublin's reputation as a regional center of commerce.

BÁRID MAC ÍMAIR, KING OF DUBLIN

As a young Viking lad, Bárid came to Dublin, where his father, Ímair, had risen to the throne. Encircled by distrustful Irish natives, the Norse enclave was often under siege. But Bárid's passionate focus on trade and commerce opened doors to surrounding kingdoms and brought him good favor with the high king.

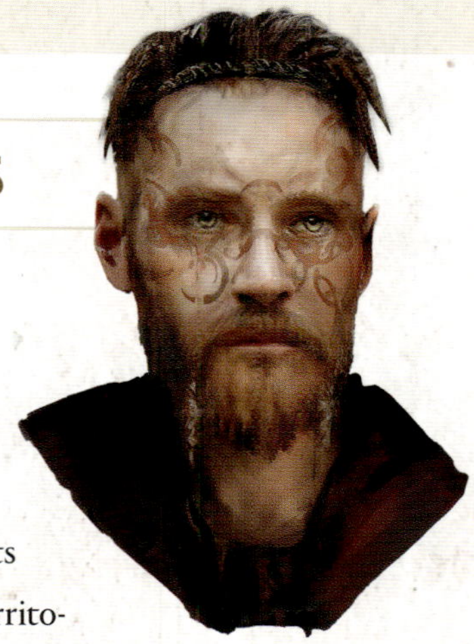

KEY EVENTS

Eivor helped Azar expand Dublin commerce by establishing a trading post at Rathdown. With this post—and later, other posts established in other Irish territories—Bárid's network gained greater access to coveted foreign goods and delicacies. For example: Eivor soon acquired a special gift of exotic spices for Flann Sinna's impending coronation as high king.

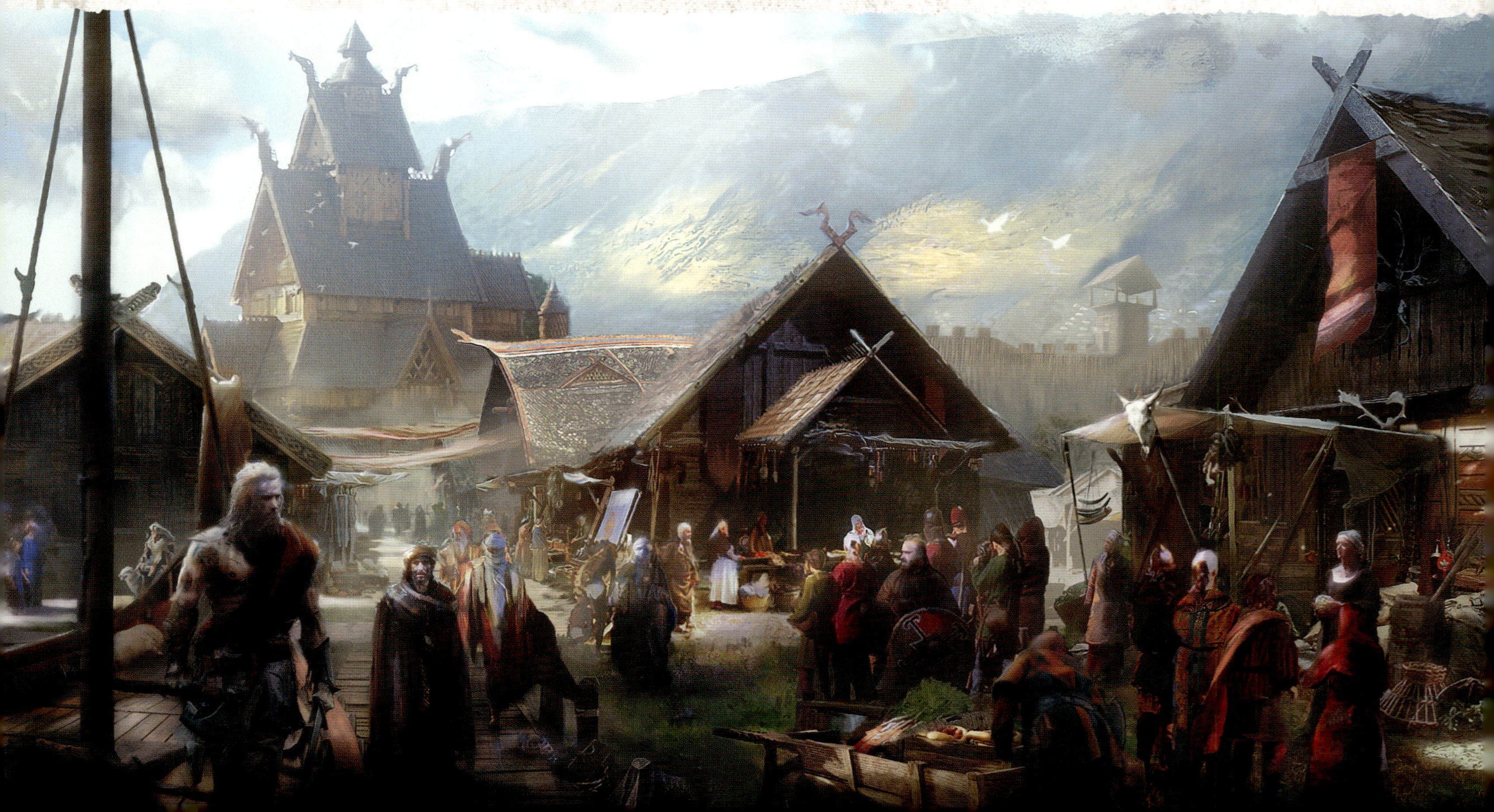

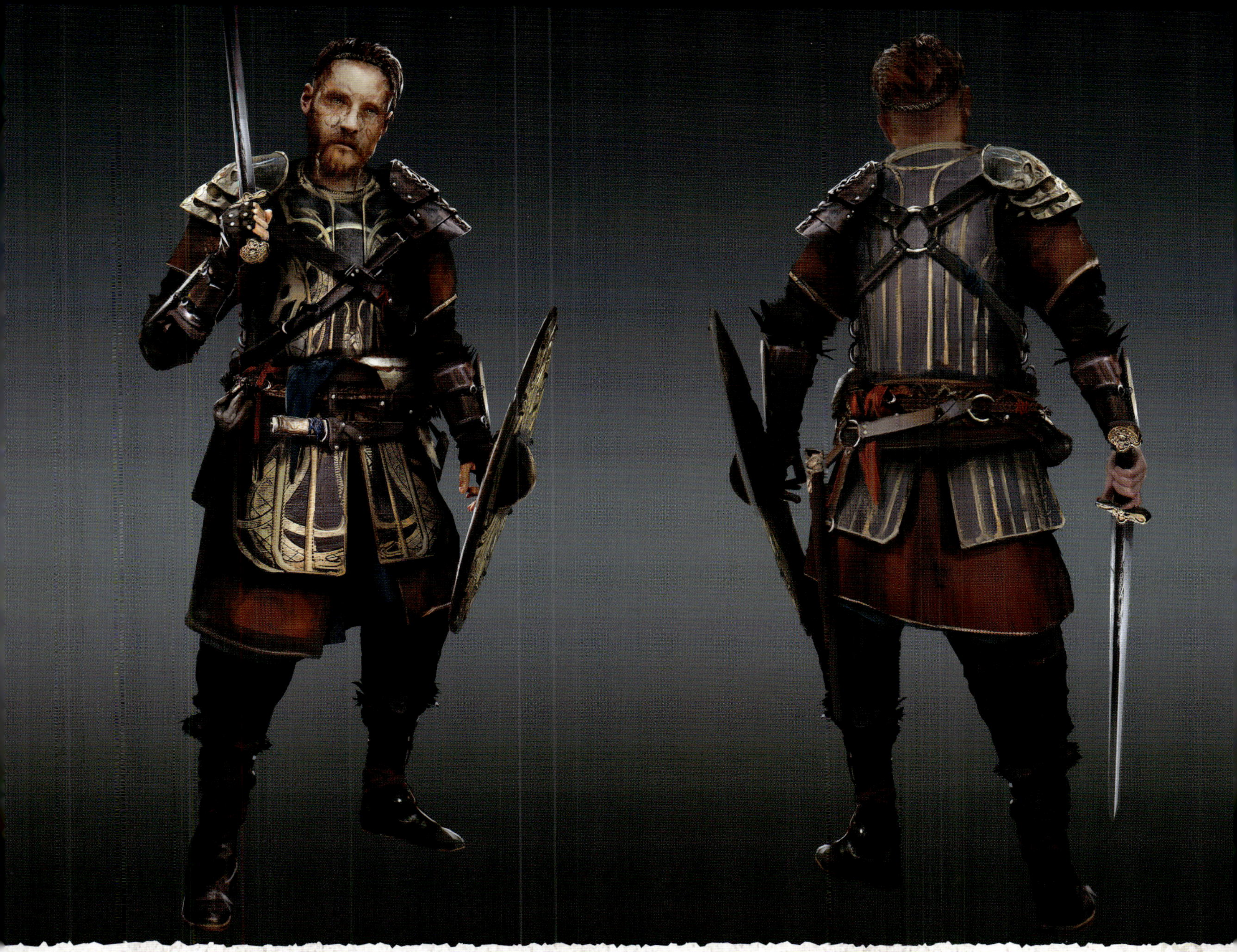

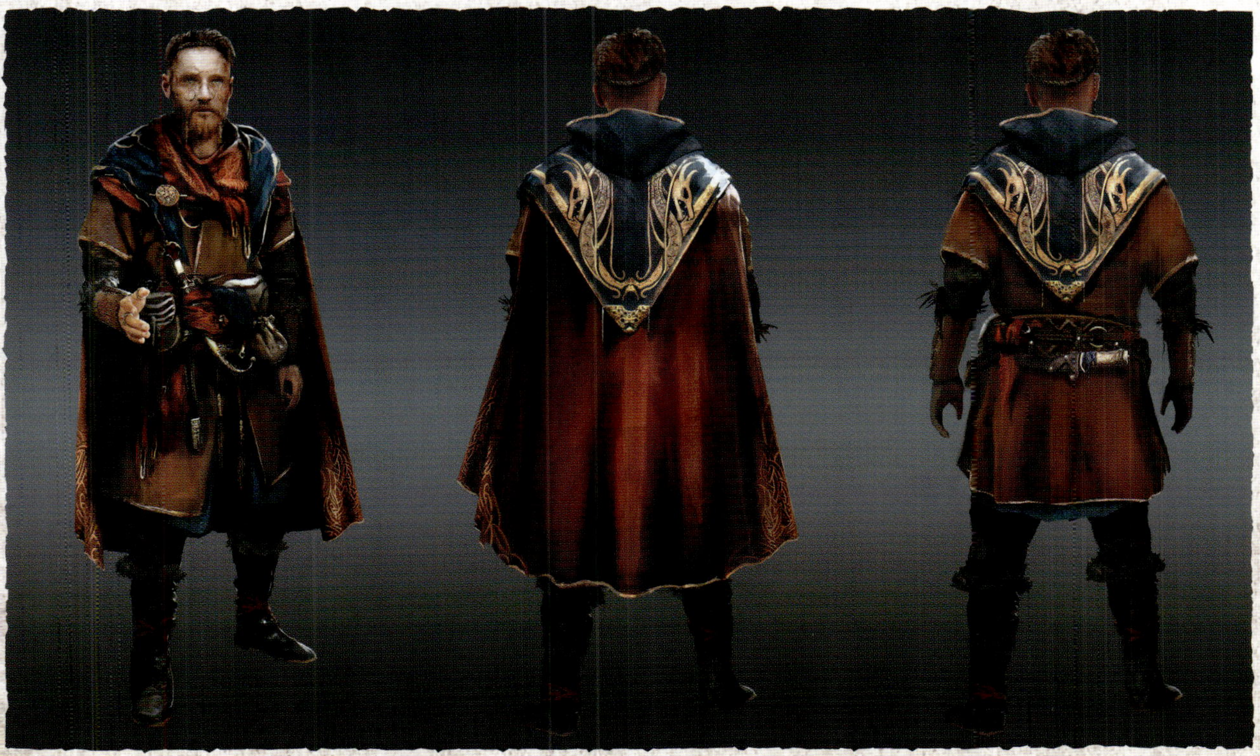

Meath

Eivor traveled with King Bárid and a woman named Ciara, Flann Sinna's court poetess, to the traditional high king coronation site on the Hill of Tara in Meath. Once there, my Viking partner thwarted one assassination attempt on Flann, then retrieved the stolen Book of Kells, a holy text pilfered by Danish thieves. These acts helped endear Bárid to the new high king.

KEY EVENTS

Eivor's next mission was to build support for Flann by currying favor with surrounding kingdoms in Meath. Her goal was to reinforce Flann's army with local troops and supplies, creating a strong counterweight

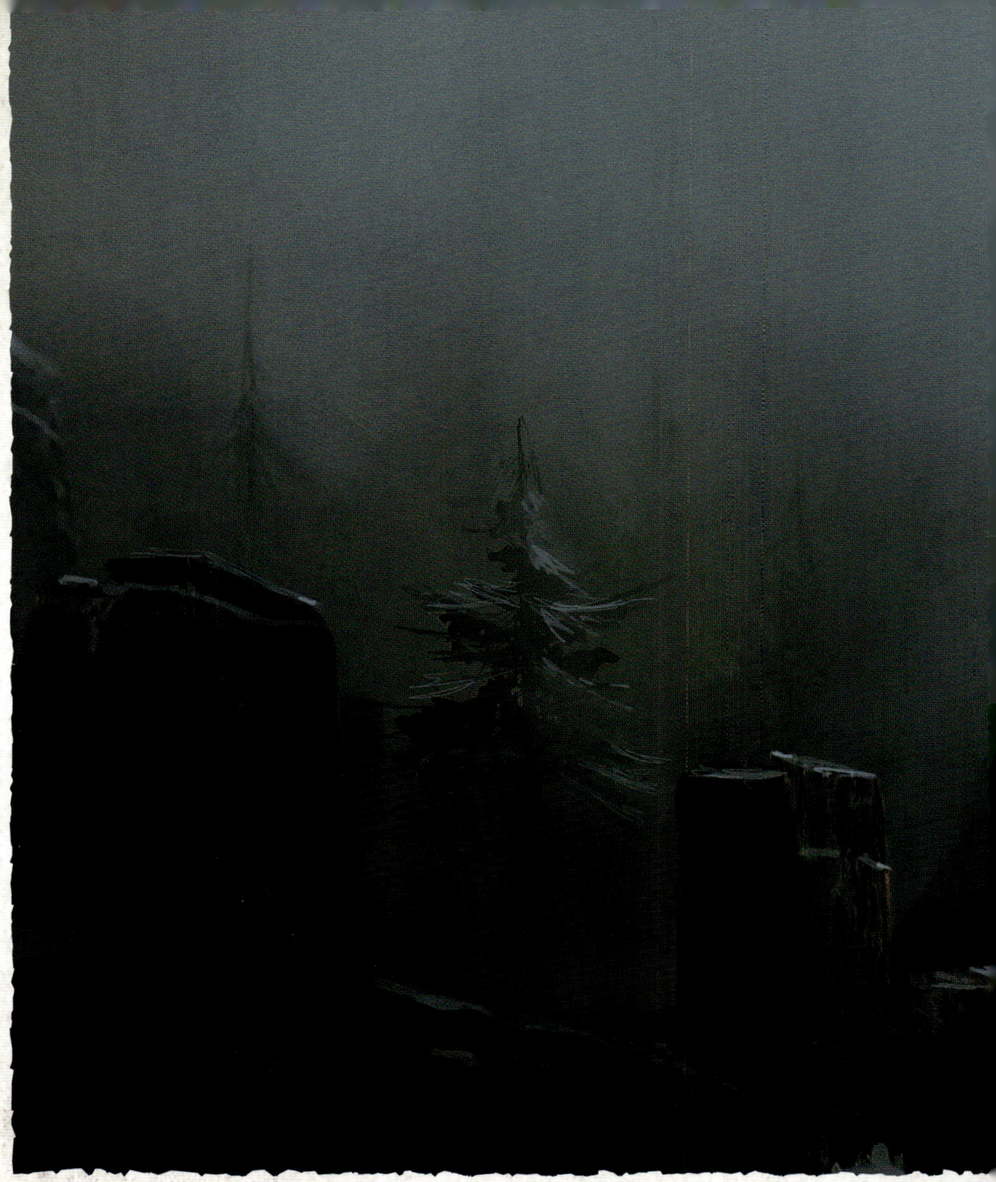

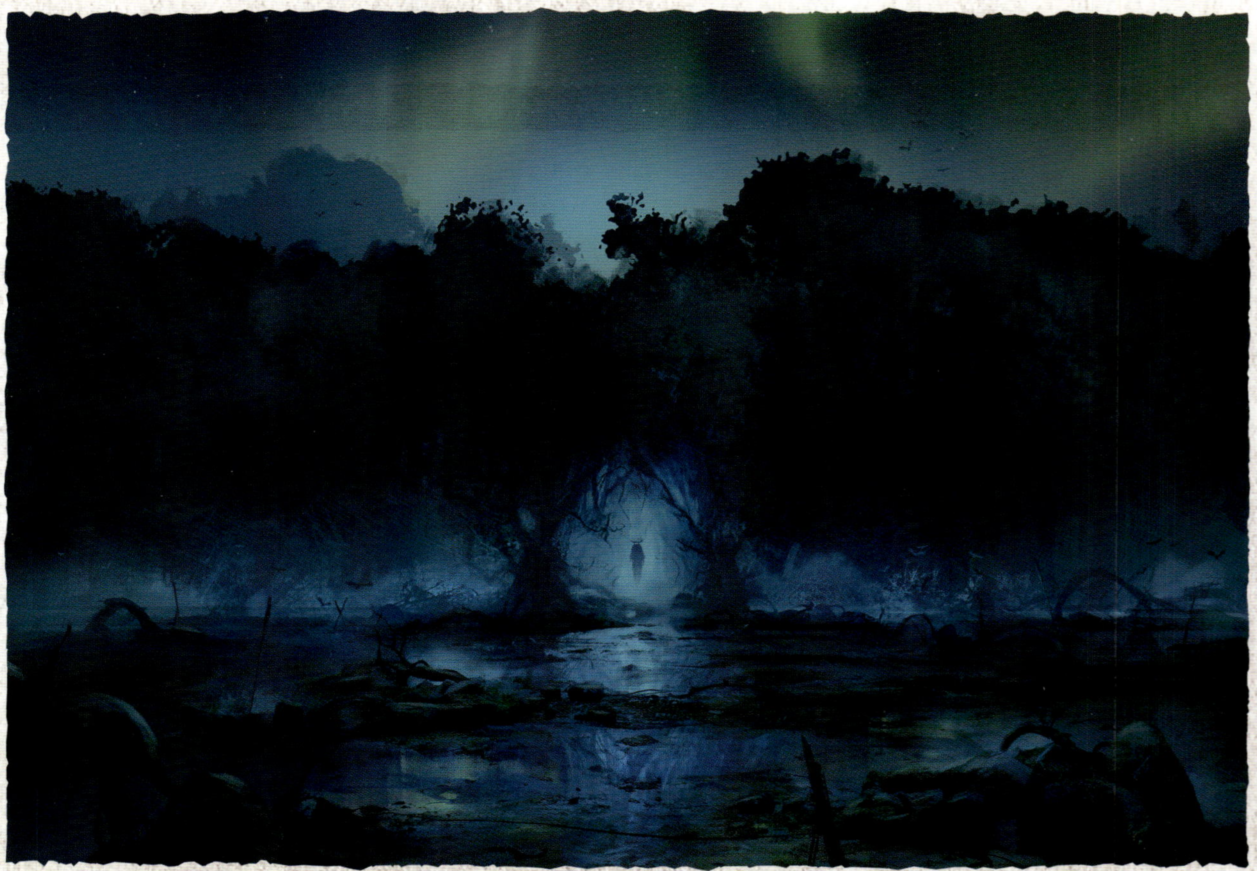

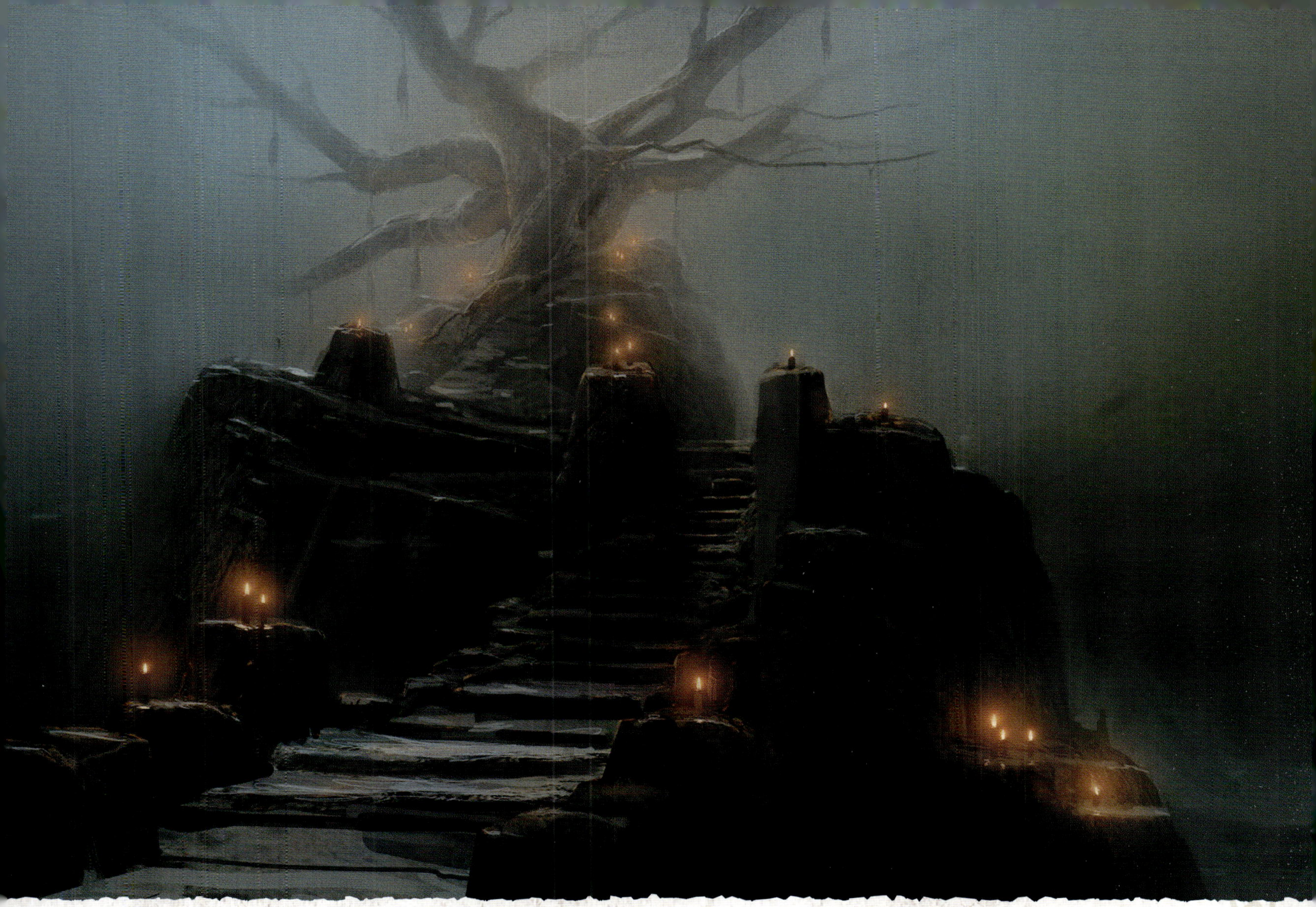

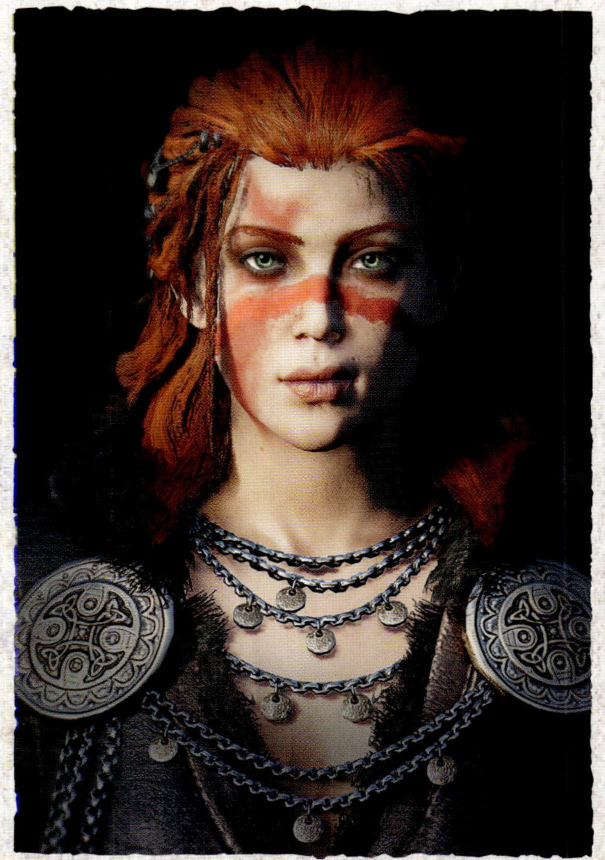

to the impending alliance of hostile Ulster and Connacht. Directed by Ciara, Eivor completed a series of royal demands from local Meath kings; in return, they sent tributes of men and resources to Flann's Southern Army, bivouacked in the town of Knockfree on Meath's western border.

In Knockfree, Eivor met the high king's war council (which now included Báríd) to plan an assault

CIARA INGEN MEDBA

Named as Ollamh Érenn—the "bard of all Ireland"—by the newly crowned High King Flann, Ciara is an important figure in the royal court. Eivor says Ciara's word carries much weight in all matters, not just cultural. Both her bond with the mysterious Lia Fáil monolith and her deep roots in ancient Connacht suggest a close connection to the old druidic ways.

Ciara ingen Medba still proudly bears the trappings of her pagan spirituality.

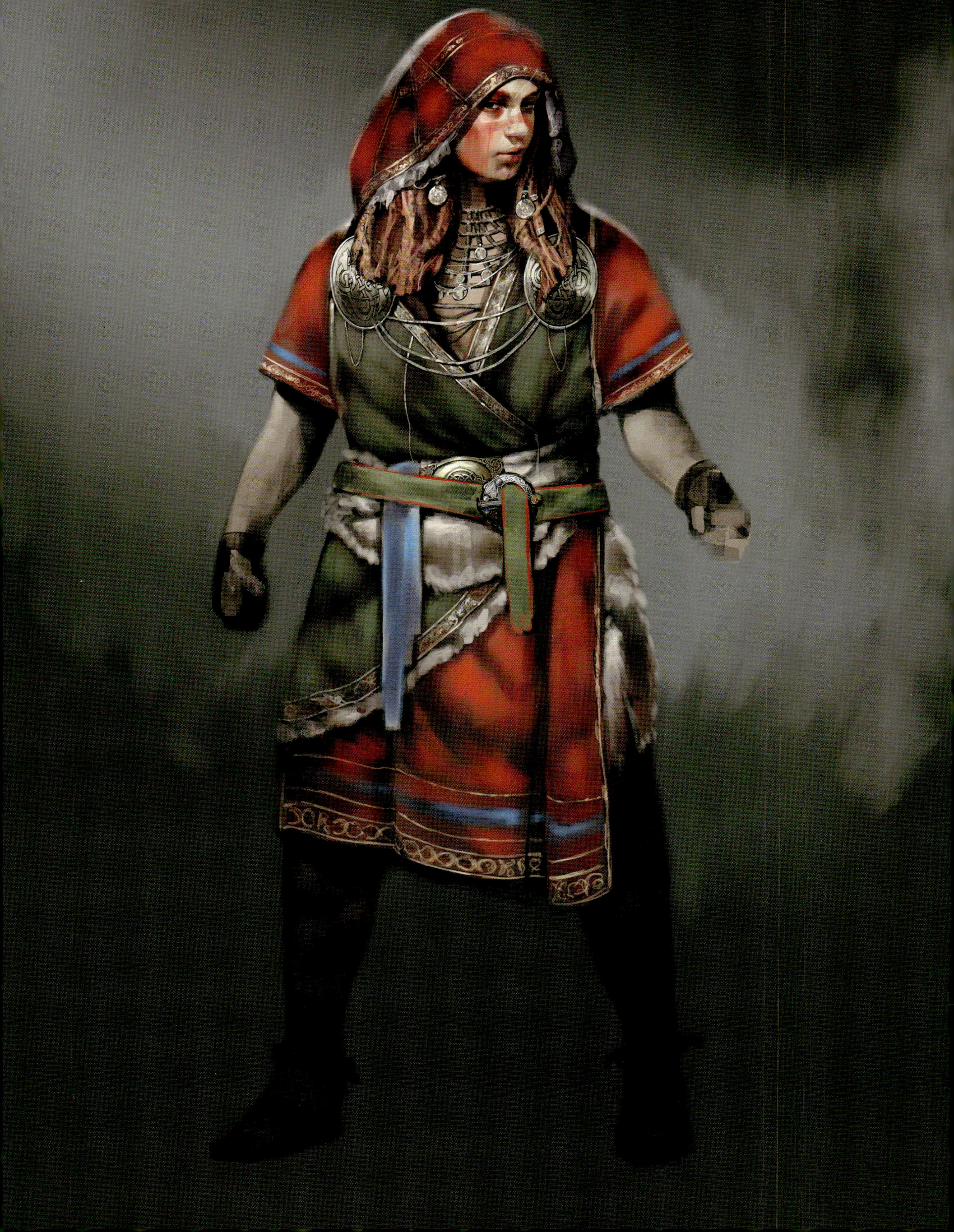

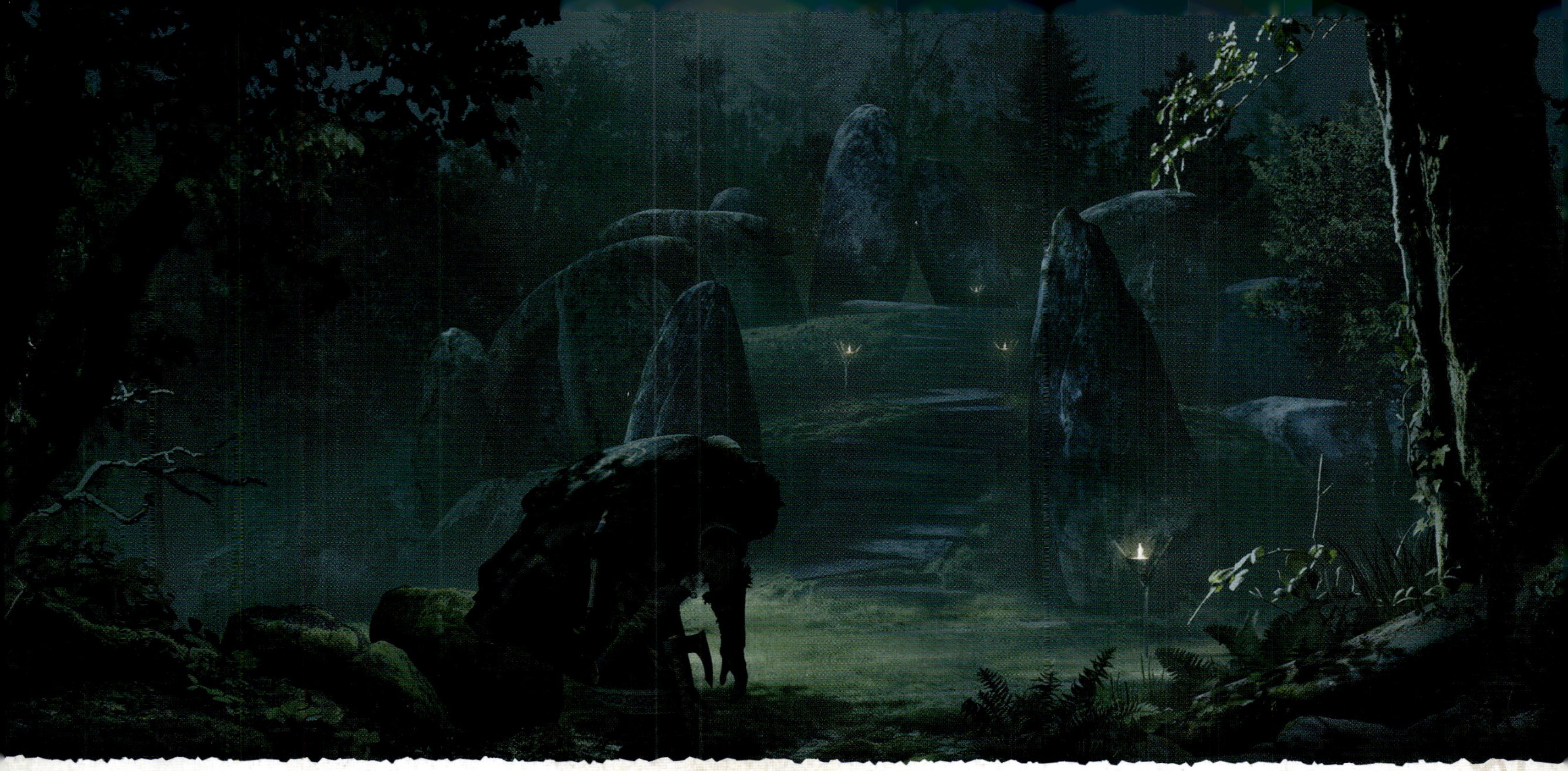

SICHFRITH

Son of Bárid, this defiant lad worships the traditional Viking values of valor and glory in combat. As a result, Sichfrith has trouble recognizing his father's genius in using trade to gain power in regional politics.

against Connacht's forces garrisoned in Cashelore, an imposing stronghold atop the cliffs overlooking the border of Connacht and Ulster. Eivor volunteered for a spy mission to infiltrate the heavily fortified castle and unlock the main gates for Flann's Southern Army to breach.

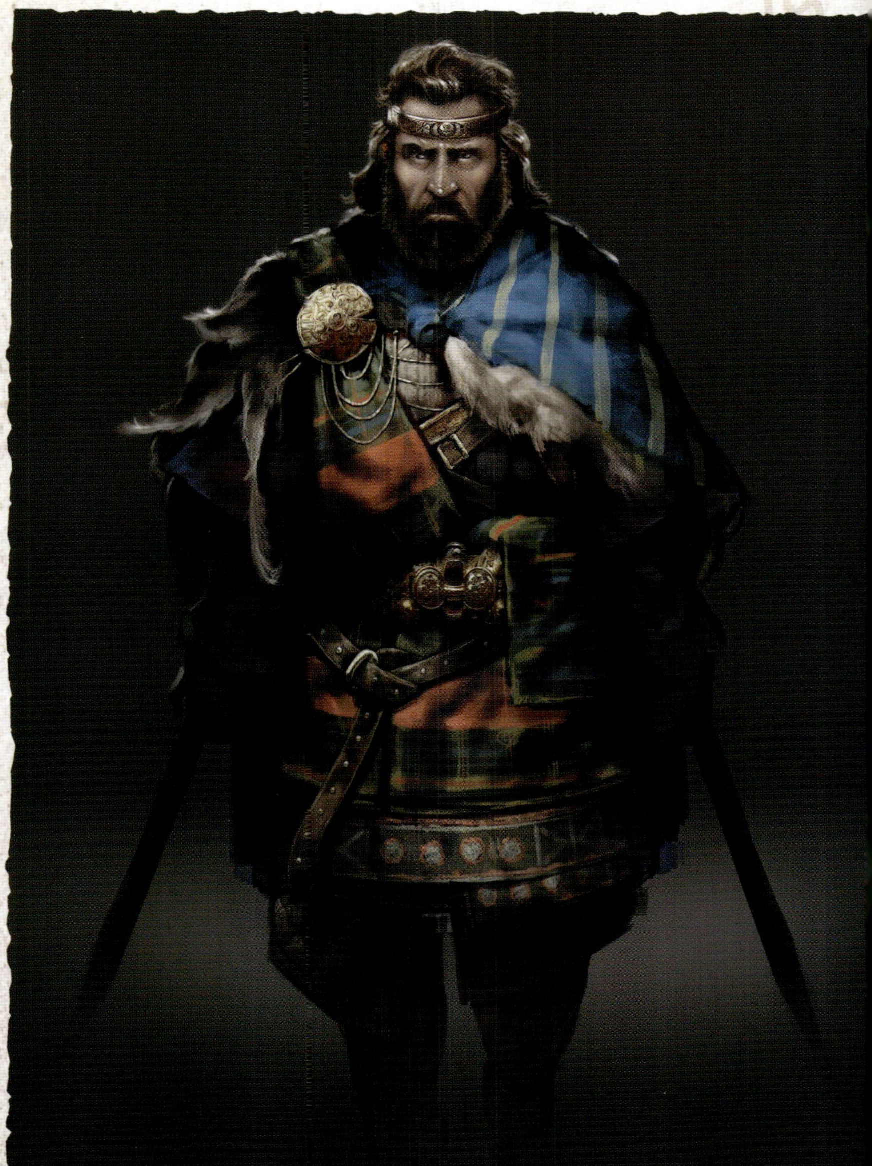

FLANN SINNA, HIGH KING OF IRELAND

Born into the ruling Clan Cholmáin, a familial branch of the southern Uí Néill dynasty, Flann was clearly destined for greatness. He was crowned high king (also called king of Tara) shortly after Eivor's arrival in Ireland. As leader, Flann forged a unique alliance of his southern Uí Néill clansmen with the Viking settlers who remained.

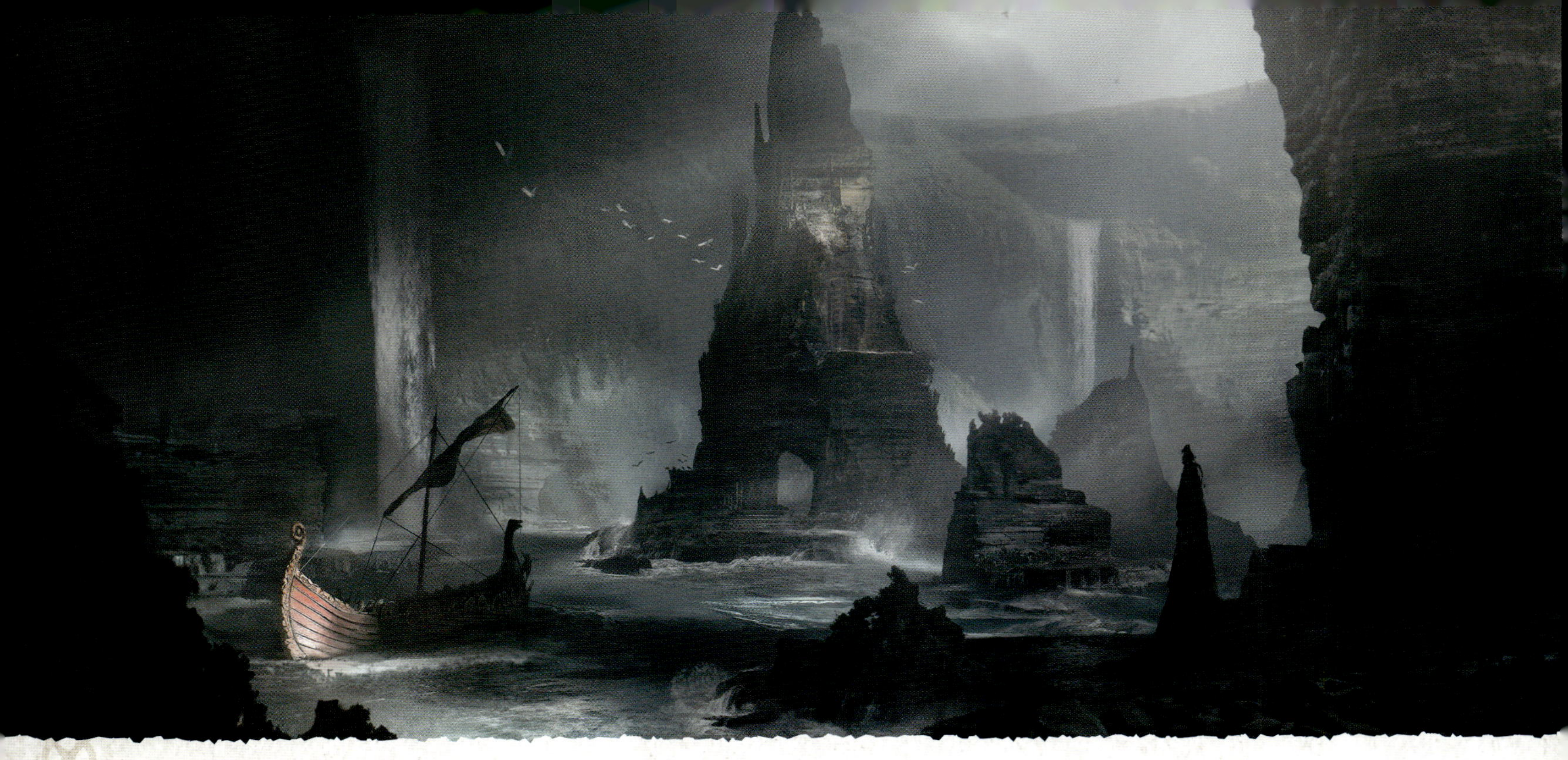

Connacht

Few I've met—even among my Hidden Ones brethren—can match Eivor's stealth and infiltration skills. According to reports I've seen of the engagement, my Raven Clan friend slipped into Cashelore Castle with remarkable ease and threw open the entry portal for Flann's combined Irish-Norse troops. The subsequent assault was a smashing success, with Eivor (as always) spearheading the charge through the twin ringforts of the great fortress.

KEY EVENTS

After routing the Cashelore garrison, the Southern Army's victory was soured by a dire complication—someone had poisoned Flann's Irish troops! Worse, a captured enemy soldier accused the Norseman Bárid of concocting the foul plot. But Ciara knew better—the toxic brew was a favorite of the Children of Danu, the murderous pagan cult. With guidance from Ciara and a druidic healer named Deirdre, Eivor hunted

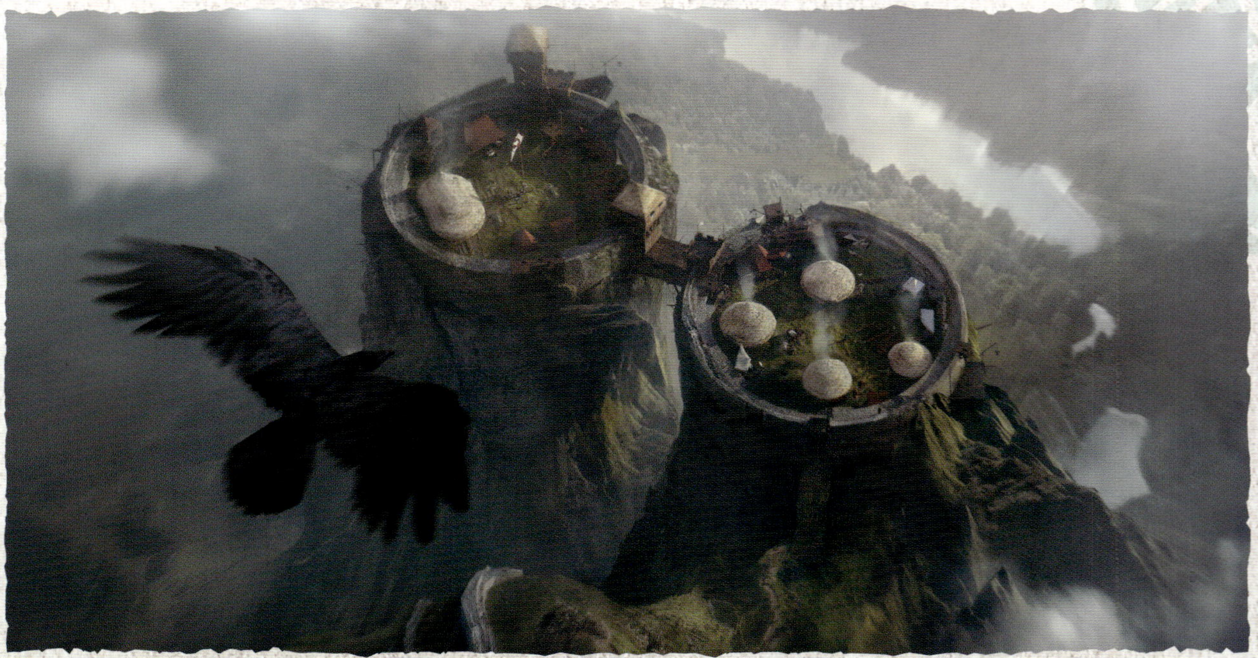

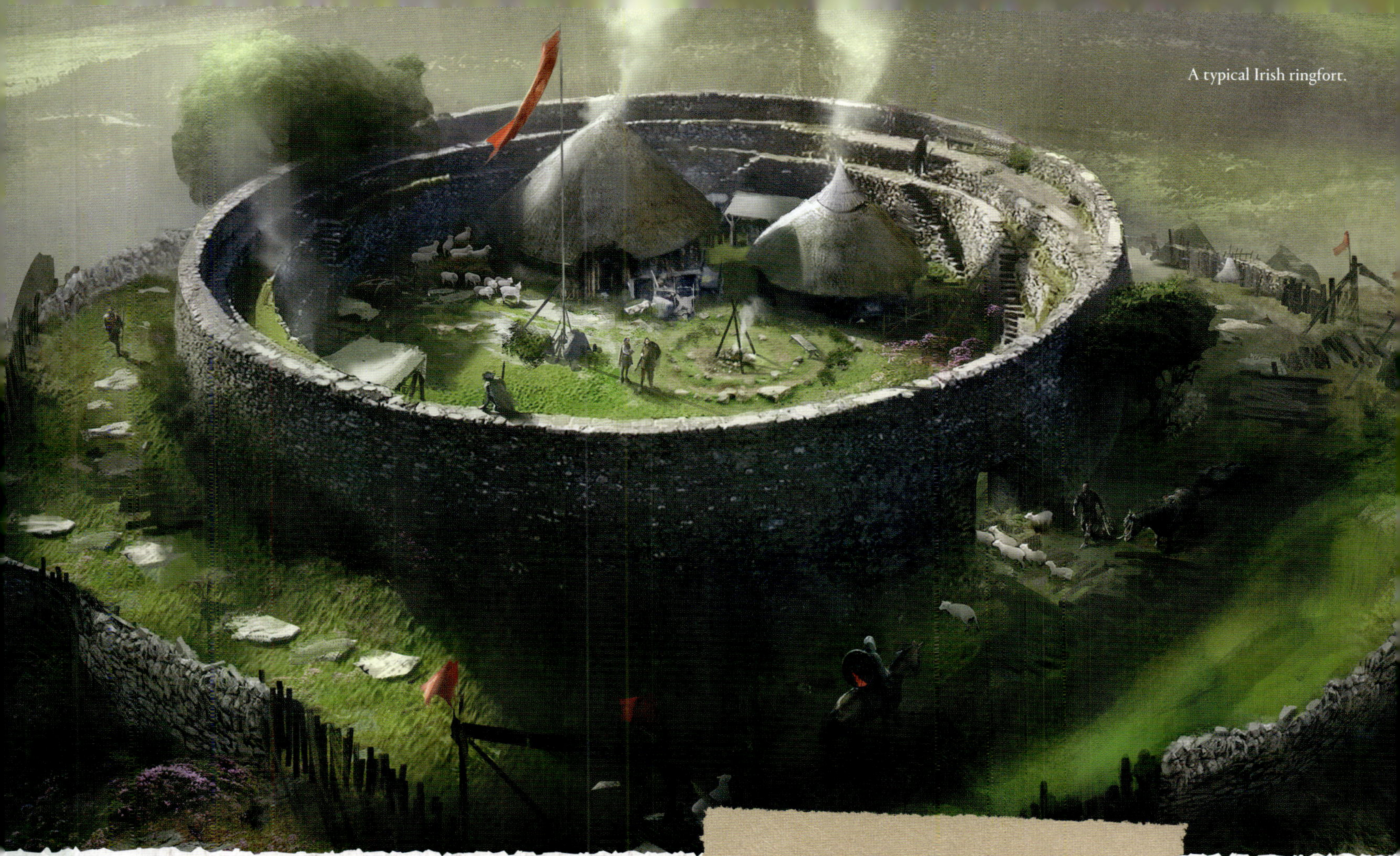

A typical Irish ringfort.

down the ingredients necessary for an antidote that would cure Flann's soldiers.

Back at Cashelore's war room, Eivor joined Bárid and the high king in planning a grand expedition into Ulster—as Flann put it, "the final jewel in my high crown." The target: the ringfort of Aileach, which Bárid called the strongest in all the lands. As Flann announced that his Southern Army would make camp at Clogher, word came that the kings of Aileach sought peace talks. Bárid offered to speak for Flann, and the high king agreed.

PÚCA

During her Irish adventure, Eivor claims to have tracked a supernatural creature called a púca. This beast is said to take many animal forms—Eivor's manifested in the form of a giant, fearsome werewolf! However, she admits her vision may have been twisted by a toxic, disorienting fog known to permeate the forested hills of southern Connacht.

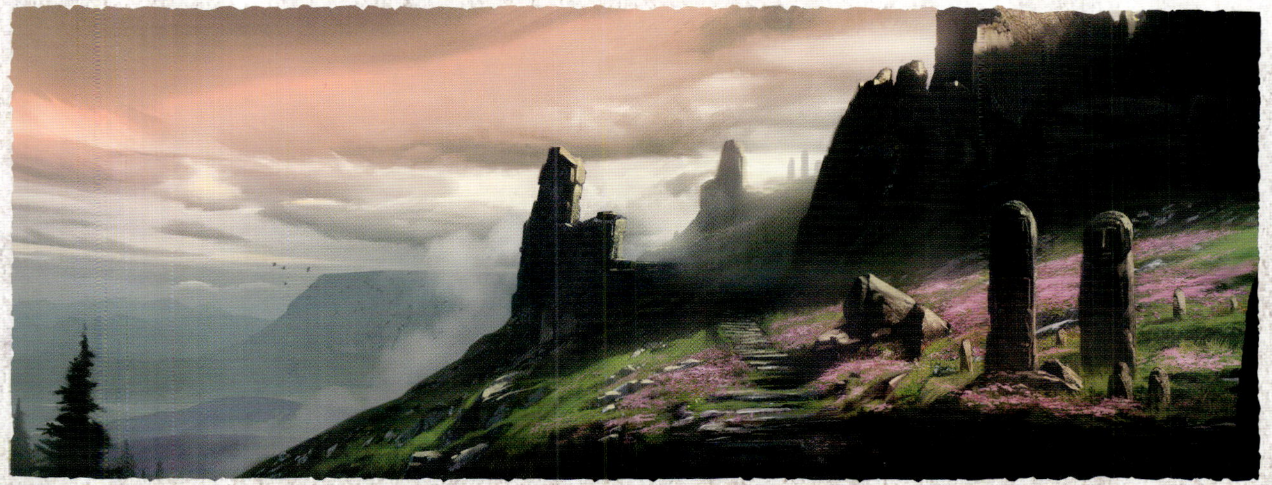

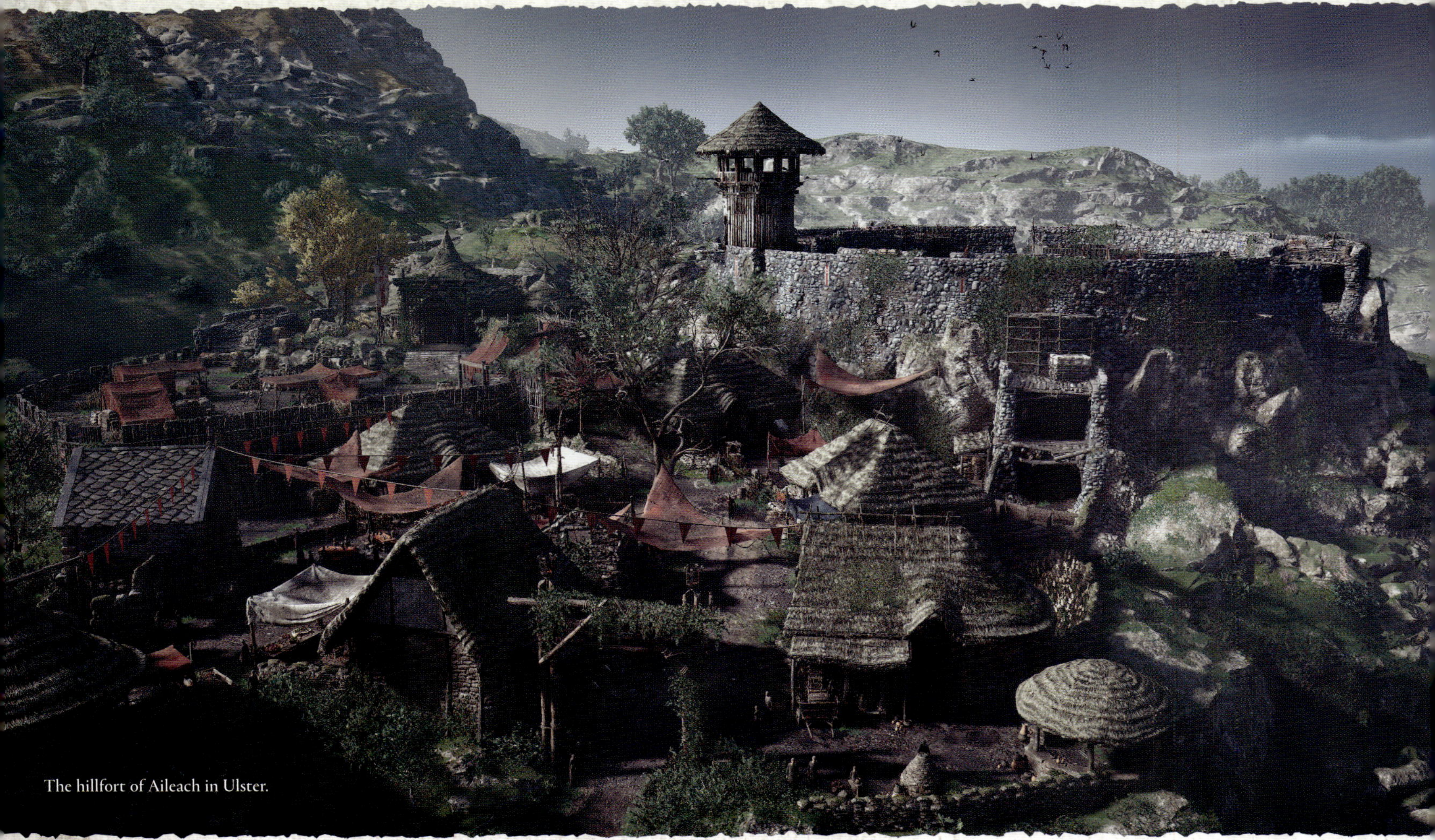

The hillfort of Aileach in Ulster.

Ulster

For Flann to be secure in the high king's throne, he needed sworn allegiance from the northern Uí Néill lords. In Ulster, Eivor completed a series of royal demands for them, earning good standing for Flann. She then traveled to Flann's war camp in Clogher and learned that Bárid had not returned from his Aileach meeting. Eivor offered to find her cousin.

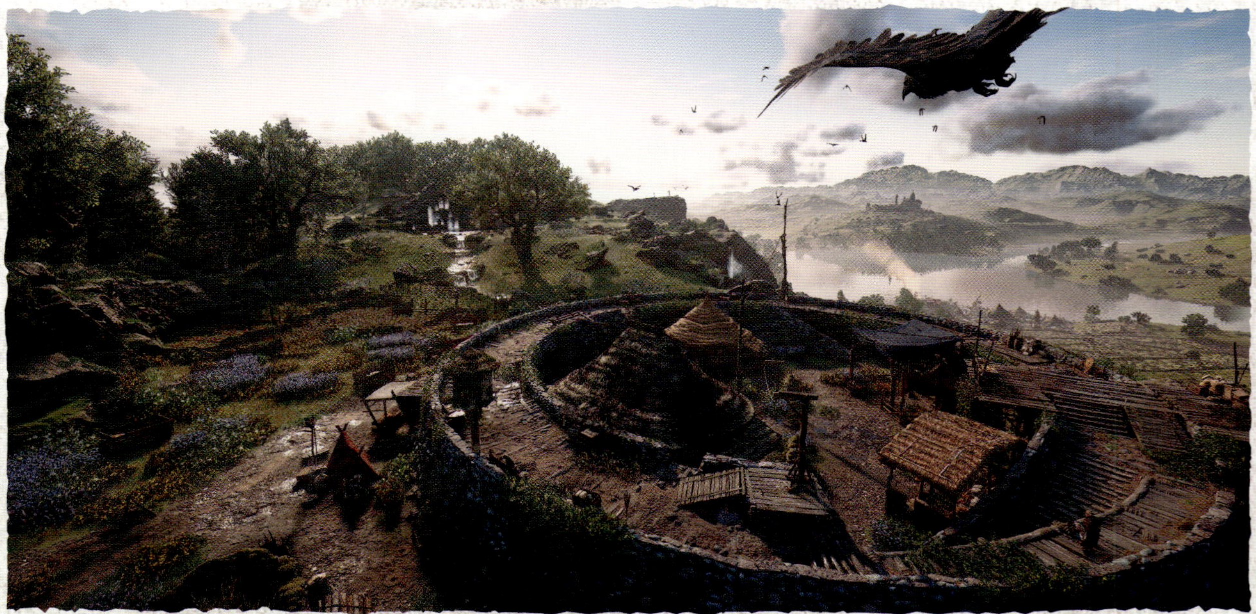

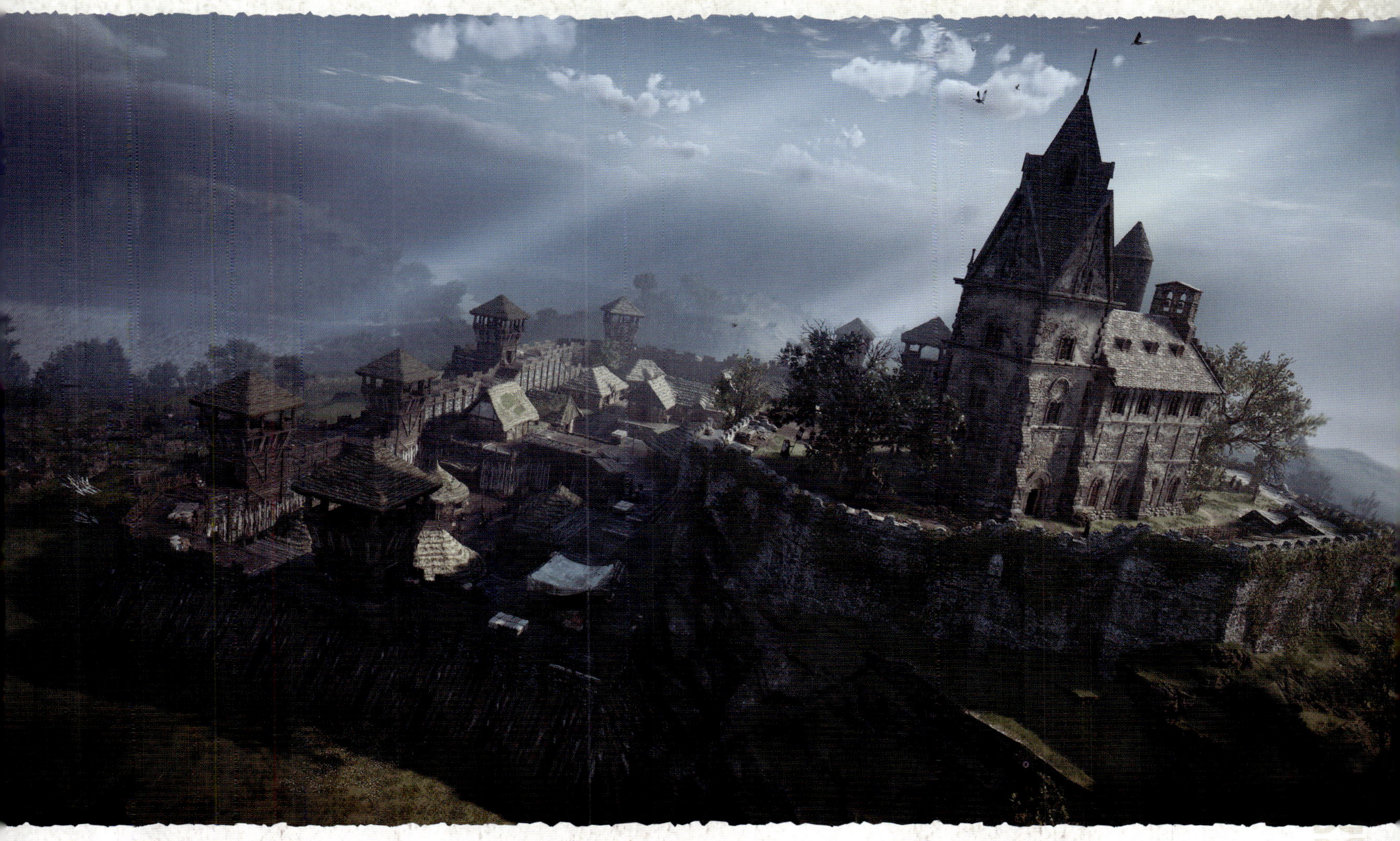

KEY EVENTS

After acquiring a king's pass in Donegal, a Norse-run trading port in western Ulster, Eivor traveled to Aileach and gained access to the main hall. There, she found Bárid feigning inebriation with two northern

ABBOT EOGAN MAC CARTAIGH

Eogan, abbot of Armagh—the so-called God's Appointed in Ireland—seemed a natural leader of Irish Catholicism, given his history of extreme piety and a knack for power politics. But Eivor managed to uncover the abbot's secret hatred of the Church and his role as founder and murderous head zealot of the Children of Danu cult.

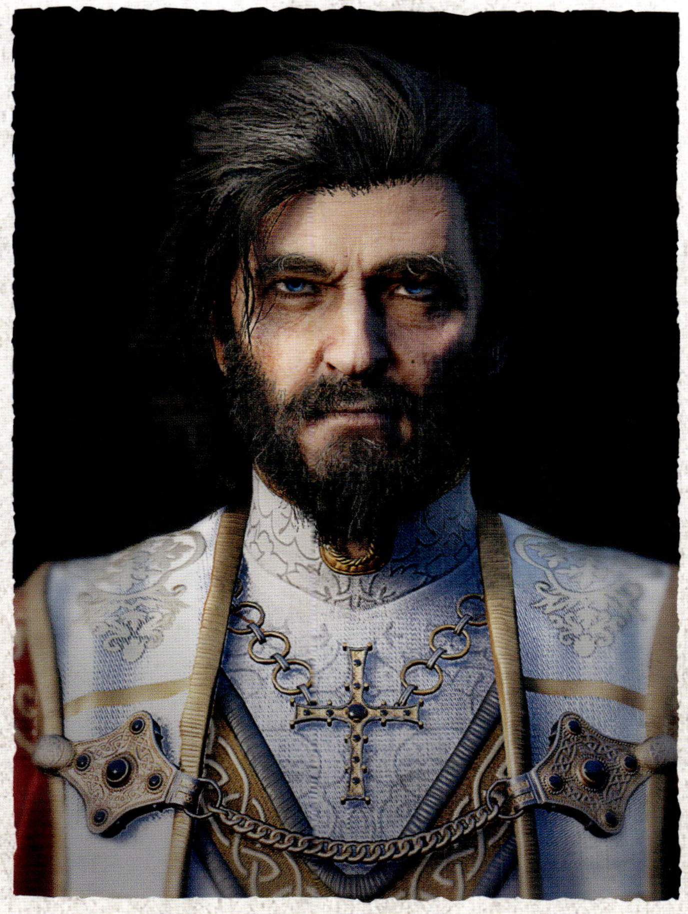

The Giant's Causeway of northern Ulster.

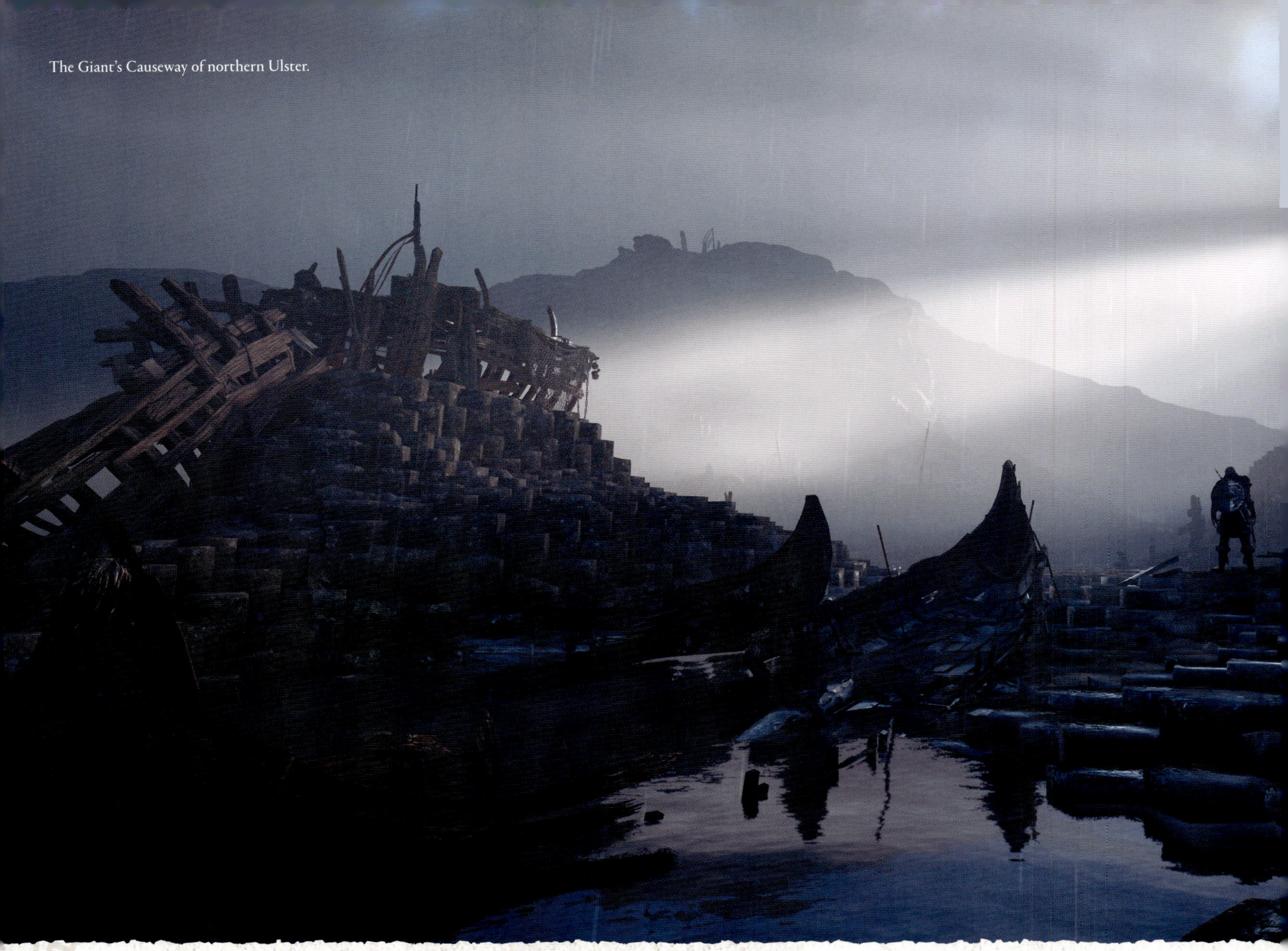

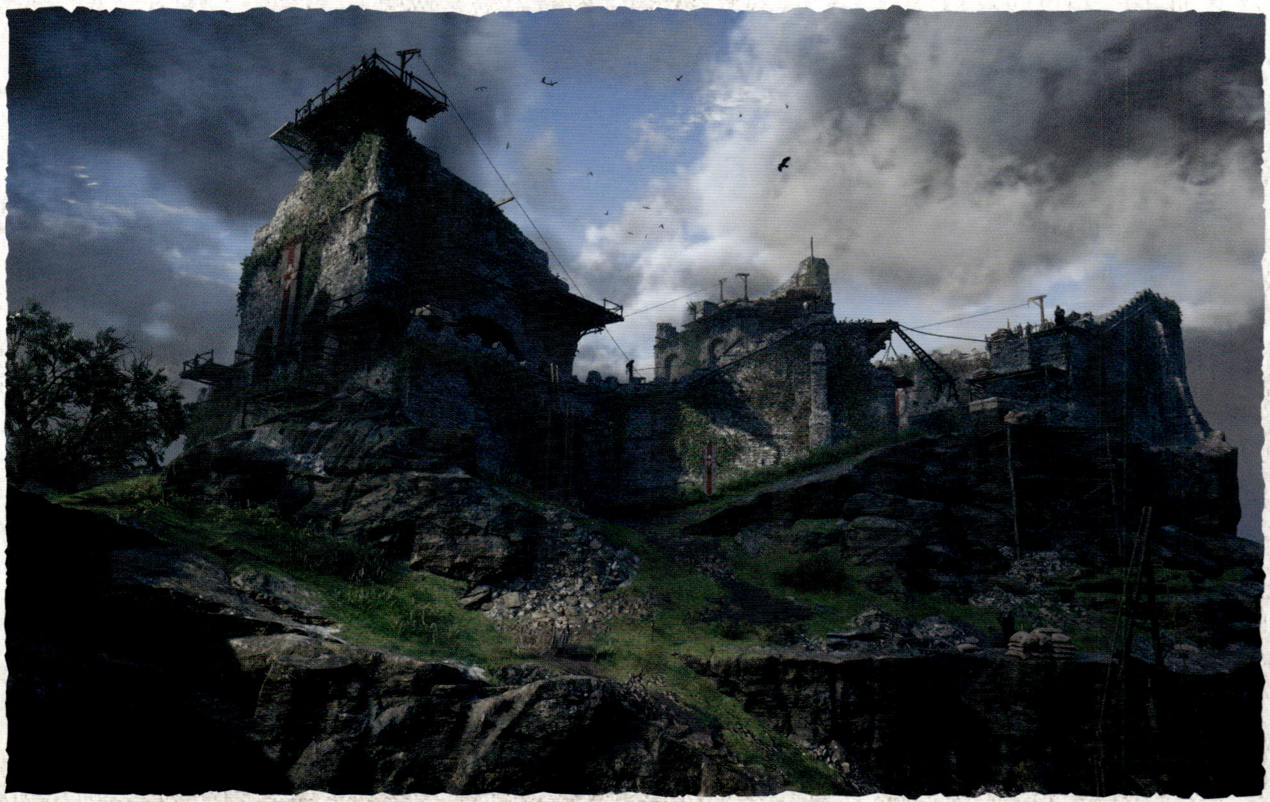

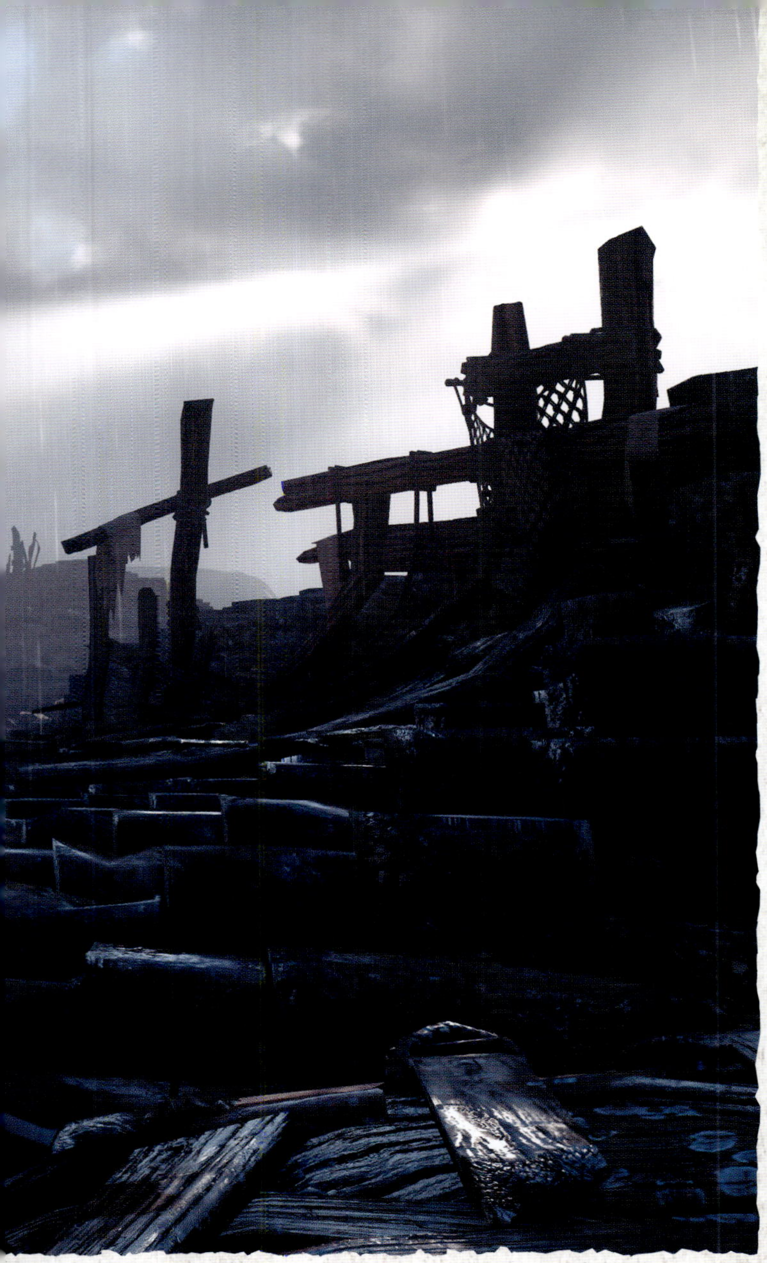

kings, Niall and Domnall. Concealing a cleverly coded message in his drunken blather, Bárid sent Eivor down to the dungeons below the ringfort. There, Eivor liberated a squad of imprisoned soldiers and, with their help, seized full control of the fortress. The defeated Aileach lords admitted that the mastermind behind the resistance to Flann's high kingship was none other than the good abbot of Armagh! Eogan had been amassing troops to ambush Flann's Southern Army.

Eivor hurried back to Clogher to report the betrayal. But war horns sounded just moments after her arrival—the abbot's troops had encircled Flann's camp and were launching a frenzied assault! With Eivor joining in the defense, Flann's forces managed to repel the onslaught, but only barely—the cost was terrible and bloody. Many good warriors were lost, including, sadly, King Bárid of Dublin.

FROM DUBLIN TO DUNSEVERICK TO ARMAGH

Eivor oversaw her slain cousin's return to Dublin for burial in Gortknaw. She vowed to carry out Bárid's final wish—to broker the ascent of his son Sichfrith to

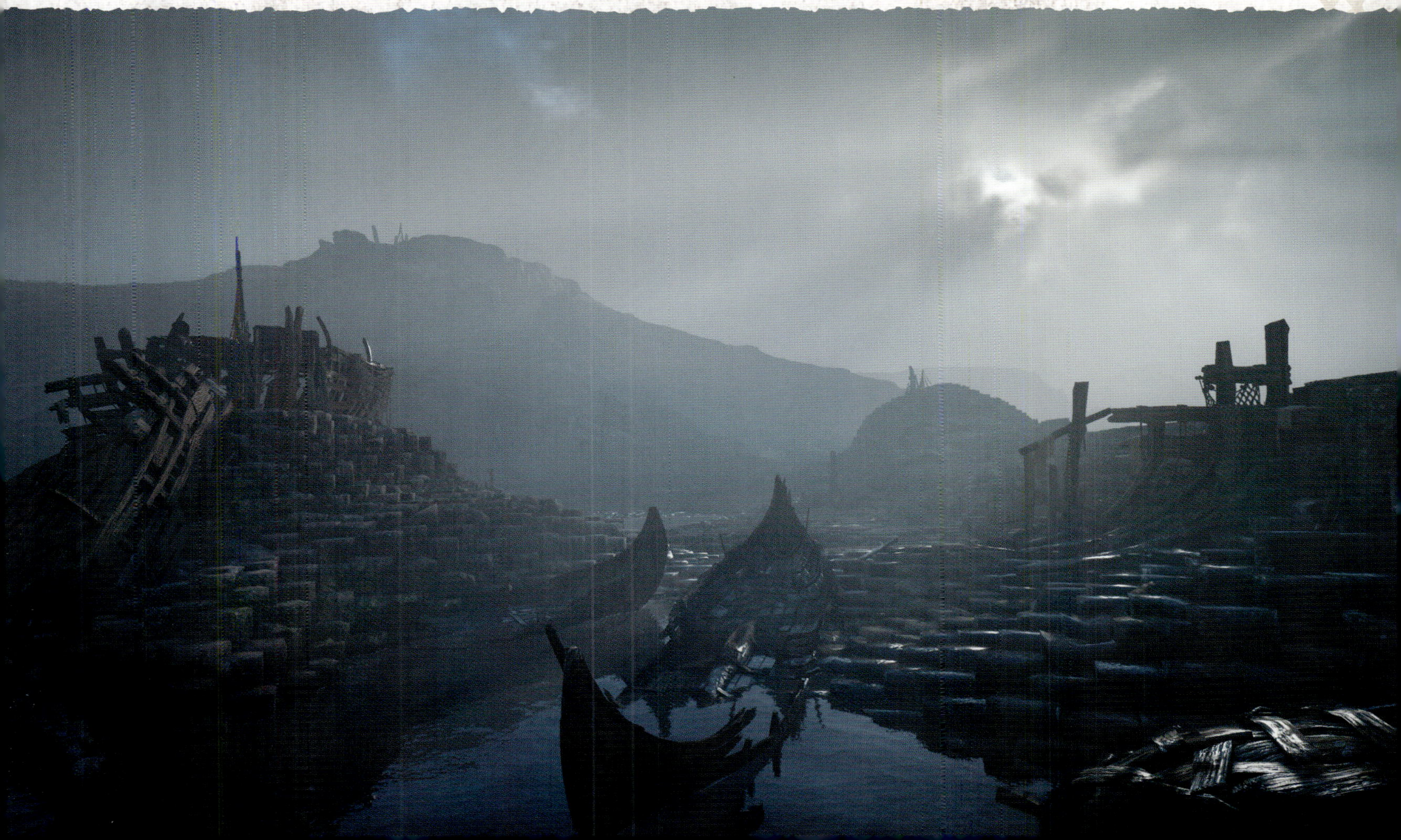

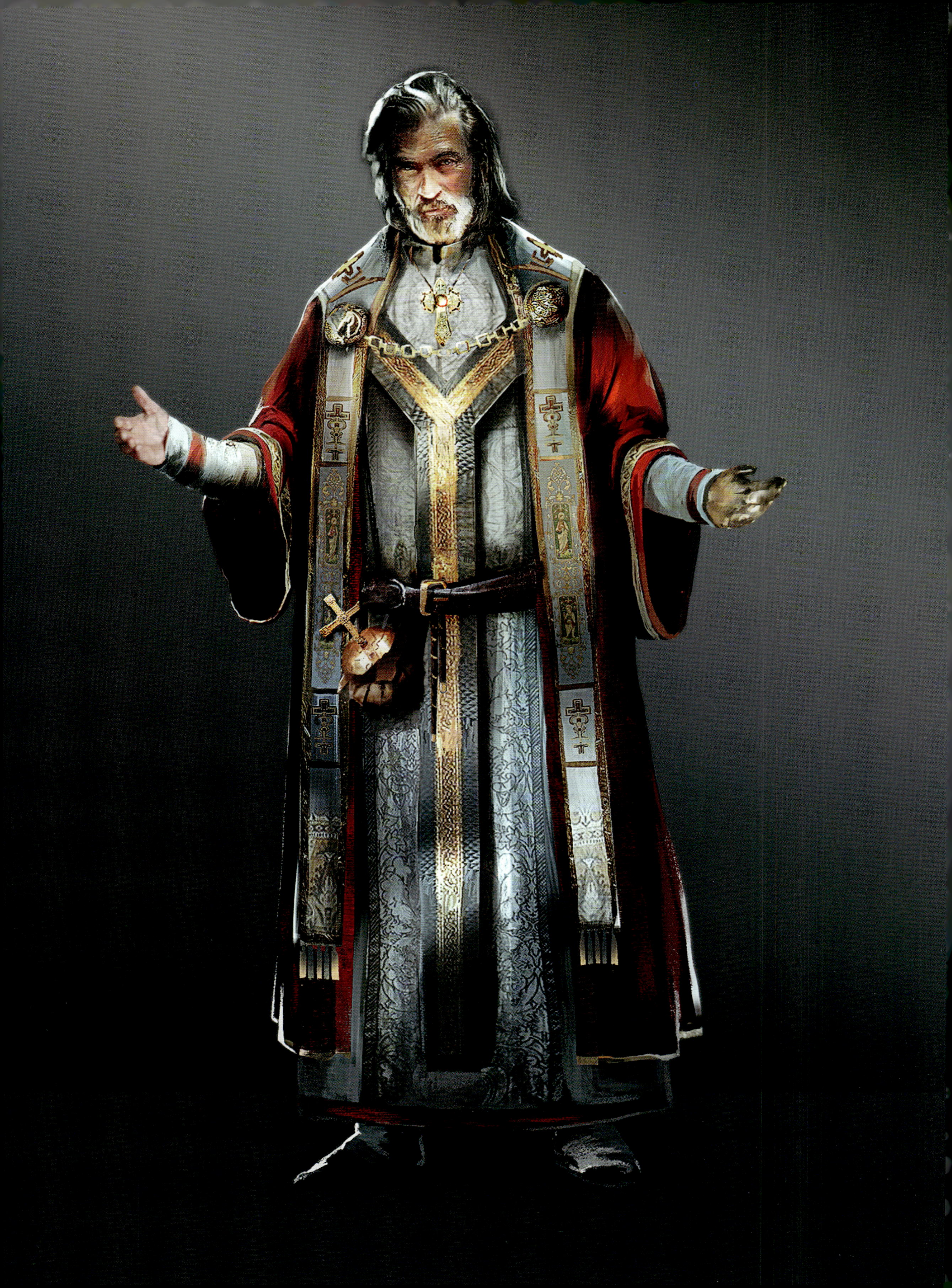

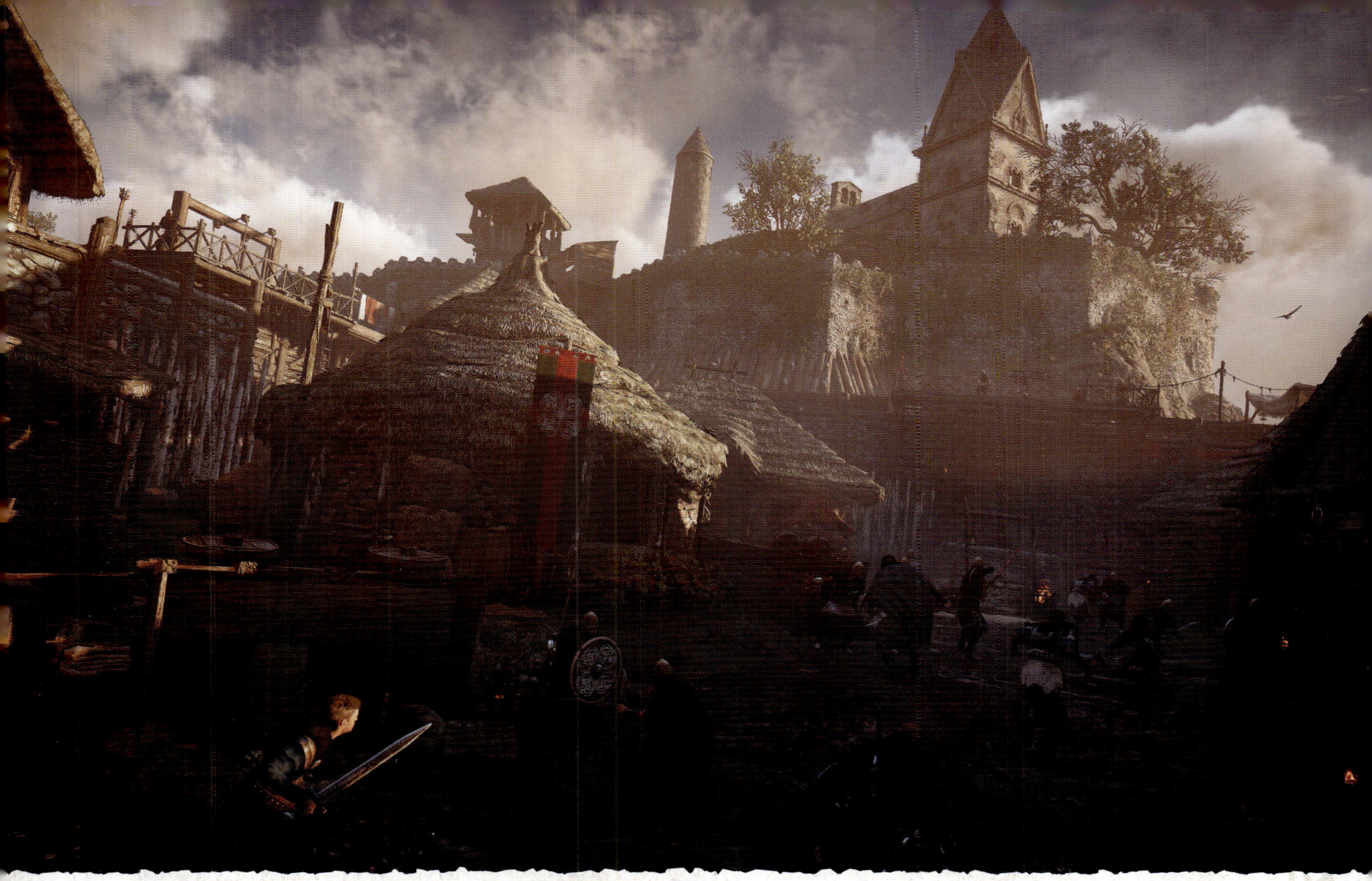

the Dublin throne with High King Flann's full blessing and patronage. At King's Hall in Dublin, my fellow Levantine Azar informed Eivor and Sichfrith that the Children of Danu—led by one called the Seed—were supplying Abbot Eogan's garrison in Armagh with powerful siege weapons and other warfighting goods.

Following Azar's tip, Eivor tracked the shadowy Danu network of arms dealers to the decrepit port town of Dunseverick on the northern coast of Ulster. There, she terminated the Seed and obtained a letter that confirmed the shocking extent of Eogan's treachery—the abbot himself was none other than the Oak, founder

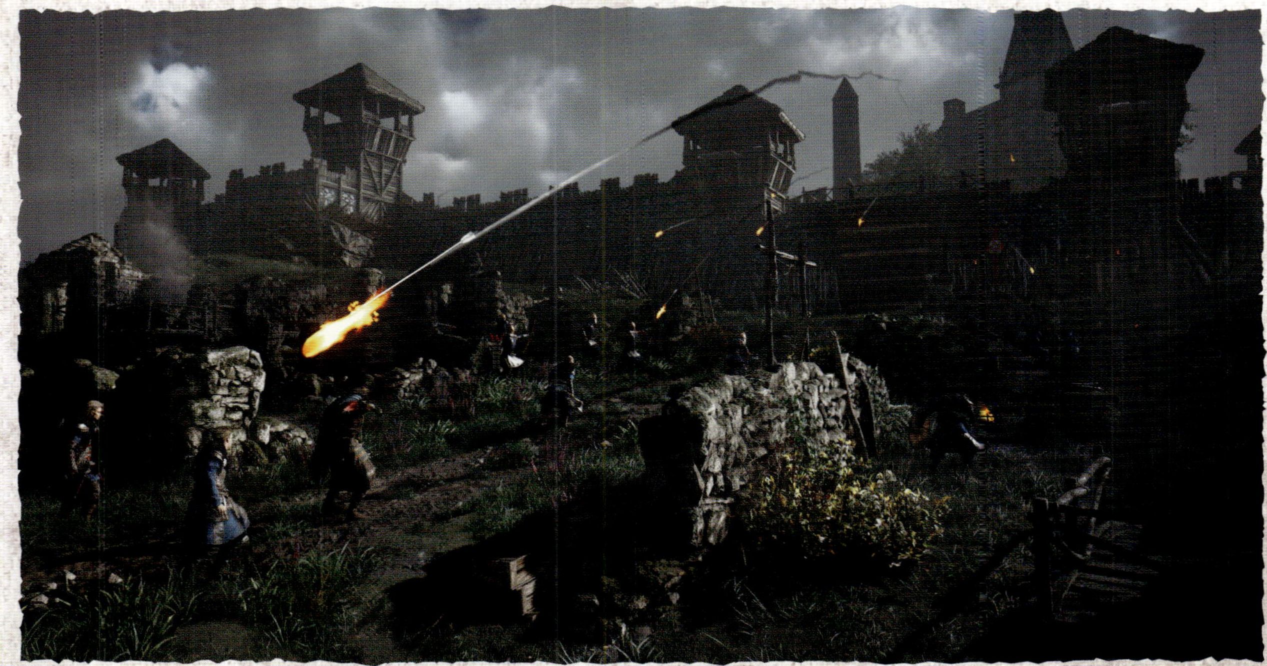

and leader of the Children of Danu! Eivor regrouped with Flann and Sichfrith at the Southern Army's staging area directly across the Blackwater River from Eogan's stronghold towers of Armagh. With Eivor in the vanguard, Flann's forces swarmed the fortress and brought the traitorous cleric to an ignominious end.

A FINAL RECKONING AT TARA

After the great victory, Eivor traveled to the King's Land meeting hall in Durrow, Meath. There, the gathered Irish lords entreated High King Flann to begin a fierce inquisition of all druidic believers, hoping to flush out other Children of Danu coconspirators. The poetess Ciara, being pagan herself, objected most strenuously. But Flann's decision was firm: "The future of Ireland is a wholly Christian one." Every druid would face inquisition and a choice: reform or exile. Such a course, Flann felt, would unite the kingdoms.

At this, Ciara stormed out of the hall. Eventually, Flann and Eivor tracked her to the hilltop of Tara, where the priestess had somehow awakened the ancient monolith known as Lia Fáil, the Stone of Destiny. The glowing stone imbued Ciara with strange supernatural powers, and she lashed out in fury. But Eivor managed to neutralize the angry druidess. Afterward, a contrite Flann promised to undo the inquisition he'd initiated.

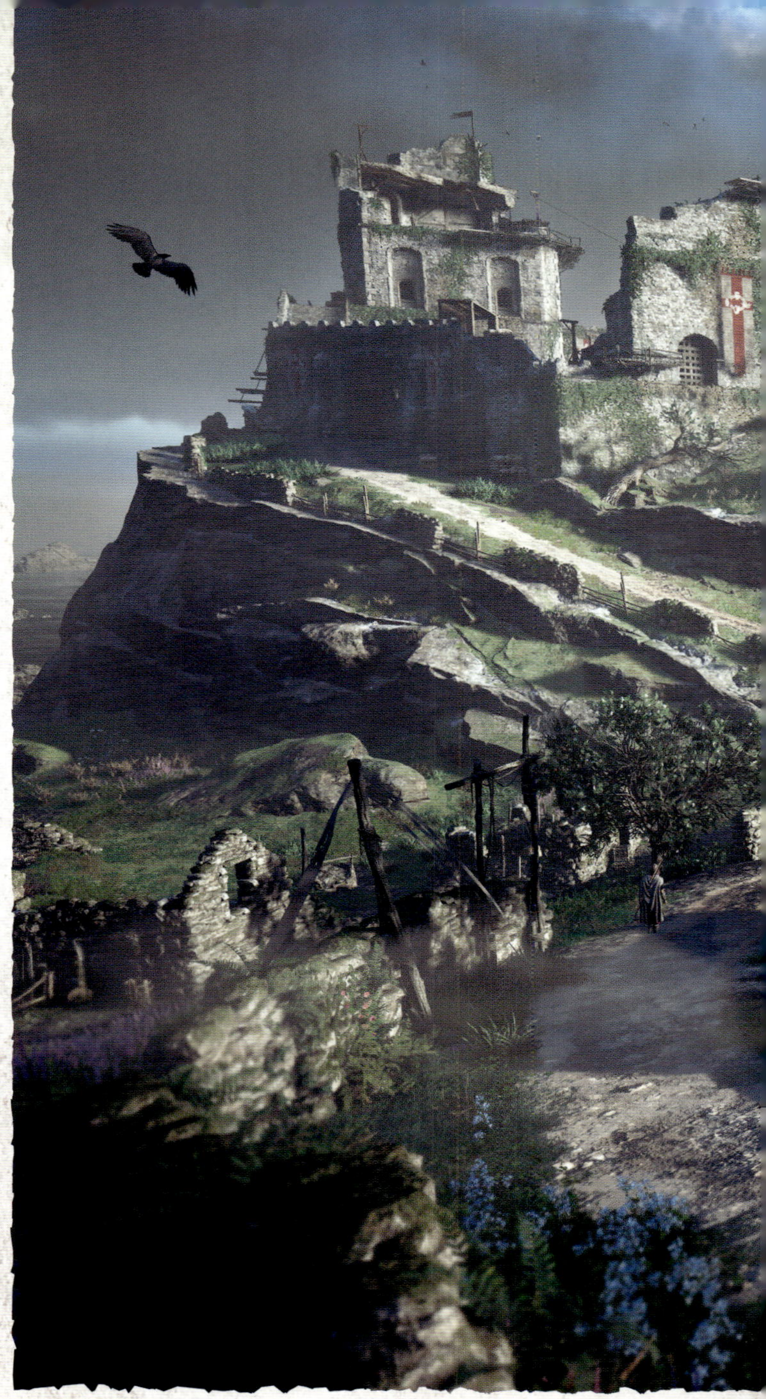

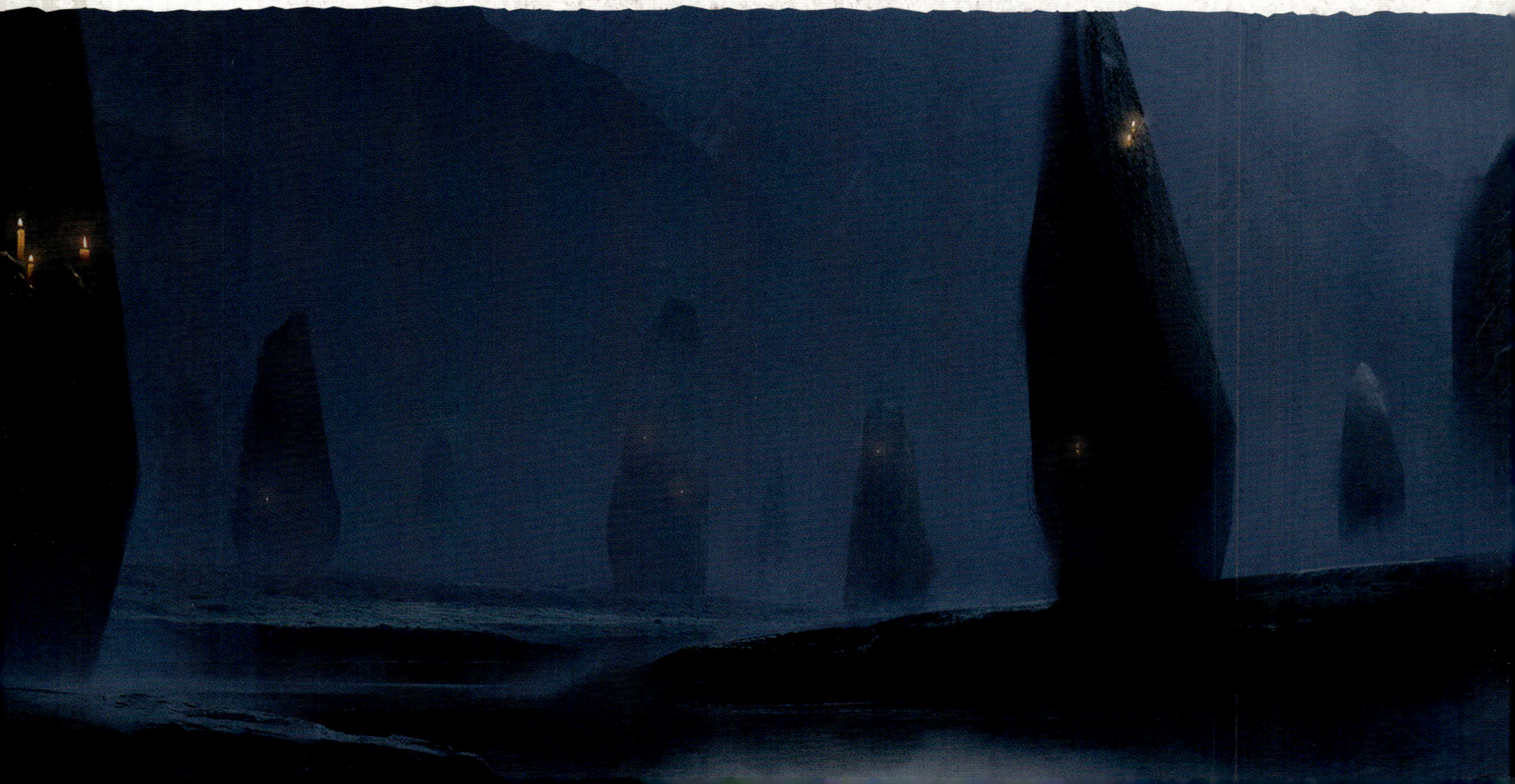

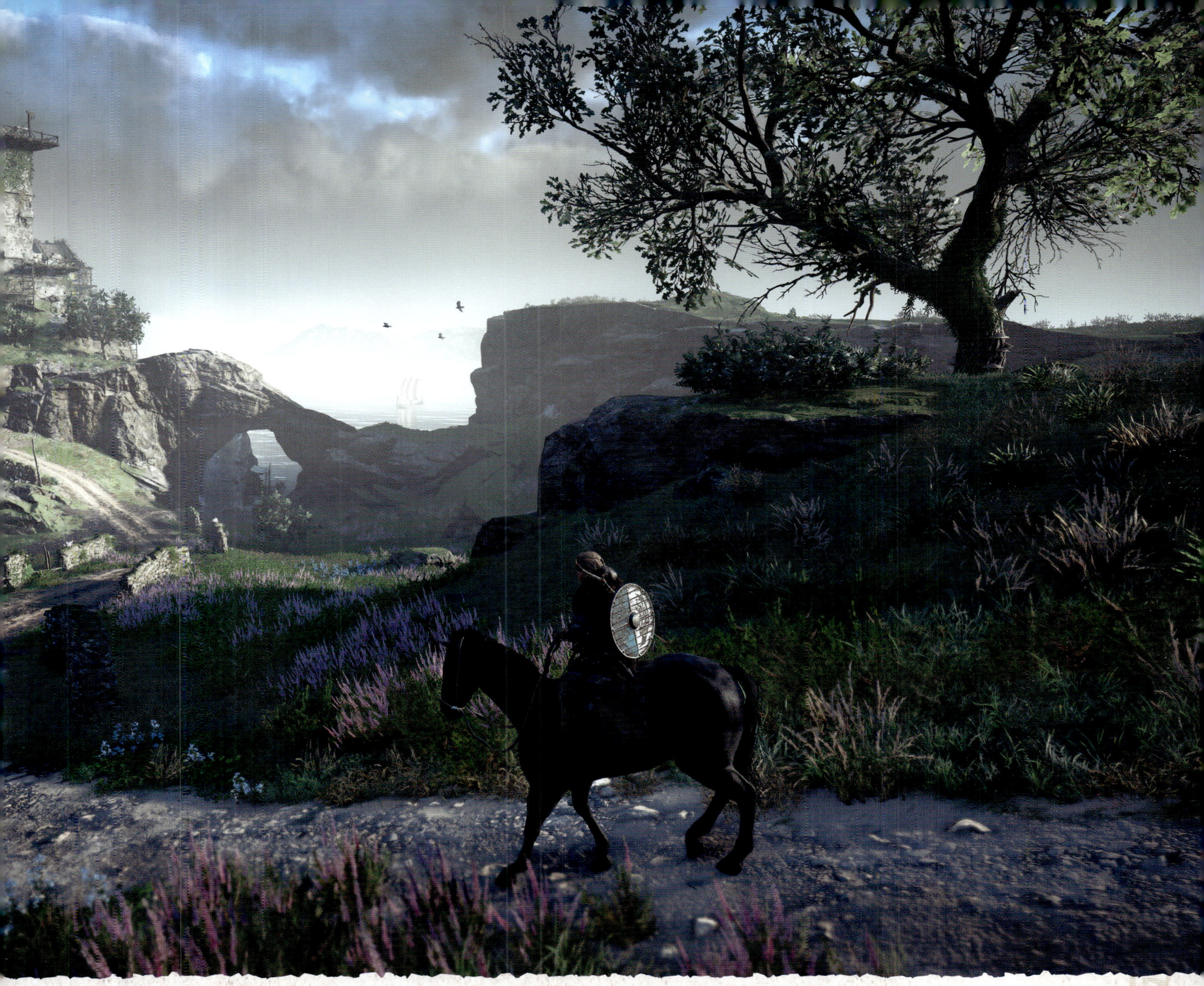
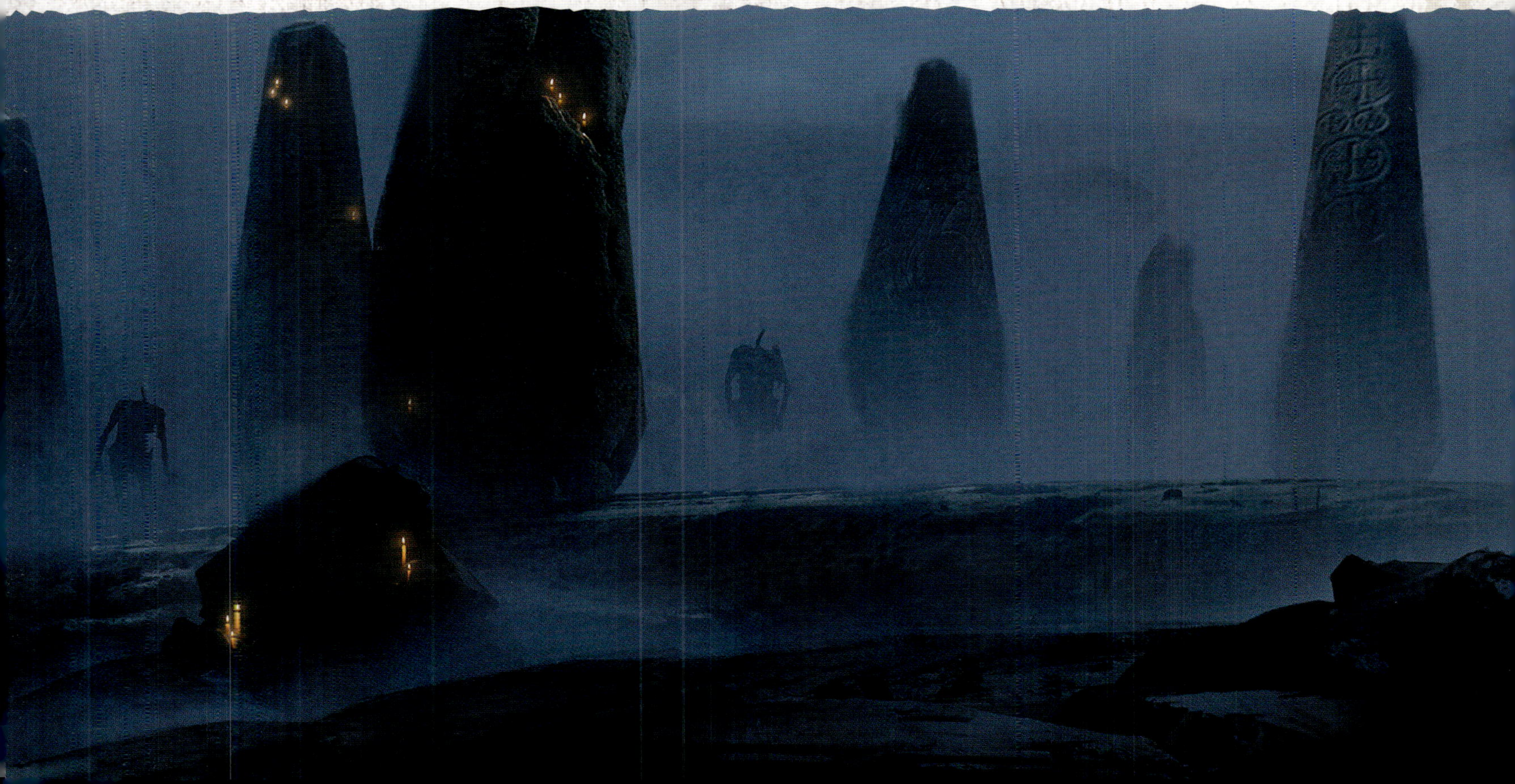

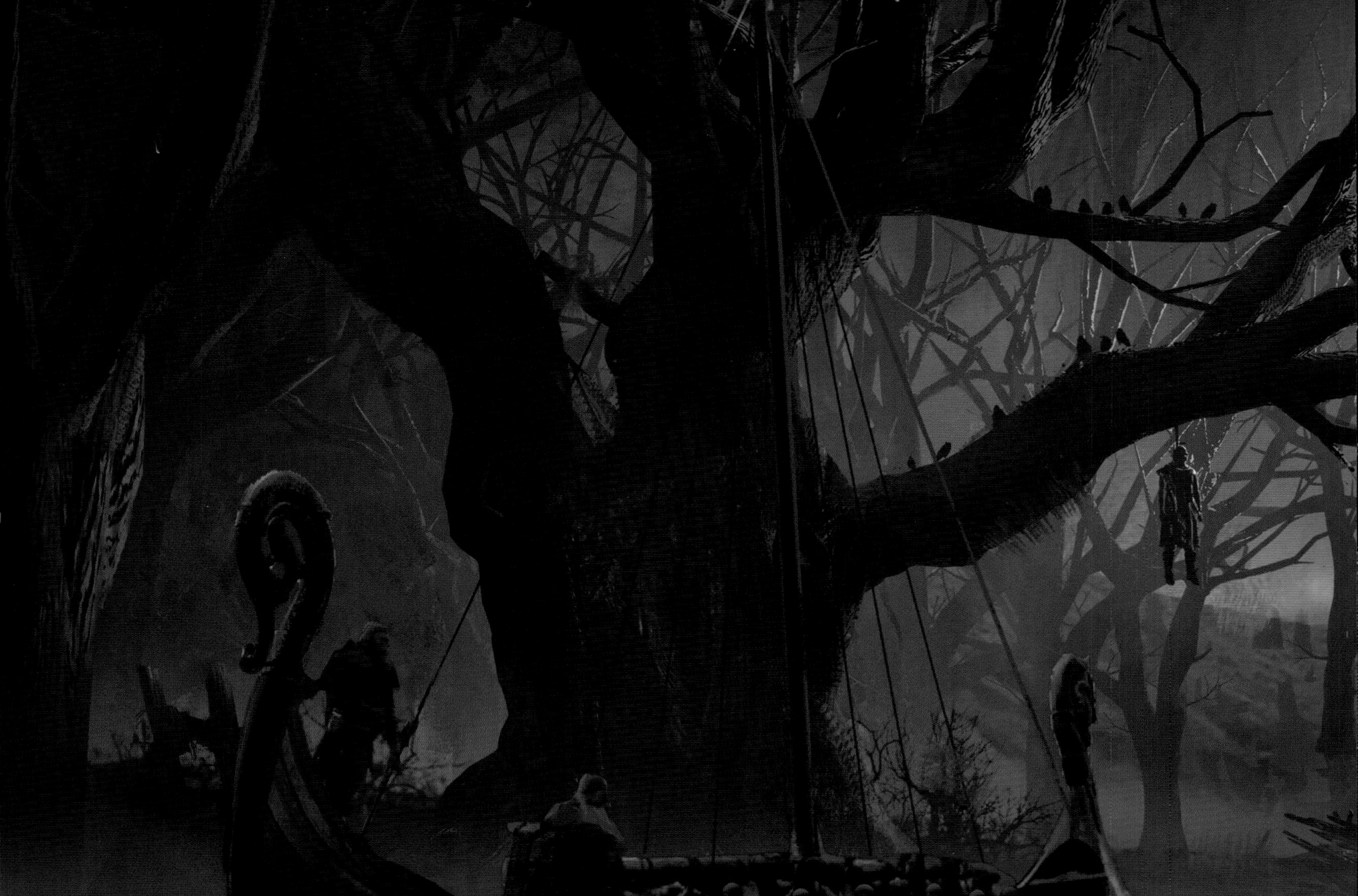

FRANCIA

During the Raven Clan's campaign to build alliances in England, two visitors from Francia arrived in Ravensthorpe. One, a Norse warrior named Toka, hailed from a Viking clan settled near Paris. The other, a Frankish fellow named Pierre, was described as her "adviser." Interestingly, they came bearing extravagant gifts of food and drink . . . and quickly built a fine new guesthouse for the village! Wary Randvi sensed a bribe and asked my opinion. In my native culture, we feel such gestures deserve a hearing, but only if one's community is secure and incorruptible—and Ravensthorpe was certainly that. Randvi agreed and sent Eivor to investigate.

As it turned out, Toka and Pierre sought help from Raven Clan in their efforts to lay siege to Paris and drive out its ruthless king, Charles III—also known, somewhat unceremoniously, as Charles the Fat. Charles was a

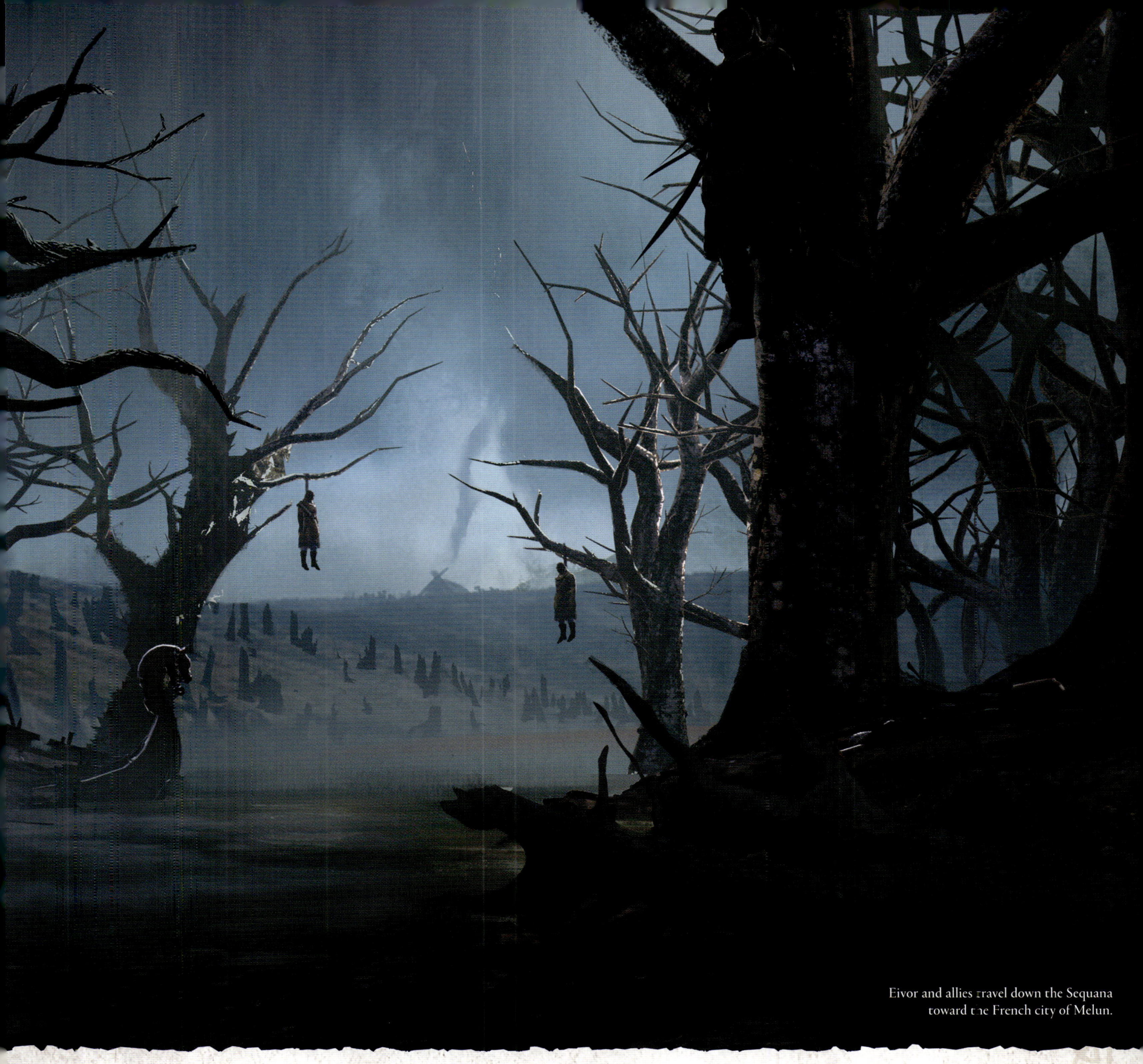

Eivor and allies travel down the Sequana toward the French city of Melun.

rising power in the region, successfully uniting the Frankish kingdoms under his rule—a grave threat to all Norse enclaves in Francia. Toka warned that once Francia was consolidated under Charles the Fat's rule, he would surely come for England next. Indeed, Randvi's scouts in Francia—and my own Hidden Ones agents, as well—had recently confirmed this growing menace.

Thus, Eivor set sail with Toka and Pierre across the channel to meet Sigfred, their Viking leader on Frankish shores. The plan was to pledge Eivor's battle axe to Sigfred's cause and help him cripple the fat king's ambition. (Secretly, I'd also asked Eivor to hunt for a long-lost Hidden Ones central bureau rumored to be buried beneath ancient Roman ruins in Paris.)

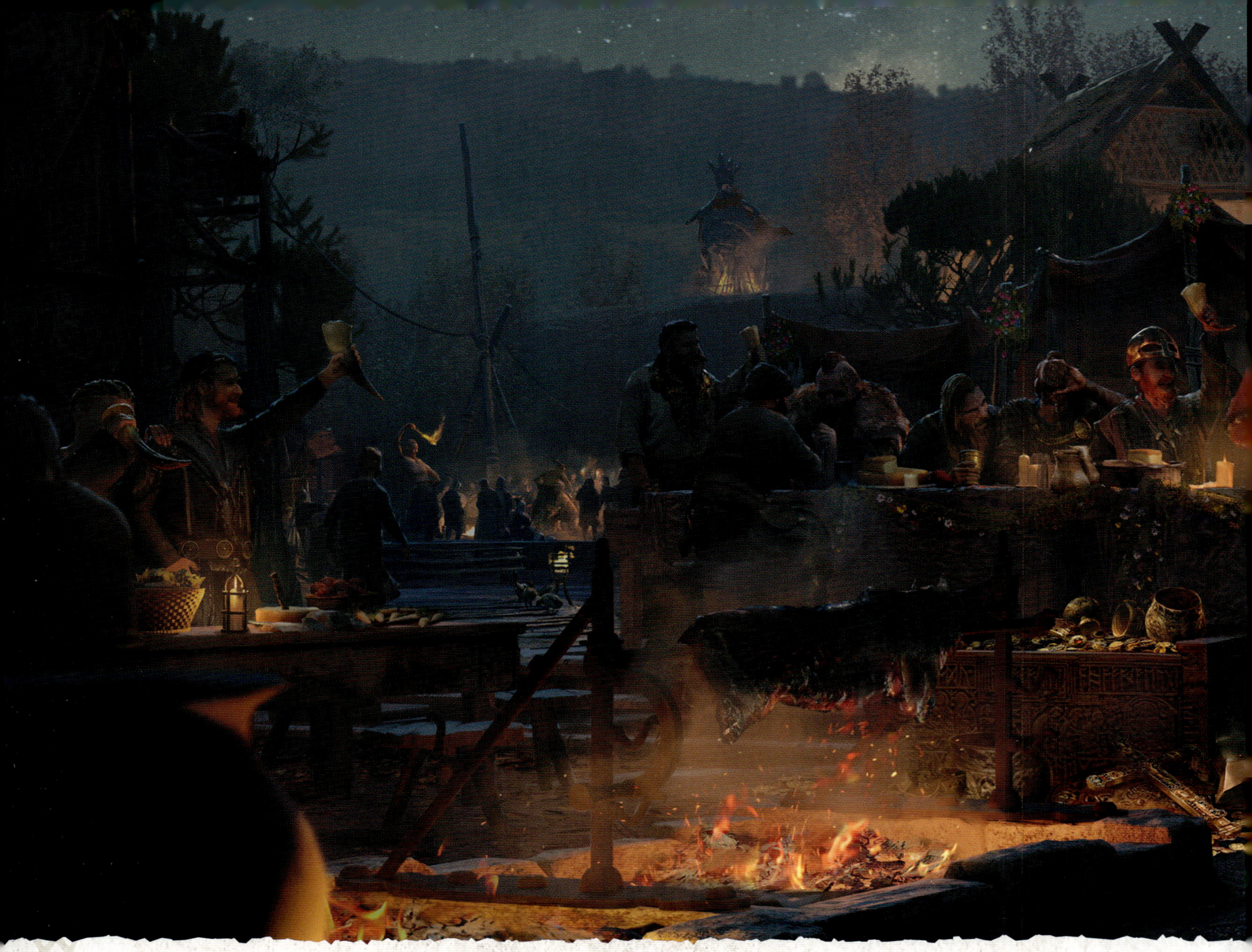

MAJOR FACTIONS & SECTS

MELUN CLAN

This clan of rugged Norsemen in northern Francia was once led by Sinric Jarl. But the Franks, under King Charles the Fat, slew him dishonorably, and his vengeful brother Sigfred succeeded him. Driven south by Charles, the clan settled around Melun and began to muster a Viking army capable of storming the gates of Paris.

THE FRANKISH MILITARY

The well-trained soldiers of Francia are one of the few fighting forces in Europe who can stand toe to toe with a Viking swarm. Led by Count Odo, right-hand man of King Charles, the Frankish infantry was tough, effective, and well equipped. The Franks also deployed a thundering charge of horsemen—heavy mail-clad soldiers wielding fearsome lances and shields, supported by light, swift ranged units, usually mounted archers who carried swords for close combat.

BELLATORES DEI

Calling themselves "God's Warriors" (their name translated from Latin), these religious zealots are big fans of grisly exorcism rituals referred to as "deliverance." Led by a demagogic scholar who went by the name Isidore Mercator, the twisted sect spread the fear of God (literally) across the Frankish countryside.

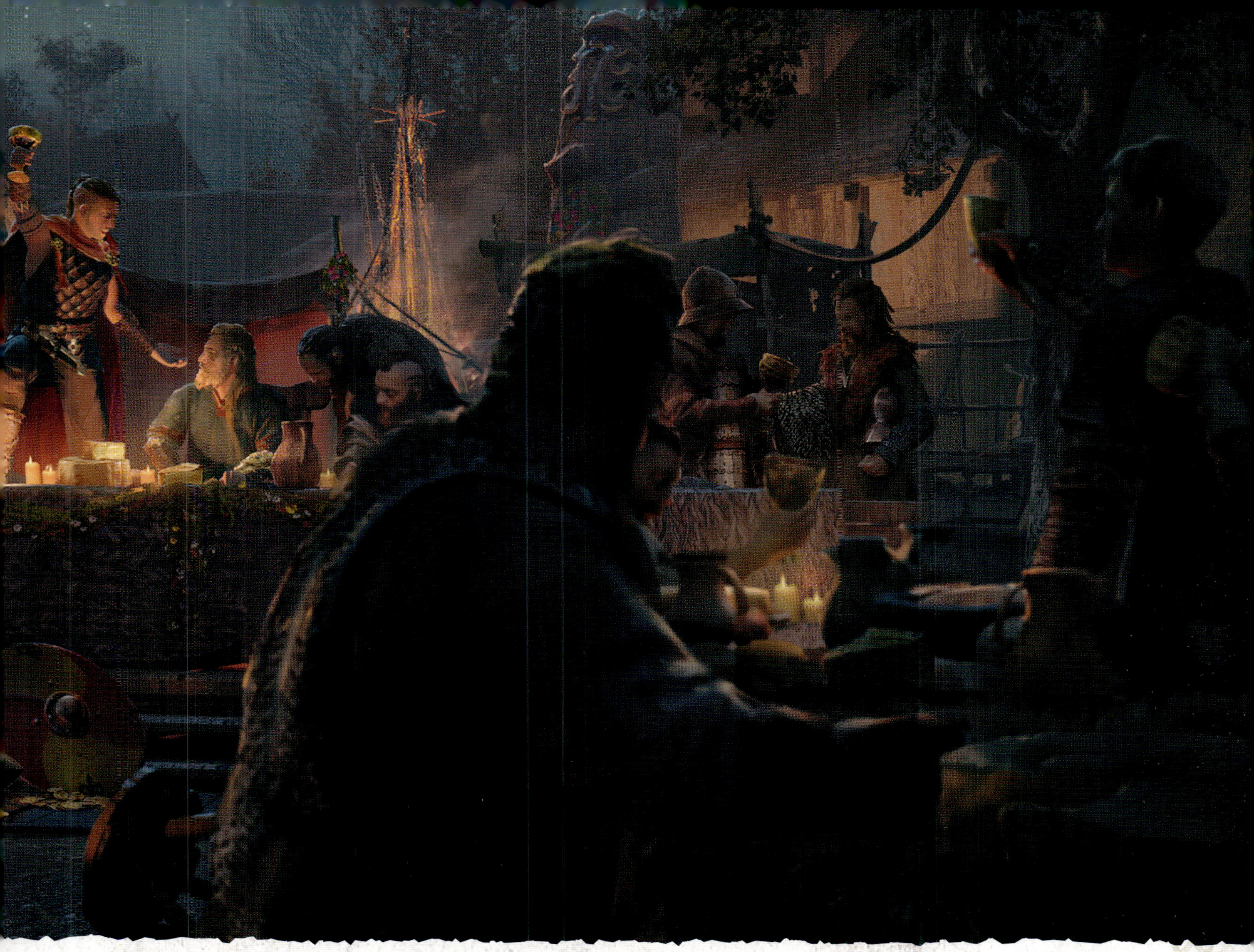

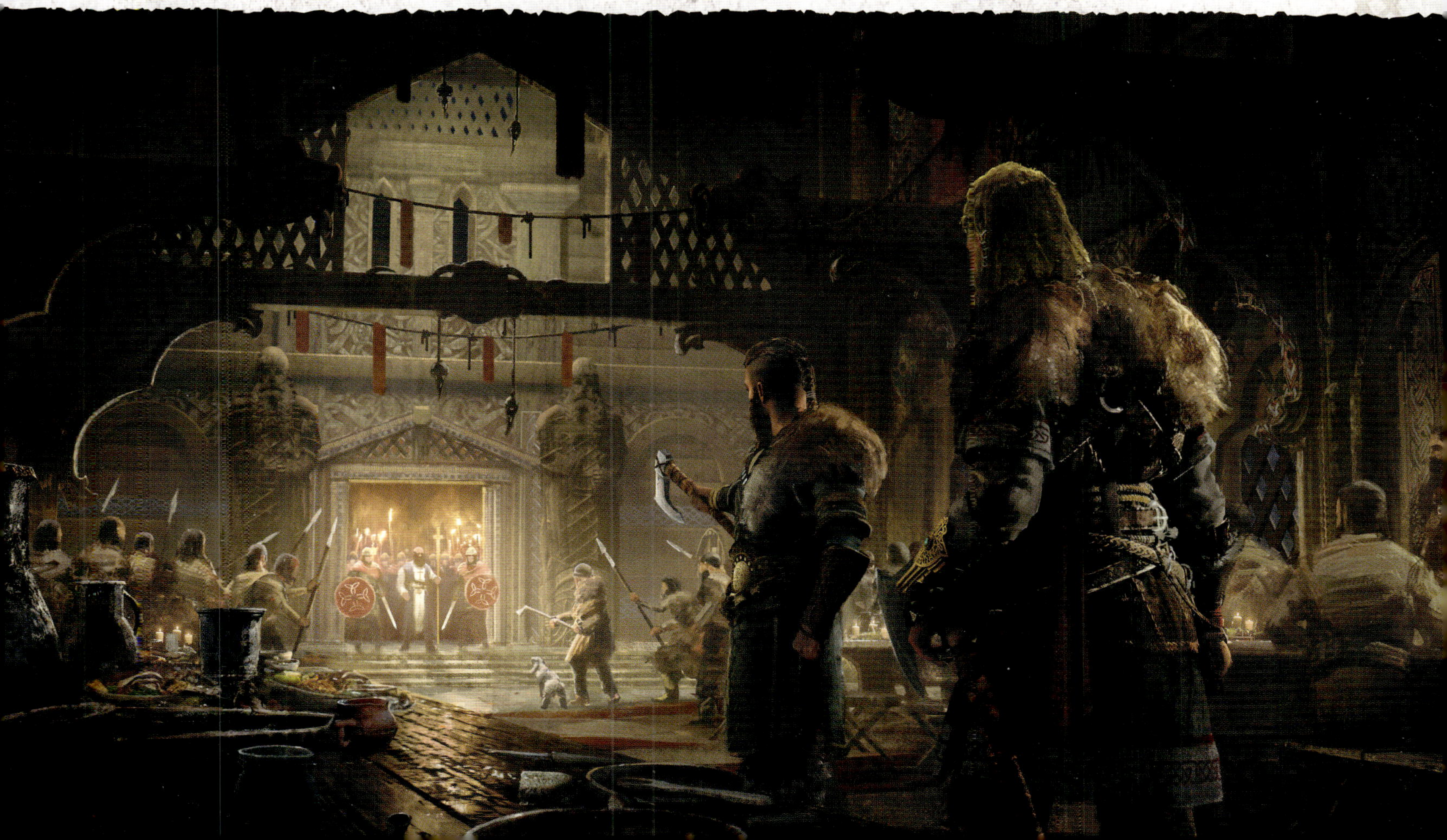

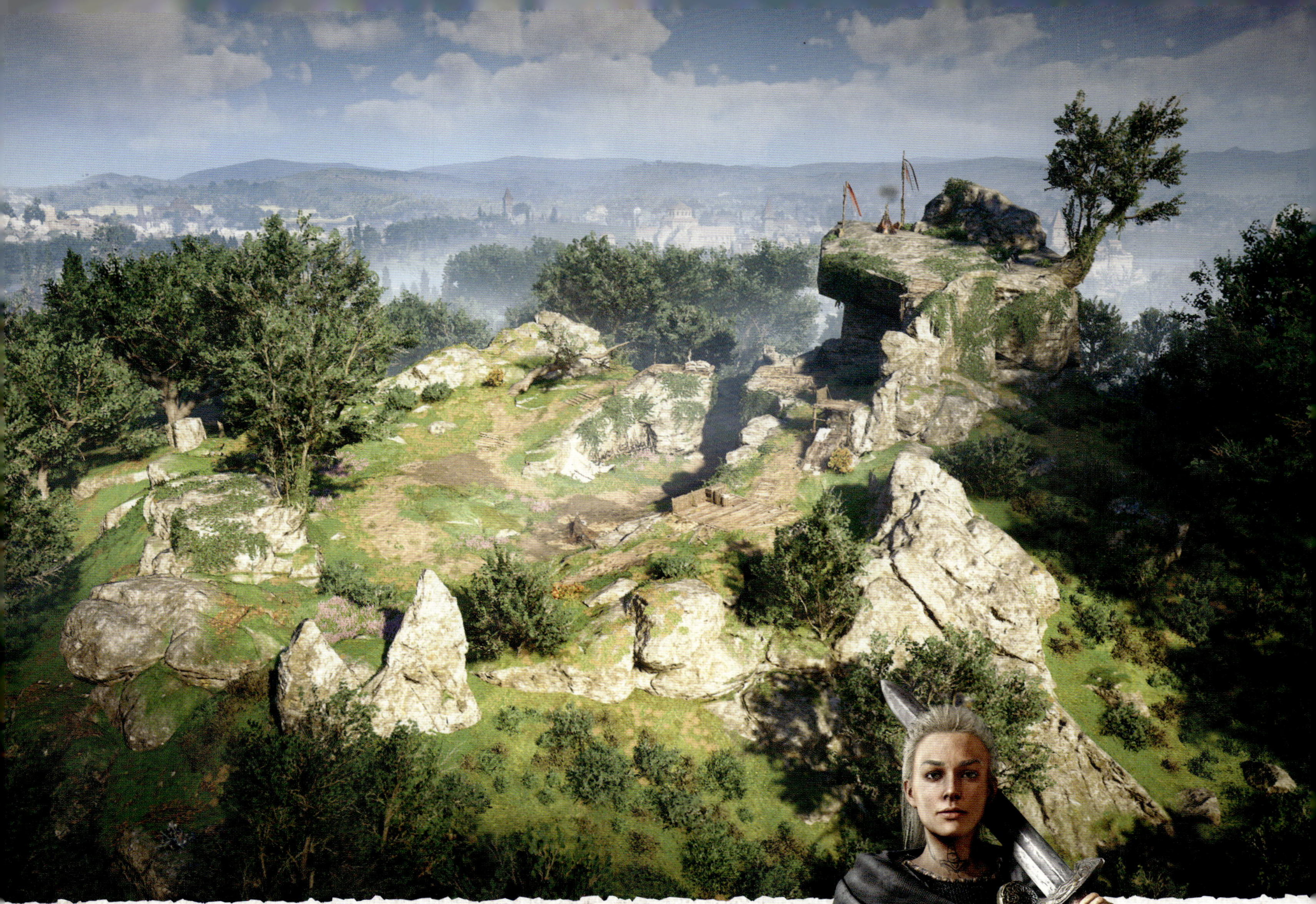

MELUNOIS

As Eivor traversed the ravaged Melunois Province, she encountered much evidence of the brutal nature of Charles the Fat's attempts to expunge the Norse presence—an unsettling glimpse of the savagery Ravensthorpe could expect if Charles subdued Francia, then turned his bloody gaze to England.

TOKA

Toka Sinricsdottir is no deep thinker, but Eivor is impressed with her leadership instincts and combat skills. Indeed, Eivor thinks of Toka as a younger sister, beloved and physically precocious. Sinric's daughter speaks her mind fearlessly, swings a deft sword, and wisely relies on the reconnaissance network and sharp-witted observations of her wily Frankish colleague, Pierre.

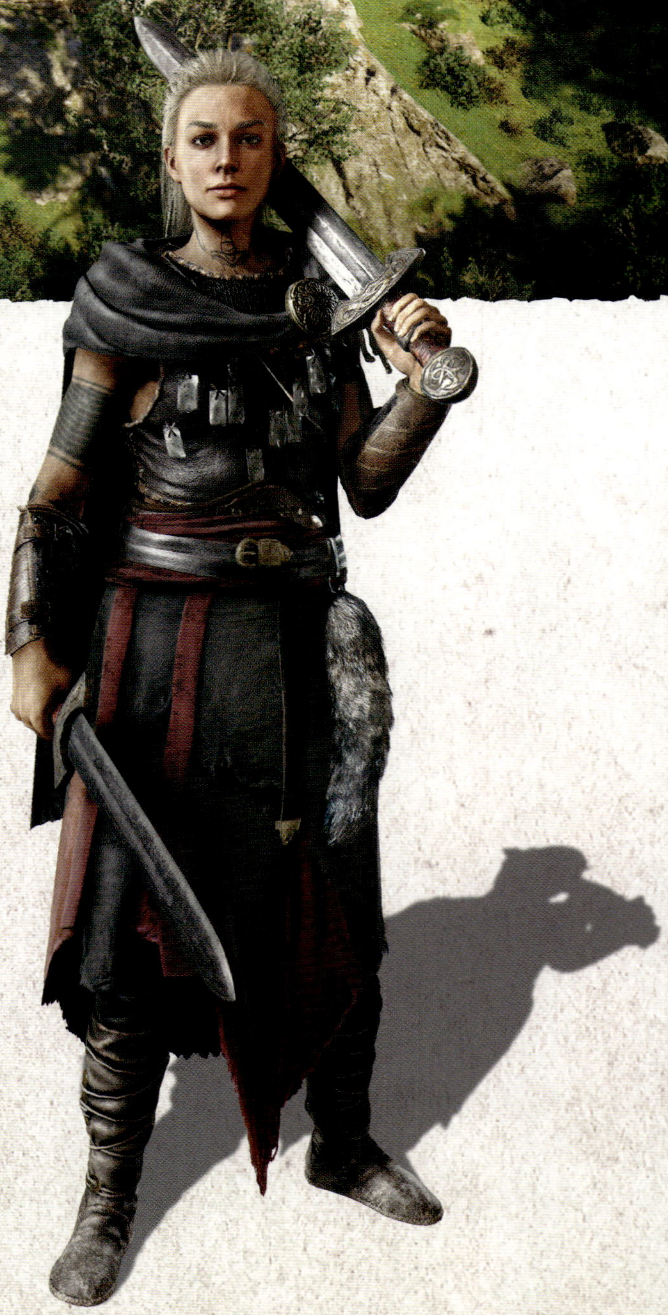

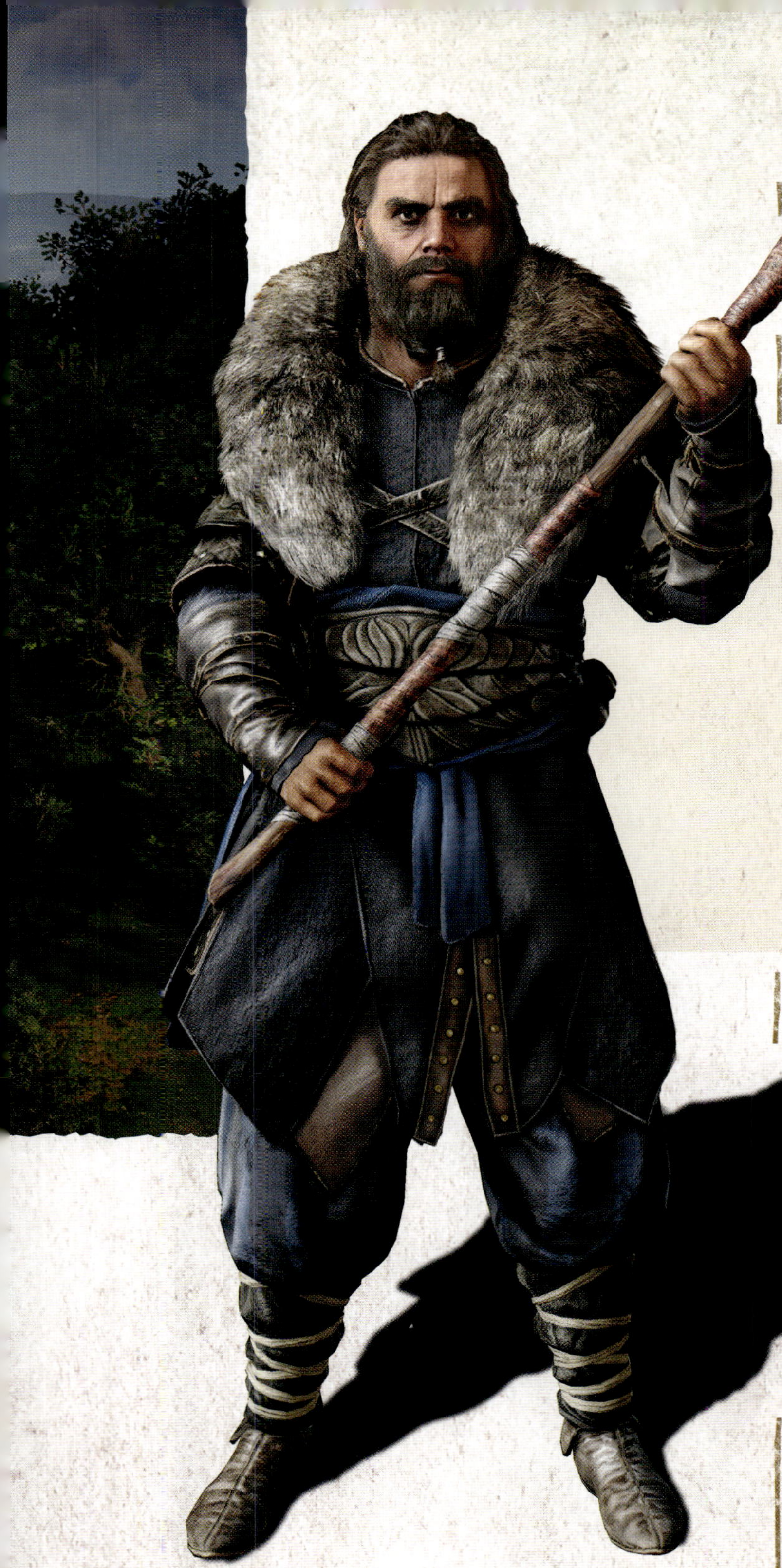

KEY EVENTS

In Melun, Eivor pledged her axe to Sigfred, warlord of that Norse-controlled town. A skirmish with Frankish cavalrymen ended with Sigfred in hot pursuit of the fleeing bishop Engelwin down the road to Paris. Eivor's report to me of the incident noted that Sigfred, although an impressively forceful commander, was prone to making impulsive and sometimes reckless decisions. I once heard Randvi describe the preferred demeanor of any Viking leader as "wild heart, level head." Indeed, I have seen this very quality in the great Viking jarls, such as Halfdan and Guthrum . . . and, yes, in Eivor herself.

SIGFRED

Reports on this Norseman—the fellow who succeeded his slain brother as jarl of the Viking clan based in Melun—portray a truly conflicted individual. A powerful warrior and charismatic speaker, Sigfred let hatred consume him in his quest to avenge Sinric's dishonorable murder. His impulsive, bloody moves displayed little long-term vision for the stability of West Francia.

PIERRE

This sybaritic Frankish rebel joined the Norse cause after his own compatriots under Charles abandoned him. Eivor tells me that Pierre "loves love" and isn't afraid to match wits or pints with anyone. More importantly, his covert network of informants has provided helpful eyes across the entire region.

ENGELWIN

A sadistic Frankish clergyman, Engelwin was also a high-ranking member of a gnostic cult of zealots known as Bellatores Dei. The dark circles around his eyes gave him an otherworldly appearance, which he reportedly exploited for full effect. Eivor took a particular relish in penetrating his sanctum at Sainte-Geneviève.

Paris

Eivor met up with Sigfred in the stinking Parisian slums. The pair observed a rousing speech by the king's right-hand man, an impressive fellow named Count Odo, the renowned protector of Paris. Sigfred also pointed out Odo's clerical counterpart, Bishop Gozlin, a fierce warrior-monk known for his stalwart presence on the battlefield. After a bit of investigation, Eivor managed to infiltrate Bishop Engelwin's fortified church of Sainte-Geneviève . . . and promptly assassinated the ecclesiastic menace.

KEY EVENTS

While escaping Sainte-Geneviève, Eivor discovered letters in the clergy chambers indicating that (1) Charles the Fat's wife, Queen Richardis, was an impediment to Engelwin's ambitions, and thus he'd sought to "remove her," and (2) the king himself might be found in a brothel beneath the Boatmen Baths Tavern in South Paris. Eivor found Charles and learned that the queen had already been abducted by an overly zealous Church faction known as Bellatores Dei—Latin for "Warriors of God." Eivor and Charles worked out a deal: the Viking emissary would rescue Richardis, and in exchange, the Frankish king would negotiate his ambitions for England.

CHARLES, KING OF FRANCIA

Like his great-grandfather Charlemagne, Charles the Fat united all of Francia under his rule. But unlike his forebear, Charles has displayed little acumen regarding *how* to rule. Rumors suggest that childhood traumas forged a fractured soul. Eivor's reports certainly portray a disturbed, devious man with dark layers of complexity.

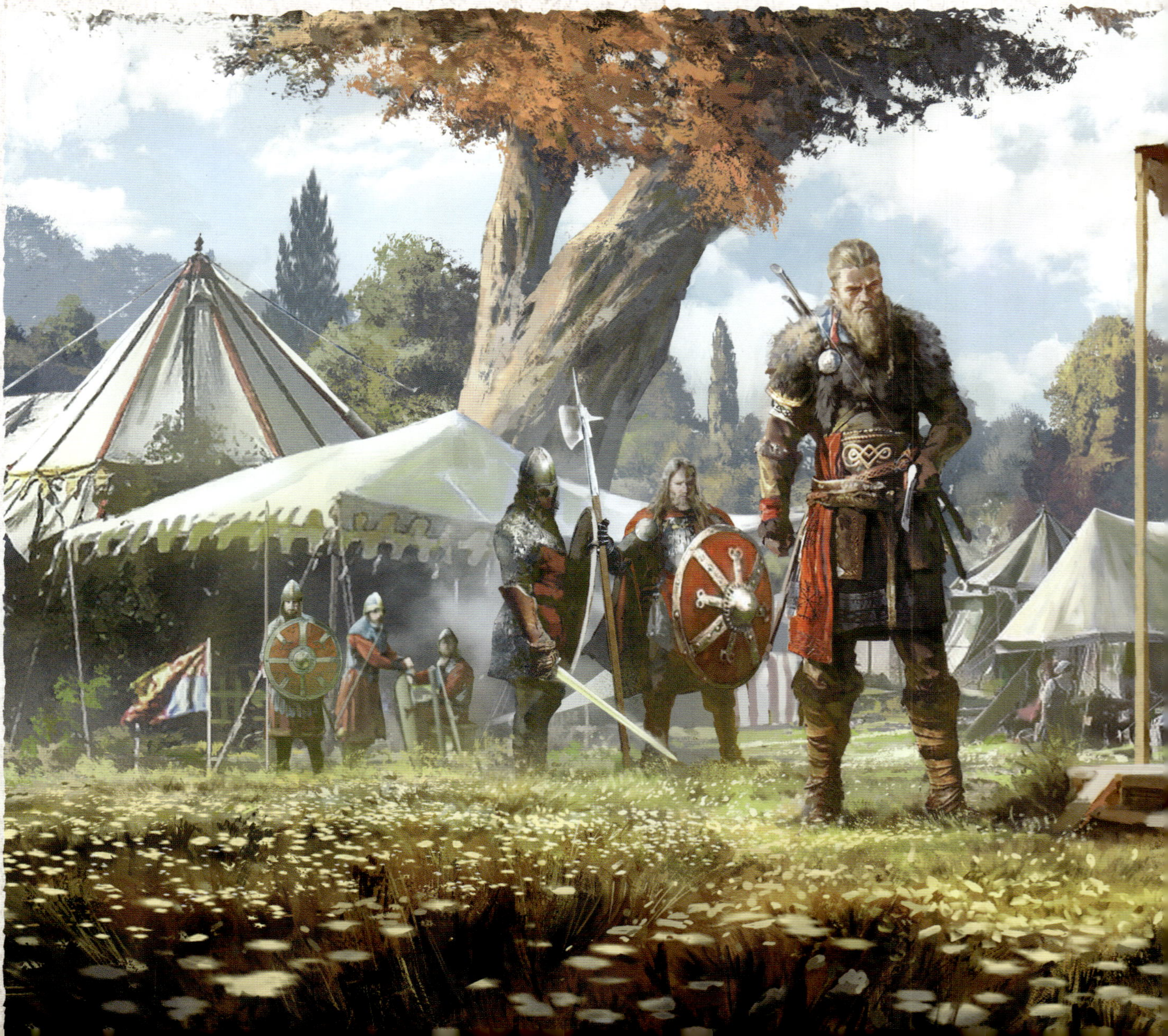

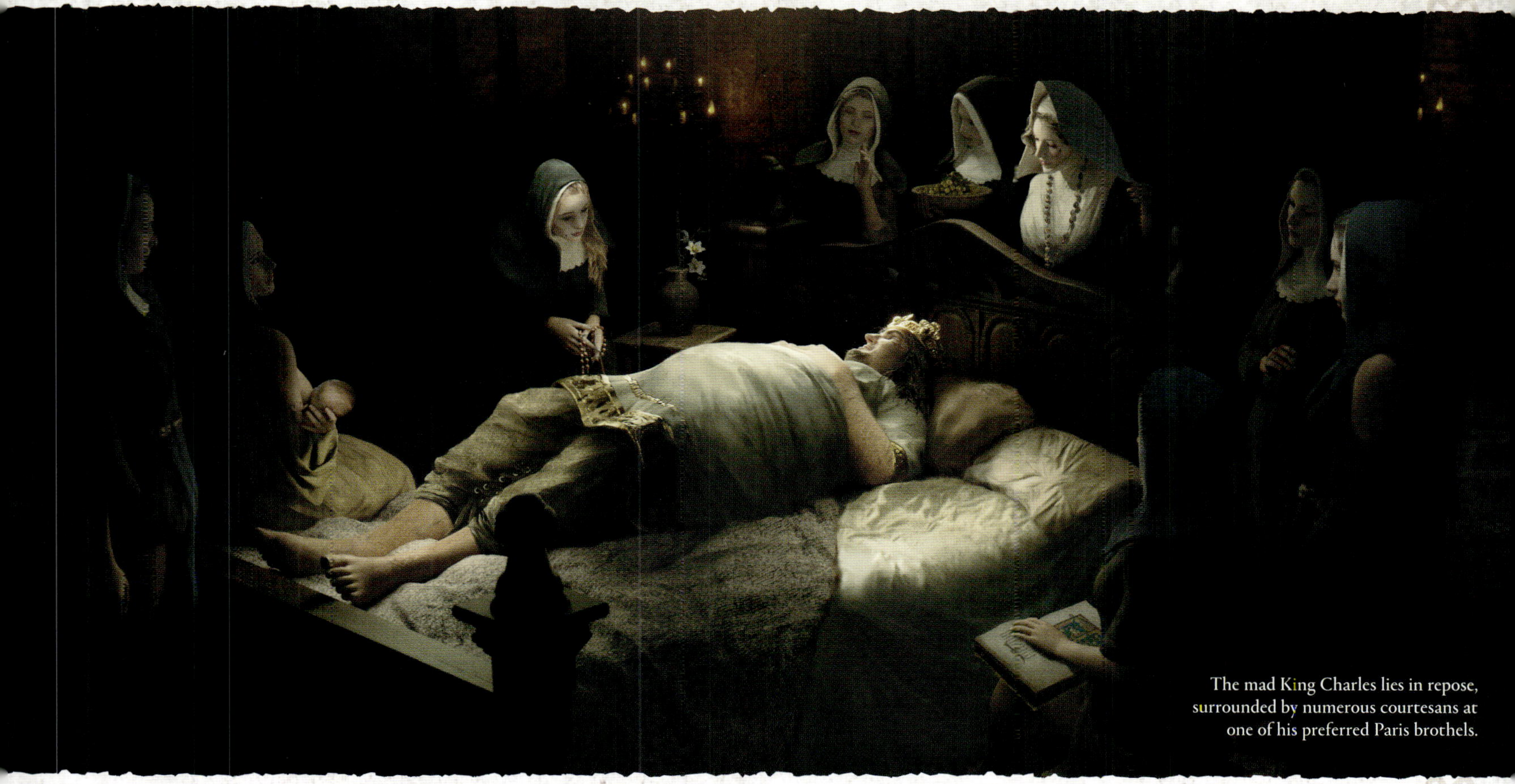

The mad King Charles lies in repose,
surrounded by numerous courtesans at
one of his preferred Paris brothels.

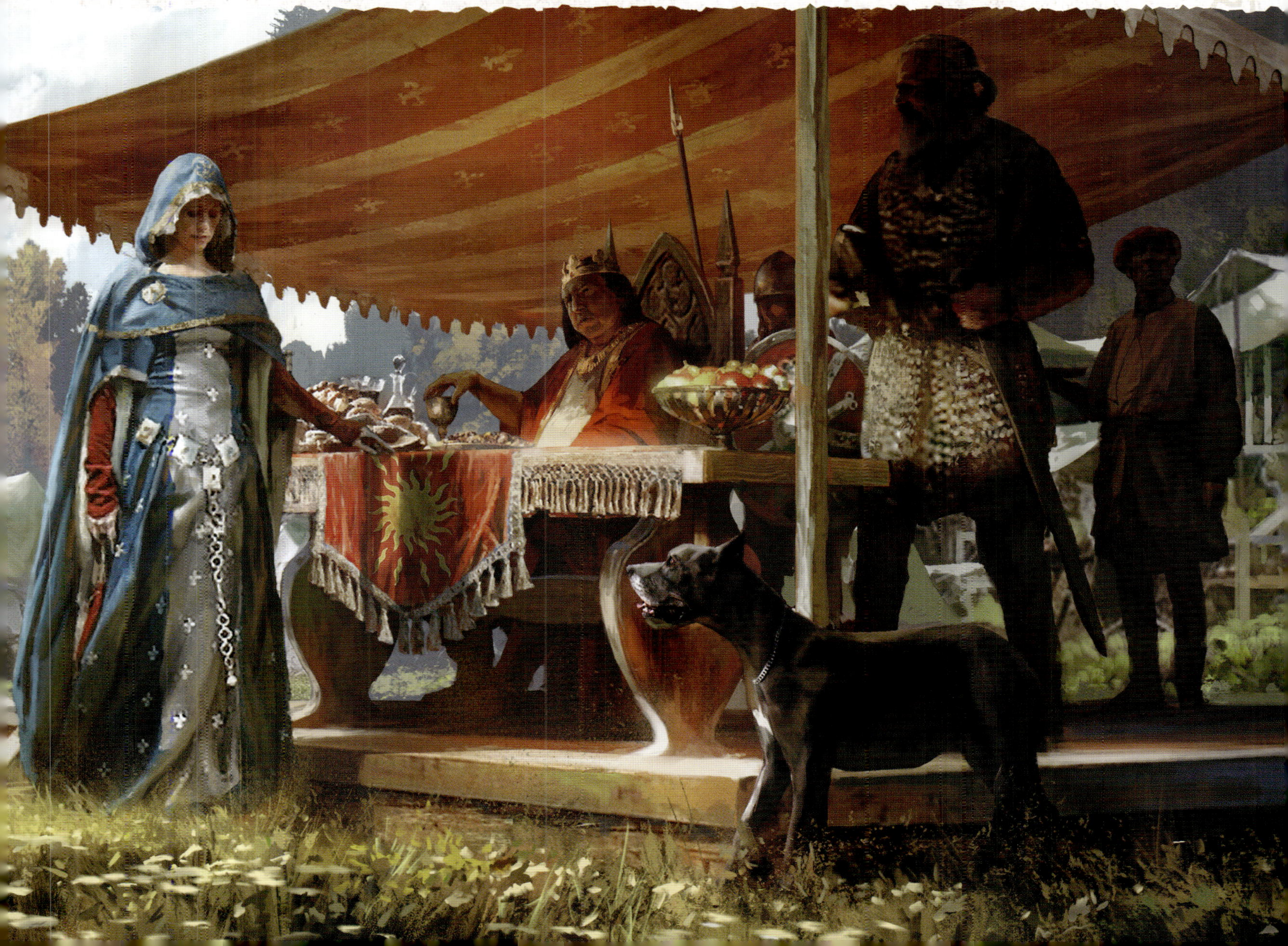

Evresin

Eivor returned to Melun to report on Engelwin's death and her meeting with Charles—Sigfred was happy with the former and not so happy with the latter. Pierre reported that his spies had just spotted Queen Richardis in the company of priests at Evreux in Francia's northwestern province of Evresin. Eivor immediately set out for that commune.

LITTLE MOTHER (EUPHRASIA)

Do you need the devil burned out of you? Go see Little Mother in Aquila for some exorcistic "deliverance." This nun's soft-spoken manner masked a cruel thirst for flaying sinners in the crucible of her secret Bellatores Dei den.

KEY EVENTS

In Evreux, Eivor witnessed a sermon by a religious figure known as Little Mother (her true name: Euphrasia) and uncovered clues about the queen's location that led south to Aquila. There, deep within a crypt most foul, Eivor found a chamber of ritual

RICHARDIS, QUEEN OF FRANCIA

Once described as "an unspoiled flower in a briar of poisonous thorns"—a depiction that Eivor heartily confirms—Richardis could spy goodness in even the blackest heart. Her husband's, for example. Devoted to her stepson Bernard, bastard son of Charles, the queen wanted nothing more than to humbly serve her subjects and help guide their souls to God.

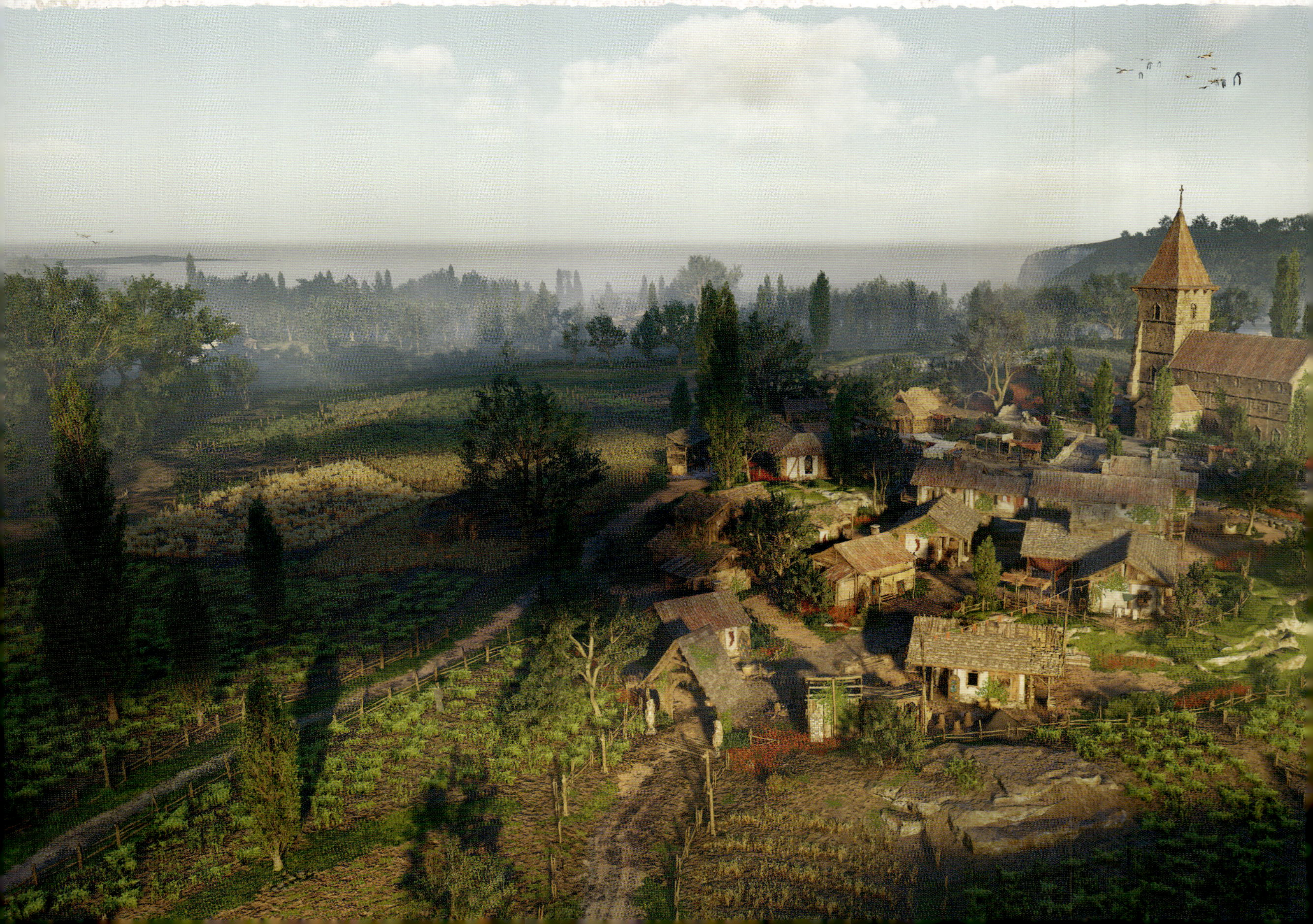

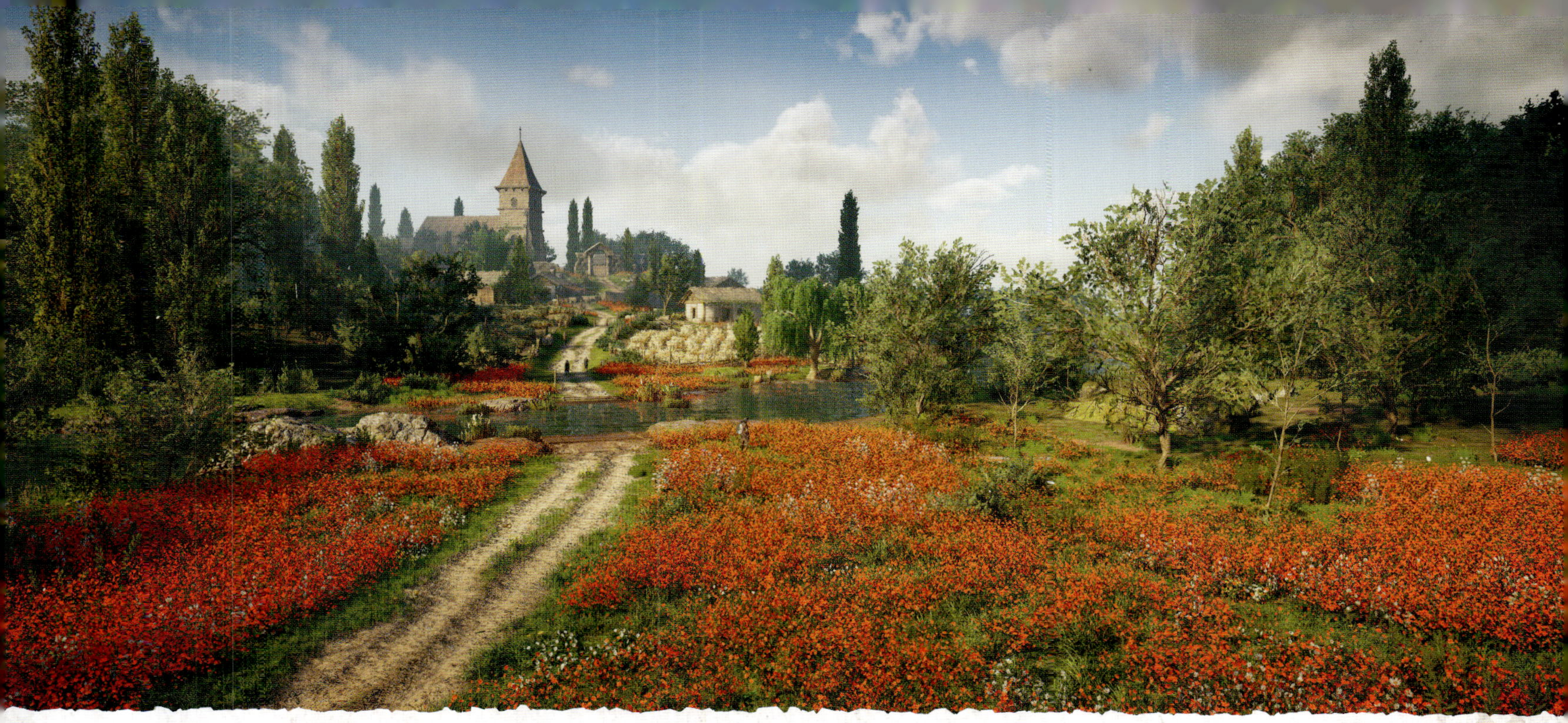

slaughter where Richardis was slated for murder. But Eivor managed to assassinate Little Mother and escort the queen safely to nearby Lisieux.

In Lisieux, Richardis introduced Eivor to the king's secret son, a lad named Bernard. From there, they traveled on to Charles the Fat's forward camp in the Arlonis Forest. (Eivor reported that en route, the queen performed a most wondrous healing of a wounded bear!) In the camp, Charles expressed nothing but contempt for Richardis and unleashed his royal guard on Eivor, a truly treacherous betrayal of their agreed-upon deal. Eivor dispatched the soldiers quickly—no surprise there—then rode to Sigfred's staging area on the Sequana River, just downstream from the city of Paris.

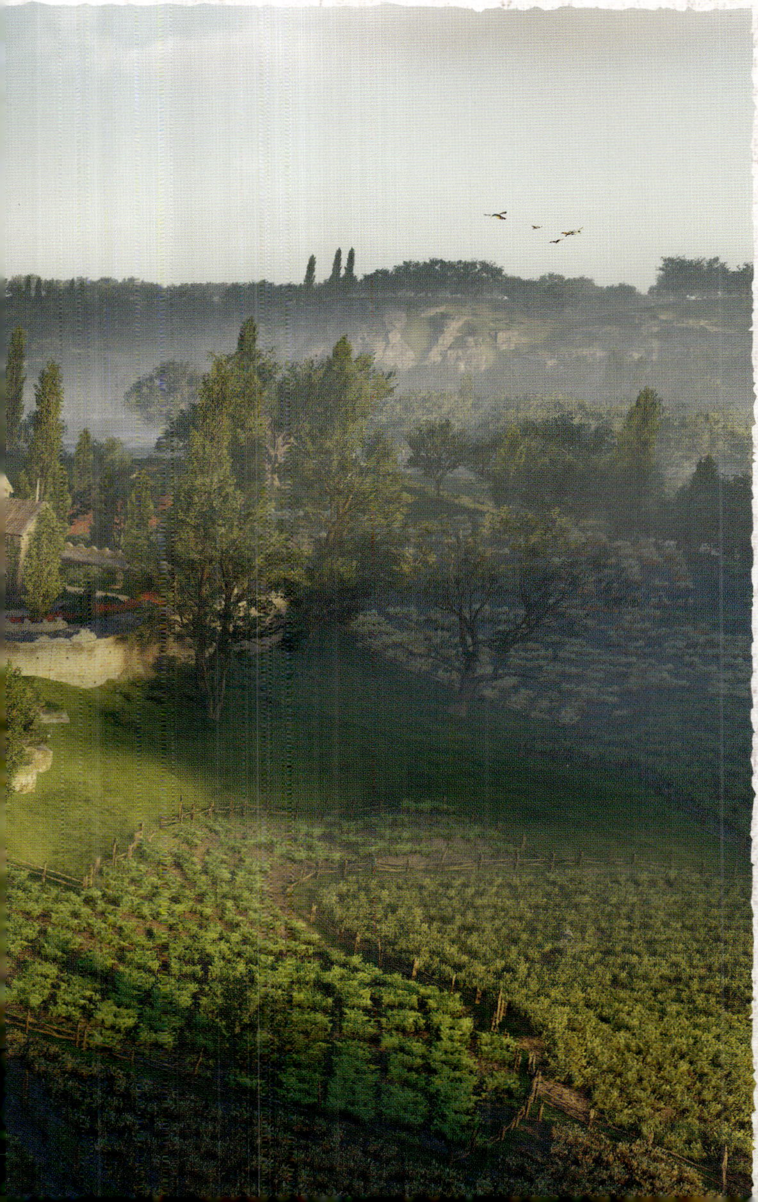

BERNARD

This bright young son of Charles the Fat has thus far enjoyed a simple life, hiding from his father under the loving protection of Queen Richardis. But Charles desperately wants an heir to his bloodline, and Bernard is all he has.

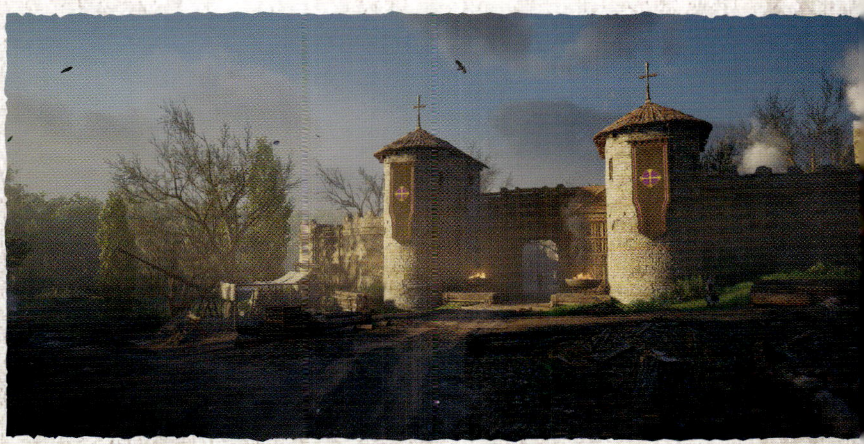

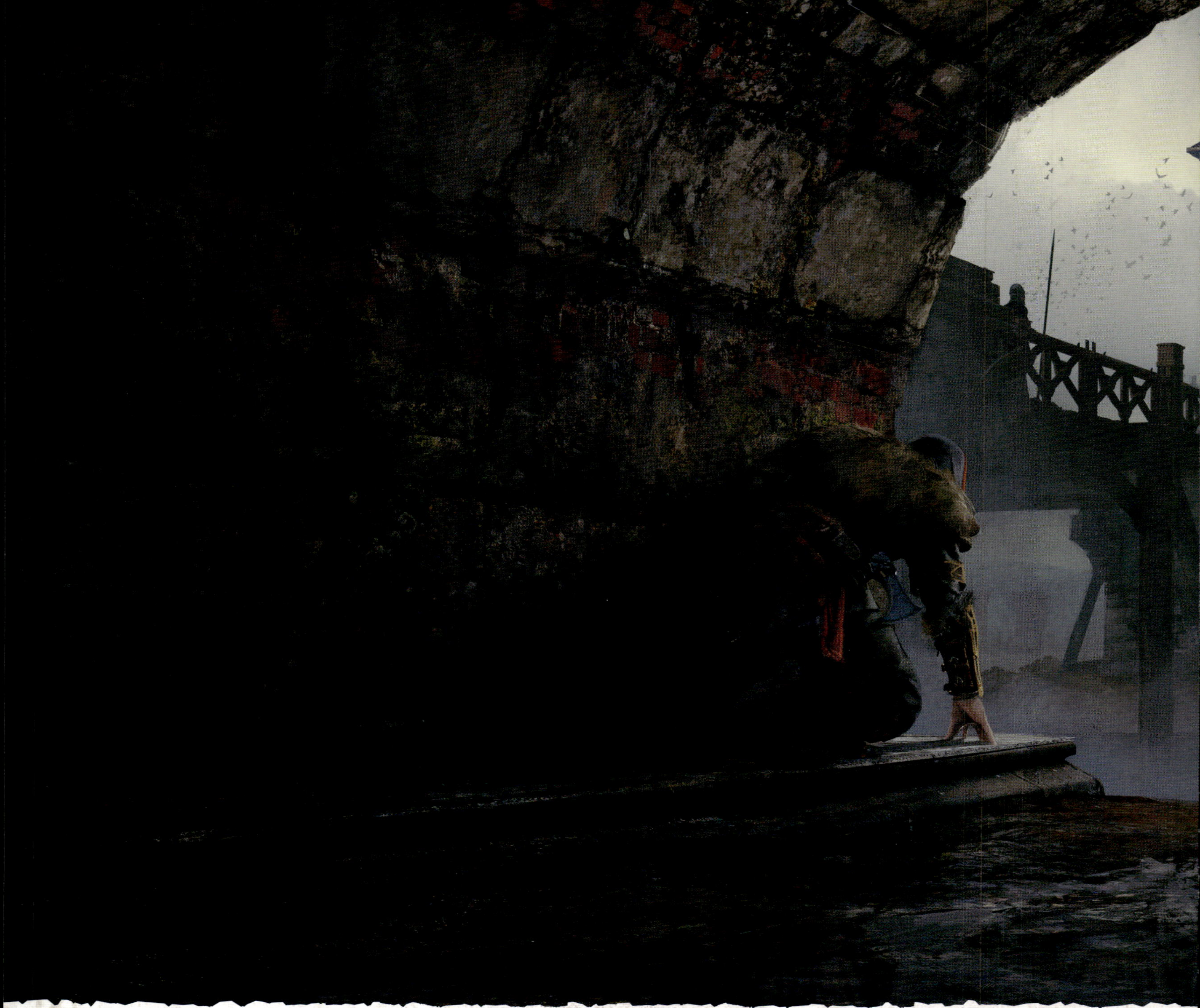

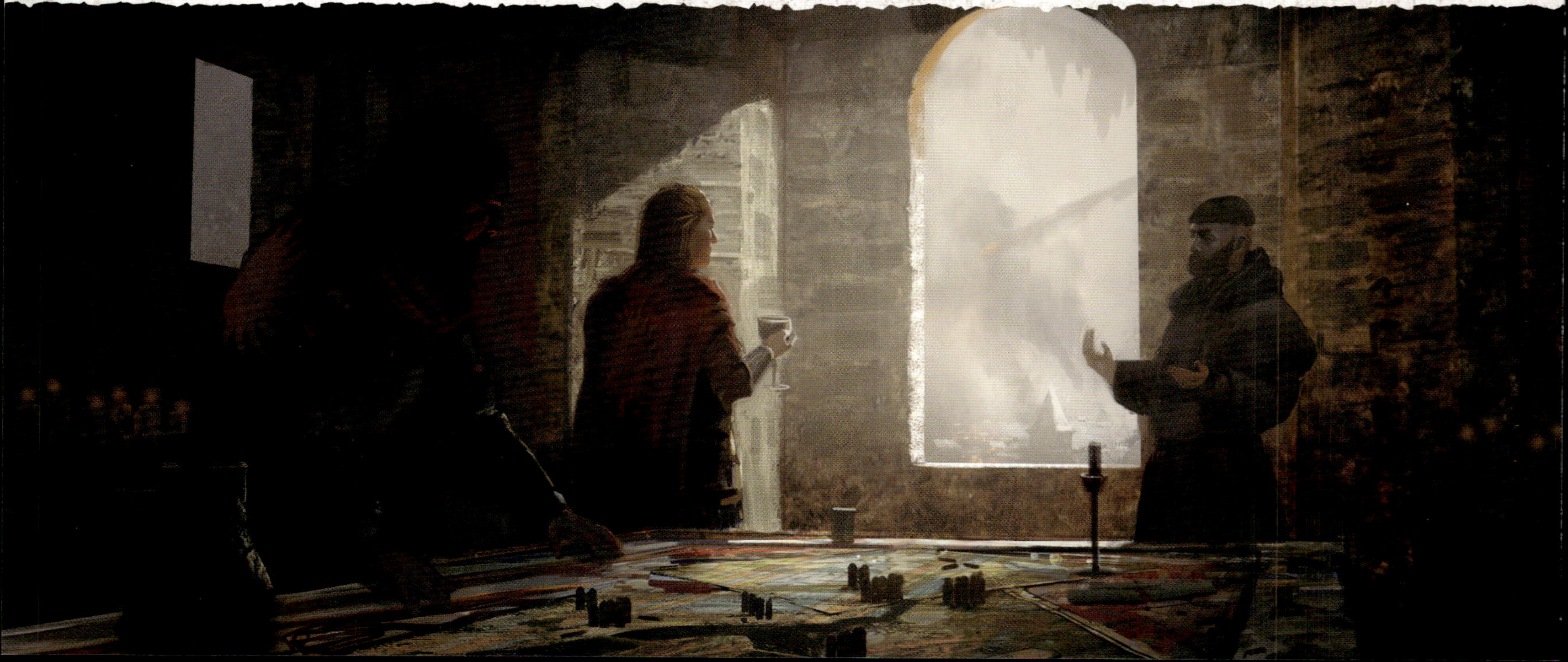

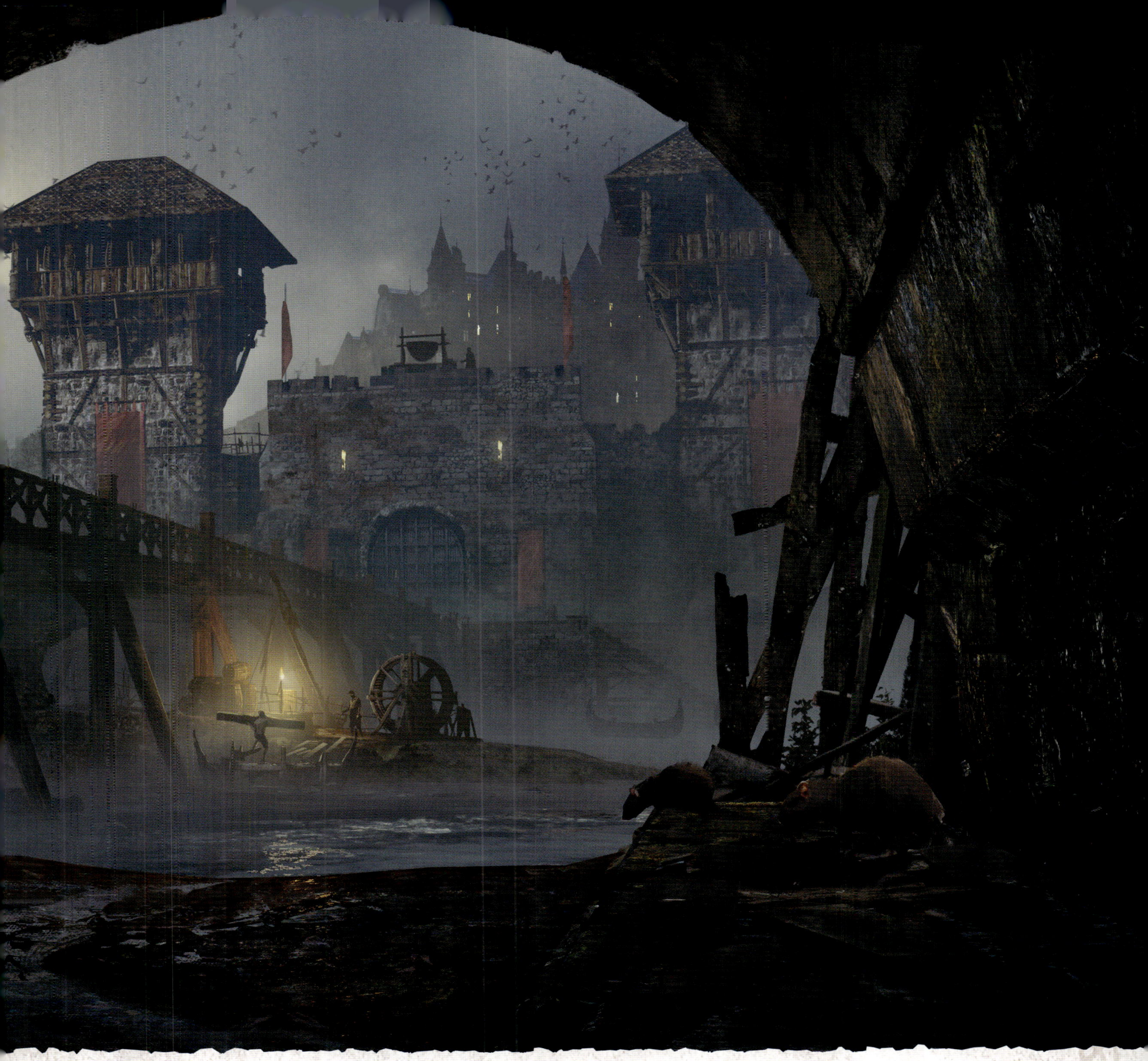

RETURN TO PARIS

KEY EVENTS

As Viking troops prepared to lay siege to Paris, Eivor tried to convince Sigfred that a negotiated settlement would be best for all: "The High One says the dead till no fields. Would you rule a wasteland?" Sigfred agreed to let Eivor try diplomacy. Eivor tracked Count Odo to his Paris manor and learned that no deal was possible—Odo would guarantee peace neither with Sigfred's clan nor with any Norsemen in England, including Ravensthorpe. A bloody siege of Paris now seemed inevitable.

To support Sigfred's siege plans, Eivor helped secure optimal placement of his heavy catapults near the city walls. She also planted explosives beneath weak bridges on the Paris defensive perimeter, thanks to intelligence from a Breton smuggler named Nolwenn. Finally, Eivor tracked down King Charles to the amphitheater in Amiens for one last attempt to negotiate a peaceful resolution. Charles demanded that Eivor deliver his bastard son, Bernard, before he'd deign to hold talks.

Eivor rejoined Sigfred's army on the Sequana, then joined the assault on the gates of Île de la Cité—the city's heavily fortified river island. There, she personally defeated the powerful Frankish warrior Ebels. But after

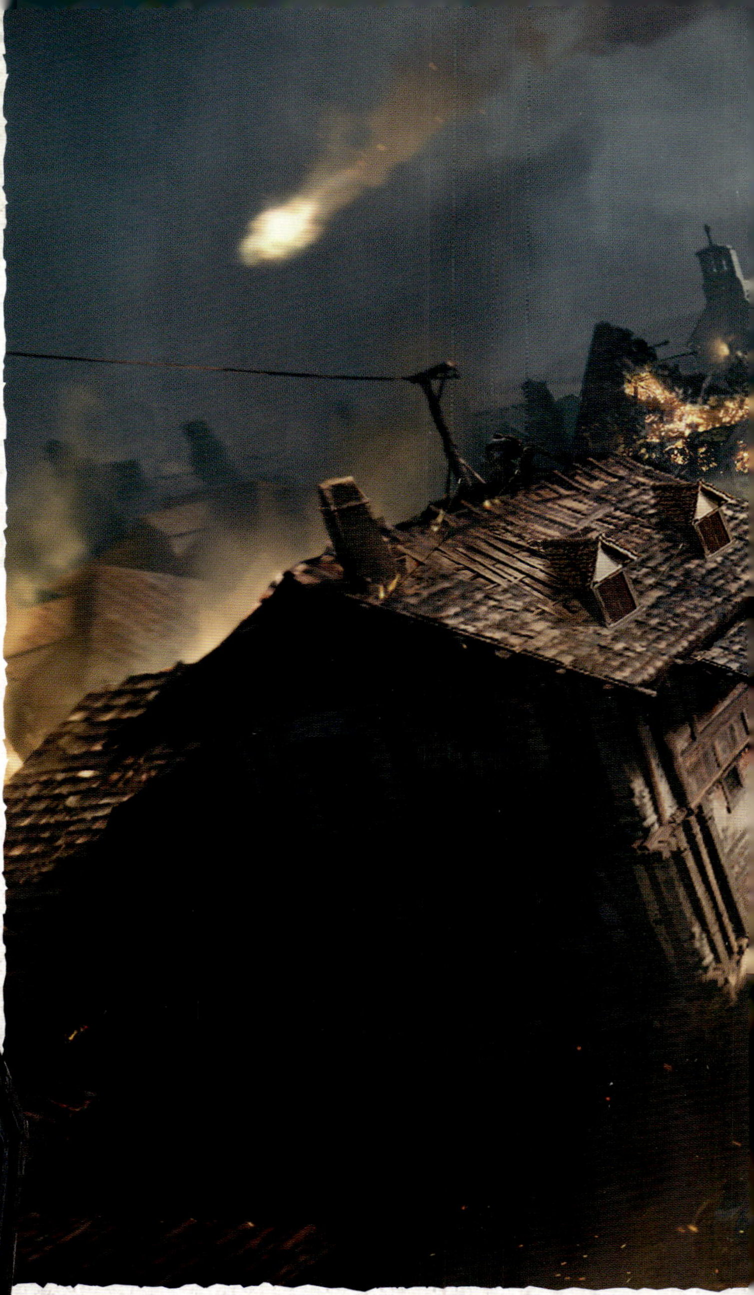

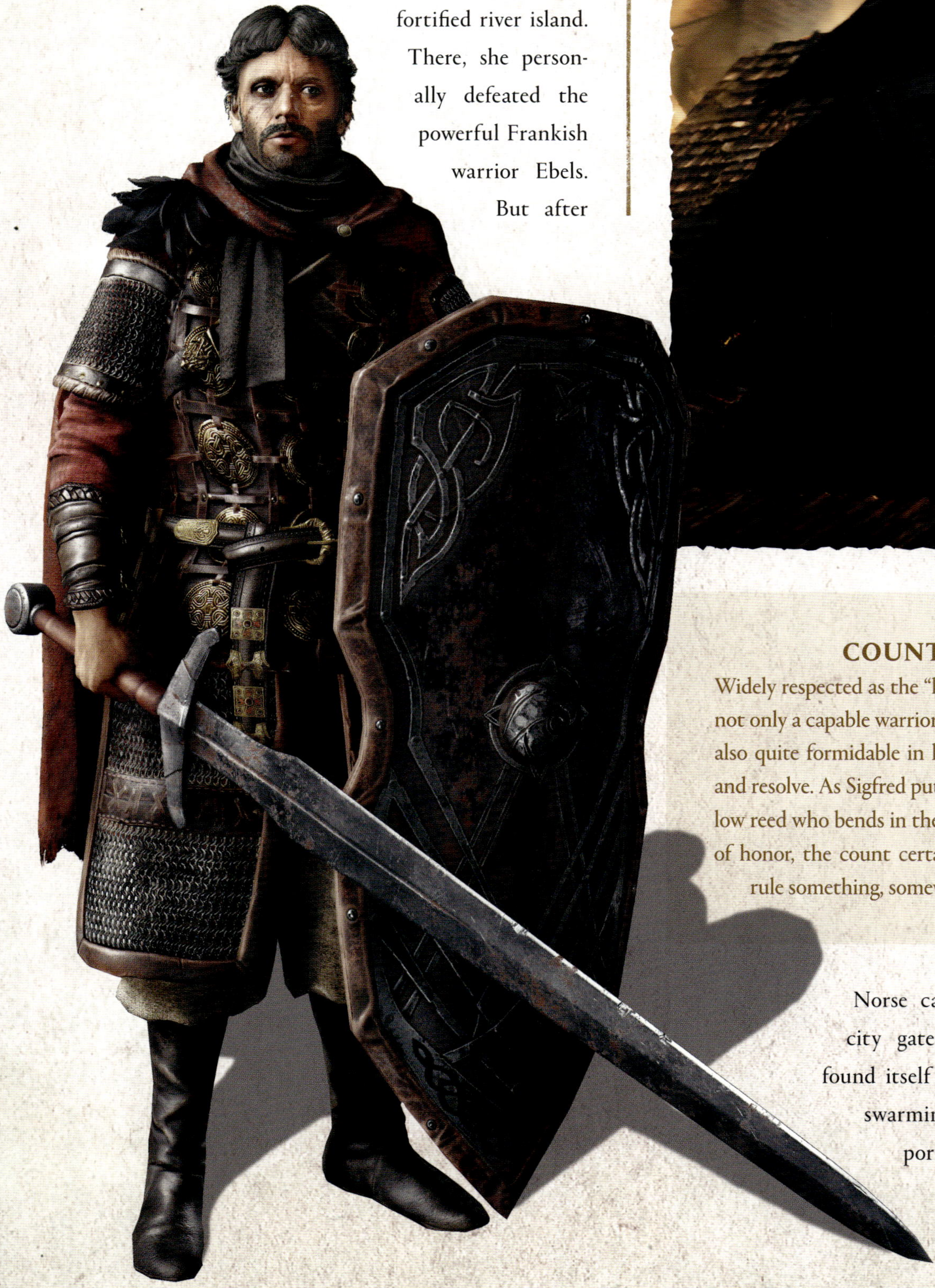

COUNT ODO

Widely respected as the "king's right arm," Odo is not only a capable warrior and military leader but also quite formidable in his political intelligence and resolve. As Sigfred put it, "This Odo is no willow reed who bends in the wind." Noted as a man of honor, the count certainly seems destined to rule something, somewhere . . . but what?

Norse catapults breached the city gates, the Viking legion found itself in a hellish cityscape swarming with foes! Eivor's report suggests the outlook was grim until Toka

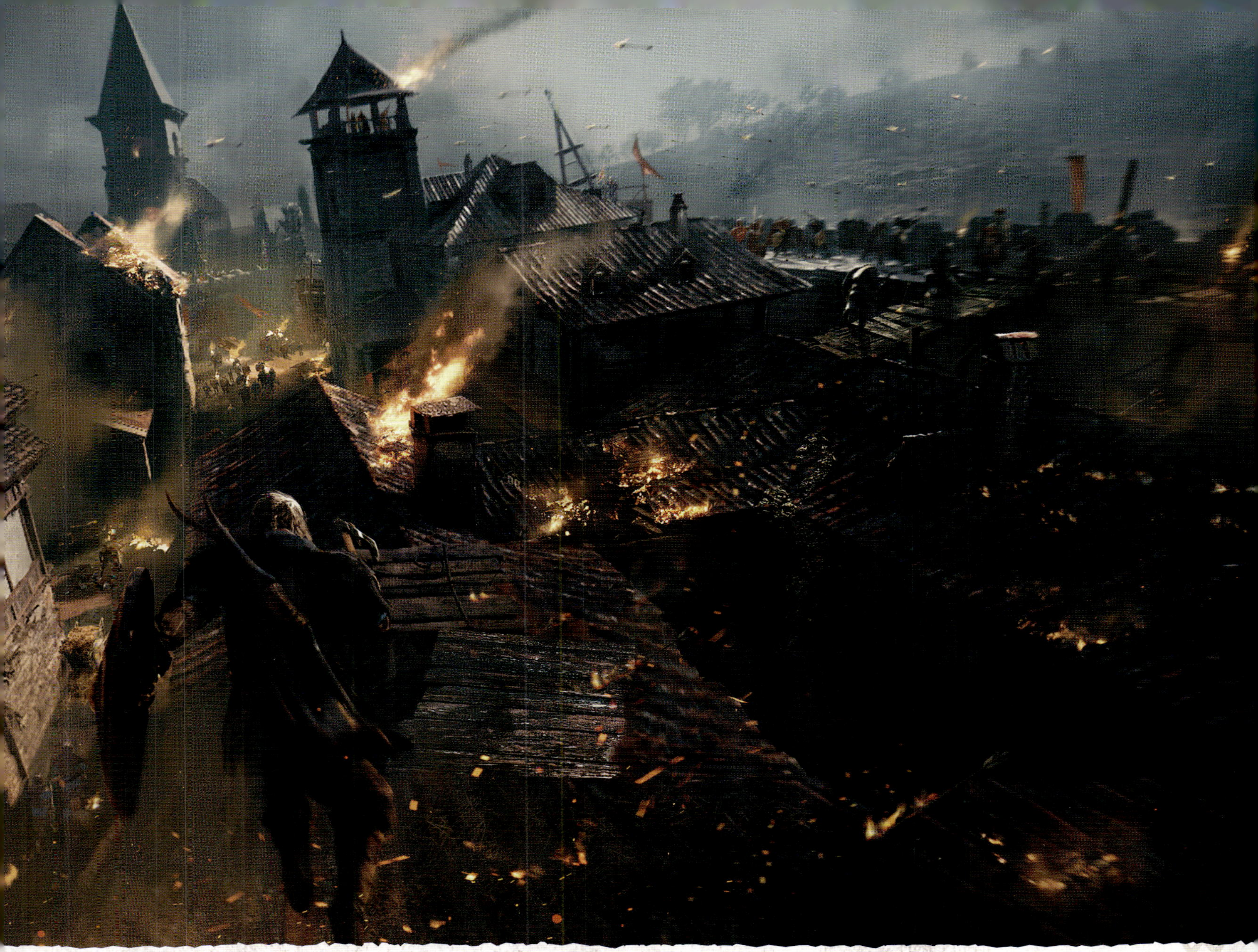

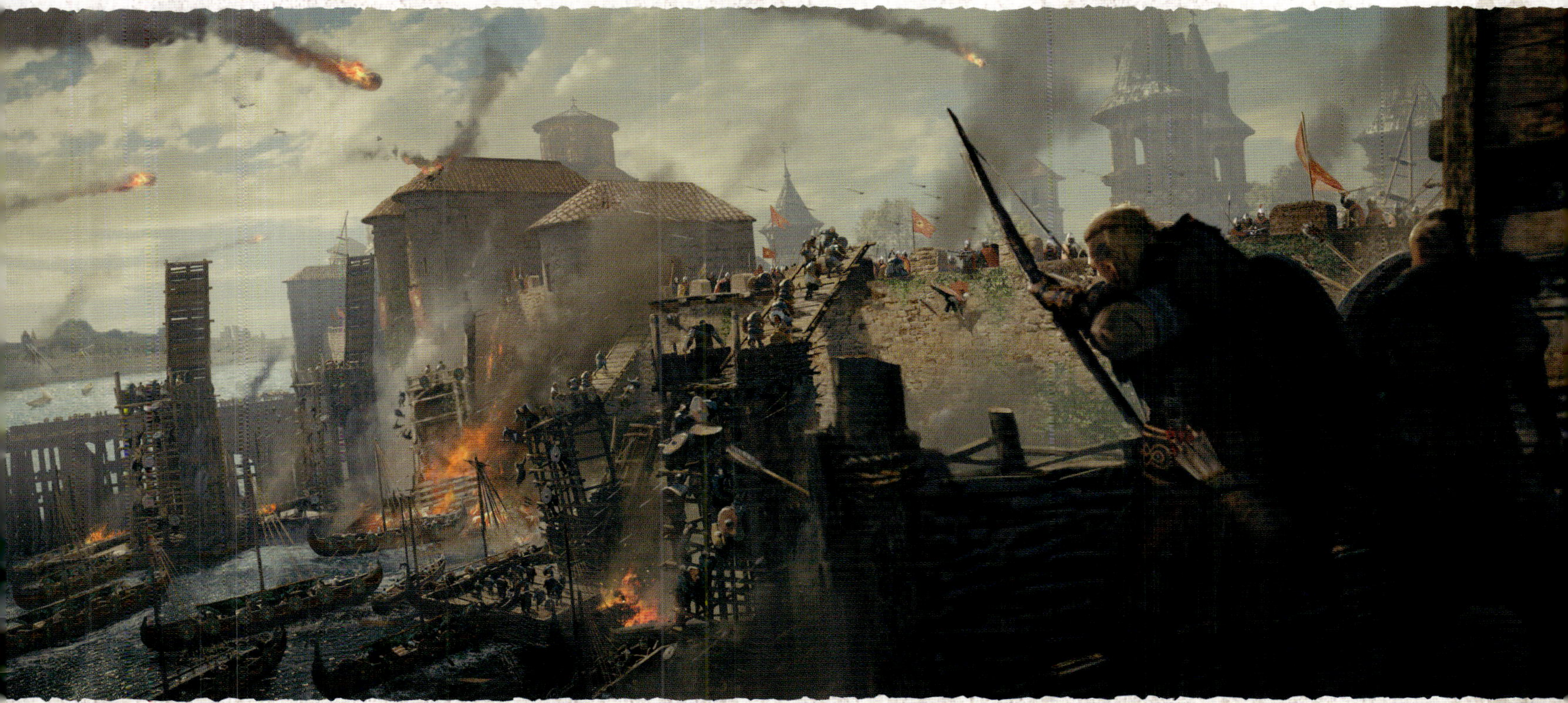

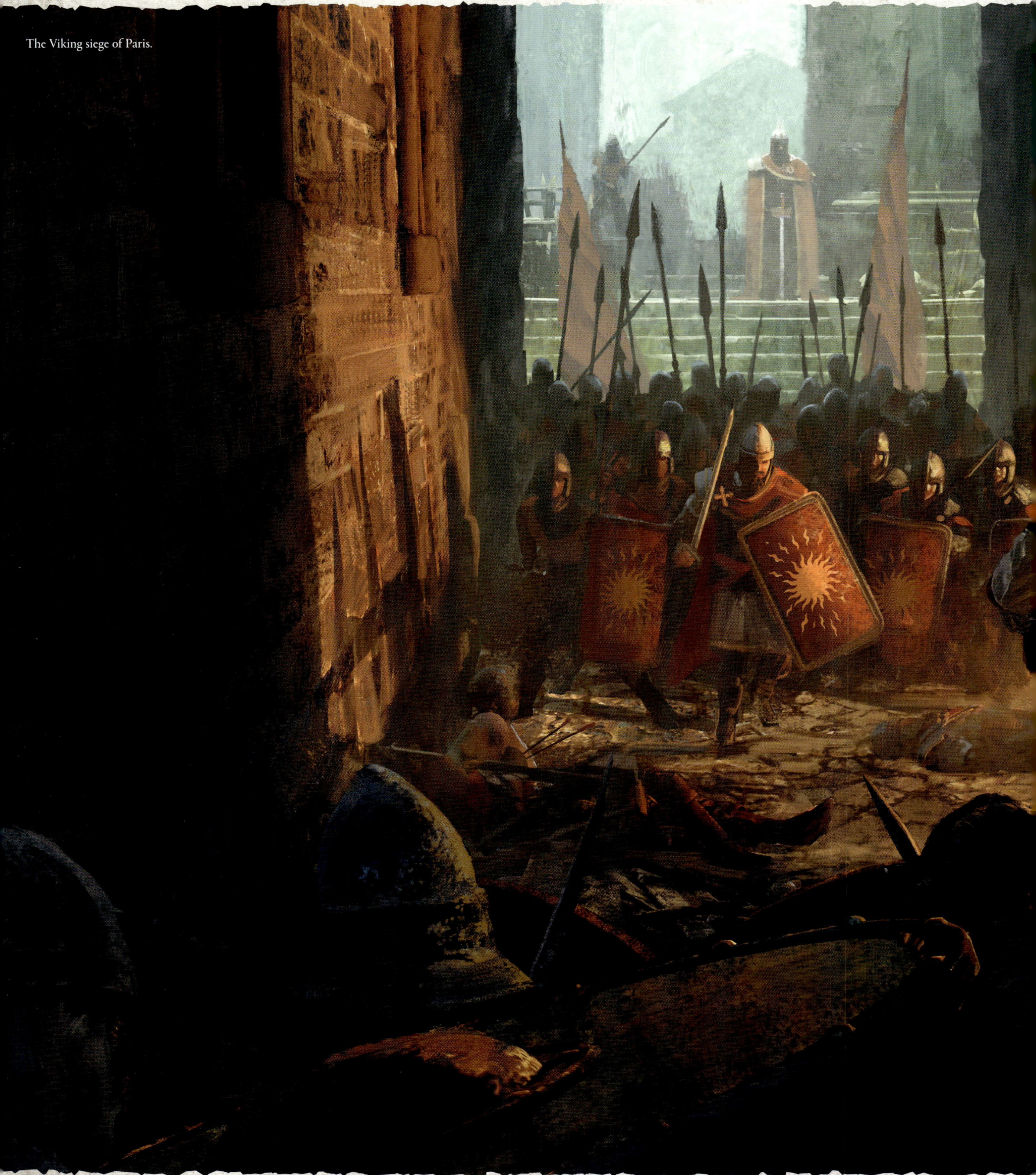

The Viking siege of Paris.

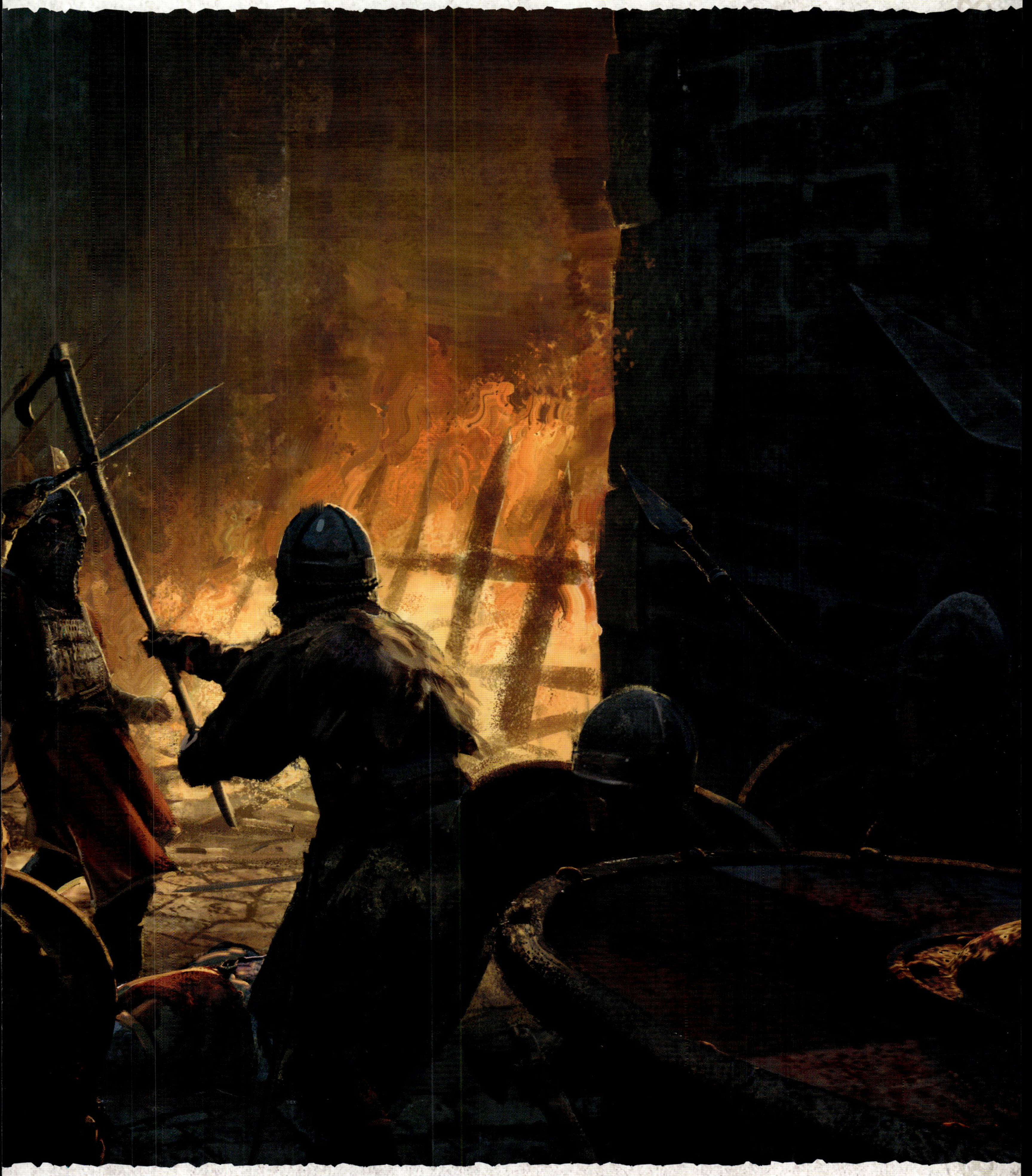

GOZLIN, BISHOP OF PARIS

Known across Francia as "the war priest," this man of God was indeed a fearsome warrior. Gozlin would plant his golden staff topped with the Christian cross on the battlefield and defend it with an unholy ferocity.

helped her light signal fires at strategic locations for the catapults to target. Then Eivor felled Bishop Gozlin (ironically by dropping a Christian cross on him) as the war priest tried to rally his troops for a decisive counterattack. This broke the Frankish will to fight!

With the deaths of his brother and soldiers fueling his hatred of the Franks, Sigfred was consumed

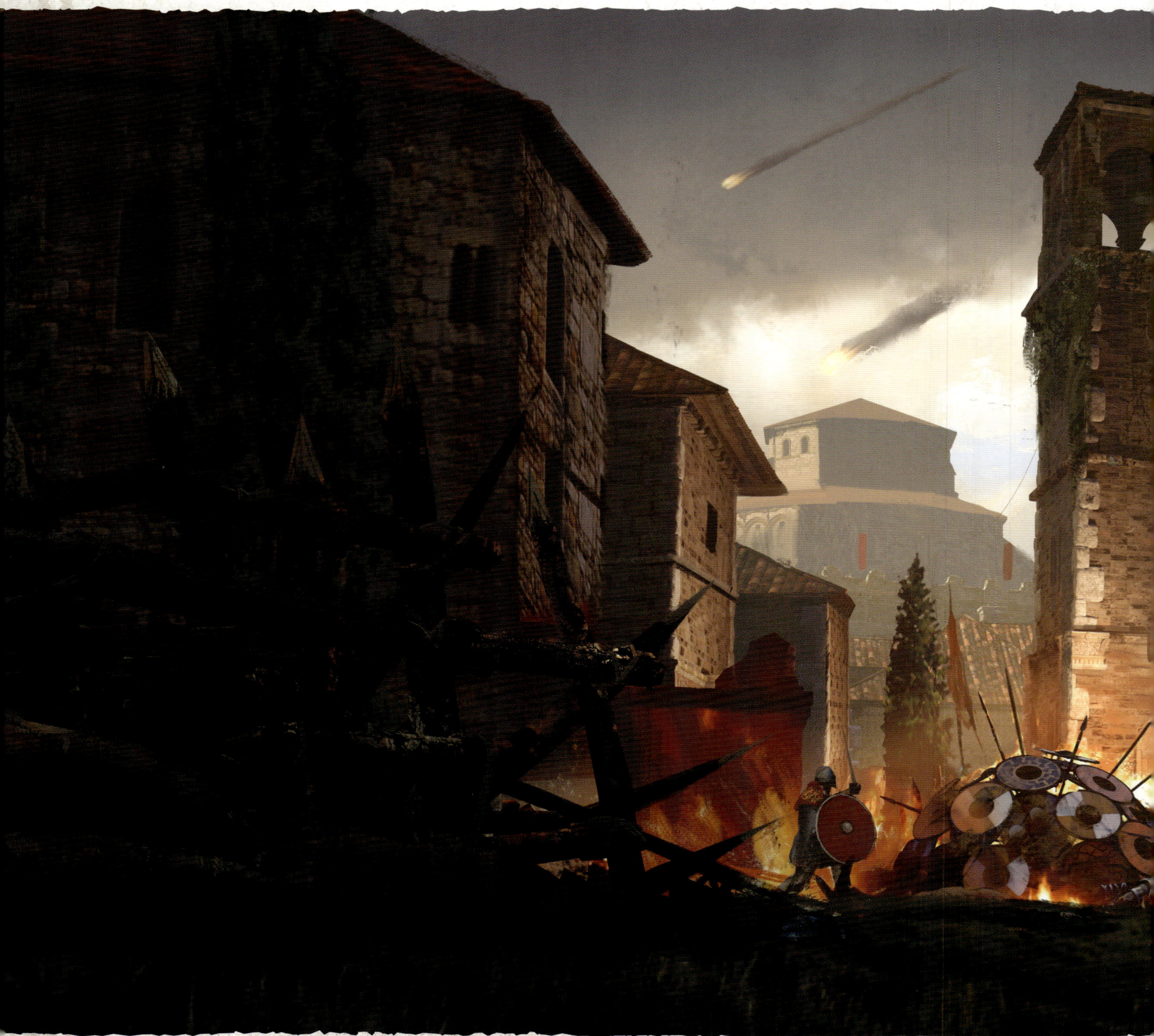

by a vengeful blood lust and began to slaughter innocent women and children . . . an act that sickened Eivor and Toka. Fortunately, Eivor managed to infiltrate the Palais, defeat Count Odo in a duel, then convince him to call a truce. King Charles arrived with his heavy cavalry but offered silver instead of combat. Fortunately, Sigfred agreed, and the hostilities ceased.

EBELS

Grim executioner of Paris and brother of Bishop Gozlin, this brutish brawler was seen as a near-invincible force of nature and a one-man salient on the battlefield. That is, until he met Eivor.

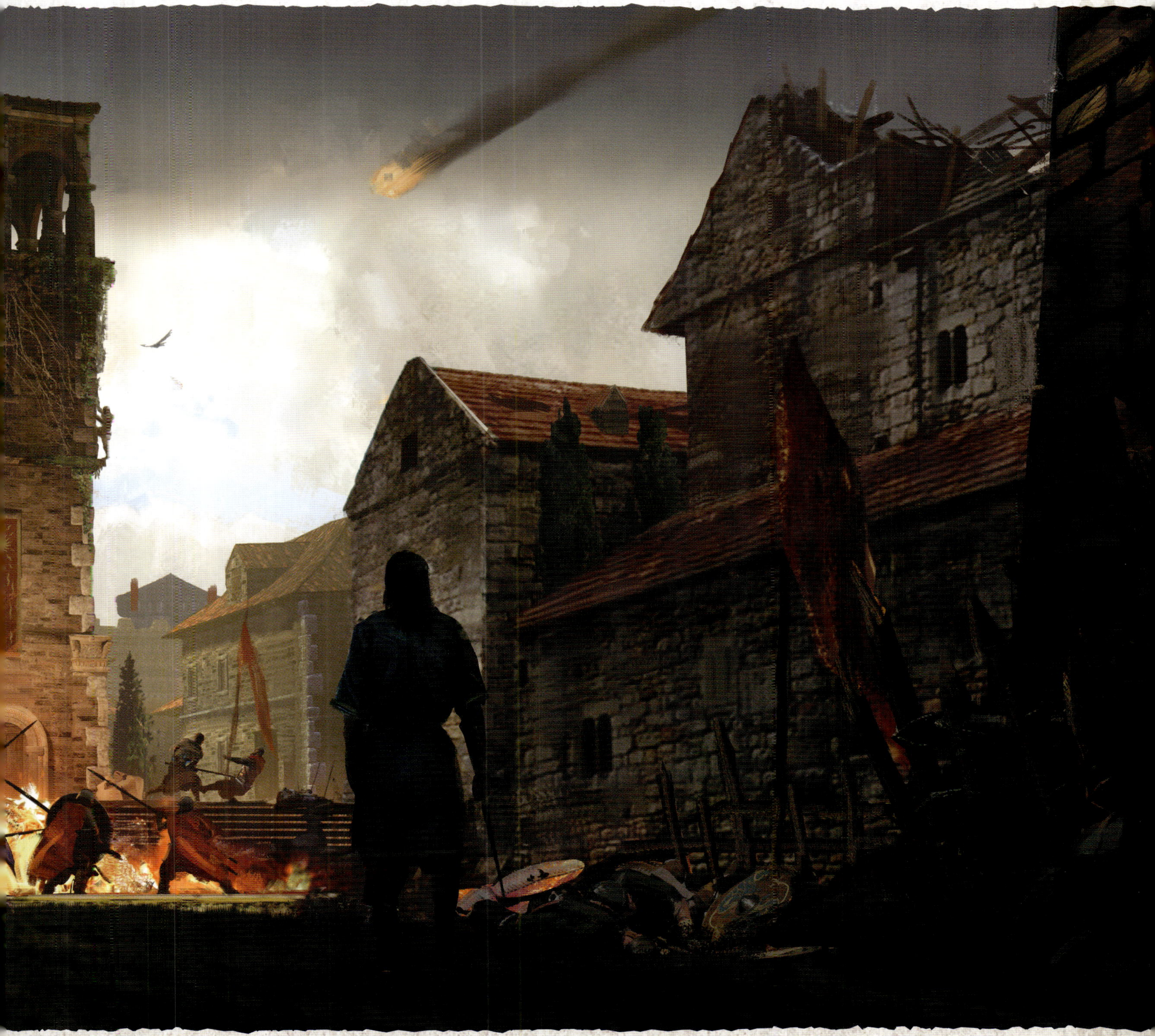

RETURN TO MELUN

KEY EVENTS

Back in Melun, much feasting ensued. Eivor tells me she even raced a pig! (Amazing what enough mead can convince a warrior to try.) But Sigfred could not shake the vengeance that haunted him, nor shed the growing cynicism his hatred had bred: "We are but a morning fog that will inevitably lift." Impulsively, he announced a bloody plan to violate the truce he'd just made with Charles. Thus, Eivor was forced to intervene . . . leaving Toka in charge of the clan.

Afterward, Pierre reported news from Count Odo: King Charles was hunting for Richardis and Bernard, and Odo believed the queen was in dire peril. Eivor immediately set out to meet Odo at Epernay in Amienois Province.

AMIENOIS

In Epernay, Eivor toured Count Odo's family vineyard as they spoke of the great threat to Francia embodied in King Charles and his reckless ways. As it turned out, Odo was mustering a rebel force to challenge Charles and seize the Frankish throne. Eivor set out to find the queen in Amiens.

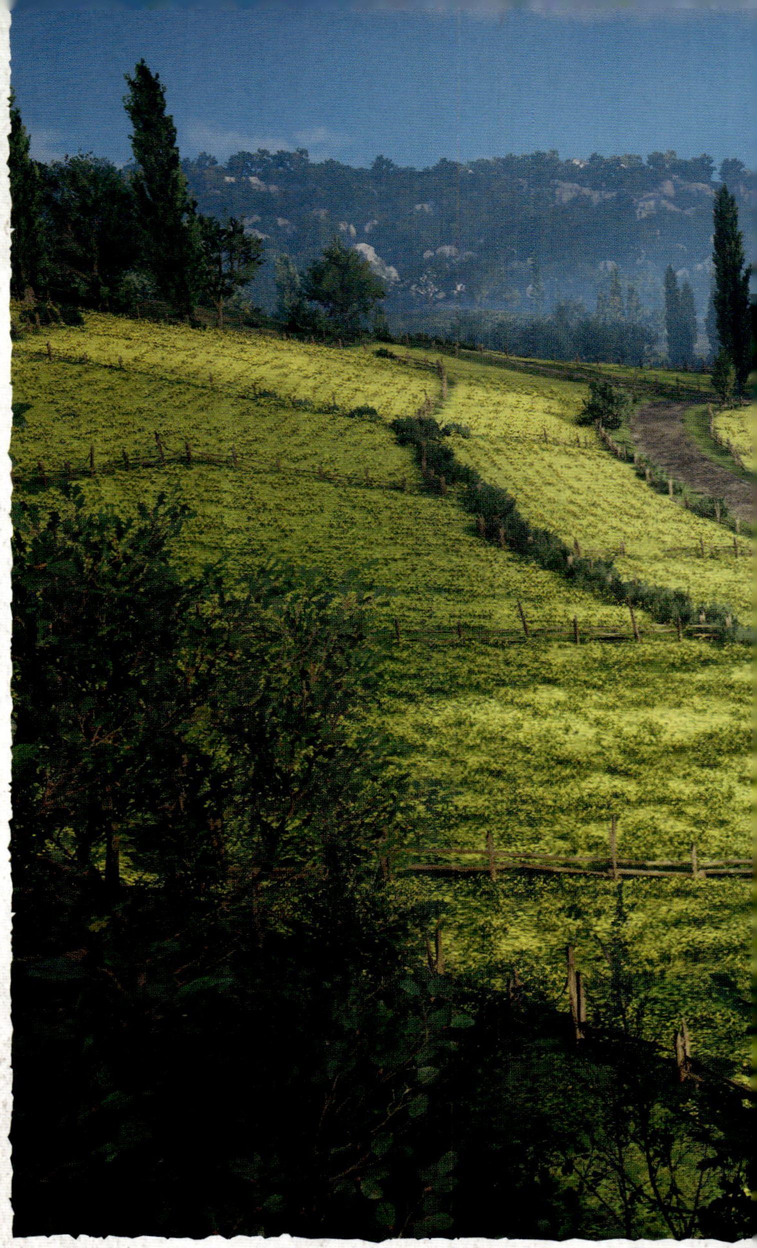

KEY EVENTS

A trail of clues led Eivor to the Slaughtered Calf Tavern in Amiens, where she came upon a most

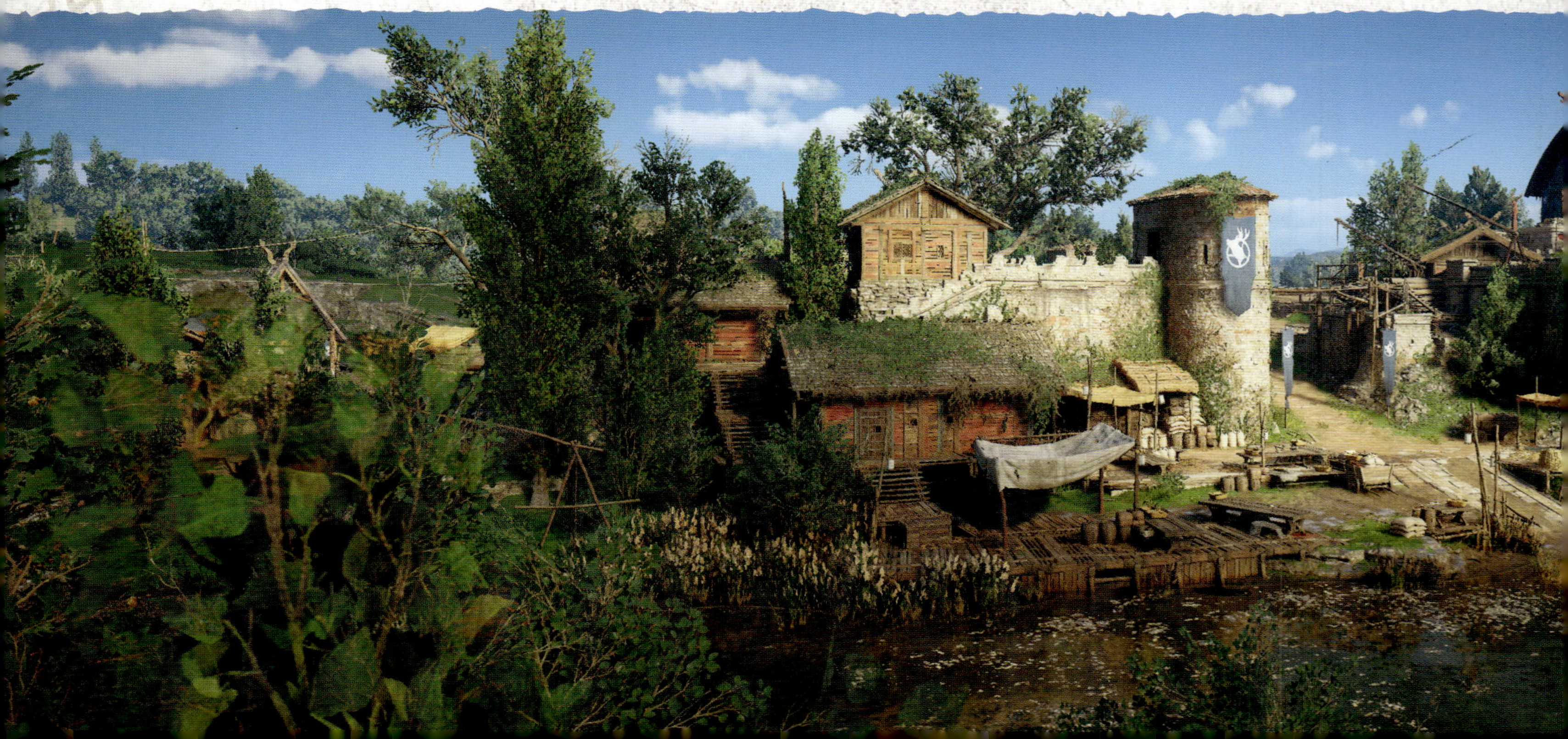

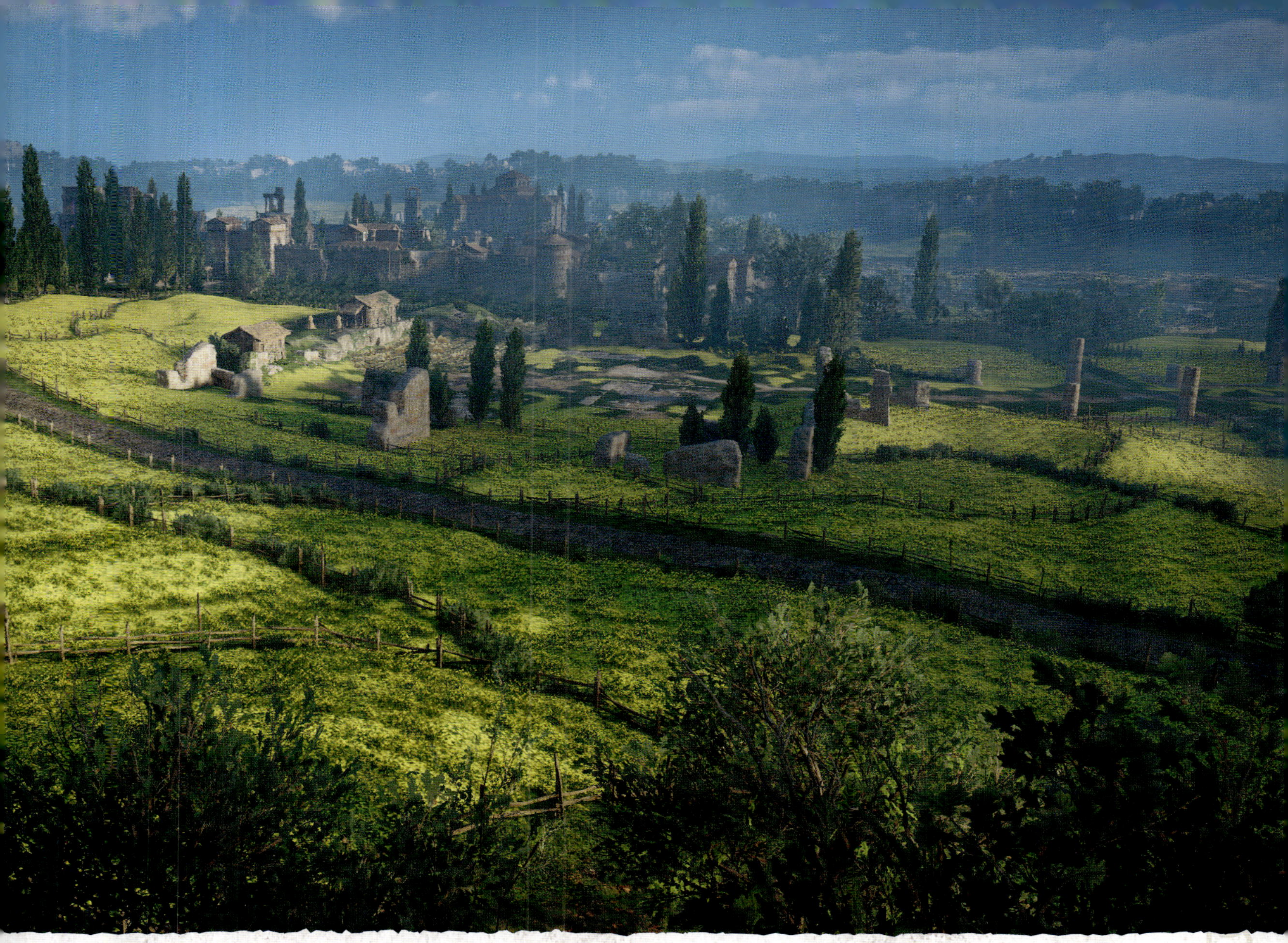

gruesome massacre of Odo's men assigned to guard the queen. Eivor found and freed Bernard from a nearby church, sending him back to his home in Lisieux. Then she tracked down Richardis to the

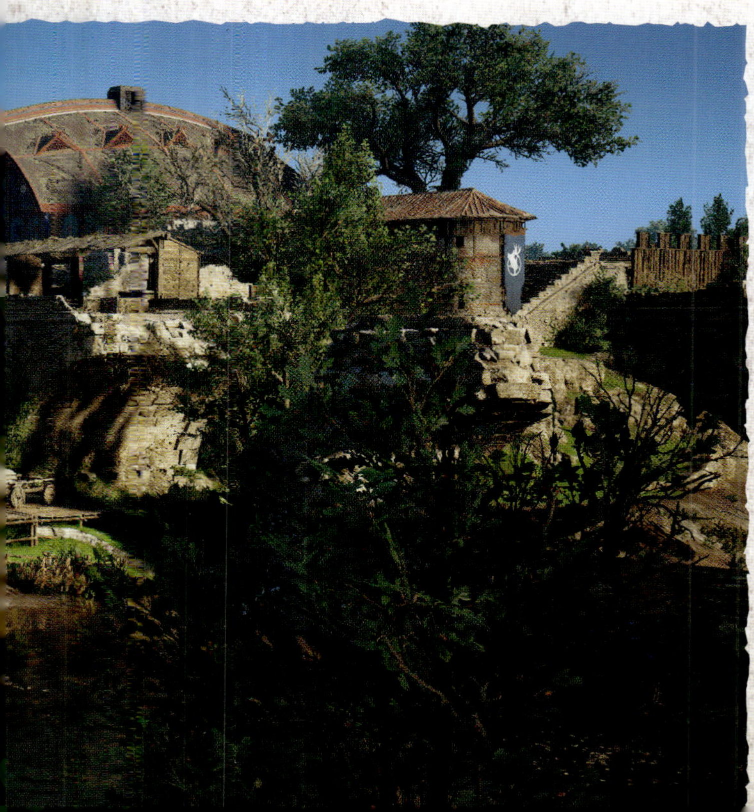

king's villa in Amiens. Charles had accused his queen of adultery and ordered a "trial by fire"—a truly barbarous ordeal. Miraculously (or so believed the onlookers), a cloudburst extinguished the flames, thus proving the queen's innocence! Eivor administered justice to Charles in accordance with his misdeeds.

Returning to the Melun longhouse, Eivor arrived just as a contentious meeting between Count Odo and Toka was escalating to the verge of combat. But the news of Charles the Fat's demise not only defused the tension but led to a general celebration . . . and to Odo's promise of having no Frankish designs on England. (Odo would be crowned king of West Francia soon after.) Before returning home to Ravensthorpe, Eivor also acquired a firm pledge of alliance from Toka's clan. All in all, a good outcome for our little town on the Nene River!

EPILOGUE

You are less mine than I am yours. And I ask of you only this: keep me honest in the times to come.

Eivor Jarlskona to her Raven Clan

I hope this record does justice to the momentous events transpiring in these northern lands—events I've either witnessed directly or had recounted to me by trusted sources. As I conclude this chronicle, I want to emphasize a central point: the spread of Raven Clan influence under the inspired leadership of Eivor Varinsdottir has been an unqualified boon to our mission here in Europe.

Indeed, my Viking friend displays an uncanny knack for nudging her allies toward what we Hidden Ones call "the light"—i.e., a more selfless view of leadership. Every land Eivor visits seems to emerge more resilient against the type of fear-based despotism espoused by the Order of the Ancients. Certainly, all alliances in this oft-brutal age rely on martial muscle for survival. But I'm pleased to report that our agenda has made headway. More humanistic values based on trust, respect, and free will are emerging even in the harsh hinterlands.

My only regret—and it is a *deep* one—regards my master Basim.

Eivor's tale of Basim's odd turn is difficult to digest. His disappearance is troubling. My mentor was a man of extraordinary skill and charisma. Son of the architect who designed the Great Mosque of Samarra, Basim was orphaned at an early age. He stowed away on a caravan bound for Baghdad and spent his childhood years haunting the city's back alleys. As a young man, Basim became a street thief of legendary skill. I've heard some refer to him as a living mirage—the one who is there, and yet is not.

But remarkably, Basim rose above that life. As Master Rayhan has said: *The way of light knows the darkness.* A born seeker, Basim was drawn to Baghdad's House of Wisdom. He told me that the wondrous works therein steered him toward justice and insight. When the Hidden Ones finally recruited him, it seemed a perfect match of sensibilities, and he rose swiftly to the rank of Mentor. Yet the brotherhood harbored concerns about his ultimate loyalties. On my first assignment under Master Basim, a protection mission in Constantinople, I was secretly directed by our leadership to observe him closely.

Despite this, I still say it was my great honor to serve as acolyte under Basim's guidance. I truly hope that whatever triggered his "personal obsessions" (as Master Rayhan described them) somehow guided him toward the peace he sought.

In the meantime, I shall continue my daily efforts to monitor the region from my Ravensthorpe bureau. I will treasure every moment in this remarkable Viking settlement—my new home, and my new kin.